Wrestling with Angels:
New and Collected Stories of John J. Clayton

Books by John J. Clayton

FICTION

What are Friends For?, 1979
Bodies of the Rich: Stories 1984
Radiance: Ten Stories 1998
The Man I Never Wanted to Be, 1998
Kuperman's Fire, 2007

SELECTED NON-FICTION

Gestures of Healing: Anxiety and the Modern Novel
D.C. Heath Introduction to Fiction (ed.)
Saul Bellow: In Defense of Man

John J. Clayton

Wrestling with Angels

New and Collected Stories

The Toby Press

Wrestling with Angels: New and Collected Stories

First Edition, 2007

The Toby Press LLC
POB 8531, New Milford, CT 06776-8531, USA &
POB 2455, London W1A 5WY, England
www.tobypress.com

ISBN 978 1 59264 202 1, *hardcover*

A CIP catalogue record for this title is available from the British Library

Printed and bound in the United States by Thomson-Shore Inc., Michigan

For my wife Sharon Dunn and my children,
Aaron, Sasha, and Laura.
And always for Josh.

Contents

Author's Preface: Wrestling with Angels

During the past twenty-five years I've published two collections, *Bodies of the Rich* (1984) and *Radiance* (1998); both are included here, as is my new collection, *Wrestling with Angels*. I've also included several stories that for one reason or another don't belong in *Wrestling with Angels* but that I find strong—"Losers in Paradise," "Night Talk," "Aaron, Personal," "Waiting for Polly Adler," and "Light at the End of the Tunnel." All but three of the stories in this volume—"Friends," "Blue House," and "Soap Opera"—have been published in magazines and/or collections. Other published stories, especially my early ones—stories which no longer interest me—I've not included.

As I reread the stories from *Bodies of the Rich* (1984), I do admire the writer—whoever he is. But whoever is he? The stories, the good passages especially, seem as if they were written by another person. I believe in the personal chaos, the sadness, this writer expresses. He's sometimes speaking through the POV of a child, sometimes of a young adult filled with existential anguish. He knows about love and the end of love—he knows divorce really well. He comes closest to who I am now when he imagines children and the needs of children; for instance, in "Old 3 A.M. Story" or "Fantasy for a Friday Afternoon."

We have other things in common, this writer and I. He and I both laugh at ideologies and the way they permit human beings to disguise their narcissism from themselves and cover personal chaos with meaning. The protagonist of "Cambridge Is Sinking" is afloat in space; the passion of the sixties is no longer able to sustain him or ground him. He enjoys the comedy and sadness of the rag-tag remains of ideological clothing used to keep people feeling worthwhile, justified. For Steve, all the hip ideologies have gone flat. He'll have to start again from scratch. The story expresses movingly, comically, the debacle of the mid-seventies, when the passion and certainties of what we call "the sixties" (actually, about 1964–1974) were no longer available. I find it a funny, moving, true story, told in a wonderful, wacky style. I can praise my own story because—well, because it's scarcely mine; that style is no longer available to me.

I do find in my early stories hints of a longing for the holy, a longing that's since become deeper and more real to me. It's part of an unfashionable search for the meaning under things. In "Bodies Like Mouths," a story that looks back on being young in New York in the 1950s, the narrator says that the protagonist's sexual longings are "intuitions of a sacred language that he could comprehend only in profane form." "Love flesh: he wanted to hold his life, shining, in his hands, and he didn't know where else to look, how else to sanctify it." Years later, in "The Builder," the protagonist has experiences of God, and, building a children's shelter, "tries to imagine that he is building a world for God to inhabit." The longing for sanctification, early and late, seems the same to me, but the later vision is deeper, more connected to the needs of other people. Even when I wrote "Bodies Like Mouths," the innocence and erotic longing of that protagonist was years behind me; distance from the young man coming of age is an important part of the story. But even the lyricism of the writing is no longer mine. The anguish of a youth trying to find himself in the city is now so remote from my life that it is as if I were reading the work of my own son.

In *Radiance* (1998) the writer is sometimes the son, looking, in quasi-autobiographical fashion, at his suffering parents, and sometimes the adult struggling with divorce and the children of divorce. Some of these stories of family had been worked and reworked for twenty years before they seemed ready. My favorite, the most complex, of these is "History Lessons." I like its sense of the discovery of the past, the past as unfinished, present, still changing.

One unchanging thing in my writing has been a spatial sense of time. In "Prewar Quality," from *Bodies of the Rich*, the young man Steve looks at a photograph in the apartment of his old, dying aunt. In the photograph his aunt is a young, beautiful woman. "Her past I see it still as a future. Her face younger than my own." In Harvard Square he sees an old man, a "Professor Emeritus he'd seen often in Grolier's Bookshop," but sees him "...as about to graduate from college (the street scene turned 1920). He himself felt seventy years old...." In "Time Exposure," from *Radiance*, Ben sees a photo of his father, now dead but in the photo a young, strong man, across the staircase from a photo of his mother, now dead but in the photo a beautiful young woman. "So young they seem. He could be their father. He could offer her advice."

Increasingly, this breakdown of the ordinary sense of time edges on the mystical. In "Glory" (*Radiance*) Avrom looks at a building on Back Bay in Boston, and "it vibrates with its existence in time so that Avrom is aware of the workers who laid the bricks and stone in the late nineteenth century...." The dead are literally present to Avrom; they are in the room. In one of my recent stories, "Vertigo," Danny's mother, senile, has lost her "normal" sense of time, but, then, so has Danny. He looks into a playground and "sees" his daughter, now grown up, and his son, now dead, as children, playing.

My own, real, son, my oldest son, died of cancer in 2000 at age thirty-two. A few minutes ago I discovered that the copy of *Radiance* I'm re-reading happens to be the very one I gave to Josh, "with my love, of course, and my deep respect." I respected him and still respect him very much as a fellow-writer, a fellow spiritual writer, though we worked in different media—he wrote and performed songs (see his website, www.joshclayton.com) while I wrote novels and stories. Though none of my writing these past seven years is directly about Josh, almost all of it derives from mourning for him. I'm not speaking only of expressing grief. It's that the way I see is different. My identification with the losses suffered by other people is deeper. Oh. *That's* the way life is. Of course, I already "knew" life was like that. I had said to friends who lost parents, "May you be comforted among the mourners of Zion and Jerusalem." But seeing through the lens of loss and grief changed my sense of how the world works, as well as my sense of what matters. I was no longer the grown son looking at the pain of the family I grew up in, no longer the sufferer of a divorce. I saw, as grieving adult, a tragic world.

I was already writing as a practicing, learning Jew well before Josh grew sick, went to the hospital, and, in a month, died. I was learning, am still learning, to use Torah as a template in my work, struggling with the world unseen behind the seen world. My protagonists long to experience the presence of God in a world filled with death, with evil, with idols—or try to cope with the consequences of such an encounter. I've been bumbling to shape a rhetoric that can bring myself and the reader closer to mystery, a rhetoric whose job is to take us deeper. This can be risky. It can so easily become hokey, puffed-up, false. But it's a tool for bringing us into moments of truth.

Here's what feels true to me, and useful to me as a writer: There's the unreal world given us by the media, by our culture, by *every* culture—by the categories in which we're taught to think, the lens through which we're taught to see. Then there's God's world. We can't live our lives only in God's world. Indeed, in my stories my characters, while they may have intimations of God's world, usually end up falling back into the world of compromise. At the end of "The Man Who could See Radiance," the protagonist "saved his heart in a safe deposit vault and brought out small sums when he could." But we can experience intimations of God's world. Christians speak of "dying to the world." The world of our exile, the false world, the world of vanity, of the mall and big cars and status and power, power lunches and power shoes—that's the world I think they mean. We Jews share this meaning. The crucial element of the false world is the separation of the self from other people and from the whole pattern of energy we call the cosmos. To leave the false world by quieting your self, attuning yourself to God, working to restore God's world, is the *opposite* of going off as hero to do your own thing. This dichotomy is a basic paradigm in my own work and my own seeing, as it was in my son Josh's songs.

In this sense, more and more I've been writing religious fiction. In "The Man Who could See Radiance" my protagonist, Peter Weintraub, perceives first a glow of energy emanating from other people, then begins to see more deeply. "If he looked too long, all the boundaries, the visible forms, would disappear. Like a computer engineer getting underneath the software, the hidden codes, underneath the program and even the machine language to the essential on-and-offs that you couldn't see." And "The Builder" begins, "So God is there. Simply *there*." In this story God is there for Michael—but Michael may be a little meshugah; he's certainly under stress.

In my recent stories, characters think about God, argue with God, speak about God with the same surety that they might speak about gravity or love. "Yisrael" means "God-wrestler." Jacob is given the name after he wrestles with the angel or with God the night before he is to meet Esau. The paradigm for prayer in the Talmud (Tractate Berachot) comes from the story of Hannah and Eli, the priest. Hannah, too, wrestles with God. Praying for a child, she makes demands on God; she is said to "attack Heaven"; it is said that Moses, too, "attacked heaven." By staying *in the ring*, staying within the template over experience that Torah yields, my characters are able to see life as tragic, not merely sad, are able to almost touch the mystery. And so my narrator Max in "The Contract," is, like Hannah, *inside the ring*. He's a pugilist, not a nihilist—a member of the Covenant, playing by the rules of Torah. He doesn't deny or negate the sacredness of the world; he assumes we're in a world infused by the sacred. This gives him the right and ability to speak to God and to Moses. To complain. He assumes that life and death are meaningful, that the world has depth and dignity. As I write at the end of my novel *Kuperman's Fire*, "The Kaddish begins: *Let God's name be made great and holy in the world that was created as God willed.* If you mourn, don't you have to grieve for the loss of something beautiful? Can't we celebrate that there is something worth the mourning—a world created as God willed?"

Loss is important only because what's loved has value.

Depth and dignity: these are no easy assumptions to make in a world so filled with evil and with suspicion. Evil I don't need to speak about here; but *suspicion*: it's become fashionable in the postmodern West to suspect any search for essential meaning, for depth under surfaces. There are only surfaces. It's not just that the world may be meaningless—this intuition can be found all through twentieth-century literature—but that the search for meaning is meaningless—that the concept of meaning is a kind of embarrassing essentialism. But my fiction does search for meaning while trying to avoid ideology—religious ideology as much as any other. I think of one of those pictures that at first seem a two-dimensional pattern but which, when stared at awhile, reveal a vibrant three-dimensionality. Nothing has changed. You're still looking at the same surface. But what seemed only surface turns out to express depth.

My fiction, secular or religious, has always been Jewish. Almost all the major characters are Jewish. But I'm thinking more of its focus on the intensely connected family, on parents' love for children and their suffering over children, on the dynamics of family, and especially on the family from generation to generation—parents of children who themselves grow up to become parents of children who become.... The stories are increasingly Jewish because of their growing emphasis, in language from Torah and Jewish tradition, on the possibility and value of living a life that is at times suffused with the holy. And they're Jewish (in, all right, a less self-congratulatory way) because of the empathy, guilt, and burden of moral responsibility that are in the stories. They're about *Teshuvah,* turning to God, about *Tikun olam,* repairing the world. Empathy, moral responsibility, guilt, *Teshuvah, Tikun olam*—are these necessarily Jewish? At least I'd claim that they are found in a great deal of Jewish fiction; when they are present, we associate the fiction with Jewish life.

Saul Bellow, whom I respect deeply, have learned from, more than from anyone, and have written about extensively, was uncomfortable with the designation of *Jewish writer.* He wanted to be considered simply a *writer*. He didn't want to be limited to an ethnic ghetto. Who does? But it's not a question of whether he wished to be called Jewish. Being Jewish often entered his fiction as a *category of being*. Just as James Baldwin and Toni Morrison are black writers, though they write for all of us, Bellow is, like it or not, Jewish. An example: in his extraordinary coming-of-age story "Something to Remember Me By," Louie doesn't just happen to be Jewish; being Jewish is a mode specifically set against the brash, tough life of the Chicago streets. Me, I have no objections to the label of Jewish writer. I believe that by becoming more aware of my Jewish roots, I've become a stronger writer. Ruth Wisse writes, "Some critics have mistaken the broad appeal of Jewish writing for proof that it belongs to no particular people, but this is to confuse universalism, which seeks to eliminate tribal categories, with universality, which is the global resonance of a tribal work" (*Modern Jewish Canon,* p. 19). I hope for Jewish and non-Jewish readers; but I speak as a Jew.

Bodies of the Rich
(1984)

An Old 3 A.M. Story

Six months now, he and the kids were without Jenny. A year if you counted the time in the hospital—and just before the hospital, when Jenny locked herself in the bedroom and wouldn't come out. Now she was in New York; Peter was on his own with the kids in Cambridge. Hustling mornings to get them out of the apartment—dropping Tony, age two and a half, at daycare, and Sara, age seven, at school. Then getting to work at the mall.

He worked as a carpenter. Even after college he'd been unable to think of anything he liked better than working with wood. He liked making things and seeing them whole. He hated the dust but liked ripping out walls in old houses and making new, open spaces, adding decks and sliders, stripping walls to bare brick; felt good building a hutch or a set of bunk beds. But these past few months he'd been working at a huge shopping mall being built a few miles outside of Boston. Who needed another goddamned mall? He could imagine himself taking part in a community protest, writing pamphlets, marching with a sign—what the hell—old muscles from Vietnam protests, nearly atrophied, twitching; and yet here he was, not just building a mall but feeling good about the work, like being a member of a collective in China—all the crews, hundreds of men, the progress visible in a single day: like watching time-lapse photography.

He spent that morning framing and sheathing a storefront, then ate lunch at the decorative fountain in the center of the mall and listened to talk about the Bruins—a "constructo" for real, with his stainless-steel thermos and shaggy moustache full of sawdust. He wasn't thinking about the kids; unless they were sick, he rarely thought about them when he was on the job. But mid-afternoon, a painter drove a small electric cart into some three-stage scaffolding, and the whole frame of pipes crashed to the cement. He was on the other side of the central square—not even *nearly* hurt—but two of the guys had, ten seconds before, come down off the scaffolding from taping the sheetrock ceiling, and one was furious.

"You asshole! Twenty-four feet, you asshole, twenty-four feet, you coulda killed me, you coulda wasted me." The guy's voice echoed through the enormous space, echoed inside Peter's fantasy—himself carted off to the hospital or maybe dead, and the kids, what would happen then? Who the hell even knew where they *were* except for him? He realized, Jesus, he'd have to write a note with his buddy Frank's telephone number, then give Frank his parents' number in Indianapolis. Not Jenny's. For sure not Jenny's. And he'd have to *tell* somebody at work. But not at that moment, not so soon after the accident.

The rest of the afternoon, he was a little spooked. The safety guard on the circular saw…hammers falling off the scaffolding…

Then, driving back to Cambridge, he listened to news of a jet crash. Suddenly, every other rush-hour driver was a maniac or a drunk. In defense, he hunched over the wheel.

He let them play in the bath together, while he sat beside them reading the *Phoenix,* looking up to answer questions, rolling up his sleeves for "some serious scrubbing," while Tony yelled in protest and all Peter really wanted was to get them to bed so he himself could soak in the tub.

The phone rang. Never able to let a call go unanswered, he dried his hands and trotted to the kitchen.

"Hello, Peter."

She hadn't called for two, three months. He was full of reproaches but didn't hand her any. "What is it?"

"Thanks for being so understanding. Jesus, Peter. I mean your tone of voice. Well, it's almost Christmas."

"What about it? I'm busy, Jenny. The kids are alone in the tub."

"Well, I got sad, thinking of Sara and Tony and Christmas. *You* know. Can't you understand that? I want to talk with Sara."

"Well, she's in the bathtub." From the bathroom, Tony was yelling for him. "Listen, I've got to get off now. Call back if you want to talk to them." Hanging up, he felt as if he'd locked her up inside the phone.

A few minutes later, she called again. "Peter—are they available now?"

He called, "Sara? It's your mother." As if it were an everyday thing. But while he did the dishes, he kept an eye on Sara. As if she were climbing rocks, he watched for signs of danger or pain.

"Sure," Sara was saying. "Sure, Mommy. Sure…sure."

What, Peter wondered, did Jenny need reassurance about? His body hunched over the pots. The Mad Dishwasher of Cambridge, furious *just in case* she had the nerve to ask Sara about their well-being.

"Do you want to speak to Daddy?" But Jenny didn't, because Sara nodded. "Goodbye, Mommy." And hung up.

Peter didn't ask. He scrubbed.

"Mommy said she wants to see us."

"She said that in October."

"She said it's Christmas and she has to see us."

"Who's stopping her?"

"Because she misses us."

"She probably does." He stopped. She probably did. He had it easy, compared. His usual line. Then—like hell she does. Needing reassurance isn't the same as missing people.

"It's almost Christmas."

"Well, maybe she'll come this time."

"She promised."

"Okay, okay."

"You never believe anything." Sara slammed down a book and marched out, brushing past Tony, who started crying.

"Oh, hell. Oh, hell." Peter sucked a deep breath and started after Sara to comfort. Stopped. "Tony—hey, you want some hot chocolate?" He went to the cupboard for the cocoa powder. Maybe the smell would get to Sara, would bring her back.

Jenny stepped down, delicate, uncertain, from the train, and Peter wanted to protect—to take her suitcase, to take her hand—the old story, family whole again, Jenny home from a trip.

"Mama, hi, Mama," Tony said, a pretty song, as if Mama had been away for the day, but then Sara ran to her as if it were a dance, and Jenny hugged Sara up into her arms and whirled her into an orgasm of reunion, and the excess of the gesture brought it all back, and he set himself, tense, against the shock of her. There she was, milking the moment, letting the pain rain down on her, defenseless, eyes wet. Goddamned if I'll let her in me. Peter lifted Tony to his shoulders and waved. Suitcase in one hand, Sara in the other, Jenny smiled, stumbled over a crack in the pavement, shook her head at her own clumsiness, listening to Sara, nodding madly at Sara's story.

"Peter, hello. The train was late."

"Not very. You hungry?"

"I wish I were. I'm getting so skinny. I used to worry about being fat."

"You've cut your hair?"

"Uh-huh. But you, Peter, now you've gained a little weight—around the shoulders. You look nice."

"It's just the winter coat," he said, not wanting to brag about the muscles he was getting as a carpenter. He took her suitcase.

"*That* coat," she said, linking her arm into his as they walked up the station steps. "One of the firms that advertise on the show makes these beautiful alpine coats. I'm going to send you one. I insist.

The head of their advertising department is crazy about me. Do you like tan suede?"

He couldn't help laughing at her act, and Sara joined in without knowing why, and Jenny blushed and hid her face in the collar of her coat. "You think I'm silly, I can tell."

Suitcase in the trunk of the VW, family filling the seats. "So your job is working out?" he asked.

"Oh, I have so much to tell you," she said. "Everything is almost perfect. I feel I'm *growing* so much. I do, Peter. And not just in the work. It's only sad because I miss you so much," she said to Sara and Tony, and turned in her seat to touch them both and giggle and cry. "It's so good to see you." Then—"All of you."

His jaw set hard against her, Peter drove across the Charles, hating her like a poison in their lives, Jenny coming back to raise hopes in Sara. He remembered her sitting in the bathroom with her wrists cut, drunk, stupefied on downers, bleeding into the bath and weeping. He'd heard her sobbing, but she wouldn't open, and he heard her and had to smash in the door; she smiled up at him like a guilty child and he wished he could turn around, stay in the kitchen for an hour, until the bathwater turned from pink to red. Instead, he'd grabbed her—"Where's Sara? Where's Sara and where's Tony!"—thinking oh my God how crazy *was* she! But she said, "With Mrs. Stanley." Innocent. A child herself. Then she wept again, and, hating her, he had to yank her out of the tub, wrap her in a blanket, and drive her to the hospital. Then go home to clean up the bathroom mess before he could collect the kids. "Your mother's sick," he'd told Sara.

That was the only day she'd tried. Unless you counted the afternoon she burned up all the snapshots of herself from their album, leaving only pictures of the kids or sometimes torn pieces with only Sara left or Peter and Tony, Jenny torn away. He'd wanted to kill her that day, but he ended mourning with her the loss of those pictures, the two of them crying and making love on the couch in the living room.

"Have you been doing any therapy?" he asked, casually as he could, as he carried her suitcase up their staircase.

She was. Oh, yes. And it was *very* exciting, but by the time he went to the kitchen to fix dinner, he'd forgotten—was it *primal* or *transactional analysis,* something like that, a therapy that permitted her to pour herself out.

A laugh, Sara's laugh. Jenny's voice. He stopped cutting vegetables. He poured himself into the quiet of her voice, imagining Jenny cajoling, lying about their marriage. He wished Sara were old enough to understand. What she understood was that her mother, who never saw her, was perfect. And if her perfect mother didn't want to see her, she, Sara, must be pretty worthless. Her mother—who had this wonderful, special job in TV (every week Sara watched the quiz show Jenny helped produce) and wonderful, special life.

"Pete—where's all the records?"

He carried his scotch into the living room. "What records, Jenny?" He knew. He remembered the satisfaction he'd felt boxing all her ugly rock music and taking it down to his car. Like getting rid of all those Sundays when he walked around the house with wax plugs in his ears and the place smelled of dope and that heavy beat vibrated through his chest and in self-defense he'd have to take Sara off to the Children's Museum. Or nights when Jenny and what was his name?—Ernst—sat up late with headphones, listening to.... He boxed the goddamned things and sold them at a record store. Bought Stravinsky, lots and lots of 1920s Stravinsky, classical, cool, to clean the air. "The records. You mean the rock 'n' roll?"

"You threw them out, didn't you? Oh, Pete."

He shrugged, not wanting to admit his profits. She poked through the plastic milk-bottle cases they used for record bins until she found *Rubber Soul.* Well, how could he get rid of the Beatles? She put it on—too loud—and closed her eyes as Paul McCartney sang "Michelle." Her curls, tight around her head, made her look like a boy—Spanish or Italian. She'd lost the long, flowing, wispy quality that had always seemed to him such a con. This new style said *no nonsense.*

Later on, the children asleep, she talked about the *realities* of New York. "I mean," she said, blowing out cigarette smoke to make her point, "they don't screw *around* in New York. They're always watching to see are you *on* or are you *off.* I try to be *on.*"

He scrubbed the rice pot. Scrubbed it passionately.

"I've been part of a women's self-help project. I've opened up a lot of the anger I'd been feeling. It feels awfully good to let go so much. I feel I can talk straighter with you. I mean you're not someone…with any power over my life. You're just a person."

Suddenly, hearing powerful, true words used to manufacture a new, fake Jenny, he grew sad; he wanted to cry for her. Well, mostly for her. "Power over my life" was a hand-me-down from a poem they both loved. Jenny was a hand-me-down from a bunch of beautiful poems. And he had been married to her. He still was.

"Make me a milk and bourbon, will you, Pete? I'm going to collect some of my plants." She took a cardboard box into the living room, and he grew instantly nauseated with fear and poured himself another whiskey.

It was the kids, of course. Her power to take away. But funny thing—it was also the goddamned plants. When she'd been with him, he could make fun of those plants, fun of the frills she brought in. But he needed a certain grace she also brought in. Croissants—even if frozen and heated up—on Sunday mornings. Espresso coffee she ground herself. Pretty dresses from the thrift shops for Sara. So he could say, "Who gives a damn? Jeans look great on her." Since Jenny went away, he found himself looking in the windows of shops. Not knowing what to buy. So Sara wore jeans. And she did look great. But he missed the pretty dresses.

Jenny came back and sipped. "Oh, Pete. I'll say one thing for you. You make a fine toddy."

Later on, he slept in his bed, Jenny on the living room couch. He had to steel himself *not* to offer her the bedroom, take the couch for himself. He compromised by taking down the clean sheets and making a bed for her while she watched. Then he lay down alone in their old bed and listened to the couch creak.

Listened to Jenny get up and wander. Imagined her slipping into his bedroom with a kitchen knife, and then the knife dissolved, she was there to make love with him, and he turned in bed, pretending to be shuffling in his sleep until she touched him and he felt her thighs against his shoulder…Christ. He shook it off and turned on the light to read. Saw himself going to the kitchen for something, and she was waiting for him, smiling up from the couch. He couldn't even leave his bedroom; imagined sitting up with her. Old 3 A.M. story.

What was she doing out there? He heard the toilet flush. Smelled the sulfur trail of another cigarette. Or was she doing up a joint to help her sleep? He saw her alone in the living room of a house that wasn't hers anymore and felt pity for her. He wanted to comfort.

Laying down his book, he tiptoed in as if to the bathroom, glancing past into the living room:

In a velvet robe Jenny was sitting up in bed with headphones on, reading a copy of the *Village Voice* she'd brought with her. Her jeans, panties still inside, tumbled over the old spool table, and on the floor, her shoe, her blouse, her other shoe.

She didn't even see him.

Peter sat on the edge of the bathroom sink and laughed at himself. You dummy! Dummy!

The next day, day before Christmas, Peter slept late. Delicious to sleep late, to hear Tony's nonsense song and not have to do anything about it. And the smell of something baking!—he never baked—and Sara's laughter. He took a long, long shower and came to breakfast with senses open and body humming. On the stereo the *Christmas Oratorio,* by Bach. How nice of her!

"The women in this family," Jenny announced, "are going shopping. Do you *realize* it's almost Christmas!—and look at this place."

He started apologizing. The work at the mall. How hard to do shopping at night—

"Oh, Peter, I'm not blaming you, you poor nut. Wow. I know how hard it's been. Sure. It's my fault in the first place, isn't it?"

He found himself saying, "No listen, Jenny, don't blame yourself—you needed—"

"We're off to buy a tree," she said. She was wearing knee-high soft leather boots, her jeans tucked inside: power clothes. He was annoyed at this pretense of strength. And excited.

"We're *just* going to buy a tree, Daddy." Sara exchanged glances with her mother. How much she looked like Jenny! Her black hair longer now, but the same wide-set eyes, high cheekbones, and broad mouth. With the same way her mother had of twisting her mouth when she got angry. The same brooding; the same high anger.

"Well, then it's you and me, Tony," Peter said. "We've got a little surprise going ourselves." And Tony sang, "Sooo-prizzze!"

Jenny looked him in the eyes. "We're family, Pete." Real tears in her eyes. And he said to himself, Aach, you crazy bitch!

"Family, huh?"

"You don't believe that? Peter! Jesus Christ!" And for a moment he expected her to reach across the round table and scratch his face as she did once. He wanted nothing but peace today. He smiled. "Okay, family. It's beautiful."

On the stereo the "Pastoral Symphony" from the *Messiah*. Strings in 6/8 time seducing the soul into a manger. A house of peace.

All morning, while he worked at Frank's on Sara's dollhouse, he remembered that manger. He hummed and he sang. As a kid growing up in Indianapolis, he'd loved to sing. He'd joined the boys' choir at the Episcopalian church downtown, and now, every Christmas, his heart was full of liturgical music by Bach, Handel, Mozart. Full of the imagination of Christ. As he worked, he sang, "For unto us a child is born," while a child born just over two years before unto him and Jenny tapped nails into a scrap of two-by-four. Then Peter wrapped the dollhouse walls and floors and tied up the cardboard carton with blocks he'd cut and sanded and oiled for Tony's present, and together he and Tony went off to the Coop to find a present for Jenny. What could you give ex-wives but maybe earrings, crescents silver like moons, an ironic gesture to Jenny as Moon Lady, gesture she wouldn't catch but that didn't matter; the point was for him to feel the gift as a humorous offering, establishing a controlled distance. Pleased with the gift, he spent his change on ice cream for Tony and himself.

"Sara! Sara!" Tony yelled when the downstairs buzzer rang. Buzzing back, Peter heard a clumping and a clattering and the same laughing, conspiratorial voices that scared him, but he opened the door, shouted "Hello, hello," and ran down to help haul in the tree.

"Oh, Peter, what a ridiculous time we had getting this home. We carried it, and it was *so* far!"

"It's wonderful. Let me help."

"Please be careful, Daddy," Sara said. He laughed and felt furious. The Women. He got the old crooked tree stand out of the closet and a box of ornaments, none special, some cracked. A set of lights with only half the bulbs working.

"We got tons more lights," Jenny said. "Oh, and ornaments and one gorgeous glass ball at the Coop, but it was so expensive so you know what I did, Peter?—I pocketed it. Like the old days."

"I remember," he said. Looking at the glass ball, so beautiful, he felt nauseated. The shabbiness of that kind of stealing! And suddenly, the tree showed itself for what it was, a skimpy, leftover, day-before-Christmas spruce that could only be faked up with a lot more lights and more ornaments than they owned.

He remembered that kind of shopping—when they were first together. He'd buy the potatoes, she'd purse the steak. So he was dull and plodding while she was magic, could produce smoked oysters out of coat linings.

They put up the tree lights, and Tony shrieked, "Tree, Sara!" and Sara wanted none of him. "He won't let me alone, Mommy!" Peter lifted him up so he could touch the lights, the star at the top, and place, one at a time, icicles of foil on the branches.

"There! Look at that, huh?" Jenny stepped back and saw, Peter supposed, a tree that could make somebody's life whole and glowing.

"I'll check on the turkey."

"Peter! Did you stuff it? I'll bet you did. You're a riot." He must have looked hurt—she touched his arm—"I'm teasing, dope. Wow. It's sweet of you. A real Christmas Eve dinner, right? Of course, I'm a vegetarian. No—I'm kidding."

Mashing the potatoes, he forgot about her. When he wiped his hands on his apron and went back into the living room, he found her sitting crosslegged in front of the tree, bawling, bawling, and Tony, on her lap, touching her face.

He sat down beside her. "It's going to be tough for a while."

"We used to have such a beautiful Christmas when I was a kid."

"And you want it to be nice for them. Listen," he said, "I really appreciate your coming up." And at that moment, it was true, although five minutes before or after, it was anything but true. Just then, he wanted to protect and to heal.

At dinner, Jenny, feeling better, sat next to Sara, and the two of them giggled, giggled, and exchanged looks. He knew these secrets weren't hostile—some Christmas present, he supposed. But then Sara wouldn't drink her milk and said furiously, "I don't *have* to drink my milk," and her eyes welled with tears, and he shrugged, he backed off—"Hey, no big thing. What's the big deal? *So don't.*" But she stayed upset, and when Tony chimed the tines of his fork against the glass, she grabbed it out of his hand. Of course he howled and grabbed, and she threw the fork down. "He *always* does that. There's no *peace* around here!" And she stormed off.

The tree lights were on; in the darkened living room the tree looked as though it belonged in a real family. Peter had taken a book of carols out of the library and got everyone to sit around on the floor and sing. For a few minutes he was in the Episcopal church in Indianapolis, practicing carols for a choir recital. Tony babbled, Sara hummed, Jenny sang in harmonies that never worked. Peter sang a tenor that was still clear and full, enjoying the sound of his own singing.

"San-a-law!" Tony sang. Santa Claus.

"Sure," Peter said.

"We have a surprise for you," Jenny said, closing Peter's book of carols. "Sara and I."

"Shouldn't that wait till tomorrow?"

"Not that kind of surprise," Jenny said. "Isn't Daddy silly?"

"We'll open presents in the morning, right?" he said.

"Not that, you silly daddy!" Sara laughed.

"Sara and I decided—to be a couple of big girls in New York together."

"Jenny!"

"Mommy says there's room now, there wasn't before, but now Mommy says—"

"Think again, Jenny. Goddamn you, how could you lay that on her? We'll talk about this later."

"There's *room* is the point, Daddy."

"I don't see what's so strange," Jenny said. "My God. I thought you'd appreciate it. I mean, I can't take care of Tony right now, but I'm getting stronger, and it's something to think about, but Jesus, what's so special—"

"Well," he said, "well, I don't see anything so terrible about it. I think that's fine, maybe next weekend for a couple of days."

"Peter, this isn't a joke."

"I'll visit you a lot, Daddy, and you can visit me."

"Well, it's certainly something to think about," he said. "Christ, yes, it's certainly something to consider, Sara."

"It'll be fun in New York, Daddy."

"Oh, sure." He munched a Christmas cookie, another.

"Do you have to freak out?" Jenny, in control now, went to the stereo and found the Beatles. "I want your help in this thing." He didn't answer.

"I can get a lawyer, you know."

"No, you don't need to do that, Jenny." *He'd* need to get himself a lawyer. Establish custody. The whole deal. Why had he thought he could get away without it? "Let's get the kids to bed, Jenny."

Jenny helped Sara wash up while he changed Tony. He sang to Tony, "Now Tony's pants are coming off…now he's getting tickled…now he's getting nice dry powder…" all the time listening to Jenny tell Sara about TV, about the subway she took to work in the morning, about the gorgeous shops along Fifth Avenue. In court he could claim desertion; she would say she was establishing a career. He could prove mental instability; but she was doing therapy, and in court she'd seem a perfect mother. And it would take years. With Sara bitter every day…

But suppose Sara went off with Jenny. Hardly aware of Tony, he got him ready for bed, rehearsing a plea to Jenny—Don't know what I'd do without her...frightened for her.... He saw Jenny in an evening crying jag, Jenny slamming out of her apartment leaving Sara alone. As if it had already happened, Peter's head throbbed with his anger. Then he became aware once more that he was with Tony—Tony in the crib now—and rubbed his back and sang him good night.

Where were they? Then he heard them in Sara's room. Standing in Tony's doorway, he squeezed tight his eyes and let the pain come, and without making a sound, he howled, he mourned in advance. Collecting himself, he went into the living room to wait for Jenny.

But Jenny didn't arrive. She wrapped presents. He could hear the crackle of the foil. So he put Sara's dollhouse together and stepped back to look, loving it, more pleased than if it had been an addition he'd been hired to build. Then, covering it with one enormous sheet of wrapping foil, he put it under the tree with Tony's blocks and with Jenny's earrings in a box so tiny it could hardly be seen beside the two huge packages.

Then Jenny came in with her boxes. "Well, *finally,* Peter." She flopped back, exhausted, on the old couch.

"Well, Jenny. We'd better make plans. So much to think out. School for one thing. And clothes. And Sara's friends. Saying goodbye."

"We're not going to make a fuss, Peter."

"No—no fuss," he said. Suddenly it came to him. What he was doing. "No. I'll leave it all in your hands." It came to him; he felt crazy with excitement. "You just tell me if you need help."

"I appreciate it, your understanding. I've got the prettiest curtain for Sara's bed, I mean you've never seen the apartment, well, it's one bedroom, my bedroom, and a kind of living room, you know, with a kitchenette? We'll curtain off a part of the living room. With a pretty red curtain. So she'll have some privacy?"

"That sounds nice," he said. "Of course, it's a little tough when you have someone over. Late at night. But you can handle it."

"There'll be just the two of us," she said. "Don't worry."

"Well, that's up to you. But maybe it'll be hard for a while. I mean, coming straight home after work, making sure there's a sitter you can trust for after school. And then, when she gets sick. Or when *you* get sick. Last month I had a wipe-out flu for almost a week. I'd hear the kids in the kitchen and just couldn't make it out of bed..." Peter sipped his whiskey. "What school will she be going to?"

Jenny rolled a joint, half tobacco, and sitting on the floor by the tree, smoked and thumbed through the records. "Hey, Christmas music," she said. "I remember," and pulled Handel's *Messiah,* a boxed set, from the shelf. "I remember this. Every Christmas. And this morning on the radio."

"I sang it a couple of times," he said. "So. What about school? Is it close by? But I guess you'll figure that out when you get there?"

"Sure. Whatever the goddamned *district* is, Peter."

Peter went into the kitchen for a whiskey, stayed to sharpen the kitchen knives on a carborundum attachment to his electric drill. He felt relieved by the steady concentration. Over the whine of the drill he heard the first notes of the overture that begins the *Messiah.* Always it thickened his breath with sadness and, at the same time, fullness of being. His fantasy—when he was an adolescent singing the music, nervous at the first bars as he looked down at the sheets in his hand and past the conductor to the silent church full of people—was of vast, spiritual dignitaries in procession, powers into which he could be absorbed, his personal indignities dissolved. Again tonight. The deep, rich breaths made him need to listen. He turned off the drill and put the knives away.

Jenny's eyes were closed; she was spinning into the music and nodding, nodding to encourage the grass to do its work on her head.

Hearing him, she looked up. "You funny man," she said. "You're being too easy, you know what I mean? Too accommodating. I dig. You think you'll scare me off? I mean, you want me to know how tough it's going to be?"

"Maybe it won't, for you."

"Peter, don't you think I have the goddamned right? Really?" He didn't answer.

"Because of a few months? And okay—I was pretty depressed for a while. I don't say I was the best mother in the world, but who the hell took care of them when they were babies? Peter? And I don't mean just fed and changed them, right?"

Recriminations caught in his throat. His temples pulsed with *shoulds, didn'ts, nevers.* He stuffed them down into himself; he closed his eyes. It was true, what she said was true. He was a Johnny-come-lately. Or almost true. True enough. The old trick of seeing from every side. During the Vietnam protests, he'd never been able to think of university administrators or police as "fascist pigs." Always he imagined himself on the other side of the police line. And tonight he found himself imagining Jenny's defense—You always made me feel crazy, incompetent. If I have to handle a child, I'll grow up…

She stood up and touched his cheek. "Peter? You know, listen, maybe we can sleep together tonight? You know, I miss you in bed. You get to feel nostalgia for another person's smells and the way he touches you. Funny Peter."

He didn't answer.

She shrugged. "Well, listen—" she smiled. "No big thing, Peter." She hummed to the music. "Nice, huh? Kids asleep. Why couldn't it be like this?" She laughed. *"I don't* mean I want to *try* it again or anything like that. Just it's too bad. Lots of things are too bad." She danced in a circle, jarring the tree slightly. A set of lights went out. Peter jiggled the lights, and, mysteriously, they flickered on again. "You've always been a good father," she said. "I've always told you."

"It's exhausting. You're never able to drop your guard. That's what's so tough. You can never stop. And then, there's the money. Sara's going to need new clothes. She's sticking out of everything. And not just the money, but there go your weekends." He laughed sharply, as if he were expelling the joke rather than enjoying it. "Yes, that's right. I'm saying all this to scare you…" But saying it as strategy, he became aware how true it was. He felt, more than he had for months, the weight of parenting.

He rambled on, as if she were taking notes. Sara's winter coat was torn. She needed new boots. Medicine twice a day for her rash. Box up her dolls and her sleeping bag. You can take a taxi from Penn

Station. As he talked, he felt a burden lifting—but leaving a pocket of bleakness. "I can take the dollhouse apart."

"Can't you bring it down when you come? Everything doesn't have to be there at once, for godsakes."

"But it's her new dollhouse."

"All right. Somehow..."

"I wanted to teach her to build furniture for the dolls. It's a nice way to learn to use tools."

Jenny laughed. "Well, that *will* have to wait." She closed her eyes and sat back on the couch. Chilly, she covered herself with a blanket. Her short, curly black hair and the shapeless blanket made her look suddenly very young, a child herself, younger than when he'd first met her. And at once his heart opened to her. As if he felt comfortable, he stretched. "I'll get ready for bed."

Lying in the dark he could hear her take a shower and paddle back to the couch. Could hear the whine of her blow dryer, hear her plug in the headphone jack and snap on the power. Suddenly a muffled, "Oh, *shit...*" Barefoot, he went to the door.

"Everything's dark, Peter. It's the fuse. I washed my hair, and I was drying it and the headphones besides—have you got another fuse?"

"Sorry," he said. "Why don't you get some sleep?"

The tree was dark. He could see her in the pale light of the street lamp through the window and the reflected light from the kitchen.

"Well, my hair," she pouted. He laughed. She got up from the couch, and he laughed some more—she was dressed in a pair of his winter long johns that flapped and bulged and bloomed over her young-girl body. *"Please don't laugh."* She waddled into the kitchen, hair gun in hand.

He went back to bed; far off, the hair dryer whined. He lay in the dark, imagining her sitting up chilly and bored in the kitchen. He heard the clink of his liquor bottles. Then she creaked across the old floor to the couch. No light, no music. But it was too early for her to fall asleep. Eleven-fifteen, eleven-thirty? She'd be up for hours, lying and itching in the dark.

Good.

Give her the time to feel what it was going to be like as a mother.

But a few minutes of listening and imagining and Peter was himself not able to sleep. He imagined Sara sleeping behind a red curtain; he buried his head in his pillow for comfort.

What's the use? Might as well be Father Christmas one more time. He got up, slipped into a robe, stood in the doorway expecting to find Jenny trying to sleep. But there she was again in her red velvet robe, sitting up, with headphones on. He could see a long black extension cord trailing away into the kitchen.

"Oh, hi, Pete," she said, overly loud because of the headphones.

"This time I didn't plug in everything at once." She took off the headphones. "Joni Mitchell. You kept her stuff at least."

"Come to bed with me," he said, not having known he meant to say it. He saw himself as powerful, protective. But his voice didn't sound powerful to himself, and he wished he could say it over again—*Come to bed with me.* But he just waited. She smiled, she shrugged and turned off the power on the stereo and stumbled to him across the dark room, and he knew at once how hungry he was for her, needing her in his cells, not having known in advance, the way he needed caffeine when he'd tried to kick coffee a few months back.

She took his hand, let him lead her back to the bed they'd shared for years. And he felt furious with her—that she was doing this to him. And furious at how short she'd cut her hair as he held it in his hands and kissed her. She laughed, then, a strange burst of laughter, and began to bite him and scratch him lightly with her nails, as if he were some new lover, nothing like the old ways, and he pulled at her to force her down and tugged open the robe, ripping off a button, wanting to wound her, to make her afraid, furious that she was going to—*enjoy* this.

Under her robe, his thermal underwear. She cooperated like a child, lifting her arms, as he pulled it off. Then she wrapped herself in her own arms and curled under the covers.

When he came into her, she was wet the way she never used to be. He didn't love her at that moment; he wanted to use the thrust of his hips to break down this new composure, this—amusement. Usually he had sweated for her satisfaction, pacing himself to her, watching her face for signs, but tonight the sign he was looking for was submission, was fear.

She flipped her head side to side, side to side. Was she with him, crazy Jenny, or inside her own rhythm? He found himself trying to reach her now as if she were down inside a deep cave and the thrusts of his body were like shouting down into the cave after her and she wouldn't answer. Louder and louder, pushing aside everything in his way, wanting to hear, Oh, Peter, you hurt me, Peter you hurt me, but he couldn't reach her, and then he himself, it was he himself, pouring out, as if wounded, yelling, "Bitch! Bitch!"

She was holding on to his hips, very, very concentrated, as if this were a puzzle and she almost, almost had the answer; and then, oh yes, she *had* it, and moaned, oh, oh, oh, and laughed, and he was furious at her easy pleasure and found himself shaking, he was shivering not from cold but from the inside, he was weeping.

"Peter, baby, it's okay. What is it?" He let her lean over him and smooth his back and run her fingernails through his hair. "My poor Peter."

He blew his nose; they both laughed at the trumpeting and then he pressed his cheek against her small breasts and she held him and he felt himself flowing away into her and didn't know why he was weeping.

Though she was curled away from him in the bed, something in the set of her shoulders told him she, too, wasn't sleeping. He imagined her with that worried-child look on her face.

He nudged her.

"Uh-huh?"

"Jenny? Are you okay?"

"What?"

She turned and touched his face. "I'm sorry for you. I feel bad for you."

He shrugged. At that moment he hated her.

"Peter? It freaks me out. Being here? And you're so vulnerable, Pete, I mean I really hurt you, and I hadn't figured. I thought you'd feel relieved, my going away."

"You're not hurting me. It's just a confusion. Jenny? Let's get some sleep."

"No, listen—what freaks me out the most is just being here. I didn't know how shaky I was going to feel. In bed with you? Jesus Christ, and nothing is finished or clear. Except that I'm getting all these panic feelings. You want some coffee? You want to sit in the kitchen?"

He remembered the 3 A.M. nights, postmortems on lovemaking, disquisitions on her insecurities, what kind of mother? What kind of woman? While he listened and nodded. Maybe she should go back to school?

In what?

Who the hell knows? Peter? I feel like my eyes always want to cry.

What does Dr. Schaeffer tell you?

His favorite word, Peter, is *appropriate.* And *inappropriate.* I'm being as appropriate as I can, Peter. Jesus Christ, do I work hard at being appropriate…

The old story. The old song. He'd listen and he'd listen. Not anymore. "Not tonight," he said. "Please, Jenny. We'll be up for Christmas as soon as it's light. Tomorrow."

"Yeah. So goodnight. Goodnight." She laughed the old laugh, really a multiple catch of breath with a tiny high ring to it, like a dog whining at the door. "Kiss me?"

He kissed her. They retreated both to their own sides of the bed. Lying with his back to Jenny, he was intensely aware of her body behind his. Until, finally, unable to sleep, he whispered, "Okay, if you want to talk…Jenny?" But she was asleep.

Christmas morning. Sara stood at the foot of the bed, silent, with eyes that denied curiosity or caring. And he, in turn, played cheerful Daddy, rubbed his hands together in anticipation he didn't feel. Over coffee they opened gifts. While Tony and Sara unwrapped their stocking presents, Jenny kissed Peter for the earrings and, tilting her head to one side and then the other, tried them on and danced, Moon Goddess, around the living room—old pine floor needing new varnish, worn scatter rugs threatening to spill the dancer; Sara clapped and Tony imitated Sara.

"I'm taking modern dance again," Jenny said.

Then Peter opened his present from Jenny—a pair of fine leather work boots. He let Sara and Tony feel how heavy, how sturdy…

"Sara helped pick them out," Jenny said, still twirling. "I mean if you *have* to be a carpenter for some reason."

"What's wrong with my being a carpenter?"

"Oh, funny Peter." She kissed his cheek.

Then Peter and Jenny opened potholders and paintings, and Sara took the wrapping off her dollhouse and screamed, "Daddy! Daddy!" and Tony wanted to play with it and began to cry, but Peter helped undo the wrappings of Tony's blocks, saying, "Ohhh, look, it's blocks, Tony-blocks!" and Tony quieted, repeated "Ohhh, blocks," and watched Peter stack them, then stacked some himself. "And Sara, honey, you and I are going to make most of the furniture for your dollhouse ourselves. I'll teach you carpentry. Do you want to learn carpentry?"

"Uh-huh." But her head was stuck inside the second floor of the dollhouse; she looked out through a dollhouse window.

Jenny stopped dancing. "Sara, why don't you open that box over there?" Sara, eyes already staring somewhere beyond the room, undid the wrappings.

"Try it on."

For a minute, Sara didn't get it. Just clothes. Then she let out a screech and ran off to the bathroom. Peter raised his eyebrows—Jenny just smiled.

Suddenly a pink ballerina twirled out of the bathroom and spun across the floor, arms raised. "Look! *Everything.* Even the ballet slippers!" Pink leotard and tights, shiny black slippers. Jenny danced around Sara, hummingbird around a flower. Peter saw the beauty and felt defeated.

"The rest of the present, baby, is lessons. Ballet. Or modern."

"Oh, Mommy!" Sara spun away.

"Lessons when you come down to visit Mommy."

That was the first sign. Peter studied her face. He didn't dare ask, afraid that if she realized her inconsistency, she'd erase it. Or maybe there was no inconsistency?

He began breakfast, hearing, as he beat up the pancake batter, the shush of Sara's new slippers. He sifted in baking powder as if making pancakes could be some kind of antidote to the poison drenching the cells of his heart. He turned on the kitchen radio—the *Messiah* again, *Messiah* for Christmas morning, but thin, tinny. He could have gone over to the stereo and heard the record over a good sound system. Why didn't he? Maybe because over the radio the music came from the outside world—as if this were a desert island and any contact was precious.

"I can't dance to that, Daddy." Sara stood, hands on hips, in the kitchen doorway.

"It's Christmas morning," he explained. "Handel is part of the deal, like Christmas trees and pancakes."

"Look," she said, and spun a cocoon of pink around herself.

Jenny was quiet during breakfast. Peter wolfed down pancake after pancake.

"In a few days," Jenny said, "I'll call everybody. Then we'll get set for you to come visit, baby."

"Come visit?"

"You'll love it in New York—we'll do all sorts of crazy things together."

"Mommy? Aren't I coming with you?"

"Well, that's really hard. With all your things? And your poor daddy—"

"Daddy? What did you tell her?" She sat fiercely straight. Tony threw his pancake on the floor, and Peter yelled, "Tony! Christ!" and Tony started to cry.

"Mommy, you said—"

"Well, I thought some more. Well, you know your mommy. Boy.

Do you look pretty in that outfit. You could be a beautiful dancer!" Jenny's eyes seemed glazed with tears. "A terrific, beautiful dancer."

"Mommy."

"Well, your mommy can't. I get scared…and then I can. And then I can't. But she will. And we'll have a good time."

Sara, scowling, scrunched down in her chair, arms crossed. Nobody had paid attention to Tony's crying; he stopped and was eating again, remembering from time to time to whine, "I want pancake." The pancake on the floor. Still on the floor. While the Robert Shaw Chorale burst into "Glory to God, glory to God in the highest…And peace on earth, good will towards men." Peter began to giggle, but, afraid of losing control, he stopped, he caressed Sara's hair. She shook free.

"Did you tell something to Mommy?"

Jenny pushed away from the table. "I'd better pack. My train's at one."

"Now for Christsakes, Jenny—"

"No, really, Pete. It *is*. Sara? Sara?"

But Sara ran into her room and slammed the door.

By the time the train stood in the station, Sara was squeezing her mother's hand.

"I'll call you in just a couple of days. I have to think about schools and sitters and then I'll call you and maybe I'll rent a car and drive up next weekend and off we'll go."

"You won't," Sara said, but she still held Jenny's hand.

"How the hell do you know what I'll do?" For a moment Jenny pulled back, livid. Then she hugged Sara, who stood like a statue, letting herself be hugged. "We'll dance together, baby. You'll love New York. There are so many…museums?" She kissed Sara and kissed Tony and gave Peter a hug. Her eyes were in panic. He looked away. She lugged her suitcase after her up the iron steps to the train. She waved from her seat.

Sara waved back solemnly.

Tony began to cry. He howled, "Mommy! Mommy!" and Jenny, not able to hear, smiled and blew kisses, and the panic wasn't in her eyes. She was a hip New York woman, very strong, curly jet-black hair, a broad, gay mouth. The train edged slowly out.

Sara wasn't talking. He ached to hold her and hear her cry it out, knowing it was as much his own tears that weren't being cried. At dinner she was sullen and polite. Later, while he was doing dishes, he heard Tony shriek and wail, and he rushed in. Sara yelled, "I know you're going to take his side," and ran to her room and locked the door. Tony's blocks lay scattered. "Sara hit, Sara hit." Peter kissed his elbow and, lifting Tony to comfort, stood outside Sara's door, tapping.

"Sweetheart? Sara? Do you think I made Mommy go away?" He waited and waited. Then the door lock clicked. Sara wouldn't look at Peter. She shrugged. "I guess not.... I don't know.... No." He stroked her hair, tentatively, as if she were a strange animal. "Your mommy went away. I didn't make her."

"Uh-huh."

"You believe me?"

"Uh-huh."

He wasn't sure what he himself believed.

He felt the silence of the apartment and put the Beatles on the stereo again. Preparing for the next day, he laid out clothes and made sandwiches, feeling the weight of making the family *run,* the weight of putting things back together. Until the next time. A month from now? Two?

"You want me to read you a story, Sara?"

No, she had homework to do. Tony asleep, Peter sat with Sara at the kitchen table. Hunching over a sheet of paper so Sara couldn't see, with his fat carpenter's pencil he wrote a note to fold into his wallet:

> *In case of emergency,*
> *my children...*

Originally appeared in Esquire, *January 1980*

Bodies like Mouths

During the winter of 1955, Chris took courses at Columbia. He came from Cincinnati; New York stunned him. Knowing nothing, he took a room in a railroad flat uptown near school: one room, 11 x 7, bed with a defeated mattress. It was cheap, and he could use the kitchen along with the three other roomers—after the Dirksons had finished.

At night, when he got home from work, Dirkson used the kitchen first. He seemed to slow down his meal so he could feel his power. After he and his wife were through, it was Mr. Dirkson who cleaned up, sponging counter and linoleum wrathfully so that no trace of their lives remained. The roomers listened, each from a separate room, hearing the scraping and scrubbing as a language of hate—all *right,* you little bastards: I want to see it the same way tomorrow morning.

Then he hollered, "Kitchen's free!"—and the roomers came in, carrying each his own paper bag. Each to his own cupboard space, own refrigerator half-shelf. At the end of their meals, each separate, everything disappeared; the kitchen belonged again to nobody.

Chris never stayed in the kitchen long. In Columbus, his mother's kitchen had been the happiest room in the house. But here: on the wall over the table with its green oil cloth, one yellowing picture—*girls holding roses*—cut out of some magazine years before and glued to cardboard. A single fluorescent light hanging from the middle of the ceiling tore at Chris's stomach. The one window was black on the outside with soot sucked into the inner courtyard of the building—a kind of air space, like a large, dirty chimney with windows. The dirt seeped into the old towel left always between upper and lower sash to keep out drafts and dirt. And, inescapably, the rancid smell, smell of despair, clung to the old paint, the ceiling plaster. Years later, remembering—that bleak room was somehow redeemed by the strength of his memory, memory like an act of love.

Dirkson in underpants and an undershirt. Annie the next-door roomer laughs and jiggles a thumb—"Some beauty, huh?" She walks around in a ragged terrycloth bathrobe. Not much of a beauty herself. Chris longs for lean, blonde angels. Her breasts are small and her waist thick—not fat, but solid. She has long, fuzzy brown hair that would look beautiful fifteen years later but in 1955 looks messy. Her eyes are shrewd—he is afraid of what they might see. "Some beauty," she says again. Chris's smile doesn't commit him. "Oh, Jesus! Another great roomer," she says.

From behind their closed bedroom door and his own bedroom door, he can hear Mr. and Mrs. Dirkson, fighting. Dirkson's voice, murderous, is muted by his throat, muffled by the doors. Sarah's voice—whatever the words—sneers. Something thuds. A curse, repeated, in a tense monotone. Chris comes out into the hall and stares at the Dirksons' door: a blurred television screen.

A key turns in the front door lock. José tiptoes in behind a short, dark-skinned kid—a kid not more than sixteen. José looks maybe sixteen himself, but he must be older—he's here on government scholarship from the Philippines. José raises a finger to his lips—Chris grins: rings on every finger—gold, brass, glass, semi-precious stones. They disappear across the hall into José's bedroom.

"YOU goddamned bitch!"—explodes through the Dirksons' door. Annie sticks her head out of her door and looks at Chris. Her eyebrows lift. She lifts a Schlitz in toast to one more brawl. They both withdraw into their rooms. From José's room Chris hears a fluent run in minor key on guitar. A flamenco strum and *ai-eee!!* He can't hear José's song—only the repeated words, louder than the rest—Flores...flores...flores...

Alone in New York: outside the apartment it was no grim prison. Secrets bloomed like sea anemones, charged, tumescent. He walked a lot, carrying a burden of terror and love-feelings, nowhere to put them down. Walking: down Broadway, across Central Park South, down Lexington. Looking at women. Legs whispered to him so fervently—aaah, the swell of calves in nylon—he could hardly stand it. Painful, the curve of coat over hip, curve in his mind, curve rushing and singing like a roller coaster. In his *mind,* though not recognized as in his mind—intuitions of a sacred language that he could comprehend only in profane form. Hungry all the time—love with nothing he knew to love, love sniffing into every dark place. His heart was touched—as if the city were an old pan-handler, old ticket-taker.

Love spilled out onto the facades of elegant townhouses from the turn of the century, houses he couldn't hope to enter, molded cornices, windows the shape of old ladies in dreams, huge windows full of green plants. Jazz clubs in cellars he wished he had the nerve to enter. Lebanese groceries, Italian groceries, bodegas. These he entered; he ate good bread for the first time, ripping off the chunks and chewing hard, as if chewing were a form of loving.

Sometimes he followed a girl in a topcoat, creating her (oh, her elegant walk, her lean body, must be wearing a leotard—a dancer—hello, I'm Chris) followed her to the 116th Street subway kiosk (hello... my name is...) and leaned over the railing while she dissolved into the undulating subway dragon, yellow hair fading into the dark crowd.

Fearing and loving, in all-night Hayes-Bickford cafeterias, talking to gamblers about women. Home again at midnight, the piled-up cushions on his bed tumbled, under the streetlight, into odalisques in leotards.

The Five Spot. I am invisible. Hipsters passing funny cigarettes. Someone named Miles Davis. I don't understand the music but I bob my head.

Dirkson, in underpants and undershirt, cut onions and complained about the tax forms he had to work on. The taxes or the onions made his eyes tear, and he cursed and wiped them with the back of his hand. "That's right," he said to Chris but really to himself, "leave it to the goddamned onion to finish the job. All day the goddamned garage door kept opening and closing you wear a coat you sweat so you take it off and freeze your ass off." Next to the tax forms were three sharpened pencils, a box full of papers, a bottle of Budweiser. "Painful," Dirkson said. "Fucking painful."

Dick is thumping some woman in the next room. The springs shriek like mice or guinea pigs, and the headboard slams the wall. Chris finds he's clenching his jaw, and he tries to relax: first thing in the morning! First thing in the morning—Christ! He gets up and sticks his head out the door—sees the bathroom door is shut: Dirkson up to go to work.

Chris puts water up to boil. Even from the kitchen he can hear Dick. The bastard. Two hours a day he swims, comes home with any of three different women, all really pretty; they groan and grapple till 11:00 and are doing it again at 6:30. Athlete's schedule. He should tell him something.

Sitting over coffee, he hears laughter, click of a door latch, and Dick comes into the kitchen with the woman. She looks flushed but her hair is neat and her white blouse is crisp and tucked inside her peasant skirt. Dick smiles good morning and that's all. Why doesn't he introduce us? Doesn't he remember my name? She boils water. Curly black hair tumbles halfway down her back.

Chris is in love with her.

Then Dirkson comes out of the bathroom and stands, arms akimbo, and glowers at Dick. Chris figures on some yelling—even at the other end of the apartment they must have heard, and Dirkson hates noise.

Dirkson glowers; then he grins, you even see his teeth: "You make one hell of a racket, you know that?"

"I can imagine," Dick drawls.

"You're some guy. Yessir!" Dirkson laughs and shakes his head in pleasure and embarrassment.

"I do my best, Mr. Dirkson."

"I'll bet. Miss, does he do his best? I'll bet he does."

She just smiles. Chris would like to obliterate this smug son of a bitch: his lecherous eyes. Both of them. But also—he's fascinated at the change in Dirkson. And this woman, her presence, is for Chris like morphine he was given in a hospital once. He is suffused with love.

He sips his coffee while these two bastards congratulate each other for being men. And didn't she mind—she was the runner's track, vaulter's pole, lane for the swimmer? Is that what women really wanted? It was 1955. Everyone winked and said yes, that's what women really wanted: to be fucked into grateful obedience.

Dirkson goes back inside to dress. Chris remembers the *look.* He knows it from high school locker room, dances of Friday nights. That look—it made him nauseous, made him drop out of the field; let them run on, around and around the track, without him.

She looks at him, she smiles—"Want some more coffee?"

"Sylvia, we've got to get going," Dick says. "He can fix his own."

Chris wishes he could lift this bastard by his hair and clamp his neck to the wall. Instead, he smiles and takes the pot from Sylvia's hand.

Love flesh: he wanted to hold his life, shining, in his hands, and he didn't know where else to look, how else to sanctify it: breast flesh, leg flesh, curve of hip into thigh. He didn't know that flesh was metaphor, metaphor piled on metaphor, and that history made and remade the metaphors. He was poisoned by the metaphors but he didn't know that yet. It all seemed his private, single struggle, personal humiliation—at being a man, at not being a man. Outside, along Broadway, mothers pushed baby carriages and walked children in a protest march: their milk, their food were being poisoned by radiation. From his bedroom window he could hear them chanting. A few blocks away, at Columbia, he took *political science* and *history.* All that was outside. Then there was the private, the *inside:* sex and love and being a man and finding something to do with his life he could at least stomach. His own pain, his possession. Ultimately—everyone told him—Man is Alone.

"Een Manila, wan I was twelve year old, the soldiers, Japanese soldiers, took me, they rape me. Ees how eet all started."

"José, you couldn't have been raped by Japanese soldiers. They were gone, the war was over, by the time you were twelve."

"Okay, okay. American soldiers then. What's the deeference?" He burst out laughing. Putting on an imaginary top hat, he danced on top of the bed, on top of the table.

"Be careful of the books, will you?"

"Oh, the books!" He bowed deeply.

Annie sliced up vegetables on the cutting board; she used her own iron skillet to saute them. While they simmered, she scrubbed off the board and opened a Schlitz with her Swiss Army knife. Chris ran the cold water a long time, until some of the poison and despair were out of the pipes. In her robe, Annie looked dilapidated and blousy, already a little like Sarah Dirkson.

Mr. Dirkson was in the john. Annie pointed with her thumb. "He spends a sweet little time in there, huh? You think he jerks off in there?"

He wanted to hush her—the Dirksons' room was two doors down. But he laughed.

"Oh. Oh, my. Was that some laugh!" Annie said. "God, what a place I'm living in."

"I'm sorry."

"He's sorry."

Vivaldi from José's record player. Suddenly the bathroom door jerked open. "Hey!—Will you keep that goddamned thing *down*?"

"You going to be living here for long?" Annie asked.

"I doubt it."

"Sure. You want to do a funny cigarette?"

"You hear me, José?" Dirkson bellowed. José opened his door a crack and Vivaldi splashed through the apartment.

"Ees poetry, Meester Dirkson."

"Shut it."

José sighed. His hands opened to the heavens and his rings—one, two, even three—on every finger, flashed. His poet brass knuckles. Dirkson and José both closed themselves in again.

Annie took the pan from the stove—she ate off it, ignoring a plate.

"Why do you stay here?" Chris asked.

"Come *on.* It's cheap. But I'm splitting for a while, thank God. Listen—you didn't answer my question."

"I don't smoke."

"I don't mean tobacco."

"Thanks—really—but no. *No.*"

"Thank God I'm splitting for a while."

Dirkson came out of the bathroom. "It's free. Don't forget to clean up after yourself."

Chris sat in his room, reading Auden. His only decent course was in poetry, with Babette Deutsch. Such a delicate, crisp lady. She touched him with the power of the unspoken at the heart of the spoken. Auden's simple speech vibrated in his mind. He wished he could make such language. With his lips he formed empty whispers as if they were real words, real lines of poetry. He wished he could reach in and pull out the words.

The doorbell. Annie ran down the hall to get it. Chris opened his own door a crack. A big guy, very black, smiled and lifted her up by the waist and kissed her. She let herself slump against his shoulder. Then they were gone. Chris heard them laughing down the stairwell, heard the front door slam. He looked at Auden's words again but couldn't make sense. Looked out his window to see Annie and her friend, but they were nowhere in sight.

Sometimes at night he couldn't sleep. Even with three blankets he was cold, and had to pile his coat and jacket on the bed. The weight felt like some other body—he didn't try to think whose. Toilet paper stuffed in the crack around his window casement didn't help much. Too much steam heat all day, then cold all night. On his ceiling feet scuffled—the children upstairs, the Iraqui student, his family. He lay propped up on pillows and stared out at the brownstone across the street. A woman's silhouette behind a window shade, the light behind her. He wanted to see her, whoever she was, wanted to watch her making love. A long scream. A couple laughing in the street. An auto horn, furious. A bottle smashing against wall or pavement. He shut his eyes. It got late, he felt panicky—so much to do tomorrow—he needed sleep. Drowsed, drowsed: birds, a tunnel, solemn dialogue with a teacher. Laughter: laughter from José's room. Then quiet in the apartment. In the cold wind he felt it creak as if this were a dark ship. A voice in Spanish—José was talking in his sleep again. The bodies, rocking, each in its own metabolic rhythms, its separate secret processes. The crew slept. Bodies crumpled, curled, as if folding around a dream stone, a stone in sleep. He heard no one but sensed them all: hungry bodies, hurting bodies, sexual bodies glowing in secret. Bodies like mouths. Sexual swimmers going deeper into longing.

"You get your goddamned bags packed, José. I want you out of here by tonight."

"Oh, please, Meester Dirkson." José got down on his knees. Skinny kid, he looked twelve years old. Dirkson like Zeus above him. José fluttered his eyelids: "Please, Meester Dirkson, José ees just a harmless fairy. You wouldn't be so cruel to José?" He clung to Dirkson's knees. "Where can I go? I am so weethout money."

Chris couldn't stand it. José was eating this up, loving the scene, overplaying it just this side of parody. If Dirkson had suspected he was being put on, he could have shoved José away. "Come on, come on, let *go*, José."

"The end of the week, Meester Dirkson?"

"Sure, okay," he said, pulling away and brushing off his cuff from something dirty. "The end of the week, José." When he was gone, José danced a tiny, delicate, silly dance, a devil dancing on eggs, and he grinned—a little boy with big, crooked, yellowing teeth. He reached his arms up and clasped his fingers around Chris's neck while he kept up his delicate dance and hummed a little tune. Chris smiled but pulled back. "Oh, don' worry. I am not pheesically attracted to you. Eet ees sad." He sighed. "But not ultimately. 'All theengs fall and are built again…' Yeats, si! He *knows.* Ultimately, what ees sad? Notheeng."

"Oh, bullshit."

"Sure, sure evertheeng ees bullshit. Eet ees sad."

Chris waved him off and went into his own room and closed the door. But a minute later José knocked and slipped in like a cat or the wind. He sat crosslegged on the bed and rolled a cigarette.

"Een Manila during the war, I learn to roll cigarettes and drunks. At seven year old I make out okay."

"But you, you're a genius, didn't you tell me?"

"Laugh at me, I don' care, Chris. I *am* a genius. Like Goethe, like the holy Mozart, like Rilke and Yeats and Chaplin. Chaplin ees a very high saint, Chris." He held his fingertips together at his heart in devotion, then grinned wickedly. "I, however, am not a saint."

"You've read an awful lot. You're here on some scholarship? The Philippine government?"

"I am as poor as the leetle cockroach in the keetchen."

"Annie tells me you spend all your money on boys and that you live on hamburgers."

"Now you sound like Meester Dirkson." He sulked.

"Oh, José!"

"Where am I going to go?" he wailed in a tiny voice and buried his head in the pillows. Real tears!

"Poor José. What about the Y? Listen, I'll help you look for a room, okay?"

"Okay." A tiny, child's voice. One eye peeked up from the pillow. "You want to sleep weeth me?"

Sarah Dirkson sits in a bleached-out, flower-print housedress, *not* reading the *Daily News, not* drinking from her quart of ale. Her skin looks puffy, her eyes red; what seems strange to Chris is that she sits back, relaxed, as if she were watching an invisible TV and weeping over a soap opera. Chris fixes himself a cup of instant and sits down. "I'm sorry, Mrs. Dirkson."

"You're a good kid. It's nothing."

"Is it your husband?"

"He means well. Anyway, that's not the point, is it?"

He shrugs and shakes his head. "Sorry?"

"I *mean,* it's my *life.* My *life,"* she says again as if it's a pun or the punch line of a joke he isn't picking up. Defeated, she keeps crying, her mouth slack, without definition; Chris finishes his coffee in a hurry and goes back inside to study.

Later he smells bread baking. In this place! Mrs. Dirkson baking bread.

He studies French grammar and memorizes vocabulary. A sinking feeling that he will never need to know that *tache* means *a stain; savant, skillful; nourrir, to feed, to nurse...*

When he hears the knock, he realizes he expected it. He remembers his bed is cluttered with clothes. "Come in?"

"Here's bread. I baked plenty. My mother used to bake bread."

"Mine too. Thanks." He feels invaded. Maybe she's trying to take him to bed, wants him to ease her life. Suddenly her blousy body and fleshy face make him feel a little nauseated. How could he make it with her? He never could. He retreats into a dead smile. "Thank you." He takes the plate and sets it on his study table, a flowering plant among the 3 x 5s. They both regard it.

"*Try* some."

"Sure. Hey..." With what knife? He looks around for help. "*Break* it."

"Sure." He feels he is violating the bread. He rips at it, catching dough under his nails. Smiling, smiling, he stuffs some in his mouth. "Wow. Wonderful."

"*Isn't* it good?" Her face is full of pleasure now. He can only nod. Stuffing and chewing, he nods. It's dry. Too big a piece. Why didn't she think of butter?

"I figured you never got any homemade stuff."

"That was really thoughtful," he mumbles through the gluten. He concentrates hard on his chewing, and his eyes close.

"You're some student, I just bet. Look at those books all over."

"I'm a slob. I'm not very neat. It's great bread." His mouth aches. The loaf lies broken apart and embarrasses him.

"You don't seem to have any friends."

"I've only been in New York a month."

"You've got to be careful of course, not to mix with the wrong people. I approve of that. Take someone like José. Christ, I don't want to talk about people behind their backs, but José was probably a sweet, innocent boy back in the Philippines. Well you look at him now—these kids he picks up, he ain't giving them candy in his room. Don't I know it—New York is a terrible place. But you can't live in your books all the time, can you?"

"You're right," he says, wanting her to leave.

"I'm not talking about a tramp like Annie. Do you realize she went off with that…colored man five days ago? Well, is she crazy?" She thought for a moment. "Well. Who the hell am I to tell somebody else a *damned* thing? I'm some prize package if you know what I mean." She shrugs and walks out; stops, her hand rubbing the door jamb. "Anyway, if you need anything…"

"Thanks, Mrs. Dirkson."

"Sarah. Sarah." She leaves him alone, thank God, but the silence is powerful, it makes him ache; like a god it pursues him out of the room into the noisy side street, onto Broadway. Smell of fried rice and beans. A tinny record in Spanish from a music store. No silence here. Men in cheap clothes, leaning against cars, are in the know. Some *know* he doesn't possess. The young women passing who glance at him live at a level of sexuality so intense it would wipe him away. But under the jangle of Broadway his love starts to come back, like a muscle in spasm, loosening. His eyes ache as he looks too hard for someplace to put the love down. He sees three children, three children walking a cocker spaniel. Loving children: always easy; always a relief.

Annie was back.

In the kitchen she sat brooding over her coffee. Dick washed the dishes and hummed a blues her way as if she were supposed to catch the unspoken words. She ignored him. Chris took a can of pineapple juice from his refrigerator shelf and poured out a glass. "Annie—you want some?"

She shook her head.

"You sure?"

She turned a sour look on him. "I'm not in such a great mood."

Dick kept up his song, the humming increasingly suggestive; he seemed to be soaping her back instead of a plate. Suddenly she turned—"And *you*—" she snapped at Dick—"just fuck off. I don't need your crap one bit."

"What happened to your big boyfriend?"

She ignored him. "*This* one—" she told Chris—"tried to put his hands on me the first day I moved in. He's real sweet.... Hey, you, why don't you go hum at the pigeons?"

Dick wiped his hands and kept humming, grin on his face, all the way to his room.

"What was he humming at you?"

"Oh. Just a blues. Because the guy I was with is black?"

"It turned out lousy?"

"Why don't you just go away? You want to suck energy out of my problems? Go away."

"I'm just sorry for you. Jesus!" He got up.

"You're good at being sorry for people. I know the type. You eat that shit up, don't you? You're such a sweet, sensitive fucker. You eat that shit up. I don't see you saying a goddamned thing to that prick, however." She turned off her eyes—a stranger.

A stranger. Foreigner. Some language I no talk so good.

Dirkson tried the door; it was bolted from the inside. With one thrust of his heavy shoe, he smashed it open. From his own doorway Chris looked past Dirkson, past José. A darkskinned kid with a lot of curly hair was pulling up his pants, eyes like a trapped rabbit's. José was still on his knees. He looked back over his shoulder at Dirkson, Dirkson godlike above him. Probably that would have been all except for some yelling. But then José grinned; he grinned, he ran his tongue across his lips and wiped them with his fingertips. As if to say, Too late, Meester Dirkson. Dirkson let out a roar, like an animal, and smashed his heavy work shoe into José's head; José went down, and Dirkson picked him up by the hair and belt, picked him up and carried him to the front door. There he held him under one arm—José didn't struggle, was probably not conscious—screamed over and over, "You fucking pig, you fucking pig!" while he managed to open the front door locks and toss him down the stairs.

José tumbled like a rag doll, offering no resistance, and crumpled, slack, on the landing. Dirkson slammed the door and turned away, obviously scared, embarrassed. He yelled at Chris, "WHAT kind of goddamned house does he think I run?"—and brushed past him.

"I'm giving notice," Chris yelled after him. "And right now I'm calling the police."

Annie went out into the hall.

"I don't give a shit *who* you call."

Sarah Dirkson had her hands on her husband's arms trying to calm him—he shrugged her off and went back to their room.

"Oh, my God, my God in Heaven!" Sarah Dirkson knotted the belt of her robe and went out with Chris to pick up José. But José, somehow, had slipped away. Annie was standing there. There was blood on the steps, blood on the banister. They heard the downstairs door slam.

"He's some tough kid," Sarah Dirkson said.

The teenager slipped past them and ran down the stairs.

"Hey, you—you stay the hell away from here!" she yelled after him. Then, turning, she put her arms around Chris's shoulders and leaned her head against his chest. Stiffly, tears thickening his eyes, he held her, gave comfort, wondered now where the hell was he going to live.

Annie went inside and left them standing there.

He got dressed and went out, forgetting his books. He had to look for a place to live. But what he was really looking for was José—he took the subway to the Village and hunted without a hope. He had the feeling that this beautiful monster, New York, had swallowed him up.

What he was really looking for…but if it was José, why did he poke into Village bars? José never went to a bar. Chris stood in entranceways. Afraid of the bartender's eyes. Of the one or two men sitting at the bar. He could imagine whole lives about them. Or no—not imagine the lives: imagine that there was something to imagine, something to feel for. So, on trust, he felt for it. He poured his own energy into half-lit rooms, then wondered at it as something foreign to him. Twelve years later, when Dylan was singing of Desolation Row, he always saw this image of men in the half light of a Village bar.

He wandered through coffee houses, looking and not looking, finally stopping for an espresso at Rienzi's. Soft Mozart chamber music reminded him of José. Then a boy flashed by outside on Macdougal Street. José? Chris swigged his espresso and hurried after. The boy was just turning a corner—a shock of black hair—or was that somebody different again from the boy he'd seen?

Where did the kid go? Chris was blocks away from Macdougal, down sidestreets folding into sidestreets. Now he was just walking. Looking for *vacancy* signs on the doorways of brownstones and graystones, looking for the mystery. A woman in a window—a black woman with a Siamese cat—grinned his way. He felt a glow of love for her, for the city, felt that, after all, it wasn't swallowing up José, but hiding, protecting him.

Somewhere there was a room. He walked until he came to Macdougal, pleased with himself that he could find it again. Over another cup of espresso he looked through ads in the *Village Voice.*

At the next table, a young man and two women were talking—incomprehensibly—about some article by Norman Mailer, about Fritz and Laura, about the Poujadists in France. A long speculation about the roots of fascism. The name Reich…Reich…Reich. Chris felt their excitement and concern and locked it into his heart as a model of something for himself. Then their talk submerged beneath Vivaldi and espresso. Walking over to a rack, he lifted a copy of *Le Monde* hanging on its wooden dowel and brought it back to his table. Struggling with the French, he tried to feel at home.

That night, three light taps at his door. He opened—José with a beret over a bandaged skull. A cut along his cheekbone had been dressed but not bandaged.

"You're okay?"

"I tol' you I take care of José."

"That was pretty stupid—" Chris mimicked José: tongue along the lips, fingertips wiping them dry. "You provoked him."

"Did I do that?" José asked in his tiny child's voice.

Chris laughed. "Well? You need some help, genius?"

"Eef you could store some boxes, I sneak back and got some boxes packed."

Chris looked around and laughed. "Store *where*?"

"Under the bed? I got a place, ees okay—just a couple days."

"I'm leaving. I gave notice."

"Ai-eee! For me? Chris!" José smiled his most delicate smile and fluttered his eyelids.

"José, please cut that out."

Under the bed was already crowded, but they crammed things in.

José hummed a song. "Thees ees from divine Mozart, the *Magic Flute.* Papageno, hees song, wan he ees gagged for hees lies."

"It sounds appropriate, José."

A tapping at the door. "It's me. *Annie.*"

She slipped in and sat with Chris on the bed. José reenacted the beating in mime.

"That bastard," Annie said. "I'd love to stomp on his balls."

Chris looked at her, dismayed.

"Mr. Sweetness here," she said.

José hummed Papageno's song. He sat on Annie's lap—Chris realized how very small he was. His bright eyes looked deep into

Chris's and he recited, "Wan longing comes over you, seeng the great lovers. Ees Rilke," he sighed. "'Those whom you almost envied, those forsaken, you found so far beyond the requited een loving.'"

"You see?" Annie said. "You see? José understands everything. Let's go down for a six-pack."

"I swear to God, I don't know why I stick around here. So I can learn to paint? I'm no painter. I mean. So why am I hanging around? It's more alive than Denver, I guess—sadder, too. Sometimes I get so I want to scream. Billy told me to split a couple of days back. I mean. I was a real shit to him. But even if I were Miss Honey Pussy of 1955, it would have been the same. So I went out on the street, I stood on the corner of Eighth Street and Sixth Avenue trying to peddle my ass. Well, first off, my ass practically froze. And then, nobody bought. You always figure, shit, what a lousy thing—to sell your ass? What you never imagine is, maybe nobody'll want to buy."

"Oh, Annie!" José kissed her ear and she brushed him off.

"I suppose if I got dolled up and went to the right place—"

From the Dirksons' bedroom they could hear his snarling, not the words.

"Poor woman." Chris felt a sweet melancholy here in this tiny room, with the one-bulb lamp on the wall over the bed, the three of them in a cabin in some floating city, a terrible ship slipping through the night, or city like a psychotic sleepwalker not knowing where—and the three of them safe. Remembered as a child taking a sandwich to bed, secretly, propping up the covers with a toy gun, sitting in the cave of his bed with a flashlight, reading stories…

Dirkson's voice became a roar. "…Bastards! …" They looked at each other wondering whom the word referred to, knowing it made no difference.

"Goodbye, Chris, Annie—I geev you a kees." Suddenly, José slipped under the bed and took a paper bag from one of his boxes. A finger to his lips; like a sprite, he was gone.

A minute later the lights went out. They looked at each other. Annie said, "Shhh…José."

They waited.

The bedroom door, the Dirksons' door, banged open, and Dirkson, barefoot, in underwear, clumped down the hall. Noise in the kitchen. Then "Sarah! Goddamnit, somebody's been tampering—"

Sarah's slippers. "Stop yelling—it's eleven o'clock." Chris imagined a malicious Ariel tiptoeing down the stairs, out onto streets where he was no less at home than here. At home nowhere, anywhere.

Then the lights went on.

"I bet the little bastard came back." Dirkson slammed the door of the fuse box.

Chris stood in the kitchen doorway. "Trouble, Mr. Dirkson?"

"You seen that little bastard? I bet you have." Then he noticed Annie. "She just coming out of your room? What's she doing in your room? You mind if I look in there?" He went in. No José. Dick came out of his room. Alone tonight, he wore his sweat suit and track shoes, but his eyes looked bleary. "What's going on?"

"That little faggot." Playing hide-and-seek, Dirkson pushed on through the apartment. Sarah took a beer from the fridge, opened and swallowed deep. Chris saw her look at Dick a long, long look, then hand him the beer. Dick grinned at her and she laughed like a young girl. "Life is funny," she said to some invisible audience—the imaginaries who really understood and cared. "Ain't it, just ain't it?"

Then a roar from the bedroom. Dirkson with his shoes in his hands. "That little bastard—he filled these up with something." He took a spoon and dug, but it wouldn't give. Annie took a look. "Plaster of paris. Just forget it, Mr. Dirkson."

He threw one shoe, then the other, against the kitchen door. The first thudded and fell, the second left a long split in the wood. "How'd he get in there?" Then he realized and rushed back inside. "THAT FUCKING BASTARD!"—Chris knew now that he had never really heard Dirkson raise his voice before. Dirkson went for the phone. "He stole my pants, my wallet, my money, my papers, I don't know what else, the little fucking thief."

But the phone was dead.

"The wire's cut, Mr. Dirkson," Annie said.

"You mind your own business." He pushed past Sarah; they heard him at the bedroom window.

"These buildings all connect," Annie said. "He must have climbed up on the roof and down some other stairs."

"I had my *pay* in that wallet, five goddamned days of keeping cabs moving, busting my ass in that crappy place, you think it's funny?"

Chris saw in his mind's eye his own father, who worked in an insurance office and never cursed, never raised his voice—but his feelings weren't all that different. Chris felt sorry.

Sarah leaned against her husband's arm. "Oh, Fred, Fred, your money." She was crying. He only half pushed her off.

"Everybody can get the fuck out of here. I mean tomorrow, the next day. I mean *you*—" he rammed a finger into Chris's chest—"and you, too, Annie. Not you, Dick, of course, but the rest of this trash."

Annie laughed and went to her room. Chris closed his door, put a chair against it, and undid a couple of José's boxes—now how could he get them back to him?

A crumpled felt hat with a parrot feather, a collection of Beethoven string quartets, an eyebrow pencil, a column of four poses of himself from a subway photo booth—grinning, malicious, terribly sad. A couple of soiled t-shirts, a notebook of poems in Spanish, a packet of ragged letters, an American flag, an old newspaper photo of Franklin Delano Roosevelt, a pile of magazines with cover pictures of nearly naked athletes with oiled torsos, a torn pair of blue corduroy pants—a child's size.

He stuffed everything back, put the chair back by the table, got into bed and waited for sleep. Tomorrow he'd be out on the street. A new room somewhere. José's things would have to go with him.

Chris lay curled up, imagining José out on the street somewhere. Someday he'd pick up the wrong boy or steal from the wrong landlord and somebody would kill him. He remembered José tumbling down the stairs, saw the blood again, felt Dirkson's shoe thud against his skull, his own skull. He prayed, though he had stopped believing a long time ago, Dear God, please protect José, keep him safe.

A tap on the door, Annie came in, sat on the bed and lit up one of those funny cigarettes of hers. Chris felt trapped. A few years later he would have seen Annie and the funny cigarette as somewhere to run to, but this was 1955, and he was already enough of a family disaster for not finishing at Ohio State and entering an insurance business, a wholesale drug outfit, a used-car dealership. It was 1955, and the smoke from Annie's funny cigarette might as well have worn horns and a tail; it took him years before, looking back, he kind of loved her for how scared and needful she must have really been that night. Remembered her with love. She sat on his bed, sat on the edge of his bed. He could see, in the streetlight, her flannel nightgown, her hair loose around her shoulders. She didn't look at him. She took a deep drag and passed over to him the funny cigarette, passed it over and he took it as if it were the commonest thing he'd ever done, though he figured—one drag and he was finished. And he said, Then I'll be finished, I want to be finished. He sucked deeply the way she did and held in the smoke. She took back the cigarette and it was like throwing himself away but he held in the smoke and Jesus he felt a hum and a buzz through his body and his head loosened. Then she was passing it back, and he did it again.

She didn't talk. Into her silence he poured the mysteries that would break his life apart. When the cigarette got too small to bother with, she swallowed the tiny dead butt and, pulling down the covers, got into bed with him. A couple of children at camp, he thought, not expecting to think that. But then he was shocked, when she touched his bare legs, at the terrific intensity of the touch or of the touch of his fingers to her nightgown, the curve of her thighs and ass. It made him gasp, and she put a finger to his lips; she shaped, with her hands, his back and shoulders. Oh my God. He pulled off his jockey shorts, he kissed her and almost got lost inside the kiss, his first marijuana kiss, his first kiss in hell. Then he was inside her body and his heart loosened and poured out, and he felt incredible gratitude and simple peace and this didn't seem much like hell. "Come on," she said, and made him move harder, so he did, almost angry. "Come *on.*" He started to come, and laughed, she hushed him, but he started bucking and roaring and bellowed and came like hell; she moved hard then, and came—or pretended.

He was nearly asleep. She pushed him to one side of the bed. "You make too damn much noise. But I'm staying. If he barges in, to hell with him. I'm not sleeping by myself tonight."

When Chris woke it was just dawn. His head felt a little light; the buzz was gone. Annie was curled up at the other side of the bed, turned away. He wanted to run his hand along the soft, flannel curves of her, afraid to disturb things. He felt—knowing, sure, that this feeling was fragile, that it would collapse like a hardwood coal that kept its fire shape until you touched it—that the city pulsed in this room, that the center of the city was here, the two of them, this bed, and that in some sense, like a spider in the center of a web, he was in touch with the extremities.

Then he must have fallen back to sleep. "Well, Jesus Christ," he heard, and woke up. Annie was sitting up, looking into the little mirror on the wall. "Look what you did to my mouth."

"I'm sorry. Is it bleeding?"

"It's puffed up. I better be careful about you." She leaned over the bed and kissed him on the tip of his nose. "Thanks for last night. I would have felt lousy sleeping alone. I don't know why."

She slipped out; he heard the door to her bedroom open and close. And the feeling—that here was the center, that the city was inside this room—dissolved. The city was *out there* again—not in his room, not even in Annie's room—just somewhere *out there.*

Hungry to begin. He'd seen three ads for sharing an apartment—none of them were in when he'd called—and he found out from a waiter at Rienzi's about the notice boards at N.Y.U. Smiling, he remembered José's boxes: he'd have to take them along—and how could José find him? He saw himself lugging José's boxes from furnished room to furnished room for years and years.

To begin. Plenty of energy, even a kind of courage. Images of windows with green plants, jazz from record players in converted lofts, the smile of the black woman stroking her cat. A room somewhere—he was very hungry to go out into the city; city, body of himself, he really understood. Body of himself—hunger for what he didn't know was already in himself, himself not separate from the life that pulsed through him.

Originally appeared in Shenandoah, *Spring, 1982*

Cambridge is Sinking!

The Sunday-night telephone call from Steve's parents: his mother sorrowed that such an educated boy couldn't find a job. She suggested kelp and brewer's yeast. His father asked him, "What kind of economics did you study, so when I ask for the names of some stocks, which ones should I buy, you can't tell me?"

"It's true, Dad."

George rolled a joint and handed it to Steve. Steve shook his head. "But thanks anyway," he said to George, hand covering the phone.

"Man, you're becoming a Puritan," George said.

"Stevie, you're getting to be practically a vagrant," his father sighed.

Susan kissed him in a rush on the way out to her support meeting. Where was *his* support meeting? He closed his eyes and floated downstream. "Goodbye, baby."

A one-eyed cat pounced from cushion to cushion along the floor. He hooked his claws into the Indian bedspreads that were the flowing walls of the living room. The cat floated, purring, until Steve yelled—

"Ché! For Christsakes!"—and Ché leaped off a gold flower into the lifeboat. It wasn't a lifeboat; really an inflated surplus raft of rubberized canvas; it floated in the lagoon of a Cambridge living room. It was Steve who nicknamed it the lifeboat and christened it with a quart of beer.

Steve scratched the cat's ears and seduced him into his lap under Section 4 of the Sunday New York *Times:* The Week in Review. Burrowing underneath, Ché bulged out Nixon's smiling face into a mask. Ché made a rough sea out of Wages and Prices, Law and Order, Education. Steve stopped trying to read.

The *Times* on a Sunday! Travel and Resorts. *Voilá!* A Guide to Gold in the Hills of France. Arts and Leisure. Business and Finance. Sports. Remember sports? My God. It was clear something was over.

All these years the New York *Times* was going on, not just a thing to clip articles from for a movement newspaper, but a thing people read. Truly, there were people who went to Broadway shows on the advice of Clive Barnes and Walter Kerr, who examined the rise and fall of mutual funds, who attended and supported the colleges and churches of their choice, who visited Bermuda on an eight-day package plan, who discussed cybernetics and school architecture. People who had never had a second-hand millennial notion of where we were heading—only a vague anger and uneasiness.

Steve tried to telepathize all this to Ché under the newspaper blanket: Ché, it's over. This is 1973. Hey. John is making films, Fred lives with eight other people on a farm. But it isn't a *commune,* whatever that was. The experiment is over.

Look: when Nancy cleared out of the apartment with her stash of acid and peyote and speed and hash after being released from Mass. Mental, cleared out and went home to Connecticut; when trippy Phil decided to campaign for George McGovern and nobody laughed; when the *Rolling Stone* subscription ran out; when Steve himself stopped buying the *Liberated Guardian* or worrying about its differences from the regular *Guardian;* when George—when

George—stopped doing acid and got into a heavy wordless depression that he dulled with bottle after bottle of Tavola—and said he'd stop drinking "soon—and maybe get into yoga or a school thing"—something was finished, over.

Ché purred.

The lifeboat floated like a bright orange *H.M.S. Queen Elizabeth* sofa in the middle of the sunset floor. Steve sat in the lifeboat on one of the inflated cushions reading Arts and Leisure and listening to Ray Charles through the wall of George's room. As long as it was Ray Charles he didn't bother to drown it out with the living room stereo. As if he had the energy. He sipped cranberry juice out of an Ocean Spray bottle and looked through this newspaper of strange science fiction planet aha.

Ray Charles whined to a dead stop in mid-song. George stood in the doorway and stood there with something to say and stood there and waited.

"Come aboard. I'm liking this old boat better and better." George: hippo body, leonine face with a wild red mane. He ignored the boat. "Steve, I'm going back to school."

"School? To do what?"

"Get a master's."

"What in?"

"I haven't got that far yet. I'll let you know." The door closed. Ray Charles started up from where he had left off.

Steve smiled. He stretched out in the lifeboat and let it float him downstream. They came to a rapids, he and Ché and the New York *Times,* and he began negotiating the white water. George. George: school? Well, why not.

George. One day last year when George was tripping he found his Harvard diploma in the trunk under his bed: he ripped it into a lot of pieces and burned—or began to burn—the pieces one by one. But halfway through he chickened out and spent the rest of his trip on his knees staring into the jigsaw fragments as if they were entrails of Homeric birds, *telling him something.* Yesterday, when Steve went into his room to retrieve his bathrobe, he found the fragments glued onto oak tag: half a B.A. on the wall. Nothing else was any different: unmade bed, unread books, undressed George, sacked out in the bathrobe. Steve burned a wooden match and with the cooled char wrote R.I.P. on George's forehead. George did.

Susan was gone for hours. Sunday night. Steve sat crosslegged in his lifeboat and made up lists on 3 x 5 cards.

It was a joke that began when he was doing his honors thesis at Harvard. On the backs of throwaway 3 x 5s he'd write

> B-214:
> Steve Kalman cites Marx—18th Brumaire—
> "Peasants shld be led into socialism
> by being asked to do housecleaning once a week."

He'd tape that to the bathroom mirror so the early morning peasants, recovering from dope and alcohol and speed, could hate him and get some adrenalin working. It was therapeutic.

Now the lists were different:

a) learn karate
b) practice abdominal breathing while making love
c) read Marx's *Grundrisse*
d) read *something* through to the last page
e) "Be modest and prudent, guard against arrogance and rashness, and serve the…people heart and soul" (Mao)
f) specifically: fight racism, sexism, exploitation
(whew!)
g) practice revolution

When he felt it might be necessary to do something about an item on the list, he closed his eyes and meditated. Words sneaked in: what he might have said to Susan, what was the shortest route to Harvard Square, would he see his guru face to face the way Sam said *he* had, how many gallons would it take to do the kitchen. Aach, you should just get into the waiting, into this time without political meetings or leafletting at factory gates. Get into something.

In his mind's eye Steve saw Susan's face. All right, she wasn't Beatrice or Shri Krishna. But who was, nowadays?

She came in late from her support group; Steve was in a gloomy half-sleep. She curled up behind him and touched her lips to the baby hairs on his back. He grunted and turned around: "And that's another thing—" he kissed her cheek, her nipple.

"What's another thing?"

"Your other nipple." Which he addressed himself to. "Listen. You come home after an exciting day at work while I've just swept the floors and wiped up the children's doodoo. Then you, you want to make love."

She held the cheeks of his ass and pressed him against her. They kissed. "Stephen, I don't have what you just said quite figured out, but I think you're making a sexist comment."

"Sexist? What sexist? I envy you your support group. You leave me nothing but the lifeboat and Chairman Mao."

"And a couple of years ago you'd have been up all night hammering out a 'position.' I think you're better off."

"We make love more, for sure."

"Let's make love, Steve."

And they did.

"Let's get out of Cambridge before it sinks. Cambridge is sinking."

Susan played with his curly black hair and beard, a Cambridge Dionysus. "You're silly. Cambridge is built on money. There are new banks all over the place."

"Then it's *us* who are sinking. We've got a lifeboat, let's go."

"Go where?"

"How about British Columbia? They need teachers. Or northern Ontario?"

"You'll get a lot of political thinking done up there."

"In exile? Look at Ho Chi Minh. Look at Lenin."

"Oh, baby. They were connected to a party."

"I love you. You're right. Let's go to Quebec and get away from politics."

"Away from politics? Quebec?"

"To Ontario."

"But baby, you're away from 'politics' right here. That's what you're complaining about."

"But Cambridge is sinking."

At night in bed it was funny and they had each other. But daytime after they breakfasted and kissed goodbye and Susan would go off to teach her fourth-grade class and Steve would go off to the library to read Trotsky or Ian Fleming or he'd sub at a Cambridge junior high and sit dully in the faculty lounge waiting for his class to begin, then he'd think again, like the words of an irritating jingle that wouldn't stay quiet, about whether to go on for his doctorate in sociology so he could be unemployed as a Ph.D. instead of unemployed as an M.A.

Susan was off at work. Steve washed the dishes this morning. M.A. Ph.D. The dishes. If you called it *karma yoga* it was better than dishwashing. But he envied Susan her nine-year-olds, even if she were being paid to socialize them into a society with no meaningful work, a society which—*watch it:* do the dishes and stop the words.

He did the dishes—then spent the rest of the morning at Widener Library reading Mao's "On Contradictions."

He was to meet George for lunch. On his way Jeff Segal passed him a leaflet without looking up.

> The press loves to boast that the student movement is dead. It's alive and fighting back. And SDS is in the forefront of that fight…

My God—SDS. (Which meant, in fact, PL.) Well, Steve felt happy that something considered itself a movement, even a handful of people using the rhetoric of 1950s ad men.

Steve passed through Harvard Square—past the straight-looking Jesus freaks and the bald Krishna freaks dancing in their saffron or white sheets and their insulated rubber boots. In the corner news store, across from the kiosk (Steve remembered when they "took" the Square and people got up on the kiosk and the cops came. So the freaks charged off in all directions busting windows—called *liberating the* Square—while he, Steve, who'd helped organize the march and rally, walked quietly *away.)*—in the corner news and magazine store there was George reading the sex books at the rear of the store.

"Hey George!"

They got out into the street and stood blinking at the noon light like a couple of junkies oozing out of a basement. George took out from his army coat lining the copy of *Fusion* he'd ripped off. He thumbed through the record reviews and he headed down Boylston to Minute Man Radio. "You stay here, Steve. I know what you think about my ripping off."

Steve watched the young women of Cambridge pass. A lot of fine lunchtime arrogance that he delighted in; but, he considered, not a hell of a lot in their eyes to back it up. One blonde on the other side of Boylston, tall, with a strong walk and no-bullshit eyes: Steve fell in love with her right away and they started living together but she had kids and he didn't get it on with them and she had perverse tastes in bed and didn't understand politics so by the time she actually crossed the street and passed by they'd separated it was too bad but anyway there was Susan to think of and so on. But they smiled at each other. Then George came out with Bob Dylan—*Greatest Hits Volume II*—and showed it to Steve when they'd sat down for lunch.

They ate in the Francaise under the painted pipes, ate their good quiche and drank French coffee. "George, I think this is a Hemingway memoir. I'm feeling nostalgia for this place while I'm still here. That's bad.

"I wonder where I'm going, George…

"I can't be Raskolnikov, George, as long as I can afford quiche for lunch. But it's the direction things are moving."

George ran his thick fingers through his wild red mane. "Not me. I decided. I don't want to be a casualty. I'm getting my M.A. in English and moving into a publishing house. I've got an uncle."

"Could you get your uncle to help you get your room cleaned up?"

"It's a pretty hip publishing house."

"I bet, George, that they make their profits off only the most freaky books."

"What's wrong with you, anyway?"

Steve bought George an espresso. "Here. Forgive me. This is so I can take our lunch off my taxes. I'm organizing you into our new revolutionary party."

"You couldn't organize your ass, lately."

Steve agreed. "I'm into getting my internal organs to communicate. I'm establishing dialogue at all levels."

After lunch Steve called Susan in the teachers' lounge at her school. "Hello, baby? Cambridge is collapsing."

"Love, I can't do anything about that. Thirty-one kids are all I can handle."

"Pretend I'm a reporter from the *Times* and you're a terrific genius. 'Tell me, Miss French, how did you get to be such a terrific genius? I mean, here the city is falling down and nobody can stop snorting coke long enough to shore up a building, and here you are helping thirty-one human kids to survive. How, how, how, Miss French?'"

"Steve, you know better, you nut."

"Steve knows what he knows; me, I'm a reporter."

"Well," she cleared her throat, "I take vitamins, and I make love a lot with my friend Steve. And I ask his advice—"

"Ha! Fat chance!"

"—and I owe it to my sisters in the women's movement."

Steve didn't laugh. "It's true, it's true. Ah, anyway, love, I miss you."

Steve went up to the raised desk at the Booksmith on Brattle Street to ask the manager whether the one-volume reduction of Marx's *Grundrisse* was out in paper. The "manager"—long mustachios and shaggy hair like a riverboat gambler, $50 boots up on the desk where they could make a *statement*—aha, it turned out to be Phil. Hey, Phil.

Phil looked up from the counter, stopped picking his Mississippi teeth and grinned. "I've been meaning to stop by, Steve. You didn't know I had this gig, huh?"

"It's good to see you."

"Sure. I watch the motherfuckers on my closed circuit swivel-eye TV set-up, dig it, and I check out the Square when things are slow. It's okay. I'm learning. In a couple of months I'm going out to Brattleboro, open a bookstore. A hip, a very hip bookstore."

"In Vermont?"

"There's a whole lot of freaks in Vermont."

"You doing a movement bookstore?"

Phil began picking his teeth like someone waiting to look at his hole card. Grinned his riverboat grin. "My uncle's setting me up, Steve. I want to make bread, man. As much as I can make in two, three years, and then I'll sell and split for someplace."

"Where?" Steve played at *naïf* to Phil's heavy hipoisie.

"Lots of time to work that one out."

Steve forgot to ask about Marx. But Marx was all right. He found a *Capital* and when the camera had swiveled away, he slipped it into his bookbag. Then a Debray. A Ché. Mao's *Quotations.* A Kropotkin. Into the lining of his air force parka. If Phil noticed, he didn't say. They grinned hip gambler grins at one another and Phil said, "Later, Steve."

Marx, Mao, Ché, Debray, and Kropotkin. A complete infield, including catcher.

Steve pitched his winnings out of his lining, into the lifeboat.

"*You,* Steve?"

"Everybody's got an uncle, George. Wow. I remember Phil when we took the administration building. He was up on a car that night doing a Mario Savio. And now—" Steve told George about the *very* hip bookstore in Brattleboro.

"Everybody's got an uncle, huh?" George grunted. "And you're pure, huh?" He assimilated it into his computer; it fit. He swallowed once, then his massive moon face, framed by red solar fire, relaxed. He went back to his room. Steve considered tacking up a 3 x 5 sign over the doorway: The Bestiary. Today he was a wall-eyed computer. Yesterday George was a griffin. Tomorrow he could expect a drunken red-haired cyclops.

What animal was Steve? Steve was *existentialops meshugenah.* Nearly extinct, thank God. Little survival value. Never looked down at the ground. Every bush a metaphor. Can't go for a picnic on a hillside without watching for a lion, a wolf, and a leopard.

He shrugged. Ask Chairman Mao. He opened the *Red Book* at random:

> We should rid our ranks of all impotent thinking. All views that overestimate the strength of the enemy and underestimate the strength of the people are wrong.

Good advice. But, plagued by impotent thinking, he climbed into the lifeboat and hugged his knees and sulked. He sat there till George, hammering up another picture on his wall, got to him. "George, will you cool it? Cool it, George. I'm miserable. The sky's falling down."

He tossed Mao aft in the boat, fitted real oars to the real oarlocks, and began to row in the imaginary water. It was smoother and easier than in real water—there was no struggle, and so, no forward motion. All things proceed by contraries. Blake or Heraclitus or Hegel or Marx. He rowed.

He rowed. Aha! It began to make sense. He was expressing precisely the "contraries" he felt in this year of the Nixon: him pushing, nothing pushing back but hot air from the radiators.

So. He closed his eyes. There was a forest on both sides. Tactical police were utterly lost in the woods. Maybe it was a beer commercial. Inside his head Steve did up a joint and floated, eyes closed. The tactical police were stoned. Then he turned inside out and floated into a deep jungle world. There was a fat parrot, iridescent yellow and green, red and blue wing feathers. It was as big as a tiger.

George had a real parrot in his room, and it was the only thing George took care of. Including George. It wasn't very beautiful, certainly not iridescent or big as a tiger. It liked dope, ice cream, and Cream of Wheat. Like George. But now Steve floated while a very different bird floated overhead like a bubble or helium-filled crystal ball. He watched for the Good Witch of the South. Or for the Wizard of the East. But before any such visitation, he fell asleep.

Cambridge is a lie. Doesn't exist never existed. I am in my cups. The moon a cracked saucer. We are hardly acquainted.

In the graveyard of the Unitarian Church, sixteen-year-old runaways slept, dreaming of breasts with amphetamine nipples. They are all the time tired. Cats prowl the graveyard lean and angry. They suck blood and fly moonwards. The Unitarians underground are coughing uneasily. They are pressed down by the weight.

He woke up. He pretended it was a Caribbean cruise; this was the ship's boat, his jeans were a dinner jacket and tuxedo trousers. Susan was off at the captain's table getting champagne cocktails.

When she came back they walked through the Square arm-in-arm with champagne glasses and a bottle of Mumm's. It was spring; they kissed in front of a Bogart poster and poured more champagne for a toast. The Beatles were on again at the Brattle. There was nobody else in the theater. All the psychedelic flowers were fading, wilting dingy, like the murals on WPA post-office walls. The submarine had faded to a rusty chartreuse. Steve remembered when it was bright yellow and Lucy looked just like an acid lady. You used to get stoned or drop acid and get into the colors.

The lifeboat was getting full. Harpo was asleep on a raccoon coat, and George and his girl, very stoned, were examining a wind-up see-through clock they'd ripped off at DR. Steve could hardly spread out his newspaper. It was a rush-hour subway except everybody had suitcases and guitars with them. "Is this the way to Charles Street?" The sign over the door said DORCHESTER.

They held on and on, the subway was behaving like a bad little boy they were disappointed and wrote a strong note home but his government didn't reply. They floated through Cambridge trying to find the exit. They shouted FIRE! but it wasn't a crowded theater, and so they were stuck, everyone with their own suitcase and their own piece of the action.

Susan's key turned in the lock.

"Susan—hey, Susan! Let's go get dinner!"

The neighborhood food cooperative operated out of Ellen's apartment. Her twins crawled among the market boxes and noshed grapes. "Stop noshing grapes!" Ellen warned. Susan put an Angela Davis defense petition on the table for co-op members to sign.

Chairman Mao sat crosslegged on a cushion slicing a California avocado with his pocket knife. He ate slice after slice of the creamy green fruit.

Co-op members started arriving to pick up their orders. Twenty-three member households came in; only five ordered Angela Davis. Steve threw up his hands: "Dare to struggle, dare to win!" Chairman Mao shrugged sympathetically. He'd had trouble of his own with Cambridge intellectual types. Ellen hugged her twins and said, "But it's people that count, not politics." She put a Paul Klee on the stereo and hummed W. B. Yeats.

Early spring. Cambridge. Torpor, confusion, scattered energies. A return to sanity was advertised in *Life* and in the little magazines. Aha, you mean sanity's *in* again. Okay! The art show Steve and Susan took in after dinner so they could drink free wine and hold hands was all giant realistic figures and giant colorful geometries. He could imagine them in the lobby of the new, sane, John Hancock Building. They said EXPENSIVE, CAREFUL, INTELLIGENT, PURPOSEFUL, SERIOUS; but HIP. And look at the long hair on the doctors and PR men at the opening. Everyone was hip.

"They're into patchouli oil on their genitalia for sure!"

"Who're you kidding?" Susan laughed. "You don't want to see paintings, you came to kvetch. You're a silly man. I want a Baskin & Robbins ice cream cone. And I'm willing to buy one for you, too."

"You're throwing your wealth up to me."

"Well," Susan signed, and took his arm like a lady, "some of us have firm positions in the world. Only Harvard Square trash does substitute teaching. This is a free country. Anyone with a little guts and brains and in-i-sha-tiff—"

"All right, I want an ice cream cone." He stopped and right there on Mass. Avenue kissed her, because she was so fine, because her tight jeans made him want to rub her thighs, because she kept him going through the foolishness.

They walked by the Charles River with their bridges burned behind them. There was nothing to do but shrug. An invisible demonstration passed them from 1969 waving red and black flags and shouting old slogans. So they marched too. Steve lifted a revolutionary fist and shouted, "Take Harvard!" Susan said he sounded like a Princeton fan from the '50s.

"In the '50s I was a kid waiting for someone to push a button and end my having to go to school. I wouldn't blow up: just my school. The walls. Then in the '60s I expected us to tear down the walls."

"Well?"

"Now? Ah, Susan, where will we wind up?"

"In a clock factory?"

On the other side of the river the business students stood by the bank with almost long hair and fat empty pockets. They bought and sold dope and sincere greeting cards with pictures of couples walking almost naked by the edge of the sea. Since the bridges were burned, Steve could yell, "You think you smell any sweeter, baby?" The business majors at the bank ignored them. When they had their stock options, where would Susan and Steve be? In the bathtub making love? In their lifeboat on a stream in British Columbia trying to locate the Source?

They wanted to make love, so they went back to their lifeboat and opened a bottle of cheap champagne. "What should we toast?" she asked.

"The river that gets us out of here?"

Steve made love with Susan on a quilt in the bottom of the rubber boat, a raft made for saving downed fliers.

Tuesday at lunch George and Steve spent a bottle of beer mourning the casualties.

"I decided again this morning," George said. "Not to be a casualty."

"Terrific."

"It's been a war of attrition. You know, 'I have seen the best minds of my generation…'"

"And some of the worst," Steve said.

"Sure. But like last night. Lynne came in to crash at 2 A.M. She didn't want to ball, just have a place. I think Paul kicked her out. This morning I woke up to the smell of dope, and she was getting sexed up and so we balled, but she didn't even know I was here. I can't get into that sickness anymore."

"Well," Steve said, "Listen: Afterwards Lynne came into the kitchen, you were still in bed, Susan was off to work. We had coffee. I asked her about her children. Her mother is still taking care of them. 'But I'm really together, Steve.' She told me that about three times this past year. 'I couldn't stay in that hospital; nobody knew anything about where I was coming from. My *supposed* therapist had never done acid, but he's telling me about drugs. But anyway, they detoxified me. Cleaned me out.'

"I asked her how much she'd been doing. 'Wow, too much,' she said. 'I was exploring heavy things, I was deep into myself. But back-to-back acid trips…too much. I think the hospital was good. But this psychiatrist with long hair, you know?…About my father.' Her voice started fading out. 'I had to split. I had to get back to my kids…' So she signed herself out.

"I reminisced about her kids—one day Susan and I took Lynne and the kids out to the Children's Zoo. So I was babbling and fixing coffee. I turned around, and Lynne was doing up a joint, and her clear blue eyes were really spaced out. She was fingering Nancy's old flute, recorder really, and she was talking to it: 'This side is blue, is

Hegel, and the lower register is red, is Marx. The point is to listen down into the tone of God. Otherwise you're condemned to repeat the cycle.'

"I gave her a kiss on the cheek and went back to my lifeboat to read. I understand you about casualties, George."

The casualties. And what about Lynne's two little girls? Today Nixon was on TV from Mars. He toasted a new "long march" of the American and Martian people. Two years ago we thought it was all set to auto-destruct: General Murders and Lying Johnson and Noxious Trixter and Spirococcus Agony and Chase Banana Bank. Now we're out looking for jobs. Peter, who put me down for getting a degree. Offered a job at Michigan if he'd finish his dissertation. He refused, lived on welfare, and organized at factory gates. Now he's still on welfare, but there's hardly a movement to support him. Two years ago he was right. Now he's another kind of casualty.

The bridge is burning while we stand in the middle. Our long hair is burning, wild and beautiful. We are the work of art we never had time to make.

I don't want to be a casualty.

Feeling restless, uneasy, he sat crosslegged on a pillow in the orange boat. He tried paddling down a magic river of umbrella trees, giraffes with French-horn necks, a translucent lady with hummingbirds flying out of her third eye. But the film kept breaking. To placate him or perhaps to make things more difficult, the projectionist flashed a scene out of his childhood: floating on a black rubber tube, a towel wrapped around the valve like the bathing suit that sheltered his own penis. He floated safe and self-sufficient past the breaker rocks. Where nobody could touch him. Meanwhile his mother stood by the edge of the ocean waving a red kerchief she pulled out of the cleft between her heavy breasts. She called and called, she tried to interest the lifeguard in his case. Steve's lips and ears were sealed.

Steve opened his eyes. They burned a little from salt water although he was twenty-four years old, although this was a make-believe boat, a living-room prop. He felt like a shmuck. Chairman Mao's face was red.

He didn't close his eyes again. "Hey, George? George!"

"I'm doing up a joint," George said from the other room. Then he came in and lit up. "Want a toke?"

"Listen, George—"

"I'm gonna get stoned and then get my room clean. Clean."

"George, first, come with me for a couple of hours. We'll wash our sins away in the tide."

They lifted the inflated rubber boat onto their heads like dislocated duck hunters. Through the French doors to the balcony, then by rope to the back yard. Steve lashed it to the top of George's '59 Cadillac. He wore a red blanket pinned at the collar, Indian style.

At the Harvard crew house they put the boat in the water and pushed off into the Charles. Metaphor of Indian so long ago there existed no Prudential Center or Georgian architecture of Harvard. Nice to push off into the river wrapped in such a metaphor. But today there was oil and dirt on the surface of the Charles; perch, hypnotized or drugged, maintained freedom of consciousness by meditating on their own motion. Even the fish with hooks in their mouths were contemplating their being and harking to a different drummer. That's all metaphor, too, for who would go fishing in the Charles? Steve played a rinky-dink tune to the fish on Nancy's recorder, but they turned belly up and became free of their bodies and of the river. The smell was nasty.

George said he felt like Huck Finn. Steve thought that was possible. They floated under the Harvard footbridge and past the site of the future water-purification plant to the River Street Bridge. Stench of traffic and COCA-COLA in two-story letters. The river curved. "I can see myself as Tom Sawyer," Steve said. "For me it wasn't quite real, getting Jim out of slavery. I always figured on Aunt Sally's investment firm to settle down into. But for you, George, it was a real plunge. You almost didn't come back out. You were almost a shaman who didn't return."

"What are you saying, you crazy fool?"

"We must steer the boat. Susan's school is by the left bank. She'll be getting out in fifteen minutes."

Kids in the playground on the other side of Memorial Drive waved at the young man in the bright red blanket. Steve leaned over the chain-link fence: "Peace to white and black brothers," he said, spreading his arms. "Tell Princess Afterglow we have come." George and a small boy tossed a ball back and forth over the fence.

"You're silly," a little boy told the Indian.

"Call Miss French. Ask Miss French to come down to the fence."

Miss French came down to the fence. Two little girls held her hands as they led her to the fence. She laughed and laughed and gestured *ten minutes* with her fingers.

George took up the recorder. It squeaked. "Steve. Those kids. That's where it's at."

"George, I don't believe you said that. Listen, George. I may dig being crazy or playing at being a child, but I can tell you that won't save me. Or being a freak. Or being an Indian. Metaphor won't save me. I got to save my own ass, so to speak. I mean, it's not any kind of revolution to float down the Charles in an orange boat."

"It was your idea. And who's talking about revolution? You're getting incredibly straight."

"And there—see—you can't make it on categories like straight. It's all over—the time you could think of *them* as bread and wine. So everything turns to shit in your mouth. Is bound to." He tugged at George's matted hair. "Except I don't feel like that this afternoon. I feel pretty manic and joyful."

Susan leaned against her bookbag in the stern and stretched back, her face parallel to the sky, and took it all in.

"Just smell this water. Don't fall in, friends," Susan said. "We'd be pickled in a minute."

They paddled upstream towards Harvard. Downstream, upstream. Circle Line Sight-seeing: on your right is Stop and Cop, and the Robert Hall Big Man Shop. Fer you, George. Harvard crews raced each other towards the lifeboat; alongside was the coach's motor launch. The coach, in trenchcoat, scarf trailing crimson in the wind, stood droning into a bullhorn. For a second Married Students'

Housing was upside down in the water; then a gust of wind shattered it into an impressionist canvas.

The shell raced by and the orange lifeboat rocked in its wake and in the wake of the launch. They shared an apple left over from Susan's lunch and didn't fight the rocking.

They rowed. They were rowing home. Home because

The cat has to be fed.
And the parrot.
Because we are hungry and
the place needs to be cleaned up bad.
There are lots of books at home, and a telephone.
Home doesn't smell as bad as this river.

No wild crowds on shore cheered this. From the footbridge no Radcliffe girls dropped white roses on their heads. Farther on, even more to the point, no marchers cheered them with raised fists, with red flags in the spring breeze, with a bullhorn dropped down off the Anderson Bridge so that Steve and Susan and George could address the crowd:

"Well, it's been a terrific five years. We've all learned how to make love and posters. We can really get into the here-and-now at times and we've learned to respect our fantasies. Yum yum. We're glad to be going home. We hope to see all the old faces tomorrow right after the revolution is over so we can clean up the paper we dropped."

After this didn't happen they paddled up Memorial Drive some more. The gulls were fishing. The shells raced past them going the other way and they rocked and bobbed, like a floater for fish. They sang,

Fish on a line
all strung out
If I cry the moon will go away.
Are you with me?
Plenty of conditions
Sold by the millions

Nice to tell you
can't hold water.

They drew pictures of fish in the water like invisible ink to be recovered later and read.

"We can't get anywhere this way," Steve said.

"Just float, man. The trouble with you is you never learned to float." George shrugged and reversed his oar, so the boat circled after itself like a dog after tail, like Paulo and Francesca. Infinite longing unsatisfied. But this was merely parody. George knew better than to long. The river stank but he had a cold. Steve and Susan were kissing on the bottom of the boat. Who knows how this fairy tale goes?

Why are the bridges all falling down? Why are the boats floating against bars of Ivory soap and turning over? It doesn't matter how the words go. They wound me up and didn't give me directions. Steve groaned, playing wind-up toy. But when he finished kissing his friend Susan, he took up the paddle and coaxed George into rowing upstream past Harvard to the boathouse.

Steve—Oh God Steve you've got to stop torchereeing yrself, Steve decided painfully. CHINA WASN'T BUILT IN A DAY. Steve closed his eyes and meditated, crosslegged in the wet lifeboat, on the career of Mao Tse-tung.

Susan and George carried in a brass tray with what was left of the champagne. But Steve was meditating.

"Join us, why don't you? We've got some heavy pazoola here on a fancy gold tray," George like a six-foot-three red-haired genie wheedled. "Cut the meditating."

"Who's meditating? I'm telephoning Mao Tse-tung in Peking. *Hello, Peking?*"

"Well, tell us what he says."

Chairman Mao, Chairman Mao, Steve said inside his head. Tell us what we can do in this year of the Nixon.

Ah yes, Mister Nixon…

It's been a long winter, Chairman Mao.

With no leaves on the trees, the wind shrieks; when leaves fill the branches, the wind rustles.

I think, Steve said inside his head, I get what you mean.

The important thing, Chairman Mao said, is to get outside your head. Open your eyes. What do you see?

The rubberized canvas sides of my orange raft and a print of the *Primavera* on my wall. My friends are offering me champagne on a gold tray. A brass tray, to be exact.

Chairman Mao supposed a difficulty in translation. You, you behave like a blind man groping for fish. Open your eyes. Study conditions conscientiously. Proceed from objective reality and not from subjective wishes. Conclusions invariably come after investigation, and not before. Open your eyes.

"Open your eyes and your mouth," Susan said. "Here it comes." She tilted a glass of champagne to his lips.

"Well, nobody can say those are elitist grapes. Those are the people's grapes," Steve said, pursing his mouth. "Connoisseur! Drink up!"

Picking up the pieces. Picking up the check. Somebody got to pay before we split and all them lights go out. Ah, well, but it's time to clean up and start almost from scratch.

Susan and Steve helped George clean up his room: Two green plastic trash bags full of wine bottles and dustballs, molding plates of spaghetti, old *Rolling Stones,* socks with cat spray, insulating felt strips chewed up by the parrot, Kleenex and Tampax and a cracked copy of Bob Dylan's *Greatest Hits Volume I* and a few cracked *ands* that broke open like milkweed pods and had to be vacuumed up in a search-and-destroy operation.

When George's room was swept and scrubbed, George decided to wash away the Charles River effluvium in the bathtub. So Steve and Susan sat crosslegged in the bottom of the lifeboat. Wiped out.

Then Steve pulled the plug. The boat hissed disapproval, deflated, expired. They were sitting in their own space, for better or worse.

Originally appeared in Massachusetts Review, *Fall, 1972*

Part-time Father

Next to him on the seat of the old Saab, a baseball, still in its packaging. Like flowers for a date. It embarrassed him, this wooing of his own son. Embarrassed him, playing the role of good-guy camp counselor—when he wanted just to be a father. Sometimes the pain of it made him want to forget the whole thing—these long drives, the planning and knocking himself out. And for what? A weekend. Not even. Why not be a father just to Jesse—his second family? Wasn't that plenty? But somehow, alternate weekends when Aaron wasn't busy with a Little League game, Herb saddled up and rode the sixty miles east to Concord—a backwards Paul Revere bringing no news, just himself.

He listened deep into the Saab's engine—too deep for his own good. Nagging anxiety about the engine, 120,000-mile engine, throw a rod and where would he be? How could he pay for a thousand-dollar repair? He imagined he heard every tappet click, felt every hesitation like a skip of his own heart. Jazz on the car stereo stopped the engine sounds. He listened deep into the music as the dying Massachusetts mill towns passed by.

At the country club courts, he stood outside the wire fence and waved. Aaron waved back with his racket, then set himself for the other kid's serve. A pasty serve—and Aaron smacked a stinger of a return down the line.

The lessons were paying off. Aaron's own serve had possibilities. It gave Herb pleasure to see his son press forward ferociously at the stroke and charge the net, hungry to volley. But the other boy returned the ball so high above Aaron's head it bounced over the fence. Herb tossed it back. As Aaron caught it, turned away from his opponent, he rolled his eyes in mock disgust. "About ten more minutes, Dad."

On the way home to get his suitcase, Aaron blabbed. Nervous, Herb supposed, like his father.

"Like the sneakers? Adidas. Same as the shirt I bought you, Dad. They're new, the sneaks. So's the racket. Mom and I picked it out last week. It's helped my game a lot.... Steve's coming for the weekend. Okay?"

"*Sure,* it's okay," Herb said. It wasn't at all okay, so breezily he added, "Hey. Your game *has* gotten stronger these past few weeks."

"Thanks. It's the lessons."

As they drove, Herb admired his son—lean, with good shoulders and a face that had begun to reveal the good-looking young man he was going to be. Small for his age, but strong. Herb remembered how his own father used to test his muscles with a squeeze and a grin. Now he was going the way of his father: hairline beginning to recede. Hint of a belly over his lean frame. Maybe that's why the kid's spunk excited him. But as he examined Aaron's Alligator sport shirt, he felt sadness in the hollow of his chest: that this boy, growing up with the expectation of winter vacations in the Caribbean, would be lost to him.

"Can we play some hardball this weekend, Dad?"

"I don't think so. I don't see how. Maybe softball."

"Well, Jesus, there must be some regular hardball game *somewhere.*"

"Don't you get plenty of hardball? With Little League?"

"Well, that's the point, Dad. My glove isn't right for softball and my arm isn't used to it and it throws my timing off."

"Aaah, you do fine."

"Maybe—you think—I should get another glove—Just for softball?"

Herb shrugged; he didn't answer. Aaron fiddled with the radio and the car was filled with the Beatles. They both loved the Beatles. Herb tapped his foot and tapped his foot, but finally he couldn't take it:

"Another glove? Christ. New sneakers, new skates, new racket. And that—computer baseball game you're fiddling with instead of being with me. Sometimes I wonder."

The rest of the ride to Aaron's, both of them were silent.

Down a street with contemporary colonials with broad front lawns, American eagles over front doors. So cornball! But just an interim street for Francine and Richard. They were looking for an elegant Victorian in Wellesley or Newton.

"I'll be just a minute, Dad." Aaron ran upstairs.

Already, Herb was regretting the boring lecture. The kid couldn't help it. That was the way they lived, Francine and Richard.

Francine met him in the living room wearing the velvet lounging robe Richard had given her for Christmas, a robe that Herb couldn't have afforded when he was married to her and now, even if he could have paid for it, wouldn't have spent that much on. She wore it a lot—maroon velvet with black piping. If he resented its opulence, he also—admit it—liked to see her wear it. It created a plane of graciousness for them to meet upon, a courtly speech that protected them both. Her dark hair against maroon velvet. Looking at her now, he saw a piece of what had made her so attractive to him fifteen years ago, and saw what had made him want to leave her. Both were there, somehow, in that one lounging robe.

"Well, have a nice weekend," she said.

"Hardly weekend. Thirty hours. Friday night he was busy, and Monday's a holiday but you're doing something. God knows what."

"Come on, Herb. I told you long ago we were going up to New

Hampshire Sunday afternoon—we're visiting the Bronsteins. Steve's parents. You said it was all right."

"Did I? Okay. Then it must be all right."

"Oh, please, come on, *please* don't make it hard for me, Herb. I'm in the middle," Francine said. "Doesn't Aaron deserve a normal life?"

"Enough, Francine."

"I'm supposed to appease both of you."

"All right. Enough."

"We'll meet you at three—on Route 2 again, okay? Like last time. Next time I'll drive him out to make up—okay?"

"Okay." He kissed her goodbye and, in reconciliation, put his arm across Aaron's shoulders on their way out. "See you at three, Francine."

"Have fun, you two," she said and stood in the doorway waving after them.

They picked up Steve, piled his bags in the trunk, headed west. Most of the way home, Aaron played computer baseball or tumbled in the back seat, laughing, with Steve. Steve was a tall, skinny kid with an annoying laugh. Polite and sneaky. It annoyed Herb to hear Aaron and Steve sharing private jokes. In defense, he played a tape of Galway Kinnell reading from his poems. The tape over, Aaron stopped kidding around and told his father about the class unit on Egypt and about an overnight his Little League team was going on and about the model of a suspension bridge across the school pond he was constructing with a couple of classmates. "We have to use a lot of math…It's *beautiful*," he added. And the way he said "beautiful" touched Herb's chest, made his body hum with delight, and he turned for an instant and grinned at Aaron. "Well, I'd love to see it."

"I'll send you a Polaroid snapshot next week," Aaron said. Taken with his new camera, Herb sighed. But said, "Thanks."

Passing through Green River Falls, he pulled up at his storefront office. Gilt lettering on the plate glass already peeling: Green River Community Action. What was the plate glass advertising? Poverty?

The store was as bleak as the next-door thrift shop. Unlocking, he saw the office as if for the first time, saw through the eyes of his son. Noticed that the drab, scuffed linoleum had worn through to bare wood at one spot; and noticed Sonia's desk—a garbage heap of crumpled paper, forms sprawled in collage over other forms (but she was, Sonia was, after all, his best intake counselor); noticed the boring, oppressive row of green metal files.

At the rear, his inner office. When he started this job, five years back, he'd refused to separate himself out as director of the agency by having his own office, his own locked door. But he got a lot more work done this way, and his staff people didn't feel his eyes on them. Still, every time he put the key in the lock of his office door, he felt embarrassed.

The report was waiting for him on a desk piled neatly with unfinished work. "I'll be done in a couple of minutes," he said, gently. They didn't mind—took turns on Aaron's computer baseball game, Herb was annoyed—but what did he expect? He skimmed the report—a ritual: he knew it would be okay.

But if he knew, what did he come here for?

Then it hit him. Sure. A kind of moral propaganda: to model the seriousness of his commitment to these people in his files. A way of life different from what Francine and Richard were teaching Aaron. That's why the computer game bothered him: Aaron brought that life along with him. And he wanted to tell Aaron, Listen, listen, back a few years we had the sense we could make new lives for ourselves—not just get ahead. New lives. Whatever phoniness went along with it, it was okay.

He didn't say this. But he couldn't help mentioning, as he placed the report in the OUT tray, "This Mrs. Skorzisky's got cancer pretty bad. We're asking for special payments. She's a special case, but it's like most of our people, Aaron—multiple problems. She's been in and out of the hospital. Her husband's in another state. We had to get her fuel payments last winter. The little girl's in Head Start, and her older boy we got a job through Youth Employment. So we do what we can."

"Dad?"

"Uh-huh?"

"Why don't you go into politics?"

"What?—Are you kidding?"

"Maybe run for Congress."

Herb just shrugged and grinned at Aaron. "Come on." He was caught between feeling flattered that his son thought him capable and hurt that his son didn't consider this job useful enough. Or important enough. And maybe was ashamed in front of Steve?

"Come on. Let's get going. While we've still got the afternoon," Herb said, feeling the time flowing out of him like breath or blood.

A few miles south of Green River Falls was the rough pine and insulated-glass house Herb had built for himself on a hill, built from foundation up with a couple of carpenters at a time when he'd hardly built anything in his life. It faced south. From the gravel driveway you could see two big solar panels that gave them their hot water and, at the edge of the driveway, the remains of last winter's woodpile, wood that gave them all their heat.

Lynn, feeding Jesse on the front porch, waved a spoon and Aaron yelled, "Hi, Lynn," yelled in his manly, uneasy, first-part-of-the-weekend voice. He carried his bag to the porch and stood hands on knees bending over Jesse in his highchair. "Am I your brother? You remember me? What's my name?"

Jesse, as always, went cuckoo. Did he know that Aaron was in special relation to him? What could *brother* mean to a one-and-a half-year-old? But he grinned and shrieked "Aaaaaahhhhnnnn!"—and tried to squirm out of the chair.

"Wait till you're done," Lynn said. She hugged Aaron and said hello to Steve and asked Herb to get the kids settled in, for godsakes, while Jesse finished eating.

"Let's get these bags up to the loft—on the double." Cheerful camp counselor, all-American roarer, circus barker, uneasy father—he clapped his hands and off they went. Herb grinned at Lynn. "We're off to the woods," he said, apologizing without saying so for leaving her.

Then Aaron was back, holding Jesse and grinning. "Weird little guy. He's getting so big," he said as Jesse manhandled him. Then Lynn was asked to admire (1) Aaron's sneakers, (2) his Little League jacket, and (3) his Alligator shirt—a match for the one he gave his father. She admired.

"Can I have something to drink, Lynn?"

"Oh, Aaron," she groaned. "You *know* where the refrigerator is. It hasn't moved, honey."

Herb started to help, then stopped in time, and Aaron said, "Sure," and went off with Steve to the kitchen.

"He's just being polite," Herb said, hunching forward on the peeling-paint rocker.

"It still aggravates me. And why is it *me* he asks?"

"Because it's you he's less sure of."

"Maybe."

"About his *place* here."

Leaning back and closing his eyes, Herb rocked.

It stayed warm but clouded over in the afternoon. They hiked through familiar hills. Skunk cabbages were unfurling in the swampy places, violets—he picked some and placed them reverently in a moist plastic bag—higher up on the trail. Often he took Aaron climbing in the mountains, serious, though not technical, climbing. It was among the best things they did together. Climb hard, feel close, not speak too much. But today was just a ramble. They wandered off the trail, cut across country—spring still new enough to make it easy to get through—hunting some miraculous meadow.

Leading the way, he played "Father." Not that he didn't love Aaron; it was as if fatherhood were a creation, something he had no authority for.

What about his own father? Had *he* ever felt that way? It was hard to imagine. His gross, lumpish, bearlike father!

"Let's you and me go see a movie, Herb," his father would say. Satisfied and sleepy on a Friday night after another hard week, he'd say, "Come on, tough guy, huh?" So they'd go, and it didn't matter what movie, because half an hour into it, he'd be asleep, one hand on Herb's knee or around Herb's shoulder, and it was nice sitting there, his father the gross body, he, the eyes and imagination, sitting close in the dark, breathing the onions of his father's breath, giggling to himself whenever, in the middle of sleep in the crowded theater, his father would let go a fart.

But by the time Herb was in junior high, that had stopped. So hard to remember just when. Or when he, Herb, began to disown his father, to be numb to his tender stuff. There had always been the yelling, but now there was nothing *but* the yelling. Fights at night with Mom. He worked late just to avoid her. Came home when she was asleep, tiptoed to escape her demands. His eyes hated the stains on the kitchen walls as signs of failure. He scrubbed the stains to death; he killed cockroaches like enemies. Or in a softer mood he'd heave a breath, checkbook and pen in hand, sag and slump, say, "The bills, Herbie. Oh the goddamned bills, the bills. She thinks I'm supposed to be a goddamned millionaire. She wants, she wants and she wants, what does she want from me?"

Herb hardened against his father's weakness. It was better to *fight* with him, because then he could feel their separation. I'm not like this—this poor bastard. This loser…

Now, remembering, he felt tenderness for him: a hard-luck householder trying to hold things together.

Aaron and Steve had brought a pair of walkie-talkies. One would "lose" himself and then, by describing his location, lead the other to him. Herb walked on, past stumps from ancient logging.

Suddenly, fording a stream, rock to rock, Herb superimposed another forest over this one. Where?

The Berkshires. He and Francine, the first or second summer of their marriage, were camping in the hills near Tanglewood. She'd come only for the evening concerts. In the woods she was afraid: of bears, of getting lost. Afraid of the earth itself because it reminded her of graves.

But she never let on. It was a fine day, and she was supposed to be happy. Herb wedged a bottle of wine between the rocks of the stream and played guitar for her. He remembered her face as the face of a too-serious child.

Being there in memory, he knew as he hadn't known then—he

had resented her serious face, her fear. But also wanted to comfort and reassure, to shore up the world for this other creature: Love, the world is as strange to me as to you. Am I supposed to be a man? I am unsure of the ground under my feet.

He plucked the wine from the cold stream and handed her the bottle. She smiled—a fake, frightened smile Herb hated—and sipped the wine.

"Isn't it beautiful here, Francine?" Herb asked, knowing that it wasn't in the least beautiful for her, pressing her to say the truth so he could be *legitimately* angry at her.

"Beautiful," she said, and looking around her as if Appreciating the Day, she sipped the wine...

Herb took one of the walkie-talkies and hid behind an old tumbled stone wall, from which he could see the boys. He lay there, directing them "twenty steps down slope, then find a clump of birch..." until they came upon him. They sat on a carpet of star moss talking Red Sox, and he felt happy. He knew these woods pretty well. He could feel, through invisible filaments threaded to his heart, Boston far beyond those hills over there, New York downriver. As if he were the center point of a map laid out through his body. And suddenly, as if a forest god had made his presence felt, his dead father, hardly a forest god, urban seat-of-the-pants struggler, entered and filled his body. And then, as if the moment were no longer locked into a niche of time, he felt himself father to Aaron and Aaron father to another little boy, and all of them here this instant. He remembered the photograph on the desk of his own grandfather, photograph of his father and two uncles impossibly as children. For an instant he was tinted sepia and framed in antique gold. His face calmed, his breath deepened, became rich: he was a photograph on a desk, a photograph in the study of Aaron's someday child.

Father and father, son and son, he smiled for the camera...

Friends came for dinner, the boys went upstairs to watch TV, and Herb was caught between. He'd hustle upstairs to sit with Aaron and laugh at the commercials, hurry downstairs listening hard to catch whiffs of table talk so he could be part of things when he sat down.

Annoyed at Lynn for having eyes to smile at his nonsense, he knew that if Aaron were part of this marriage, lived here with them, he'd let the kid *be* for the night. But having so little time, he pressed it unnaturally, and the wine was sometimes bitter.

Next morning the same: Herb wanted a few minutes to sip a cup of coffee and play with Jesse on the living room rug. But outside Aaron practiced pitching to Steve. Aaach. He should join them. But Lynn wanted to shower and wash her hair. In compromise he watched Aaron through the window and from time to time trotted to the door to yell out, "Great pitch."

"Thanks!" Until finally Lynn came in, rested, clear, calm—he could see it in her eyes, not haggard, tense, driven by the schedule of her work week—came to him, her hair in a towel above her head, wearing his terrycloth robe, and slipped the robe down off her shoulders, turned her back to him: "Lotion me, okay?" He did.

"I'll be a few more minutes," she said, and gathering up her robe, went upstairs.

"Take your sweet time," he said, not meaning it, because it was after nine and he wanted to spend the morning playing ball with Aaron. No game this morning—part-time fathers had a hard time finding pick-up games—but he could take them down to the town field for practice. Even hardball practice.

He wrestled Jesse around the rug, but Jesse decided he wanted to play by himself—stack block on block on his own. Herb was amazed to see his fingers working, this little creature. He went off for his shine kit and brown wingtip shoes and shined them up while watching Jesse build.

From outside, a high yell: "Strike *one*!"

As he shined his shoes, again Herb became his own father. His father had, of course, been more intense about getting a high shine on his Florsheims. Near bursting, face flushed and sweaty, he used to brush his shoes the way you might cut cordwood with a hand-saw, so much power went into those shoes, then slap the leather with a cloth, wipe the sweat from his face with a pocket handkerchief, unfold a white shirt just back from the laundry. Herb had two pairs, black and brown, of his father's Florsheims, twenty, thirty years old now, still in good shape, and when he wore them, he went through his father's ritual. Gentler about it, but still he could feel his father enter his body, his own face fill out with his father's heavier face, his own back thicken into his father's muscular thickness; it was like possession, and he couldn't alter his own body feelings to dismiss, to exorcise his father's flesh. Hell: didn't even want to. He felt himself part of a long continuity of fathers lifting up sons.

"Strike *two*!"

At last Lynn came down the stairs with Uncle Sam, their blue-fronted Amazon parrot, on her shoulder. Green smock, green parrot and her blonde hair. "Well," he said. "Good morning, love." She was *back,* he said to himself. Meaning? Oh, that weekdays were tough and often her eyes were elsewhere and he, too, was under pressure and Jesse would kvetch and howl and he and Lynn wouldn't be there for one another. Now, she was back.

"Hi, parrot lady." He nuzzled her. Uncle Sam nibbled and nipped his ear.

She smiled at him, then she sat down with Jesse, and Herb was free. He waved from the doorway, zipped up his windbreaker, and trotted out like a big league ballplayer at the start of a game. "Okay, let's get some action started here," and Aaron threw him the ball, and he realized, as he threw it back, Ah, dummy, the action had already started without you, you're not the action, and he realized that the surge of guilty energy was very like his own father's. But that was all right, it was all right to let his father play some of the ball. At this moment, he had room for both of them…

Driving Aaron to meet Francine halfway to Boston, Herb didn't listen to Aaron and Steve talk baseball in the back seat, baseball and baseball cards, voices over the hum of wind higher as the talk grew hotter. Herb felt the usual Sunday-afternoon-pain-behind-the-eyes, taking-Aaron-back pain. He resented him a little. Twenty, thirty minutes before he met Francine at Howard Johnson's for the changeover, he began to cut himself off. It felt like a dream: he was chauffeur. Aaron ignored him. Weekend father, he was near tears. How's school? How's your Little League team? Questions like those fell into a pit and died.

A couple of years back he could have played an alphabet game with road signs or billboards, but that was too young for Aaron now. Almost a teenager—my God. There'd be secrets and private pain, soon, maybe already, and he wouldn't be there for Aaron the one moment late some night when, after stirring stuff around for a week, he could talk to a father.

So.

So. So that's the way it was.

"Hey—you remember Twenty Questions? I've got a Twenty Questions for you guys." So they played. Herb had Carl Yastrzemski's Red Sox cap in mind, and the boys got it in seventeen—with a little help.

"So," Herb said, "you got to play hardball after all."

"Not really *play,*" Aaron shrugged.

"Well, it was the best I could do."

"Sure, Dad. And I wouldn't mind playing even softball—you know, a choose-up game?—I mean next time. Maybe I can get Mom to buy me a softball glove."

"Oh, Christ, Aaron. Get what you want. Get whatever the hell you want."

Up ahead was Howard Johnson's, and he slowed down. Whatever he was carrying, he could lay it down and breathe.

Francine, sitting in her car, reading, got out and waved as they pulled up. Left rear fender crumpled a little but he decided not to ask, knowing without putting it into words that to ask would have meant restoring a piece of their old relationship, a piece that was never any good—he the critic, she the dolt about machines. He waved back, the boys got out and Aaron started telling her about the Red Sox game the day before, and she nodded, nodded, wasn't hearing, stood looking at Herb in that vague way of hers, as if wanting to be in conversation with him but distracted by the boys, transferring gloves and bat and backpack to the trunk of her Buick.

"Richard's inside making a telephone call," Francine said. "If you want ice cream, he might just buy some for you."

They cheered and ran off.

She wore jeans and a sweater. He remembered how she'd been

contemptuous of jeans, how she'd worn tweed skirts and forced her hair straight while they'd collaborated, without revealing it to one another, to grow far enough apart to separate. Now that they were separate, it didn't matter what they wore.

"How was the weekend?" she asked. "Everything okay with Aaron?"

He shrugged. "It was a nice weekend."

"We had a nice weekend, too."

"Good." He stretched and yawned to show her he wasn't tense or depressed.

"Oh—" she remembered—"do you have your check? If you don't, it's all right," she added in a rush.

"Oh, *sure.*" He fumbled for his checkbook, wrote out her check against the hood of the Buick, ashamed she had to remind him. "Cash it quick," he said.

She laughed her tense laugh and folded the check into her purse. She stood by the car and they were quiet, as if taking the air.

"I was walking in the woods yesterday," he said, "and I remembered the time we went camping in the Berkshires. You remember that weekend?"

She nodded. "We went to Tanglewood. Sure. Of course I remember. I was eight months pregnant with Aaron and sick to my stomach."

"Pregnant. No kidding. You sure?"

She could hardly forget *that,* she said.

He felt ashamed. His memory seemed like a fiction—designed to give him a version of the world he needed. That she was pregnant! He looked at Francine's face to let it remind him. But she seemed, for a moment, like some new acquaintance.

"What I remember," he said, resenting her for making him feel ashamed, "what I remember *best,* is feeling I was supposed to be a Man. I was supposed to be strong and reliable. A...*man,*" he said again, waving his hand in the air trying to shape for her the significance of the word. "I don't know if that was just *me* or if you really laid that demand on me."

"You weren't misperceiving. I imagined life with a fantastically wealthy older man. You know—yachts, power, invulnerability. He would take care of me. Remember—I'd lost my father a couple of years before."

"That's right. Your father."

"We were little children. You and I."

"Sure."

"The fantasies," she went on. "I could never tell you. I guess I wanted a nineteenth-century husband."

He smiled. "You think that Richard is a nineteenth-century husband?"

"I've grown up a *little,*" she laughed.

Out came Aaron and Steve, licking ice-cream cones, Richard behind them, his hand on Aaron's shoulder. Herb waved.

"Ice-cream cones are up to half a buck," Richard said, coming up to Herb and shaking hands. "How the hell do poor people survive?"

Balding, smiling, handsome in his belted suede jacket and Basque beret, Richard was and was not the protective nineteenth-century husband Francine had wished for. *Was* because he had some money—ran an investment counselling firm in Boston, found tax shelters and leasing gimmicks for the rich. Was *not* because you could see right through his stance of tough practicality to a decent, vulnerable man.

Aaron hugged Herb goodbye and sat in the back of the Buick with Steve.

"Well," Herb said. "So I'll see you in a couple of weeks."

"But Herb?" Francine said. "Remember, we talked about it? We've been planning to go sailing—on Arthur Quint's boat—with Aaron and Arthur and Lisa and their son? It's a little tradition of ours, getting the boat ready for sailing in the spring."

"Oh, Christ."

"Please, Herb."

"Then—what about *next* weekend instead?"

"I'm afraid next week is impossible," Francine said, looking over at Richard. "Sunday's fine, but Saturday night he's going to a class party or something."

"But Sunday is fine," Richard underlined.

Herb started to feel choked. Tears thickened unreasonably behind his eyes. "Well, it's always something, isn't it? And here I am, busting my hump to pay for it." Using the idiom like a slap. But it was his own face that felt hot.

"Oh, Herb. Here we go. Please don't make it hard for me. Doesn't Aaron deserve a normal life?"

"Normal! You keep saying *normal.* So I have to pay for him to go sailing or buy twenty-dollar tennis shorts or some fancy softball glove?"

"Excuse me," Richard said. "I think I'll go sit in the car." He climbed in and started the engine so he could play the stereo to cover the quarrel.

"Do you really believe," Francine asked, "you pay *half* of Aaron's support? Do you, Herb?"

"Probably not. Of course not. In a house like yours? And summer camp? But in relation to my salary—"

"You're a trained *lawyer,* for godsakes. You talk as if you're poor, Herb."

"Compared to you and Richard? Do you know what I make at the agency?"

"But that's your choice," Francine said. "It's fine if you want to work for people in trouble. Somebody has to. But is it fair to make us pay for your choices? Now, listen—do you know what just his tennis lessons cost us?"

"That's the point."

"What's the point?" Francine's voice had grown raspy, monotone, brittle.

"This life," he said, biting off his words. "I don't mean to put down your life for *you.* But I give you my money to turn Aaron into an alien. An adult who'll look down on me as strange. But *he's* going to be the strange one. In the world as a whole? Not knowing what's really up—"

"Oh, when you get self-righteous like this—"

"—thinking the whole world is a suburb with tennis courts and sailing lessons and that Betamax of yours—"

"What sailing lessons? Oh, *boring*!"

"Sure, he's been to London and Los Angeles. But he won't care a goddamn what people have to go through."

"Give me a little credit, for godsakes. I think he's learning a lot about other people. Oh—you can get to be such a sadsack sometimes. You can get to be such a loser, Herb. You think I want him to grow up like that?"

He turned from her, leaned down and tapped on the window of the Buick. Aaron waved; Herb waved back and grinned. Francine stopped at the car door. "I'm *sorry.*"

"It's okay."

"Call me later in the week. All right?" He got in the Saab and casually turned the key, and the goddamned engine wouldn't turn over and it wouldn't start and it wouldn't start, old car, no money for a new one, and he kept his eyes straight ahead and his face deadpan—and suddenly it kicked over. He breathed, gunned the engine, and drove off, past the service island, into the lane that led back to the highway.

Jesse pulled his wagon filled with hats and scarves across the living room floor. Lynn, curled up on the sofa, read a book on two-year-olds, getting ready for Jesse's next stage. Herb didn't feel like talking. He went into the kitchen to fix dinner. Sipping wine, slivering chicken raw from a breast, he listened to an old Brubeck reissue over the stereo. And then, for just an instant, he remembered his father again, his father fixing a sandwich to take with him to work, and it's maybe 6:30 in the morning, a Monday morning, and his eyes are half open and he's slugging down coffees to get started. Pop looks up, grins, yawns comically, theatrically, as if to acknowledge that he's a communicant in the ritual of getting up, going to work. A workingman. No. Something more: being a person who handled, somehow, the pressures.

Herb grinned back. He started cutting onions.

Originally appeared in Virginia Quarterly Review, *Fall, 1977*

Prewar Quality

It was hard times.

At night Susan massaged his neck and shoulders as if he were a warrior or a ditch digger. His hard work!—writing reports on Services to Juvenile Offenders. The massages were light-hearted, a form of irony. What, baby? What's the story? He didn't know. The job, he supposed, was a lot of it. Still, it was better than bumming around Harvard Square. And the want ads in the *Globe* were no better to read than the mail.

He was preoccupied with the mail and with the telephone. He scribbled lists of calls and made them and checked them off his list whenever he doubted that he had any right to his life. Of incoming calls, he was suspicious.

A call from his mother as he was leaving work; Aunt Miriam had been taken to Mass. General. "And I wondered, Steve—you're in the same city, and she was so close to you when you were a little boy."

"Sure. But we're planning to go off for the weekend."

"Oh, Steve. Aunt Miriam."

He brought along a book for the waiting room.

She was in intensive care; he had to talk his way in—a "nephew." Then the doctor was generous; he explained that every night she survived the odds grew better. But it wasn't likely she'd live through the weekend. The vascular system of a woman of eighty. How does it happen, Doctor? She's not even seventy. The cigarettes? But she hadn't smoked in years. Pollution, tension, disease? Is it inherited? Arteries harden till the heart bursts. A punctured aorta and nothing strong enough to sew a dacron tube to. Jeans too worn to patch. You can go in now.

Miriam lay fourth bed down in a jungle of tubes and wires. So small in the hospital bed. And he remembered her a big-boned woman. The covers rose hardly at all over her frame. He didn't want to look at the bones sticking up through the sheet. He realized he was holding his breath and that the tension in his belly was making him nauseated. He let go; a hot wave of blood rose to his throat and face: Hey, Aunt Miriam!

Her hair they'd left alone; it flowed over the pillow; her small head floated within it. He remembered her eyes, but her eyebrows had grown thick and unkempt, manly. Peasant-from-some-other-century's eyes. It had been ten years. He had been fifteen.

A stool by the bed. A nurse carried it over for him and touched Aunt Miriam's shoulder. "Mrs. Rose?" Was she asleep? What was the good? Her eyes (he remembered them) were open.

"I'm Steve. Stevie Kalman, you remember."

She lifted a hand light as a bird and laid it on his arm. A disattached hand, like a word, so light. "You see how it goes," she said, slurring the words a little. "I can't offer you anything."

He waved the suggestion away.

"They took my cane." Then, an idea—"Will you see about my cane? Make them give it back. I can't even make a cup of coffee for myself without my cane."

"Do you know what place this is, Aunt Miriam?"

"Where we are? The *hospital.* I don't remember which. They told me after the pain. But what about dinner?"

The cane. He'd heard about her accident of six years ago. He couldn't imagine Aunt Miriam with a cane. Always so strong. When he was twelve and she must have been more than fifty, she could outrun him. Where was that? The beach, the beach. They ran the hard sand along the tide's edge. She wore a simple black bathing suit with a white handkerchief to hide the cleft. I used to be quite the runner, Steve. Want to try me?

Instantly—sitting on the hard stool looking at Aunt Miriam dying—he knew why he'd chosen to remember. Because he felt right now an embarrassed winner. He felt healthy, an ashamed god, in this terrible place. The old blind man groaning among his tubes in the next bed, the...person—man, woman—mummified in bandages. Burned? Burned horribly?—across from the foot of Miriam's bed. How could she stand it? But she must be hardly aware. He, Steve, wore a clean white shirt open at the neck. He crossed his legs and felt superficial, effete, a dandy. He felt embarrassed in front of the nurse who hurried from bed to bed, checking tape and bandages.

Deep into her nose, translucent plastic tubes. Another into her mouth. From under the bedclothes more tubes, connected to a plastic sack pinned to the bedding. Tubes for intravenous feeding were taped against her arm; plastic-coated wires taped over her chest fed data into a small oscilloscope measuring pulse rate and pattern. As he sat he watched the screen in fear that the rate would jump past the DANGER setting. He didn't know what would happen then. He spoke softly, as if Aunt Miriam had a tarantula on her neck and must make no sudden movements.

"Aunt Miriam, it's been so long, such a long time. My mother sends her love."

"Then shouldn't she be here?"

"She will be."

"I never completely trusted her. Not completely. It's your father's fault, of course." Vacant for a moment. Then she confided—bringing her face up from the pillows—"I'm very sick, you know. They tell me it's back pains, the dummies. It's back pains all right, there's blood burst through something and it *hurts.* They don't put you in this torture machine for *nothing.*"

She tried sitting up (Aunt Miriam! The tarantula!), tried

ripping away the wires and tubes, and he had to grab her hands and hold them as if just in friendship. "Aunt Miriam, Aunt Miriam, just relax, we'll talk."

She sank back; her body disappeared under the sheet.

"Well, what's to be done? They took me here in an ambulance. I was *very* sick. I'd hate to tell you what I did in my bed just before..."

"Never mind. You get strong, Aunt Miriam, and Susan and I will take you out to Jimmy's Harborside."

"Oh! I know the place. Shellfish! No thank you!"

"Sure. The Sanae, then. We live on a vegetarian diet too. Mostly." And Steve was amazed—the confluence of cultures! She—oh, a food faddist for years now, a frequenter of health-food stores; he and Susan—eaters of brown rice and mung beans.

She looked at him and winked. A conspirator. He drew very close. "Stevie—what does *Monsieur le Medecin* say?"

"The doctor says you're a very sick woman. You've got to rest yourself."

"I've been busy all my life, Stevie."

"I know you have. You've worked very hard."

"You can't imagine what a dog-eat-dog profession fashion is."

"You were always successful," he said, tuning in on her need.

"Always! Even as a young girl just out of high school—with no...connections—" She said *connections* as if it were a foreign word she had to work to recall. "I was an *unusual* woman, Stevie. I was never your run-of-the-mill young woman rushing after a husband and security. Security! I never had security. I never wanted security. I took chances, and I was a success." She quieted and closed her eyes. "Of course, to be close to God is the only real success..."

Then he remembered all at once: the wild Aunt Miriam; then, when he was a teenager, the totally reformed Aunt Miriam—Aunt Miriam thc Rosicrucian.

She came for dinner twice a year; she led them in silent meditation. Old Stick-In-The-Mud Miriam. His father wouldn't close his eyes but no matter. Then the battle over the white bread, the sugar, the meat.

You know, his father barked, the only decent meal you eat is when you come to New York and eat with us. I never see you leave anything on your plate.

Miriam chewed carefully, chewed up and swallowed her anger. Finally—"Waste is a disgrace to God."

Why did she still come to visit? To renew contact with a reflection of herself from ten, twenty years before? But now she talked about spiritual exercises and profound meaning. And when Steve was fifteen and horny just all the time, she told the family that she had for some years now *achieved celibacy.* Steve caught her alone as she was putting on scarf and galoshes. Aunt Miriam, why? What made you—achieve celibacy?

She laughed.

You don't remember, she'd tell them, but once I was a beauty. That sort of thing doesn't matter to me now, you see—but once—Oh!

Once, just before the war, she sailed the *France* to France. The scales of the fish were gold on her gold lamé blouse; there were diamonds for her rings, a ring for every finger. She was commanded, *bien sûr,* to the captain's table. Where a Du Pont, imagine, fell in love with her. But that...sort of thing stopped mattering, it stopped mattering so long ago. I was twenty-eight, it was so long ago, I lived with Chikalaiov on the left bank, the whole world was topsy-turvy—communists, fascists, you had to be *some*thing. I was—I suppose—a communist, but I didn't really care. I was even hit on the head by the French *gendarmes.* Oh, *bien sûr,* it was an accident, an *erreur,* but there it was. So I called myself a communist until after the war...but I NEVER trusted those Russians...this was the 1950s. She tapped her fingers on the kitchen table to add credibility to what she had to say. The nails were blunt now—the scarlet tips were gone!

"But you were a success in worldly terms, too," he told her, brushing back her hair so he could touch her cool forehead.

"I was!" Her voice was clear and musical, somehow innocent. "Oh, Stevie, how you loved it when I came to see you, you were such a sweet little boy, 'Auntie Miriam, Auntie Miriam,' and your father tried to hush you. He never thought I was good enough. But you loved me. And I'm not even your real aunt. Though I was close as a sister to your mother. Please Stevie—" she whispered—"Don't tell her to come in yet. Let's be quiet and not bother her. Until they take away these awful tubes!"

He nodded and took her hand. She must imagine his mother was just outside, in the waiting room.

She arched her brows: "Stevie, you see, I always knew you'd be a big man someday."

"I'm some big man! I just work in a social agency."

"Well, it's just a matter of time. You're going to go places, you mark my words, *mon petit.*"

Subway through Cambridge, rush of the wheels. Feeling let down and empty after all that intensity. Remembering Miriam's child-face nested in her hair on the white sheet; should he call in sick tomorrow, stay with Miriam? Numb, helpless in the rushing subway, remembering Miriam *before* she'd changed, before she'd turned "spiritual." I was a little boy. My father roared after she left—that piece of tinsel, of fluff, pipe dreams she feeds you and you swallow them down. Forty-five years old, she's still a little girl. And *you're* still a little girl.

She's been all over the world.

Sleeping around like an alley cat that's no trick.

She's a famous designer. A brilliant woman.

Aunt Miriam's lipstick smelling of pipe dreams on my cheek. Off again to Europe on a buying trip.

What do you need her for?

What do I need *you* for?

The train hissed to a stop at Kendall Square.

Steve remembered that Miriam of his childhood, her reddish blonde hair fluffed up and careless, dark at the roots; her spangled hat and two-inch heels. Steve remembered the long black limousine that met her at Grand Central, brilliant, magnificently clean against the dirty street they lived on—a Venetian gondola carrying a princess, an aging, mad princess, past kids playing stickball, mothers sagging on stoops. Auntie Miriam!

Times a' gettin' hard.

Old Lady Stick-in-the-Mud. Rosy Cruisin'.

A set of tin soldiers from Paris. Prewar quality, she said. Set up the castle and opposing tin armies, tiny silk flags for the battlements; castle smelling for weeks of perfume from Paris.

It was raining when he trudged up the kiosk steps into Harvard Square. Drab late-fall cold rain for Miriam. And it was Thursday evening, which made him especially depressed because it wasn't Friday evening. He bought flowers at the corner so Susan would have something to see besides his face.

Susan attended to his flowers; she attended to his pain. Attention without tension, so that the pain eased and the situation itself stood out, cleared of entanglements. He looked up at her clear brown eyes and tried to imagine her old, entangled in tubes, her arterial system a clog of scabby, rotten stuff there was no way to operate on.

"Susan, her face—it's so young."

"You want some wine, honey? Before we eat?"

He shook his head; he held Susan very, very close.

"Hey, I'm not going to fall apart this soon," she laughed. "I'm only twenty-four, you nut."

After dinner he called his mother in New York. *Aunt Miriam is dying.* She cried and Steve soothed. "Steve, I'll be there as soon as I can in the morning. Oh, my God, Stevie, what a gorgeous woman Miriam was. You'll never know.... Listen—something important. *You* know these hotels. The first thing they'll do is padlock the apartment until they get a court order appointing an executor. Call Francie, Steve—Steve, call Miriam's sister Francie. Get the key from the nurse. Go and see if you can find the will. It's for Francie, she's poor, and godforbid...see if there's a will. And small round keys to safe deposit boxes, bankbooks. You understand?"

"We'll go together," Susan said.

In the foyer to Miriam's apartment one small red bulb had been left burning, turning the living room into a cave or tabernacle. He couldn't find the overhead lights; Susan went from lamp to lamp. Half the bulbs were out, but there was enough light. The walls were full of family pictures; Susan looked at the pictures while

Steve looked through the desk. A big hotel desk, it was practically empty.

"Steve, look—is this you?"

A photo of himself and his cousin at the beach: Miriam's eye must have been behind the camera. He imagined her looking at him, became her looking at this kid, perhaps the day they'd run the beach together. In the picture he looked about twelve.

The dim walls, dusty glass over the pictures. It was hard to see who they were. Family. He wouldn't know. Soldier from the Second World War. Women in one-piece bathing suits with children on laps. The same children older and older, then teenagers at a photographer's studio in suit and tie or graduation dress, then adults with their own children on their laps.

A photograph of a crowd of young people in a brand-new open touring car of the early '30s; in the background the apartment buildings of Central Park South. His eyes were getting used to the half light. "Susan, look." That woman next to Miriam, he knew *her,* she'd given him these eyes, these words.

"Beautiful!"

Except for photographs there was little in the apartment that didn't belong to the hotel. The meagerness made him shudder. One book—a dictionary—a pile of Rosicrucian magazines on the coffee table.

They watered the ivy, the jade plant, the geraniums.

In the closet, a line of shoes, so many. Didn't she ever throw old shoes away? Shoes, a fallen cape tumbled in the corner. Maybe it was false memory: Aunt Miriam sweeping once into their kitchen in a cape like that. Story about a cab driver who tried to seduce her and drove her around Central Park seven times with the meter running.

At the back of the closet, on the floor, there was a fine old steamer trunk, elegant with fleur-de-lis designs. They lifted it out carefully and set it down under a lamp. He felt very close to Susan. On their knees they were mourners or worshippers, archeologists, detectives, conspirators, lovers sharing a world.

In the silk side pocket of the trunk was a pair of mother-of-pearl opera glasses in a suede case; a 1929 *New Yorker* with a cover, slightly torn, of Fifth Avenue on a Sunday. Stylized to look quaint. To produce nostalgia. Now the cover itself, its particular style, looked quaint. He thumbed open the magazine to a paper-clipped page—a circle in red pencil around a fashion note—

> Miriam Rose, whose smart afternoon things we didn't see, is showing sports trousers of plus-four length... Mainbocher is the latest...

At the bottom of the trunk was a cardboard file. Steve found two tickets, untorn, to a play he'd never heard of. He put into a manila envelope a key wrapped in a slip of paper with a number and the name of a bank, a storage ticket for a fur coat, a long white envelope with Miriam's careful printing: Last Will and Testament, and dated July 26, 1942.

He and Susan spent an hour looking through the trunk. Old letters they left tied in velvet ribbons. But they read through a folder of Aunt Miriam's love poems. Had she showed them to anyone? Then—"Susan, look!" A framed photograph from the 1880s—from Russia? From Austria?—a family about to split up, one branch to the New World: a conventional studio tableau, posed grief-at-parting; brother with a handkerchief-of-sorrow to his cheek; young woman, maybe Miriam's grandmother, stretching her hand in farewell to an old man in a frock coat. A new life in Baltimore.

Then a photograph of Aunt Miriam in a velvet gown and white silk shawl—long fingers in her lap, diagonal over long fingers. "Younger than this, Steve?"

She is so young again. She is living in 1936 looking forward to years of glamour. Or is it me doing that? But her face, I didn't make it up, it is a child's face, looking forward. It is 1928; she is a Baltimore girl coming to New York! She spends half her salary on rent; she is only twenty years old. Writing long letters Dear Momma, her parents Orthodox Jews, Jews of the "old school." A virgin; brought up to be someone's future wife. *I took chances. I had courage. You think it was easy? Spagnoli was my friend. He taught me and taught me....* Her past I see it as still a future. Her face younger than my own.

Tired, late, another call from his mother. He asked her if the will was still operative.

"If there's no later one. 1942! Because of the war she made it. She wanted to become a nurse…"

Susan was working on her lesson plans; Steve put down the phone and hummed "As Time Goes By"—as if he were Sam in *Casablanca.* "I'm in love with the good ol' days. Good ol' bread-lines, good ol' Hitler."

She laughed. "Well, it would be nice to go to Paris together."

"I'm going to buy you a long feathered boa and a double string of pearls. We'll stroll the Champs Elysees just as soon as my unemployment insurance runs out."

"You're not getting unemployment insurance."

"We'll see about that."

A juke box woman, she danced to Glenn Miller. The old razzamatazz. Ticket stubs taped inside a program—Ziegfeld Follies 1937. Glorifying the American Girl. Miriam in lipstick, Miriam in heels, one knee bent, heel resting on a boardwalk railing. Huge flopping hat framing her face. The Spanish Civil War was going on. She hated fascism. I am a remarkable woman, Stevie.

"On the phone tonight my mother was remembering champagne at the Plaza in 1939. My God, 1939!" And was it any different for himself? The 1950s weren't a time of McCarthy and reactionary cold-war politics. They were summers at the beach, they were Miriam bringing him curious antique keys, taking him to the Statue of Liberty.

"Well, you're a delight," Susan said. "Bother me when I'm working, then go off and dream."

Not being able to turn himself into a delight, he kissed her. He was a sailboat his mother had launched at the small pond in Central Park. But where were the cement walls? In every direction was ocean.

She had been asleep, but her eyes focused sharp on his face. "You've gotten to be a man, I suppose.… So? What can you tell me about these smells? Well…do you think I'm going to be all right?"

"You'll be fine."

"You'd say that one way or the other." She drifted away. Then back again. "How's your mother?"

She didn't stay awake for the answer. Her mouth opened askew. He examined the soft, only slightly wrinkled skin of her face. That she had danced with a Du Pont. That she had serious ideas about the spiritual life and had become a stolid, drab businesswoman. He couldn't tell her that he had seen her in her apartment last night, that he saw her past as a future.

She lay with tubes in her nose, in her mouth, in her arm; wires to her chest measuring the beat of her heart. She is a delicate business. Years of designing herself, of diets and vitamins and making love on buying trips to Paris. The RAF pilot she married and divorced. Henry Wallace—in 1948 she worked for his campaign. I was born that year. *Alexander Nevsky* and Paul Robeson a benefit at Manhattan Center.

Layers on layers. Miriam opened her eyes and looked at him a young girl, flirtatious, arriving at Paris on the train from Le Havre. Younger: a child looking at her father from a sickbed. Then she clouded over with pain. She stopped being with him; he stared at the oscilloscope.

It was all right. She smiled up at him and sighed, "Stevie! *Tu es trés, trés chic, trés charmant, mon petit."* She laughed and shook her head, wrenching at the tubes. He held her hands. He remembered the Christmas day she fluttered in speaking French, French, French. His father walked out of the room. Mother had lost most of her French, but that didn't stop Miriam. His mother's present that Christmas had been a set of Edith Piaf records.

"I'm not afraid if this is dying, Stevie. It's all right. You look at me so unhappy, *mon petit.* If the dying doesn't take too long, it's an adventure."

"Oh, Aunt Miriam—"

"It's an adventure, in a way." She squeezed his fingers. "Did your mother ever tell you how brave I was in Paris—the one time we were in Paris together? I let an *Apache*—that's a street person, a local tough—pick me up in a bar! (You're old enough to hear this, I should hope so!) I hadn't twenty francs in my purse, so what could he do to me? Sarah was afraid he'd kidnap me into white slavery. *Well, not at all.* I was *never* a coward."

"You're a strong person, Aunt Miriam. You really are."

She smiled. "And you—what a big man. You have a career?"

"I have a job. Trying to help young people in trouble."

"Well, I knew it. And you're married?"

"Almost." He remembered the long love poem he found, yellowed carbon copy in her trunk. He'd memorized the first stanza—

> Why deny the sacred duty
>   of a love both free and strong
> Who can hope for grace and beauty
>   without faith to guide along…

Old lady. Proud young woman full of romantic bric-à-brac. So young now and dying, she was old, it was 1929, collapsed veins and images. As if he were watching a friend, as if he were watching Susan, go through the loss of her youth in a few moments; then return to that youth with its promises known in advance to be empty. Oh, Jesus.

"I'll let you sleep, Aunt Miriam."

"I'll have plenty of time for sleep, *mon petit.*"

She was being romantic; the French. Romantic about dying? Come on.

Woman in her terrible boat, condemned. A certain shipboard adventure lying there, a certain hope that a war would lead to a socialist world, a Ziegfeld Follies performance: alive there on the bed.

"Miriam—how do you feel?"

"Strictly between us, I think I'm feeling better, Stevie. They'll take me downstairs soon."

"Downstairs?" Then he understood—she thought this was a part of the hotel. "You mean take you home?"

"Home, downstairs. It's the same thing, isn't it? Did they lock my apartment? Who's going to make dinner?"

He guessed it was the sedative. Or too little oxygen in the brain. He wanted to ask, What is it like, to look back…Miriam the young woman.... But his mother was at the door of the ward. "Only a few minutes," the nurse told them both.

"Miriam, it's Leah." His mother looked beautiful too, not haggard as he'd expected. He kissed her cheek. She wore a wool cape with Persian trim. It went well with the 1930s hat she wasn't wearing, with the bobbed hair of her yearnings, with a double string of imitation pearls: two young women, one thirty, one twenty, posing for a friend (perhaps Chikalaiov) at a sidewalk café.

"I'm sick, did they tell you?"

"You're wonderful. Dear Miriam."

"Your boy is sweet. Stevie—I can call you Stevie!—what a sweet boy. He hasn't left for five minutes." Then she said, "If I had children, that would be an entirely different story...Stevie, I remember when you were born, what a beautiful baby."

"You were always good to him."

"*Wasn't* I good to him? Well, and shouldn't I be? Look at him now. He's going to be a great person. A big man. You *never know.*"

"How do you feel?"

"Better. Much better."

His mother remembered: The beach days. That crazy artist you lived with. Your rich friend in Paris. The morning we sailed on the *Aquitaine.* Do *you* remember McCory, old man McCory, he wanted to marry you. Champagne at the St. Regis...

And Miriam: I went to the St. Regis to dance, I went to the nicest supper clubs. The waiters were gorgeous Italians. Or maybe that was a boat, I forget... "You know, Stevie, I almost seduced your mother away to an entirely different life!" She remembered: "Oh, Paris, trying to make a comeback after the war. From all over we were invited, there were skinny children begging food, but in the showrooms it was another story entirely: high fashions and champagne—the best! Where is New York, really..."

She held his mother's hand, it was an old story, her voice wasn't strong enough to carry the energy.

"Oh, what *show* they had! I looked up Chikalaiov at his old address. But, with a Russian name—I had little expectation. His concierge sobbed. *'Allé, s'en allé, it ne reviendra jamais.'* I ordered just a few good things. But when I returned to New York, I interpreted the French fashions with an American woman in mind…"

Steve slipped away. He found Susan and they waited together. Parts of the *Boston Globe* and out-of-date *New Yorkers* to thumb through. Meditation on the 1930s. Flowers for Miriam, her hopes sparkled. The breadlines vanish, she is a queen. You surprise me, sir. Oh, Lady, the old ladies who could speak a line like that are long gone. I am nearly long gone, she reminds me. Wait for me, I'll join you.

They waited. Steve's mother came to wait with them. I remember, I remember, did I ever tell you the time. I was eighteen years old, a baby, and she was in her late twenties. Four flights of stairs, she was living with an artist. I remember.

Steve wanted to see her once more before they went home. They were changing her sheets, they were washing her. Just a few minutes.

"You're Miriam Rose's family?" The tall, athletic doctor stood in the doorway; it was a courtroom—they stood up. "I'm afraid I have some bad news…"

"Oh, my God." Steve's mother started to cry and Susan held her.

"Mrs. Rose passed away as we were changing her bedding. The aneurysm burst again. She was gone without knowing anything."

"So fast!"

"We thought it might happen like that. Do you want to see her?"

Steve did want, although he felt that what he should want was to walk away from the dead. But his mother…if Susan could take care of her a minute while he slipped off…

They'd finished cleaning the body; the nurse drew the plastic curtain around the bed. He kissed her cheek, he loved her. Aunt Miriam. He wished he could cry.

At the funeral he avoided the body in the coffin. He sat with his mother and Susan very apart from the service. Seven or eight old ladies, older than Miriam, came in and sat down. By the time the service began the room was half full of people in their sixties and seventies.

Whenever he went to a Marx Brothers movie or an old Gary Cooper-Marlene Dietrich movie, he felt the question, Where was that pretty supporting actress now? An old woman somewhere in L.A. cooking eggs for herself on a hot plate? Now he wondered who these old people were. What had they been in the twenties and thirties? He looked into their faces and tried to imagine them imagining their futures. But they were masks, unapproachable, sacred ritual figures.

"Over there, that's Frances, her sister Frances." Paralyzed, in a wheelchair. Tiny withered bird with claws for hands. Next to her wheelchair a huge black woman, rhythmically stroking her back through the blanket.

His mother turned for comfort not to her son but to Susan, another woman. He saw her face deeply; lined, tired underneath her charm. She was only middle-aged. But he saw her lying in a hospital bed tangled in tubes. Old dying woman. But at the same time or a moment after he saw her as a young, life-hungry woman who could *never* fall into the traps laid out for her. And then he thought of Susan; and of himself. The inside of his body hollowed out—a plane hitting an air pocket—he had to suck in breath to keep from sobbing.

And still to keep on putting a life together!

He walked home with Susan and his mother, holding them both around the shoulders, seeing in a new way. He couldn't talk to them about it. Seeing an old man, Professor Emeritus from Harvard he'd seen often in Grollier's Bookshop, seeing him as about to graduate from college (the street scene turned 1920). He himself felt seventy years old; he couldn't talk to Susan. But alone with her, that night, after they'd seen his mother off on the train to New York, he told her, "I guess I'm crazy. I keep seeing you as seventy years old; we've been together all this time."

"And we're still together? That's nice."

"Oh, we still love each other. But where have the years gone?"

"We have the children."

"But they're older than we are."

Up over the vanity a Chinese poster of Marx strokes his beard. He has just finished his early philosophical manuscripts. He may write an analysis of the development of capitalism. He strokes his thick beard and tries to undo this idealist nonsense. The revolution is at hand! But Steve watches Aunt Miriam step out of a taxi and wave—her hair is long, she wears a smart white silk scarf tossed over one shoulder, rakish hat angling over one eye. Lipstick and pencilled eyebrows. Hey, Miriam, hey, Aunt Miriam, it's 1929—I *know* there's a crash coming. But Miriam is full of bustle. And now Susan is nearly asleep, curled up against me. We're two overlapping question marks in a bed, but it's only me doing any questioning.

Susan, you're so warm, love, my body next to yours thaws, I stretch into a kind of exclamation point; hey Susan, don't let's sleep yet. But Susan is asleep.

Big man. Big Man.

He remembers her face, Miriam's dead face; remembers that he kissed her cheek; it was so soft, only a little bit cool. So much like a girl. Younger than his mother, younger even than Susan. Her skin soft and delicate, the capillaries lining her face like a leaf with sunlight coming through, a stained-glass leaf, a church.

Originally appeared in Colorado Quarterly, *Fall, 1977*

Fantasy for a Friday Afternoon

David fishtailed the old bug down the icy creek road to Route 2, out of Heath, out of the hill towns, barely in control, but who knows—Jamie could be really sick, he could be dying with a burst appendix for all he knew, and the poor kid was never in on the decision to live in the hills twenty miles from even a second-rate hospital.

Wool hat itched and sweated David's forehead. He hunkered down over the wheel, brewing a headache, almost *wanting* the headache, as if that at least would be making an effort. Jamie in a sleeping bag across the back seat, and not even decent heat in the car, loose door rattling and wind hissing in the crack.

Jamie groaned.

"I'm *hurrying,*" David said, as if the groan were an accusation. He skidded a turn and nearly slid off the side road across the highway. "Son of a *bitch!*" Then, closing down his terror, breathing mechanically to shut it down, he became solid, purposeful. "Hey, Jamie. You didn't know your daddy was a racing driver, did you."

No traffic on Route 2, thank God. He climbed a long hill, smooth highway broad as eight country roads, VW engine whining and tapping in third.

"DADDY! DADDY!" Jamie was suddenly screaming, howling. David pulled over quick and skidded against snow the plows had piled up.

"Okay, okay!" He spun in his seat. "What? What?"

"I made in my pants." Jamie howled.

"You made a movement?" Now he could smell it. "Loose?"

"I wet the sleeping bag, Daddy!" Jamie was in spasms of sobbing.

"Do you hurt, Jamie?"

"I'm dirty!"

"Thank God! Thank God that's all it is. You had to poop is all." Then, relief over, he sighed, "Just climb out of the bag, okay?"

"It's cold."

"Yeah. It's cold. Never mind."

David kissed his son's forehead and turned around in the road. "We'll take care of it at home, you dope. It doesn't matter about the bag."

"I'm not a dope."

The engine missed a couple of beats. David had a vision of its heart breaking down, father and five-year-old shit-in-his-pants son stranded at maybe ten o'clock on a freezing night, not much traffic and who'd be willing to stop?

But the bug kept trudging along okay. Onto the country road for the five-mile climb to Heath.

Jamie was brooding. I would be, too, David sighed. Moon-filled night. Sap buckets like devotional candles catching moon near the base of the sugar maples, evidence of faith that the winter would break down soon. Hard for him to believe.

The sleeping bag was stained, but not bad. "Now out of those clothes and I'll wipe you." Thank God the washing machine was working again. Out of nowhere he found himself singing Cole Porter—"I Get a Kick Out of You"—and when, unexpectedly, the lines came through—about ennui and champagne—he began to giggle and had to sit down, wet sponge in one hand, to laugh it out. "Hey, Jamie, what *am* I doing here?"

Jamie shrugged, sleepy now.

"Old city kid like me?" He scrubbed Jamie down. "The joke has gone far enough."

He heard Anna's car squeal to a stop on the frozen gravel. "Don't you think so, kid?"

Cleo heard the Saab and barked like hell. Then Anna called from the mudroom, "Come and take Sara." He took the baby from her. Pulling off her boots, she asked, "Anybody call? Anything happen?"

David was maybe too tired to make love even if Anna had wanted to. But he supposed she didn't; the question wouldn't come up. The vocabulary of their life together didn't include much love in the middle of the week. Waiting for her to settle Sara in her crib and come to bed, he lay looking through Anna at a list in the air: Hemingway in period E, discussion in period G of a few dittoed papers...On this side of the list, Anna was down to her longjohns. Over that she flipped a flannel nightgown.

"That cold it's not," he said, somehow annoyed.

Because they weren't making love. Because the longjohns made her body look thick, doughy, untouchable—no longer the sensual peasant he first saw eight years ago in the light of hanging kerosene lanterns at a barn dance.

He turned onto his side away from where she'd be.

"Sorry you had all that hassle tonight," she said.

He shrugged. "I panicked."

"Are you angry I wasn't home?"

"You couldn't be home."

"But are you *angry?*"

"Not your *fault,*" he mumbled, angry at her for running her therapy number on him. He began to tense up and became fearful he wouldn't be able to sleep again and he needed it so *bad.* He didn't want to quarrel. After all, therapy was what she did. That was also not her fault. Neither were the faded longjohns.

In bed behind him, she smelled of the woodstove she'd just tamped down and of the skin cream she wore against the air dried out so by the stove. "Good night, David. Thanks for tonight."

Most days the long, long drive to the regional high school served as a buffer: at school he didn't think much about Anna and the children. But today was Friday, and, hanging up his coat, he found himself listing jobs for the weekend: taping and painting the drywall in the bathroom, installing a new damper on the woodstove. As if he'd already bartered away the weekend before it began.

Turning from the teachers' closet, he noticed Diane Holmes sitting in the corner of home room, and suddenly he was fully present. Diane was early, as usual, writing as usual in her leather-bound journal, brooding as usual, with what seemed an intelligent sadness he was a sucker for.

But this morning there was something that wasn't usual. Something about her clothes. The crisp white blouse and beige slacks, just the usual ugly polyester clothing that made him feel so hopeless because the locals thought of it as *fancy* clothing and shopped for it Friday nights at the mall, and he, projecting himself unfairly, inaccurately, into them, felt how little it must appease their hunger. But the point was that, in the vocabulary of Diane's wardrobe, these were *good* clothes. On a schoolday? So he went up the aisle in the small room, smiling at this small, nervous, very pretty girl with amazing eyes, and, not wanting to get too close, sat on the edge of a desk halfway to Diane and said, "Hey. *You're* all dressed up."

"Not really," she shrugged.

"You look nice." And didn't say, That's a good sign—I worry about you…He shrugged, turned to greet his little buddy Phil Gamboni, pudgy Phil who edited the school paper under David's direction. "Hey. How'd the game go, Phil?"

"Nothing spectacular, Mr. Frank. Nothing sensational. We won. Smitty scored 22."

And then they were all on top of him, Tony and Pete and Elena and Sukey—and the day began. He passed out slips for library, information on the school carnival, handed out a couple of free paperbacks he'd scrounged from publishers—his final ties to rip-off days when, ten years ago, he'd left Boston for the country, moved to the commune in Western Mass. and stole items from a long list that hung in the kitchen—a rip-off list—and felt righteous doing it because the benefit wasn't his and the loss was some chain store's. What bullshit, after all. This paperback giveaway was the last vestige of those Robin Hood days—publishers' freebees, no longer free, either, fifty cents now. Well, it was the only way most of these kids—children of mill workers, part-time farmers, cashiers in K-Mart, businessmen in town—would get to own a decent book. Left on their own, they'd buy a record, go see a rock concert. But given books, they often loved them.

Looking up, he noticed that Diane had slipped out. While he blabbed to the others about college—they were juniors and should start thinking soon, though he knew that less than a third would go—with one antenna of his mind, he felt through the school for Diane.

Mr. Armstrong had asked him to keep an eye on her.

Twice she'd left Green River Falls, run off, once to New York, once to Boston. Once there'd been a rock singer involved and the kids had her labeled—though at school she kept to herself—as wild. Each time she'd come back on her own, but not until her parents had called the state police and the school had had reports to fill out and a social worker had taken up an hour of Mr. Armstrong's time and Armstrong hoped it could "be avoided in the future."

"She's a funny girl, George." David could say that but couldn't tell George Armstrong about her big, serious eyes, sullen, sad eyes, her look of knowing something she didn't want to talk about. "I like Diane," he said simply. "I like the seriousness with which she talks about a novel. Hell, George, she *reads.* That's something. Sure—I'll keep my eye on her."

So this morning, before the bell rang for first period, David left his home room and went down the hall toward the library.

Turning the corner, he saw her halfway down the empty corridor. Open locker door between them, so that all he could see were her canvas shoes and the curl in her long brown hair.

"That you, Diane?"

"Sorry, Mr. Frank. Something I forgot." She closed the door before he got to it. Maybe she *had* forgotten, but he saw her carry away nothing he hadn't noticed before—the same journal, her loose-leaf, and a text.

"It's okay. I'm not policing you," he said. "But it would be good if you could hang in there with us."

She nodded.

"You understand?"

She shrugged. "Because I'm alone a lot. You want me to be more social."

Saying it like that, she was right in such a way as to be all wrong. How could he set her straight? She lacked the categories. *Social.* Christ, no. "Not *social,* Diane. Look: I like who you are. I like it that you're alone and read and think about things. But if you could be more connected. Connected—not social."

She tucked her books under her arm and walked down the hall with him. For the moment, they were connected. "You're about the only one around here—" She stopped.

In the middle of feeling sad for her, he glowed.

"Is something going on at home, Diane?"

The bell rang for the first period. Energy, suddenly, in the deadly empty green corridors. She shut her eyes and laughed, and he laughed with her.

"Got to go, Mr. Frank."

"See you later." He wanted to pat her arm, her shoulder. He was an easy toucher—liked the physical contact with the kids. With Diane he was more diffident. He waved, he smiled—he felt false.

As the day went on he forgot about Diane. Forgot until he slipped in the teachers' lounge for a cup of coffee and overheard Jameson hold forth to Stanley Ford: his potbellied interpretation of inflation, a sermon delivered in a pontifical singsong that let Jameson soar above this regional high school, above the "tedious" students he taught—students who knew Jameson for the ass he was. Overhearing, David remembered Diane. Why *wouldn't* she run away?

Stanley, Jameson's victim this morning, you couldn't help but like. Sure. But the both of them made him wonder, What *could* come out of such a place? Suppose you had a potentially terrific tennis player—world class—and all he got for a coach was Mr. Skibiski. A sweet blusterer, Skibiski, not a bully, not a little Mussolini of the tennis court. But no coach. Then wasn't it the same for any potential musician, historian, future person of affairs? This school bred millworkers, office workers, bored mothers, Sunday snowmobile drivers, submissive citizens, men and women ashamed of themselves, who considered themselves third-rate, deserving of whatever governments and corporations needed to do to them.

Before Jameson could catch his eye, David carried his coffee back to his home room.

Diane was in his last class of the day, a class of juniors, most of them community college bound. She sat in the back, and all at once he recognized that he was trying to get her to look up from her journal.

They talked about Hemingway's "Hills Like White Elephants," and halfway into the period he stopped and asked them to write a dialogue in which something powerful was going on between two people and neither wanted to speak about it, and yet the thing lay beneath every word they said.

"Like sex?" John Flynn said, coolly.

"Sure. Or what else?"

"Somebody dying. Or leaving," Ellen Skinner said.

"Or people really pissed at each other," Ervin Price said.

"Go on. Write it. Try just a few lines. A page."

Hunched over her journal, Diane wrote, but he didn't suppose it was the assignment. He guessed that *what* she wrote hardly mattered. Just *that* she wrote, and could keep out of things. He let her be, but he felt the pulse of her sadness.

It touched off his own. Tears started up just behind his eyes—something that had been happening these past months. Winter months. New England winters. What's to be sad about?

Hadn't he gotten just about what he'd asked for?

Ten years back he'd finished college and a month later fled the city. Like Babylon. His draft board had classified him IY—troublemaker, weirdo—for the speech he'd made at his physical; naked, he'd stood on a wooden table and taught a "class" on racism and genocide and imperialism. He'd been pulled down and kicked out, but he'd won. When he left for "the woods"—that was the way he kidded about it then—he never got reassigned to a new board. He dropped out, ran from Babylon to the commune. And wasn't it a good move for him? He knew nothing when he arrived, but he stuck it out. Now, living just with Anna and the kids, he could handle country things—could sharpen a chain saw, cut up and split logs in an easy, hours-long rhythm, set fence posts, cultivate asparagus and cucumbers—cash crops—keep up, with Anna's help, a decent garden that provided them with most of their vegetables. And when he looked at the split wood he'd stacked outside their door and, inside, the woodstoves were stuffed and stoked, he felt proud of this life he'd made. Proud again in spring when he'd rototilled the garden for another planting.

This season was in between: winter's end. In the hill town where he lived, spring hung back a week or more behind this county seat where he taught. Maybe that was all it was...

He left just ten minutes at the end of the period to listen to a few of the kids' papers. Diane didn't take part. A couple of minutes before the bell she slipped out of the room. He let her go; after the bell and he'd collected the papers, he sat watching the buses load. Due at a meeting in fifteen minutes, normally he would have swigged a couple of fast coffees so he could stay awake through George Armstrong's speeches. Instead, he watched for Diane. Knew which bus she took. Knew she wouldn't be on it.

The buses, one by one, pulled away. A few kids had begun using bikes already—streets icy in patches still, too dangerous—and a few cars stopped to pick kids up. He didn't see her.

David shrugged, went for coffee, and looked down the corridor where Diane's locker stood. What the hell. Went back to collect his books and head for the meeting.

Then he saw Diane.

She was crossing Winthrop Avenue, backpack on—daypack,

really, a pack with no aluminum frame but huge bulk humping over her lean body, long green scarf trailing over her shoulder.

He could explain to Armstrong later. He shoved books into his briefcase and, coat still unzipped, was out the door, across the parking lot to his car. Diane was already out of sight, around the corner. Heart thumping, he went after her.

School was just one long block off Stevens Avenue, the main street that led at one end to the interstate (New York? Montreal?) and at the other to the highway (Boston? The West?). Figuring *Boston,* he cruised north, and in less than a block he saw her.

"Hey, Diane!" He pulled over, rolled down the window. "Need a lift? It's too cold to walk very far."

"No thanks, Mr. Frank."

"Hey—no trouble," he said, opening the door for her. "I'll take you up to the highway."

She stared at him a long few seconds, thinking, he supposed, that now her plans would have to change. Struggling out of the straps, she heaved her pack in the back seat and climbed into the front.

"Where to, lady?"

"I'm going to visit my aunt in Orange."

"Hitchhiking?"

"I've got money for the bus but I figured I'd hitch and save it."

The fullness of Diane's explanation told him it was a lie. She needed, he guessed, to avoid the drugstore bus station where everyone would know her and remember where she'd gone.

"Well," David shrugged as he turned onto the highway and the old bug picked up speed and the loose door rattled like dice, "I'm heading past Orange. I'll take you."

She shrugged, folded her arms over her winter parka, and sat back. "Bummer," she sighed.

A trickle of heat hissed through the old car. Tick of the tappets and tiny, high-pitched whistle that Anna could never hear quieted as he reached 55 and leveled out past ice, blue on the rocky cliffs that overhung the road, cliff slashed through to make the road. Thawing, freezing, always blue, late winter. He watched for icy patches in the road. Diane slumped in her seat, arms folded, mouth set hard against his interference.

"Look, Diane, if I take you to Orange, you'll just have to hitch again or spend good money on a ticket for Boston. And what the hell. Even if I fink on you—and I won't—you can lose yourself pretty well in Boston, right?"

"What's *fink?"* she asked, suspicious: no—*irritated* at him for using a word she didn't know.

"Squeal. Rat. Stool. Turn you in."

"You're going to Boston?"

"Now I am. Okay?"

"Nobody's making me go back."

"Who? Me? Who said anything about going back? Listen, you're sixteen. Legally you can drop out, right?"

"Look, Mr. Frank—"

David, he wanted to say. My name is David. But he contained himself. "Let me waste the gas," he said. "You matter to me. Okay?"

She copped a quick look at him and he couldn't look back, embarrassed that she might take that the wrong way. Or that he might *mean* it the wrong way. With peripheral vision he watched her watch him. He wanted to smile. He wished he could put a paternal arm around her.

"You meeting anyone in Boston?"

"I'm *not* running off to get *married,* Mr. Frank."

"Funny. The way you said 'married,' you make it sound pretty revolting."

She shrugged.

"I see you at school. I keep wondering about you and your parents. Look—I mean, do they knock you around? Anything like that? Some funny things go on in families."

She lit up. She laughed and unzipped her heavy parka and whipped off her long green scarf and let out a spurt of laughter. She snapped on his tinny radio. Crappy top 40 under a sea of static. She fiddled with the dial. Heavy energy DJ's who made him wince. "Oh, Mr. Frank, is that funny. Boy. Nobody beats me," she said. "We don't say ten words to each other. They're afraid to talk to me. They figure I'm weird. I stay in my room with my music and my books and come down for meals."

An old, old story. But he said, "Sounds awful."

"If I *do* say something, I'm not a person. Just somebody peculiar. So I don't talk. We eat together. You know—Pass the salt. Then I wash the dishes and run upstairs."

"You read a lot."

"Oh, sure. Always." She sat back again.

"So it's dead at home—and dead at school."

She switched off the horrible music and turned to him: "Your class is okay."

"Thanks."

"But Mr. Jameson in history? He's more out of it than my father. I can learn more by reading on my own."

She was, he felt, taking a chance, trying him. He said, "Jameson's a nerd. Contini's a shmuck. I see them in action in the teachers' lounge."

"Teachers' lounge," she laughed. "But you don't have to sit and listen to Jameson and listen to him."

"I count my blessings…" He guffawed.

"What's funny?"

"We're both running off from school, that's what."

"Are *you* running off?"

"Yes. Yes, maybe I am," he said, surprised. Then added, "For the afternoon." And at once he had the fantasy of spending the weekend with Diane. Little hotel where he'd spent a night with Anna once. Running off with her, this sexy young girl, lithe like a gymnast, girl without drudgery.

His head felt giddy. Oh, just a kind of waking fantasy. Fantasy for a Friday afternoon.

"Green River Falls," she groaned.

"*Boston*," he sighed.

"Did you ever live in Boston?"

"I grew up in Boston. Brookline, really. I went to Tufts. My father owns a couple of bookstores. My brothers are in the business, and I was supposed to come in with them. But I dropped out. Came to Vermont and then to Western Mass. to live the Good Life. But the Good Life got a little boring, so I started teaching.... And now, teaching..." He didn't finish—wiggled his hands back and forth, *comme ci comme ca.*

"I want to visit the museums."

"Me too. And I want to go glut myself on foreign films," he said, grinning, "and eat croissants in little cafés and have intense, phony discussions about art. And, especially, I want to go roller skating along the Charles. We saw them do that one weekend."

"Roller skating?"

"Sure." Saying it, he flushed, feeling Diane's quilted shoulder pressing his own, and he felt his fingers stroking her lean, naked back and hips—like a mill race it rushed through him, making him churn, making him say, To hell, to hell with it, to hell with being ashamed of this, to hell. He didn't care that she was a kid, didn't care that her face was beautiful but only half formed; he didn't care that he could feel her unease, her forcing herself to be grown up. To hell, he wanted to hold her, as if she held some terrific power that could free him or anyway soothe him. But, quietly, he just sighed, "Boston...Boston." He sighed again. "I could dig it myself." *Dig it* maybe didn't mean anything to Diane, but she caught the tone, and her face brightened.

"I've been putting away money in a bank in Boston," she said. She tossed it out casually, the way a child makes light of something she's most proud of.

"Hey! A thousand?"

"Four hundred."

"Well, that's enough for a while. And then—what?—a waitressing job?"

"Maybe. Sure."

"Sure.... And then what?"

"I don't know.... Eventually..." she stopped, said again, "*Eventually*, I mean, I want to do something. I mean *really* do something. Maybe become a journalist." Then a shrug—no big thing.

"Hey. You've never told me that before. You know that?"

She didn't answer. He took the miles at an easy 50. At the crest of a hill above Fitchburg, he switched on National Public Radio from Boston—late afternoon Mozart without much static. He raised his eyebrows at her, meaning, Okay?—but she was into her own thoughts. He imagined her life in Boston. Who she'd get involved with. Conned by. He saw her imperceptibly drying up with cynicism, her spirit watered down by banality. God forbid.

"Well, *why* should I stay?" She asked him in sudden anger. "Am I going to learn anything?"

He breathed a great breath and, exhaling, his spirit balloon sank to earth again. In her pout, in her slight whine—in her need—he understood with his heart: She was, of course, a child. Beautiful because she was a child. Not that he didn't want to touch her. Oh, Jesus, sure he did. But he knew he wouldn't now. He was both disappointed and relieved.

"Ah, you're right," he said. "You won't get a lot at that school you couldn't get on your own. A little math. Practice in writing. Talking about books with me and with Linda Krantz. I'll tell you, if you hang in there, I'll bust my hump to get you a scholarship at a private college—or help you make the right contacts at the university so you don't waste more time. Because if you're going to be a journalist, you're going to need to *know* things, Diane. Experience *isn't* enough. With no education you'll be taken in by simple-minded formulas. That's the problem."

"It sucks."

What sucked? Everything, he supposed.

Even *with* an education, he wanted to tell her, there was the likelihood of getting suckered in by simple-minded formulas. For instance, himself. Dropping out, running from the wicked city to the virtuous land. Another version of pastoral. And then, imperceptibly, the place he ran to as a refuge became a place to run from. Not that there *wasn't a* poetry about splitting kindling on a frosty morning. To eat—at a table he'd built—bread Anna had baked, warm from the oven, it made him slow down and feel the nub of life between his fingertips. But the phoniness! He hadn't understood ten years ago that his retreat had been a kind of aristocratic gesture—a younger son, in England, say, preferring a quiet life on the family estate to the vulgarity of a "trade." He hadn't understood how much his retreat depended on the ordinary local people—that cousin of Diane's who owned the service station, for instance—people who didn't have time to care about the texture of wood and mildewed stone and late afternoon sunlight on young leaves and the comfort of radiant heat from a woodstove as you dressed in the morning.

Nor had he understood how much he was *dependent* on Babylon. Cheap gas, for instance, that used to permit them to drive fifty miles to a movie, run off to Boston for a weekend, go to Tanglewood for a concert. They did that less and less as gas became more expensive. It had become a luxury for them to have two cars, to live twenty miles outside of town. The farthest thing from simplicity. And without cheap gas their country life was closing in on them.

He ached to tell Diane how tired he was of his country life, his teaching life. He contained himself.

"Suppose I lived in Boston," she said after a long silence. "Couldn't I take classes? At Harvard? At—where was it you went?—"

"—Tufts—"

"—Tufts? And couldn't I finish high school in Boston?"

"How, if you're working? And to get into college? No way, without graduating high school first."

"There's a rest stop up ahead. Please pull over, okay?"

He flashed his turn signal. He knew he'd won, so he found his heart sinking, sinking.

He pulled off the road and cut the motor.

"I just don't know," she said, playing with the fringes of her scarf. "I need to think a minute."

They were silent together.

"It's just this spring—and then just one more year, Diane," he said at last. He felt tears well up. He wanted to put his arm around her. *Just that.* Jesus. So *much* wanted. And couldn't.

She began to dry heave suddenly as if she were throwing up—he even moved to roll her window down—then saw it was just tears she was holding back. So, as he had done with one kid or another more times than he could count, he put his arm around Diane and held her against his chest and let her weep, and felt his own need to weep—the loss of her as imagined lover or rebel as she metamorphosed fully into a child he needed to care for.

When they got back to Diane's it was after five. Half a block from her house he dropped her off.

"Have a good weekend."

She laughed. "Yeah. You, too." She shifted her book bag to her left shoulder, held out her hand and half shook, half squeezed, his own.

He watched her walk away. For maybe five minutes he sat with the engine running, gas getting used up, and then he headed home along Route 2, but so slowly that soon a line of cars was stuck behind him and a big trailer truck shot past, diesel horn honking. He pulled off the road, switched off the engine, sat and thought, eyes closed.

He found himself sweating, his stomach doing butterflies as he understood what he wanted to do. He was heading home—but home just to pack; it was Anna's late night at the center. She wouldn't be home till seven. He was supposed to pick up the kids from Sandy, but they'd be fine. By the time Anna came back, he could be on the road again, city clothes packed.

He'd pack just enough for a few days. He supposed, whatever revulsion he felt, he'd have to come back to finish his contract. But at least the weekend—and maybe a couple of sick days.

Nowhere near enough gas to get to Boston. He stopped at Tom Christopher's service station.

"Fill 'er, Tom. Thanks," David called, and at the same moment noticed the scarf, Diane's scarf, caught in the passenger door and making the cold hiss through the car even worse than usual. Diane's green home-knit scarf. As he rolled it up and stuck it in the back he remembered that Tom Christopher was Diane's cousin, and for a crazy instant he imagined him recognizing the scarf. Uncovering David as the Child Molester of Western Mass. Crazy—but David's face felt hot as he paid Tom for the gas and, waving goodbye, pulled out onto the highway.

"Bummer," he said aloud. He was flooded with imaginings:

Diane taking off for Boston to look for him, turning up at his parents' door. And he knew that coming back had nothing to do with his contract: he was stuck, at least for the rest of the year. He couldn't walk out on Diane now. Couldn't desert Phil Gamboni, for Christsake. And as he turned off onto the rough hill road home—washboard dirt and cracked blacktop, his body tensing at each ridge and hole that wore down the shocks—he felt more than ever bound to that road. Bound by his imagination, that saw Anna having to split wood and tend the fire and the kids by herself, and Jamie waiting for him, not understanding. He was furious.

Trapped by ten-year-old gestures of freedom that had turned into loving obligations.

He took it out on the car, revving the engine, soothed by the high whine and whistle as he skidded the turn past the peach orchard and the church and general store up to his own driveway.

Anna's Saab in the driveway—she was home early. He trudged over the caked snow, took off his boots in the mudroom, and walked into the kitchen.

And that would have been the end of it, if Anna hadn't been annoyed at him for not picking up the kids—for making her pick them up after she'd ended her day with a long battle at a staff meeting—so that when he came in she didn't even turn away from the sink. "You're *late,"* she snapped—

—And that did it. David, without a word, pounded up the stairs to their bedroom, yanked and scraped his old valise out of the closet and dumped into it his only suit, a good sweater, a couple of fancy shirts he'd never opened, and black wing-tip shoes—his father's castoffs. He left in his drawer his second set of winter underwear, jeans, overalls, his everyday wool shirt with the paint stain over the heart, and was down the stairs in two minutes. Sara was shrieking in her high chair. Jamie gawked at him from the foot of the stairs. Anna stood by the kitchen door. "You're going somewhere?"

He slammed down his valise. "I'm going to Boston! Screw all this!" And everything his eyes lit on filled him with loathing: the washing machine they had to beg a repair man to come twenty miles to fix, the never-quite-airtight stove, the sleeping bag, clean and dry again, folded over the back of the kitchen rocker, and, most loathsome, left open in the middle of the kitchen table, a pompous, unnecessary letter from Armstrong to the faculty.

"And you think *I'm* staying?" she said. "You think it's so sweet for me?"

"If you're coming—then come on!" he shouted.

Too furious to answer, she went to the phone and called Herb and Sandy—would they mind coming by this weekend to keep the stove stoked?

Of course they'd do it, Sandy promised. Well, David had done it for them last month.

"I'm not so sure I'm coming back this weekend," he yelled after her.

She turned to give him a filthy look and went up to pack.

His rage temporarily fizzled, he snorted a big laugh. Jamie picked up the laugh.

"Crazy Daddy," Jamie said.

In half an hour, working in silence, they had the Saab loaded with luggage, baby gear, toys, dresses hanging over the rear seat, Sara in the carseat, Jamie jiggling with excitement. Anna wasn't talking. How long, he wondered, before he'd break the silence? He knew he would, knew they'd be talking again soon. The inevitability relieved and saddened him. Ah, he thought, looking at Anna out of the corner of his eye, she's been working goddamned hard. It'll do her good. Sara whined for juice and Anna scribbled notes in her small black journal and Jamie jiggled and the Saab rocked over the ruts. And David was lugging it all to Boston.

Originally appeared in Agni Review, *Spring, 1983*

Bodies of the Rich

I was fourteen the last summer we spent at Feingold's Manor.

Feingold's Manor—past the lights of the boardwalk—and I still think of it as cast into darkness, old three-story beast. And why beast?—Its clumsiness, clunkiness, iron fire escape askew and gritty stairs that smelled of family cooking, of ocean tracked up every day by mothers and children.

We had, my mother assured me, too much class for Feingold's. Too much class—but hardly enough money to pay our way. In spring my mother haggled with Mrs. Feingold, sighing poverty and years of loyalty to the manor. Mrs. Feingold wouldn't answer; she cleaned her glasses on her sour-smelling skirt. Finally a curt snap of the shoulders: disgust but agreement. Feeling like a beggar, I smiled a lot at Mrs. Feingold and didn't overuse the toilet paper in the hall "facility."

Mornings I ran barefoot past the hot dog stand, through the parking lot dangerous with broken glass to the sand, still cool from the night. Plunging like a horse into the waves, I broke through the whitecaps, a wrestling match, love match, my only sexual combat.

Out to the calm water, where I floated, my baby fat not a problem, our lack of money irrelevant, king of the deep, rolling ocean.

One morning my mother joined me early. "So," she said as if in the middle of an ongoing conversation, "shall we go for a walk?"

I waited for her, and we finished the walk together. Half a mile, jetty to jetty, from the beach near Feingold's Manor to the beaches of the great hotels, red brick or white stucco hotels from the 1920s with their roped-off plots of sand raked every night by beachboys, wooden reclining chairs awaiting the bodies of the rich. Maybe not so rich, but to me then, prince of a family that couldn't afford Feingold's, rich enough. That she was willing to walk all that way to be surrounded by these rich bastards who kept us roped off their sand!

We sat halfway between the roped-off plot of the Ocean Royal and the ocean, far enough from the ropes so as not to seem envious. "The ocean," I told her, "they can't rope off."

"With money, my dear, you can rope off whatever you like."

I swam, then read—but only with one eye. With the other I watched the guests of the Ocean Royal come out in rhinestone-edged sunglasses, bellies distended from hotel breakfasts. Fat matrons in gold lamé one-piece bathing suits fell into reclining chairs. Kids my age formed a circle around a huge portable radio. For no reason, I hated them.

But loved the young women with yellow hair who lay like roasts, first on one side, then, for even tanning, on the other, wearing tiny eye-lid covers to avoid the untanned ovals left by sunglasses. Women I could touch with my eyes without fear of being touched by their eyes. I could watch their breasts rise and fall—such beauty to walk around with, those breasts. And, still reading, I waited, as I had all summer, for a girl. All summer inventing her. She didn't have to have breasts yet, please, dear God. Or small, new breasts would be okay...

Then, looking up from my book, I saw a girl nearly my own age. Hopping on one foot at the edge of the ocean, she did an Indian dance to shake water from her ear: lean-legged, slight, with long brown hair and animal eyes, troubled eyes.

And she had breasts.

Standing up and stretching, I put down my book and pretended to hunt shells along the edge of the incoming tide. I think I picked up a shell, any shell, and rehearsed: Did she know what kind of sea animal—but she was gone, up to the roped-in beach front. I saw her with towels and beachbag and mother, leaving. For the morning? The day? The rest of her life?

At once I resented her for being rich. I hated her mother, who would be cross, bored, middle-aged, face smeared with protective oils she would in turn have to protect by staying out of the water. The fancy hotel was a castle, the beachboys castle guards. I was the peasant at the gate.

I didn't tell my mother. Peasant turned spy, I trailed them. I slipped the rope and trotted up the sand. Waving casually to the beachboys who leaned against a post, I jogged along a planked walk, past a shut bar, down a damp corridor. I could hear their voices, the daughter's murmur, the mother's soothing, lyrical comfort voice I'd soon get to know so well. But turning the corner in panic, I found they'd escaped—I stood watching the indicator arrow above the elevator rise along its half-circle to 3.

I turned away, suddenly washed through with a floating, high-pitched craziness: What was I doing here? Suppose I'd met them. What could I have said?

I whistled my way back towards the beachboys. "Hi," I said, stretching and scratching and yawning. Then I ran, young athlete in training, to plunge into the ocean.

When the girl didn't return after lunch, I waited for my mother to take her nap, then slipped the rope again. "Some terrific waves," I said to reassure the single beachboy. He didn't care. Jesus, he said, he wished he could go for a swim. "Great waves," I said, passing on, towel over my shoulder, to the hotel basement, feeling callow, spoiled, that I could swim and search for a girl while he had to work. As if I were in *fact* the rich guest who belonged at the Ocean Royal.

I'd invented a friend, Arnold Zweig, in case the management asked what I was doing there. Still, it was hard to get up the courage to walk up to the lobby. So I wandered through the basement. I opened a door wide enough to see a huge laundry room, hot as a steam bath, where two black women were ironing sheets. I could hardly believe it: to be ironing in such heat? One of the women looked up and I smiled a cramped, false smile at her, as if to say, I'm not one of those who put you here; she didn't smile back. Closing them in again, I considered calling the Department of Health.

Then, from the end of the corridor, I heard echoing voices.

Forgetting the laundresses, I snooped on. Found a pile of old newspapers and took one. I think my fantasy was of finding a castle dungeon. But, turning the corner, I came upon an open doorway, daylight so suddenly bright I couldn't see. Stepping through I found myself at the hotel swimming pool.

I hadn't known about the pool—a small guest pool in the courtyard, not visible from beach or boardwalk. Surrounded by a low brick wall, tiled in aquamarine, it was, except for kids, empty. Easy work for the lifeguard, who sat by the little kids sunning himself. But the patio surrounding the pool was full of guests in loungers. A waiter in white uniform was serving drinks. At one table, women played bridge; mah-jongg at another.

I dropped my towel and dove in, dove deep, came up and sat at the edge of the water, delighted with myself for finding the pool. Then, as my eyes cleared, I saw the girl and her mother standing in the entranceway, looking around for a place to sit.

The girl pointed to a pair of lounge chairs; they carried bags and towels over and sat down. The girl walked in halting, rushing, delicate, embarrassed steps: I loved her. But the mother—she was the surprise.

She wore a white bathing suit that was almost a bikini. This was ten, fifteen years before bikinis came to the United States; maybe I'm remembering badly. Could I really have seen the bony points of her hips, the cleft of her full breasts, even her belly button? I saw the other women around the pool look up and stare. Resenting. But she smiled, self-consciously, blissfully, as if to say, My my, what a lovely day! She was the first mother I'd ever seen who was beautiful. Not beautiful, really: a sweet-faced, slightly fleshy woman. Beautiful isn't the point. *Sexual.* Mothers were never sexual. Mothers were mothers. Was she the girl's *sister,* then?

I went back to my towel and my newspaper, unable to finish a column of print without looking up. The girl stood, put down her sunglasses, and ran in quick little dance steps to the water, stopped cold, eased herself down the ladder and floated away.

I felt misery, felt my own fear like a cripple's gimp, imagining it visible, knowing she'd swim and I'd hunger but say nothing. Just haunt them both with my eyes, while I felt them watching me watching.

The girl swam so clumsily—sidestroke—it made me want to protect and teach, though I was no special swimmer. I stood up and jumped in. I swam the width of the pool in perfect form, as if a March of Time newsreel camera were looking down, then turned over to float gracefully near her serious sidestroking.

"Mother? Come on!" she called. Her voice wasn't nearly so elegant as I'd imagined: an ordinary New York whine, the kind of voice my mother loved to parody. But I erased the criticism. "Come *on,* Mother!"

So it was her mother! "You know I'm no swimmer," her mother laughed. But she put down her glasses and came over. The other women poolside stopped playing cards, sat up from sunning themselves, to stare as, in all her bare skin, she slipped into the water.

Three of us now. Easier for me to talk when there were three. I swam forth, I swam back, I yawned and called out, "Isn't it funny—nobody but us in the pool?"

"And the water is just right—so warm," the mother said, feeling it with her fingertips as if it were a pet animal.

"But I like the ocean," I said, playing Male. "You get used to it."

"Are you staying here in the hotel?"

Hot-faced, I shrugged—"No—a friend. At least I think he's supposed to be staying here—"

"What a lovely day," she sighed. "This is Sandra," she said. "I'm Arlene Koffman."

"Richard Stein," I said.

"Thank God," she said. "Company for Sandra."

"Mother!"

Arlene Koffman laughed. Sandra pouted and splashed off for

a Coke. "I think I said the wrong thing? Oh, but Richard, Sandy knows nobody here—it's so boring for her. She's exactly the way I was at thirteen. A little shy. Always alone, reads too much, I feel sad for her. It's nice to find somebody she can talk to."

"Sure," I said. "Great." But I had been trained by life with my mother to know that it was Arlene who needed someone to talk to.

Of all the adults I knew, only my mother ever exposed pain to me. My mother thumped her chest and wept: her brother, flesh of her flesh, was gone—up in smoke or turned to soap, God knew where.... And wept—equally—at her lot in life. A side-street apartment in Washington Heights. Feingold's in the summer. But what got to me most was her loneliness. "Your father is a decent man," she'd say. "But is he company for me? Tell me." He wasn't. I had to try to be.

"So are you staying here all summer, Mrs. Koffman?"

"Two weeks. They fatten you up here. More than two weeks, I'll be ready for the meat market." She laughed. We were out of the pool, drying off. I had to notice her tan torso, breasts exposed halfway to the nipples, and my breath bulged inside me. "But before the meat market gets me, I'll be bored to death."

Now a curious thing happened. I felt Arlene stiffen and stir in her chair and I followed her eyes. A distinguished, well-built man came out of the hotel. The man looked like an ambassador or—still more impressive to me then—a movie star—Cary Grant, say. Handsome, hair waved, with more than a touch of gray at the temples. James Mason, say. He stood by himself, towel toga-like across broad, tan shoulders, smiling at Arlene Koffman in a way that made me hold my breath. I'd never seen a look of such intimacy and tenderness between adults—except on the screen. Real adults seemed to have very little tenderness for one another. On weekends my mother and father would smile at each other—his smile expressing guilt and a desire to be approved, hers expressing affectionate, mocking irony. Those looks I turned away from, not comprehending the precise nature of her irony or his guilt. But the look of this handsome man I understood enough to bulge the front of my bathing suit and have to cover up with the *New York Post.*

Then Sandra was back, with three Cokes, and Arlene waved to

her. Just behind Sandra, a mammoth woman in a one-piece suit like the cover of an overstuffed chair came out into the sun and stood behind the handsome man. She pointed, he took the beach-bag from her and led the way to a pair of recliners, while she, certainly his wife, followed like some proud bird, examining the other guests. I imagined it a look of challenge: You see me in this enormous cage—I dare you to laugh!

Three hundred pounds. Maybe more. Was her face calm or furious? Somehow, I remember both. Calm I suppose but I presumed a hidden fury—to walk across a patio dedicated to the glorification of women's bodies, to be appraised by these jeweled, creamed, bleached, tanned women-without-men and your husband is gorgeous and you look like an overstuffed chair—how could she be less than furious? I felt bad for her. I guessed—and I was right—that she held the purse strings, and I imagined a Hitchcock plot of romance and murder.

Sandra handed me a Coke. Turning, I saw that Arlene had lowered her chair and was sleeping or pretending. I invented tears for her.

"You want to take a walk?" I asked Sandra.

"All right."

We walked the beach, kicking wisps of sand and staring at the arc the mind made of their fall. I was dying to ask about James Mason, but did Sandra know? Did I know—maybe I'd invented the whole encounter. We were halfway to the next jetty, done talking about where she lived (Central Park West, the expensive street facing the park) and where she went to school (Ruxton School for Girls). I yawned and asked, "Did you see that gigantic woman at the pool?"

"Her? Sure. That's Mrs. Cole. She's very rich. I think it's sad. She's not very nice. I think it's sad."

I stopped playing detective. I imagined taking Sandra's hand and looking at her with the look James Mason gave her mother. Instead I found a bronze stone for her. We examined it on my palm.

"Beautiful," she sighed, a breathy *beautiful* that I thought I could feel tickle my palm. I shivered. I placed it in her hand, the stone.

I led her to the jetty, rocks stretching out into the ocean. Here I had the courage, somehow, to hold out my hand. "Let's climb, okay?" As we touched, the first hand, first girl since I'd slipped over the line into guilty adolescence, I grew hot and hard and had to hide my body—but casually—from her eyes. We walked to where the waves crashed around us, then sat and took the spray. I told her about Hemingway and Steinbeck. She told me about her flute lessons. Next summer she'd be at music camp. She took art classes at the Metropolitan. She was reading *Lust for Life,* Irving Stone's novel about Van Gogh's life. Her mother had given it to her, but it was really good, really sad. I asked, did she know *Starry Night*? I didn't say, Can I see you tonight? I didn't say, We live in a roominghouse past the end of the boardwalk. I didn't tell her, I have baby fat around my waist so that all this time I've been sucking in my belly and throwing out my chest.

"And your father?" I asked, walking back.

"He's in business for himself. The dress business. He's only here on weekends."

"I think it's terrible the way husbands only come out on weekends."

"He doesn't even like his job," she said.

"I feel sorry for husbands," I said.

"But they love each other," Sandra said. "Whatever happens."

"Whatever happens?"

"I mean it's not like some parents. They'll never separate. They fight, but they love each other."

"I wish," I told her coolly, "my mother would leave my father. He'd be a lot happier. She would too." Actually, it was the last thing I wanted. The night my mother packed her suitcase and left for my aunt's, I begged her to come back. "It's terrible," I said, "how miserable people make each other." I liked sounding free; it let me take a broad view of her mother's romance with Mr. Cole. If there were a romance.

My mother was waving her handkerchief at us. "I'd like you to meet my mother," I said, not in the least liking it.

"Aren't you going to introduce me to the young lady?" my mother said from some yards away. Her cultured voice. British.

"Sandra Koffman, this is my mother, Mrs. Stein."

"You did that beautifully," my mother said.

"I have to go now," Sandra said. "Nice to meet you."

"I'd love to hear you play the flute," I said quickly.

"I'll be at the beach tomorrow." In a stumbling, jerky, delicate dance, she ran through the sand back to the hotel.

"Charming," my mother growled. "That's what they're like nowadays."

"Tomorrow" was a rainy day. I moped at Feingold's Manor while my mother tried to interest me in books or food. After lunch we played a few hands of gin rummy but before the game was over, I threw down my cards, got my raincoat, and ran along the slick, deserted boardwalk to the Ocean Royal. Leaving my raincoat folded up behind a potted plant, I ambled through the lobby, the card room, the solarium. Nowhere. At the front desk I said, "Arlene Koffman—that's 322, right?"

"305," a bored voice answered. The clerk never even looked up.

I took the elevator, heart in my ears. Down a plush-carpeted hallway, 309, 307, 305. Flute music in my ears. I knocked.

Arlene Koffman in a peignoir. I remember translucent white with raised flowers. Probably some other woman, at another time. And through the lace at the front, her breasts.

The flute kept playing. Then I noticed the record player, turn-table turning. "Hello, Mrs. Koffman. Is Sandra in?"

"She's at the movies. The one downtown. Maybe you can catch her."

"Sure." But I had no money for movies. Arlene Koffman kept her hand on the knob. Suppose she asks me in? I just stood there. Finally—"Mrs. Koffman, I wonder, what was the name of that book she's reading? About Van Gogh?"

"*Lust for Life*? Would you like to borrow it, Richard? It's Richard, isn't that right? Wait there a minute."

"Yes, thank you." What was I thanking her for? Getting the book? Remembering my name? She opened the bedroom door and

I heard a shuffling. And another voice, a man's voice. I found myself getting hard while my eyes looked at the record player and my face pretended I was just a kid and what did I know?

She came back, book in hand.

"If you're short of money for the movies—"

"No, nothing like that, Mrs. Koffman. I just want to read it so I can talk to Sandra—she was telling me—"

"Wonderful. Well, goodbye, Richard." I was cut off by the door. And did I really hear laughter from inside?

I protected the book under my raincoat and, back at Feingold's, read *Lust For Life* the rest of that dreary afternoon, read it as a gospel of spiritual adventure, a message from both daughter and mother.

Next day, thank God, was clear, dry, hot. Again we walked up the beach to the Ocean Royal; again my mother lay out our blanket halfway between the roped-off hotel beach and the ocean, reading Winchell, then turning to a book of Chekhov stories in translation. I followed Van Gogh to Arles.

It wasn't until after lunch that Sandra came down to the beach. I put down her book and yelled; she smiled hello. I ran up to her, but, approaching, I felt her mood and slowed my pace to hers. We swam for a while, touching as a form of play. Floating together, we agreed that Long Beach was *boring.* "Can you even imagine Vincent Van Gogh in Long Beach?" I said. "Oh, God," she said.

Later, I followed Sandra through the roped-off beach to the plank walk, along the basement corridor—I didn't mention the laundry women in the terrible heat—to the pool, where her mother sat writing letters. I invented loneliness and sorrow and an ugly husband for her, so I could accept her taking an elegant fop for a summer lover.

Her lover sat with his wife on the other side of the pool, a *Wall Street Journal* on his lap, a drink in one hand. Once in a while he looked up to smile—ahhh—at Arlene Koffman. On behalf of husbands cooking in the city, I resented him—but I sympathized with her. And Arlene sighed. Up to that moment I'd heard only my mother sigh so deeply—and that to indicate the depth of her daily suffering. But this sigh of impossible love! There they were—separated by that ocean of a pool—he a gallant flyer, she a wartime nurse, their love hopeless.

Or, perhaps, not all that hopeless. In the middle of the afternoon, I saw Mr. Cole get up, slip on his terrycloth robe, and, leaning over to say something to his wife, go back to the hotel. Five minutes later, Arlene yawned and stuck her lettercase and cigarettes into her beachbag. "Dearest, I'm going up for a nap. I'll see you here later on. You don't mind?"

"We'll be at the beach, Mom."

We watched her go. "Mother and her naps," she laughed. Was she covering up? Or didn't she know? Walking along the beach again, we traded secrets like kisses. Hers: I don't really care about the flute. Mine: my father wishes he had a football player instead of me for a son…There was one secret I held on tight to, but I couldn't stop visualizing a cool bedroom, shades drawn and sheets scattered, ecstasy tumbling hot in the center of the world. Imagining the mother, I could scarcely concentrate on the daughter. But I took her hand—and ached, trembled, at the contact, ashamed that I wasn't the hero who had the right. The golden flyer.

We ended the afternoon reading together by my mother. I held the book, Sandra turned the pages, until, looking up, I saw Arlene Koffman: her nap done, there she was, waving at us. My breath locked inside my throat.

"This is my mother," I said. "Myra Stein. And this is Mrs. Koffman—Arlene."

"How *nice,*" my mother drawled in her British charm voice. She reached out a hand. "My son, it seems, is very taken with your family."

"Richie is very sweet," Arlene said. I rolled my eyes to get a laugh from Sandra. She wasn't a laughing girl. I stopped. I couldn't stop looking and imagining. Mixed in with the sea wind must be the perfume of Arlene's lovemaking. But they were talking about Long Beach in the 1920s, "when it was really *something.* I remember when the Ocean Royal was built," my mother said. "But what hasn't come down in the world?" Arlene sighed—in agreement? I thought I detected something else in that sigh.

My mother was maybe ten, fifteen years older than Arlene, who must have been young, very young, when Sandra was born. Although she came from Feingold's Manor, my mother played the older *grande dame,* but it seemed to me that Arlene only half listened. Was she sad because they could be together so brief a time? How strange, how immense, that afternoon lovemaking seemed. But my mother just chatted to Arlene about the brilliant, wealthy people she used to know before she married and, like Long Beach, came down in the world.

I noticed that Sandra had dug a little hole and was burying her foot. Instantly I grew panicky she'd felt me neglecting her for her mother. I added sand to the hill above her foot, then burrowed down, my fingers a strange animal, to touch the underside of her foot and force her to explode her hiding place. "Come on," I said. "One last swim?"

"We're invited to the pool tomorrow," my mother said on the way back to Feingold's. "A spoiled woman. Not an ounce of class. But very sweet. And *tres jolie,* don't you think?"

I *did* think.

"Believe me, I was a lot prettier at her age. She's a child herself."

She heard me not answering.

"You don't think so? You think your mother was always a frump? Aach! As God is my judge, I could have married a millionaire. Many millionaires."

"Well, you didn't."

"No, I had to marry for love. Love!" She lit a cigarette in the wind and exhaled all her aspirations. "Love is a luxury, my boy.... Now, in all seriousness—will spaghetti do for you tonight? For tomorrow, when your father gets here, we have lamb chops. You're pleased?"

Friday morning. My mother took her sweet time at the mirror. She dolled up: creams and mascara. Didn't fix lunch. And instead of the old, patched beachbag, she carried a fancy Italian straw bag she'd bought in the city for just such a purpose. Down the sad staircase at Feingold's.

We walked the boardwalk. I didn't like her eagerness. "It's just a tiny pool, Mom. No big deal."

"If they ask us for lunch, leave the answering to me."

We entered the Ocean Royal from the boardwalk and asked at the desk.

Arlene had left a message: *We're at the pool.* I started for the stairs—my mother tugged at my shirt. "The *elevator.*"

We walked along the basement corridor that led to the pool. "You see this door?" I said, stopping at the laundry room. "I want to show you something." I opened the door; the room was dark. "The other day—two black women were working in this terrible heat. Like a steam bath."

"People suffer," my mother explained. Dutifully, she sighed. "But you—you shouldn't go near laundry rooms. That's not your business."

She was, I knew even then, being contrary. If I had said I cared nothing at all about poor people, about suffering, she would have said, I can't bequeath you a heart, my boy. I knew she had a heart, but I preferred to let her take the role of social climber, leaving the good stuff for me.

We stood in the sunlit doorway to the pool. Sandra and Arlene Koffman waved from the far corner. My mother stood a moment, hand on hip, taking in the canasta players, the mah-jongg players, the sunbathers. I could feel her contempt.

We sat together, the four of us. My mother sighed with pleasure. "I've always loved a good pool."

Someone's husband arrived early from his week in the city. So pale he looked. Laughing and an embrace. Arlene was nodding without listening. She watched the doorway, seemed upset. I invented a lovers' quarrel. Had he stopped caring about her? Oh, that bastard!

My mother was telling Arlene about Paris. Oh, how she used to love Paris! The magnificence of the Louvre. And that "pretty little jewel of a chapel"—Sainte Chapelle. And the great synagogue....

That darkened her mood, and she talked about her cousin, who'd lived in Paris. Who knows where she is now?

"Yes," Arlene said. "It must all be very different." But she wasn't really there. She looked past my mother toward the hotel.

Sandra and I swam in the pool. Stopping at the ladder, I laughed. "My mother doesn't always talk that much."

"It's nice for my mother," Sandra said. "The only other people she knows at the beach are the Coles. That fat woman and her husband."

"You're friends? You didn't tell me that."

"Oh, personally, I can't stand her. He's okay. Not exactly friends. They just eat at our house once in a while. Or my parents go to their parties. But that's not why we're here. Why we're here is my mother thinks I care about the beach."

"I'm glad you're here."

"Thanks." Sandra kicked into a sidestroke. I followed. Then, bored, we sat down by our mothers and let the sun dry us.

We were hardly dry when we saw Mrs. Cole. She filled the doorway, scowling. I imagined what she must look like without that sack of a bathing suit around her. And instantly I groaned inside for the pain I imagined in her. The laundresses in that hot room were in a palace compared to her prison of fat. I touched my own belly—belly I was too vain not to suck in—and imagined what agony it must be for her to walk past all those women.

She carried herself her lumbering way along the side of the pool. Sandra said, "Here comes Mrs. Cole, Mom. I guess she's got to snoop about our guest.... Want to go to the beach, Richie?"

But Mrs. Cole was upon us.

"Please sit with us," Arlene said—and stood up to introduce her to my mother.

"Sit with *you?* I came to tell you what you are," she said, loud enough for all the women at the pool to hear. "You—a tramp is what *you* are. You're nothing but a tramp!" Very formal, her delivery. A public announcement.

Then, in slow motion she pressed forward, a tank, her arm pulled back for a slap, and Arlene tripped backwards over the leg of her lounging chair. Finally, Mrs. Cole slapped—but she was too stiff or too proud to swing with her whole arm. Thank God. The slap became a swing of the fingers, as if this giant beast were swatting a fly. The tips of her fingers grazed Arlene's face. A ritual slap. But Arlene screamed twice and cried behind her own fingers, leaving Mrs. Cole on stage.

"I'm very sorry to do that in front of you, Sandra. I thought it was all over a year ago. They kept on behind my back."

Sandra had been standing, stunned, gawking. Hearing her name, she came alive, shoved at Mrs. Cole but couldn't budge her. I took her enormous arm and pulled. She stood her ground. "A tramp!" she said again. Then, satisfied or embarrassed, she turned and walked away.

The women around the pool stared. They stared and then they talked. I helped Arlene into her chair—she was still weeping. My mother said, "Garbage like that. Lice! Don't worry."

Arlene shook her head.

"I'd sue," my mother said, holding Arlene around the shoulders. "I knew a doctor once—" then she stopped talking and just held.

Sandra was brooding. Her eyes wet, she looked like a hurt little girl. I rubbed my hand along her arm. Downy hair. "It's okay." She bent to her mother and kissed her and put her arms around her mother's neck and took a wet kiss in return.

"Oh, he's such a coward," Arlene sobbed.

"Oh, Mommy," Sandra said. Then she was crying. Then she was off—walking fast by the pool. I followed, caught up to her in the corridor to the beach. She leaned against a column, weeping. I held back, but finally I held her shoulders and loved her.

"You want to take a walk?"

"I've got to see Mommy."

"Sure—you want to go back and see your Mom?"

"Why did she do it?"

"To get back—revenge, I guess."

"I mean Mom."

"I guess she loves him. I'm sure she loves him."

"But she didn't tell me. Why didn't she tell me?"

We both knew why. I kissed her cheek. Somehow, that got me excited and I didn't feel I ought to be.

"Daddy's coming tonight," she said.

"So you want to go back?"

"No. Let's take a walk," she said. We went past the beachboy, past the ropes, to the water. Sadly, we walked down to the jetty. The tide was out, leaving small pools in the depressions between the rocks. Sandra lay belly down on the hard, wet sand and, head in hands, stared and stared until the big world had maybe disappeared for her. I lay next to her, self-conscious, awkward, until I was able to make the rock seem a giant cliff and the pool a lake and the hermit crabs and starfish giant sea creatures. A string of kelp became the jungle of some other planet. We hiked the landscape together. But it was impossible to live there. "Richie? Want to go back now?"

But we didn't have to. Turning, we saw that my mother and Sandra's mother had come down to the beach. They sat on towels spread out near the water. As she talked, Arlene was drawing with a stick, patterns in the sand. My mother listened. "Yes," I heard her say as we approached. A breathy "yes."

Like a trial lawyer, my mother extended an open palm toward Arlene and offered her to me. "Why does Mrs. Koffman have to put up with trash like that? So—we decided—this noon we'll eat lunch at *our* place. Decent, simple, home cooking. Tell me, Sandra, do you eat lamb chops?" My mother gave me a Look.

Back at Feingold's Manor, my mother broiled the lamb chops and reheated last night's vegetables. Not once—not climbing the Lysol stairs, not showing Arlene the hot-tar terrace nor opening the old, shaky, wooden icebox for food—not once did she criticize Feingold's. Queen reduced to this broken-down flat, she simply moved in the old kitchen with the grace of one used to better things.

"My dear, you want a cup of tea?"

"Oh, Mrs. Stein..." Arlene began to cry. "Mrs. Stein, I love him..."

"Life," my mother sighed. From the O'Neil apartment below

came an infant's shrieking. Without undue haste my mother closed the door to the porch.

"Sometimes," Arlene said, "someone comes along in your life and you can't help loving them."

My mother provided a Kleenex.

Arlene and Sandra picked at their chops. I ate my own, then ate their leftovers. Arlene fumbled for a cigarette. "Mrs. Stein, what you must think of me…"

"Nothing of the sort. Call me *Myra,* my dear."

"Myra, this is the romance of my life." Arlene looked beautiful in tears. I felt a furtive pleasure at being in the presence of such high emotion. "Oh, we've been in love for years."

Sandra, slumped in her chair, poured salt from the shaker into a tiny mountain on her plate, then etched with the tines of her fork in the salt.

"Sandra," her mother said. "What are you *doing*?"

Sandra shrugged.

"Sandy? Please."

"So does Daddy know?"

"No, Daddy doesn't know. Sandy—I love your Daddy. I do. But Stan…is the romance of my life," she said again. "We tried to stop seeing each other. We just couldn't, that's all."

Sandra shrugged. "Then *that's* why we had to come to Long Beach."

"Sandra," my mother said, "your mother is an angel. I know an angel when I see one."

"Isn't it, Mother?"

"Partly, yes."

Furious, Sandra turned back to the salt. Arlene cupped Sandra's face in her palm. "Please, Sandy?"

"Well, what's Daddy going to say?"

"Do you want me to tell him?"

"I don't know. No."

"I will if you want."

Sandra shook her head.

"Would anyone like some nice fruit?" my mother asked.

"He's my heart," Arlene said and was touched to tears by her own words.

"That isn't a woman," my mother said. "She's a Hitler. A Nazi tank. To make such a scene. Would a lady make such a scene?"

"Mommy? How did she know?"

"She was waiting in the corridor yesterday afternoon. We weren't thinking. It was such a beautiful hour together. That's all we have."

"I knew a Very Rich Man once," my mother said, slowly, so we'd know this was wisdom, "who was married to money. 'Myra,' he said to me, 'you want to know what hell is? Married to money is hell.' Finally, he divorced her. Of course, she didn't give him a penny."

"How can I go back there, Mrs. Stein?"

"With your head held high—that's how," my mother said triumphantly.

Watching the sway of Arlene's body on the way back along the beach, I felt cut off within my adolescence from a depth of sexual life she knew. And cut off from Sandra. As if to touch her now I would have to be a man. I felt unable even to imitate manhood.

When they went back to the hotel, Arlene's arm around Sandra's waist, I sat with my mother outside the ropes, looking out at the ocean. It seemed, the ocean, drab. Boring. I fell asleep. Woke to my mother's "Well, how *nice.*"

A tall, good-looking man with tan face and pale chest stood above me. Athletic. In his thirties. Arlene, in gold lamé swimsuit, hung on his arm. "Mrs. Stein, I wanted you to meet my husband. This is Harry. Mrs. Stein has been wonderful to us."

"Oh, my dear—"

"You have. Saved us from those boring people at the hotel. And we wanted to say goodbye."

"You're leaving?"

"We're checking out today. I can't stand it another day."

I was fully awake now. Sandra stood behind her parents. We looked at each other; she turned away. "Richie—you want to go for a swim?"

I ran after her. "Wait up. Sandra?"

She stopped. "Don't say anything in front of my father."

"Of course not."

"She has to go away from him. She loves him so much. And she loves my father too. She promises she'll stay away from Stan. It's so sad. He won't leave his wife. You know—money. I think it's disgusting. But this way it's better, really…" So much talk bursting out of her silence. I followed her into the water. We watched the waves heave and explode into white, then die around our ankles. "If I write you," I said, "will you write back? Will you see me in the city?"

"Of course. Come on, Richie—last swim for the whole summer."

We dove into the same wave and I imagined her tumbling lost inside the roller and me saving her and her father inviting me into their lives. But we both spluttered through to the other side and smiled. My smile was phony. "So goodbye," I said, wanting at least to sip the pleasure of tragedy from the moment. But she swam a couple of strokes and said, "So have a terrific rest-of-the-summer, Richie. We're going with Daddy for a week to the mountains. It was all arranged so fast."

"I never heard you play the flute."

"Well, I'm awful anyway. Richie? Don't think bad about Mommy."

I watched her skinny beauty almost catch a wave. She danced, stumbled, ran the rest of the way to shore. I floated till they were off the beach.

"Well," my mother sighed on the trudge back along the beach to Feingold's Manor, "so it goes. Now I have to get more lamb chops. Do you think your father would mind hamburgers? Maybe meatloaf? I'll make a nice gravy."

"Sure," I said, feeling, somehow, sorry for her.

"You know, my dear, I felt in my heart for what that poor woman is going through, but you know, a high-class woman doesn't follow her boyfriend to hotels. That's not high-class people."

But the further we got from the Ocean Royal, the emptier I felt. Whatever my mother said, high-class didn't mean meatloaf and fidelity; it meant money and romance.

As we passed the end of the boardwalk and crossed the final jetty, we saw my father waving. He'd just come out from the city, down to the beach, a few hours early. Still wearing city pants, carrying his shoes, his big belly and chest pale, he looked so out of place that I felt ashamed, then ashamed of myself—remembering that his labor kept my mother and me there at the beach, gave us our tans.

"Well, what a pleasant surprise," my mother called across ten yards of beach. "We didn't expect you till dinnertime."

"I worked late last night. Max let me out at one o'clock so I could beat the rush."

"Well, my dear, *aren't you taking a chance*?"

But not listening to her, he said to me, "Well, look how brown m'boy's getting. Another couple of years, you'll be knocking 'em dead. Like your old man."

"Aren't you taking a chance?" she said again. "I remember Bea Altman once saying, 'If you want to find a faithful wife at home, make sure first you telephone.' "

"Your mother's kidding," Dad said.

"Don't you think the boy knows *that*?" she snapped.

"So how's the water?" my father said.

"Seaweed," she said. "It's nicer down the beach." She pointed back at the great hotels.

"The seaweed's gone," I said, fatigued. "Let's just stay here." But here—the beach near Feingold's Manor—seemed drab, less in the sunlight than it once had.

"You look tired," she said to my father as we stood by the water. "It was a hard week?"

He admitted it.

"You'll rest this weekend. So. So tell me," she said, as they both looked out at the waves, "for tonight will meatloaf do your majesty?"

Originally appeared in Shenandoah, *Spring, 1982*

Uncollected Stories

Losers in Paradise

We were gathered together for the reading of the numbers. "Eleven…twenty-two…three…nine…" Morning coffee break, every Thursday morning, Steve called them out like a minister announcing the number of the next hymn or reading from a Psalm, slow and solemn, and members of the congregation answered, "Yes!" or—most of the time—"Oh, bummer." "That does it." "I'm wiped."

Three years ago, Randy Skibiski won Mass Cash—$100, 000. I wasn't around back then, but it's still talked about with reverence. Randy works, like he always did, in the company mailroom, I mean what the hell, $67, 000 after taxes? Nice bank account, couple of trips, that's all. But it shows you. And every once in awhile someone wins a few hundred, maybe the Daily Numbers, no big deal. I never won a thing, and I wouldn't keep playing only for the socializing.

Everybody gets into it, plays their Megabucks number, then whatever else—Mass Cash, Mass Millions. Tony is addicted to scratch tickets. Me, nothing. But everyone does Megabucks and swears not to listen at eleven the night before, so before first delivery on Thursdays we drink coffee out of travel mugs with store logos or team logos and, ticket in hand, sit on the counters and wait to hear the numbers from Steve, slow, number by number. Juices everybody up. That's the point. Not much pleasure, picking up mail, delivering mail, what the hell.

But what happened was that one afternoon Alice Krause sees Patrick Conway's ticket on the desk—he bought it at lunch—and she's always kidding him anyway, so she jots down the numbers, tells Steve, and he dug the idea. Patrick is something of an asshole. This job works or almost works when it feels like a team, like you're part of a team, a crew on a warship, so you throw showers or bachelor parties somebody gets married, one of the girls makes a cake for your birthday, and you gripe together, Hey, son of a bitch in the Vice-President for Marketing's office with his express mail pick-ups, well fuck *him*, and the crew is down to seven plus some part-timers, sorting, pick up, courier stuff included, so most of the day we're hopping and if it's a team thing it's okay.

But Conway, Patrick Conway, tall, skinny guy, glasses, early thirties, who picks his nose when he thinks nobody's looking and sticks the boogies on the junk mail, he just does his job deadpan. When Joe retired Conway gave his share to the cash pool for a present, but grudgingly—and he eats lunch alone, he's into remote-control race cars I figure, cause that's the magazines he reads, but he won't talk about it unless you ask, and I don't ask, because when I told him about my trip to the Keys, diving deepest I've ever gone, 100 feet, he grunted and kept on sorting mail.

So maybe that was part of it, and maybe Steve was feeling not exactly nasty but maybe just a little hostile and so next morning he droned out, "Eleven…twenty-two…three…nine…seventeen…" and then came the usual groans—except Patrick was silent. Well, he was always silent. Steve didn't look his way, Alice too. Me, I didn't know a thing. Nobody else knew—that was one of Steve's bright ideas—"It'll be more convincing that way," he'd told Alice. "Like, you think Tony's a fuckin' Academy Award actor? He'll roll his eyes or ham it up or something. No. Nobody else."

Steve is boss of the mail crew now that Joe's gone. Right under the supervisor—supervisor's management and isn't part of the crew.

Steve's a slightly out-of-condition ex-jock who once had dreams of playing pro ball, made all-State as fullback twenty years ago, and it was the last win he ever had, because now, yeah, he's boss, but what's it mean? A few more hassles, a few more bucks, nothing. Nothing is what most of them got. Me, I figure on saving some money, go back to school full-time, finish up, major in Hotel and Restaurant Management, and go where I want, Europe, Japan, wherever. My dream is run a scuba operation for tourists on some island. Maybe even a resort. They kid me in the mailroom. I'm Mr. Fish. *Hey Bobby, you somewhere else? Bobby's dreaming again, must be in deep waters with the angel fish.*

"Eleven…twenty-two…three…nine…seventeen…" Steve paused. "Six."

"Say the numbers again." —Patrick.

"Why? You got something? How many?"

"Just read them."

Steve read, kind of bored, kind of curious, and Patrick went stiff. "Give me the paper."

"Fuck you, you think I can't read numbers?" And Steve ripped up the page and crumpled it up and tossed it in the big canvas bin and said, "Go buy your own paper."

"I think I got it. I mean all six. All six. How many millions?"

"I don't know, I didn't look."

"I'm going out to get a paper."

"Yeah. Go ahead," Steve says. And Alice says, "Or you *could* call Physical Plant, Patrick—" We all know Constantine's crew does what we do with Megabucks except they pick numbers together and share if any number hits.

So Patrick picks up the phone—everybody knows the number for Physical Plant but he fumbles and has to start over—and must be Stan McClosky answers and Patrick goes, "It's Patrick Conway. Listen, can you read me the numbers, the numbers for Megabucks?" And of course Stan's in on it and reads out the same numbers, right?—and Patrick doesn't even ask how many millions, he's like, "Oh my God, oh my God," and Joannie's shrieking, everybody's laughing, and Patrick rushes into the supervisor's office to make a private call home. And that's when Steve tells us the gag, and reads the true numbers and everybody goes, "Oh, bummer." "That does it." "I'm wiped."

And everybody's goofing, except Randy Skibiski, who doesn't think it's so funny, but that's because it really happened to him, at least on a small scale, and I think it's funny but I'm feeling uneasy, too, because what about the guy's wife, suppose he reached his wife, suppose he goes and quits or says fuck you to the higher-ups, because I tell you, you could give somebody a mouthful the way they treat people, like shit basically, and I'm thinking *That's plenty*, and Joannie says it aloud, "Steve, you gotta tell him, that's enough," and then I'm like, "Yeah, you can't let it go too far, we got to work with the guy."

And that would have been it, but Patrick comes back, and before Steve can say a thing, Patrick sees us all laughing and weird and he still doesn't get it, because that's what we'd be like if it happened for real, right? And he says, "I'll tell you the best thing—I can *walk* from this shithole office—"

"Hey, Patrick, Patrick, hey Patrick!—"

But Patrick thinks—well, who knows what he thinks but he's on a roll. "I got nothing against you guys, but it's like being a pathetic loser, working here. You know how sad it is, this place? Losers, all a'you. I'm even gonna give you some money, I am, a few hundred each, because I'd'a never bought a ticket in the first place it wasn't for you. But this place is Deadsville, Losers' Paradise. Thank God I'm getting th'fuck out."

It was the most we'd ever heard him talk at one time. And the feeling—the feeling was so full of contempt it was scary. I flashed to those guys who get fired from some Post Office and come back with a shotgun and blow everybody away, guys with a terrible grudge. Only in fact *he* wasn't saying he hated us. In fact, *I* was the one feeling the grudge. I don't mean I wanted to kill him but still. And I guess everybody…because the mailroom got quiet, and nobody tried to tell him the truth, not now. We all turned to sorting, to loading the trucks, and he stood around in the middle of the long room with its stained plywood counters and machines and bins and nobody even looked at him.

It was like it really happened, like he really had the winning ticket and we were pissed. Only, see, I think if somebody for real hit the big one, I'd say great, great, and maybe I'd wish it was me instead, but I'd be happy for the guy. But here I'm depressed and can't figure, I'm talking to myself, inside my head I'm saying, Fuck you, Conway, you can just live with it. Next twenty years you can fuckin' choke on it. I wasn't going to tell him a thing.

But now, now all of a sudden this room feels like a prison, the crew like prisoners, and Joannie, Alice, Steve, Randy, Tony, me, we all go through the motions, our morning routine, nobody looks at anybody, the joke has turned to shit in our mouths, the joke's on us somehow. And *why*, when Conway makes a jerk of himself?—it's a natural pay-back, right?

I make my special run for Express mail through Finance. I'm taking it out on my transmission, jerking the clutch, backing up like a guy parking cars at a restaurant. I come in with two big bags of mail, and there's somebody I don't know taking flash photos of Conway, and everybody's out of the way, I mean at a sorting table, fixing records, or out of the room, just Conway standing up smiling a crooked smile, your basic high school geek grown up, guy you meet at a high school reunion and say to yourself, You're still the same asshole, same geek from home room, Conway with glasses in one hand and other hand on the big Pitney-Bowes machine, this lady asking him questions and taking pictures, and Joannie comes up, takes a bag of mail from me and, her mouth not moving hardly, says, "Guy from the company news bureau for the paper. Steve says Stan must've called. Or Conway's wife."

"Jesus." Now I start feeling sorry for the guy again. Or uneasy. They got to check, they find out it's a gag and we're gonna look like awful pricks. What kind of explanation, to say the guy put us down, he made us feel like shit, so we let him stew?

But the feeling was strange. Here it is: every job we did that morning seemed like it was done for a video camera, like we were so conscious, it got sick, nothing done any different but like we were imagining it played back to us in slow motion. We did the work and avoided catching anyone's eyes.

Then a call comes in for Patrick, and when he comes back

from the office, he knows, you can tell, because he's dead-faced—maybe the news bureau, maybe his wife, and he doesn't complain and nobody says, *Hey, we let it go too far, sorry, but you were such an asshole*, nobody says nothing.

What I think now is, it must have felt for Alice, for Steve, I know it felt for me, like *we* were the ones—all of us—with the ticket that turned to shit, like we'd banked all these dreams and the bank went under. People didn't look at each other; they went their separate ways for lunch. But on his way out, Steve turns in the doorway and spreads his palms, says, "Hey. Sorry. Not such a great idea, huh?" He apologizes to *us*, not to Conway, who puts on his windbreaker and goes out with his lunch bag and his magazine.

And my stomach is doing funny things. I keep looking at the door like I'm afraid I touch my pocket I'm gonna find somebody just ripped off my wallet. Before I think about it, I pick up my lunch, pull my sweater over my head and follow Conway.

I keep my distance. I know where he's going anyway—new employee cafeteria in the old manufacturing building. Those manufacturing jobs gonc, parts milled somewhere else, the building a fire trap and somebody got the idea of giving the survivors of the layoff a cafeteria and naming it after a guy everyone knew, Larry Kroll—security guard on the gate who knew everyone's name, said hello to you, guy died last year of emphysema. Got the new energy-saving lights that look a lot nicer than the old flourescents, new linoleum; same machines, same food. I bring my own. Patrick, too.

I put my feet up on a cafeteria table, sit back picking at my sandwich and staring at him across the room. Not like I want to talk. Maybe—well, maybe just say I'm sorry so he won't kill himself, but not *talk*, you know? But it's weird, it's like he's got the clue to something, a puzzle. It's sick, like gawking at a burn victim or a thalidomide baby grown up, arms like hands, or the old drunk I used to watch outside the saloons of Medford, his pocked, fat, red nose. "Hey Rudolph!" kids used to yell. I never yelled. He scared me, how far down he got and still kept going. Like he must know something I didn't want to *know* exactly but wanted to see *him* knowing, like a kind of holy mystery, like a sacred leper.

I'm also a private eye watching a suspect. But doing a lousy job it turns out, because when I'm about finished with my sandwich, Conway stares straight into my eyes, and I grin and open my palms. I try to communicate something in my face, like, Hey, I'm sorry, I'm not your enemy whatever you said to us. Fuck it, what you said, it's what lots of people feel, maybe me, what I feel. Fuck, I guess that's it, that's what's chewing at me, it's what he said: *Losers' Paradise*.

And then he takes off, leaving me sitting. And I'm up in my head but there are no words going through me. And then for a time outside time I'm fifty feet down looking up at huge sea turtles against the light of the surface, playing the air in my buoyancy compensator to float just where I am, and the people in the cafeteria become weird species of sea life.

After work, I pick up my mother at manufacturing and we head towards Boston and I tell her about it. She says, "You ought to know better. Don't let the higher-ups hear about it or you'll be out on your ass next round of cuts." Which kind of misses the point, my point, point I was making—the funny way it made us feel about things. In fact, maybe that's what I wish for, to be out on my blessed ass. Then I remember the mortgage. In my mind's eye I see the papers, my mother hunched over the lawyer's table, signing. After my dad died, we remortgaged. Her income alone would barely handle it. So I shut up.

I'm feeling low. I think about the time I was twelve and Dad took me to the woods to hunt deer. I pretended to care so he could see me caring. He was no hunter; he borrowed the guns. We wandered around in the snow till our fingers and toes went dead, and there were plenty of deer tracks but no deer. The tracks went in circles, then nowhere. Us too. Every once in awhile we'd cross our own tracks. He felt stupid, so he got pissed at me. We didn't talk the whole way home.

I've got friends, I grew up here in Medford, I went to Medford High, did sports, got all the friends in the world. After we eat the soup Mom cooked on Sunday, I go over to Gerry's house, we shoot some hoops till it gets dark, and I tell him what we did, but he doesn't get it—thinks the guy deserved it, and that's not the question. I call my girlfriend Jeannie, and she tries for me. She soothes me with her sweet voice, like singing, saying, "Bobby, don't be down, this is just a temp job, honey."

And I say, "Sure, I know, I know," and I don't know. My mother keeps asking when Jeannie and me are getting married, she wants us to move in, and I can see that, it would *make* things for her, she could help take care of a kid, there'd be a real family in the house again, and she's a good person, my mom, she wouldn't get in the way or anything. But Jeannie and me, we get married, what's the odds of my finishing a degree and moving on? Like zero? My mom says she can maybe help me get a training position in the main office. And the thing is, I kinda love Jeannie, and she's got a desk job, it would be okay. Better than okay.

But times I feel like a fox sniffing at a trap.

I think about calling Patrick, but I don't, I keep Mom company awhile in front of the TV and go to bed early and for a long time can't sleep. Next day, Patrick stays out. I figured. We none of us talk about it till we're sure, then we can't talk about anything else. At break Joannie says, "We got to call him up, maybe send something funny, balloons or a belly dancer, you know, like for birthday parties? Or just all of us call?"

Alice rolls her eyes, real hostile, like *Give me a break*, and goes back to sorting. But Randy says, "Fuck it. I'm calling. Anybody wants to talk after me, tell me." He sits on the sorting table and calls. But Patrick's not home or he's home and not picking up. Randy leaves a message. "…Get back to us. Sorry, good buddy. We feel like shit…"

And we do. All day I'm expecting the guy from Personnel to come in and chew our asses good. Nothing happens. But it's a pretty bummed-out mailroom.

After dinner, I look up Patrick Conway in the company telephone book. He lives in Arlington just the other side of Ball Square in Somerville. I'm feeling embarrassed, I rehearse, like a teenager calling a date. The guy's wife answers, and I say "Mrs. Conway, I'm calling to apologize to Patrick, I work with him, everybody feels bad…"

And the woman bursts into tears. Right away I fear the worst, like the guy jumped off a bridge or went into the garage and sucked the exhaust pipe, but then she says, "He's not here. Try later maybe."

"What's the matter?"

But she's crying again. "I think the bar down the corner."

"Is he okay?"

Now she starts yelling. "That son of a bitch? *He's* okay! I'm the one with the bruises all over my face!"

"What bar?" I ask.

It's a narrow saloon smelling of sour beer, with posters stapled over the plywood paneling, TV in the far corner, kind of place I stay out of. Stinks of cigarettes. I gave up smoking a couple of years back. I don't mind when my friends smoke—sometimes I suck it up for old time's sake. But I can't stand the stink of old smoke. Six, seven, guys in a clump, two couples at a table, pool table under green-shaded light in back. Patrick at the end of the bar not watching the TV. He's got beers lined up.

The way the mind works, in one second all this:

(1) I'm surprising him. He's got no time to build up righteous wrath.
(2) If he does, I'm a lot bigger. I can take him he goes bezerk.
(3) I wasn't part of the con—he must know it was Steve.
(4) I feel for the mess he's in. I feel for the guy even if he did go crazy with his wife.
(5) This is still a geek. This is not a guy I want for a buddy. What am I doing here?
(6) What a boy scout asshole I am.

And buzzing under all that, I've got the feeling there's things I need to talk about with Patrick, geek or no. What? I honestly don't know. But I go up to him.

"Patrick? Look. I'm sorry. We all are." He's not tuning me in, so I shut up. I sit next to him, I glance down at his fist on the bar and see the swelling and cuts, and I imagine his wife's face. He doesn't look at me, and there's nothing on his face. I order a beer for me and one for him and we sit quiet and drink.

It must be five minutes goes by. The Celtics game on the screen and the laughter of the guys behind us in the bar fills the space so I can stand it. Finally, I say, "So. Pat. You coming in tomorrow? No more hassles, I promise."

It's like I just walked in this second. He turns to me, I wouldn't swear to God he even *knows* me exactly. "*Who gives a shit*? The lottery? Who gives a shit?"

"That's it," I say. "Hey. You're no worse off than you were before."

"No. Worse. Because the difference is, I *know* it."

"I know what you mean." I'm humoring him, but also I'm thinking, sure, he got all these hopes going, and now he's back to the mailroom.

But no—that's not what he's saying. "Because," he says, "now I *see* it don't matter, *it's my life*. I mean. Even I win the lottery, what's the difference?"

"The difference?" This I don't get, but it interests me. "If you *win*?" I figure it's like when my older sister couldn't cry at our dad's funeral. The shrink said she was in denial. "What d'you mean, 'What's the difference?'"

"The same, *I'd* be the same. Bobby? Say a guy like Steve Shoda, what's he gonna do he gets a pile of money? Drink a better brand of beer? Gamble it away at Foxfire? I mean, is his *life* gonna be any different? What's it done for Randy? And Alice?—Alice'd go buy expensive ugly furniture. And I'd still be a guy without any brains and what do I *do* with my goddamn life? Like I could put leather upholstery and a new paint job on my Chevy and it's still a Chevy, same engineering, sloppy tolerances so the parts rattle loose and wear down. And I'd have the same pathetic wife."

"Well, maybe she wouldn't feel pathetic with a few million bucks. Maybe? Maybe you wouldn't have to beat her up? And Alice?—she wouldn't just buy furniture. She'd get her mother a nurse so she could live at home and Tony wouldn't be breaking his ass to pay child support. And Joannie's kid needs braces, it's fucking painful to look at her when she comes in to visit."

"Who told you I hit my wife?"

"Look at your hands, you son of a bitch. You want to beat up on somebody, try me, asshole."

"She was bad-mouthing me, she said…I was a lump of shit."

"Exactly! That's it!—that's what you feel like."

"Well, you think you're any different, Bobby? You're the same."

"Maybe. Maybe I am a lump of shit. But I don't beat up on people."

"Maybe. But suppose you win the lottery, what're *you* gonna do? I been thinking and thinking. All day. About everybody. You'd get great scuba gear. You'd spend a few months with the fishes. Then what?"

"How about I pay off my mother's mortgage and let my little sister finish college? Okay?" And just for a few seconds, maybe milliseconds, it was as if I was wrapped up in the glow of those possibilities. Then it faded out and I was drinking beer in a dark, stinking bar with a geek. I'd won nothing and wasn't gonna win nothing.

"Yeah," he says. "But what are you gonna do for *you*?"

I don't answer. Now I'm drinking alone and he's drinking alone. He rankles me. It's like he gave *me* a winning ticket. And took it away. And tore it up. And all I'm left with is what I am, what I always was.

Then he starts in on Steve Shoda again but stops, just like that, and says fuck it, and like we're friends starts telling me about a car he's building in his basement, remote control race car, spends hours and hours doing it right, putting in his own high performance electric motor, pushing it to 45, 50 miles an hour real speed, and I'm nodding, I'm not exactly listening; and looking up into the computer-generated color swirlings of a time-out commercial, I'm down twenty, thirty feet by a reef, the reef is one I remember, the Cayman Islands, and I see the legs of the dive leader just below me, I'm watching butterfly fish and a school of angelfish, yellow-blue, and then a purple gramma hovering above the coral, or it's not exactly watching, it's like I take his hovering inside me, I take on the same glowing color, and then I'm following a giant sea turtle down alongside the reef, the light growing dimmer and the fish bigger, and now we're alone, down and down, me and the dive leader, eighty, ninety feet, using our lights on the coral, and the crowd is screaming, commercial break is over and somebody sinks a three-pointer.

Patrick puts his hand on my arm. "Bobby? You come back home with me? A few minutes? Okay? I don't want anybody else to know. You just be around so Terry and I, we can talk and make peace?"

"Okay," I said. "I guess. So you coming back tomorrow?"

"What the fuck else *can* I do?"

Throw yourself under a train?—this I don't say. We don't talk the two blocks to his mansion—top floor of a firetrap three-decker.

Terry Conway is a skinny little thing with a baby on her hip. It scares me, the smell of baby shit and the mess. As she opens, I see her face is all puffed-up and mascara's smeared down her cheeks. "What the fuck do you want? Keep your mouth closed. Tim's asleep, it wasn't easy after the yelling."

"All right, I'm sorry. I'm sorry. This is Bobby Sanford. Terry, you tell him: I ever do anything like that before?"

"And you never will again. I'm getting a weapon, you son of a bitch. You just try to touch me."

And now I see that in her other hand she's got a wicked chef's knife, and I back off. Hands up, meaning like *peace, peace*, I say, "Hey, please Mrs. Conway, you put down the knife, let's go talk, Patrick here feels lousy. He's got a right to be pissed at *us*, he just took it out on you."

"I mean I'm getting a real weapon. He better not touch me."

"What about the things you said to me—" But he's not mad, he's sounding gentle and sad.

I sit them down in the living room. "You said some things, he said some things, then you started swinging. My own father…look, Terry, really—if this is what he's like a lot of the time, let me kick his ass down the stairs and you go get a cop and I'll wait. Okay? Is this what he's like?"

"My Pat?" And all of a sudden she's crying hard and he puts his arms around her, knife and all, and I shut up, I sit there, I figure I'm doing okay but I don't want to be there. The smell of baby shit and stale food is everywhere, furniture is scattered from when they were fighting. I think, Jesus Christ, is this me in a few years? I'm wondering maybe I can be home in time for the end of the Celtics game.

And I'm remembering my father. Just two, three times. Last time, I picked up a baseball bat and he saw I was serious and he fuckin' backed off and kicked over a lamp and was out of there for a couple of days. He came home like a lamb. I know they say this thing is like an addiction, guys get hooked and it escalates. But my dad, it was only when he felt what his life was really like, once in five years, he'd get wild, and Mom and the house would feel like his enemy, and she'd have to leave or lock herself in the car. I try not to think of him that way, because he was no abuser, he worked his ass off for us and it was like rowing against the current, it was like following tracks in a big circle your whole life.

Now I'm definitely a third party. I say, "Sorry again, Patrick. We'll talk tomorrow. Okay, Pat? Goodnight, Mrs. Conway." And walking down the stairs, squeezing between the baby strollers and bicycles, I think, tomorrow, yeah, I'll ask him about the remote-control cars and let's see what happens.

So driving home, I should feel pretty good. Maybe I helped keep a husband and a wife from messing each other up. Maybe I helped keep that poor fucker from going down the tubes. So why am I not feeling good? Not even *okay*. In fact, I'm fucking depressed.

I start thinking about the lottery. I think about what Patrick said. What I'd do for *me*. I guess buy into a resort in the Caribbean or open a scuba club, something. But the God's-honest-truth is, I'm no businessman.

When I get home, my mom is still up, fixing our lunches for the morning. We take turns. After the Conway mess, this place feels calm and smells good. It's nothing fancy. Lace on the table tops is yellowing, floors need new carpet. Armchairs old, but so what? I think about calling Jeannie.

I say, "Ma, I just decided, I'm not doing Megabucks anymore."

"Just as well. I always told you. The odds are lousy."

"That's not exactly the point."

"You know, nothing's ever *the point* with you, Bobby. Jesus Christ."

"No, Ma, listen. It's like paying to get spit on. It's a sign of what my life is without it, always missing something."

"Yeah? Go on." She clamps the lunch boxes shut and sticks them in the fridge, laughing to herself.

"It's like, the lottery isn't even about money. It's about humiliation and so you want to become…splendid. I mean like the glowing around an angel in the old pictures, what did they call it?—all the colors. Except I'm not talking about angels. Remember Dad? Dad is exactly what I mean."

"Your father may he rest in peace never played the goddamned lottery. And," she adds, "he was no angel."

"My father had a disappointed life. Maybe everybody—and the goddamn lottery cashes in on that disappointment. The promise isn't money, it's this other thing."

"So?"

"Some time soon, Ma, I've got to get out of here, I'm gonna do it."

"Okay. I mean it, Bobby. Okay. Don't think I can't get along without you, honey." But she turns her face away.

"I don't mean I'm leaving right away. You understand? I gotta finish school." I kiss her goodnight, and she gives me a funny look I pretend I don't see. I forget the Celtics. Up on my bed, room I've lived with all my life nearly, I lie on my back with my hands under my head and my eyes closed. And I don't sleep and I don't sleep.

The house makes a clanking sound, like groaning in its sleep. When Dad died we put in a new furnace with its new sounds, and I remember feeling bad because he wasn't here to get the benefit. He always griped when he had to go down to the cellar middle of the night to reset the burner. Money from the new mortgage. We fixed the roof, put in a bathroom upstairs, that's about it, but it felt like the old creature we been living with all these years was being twisted and tortured and shamed.

I wish Jeannie were here. I try planning, but nothing comes.

After a long time, I'm dreaming awake, kind of knowing I'm in a dream, I'm looking not up but down into blue-green water, floating down to hover above the yellow-fins and fan coral. I follow a school of translucent blue fish I never saw in my life, follow under a coral ledge and now there's a great sea turtle as long as me, and I stretch out to take hold and ride it—and jerk awake.

And it's morning, and the whole drive in, I'm thinking about the colors in the sea. If I dreamed it, where did it come from, all those colors? They must be in me. Where else? Already, always, in me. I grin at my mother and talk about stuff, but I hold onto that. It's not gonna last past the door of the mailroom, I know that. I wave goodbye to my mom and I store it away where it can't be touched. And I think, okay, that's where I am. That's the winning number.

I see Patrick coming from another parking lot lugging his usual gray lunch box. I catch up so we can walk in together. "Pat, how's it going, m'man?" He slows down, shrugs, kind of grunts hello, but I can see he doesn't want to acknowledge last night. And hey—that's okay. I'm still going to walk in with the guy. He needs it even if he can't look my way.

And coming into the mailroom, I say, "Hey, Steve. Hey, Randy. Joannie…" And I count the baskets of first-class and get down to work.

Originally appeared in Witness, *Spring, 2001*

Night Talk

"The dream of reason breeds monsters."
—*Goya*

We've been, you and I, through too many of these two-in-the-morning scenes of mutual humiliation and disgust to think they can change our lives. We keep on, a ritual, to squeeze some last poison out, like adolescent pimples; I mean the way a teenager hates his skin sometimes, squeezes the flesh between his knuckles to clean out the pus, and it doesn't work. It builds up more fluid, leaves the face blotched, ravaged, and you think it's hopeless, now there's nothing to lose, and you go at it almost pressed up against the mirror.

At two in the morning, even here in Orvieto on desperate vacation, we're each other's mirror, picking away, squeezing the last drop, that never *is* the last drop, of rancor. As if hoping finally to clean it out, leaving our faces in their original purity, infant cheeks.

Two-in-the-mornings you become a lawyer, "you" meaning me as well, arguing a case before the judge of marital righteousness, laying out your arguments absolutely rationally with a child's insistence on logical alternatives. Now, there are three possibilities. Either X…or Y…. You count on your fingers. *Or else Z*, you say, and it's on *Z* the ante gets raised. Madly rational at two-in-the-morning, I put you on the witness stand. Tell me, really, when you said Q, you must have meant one of two things. Which was it? And when you ran your fingers over my shoulders and down my back, what *was* I supposed to imagine?

And you: Why did you think, when I touched you, that it meant R? Well, *didn't* it mean R? Not necessarily, you say, and why do you always *do* this? You always leave me ragged in the morning on just the wrong days. Always? When was the last time? Last Tuesday. No, I say, that was totally different. Totally. That was about the children. Are you telling me I shouldn't talk about the children before we sleep? Before we *don't* sleep, you say—I was ragged in the morning. I slept fine, I say.

Claiming your privilege to postpone cross-examination, you fold away your brief with your glasses and lay them down by the tour guidebooks, on your overnight bag next to the bed, the *letto matrimoniale*. I'm dying to end this *right*, in lovemaking, but I don't dare start anything or the recriminations will begin: So you think you can say things like that and then make love. You want me to understand that night talk doesn't stop *costing*.

And all this time we're actually dreaming, all these logical steps are dance steps in a dream we're sharing, two-in-the-morning dream make up of logic, logic blocks stacked up like Jonah's wooden ones into an architecture of pain. You see what our lives are? You see what marriage is?

Tonight in Orvieto you put in ear plugs and sleep, and I give up and lie in bed listening to street sounds and then no street sounds, and I go to the French windows and I can see a corner of the cathedral, moonlight, all white marble, the color of the facade bleached out by the moon, and I think, This should be making us incredibly happy, we should have made love a couple of times already and be holding hands at this window looking out at the old stone houses and shining cathedral, but there you are in bed, full of sadness, thick with the clear white wine of the region to dull the sadness. I think your sadness is a cover to keep you away from me in bed. Your sleep walls me out. I cough, groan, stretch; you sleep.

I'm cooped up, no other room to go read in, afraid to walk

the streets of a strange town, two-in-the-morning, and where's to go? I pull a chair to the window and get angry at you, thinking how tired I'll be in the morning, when we're supposed to drive to Assizi over the rough mountain roads and be capable of opening ourselves to the frescos of Giotto and the Lorenzettis. I want to express to you your unfairness, I want you to accept my catalogue of your failures as a wife so I can ask pardon for my failures as a husband and we can both breathe again, because all day since we left Rome we've taken breath as if air were hard to come by or were habit forming and suspect. We are afraid to breathe lest (how long has it been since I've last used *lest*) it feed our fires and the fires consume us.

Finally, I pull the standing lamp over to this chair and turn on the light, shutting out Orvieto, draping a towel over the shade to make it seem legitimately, even to myself, as if I want not to wake you, but of course, that's what I *do* want—need—to wake you. You keep sleeping. Tension gone from your face, lines of character blurred soft, and I feel tenderness and want to wake you to start again.

But I read. Or don't actually read but float above us both to the high plaster ceiling to look down with amusement at this middle-aged American couple, he, the husband, with head buzzing, asleep-awake, playing with dangerous words—*final* words—like someone toying with a gun. I try to coax him to join me on the ceiling; he refuses. Humorously, he insists: My life is stuck forever in this nowhere room. And she, the wife, sleeps shut off from his vision of their lives, a vision that grows, every quarter of an hour, darker, more absolute, congealing until he can't imagine her ever waking, it's morning, imagine them eating breakfast and driving off to Assizi from this room. Forever he will be sitting awake and she walled off with earplugs, her back curled away from his side of the bed. I want him to see the comedy, marriage comedy, it's nothing personal, this genre called *marriage.* He refuses.

And now you turn, you twist like a caught fish, you wake up, notice the lamp, avoid my eyes, go off to the bathroom, and when you return, lie down with a pillow over your head. I say, "Sandra? I know you can hear me Sandra. I want to know what that pillow over your head *means.*" I see you stiffen, only a husband could possibly see that, you're not quite breathing, you're listening through the earplugs and the pillow but not admitting it. "Now," I say, "there are two possibilities I can see…"

You sit bolt upright. "All right. Now I can't sleep, you want to talk, listen to this. You want to know why I shut out that voice of yours? There are times I can't *stand* your voice. Just for instance—do you know how phony you sound when you talk your elegant Italian?" I don't answer, so you go on to tell me how my moustache makes you cringe. "It's so false, like your voice, oh, you can be such a poseur," you say. "You stroke it, your moustache, when you talk to a woman—*any* woman—do you know that? And. And I can't stand it against my skin, *especially down here*, it makes me feel dirty, as if you cleaned your boots on me."

"No woman ever minded before," I tell her, stroking my moustache clean.

"And *what* woman are we perhaps hinting at? Oh, don't you love to see yourself the macho lover! You want to talk?—all right, frankly it makes me sick, you, you squeeze a nipple and you push and grunt and that's love? Why bother with *other women*? I might as well be anyone."

"Not anyone."

"Anyone."

"Not anyone. Anyone else would move her body more than a stone. That's your unique contribution to the *Kama Sutra*."

"If I don't move, perhaps it's because I'm not *moved*."

We get down and dirty. It's two-in-the-morning talk, what do you expect? But there are things we don't say. You don't ask how I expect you to make love with someone who's let himself go the way I have. You don't remind me of the deposits of fat along my hips. I don't speak of your fallen breasts and the slackening skin under your eyes. And all this not-speaking is a subtle expression of generosity, not to do real damage, not to go too far, not to press upon the other the facts of getting old. Those facts. We are, after all, sitting in a bare room in a foreign town, we're all the other has. Not-to-speak about these things is prudence but it's also compassion, even tenderness. We both know it.

Then, as you attack me for the cultural gaucherie, the insult, of ordering red wine in Orvieto, so that you were forced to drink a whole bottle of the white yourself, and as I accuse you of getting drunk to evade me, you *don't* speak about my relative failure in business, and I *don't* speak about the career as a research biologist you've never gotten off the ground (performing instead grunt work for a pharmaceutical firm). We don't blame one another that Tina can't make friends at school or that at three Jonah still isn't toilet trained.

At three-in-the-morning as I cross the room to sit next to you on the bed, I attack you for your lack of enthusiasm yesterday at the Vatican museums. And as you laugh at me for refusing to trek this morning to an Etruscan grave site, you touch my arm. At once a little flame rises in my arm, in my groin and thighs. This makes me angry at you, for you've deadened yourself to me. And I want to touch you but I don't want to reveal it. Or, rather, I *want* to reveal it, want you to know that I need to touch you—but without incriminating myself.

And your touch on my arm, is it shy desire and a hint of renewal? Renewal, renewal! Suppose you're feeling sorry for me instead? I lock my jaw and turn away. Now a motor scooter growls in the street; it passes, and the growl rises to a disappearing whine, and a dog barks in Italian and I stop and pat your hand, as if I'm the one doing the comforting—against the night, the dark at the bottom of the dark.

You crumple against me, and ahh, now I'm able to turn this into a story of reconciliation, cramming away in a pocket of my mind the embarrassing knowledge that it's after all only a story I'm writing, so that I don't have to know it as I take you into my arms and undo the buttons down the front of your nightgown and pull the silk from your shoulders and press myself to the warmth of your breasts and lie beside you. And did I tell you, have I ever told you, that I've never known lovemaking so sensually rich. I want to *go* nowhere, it's the touch itself, that's where the music is. Ambient Being becomes dense, like warm rain forest as I breathe you in, and the wounds flow and heal, and nothing mars or has ever marred our original selves.

In the middle of this, the middle of *you*, it comes over me all the *work* it took to bring us here. I feels as if I'd struggled to lay stone on stone and I wonder do you feel all the work and feel it was worth it, you *must* feel it was worth the loss of sleep and the loss of breath. And the humiliation. Now you understand, don't you, and for the moment we stand above the ugliness, the agony.

And you, you *come* with me, you come again and again, it's a celebration in Orvieto, middle-of-the-night, making the whole trip a victory, and you hold me and, slacking, breathe easy and lie beside me, and I'm sinking towards sleep. And then you say to me,

"*Now* can I sleep, please?"

And at first I don't get it. Then I do. "Are you saying you made love just to get some sleep?"

"Please. We've got to drive all morning. I'm so tired of this," you say. "I can't take much more."

"Are you saying—"

"Please, please, for godsakes, no more 'saying'—do you mind? I'll listen tomorrow in the car. All right?"

And out of that pocket in my mind I pull my story, "Reconciliation," and tear it up. You weren't consoling me, you were *appeasing*, as if I'm a kind of madman needing to be calmed. We've been through, you and I, too many of these two-in-the-morning scenes of mutual humiliation and disgust to think they can change our lives. We keep on, a ritual. Sleep, we sleep.

Originally appeared in Virginia Quarterly Review, *Winter, 1992-93*

Aaron, Personal

I

He could predict, sitting kitty-corner to her at another Wellesley dinner party, what it would be like to make love with Kate. She'd be ironic at first, nervous and quick with her mouth at his mouth, impulsive, excited more by the idea than by him—by her own demonstration that she wasn't just a music teacher and the wife of one of the partners at Bennett and Lowe. She'd need to show herself as this secretly passionate creature so she could permit herself even to *imagine* slipping outside her marriage...like waking at night and walking into another room, half asleep, all your skin like lips, and the other room is a bedroom you've never seen, or it's a silken tent and someone's there, propped on a silken pillow, and you touch fingertips to fingertips.

He imagined her tense fingers and stiff arms loosening, she'll let go of herself like a coat too heavy for spring...but now, now she was laughing her spurting social laugh across the table, straightening her paisley skirt, mauve, silk, and he felt as though he had a gift for her and she didn't know it yet.

I have a gift for you.

Artur Rubinstein was playing Mozart too low to be heard, there to take the edge off silences. Joe Bennett, Kate's husband, was kidding the husband of the other couple about his squash game. And he, Aaron Kern, was half listening to the three wives talk about summers at the Cape but he was in the middle of summer here in this candlelit room, for all along his right arm and shoulder and his right cheek, he could feel Kate, Joe's wife Kate, the heat from her, and he wondered was it really Kate's warmth or just his own blood swimming to the surface of his skin to be close to her.

He smiled diagonally across the table at his wife, smiled at Sylvia to give himself cover, while he touched Kate's arm and whispered, "I can hardly stand the way he plays this passage, I mean it's so gorgeous, here, here…." It was true and not true. Rubinstein played the *andante* so that you wanted to split yourself open and take the music inside, but why did he say it?—he said it because Kate was a serious classical pianist and saying it was a kind of propaganda for the life she could be sharing with him. Though she didn't know him yet.

Though this was only the third time they'd met—once at a company picnic, once at a dinner party, now here. He wondered: would I be thinking these things if she weren't my boss's wife?

Not exactly a "boss"—but Joe was one of the partners at Bennett and Lowe; Joe could make *him* one of the partners. He liked Joe, respected him as an architect; he liked his design sense, his clarity. And while Joe wasn't much of a communicator—a shy man, always preferring to sit by himself and sketch a detail than to charm his people—he ran a friendly office.

Maybe nothing's going to happen, Aaron said to his wine glass. *I'd have to be out of my mind.*

He refused to think of himself as a womanizer. Before and between marriages, he knew many women, but never to count them up. It's just that always in his life he'd been a lover. A husband briefly; briefly this second time, too, he could see. His seven-year marriage to Sylvia wasn't working, not for either of them, though they were both good with their daughter. But what he was really good at was loving women: loving them deeply for a time, attuning himself to their sorrows, feeding them. He felt like an anachronism, taking love so seriously. You could say *devoutly*. When loving was out of his life, he could hear the seconds tick his life away, waste and waste as he got older and older.

He drew close to Kate to let her perfume enter his open pores—all his pores open to her as if they were lying in bed together, already lovers, and all the petals of their skin folded back. And sitting at the table in all their clothes they made pillow talk, talked about Artur Rubinstein, who, according to gossip, often made love in his dressing room between halves of a concert. Probably untrue, but it was the language of eros, and sharing the language was like sharing the same humming in the blood.

It's eros, he thought, that made the thing go, this tenderness; it was what let him understand that the skin of Kate's arm was holy ground, her shoulder a mysterious landscape of clavicle and silk. It's the electric power in the wires—but it isn't what the wires *do*. It's like this: a computer system needs a power source. But the power isn't what the system is *about*. Eros just opens all the switches and lets information flow. So now. So now. So she breathes and my own breath comes hot and full to my chest, tangles with the music and tastes so sweet that the simple veal in sauce becomes sweeter, part of a rich fabric of meaning.

Meaning *what*? He didn't need to know. He felt the meaning between his fingertips.

At the head of the table, Joe Bennett opened another bottle of wine. They all lifted their glasses. Watching her, kitty-corner next to him at the foot of the table, he saw her almost indiscernibly lift her glass another half an inch and catch his eye and cover over the gesture by laughing at something somebody was saying. But now it was as if they were sharing the same glass and it was a potion, the wine of desire, and it was filling them with a common blood.

All he knew was her long black hair. He could imagine loosening her hair, letting it tumble around them. And he knew her long neck and knew her beautiful dark eyes and knew that he was causing those eyes to metamorphose into the eyes of a woman deeply wise and so strong she could be graceful and amused. He felt foolish. Nobody was as free of confusion and self-torture as the woman he imagined. For Godsakes, he was forty—ten years older than Kate, though five years younger than Joe. Never, through years of loving, had he ever had an affair with a married woman. Let alone, his boss's wife! Kate and Joe had a girl and a boy. He and Sylvia had a five year old girl.

But it was as if they had discovered by a sign that they were both secret votaries of a mystery cult—Rosicrucians, say—and no one else knew, and every moment they were aware, one of the other. Speaking to everyone else, but aware to trembling.

Aware of so much happening—this subtle drama with no one else in attendance. Would she slip away to speak with him? If he called and asked her to see him, would she be amazed? Breathing her in, he wondered how much she knew. He felt panic that he might be making it all up. That was the worst. It would be hell to find himself alone inside the mystery—isolated communicant.

After dinner, Kate went to the piano and played Chopin on the Steinway Joe had given her for Christmas, and he knew that only the two of them understood how grand it was for her to have worked up the Ballade in G minor. The others took it as a demonstration of skill, like juggling. Sylvia liked Chopin, but after dinner and wine she grew sleepy. Joe sat with arms folded, watching his wife do him proud. Joe's real music, Aaron knew, was cool jazz.

She's playing this for me.

He felt the music as if her fingers were weaving secret messages into the strands of his body. They told him his life was collapsing.

Afterwards, there was some kind of playoff game, basketball, and Joe and the other husband went into the TV room to watch. He knew Joe didn't care about basketball anymore than he did—Joe was being polite to the other man. He should watch too, but he couldn't. The wives talked about the destruction of forests and lakes through acid rain; Aaron sat on the fringe for awhile, then slipped away, went outside onto the terrace wishing and afraid she would follow.

It was a warm, damp night, no moon, air thick like a medium to swim through, and he so heady and alone, as if he could lift off from the deck in his black Italian shoes and blue blazer and float over the garden and away, until this love sickness dissipated.

Mosquitoes; he slapped them away.

He heard the screen door open and shut, and he could hardly breathe. Then she stood next to him. *You're so lovely*, he didn't say, though it was hard not to say; easy enough to take her hand in the dark but he didn't touch her. "My garden," she said, and she waved her hand over the darkness, sculpting vague shapes into pale blue delphiniums, golden lilies. Together in the dark they made up the garden.

II

Now, fifteen years later on a gray Sunday in September, Aaron was sitting cross-legged on the attic floor looking through a box marked AARON, PERSONAL of old snapshots and letters and half listening to voices from downstairs, laughter and busy noises. This was the day Sonia, the last child, was off to college. They'd be driving her together, a family. It was going to feel strange around the house without her awful rock'n roll.

He heard their laughter.

Between his fingers was a picture of Kate in New York, he'd taken it one weekend of lovemaking and anguish. She'd wept—that was the word, not cried—all afternoon, while he rubbed her back in slow circles, and the afternoon, so precious, slipped away and they had to take separate shuttles for Boston.

Something fell to the kitchen floor and smashed; a vase: the blue porcelain flower vase. It was amazing how you could discriminate the sound. His mother's vase. Sonia would feel bad—he had to prepare himself to shrug it off. They were in such a frenzy, the two of them, wife and daughter. He was a male, he was relegated to his study to work until they needed him to lug boxes; instead, he'd slipped up to the attic to look at old pictures. He felt adulterous.

This one showed Kate from behind, in a Japanese bathrobe, looking over a balcony somewhere. Her hair was loose around her shoulders, it must have been a hotel room with a balcony, maybe the day in Boston he was supposed to meet her at the Museum, and parking was a problem, he was late, and rushing there he saw Kate rushing too, knew her by the lovely lean swaying music of her walk and her long neck and her black hair—and for a hundred yards he didn't call out, wanting the pleasure of her beauty. *We're going to make love all afternoon*, he told himself. "Kate! Kate!" She turned, already laughing, and they were giddy and never mind the Museum, oh, save it for another day....

"Aaron! Aaron!" He was being called downstairs to carry out suitcases and boxes and load the station wagon.

She was letting the gray grow in. He didn't mind. But he thought, maybe now that Sonia is off to college, we can trade in the other car on a little sports job. We can spend some time together. Because look how little they saw each other. She worked, he worked. He got home nights at eight, nine o'clock, still absorbed in his designs; they ate whatever they could put together, made calls, slept. Only weekends did they make love or take a walk together, or go to a dinner party, where he'd be charming to some young woman who'd think he was special.

"My roommate's going to absolutely kill me," Sonia said. "All these boxes!"

"We can always bring things back. Don't worry," he said, rubbing her back in circles, and then he realized she was more pleased than worried, pleased that all this was *hers*. Her hair was wild around her shoulders, and as she grinned and helped him lift another box, he stopped breathing a moment and realized how he loved her, Sonia, how he wanted to rush out ahead of her to the university and tell them to be kind to her, to treat her as somebody special. He had a gift for her, a heavy wool sweater she'd coveted this summer in England. Too expensive, he'd grumped, and then when they'd all stopped for tea, he'd slipped away "to get a paper," and had the shop girl hold it for him. Last night he'd sneaked the box under the driver's seat to give to her at the dorm.

Suitcase and duffel, sleeping bag and back pack, skis and stereo, the house was opening up and tumbling out until you'd think the whole thing would all be inside their station wagon except for sofas and tables and beds. They waited by the car for Sonia to take one last rush through the house hunting its comfort to bring with her.

"Did you have to pack right at my feet?" Kate asked, annoyed. "It's such a long ride."

"Sorry. We'll put it where you want. I'm sorry."

He knew that when they said goodbye to Sonia at the dorm, Kate was going to weep. So he'd bought her a gift too, a string of pearls. He'd wrapped the pearls around a two-disc CD of Rubinstein playing Chopin and put it all in a pretty little painted box. *Dear Kate*, he'd written, *this is a bribe so when we get home you'll play for me*. Play *with* me, he meant. We're what each other has.

Because this morning, looking through old pictures, he became aware of how much was missing. The early fighting had bled it out of them until each of them was scarcely recognizable as the lover for whom the other had broken up a life. Broken up a life and put three children through confusion, and it cost him a good job, almost his career, and he had to start again, and he blamed her and she blamed him only they weren't permitted to blame for those things—they'd signed on the dotted line, eyes wide open, for those things—so they each blamed the other for everything else.

He remembered those terrible mornings when Joe would pick up Sonia and Chris for the weekend; the terrible Sunday evenings when he would drive to Sylvia's place to drop off Karen. The summer vacation when the three kids couldn't get along with each other and were audience to Kate and Aaron, who blamed each other for living.

Blamed and fought until that Kate of those early photos and long, anguished letters of love was more real than his *wife* Kate, and sometimes he'd slip up to his box of AARON, PERSONAL and read the letters or skim his journal and feel amused at his old intensity. And sad. And eroticized. And adulterous. And ashamed.

In this moment before Sonia brought down one last hairbrush or teddy bear and they set off and their lives changed again, he looked into Kate's eyes, still for him beautiful, wanted to take her hand and walk through the September garden, remains of a garden—Kate's garden (though he helped her do the digging). But he repacked the car to clear the space at Kate's feet.

Still, he wished she'd turn to him and take his hand. For courage. Not for reassurance about her feelings. That he really didn't need. The fighting had ended a long time ago, leaving them scarred, but kind to one another. Maybe they outgrew it. Maybe they simply became less the object of the other's obsession. When she was irritated, touchy, he stayed in his study. When he was cranky, she retreated to *her* study. They had separate lives and no energy for fighting. More and more, it was his work, not love, he turned to. Kate, too, to *her* work. Ten years ago, Kate had started writing reviews of records and concerts for a local paper, and it turned into a career in music journalism. He was proud of her, though it was frustrating, how busy she was. She rarely touched the piano now. Sometimes, on a Saturday.

Making love—it was strange—had grown deeper, certainly easier, like floating a slow river in erotic tenderness, easier than on those tortured afternoons, or, say, that weekend when each had invented excuses—a concert, a conference—to be together in Washington. And then ruined the weekend with the question, *What should we do?*

But the drama of desire, the one blood he once imagined they shared, the terrible openings to each other, the mysterious landscape of flesh so sacred, all that was shut away in the box marked <u>AARON, PERSONAL</u>.

Now Sonia slammed the door behind her, a silk pillow in her arms, and she calling, "Don't worry, I'll just *sit* on it if I have to." But she didn't have to; they jammed it in, and Kate squeezed his hand and tears came to *his* eyes and they were off. In the rear-view mirror, Aaron could see Sonia fiddling with her Walkman and deciding against it—it wouldn't go over well, better spend time with the family, etcetera. She leaned over the seat back to tell them, again, which courses she hoped she'd get and what she'd do if she couldn't get them.

Somewhere halfway, Kate reminded her to call her father. "Joe says he'll be coming down to see you as soon as you're settled." It reminded Aaron he'd been forgetting to call Karen. His own daughter, a junior at U.C. Santa Cruz, he got to see only a couple of times a year, and it was easy to neglect to call her as she neglected to call him. They talked every two, three weeks, and then there was too much to say so they said little, and she barely knew him and he barely knew her. Love at a distance. Sometimes—now, for instance—it made him uneasy to love Sonia, a stepchild, so completely. So completely, and he knew she loved him too, but her mother was her mother, and her father her father, and he—he could only be the *other* father, as he was to Chris. Suppose he'd never left Sylvia. He would be Karen's father. Thinking this, he saw behind his eyes the disheveled room of his life, jumble and breakage. His mother's blue vase.

Kate was talking about clothes—how to manage with a limited wardrobe; how important to keep things off the floor and in the closet. "I suppose you'll have to learn on your own," she sighed. Then, to Aaron, "Want to stop somewhere for lunch so we don't get cranky?"

He knew a place, he said. Sure. There's plenty of time.

On the way home, Kate wept. He drove in cruise control with his arm around her. "Don't you think you ought to keep your hands on the wheel?" she asked, not wanting him to let her go. With Sonia gone, he could put in a cassette of the Beaux Arts Trio playing Schubert, and stroking her face, he said, "Just think—no rock'n roll for at least a month."

Fingering her pearls, his gift, she stretched up to kiss his cheek, blew her nose, turned up the Schubert—and wept again. But he could predict that when they got home, she'd say, "Let's leave the phone machine on…" and they'd take hands and slip upstairs to make love. He could predict what it would be like making love with her: it wouldn't be a playful time; she might even cry. Her fingers and her body would be telling him everything, and he'd be kissing her, saying, *I know, I know, it's all right, I'm here….*

Originally appeared in New England Living, *June, 1990*

Waiting for Polly Adler

It's Sunday morning, sun barely up over the sea; it's early summer; in the movie in my head we're in Long Beach, Long Island, and it's 1927, so Long Beach is kind of chic, with huge, white stucco houses and expensive hotels that by the time I was born had come down in the world. And my uncle, Lloyd Clayton, is maybe thirty, thirty-one, killer-handsome, not yet rich but getting there fast, and he's waiting in bed in the best hotel in Long Beach for Polly Adler, madam of the most successful whorehouse in New York, to close up shop and drive out from the city to meet him for a convivial Sunday. His Stetson hat, mirrored in the pink morning light from the mirror over the dresser, is hanging on a clothes-caddy that holds his white linen suit, his two-tone brown/white sporty shoes. He can't sleep. He's been unable to sleep all night.

I know about this from long talks, early 1970s, when he was in his mid-seventies and I was in my thirties. Or not so much *talks*: he talked, I listened. He loved to recount the stories of his youth, the Story of his Youth. We'd walk along Central Park South, both of us hot-shot walkers who loved gobbling up sidewalk. I remember being amazed by the way young women would turn their heads to look at him, not at me—Uncle Lloyd in his cashmere coat and that brushed felt Stetson. When I imagine that morning in Long Beach waiting for Polly Adler, I'm inventing the Stetson hanging on that hook on the clothes-caddy, because I can't remember Uncle Lloyd without his hat. In the picture above my desk, his beautiful head of hair, wavy, silver ever since his late twenties, is hatless, but the perfect Stetson is in his hand. He's just lifted it off for the snapshot in front of his black 1934 sixteen-cylinder Cadillac. Phony grin. Click. Dressed in crisp white shirt, beige linen slacks and two-tone shoes, he stands on Riverside Drive squeezing the shoulder of his "Pop", my grandfather who died when I was eight, a little man with a brushy white moustache, a tough little man who beat his children with a belt.

It was a pale gray Stetson, not a cowhand's hat but something an oil tycoon, a cattle baron might wear, or the governor of a western state. He'd become a westerner at home "in the concrete canyons," a wealthy sport with a big racetrack watch—every year he'd take the Hudson River Day Line and then the train up to Saratoga for racing season. He didn't want you to think he was old-money, East Coast American; he was a gaudy spirit from the West and spoke with movie-Western accent—though he'd grown up in Chicago, and the only "West" he knew was Palm Springs, California, where he eventually settled my grandfather. Always on stage, his voice resonant, he sustained his vowels, let them echo through his chest, as if he were a cantor chanting Torah.

This is about a self-made, rich American. Born poor, he made himself *rich*; born the son of a Russian-Jewish immigrant, Yiddish his first language, he made himself *American*, a man-about-town in prohibition New York, acquaintance of Mickey Walker, His Dishonor the Mayor, and pal of the police chief. What was it, when he was growing up, that let him see past the models of adulthood around him? After all, he was born poor in Chicago, 1898, born Louis Cohon—his father (my grandfather) a rebellious Jew from Odessa. You hear stories of Jews tossing their tefillin overboard when they passed the Statue of Liberty; my grandfather had discarded all such trappings years before he came to America. By the time I knew

Grandpa, just before World War II, he'd discarded Yiddish. "I'm as American as Uncle Sam," he loved saying in heavily-accented English. My grandfather never looked back. Later, if you asked my father or my uncle about their history, they'd say in exactly the same words, "Ahh, what do you want to hear that old-time crap for?"

Old-time crap meant anything before Uncle Lloyd's rise to glory. Meant history. He'd have agreed with Henry Ford, that old anti-Semite, who said, "History is bunk." As far as Lloyd was concerned, the world before he started fighting it, climbing it, didn't matter a damn. He was sure that's what America was all about—dumping the way things used to be. Starting fresh. But the rise itself, oh, that he loved to talk about. We'd be walking past the Plaza Hotel and he'd grab my arm and point up to the green-streaked copper mansard roof as if it were challenging or confirming his power, and he'd say, "When I first came to this burg, I'd walk these concrete canyons and yell up there, 'You don't scare me one damn bit. I'm the boy for you. You watch. I'll have you eating out of my hand.' And didn't I do all right? You bet your ass."

So Uncle Lloyd made himself up. *Lloyd Clayton*: much too phony a name, and if in 1919, coming out of the army, he'd been a little more sophisticated, as he would be just a few years later, he'd have changed *Louis Cohon* less obviously. But that's the point: he learned so fast—but had such a lot to learn. What was he, after all, but the youngest son of greenhorns from Russia, poor as hell, his old man a Jewish, atheist, angry socialist who worked in a loft in Chicago rolling cigars, his mother a terrorized, submissive woman who took in boarders? He'd graduated eighth grade, Louis Cohon, and that was the best any of the brothers could do. His younger sister, such a smart girl, Annie Cohon, not only went on to high school, she eventually put herself through college and law school—but the three boys took jobs after seventh grade or after eighth. That's how they could afford to keep Annie in school.

There are people who parlay advantage into advantage. Lloyd worked all day in a stockroom; then, saving the nickel carfare, he walked to downtown Chicago to study. His salary went to his mother—but he kept back enough to pay for classes. At fourteen, my uncle learned stenography, then court stenography, and by fifteen, pretending to be older, he was working at a Chicago courthouse. Everything proceeded from that. But suppose it hadn't been stenography—wouldn't he have found another way?

It was the stenography that, when the army needed men who could take dictation and type, gave Louis—still Louis in 1917—entrée to a commission; commissioned an officer straight from civilian life, he lived in Washington in officers' quarters and was secretary to a general. And that's where he must have learned a smattering of manners, of proper English. Because how could he have learned to speak so well among poor kids in the public schools of Chicago?

By 1923, Lloyd was making a lot of money as a tire salesman in New York. He was already a young man about town. Yet he was shy with women, scared of women—fifty years later he laughed at "what a pusillanimous fellow I was. You didn't know I could use ten-dollar words like *pusillanimous*, did you?" He went to Polly Adler's not for the girls but for the talk, for the laughs. It's where the big shots hung out. And he liked Polly, and "she made a big fuss over me."

But when he got to New York right out of the army, he had no job, no friends. He used to brag about how he got the job selling. He was staying in a cheap rooming house on the West Side, pinching pennies while he looked for work. And he thought to himself, *Here I am in a brand-new world. We own this sonofabitch world. There ain't no country like this country.* He knew enough by the time he told me this story not to use "sonofabitch", not to use "ain't". In fact, he was vain about his "grammar" and "ten-dollar words". But he loved the panache of that tough-guy language.

"You'd think it was a cinch, wouldn't you, getting a job after the war. But see, the economy hadn't kicked in. Guys on their knees for jobs, took what they could get, the poor bastards. And I said to myself, *What are these shmucks gonna need? Where can I get in on the ground floor?*" So he took his sweet time, squeezing the time from his war bonus, from his savings, living stingy in that rooming house. How many soldiers came home from that war with money saved up? He looked at ads, he read the papers.

"Then one day, I got dressed up in my only suit, and I walked into a store—where they sold tires. I'd been casing the joint. Plate glass window, bare linoleum floor, tires sitting on little wooden stands, a brand-new store sign in the window. And I asked for a job. 'What do you know about tires?' the boss asked. He was a hard-assed guy. *I* was a hard-assed guy. 'Not a goddamn thing,' I told him, 'but I'm a smart guy and a good salesman.' And I could see his eyes staring past me—he was thinking how to get rid of me politely and maybe three other things at the same time—and I said to him, 'Look here. Just try me out. Next guy who walks through that door, try me out. If I make the sale, you give me a job.' 'But you don't know tires,' he says. 'I will when you spend five minutes and explain.' Well, right there I had the sonofabitch, because I had him investing in me, you get what I mean?"

It could have gone lousy—he admitted that later on—but as soon as he saw the man he had to sell, he knew he'd be all right. It was a little man with a swagger. "The combination," Lloyd said, "was unbeatable." Five minutes, he had a hand on the guy's shoulder and hush-hush, as if it had to be kept from the boss, he was offering him the best deal in the store—only of course it wasn't the best deal, it wasn't a deal at all.

"'I guess you've got yourself a job,' the boss said to me. 'I'll start you off at twenty-five dollars a week—right after the training period.' Now, twenty-five a week was a damned good salary those days. Better than the most money my pop ever made. Here's what I told him: 'I want fifty dollars a week.' Ridiculous! I knew I'd never get it just like that. 'Here's the deal. I work for you for six months at twenty-five bucks, and then if you think I'm worth it, you pay me in back-wages the other twenty-five bucks for the whole six months, starting today—or you don't, fine!—I walk out, no hard feelings. What d'you got t'lose?'"

Six months later—of course, because it's that kind of story—the boss was glad to pay him back wages of $25 additional a week. In another year, with commission, he was earning $10,000. By 1925 he was making $25,000 a year, and when he said he was going to leave, the boss was willing to double it for the following year. Imagine? Walking away from $50,000 a year?

He walked away—and started his own tire company out of a little office on Tenth Avenue and had cards printed up:

TIRES, INCORPORATED:
WORLD'S LARGEST DISTRIBUTOR.

The world's largest distributor didn't have a tire to his phony name. In his office he had little models of tires circling ashtrays or set vertically in lacquered plaques advertising Goodyear or Firestone. But the country, he knew, was in greater and greater need of tires. More and more cars in every little town in America, and they all needed tires. So he took the train out to Dayton and Akron and made deals to buy up factory seconds. That's all it took—those deals, and the willingness to sleep on a mattress on his desk because it was too late to go uptown, willingness to grab some sleep on an overnight coach train to save the cost of a room.

"You know how I got where I am?" he'd ask me, again and again. "I worked twenty-five hours a day eight goddamn days a week." He'd take the train town to town or drive town to town and stop in at all the little one-pump gas stations, auto repair shops, and show them pictures and take down-payments—enough to cover the cost of the tires—and then he'd send in the orders to the factories. West as far as Chicago, south to Lexington, Kentucky, and all through the Northeast. He wore his Christian name and good, conservative clothes. The Stetson, that came a couple of years later. He stayed away from "booze and broads."

A couple of scotches in the evening at Polly's he didn't think of as booze. And Polly Adler was not exactly a "broad".

When he was in town and not working in the evening, he went to her apartment—she moved her fancy brothel all around New York: West 50s, West 80s, East 50s—but kept the same telephone number, printed on a card with the logo of a parrot, a card that was in the pocket of stockbrokers, gangsters, ballplayers, politicians. According to Uncle Lloyd, she made each apartment a home, in good taste, with sofas and tables, warm wood, good liquor—this was Prohibition; people knew they could trust Polly's place. She paid off the cops—though they still bounced her around. And she was fun. Dorothy Parker and Robert Benchley from the Algonquin spent evenings at Polly's. "It was a hell of a place to make business contacts," Uncle Lloyd said.

And Polly Adler, who was, in spite of her razzmatazz, as much a cautious loner as my uncle, "took a shine" to him. Well, I've seen the pictures—Lloyd as a young man. He was gorgeous, chiseled face with sharp nose, nose of a Mohawk more than of a Jew, strong cleft chin like Kirk Douglas. He dressed well, came in alone, wasn't brassy. He never got drunk, never took one of her "girls" to a bedroom. Or so he said, and I believe him. *Contacts*, yes—but he also liked to charm Polly, precisely because she was out of bounds. I think that's it. And here's the funny thing: while Polly Adler was part of sophisticated New York and my uncle was becoming a man about town (I just saw in my mind's eye the white silk cravat he wore when he took us out to dinner), they were both Russian Jews. He was born in Chicago but his father was just off the boat from Odessa; Polly (really Pearl) was born in Russia, came over as a young girl. They'd both come a long way.

By all accounts, Polly brought kindness and good humor along. For my uncle, kindness felt like weakness. He could be generous as hell. He loved being generous, magnanimous, a big shot, loved to spend money on people. But when he felt his control threatened, a rage sprang up. Did the rage come from his father, from his father's belt, that came down on all the boys, although least on Louis? As a kid, my uncle learned to make himself someone too important for a beating. And he succeeded. By fourteen, fifteen, he ran the household.

He saw himself as shepherd of the family. In 1926 Uncle Lloyd brought my father to New York from Chicago ("Got to have somebody I can trust, Chuck."). As a yes-man he could boss around? That's not how Uncle Lloyd saw it. He was being responsible, taking his brother along with him on his rise to glory. As a child, according to my father, Lloyd (Louis) was a "namby-pamby" (my father's word), a "sissy", no athlete; a soft, scared Jewish kid chased by the anti-Semites. My father tells how he and the middle brother Jack protected Louis on the street. Uncle Lloyd must have liked the turn-around, putting his older brother under his thumb. "Of course, you've got to change your name, Chuckie. You're known as my big brother, am I right? Can't have one brother Clayton and the other Cohon, am I right?" My father became Chuck Clayton. Within a year Louis, his sister Annie, his brother Jack, and his parents had all become Clayton. Lloyd paid them for the inconvenience.

All the grandiosity! The humiliation and rage and grandiosity came early. Without it, he'd never have made it out of Chicago, surely never have bought up a square block of midtown-Manhattan real estate. I'd bet there was someone in Chicago, a mentor, a model of possibilities; I'd love to know. By the time I knew him he was an angry phony. My mother begged my father to leave him. They fought about this all the time. "Why do you stay with a man like that?" I remember when I was a young boy, in the 1940s, how afraid my father was of Lloyd's temper, of his judgment. Before we'd visit my uncle, Dad would get me a haircut and dress me up, find a stain and make me change my shirt, and on the way downtown in the subway he'd spit on his handkerchief and scrub my face one last time. "The big guy ready for us?" he'd ask the receptionist. Then he'd clear his throat, my father, put on a big grin, and knock at his brother's door.

Sometimes Uncle Lloyd was expansive and charming. Sitting at his oversized mahogany desk—it must have weighed three hundred pounds, that desk—he'd teach me about money, philosophize about responsibility, then call for his car, and a tire changer would have it running at the warehouse door. And he'd say, "How you like this beat-up old cigar box I bought last week, Jackie?"—always his name for me—and jam his foot down on the accelerator and the new Caddy would spring forward, jamming us back into the plush seats. We'd go to Lindy's, where he palmed the headwaiter a tip and we sat with "the big shots."

"See that guy over there? Jimmy Durante," he'd say, his lips still, like a movie gangster's. "Jimmy Durante." And he'd wave the waiter over for more pickles. When my father wasn't looking, he'd jam a ten-dollar bill into the handkerchief pocket of my jacket.

Other times he'd be in a lousy mood—yelling at one of his salesmen, at his secretary, at a tire changer. He'd kick his way through the aisle at piles of tires and snap at my father, "Get that crap cleaned up. What kind of shit hole you want to work in, Chuck?"

"You bet, Lloyd. I'll have them get right on it!" And, his beefy face hot, red, my father would storm back to the huge warehouse and roar, "Andy! Goddamnit—you get the hell in here!"

Later my father would tell me, "He's a disappointed man, my brother. He's not very happy at home. Frankly, your mother thinks my brother's jealous because he has no kids."

Jealous—of my father? That I couldn't believe. And not being happy in his home on Park Avenue? To a child it was a little palace, Uncle Lloyd and Aunt Bernadine's, full of mirrors in ornate frames and delicate period furniture that I knew Aunt Bernadine had chosen, as she chose the eighteenth and nineteenth-century books that lined a wall of the living room. Real books—Alexander Pope, a first posthumous edition; Hazlitt's essays, Thiers' *History of the French Revolution*. Pretty leather bindings, just décor, never opened. I know that because Aunt Bernadine was interested only in clothes and bridge, my mother told me. She was never home. And Uncle Lloyd *bragged* he never read a "goddamn book."

"I know what a great student you are, Jackie, and that's swell. Keep it up. Me, I had to go to work when I was just a little older than you. School of Hard Knocks, you get me? *My book is this city*," he said, the words resonating like prophetic utterance.

"Well, you sure know the city like a book, it's true all right, Lloyd," my father said. "You own this goddamn city," my father said.

"Cut the crap, Chuck. I own one lousy block is what I own. You get me, Jackie?"

I laughed as I was supposed to, as much in his hands as was my father.

"*But*," he said hoarsely, with a wicked grin up one side of his cheek, "ain't no saying what I'm *gonna* own at this rate."

Was he like this twenty years before, back when he knew Polly Adler? He must have been more affable. The caricature on the wall of Leone's, a famous restaurant that started as a speakeasy, shows him grinning above the shoulder of a blonde beauty with a comically long cigarette holder. When he retired, he grew more affable again. To me at least. "Cause I got money," he'd say—we're sitting over a whiskey at Trader Vic's, "I'm a 'funny guy', an 'eccentric'. If I were a poor sonofabitch, they'd call me *crazy*." Then he'd hunker down. "Say, Jackie, did I tell you about the time I was friends with Polly Adler?"

When he was in the city, 1927, Lloyd would get through a long day at work, stop for a bite to eat, then drop in at Polly's. Early in the evening for her business. And when she wasn't on the phone or talking to customers and women, she'd sit with him and listen and sympathize. "I told her things, you get me, Jackie? Not secrets exactly. Sure as hell not business. I told her what it was like, working so hard. Well, she worked just as hard. She did. You think that's not work, running an establishment like that, paying off cops, handling the drunks and the mobsters? I told her how I got where I was. Polly was a sympathetic lady. And I guess she was soft on me. I guess she was nuts about me. Sometimes I even went to sleep in her room—she was out working the clients, you get me? Time she'd come in, I'd be out of there, back to the grindstone. We became friends."

Was he just a handsome, classy guy, full of power and charm? I don't think so. She was a woman who knew how to listen, and I think he felt safe being vulnerable, telling her how lonely he was in "the rat race", how tough he had to pretend to be. And it moved her. She cared about him. That's my story—but who knows?

I've seen Polly Adler's picture—though it's a picture taken years later, when she'd been through a tough time with the Seabury Commission, with the New York Police Department. She had to spend a month in jail. The *New York Times* has a story on Polly Adler as a prisoner, scrubbing floors. Well, that would have been nothing new; she came from as poor a family as Louis Cohon, got sent to America all by herself at thirteen, worked in factories. In that photo Polly has a sweet, soft round face, big lips, puffy nose and cheeks. She called herself Donald Duck and made fun of how she looked entering a nightclub with some of her tall, gorgeous showgirl whores.

She was no beauty, but she was kind and funny, funny and practical. And Uncle Lloyd liked hanging out with the crowd at Polly's, the rich and the smart and the very, very tough. The ballplayers would win a home game or the gangsters would make a killing off some shipment of whiskey, they'd hang out at Polly's and the women would be busy. Al Capone dropped by, though not when my uncle was around. Polly hated the mobsters, but—she said—"business is business." Uncle Lloyd liked the panache, he'd pal with the guys, playing a man's man. When things got really rough and bric-a-brac started breaking, he'd put on his Stetson and leave the rodeo.

But usually he'd listen to the music. He'd sit with a drinking buddy and when Polly was free, he'd kid with her, he'd talk real estate, listen to her worries about a nasty detective. And a couple of times, when she came in her bedroom next morning, he was still there, and my guess is they smooched a little, and maybe she needed special comforting, maybe the night had gone sour, some jerk beating up on one of her "girls". I'm filling in here, because there must have been something before she put it to him—"Why don't we spend next Sunday out at Long Beach?"

Sure, she'd be tired when she drove down, but the drive would be a cinch at that hour on a Sunday morning, and he could take the room the night before. And they could be together and then get some sleep and go down to the beach, and she'd treat him to a big shore dinner before she had to get back.

"I was flattered, Jackie," my uncle told me almost half a century later. "Imagine your old stick-in-the-mud uncle as a fancy-man?"

On cue, I said, "Ah, that's one thing you never were, Uncle Lloyd—a stick-in-the-mud."

"Maybe not. Maybe not. They tell me I was quite the boy," he laughed, barked a big laugh.

"So what happened?"

"Well…" He hunkers down over the big table at Trader Vic's and I lean toward his guttural whisper. "So I make the reservation, and Saturday night I get down to Long Beach early, sun still up, and I check in and I walk the boardwalk. I remember what I was wearing. I had this gorgeous cream-colored linen suit, it was something. And my two-toned shoes. And I had a goddamn good dinner in me and the Queen of Sex, you get me, from the greatest city in the world, was driving out to have a little rendezvous" (he pronounced it, intentionally, *renn-dayz-vouzzz* in broad western accent) with the Kid from Chicago. And okay, she was no great beauty, I admit that, but she was a swell lady, Jackie. I kind of felt—" and he tapped his chest. "I felt pretty fabulous that evening. A big shot. I liked the feeling...but I was still a little wet behind the ears, those days. No—I *was*. What the hell did I know? Nowadays, Jackie, you don't have to tell me—you're an experienced guy. Every little hippie punk is experienced, you get me? But I didn't get where I was by bumming around. I was in Indiana knocking on gas station doors to get orders. I was taking the boat train to Boston or the train to Chicago and putting together a customer base. This was before we had the big place in New York. Now, I was a stunning guy, I've got to admit it. But I wasn't exactly used to this kind of thing. People believe what they believe. I looked the part. But as the evening went on, see, I grew uneasy. Uncomfortable. I looked at myself in the full-length mirror in the elevator, and you know who I saw? I saw a gangster. In a cream-colored suit. I stuck my hand in my pocket and pretended it was a gun. Lots of laughs. But then I was alone in my big room with the moon up over the great Atlantic Ocean, and I was in silk pajamas, and the windows were open—it was a hot night but a breeze off the ocean helped. And I lay there. And I lay there. And I started to sweat...."

What is he getting himself into? Suppose he catches some disease off her? Suppose one of her gangster pals follows her this morning and barges into the room and sprays him with lead and the cream-colored pajamas get drenched in blood and next day his picture is all over the tabloids? Suppose he tries to get away from her and she threatens to let everybody know or gets a tough guy to break his knees? And lying there in the big soft bed in the dark, he says, *I must be crazy. I could lose everything I've worked for.* Lying there in the dark he thinks, *I'm a good Jewish boy, a hard-working Jewish boy and look where I am.*

He said "boy", not "man". He said "*Jewish* boy"—the words letting him hide in an earlier version of himself, one he'd given up even before he became Lloyd Clayton. When he said this to me at Trader Vic's, he had a sentimental quaver in his voice.

"And what happened in the morning? What did you do when she drove out?"

"When she drove out, sonny boy, I wasn't there."

"You weren't there?"

"Before the sun was up, I got my things together, I hustled down to pay off the hotel, and I drove the hell away from Long Beach. We probably passed each other on the road."

"How did you explain it to her? She must have been furious."

Lloyd sat back and folded his arms across his chest. "She must have been. I felt like I'd saved my life."

"You mean you never talked to her again?"

"You're damned right. It was easy. I stayed away from Polly's."

I shook my head. I closed my eyes. I couldn't even pretend to take the story as a joke or a moral victory. It seemed sad to me—more for him than for her. Polly Adler—from what I've read, she could handle rejection. But my uncle—what did the flight from Polly do to him? He stayed away from Polly's place. And next year, he married his cousin Bernadine, and they made each other miserable until she left him—left him because, she told my mother, he "wasn't a *man* for her. You understand me, Jackie?" When my mother told me that, I didn't understand. Now I do.

Scared, scared, Lloyd grew more covered-up, more intensely, solely, the successful businessman. And what about the "good Jewish boy"? No, that he could discard again, no longer useful, leave it behind in the hotel in Long Beach. He was the city sport, who took in the racing season at Saratoga, ordered Tattinger's champagne at the Stork Club. He was the boss who made everyone around him unhappy.

Am I making up the connection between his running away that morning and his becoming a dictator? Would it have been different for him if he'd stayed that morning, if they'd become lovers, at least for awhile? Maybe not. Maybe by 1927 his fate was sealed. The stuff it took to get him where he was, it had already done its work. But I like to think of him there in that big sunny hotel room, when the bedraggled Polly comes in, and she says, "What a tough night, Lloyd."

And he says, "Well, you come here, little woman, and I'll make it go away." That's the ending I want.

She laughs. And she removes her brash, funny self along with her dress. She's a little squat, not tall and elegant, but she's pretty and she's a little in love with him. And this warm, corrupt, kind-hearted Russian-Jewish woman takes him up on his offer.

Light at the End of the Tunnel

Because it matters so much whether the train comes through the tunnel when the children are still inside, in another sense it doesn't matter at all: either way, nobody's life will be the same.

Certainly not mine.

The Hoosac Tunnel, four and a half miles through the Berkshires, east to west.

Either six sets of parents—seven including the counselor's—mourn their lost children the rest of their lives, and brothers mourn brothers and friends mourn friends—or else they're made aware how close they were to mourning. And so, how close they *are*, how close we all are. I think about my brother. I think about the brother who grew up…or brother lost. And I think about the future mates of those children, and the children of those children. And suppose a great-great grandchild will find, or might have found, a way to extract hydrogen cheaply or to cure childhood leukemia, and suppose a child who would have died from leukemia will live to make great music, or would have lived to make great music—a Mozart.

So either way the same: no one can forget the fragility of a child's life, lost or not lost, nor the way moments reverberate.

Or maybe it's not true the parents can't forget. Imagine that the train stops outside the tunnel, held up by the State Police. The light is from the State Police car that has driven into the tunnel. The children are safe. And now it's fifteen years later and the original terror has dwindled into laughter over an anecdote. Everyone safe, essentially nothing happened. And some parents *do* forget, forget the original terror. The call from the camp. They complain, oh, that their grown children have moved away; they feel insulted by a son-in-law. They worry about their stock portfolios.

Or else the children were there in the tunnel when the train roared through, and in terror pressed up against the wall, and one, then another, was sucked into the train as if the tunnel were the tube of a giant vacuum cleaner, and others were suffocated by carbon monoxide from the diesel exhaust. And the parents of those children died too; nothing will ever be the same. And what about parents whose children barely survived? Oh, they say, oh, now I see what life is.

I think of that tunnel often. My brother Joel, twelve years old, was one of the six children, four girls, two boys, in the group from camp.

"Who wants to go take a look at the Hoosac Tunnel?"

There were two counselors. The older one, who'd thought it up, had heard about the tunnel, not far from camp. Until they brought the railroad through the Rockies, the Hoosac was the longest tunnel in America, four and a half miles eastern to western ends. What an adventure—walking over four and a half miles in the dark while sunlight withdraws to a pinprick you can see for almost a mile, and maybe ghosts appear. I don't think the young man knew the mileage, and I don't think he'd heard about the ghosts—he was from New York City. Tim, the counselor, he's like the pied piper who led the town's children into the mountain, seducing them to follow. But Tim seduced them out of curiosity, a sense of fun, not revenge (in the original story, the townspeople wouldn't pay the piper for getting rid of their rats, and the piper called their children under the mountain).

I see them straggling out of the beat-up camp van down the bracken-thick trail and along the tracks, the kids hot and sweaty and half wondering what they're doing there and half excited, and the counselor, Tim, embarrassed: he's got them there, but why? Just to look at a hole, entrance to a tunnel for trains? He hadn't planned to go through, but now it seemed an adventure, and he'd brought along a flashlight. And of course trains don't use these tracks anymore, do they? And then one of the kids walked in and yelled to raise echoes. So the young man told the younger counselor: "Why don't you drive the van over the mountain and meet us at the western entrance? You'll find it. Just ask. I think it's in North Adams." Maybe he had a map, but if he did, wouldn't he have seen how absurd the distance for six kids in the dark? The van drove off; now the young man was stuck. "All right. Come on guys, let's *do* it." The children followed; he led the way with a flashlight.

Early in the nineteenth century a project was approved by the Massachusetts legislature to open the west to Boston by creating a railroad tunnel through Hoosac Mountain in the Berkshires. Work began in 1851, and after delays and false starts, was finished long after the Civil War in 1874. A great feat of nineteenth century engineering, it involved drilling and blasting first through hard rock, then wet schist—the men called it oatmeal. The tunneling from east and the tunneling from west met beautifully, with only 9/16 of an inch error. But there were other errors. Out of eight or nine hundred men who worked on the tunnel, one hundred ninety six died—died from rock slides, from asphyxiation, and from explosions of nitroglycerine, used commercially for the first time. It's their ghosts said to haunt the tunnel.

Soon forty trains a day were coming through. Then fewer, fewer, as trucks carried the load and railroads grew less important. The technology of one age becomes the romance of the next. It's romance the young man is after. Caving through the dark hill. Poking a light up to see the brickwork used to surface the walls when the solid rock turned to schist. The young man, in anthropology at

Columbia, imagines men sweating down here, imagines the dust and damp as they embedded the brick.

The tunnel, he can see as soon as they walk in, wasn't built for foot traffic. It's too narrow. *What do we do if a train comes? Press against the wall? Will there be room? Of course a train* won't *come, but what if?* They walk on tiptoe through mud, through pools of filthy water. *God. We should have hard hats against falling bricks,* the young man thinks. It's clammy. But he's sweating now mostly from anxiety. As the pinprick of sunlight dissolves into darkness, all of a sudden he knows: he'll lose his job. Nothing to do about it.

After a while they can see pretty well in the dark, avoiding the litter between the tracks. Bricks, garbage, detritus from trains—not much romance after all. Clammy: breath comes cold and thick. "Yuck," a girl says. And someone else: "How much further?"

As a kid Joel liked backpacking; when I was home from college he made me go wilderness camping with him. He loved climbing—rock climbing, tree climbing. By twelve he was a Star Scout. He was an imaginative child, a storyteller, an explorer. This was his kind of adventure.

Ahead, a white light. "There, that looks like the end!" The children run ahead, and Tim calls to them, "Wait! Wait up!"—but voice dissolves into drone in the dark. And he can barely see them. With flashlight he sees shadows.

The light is closer now, and they can see it's just an electric light high up on a wall.

As they go on and on, an hour, two, they begin to look over their shoulders. There's another light up ahead. And they walk on. Again it's a lamp. But what's that up ahead?

The tunnel is absolutely straight, end to end. Yet in another sense not at all straight; a dark maw of possibilities swallows sound and shape; and within, invisible branches lead to invisible branches. From time to time, the children come upon niches carved in the wall where track walkers used to flatten themselves for trains to pass in case they were caught in the tunnel. The engineer couldn't see much, couldn't hear much: sound is swallowed up. If something went wrong—say rock or brick on the tracks—the track walkers would affix small charges to the rail, to explode when the train passed over; that would make enough noise to get the engineer to stop the train.

What can stop the train now? Maybe someone sees them walking in. There are no houses nearby, but cars pass pretty often on the two-lane road that goes along the Deerfield River. Maybe there's a fisherman or a kayaker looking for a spot to put in, and he thinks, *What are those kids doing?* Or the other counselor finds the Western entrance in North Adams, and he waits, he waits, and waiting, he begins to get uneasy. And he goes to the tunnel mouth and yells. And someone, an old man, a local, notices and stops. Says, *They're doing WHAT?* And the counselor drives to a phone, hands shaking so hard he has trouble dropping in the coins, but finally he calls the Police, and the light that the children see in the tunnel, it's strobe light, red and blue and white. The State Police have called to block the train that's nearly at the Western end of the tunnel. And it's a State Police car that greets the kids at the mouth. And no one's known enough to be really scared. "Most of you would have been killed," the cop says. "Sucked into the train or suffocated." He backs out of the tunnel and the kids follow him. Into life. And the counselors are both sent home.

Or no one sees. No one stops the train, and the other counselor, standing by the Western mouth, tries to flag down the train that's creeping around a bend towards the tunnel. He screams, he waves his arms, he points, but the engineer doesn't see him or doesn't understand. And now, fifteen years later, living his life, playing with his son, the counselor replays the afternoon, and in this replaying he realizes what's going on and calls the State Police in time.

But he didn't call. And somewhere in the last mile of the tunnel the children feel the vibration and the pressure of air; there is no roar until the train is upon them. The engineer hears nothing, doesn't see the flailing of the hands until too late—or not at all.

Or did he really call? Suppose he did. If so, playing ball with his little boy, he thinks back to his humiliation, losing his job that day; but at least the kids were safe, thank God.

Why can't I tell you? Because there is no closure for me. Everyday, you decide to drive by *this* road and not *that* road, and on *that* road there's a seven-car pile-up. Joel got married last night, and me, I'm a little hung over this morning, a little depressed, and I think what might have happened. Or there is no Joel; I grew up with my missing brother more real in my life than anyone.

It matters so much whether the train comes through that tunnel when the children are still inside, matters so much that in one sense it doesn't matter at all. Accident not happening is accident. Either way, the same: nobody's life ever again the same.

Originally appeared in AGNI on-line, *2005*

Radiance
(1998)

Talking to Charlie

It begins as the old story, I've told so many stories of divorce and pain: six months back, David Kahn read by accident the wrong letter, and it was as if he'd already known, as if he finally had to open the door to the closet where the monster squatted. His wife in love with somebody, somebody brilliant, supervisor of her cases as a therapist. This guy also happened to be David's tennis partner. And in a rage, as if surprised, as if betrayed, as if such a thing had never entered his mind, he packed up, moved to a motel, drank—and fell apart.

The usual divorce story, dismal, of pain and humiliation, his family broken, ahh, you could write it yourself. Then David takes a leave from his high-powered job—selling main-frames and networks for corporations—drops everything, to live the winter like a monk at his cottage in Truro, on Cape Cod.

Why is he leaving? Revulsion, he'd tell you for the whole *meg-illah*. Secretly, he's in panic for his life. And maybe, too, he knows, could even tell you, he's leaving out of spite; he's punishing Sarah. All these years, he's been a Good Provider. While she became the intellectual, the PhD psychologist, he provided. Let somebody else do the providing.

But there's more to it. There's this. He isn't willing to be bullied anymore by the vague dream of making it, sick of working so hard—working not just to succeed but to make himself worthy in his own eyes, or really in his dead father's eyes—ghost father from childhood. What he really wants, David, is just to clear the books, to live an honorable life.

In my story he stops drinking, gets into shape. In Truro, early spring, he plants a garden: It makes him happy, on knees in old jeans, to break up the cold, sandy soil with garden fork, mix in bags of peat moss, top soil, manure. Occupational therapy.

Big chest, heavy shoulders—funny to think of a guy like him on his knees with a young plant between his fingers, planting, then patting down the soil. A big man, David played high school football, went to Deerfield Academy for a thirteenth year on football scholarship. Though it was track he was really good at—always a man who lugged weights: the hammer throw, the shot-put, the discus. A lot of guys still take him for an athlete with his big frame and heavy neck. But since the time in the hospital for his back, he feels like a sandcastle against an incoming tide, like the way his chest has started to slip and sink. Bags under his eyes, and the skin between eyelids and eyebrows beginning to go limp; hair graying and the gray strands lightening, growing light as smoke, angel hair—silly when it isn't combed into place.

The gardening calms him, the beach runs clean out his head. He doesn't think so much about Sarah and Nick. Gulls and terns and the spastic little sandpipers rise up as he lumbers their way. He watches for seaweed hiding glass or shells that could cut his feet. But soon his mind falls away, the watching happens without him. A dream is how it feels. And now he begins to get peculiar intimations, as he's chopping onions, say, that everything has happened beyond his willing. Intimations that these past months of pain, the dream-maker, dream-writer, knew all along where David was going.

Climbing to the top of the dunes, he can see more than a mile of beach. Cracking explosions of surf—small charges going off together all along the beach—and then the hiss of water rushing to the high tide line.

It scares him a little, becoming aware of this...presence, this dreamer of David's own life. His script writer. Night of a full moon, and David wonders whose hands he's in. If, just maybe, the hands might be tender, holding him, not dangling him like a puppet but holding, and he could relax and let the guy take over.

The point is, David says to himself, that if there's a script beyond my making, he, the script writer, has never *not* been in charge. It was illusion, that I, David Kahn, was accomplishing anything with my struggling. I enacted, I never acted. My whole life, the dream provided a script. That's it, exactly, he thinks, as he hunts driftwood for his evening fire.

And so, walking the dunes, David becomes aware of this presence he's joined to as if there were an invisible filament carrying messages between them. He talks to the presence. It's a little like the times he used to talk to God. His mother would take him to the synagogue after his father left for work Saturday morning and he'd get sleepy and ride the waves of the old men's chantings. He didn't mind staying. But when she recited the Kaddish for her mother and father, she made him leave. Why? Was it superstition that she herself would die if he were there when she remembered a parent? Or did she not want him to see her weep? When he came back, he found her eyes red. Was she crying for her parents—or for her failure of a life? And he, unable to change her life or be her life, he stood in the marble lobby talking to God.

Now he talks to nobody, to the sky. He ought to be talking to Charlie, negotiating with Charlie Bausch, his immediate boss and his mentor at Data Management, to go back to work. Sooner or later, he'll need the money. And he'll need the work.

I tell about David, this man struggling then letting go of the need to struggle. He's ruined his days and nights trying to be worthy. Now he knows, it's this trying that is the problem, his belief in his sickness that is his sickness, the belief that his life is in his hands. And feeling now that his tense hands on the wheel give only an illusion of control—like "driving" a roller coaster car—ahh, he lets go.

And now, magically, the story wants to move towards restoration: his family restored to him. I can feel that kind of story humming in his head. I can sense it in my own prose, sense my tenderness for David. Peaceful, he'll return to Boston, win back his wife—as if he's getting into shape for *her*—and enter a new life.

I don't trust this story.

He imagines himself at peace, imagines himself *into* peace. I write wanting—who wouldn't?—that peace for myself. The story is my own prayer to let go. To put myself in God's hands. I've never been able to let go, to quiet myself. Peace? You wish, buddy. You wish. Still, the story is true; I've felt the way David feels; there are times you float above the issues that have been clinging to you like a thick web; you know, deeply, that you've spun the web yourself, and it's not even real, it's a hologram, you can step through it and away anytime you feel like it. You needed the web. For what?—for something. I remember I sat once with a friend and felt touched by the sunlight, greenly iridescent through the plants at the window, and I didn't have to do a thing, nothing, just *be*. But a feeling like that, it comes, it goes, it's not final—New Life—God knows.

So David *wishes* it were his new life. I've wished it for him. In a sense, I'm the dreamer he's thinking about. And I'm imagining a dreamer dreaming *me*. I understand why they're so seductive, David's imaginings: they let me see the scripts of the culture as God. No need then for a ride into the dark.

But I have to take courage and ride whatever words I can find down into the dark at the bottom of the dark. I take to my heart the old myth, everybody's old thumping heart-hunger turned myth, that there be a quest. Saying that, I see myself with a paper sword on a horse made out of words. I must want to mock this quest, its pretentiousness. But that mockery is like the dog at the mouth of darkness. One more thing to get past.

Riding down into the dark, not up towards the light. But believing in the light, that the light is there, crusted over, a pulsing jewel down at the bottom of the dark, hidden to keep the searcher safe—its danger is its core; it's nothing if not dangerous; hidden also to keep the jewel itself safe, keep it from being ruined by the wrong finder.

I'm talking about the wrong finder within my own ruined self, the fat one, the exploiter, willing to turn anything into grub. The point of the hardship in the quest is to force the self to burn in a refiner's fire, so that the soul that finds the pulsing jewel is worthy of receiving it, will make good use of it. As I pray I may be, pray I will make.

And so I find my story changing. I'm telling you not about David's falling-away of self but of his longing to *believe* that he can disentangle himself from himself by himself, can ride the tails of some holy Presence. How can he, anymore than I can? But the quiet is something good. He stands, thick-bodied ex-jock, winded from his morning run, highest point of the dunes in Truro, looking like a god over the world south towards Wellfleet, the world north towards Provincetown, beach and ocean spread out eighty feet below him, and he doesn't need to make a single business call or smile a single business smile.

And the feeling he had just a few weeks before—that his whole life was over, this fabrication of marriage and family fallen like a house of cards, that it would be a relief to jerk the wheel of his BMW just slightly, ah, just the least bit—why, that feeling seems now as if it belonged to somebody else. He, David, is the actor who played that role, suffered through those pages in the script, and now he's inside his own skin, open to the next scene that's handed him before the shooting.

Last night I dreamed I was at an AA meeting—it was called that in the dream, but the room was filled with the wrecked, with hopeless alcoholics, not recovering alcoholics, and I, though not in my awake life a drinker, was on my knees in prayer, saying "I can't do it alone, I'm in Your hands." And that's it: different as I am from David, I long the same longing, to reshape my clay. But I can't do it alone, David can't do it alone.

Not completely alone, David goes to the next town, to Wellfleet, for dinner, sits at a bar drinking seltzer and watching the Celtics. He talks trades, injuries, coaching, with some of the regulars. But that's not people you work with or live with. If I'm going to imagine him into peace, and so imagine my own peace, it will have to come because he works or lives or prays peacefully with other people. Then who? Maybe a woman he meets?—but no—he did that when he was first separated.

He remembers the turmoil after he found out about Sarah, the nights of no sleep in the expensive motel, the drinking, the wreck he needed to become in order to dramatize and therefore feel some control over the pain. And then that terrible night in New York when he went to bed with a lovely woman, too young for him, thirty years old, a lawyer, thinking he was fooling them all, the gods of middle age, making a sneaky end run into a second youth without mortgage or two A.M. squabbles or back problems. Wild man again. Carol could save him. They made the bed rock.

But then he was awake and it was three-thirty in a morning in an unfamiliar New York apartment, and he was sick as hell, head thumping, mouth dry, not saved, a scared sick man of forty-five is what he was, in a strange bed, a stranger's bed. Tiptoing into this stranger's kitchen, he drank orange juice out of a foreign glass at three in the morning.

So suppose it's a man at the bar he meets, big guy with red hair who asks him to help him out a couple of weeks, help him build an addition, kind of work David did summers when he was at college, and David, who'd earned a hundred thousand, hundred and twenty thousand a year plus stock options selling computer systems, likes the idea of working with his hands again, framing a building, putting in windows.

So he puts off talking to Charlie, Charlie Bausch, his boss. He works with this refugee from the sixties, thick red hair halfway down to his shoulders. Terry has a Masters from Michigan in archeology but makes his living now as a carpenter.

The next week, he works with Terry on an addition that has to be finished this spring. By Thursday, they have it framed and sheathed. End of each day, he comes home aching, ragged, old jeans and workshirt musky with sweat, dusty with sawdust. Rock and roll in his head from the tinny radio that's always blasting under the whine of the circular saw. Maybe he'll live this way. He's surprised how much he cares to do a good job; surprised how much he remembers. He isn't surprised that Terry can keep working full-steam a lot longer than he can.

But sometimes, hefting two-by-fours, measuring and cutting, hammering, sweating, he realizes his body has taken over, he's home-free, humming along on cruise control, something like that. This is nothing to do with *listening*. It's this presence, expressing itself through his hands, his shoulders. He's riding the waves. Secretly, he thinks that working with two-by-fours will help him find the jewel hidden in the dirt. For years he's been a *luftsmensch*, a man living in the air, living by phone and by phoniness, making money—just numbers—nothing you can touch. So now, as he measures and planes, he is enacting a metaphor, a ritual, making a new David,—till he imagines himself changed by the ritual he's hammered out. But David is still David, nothing to be done. He's a rough, kind-hearted, lonely man, tired of pretending that he likes lugging two-by-fours all day. And he knows that if he came out here to live, he'd turn Terry's catch-as-catch-can operation into a serious construction business, he'd wind up selling houses instead of computers. Why bother? But the work has been good for him.

One night David looks into the mirror and sees less flab around his face, his body firm, old jock returning to jockdom. The sadness is still there in the bags under his eyes, sadness that he's lived the wrong life—his whole life he's worked like a horse to feel like a human being. But the peculiar understanding has calmed him—or the calming *is* the understanding: that not only does he live his life—he's been lived by it.

With this understanding, he returns to Boston quieted. No more boozing, no more catting around to show he still has the stuff. And with this quiet his new life begins.

Only begins: he has to find the way to the dark at the bottom of the dark, where long ago he buried someone with his true face, shining. Once in awhile he has a glimpse of the face he buried long ago, as I have of my own self at the bottom of myself. Maybe it's easier for David, for he has less to lose. That's the point of being stripped naked, like Lear on the heath. Maybe I envy.

If I knew how to imagine David going on from there, finding the jewel, changing in the soul, maybe I'd know how to make my own peace. But back in Brookline, in the apartment he finds not a mile from the old house, he feels less peaceful and more alone. The lovely quiet of the dunes, the sense that he was held in the hand of that benign Presence—it's hard to get it back. There's no ocean to sing to him, and sometimes he wonders, was it just a trick of consciousness, his imaginings of a presence supporting him, being spoken by his life?

He thinks about work, about talking to Charlie. Sitting at a deli on Beacon Street and poking through the want-ads in the *Globe*, he finds the good jobs not all that different from his work at Data Management. Why lose what he's built? Why lose colleagues he cares about? He's watched their kids grow up.

I'm listening on headphones to the music of Thomas Tallis, mid-sixteenth century English composer, choral music of peace and harmony, written at a time of chaos, struggle, murder, torture, poverty and oppression. Well, what time hasn't been like that? Tallis was composing within a tradition, even while he was changing it. And underpinning the tradition was a separate world, a world of the spirit, on which he could stand while the world around him was full of murder. Where can David stand?

There are times he stands on a street corner on his way to pick up Beth at school and watches a couple of MTA cars glide by down Beacon, and suddenly he feels a hollow rush in his belly, as if he were riding a roller coaster. And he realizes there's a piece of himself standing high up above Beacon Street, looking down from a high haven.

Every other weekend, he sees Beth and Noah from Friday afternoon until Monday night. Sarah, who has a full case load and then works at the Boston Institute for Psychotherapy some evenings, is grateful for the help. When he doesn't have them on the weekend, they're with him two nights midweek. When the kids complain about all the changing, they begin to spend alternate weeks—one week with Sarah, one with David.

Now, half the time a single parent, responsible for a ten-year-old boy, a four-year old girl, he's got to think about making dinner for them every night, think about whether they have clean clothes for the morning. He's got to have their friends over and drive them home. Now he sees what it is to be a father.

Slow, patient, a yoga of steadiness and devotion. This is a story I trust and understand. A person changes by doing the laundry on a daily basis, by picking up the kids at school and taking them to gymnastics. This is the work. No mysteries.

But David resists this story. His new life feels full of mysteries. Something's happening I don't understand, a trick of consciousness, maybe, but it lets him float above his pain. I've always thought that the dark body, of which the person you look at in the mirror is merely an emanation, had to be restored in battle. You have to wrestle for the prize. Deny and deny until you can't deny and your face is rubbed bloody into the dirt; then, raw, burnished, it shines with darkness. But as he gets used to being back, and being with the kids, David doesn't do battle: doesn't go back to work or into therapy. He hangs out; he wanders. He finds himself in a city with…reduced gravity. He doesn't need, the way he used to, to be weighed down, doesn't need his pain. He thinks, *It's still there, the pain. Just not so much* mine.

He takes long walks through Boston, feeling the strangeness of not working. And the part of him that's free of gravity and in touch with something beyond himself, that part begins to occupy his shoes. At this rate, he says, I'll never wear my shoes out. Someone leads, he follows, perfect dancer.

Sitting over a cup of decaf listening to Miles Davis after the kids are asleep, he gets a sudden urge to call Sarah. He doesn't call—afraid she'll take it wrong, as a sign of his longing. And he's doing all right. That same night, *she* calls, needing to talk. Can we meet? Sure, he says, I'd like that.

Is she, he wonders, going to insist on couples' therapy? Sarah is one tough insister. Well, he's not eager, but willing. He makes a mental note not to make fun of therapy, therapists, psychology in general. He and Sarah will have to be especially careful of one another's bruised places. David goes to a barber, he buys a new suit, dove gray; he's like a bridegroom getting ready for a wedding. Looking into the mirror, if he doesn't peer too closely, he likes what he sees—a ruddy, strong man in his prime. A little beefy, okay—and crude for a woman like Sarah; still, women go for him. And okay—there's the wounds: terrible, humiliating nights like the night in Bermuda when (they were making love) looking into her eyes, he saw she wasn't at home. Not even a message machine on. He ended that night alone, talking to himself in an outdoor hot tub. Marriage! The wounds and, worse, the bruises. Why else is it that before marriage and kids, we can meet each other and dance together with words, everything is tender music; then we marry and can't even buy a ticket to the dance hall?

But driving Sarah to a really good little French restaurant they both used to like, slipping the little BMW between lanes like a great jockey maneuvering a thoroughbred, he feels optimistic. He tells her how nice the garden in Truro is turning out, and she asks about those lovely words: *hollyhocks*, *columbine*, *delphinium*.

In a dark corner of the restaurant, he sits across the table with its checkered tablecloth and sips wine and leans his chin on his hands and his elbows on the table and grins like a fool at Sarah, listening to her story about Noah at gymnastics. This woman, he says to himself, so beautiful to me even now, Jewish Indian with her olive complexion and prominent nose, the heavy, lovely breasts I see with my hands' eye, and black hair curly and turbulent no matter what she does to tame it.

He sees her face now and it becomes her face at the instant after she'd given birth to Beth, and her hair, oh, was stringy, her skin bloated and her eyes giddy with joy. He'd been crying too, crying for the newborn they lost two years before, crying with relief that this time it would be okay, the birth okay, Beth was going to live.

"You're looking good," he says. "Been working out, I bet."

"Not much. You look really good yourself."

This woman, he says to himself, she's still my life. His eyes mist, he blows his nose in his table napkin, then remembers how she hates to see him do that. He laughs to make it a gag.

"So," he says after they order, "you called the meeting. You need a new computer or what? Kidding, kidding—hey, tell me, how are we doing with the kids? Pretty good, I think."

"Really, really good," she said. "It's some change. God. You remember, Davie—I'm not saying this to start anything, but—when you were home you were never home."

"I know, I know," he says.

"You were always somewhere else, always at the office, on the phone all weekend."

"You're right, you're absolutely right."

"Really, I'm happy about it—especially for Noah. He's been needing a father bad."

"I don't think I ever realized, so help me God. The kids, they've been a lot to me these past months." Been *everything*, he would have said, been my script—but he wants to come on like a man of strength, a grownup.

"Well, it's wonderful, Davie."

"See? I can learn, Sarah. I guess I'm never going to talk about French feminist psychoanalysts, but I can learn about being a father. Maybe a husband."

She sips her wine, he's afraid to put his hand on hers. "So what do you think?" he whispers.

It takes her time to catch up to him. Then she's there, and she drops her eyes. "Oh. David, I'm a fool," she says.

"No, no—"

"Listen, you don't understand," she says. "I'm really sorry. I mean, that's not why I wanted us to talk."

"Okay. Okay. That's okay." He holds up his hands, palms out in surrender.

"No—I'm sorry. I wanted you to know—I wanted to say it face to face—I might get married again," she says. "I'm probably getting married, Davie. Married to Nick. So…we need to begin proceedings, you and me."

There's a hollow rush in his belly, and he breathes in a deep breath and his eyes lift involuntarily into the ceiling. Only he can't lift up into a safe haven above himself, looking down on the poor sufferer. He *is* the sufferer. He's falling through a hole.

"Sure," he says. "My lawyer and your lawyer. We'll get a letter of agreement ready." Falling through a hole—or it's like his real life is a train leaving the station without him. He smiles his salesman smile and wants to drink his wine but he's afraid the glass will be shaky in his hand. At the same time, another piece of him is thinking shrewdly that if she needs an agreement so quickly, then okay, good, he'll come out of this with more than his shirt. Is she afraid, he wonders, that too long a delay and Nick might back off? Could Nick do a thing like that, the prick? He finds himself feeling protective, like a father worrying that his daughter might get hurt by a suitor. It must be a cover-up feeling, he thinks. He must be full of rage. Down and down and down he looks for it, for the rage, but all he feels is protective and full of grief and afraid she'll see. He says, "Don't worry, Sarah. I'll get my guy on it right away."

The only way he can keep from drinking now is to work out hard. He does Nautilus, takes a daily swim. The worse he feels, the more he needs the discipline. His life has imploded into a core of pain. There's nothing in him to resist gravity, to lift himself up above himself. He dances to no strange tune. His *story* collapses, and with it the David who wasn't burdened by his life, the David who enacted a dream, a script he'd been handed. It's no script. All morning he sits, like stone, like one of those meteorites in the planetarium—hot rock melted into dense, cold stone, pure weight—sits over coffee and fingers his lower lip and looks up his stocks in *The Globe*.

This isn't what he had in mind. It's the wrong story. He's supposed to have suffered and become a changed soul with a new life. *This* grief seems a waste. There are ways to use grief, taught for thousands of years, but none of them David knows. Alone, the soul, awash in grief until half-drowned, grasps any rock it already knows. Change it wants, though still—still to be somehow familiar to itself. Maybe what is being asked instead is that the soul let go, that it become a sea creature; and it would rather die than grow gills or turn dolphin, so strange! Instead, it will pretend to change, like Proteus, the Old Man of the Sea. Wrestle with him, Menelaus was told; don't let him go no matter how he seems to change form. David, not knowing how to wrestle, sits and fingers his lower lip.

Mired in pain, maybe it's a good thing he has to begin thinking of money. He's just another guy in Massachusetts out of work. He's got money put away for the kids' education, money in an annuity, but he's been cashing in CD's and Treasury notes, and it doesn't feel so romantic, so life-renewing, as it did at the beach. He can't keep stringing Data Management along, they won't hold his position open forever. Finally, he has to go back to Data Management and talk to Charlie Bausch. Driving out to 128, just as if this were a year ago and nothing had gone down, he finds himself lifting out of himself, high up above the BMW, above Route 9, and he looks down on a guy who couldn't make a new life or fix up the old one, a guy who was broken the way everybody gets broken.

Everybody, everybody, it's like being popped onto the board of a pinball machine and—whew!—missing the holes, one, two, three. Hey!—You don't die in somebody's war or gas chamber, you don't get cancer or AIDS, your kids don't Godforbid get childhood leukemia, you don't wind up in a dead-end job and some roach-infested apartment in Chelsea, but the board is slanted, and sooner or later—wait—there'll be a hole for you.

DM feels strange to him, maybe most strange because nobody seems to notice anything unusual about his being back. He waves at Ed McKitterick, at Ginny Shepherd with the lovely doe eyes—all these years he's wanted just to touch her face and to bless her or be blessed. He keeps walking, successful-salesman grin stuck on his face.

Sales works out of an open-plan office, half a football field of space, columns at regular intervals but cubicles every which way, a maze of cubicles. As he threads his usual path, he hears a guffaw. Stephen Anapulsky bursts out of his cubicle laughing, Sid Langdorf out of *his*—

"That clown he turned the messages on my screen upside down, the clown!"

His office is still untouched, the drawers still stuffed with his papers, with old snapshots of the kids. He writes a note to the custodian: PLEASE CLEAN UP. THANKS! And he heads for his meeting with Charlie Bausch.

Too heavy still, though he's lost maybe thirty pounds, Charlie carries his weight like a tired old sailor lugging a duffle. He limps a little, but David's always thought of it as a royal swagger. As if there's something dignified the way Charlie Bausch hefts the extra weight and the tired bones.

They've never really become friends, but for fifteen years, now, Charlie Bausch has been his mentor in the company. *I made some success, where did I take it but to Charlie?* Old salesman himself, Charlie taught him shrewdness, and often, middle of a sales presentation, David finds Charlie inhabiting his body, finds himself mellowing down, slowing his gestures, slowing his voice like a record going from 45 rpm to 33, down to Charlie's courteous gravel tones. I think what he does is he gets clients into a kind of hypnotic trance, a place where they feel so comfortable that they're open to persuasion.

Especially since Charlie's heart attack a few years ago, David has found his own heart open to him. The guy can get a little boring, but boring isn't so bad. If Charlie can't stop talking about the international bond market or about his granddaughter in Phoenix, what the hell.

He looks puffy and dark under the eyes, Charlie.

They talk, as they have a couple of times over the phone, about the sales that David left unfinished. "You know about Polaroid coming through," Charlie says. "That commission is yours, you know." Then Charlie tilts way back in his chair, feet go up, pencil between his two forefingers like a bridge over a precipice—a posture that means, *I'm gonna philosophize, Dave*; that really means, *I'm gonna sell you something.*

"Dave," he says, "I can understand a guy going through confused times, he goes off and puts himself together. I respect that. A retreat's a great thing. The Catholics are no dopes, they've been successful a long time with this retreat business."

"You've been very kind to me, Charlie."

"Kind? I've been grooming you. You know that. I don't want to see you lose it all. Forget the Catholics. Think of it this way," Charlie says, his voice slowing down and, like the voice on a tape recorder, dropping into a lower register. "You got knocked around the first half, so you rested in the locker room. Now you suit up.... You used to play fullback, am I right?—you get back on the field and you play to win."

"But suppose," David says, falling into the slow melancholy of Charlie Bausch's talk, "suppose you don't care about the game, suppose it's the wrong game?"

"Dave, listen, listen, Dave: it's the only game in town."

David considers this. He wishes he could ask Charlie why it was a game worth playing, but Charlie doesn't have answers like that. Besides, David knows it's a ritual, this talk. There's really no need to convince him of anything, he walked in here convinced that he has no other option. Just walking in, no matter how kind Charlie is, has got to feel like a defeat.

"The way I see it," Charlie says in a kind of sing-song, "everything got sour for you when Sarah kicked you out. Your work, whatever. Are you kidding me? If you really hated your work, you couldn't do the job you do. Am I right? Tell me, 'You're right, Charlie.'"

"You *are* right, Charlie. I'm a salesman."

"I know I'm right. How many times you win the special parking place, Salesman of the Month? For christsakes, you practically owned the slot. You're a better salesman than I ever was."

"That's bullshit."

"But you're forty-five years old, maybe it's time to get you out of the trenches. Like me. Okay, here's my offer. Regional Sales Manager is opening up. You want it?"

David looks into Charlie's tired eyes and solemnly nods.

"Surprised you, huh? See, the only way I could sell your goddamn desertion to the big guys, I said, 'Kagan is sniffing out a management position.' They came through. We'll talk details another time," Charlie says, voice lifting. "Let's you and me go get some dessert to celebrate. To hell with the cholesterol."

David drives Beth and Noah down to Truro. They're lucky: it's a sunny Friday afternoon and promises to be sunny all weekend. Late June. Cape light. A few of the tulips are still blooming, waving in the wind, making the old house look as if somebody lives there, it's not a summer rental. A pioneer columbine is flowering, and the bleeding heart is fuller than it has a right to be this first year. Look, look. To humor his Dad, Noah looks—and sighs ironically at the way his Dad always makes him look at growing things. He's developed a half-scowl David feels partly responsible for putting there, as much a defense as the squint of eyes against the sun. But his eyes—dark brown, deep—are still exposed, tender. It's why he needs the scowl. Beth sniffs a tulip and comes away disappointed. But she spots a toad and, exploding in one of her thick, hoarse laughs, she makes a grab. It's a wonder to David, the delicacy of her skin, so fine you can see the vein, blue, of her forehead, and then her heft and this laugh of hers.

They carry in suitcases and groceries, soon they're hiking the sand trail over the dunes to the beach. Noah adores David's cellular phone. "Can we take it along? Will it work from the beach?"

"Can I call Mommy and she can listen to the ocean?" Beth wants to know.

"We'll try." David hooks it on the belt of his jeans.

At ten, Noah isn't too old to be excited about his Dad's new job. He asks, "Will you be on the road a lot?"

"Less than I used to. The money's less, too.... Beth?—Careful of the prickers on the bushes, Beth."

"How come?" Noah asks. "You'll be top guy."

"But I'm not out there as much doing the selling and pulling down the big commissions. You know what commissions are?"

Noah nods. Beth says, "What are commissions?" But before he has to answer, she sees a rabbit and runs after it, yelling "Bunny, bunny, bunny!"

"Still, it'll be better, Noah. There's stock options. And I'll have more time with you and Beth."

"No-eee, No-eee!" Beth calls, her name for her brother since she could speak at all. "Find me, No-eee."

"Regional Manager! *Yes*!" Noah says, doing a victory dance for his father.

"I'll tell you the God's honest truth," his father says. "I wouldn't be disappointed if you did something else entirely."

"Like what?"

"Like...anything. What can you imagine yourself doing?"

Noah, not wanting to think, runs off through scrub oak and squat pine of the outer Cape. He pretends to search for Beth.

When David gets to the top of a high dune, he finds a strong offshore wind that drives through his zipper and down his neck. He can lean into the wind; it holds him up. And he closes his eyes and imagines he's hang gliding, all 200 pounds of him floating on this wind. He hears Beth's singsong and Noah's shout.

And his elbow bumps the cellular phone, so he imagines it's ringing, because how else *can* he get in touch these days? The presence he'd listened to, it hasn't been present, maybe he's been too busy, moving into his new office, making calls, making meetings, making a living if not exactly a life. So it makes crazy sense to him, that if he wants to get in touch again, it should be with this phone.

When it rings, wherever he is, it connects him to his ordinary world, there's no getting away from it anywhere anymore. So he imagines a different ring, oh, it's like little bells, and looking around to make sure the kids aren't in sight, he takes the phone off his belt and says, "David Kahn here." But there's no voice from some other end. "I know," he whispers over the rush of wind, "that even when I hear nothing, I'm saying what you're telling me and doing what you'd have me do. Isn't that right?"

"What, Daddy?" Beth's there; she holds onto his leg, this small chunk of wild-haired girl, attaching him solidly to the dune.

"I'm just pretend-talking.... Hello, hello," he says into the phone, "you want to talk to Bev? *Bev*—I don't know anyone by that name. Sorry."

"*Beth*, it's for *me*, I'm Beth."

"Oh, it's *Beth* you want. Well, here."

"Hello," Beth says, taking the phone. "Well, I'd love to come to your party.... All right.... They want to talk to you."

David takes the phone. "Oh, I see. Well, we will," he says to the phone. And to Beth he says, "Dance. They said we have to dance." Still holding the phone, David dances his daughter at the top of the dune, round and round, oom-pah-pah, as if he's got no choice; and in the middle of the dance he feels it coming back, the connection, the presence, as if he's a fish at the end of an invisible line, and he's so into his dance he doesn't know Noah's there till the kid says, "Who're you talking to, Dad? You talking to Mom?"

"No," David says, phone to his ear, "I'm talking to Charlie. Just talking to Charlie."

Because it's the same, he thinks, as long as you do the dance. David dances, and me, I watch him do his dance, while I do my own, hoping that I can hear the music, and that, at least for awhile, David's dance can take me home.

Originally appeared in Fiction, *Spring, 1994*

History Lessons

Peter at my side, I walk up Columbus Avenue, where I walked as a child—only then, what was it but a grubby street of bars and walkups with black iron fire escapes over their facades, deli on one side (smell of brine of the pickle-barrel) and, across the street, huge seedy residential hotel everyone knew was seeded with whores and dope fiends. Close my eyes, I can see Columbus the old way, bleak but exciting, two-way traffic those days, my father holding my arm to steer me past the drunks. I remember a man flung out horizontal from a saloon. He flew slow-motion high through the air like some anti-Superman and ended in the gutter, blood turning his face into a mask, as if all the skin were stripped away. I even remember his giant nose—well, I'd seen him before, poor bastard, the nose swollen, deeply pocked, and my mother, I remember I was walking with my mother, she nudged but didn't point and whispered, "You see? That's *syphilis*. You wouldn't understand. Godforbid *you* should end like that."

I don't tell any of this to Peter, my seventeen-year old. Both of us in casual slacks and good sweaters, an adult victory—he's usually in torn jeans and rock-band tee shirts. As far as his mother knows, we're in New York to look at colleges—and we have been to Columbia, my alma mater. But in fact, I'm walking down this new Columbus with him because he asked to see where I grew up. I tell him that these stores and restaurants are all new, but I don't tell him how *much* the street has changed. How dark it was. How dirty and exciting. I don't tell him of the Irish kids who beat up the Jewish kids from the big apartment buildings. I walked wary.

He's wearing a book bag on his back; he's holding a micro tape recorder in his hand, his stepfather's. Making it an *interview* lets it be comfortable for him; he knows I don't talk about my childhood. But as a project in family history for his high school history class it's okay, he's not just asking intimate questions. He's heard "everything," he says, about his mother's childhood in Colorado, about his grandparents—his mother's parents—and about *their* parents, a merchant family in Sweden. "Now it's your turn," he kidded me on the phone. "You know, Dad—I don't know a whole lot about you."

I laugh on cue. I've heard his mother's stories about family skiing adventures in Colorado. I don't have such stories.

Columbus, I tell him, it's the street I knew, a street strange to me. "The old neighborhood's gone—and just as well, Peter. But I still know New York. You stick with me, we're going to cook this town up for dinner. You're with a native." I don't tell him how the glory dreams brewed in my childhood Manhattan are gone too, along with the brewers who stirred those dreams. I don't tell him I'm a native who never comes back; if I have a business meeting in the city, I'm in and out the same day. I don't talk family; I give him a history lesson:

"A hundred years ago, this was way out of town," I say into his tape recorder. I can feel myself making grand myth out of history. "*Sheep grazed in Central Park. Then they built the Dakota and a couple of other big apartment buildings on Central Park West and Broadway. Then rows of brownstones for the people in the offices. Later, Columbus went downhill. When I was a kid, it was a peculiar kind of slum, because the stores still catered to the fancy apartment houses. Mostly Jews. Walkups housed the Irish and Greek and Italians; later, Puerto Ricans. Then, 'urban renewal'—a phony name to cover up what they were doing—getting rid of the Hispanics by getting rid of their homes. When I grew up, it star-*

ted to get chic, Peter. It's gentrified now," I tell him. "*Ethnic restaurants, fashions. The gentry. Same beer's expensive now. There's history: price of a beer went up."*

He laughs. "Dad, I don't call Columbus exactly fancy. I mean *look*."

I look. Sure. Street torn up, stores out of business, same black fire escapes with dead plants, filthy windows, shabby walkup rooms behind. Still, there's a Laura Ashley on 79th, there's a twenty-story apartment building.

I thumb the ponderous brownstone original building of the Museum of Natural History. Peter's got his eyes open. Seeing through his eyes or what I imagine to be his eyes, I try to dream a kind of city radiance into being.

Not glory—it's something else I hunger for now. Imagine you're walking along Columbus thinking, say, of buying apples at a corner fruit stand and a woman walks by holding spring flowers (although it's fall, a clean bright day) and takes you with her by the heart so that you follow her with your eyes, forgetting to be embarrassed in front of your grown son. And you're nudged awake, especially because you imagine *he's* nudged awake, and now the street begins to resonate in you, bus groans and stench and a little boy yelling *Hey, Mommy, Mommy, wait*!—while Mommy, fed up with his dawdling, hurries on ahead. You hear the thump of hip-hop, full bass beating out of the open window of a car; the throbbing cry of an ambulance. Somebody should make music of it, like the Elizabethan songs based on street cries of London.

Of course, that music isn't radiance, I don't mean that—but as the city comes real and suddenly you forget all about your apple, that's the way radiance dissolves desire when, for a moment, wings brush your face, when for a moment you recognize that the ginkgo tree bends just that way, no other, that even a dog on a leash walks in inward pulse of Being; that everything, even that woman talking so intently to herself, is charged with the life of its own making, life beyond your making and using.

It's that sense of being inside Being that Peter lends me as we walk. I feel a flowering of my spirit usually inaccessible to me—now it's gone again, because there's so much I'm not saying to him it crams up inside, gridlock, not all that hard to say, but no need to dump it on him. How sorry I am we don't see each other much. At the Stage Deli I asked, "How's Emma? You still close friends?" "Emma?" he laughed. "Dad! She's out in California. I haven't seen Emma in over a year." So I'm afraid to ask questions I should know the answers to. I moved away. We live in different cities and what the hell, I know, weekends a teenager needs his friends, but how sorry I am. So I bore him with questions not my real concern—whether or not to apply to Cornell, is he getting behind in his AP class in calculus? He rolls his eyes, good-humoredly enough. "Dad, come on—will you please get off my back?"

I hold up my palms in surrender, I smile but feel I've failed us again. I don't say how much I love it that the idea for this trip came from him. I was the one who called up and said, "What about a weekend in New York, Peter? We can do a Broadway show?" But he was the one said, "Sure. Great. But, Dad, what I really want to do, Dad—I want to see the places you grew up."

It's late; we spent too long at the Stage Delicatessen over pastrami and pickles, then walking past Lincoln Center and up Columbus; so before we get to my old street I veer off at 81st and cross Central Park, past my playground surrounded by black iron bars, past the runners, bikers, roller bladers—Central Park parade. Past the pond, little castle I laid siege to; past Cleopatra's Needle to the Met. After school, those days my mother stayed in her room, cursing, in Yiddish, Hitler or her life, when the apartment felt as if all the air had been sucked out, here is where I came to breathe—even as a nine year-old. A city kid who'd never seen a harvest, still, I felt home when I climbed the grand stairs to the sunlight of Breugel's *Harvesters*.

Peter looks up at the great triple-vaulted ceiling as if this were St. Peter's in Rome, grand and somehow sacred.

I cop a look at him aslant. He's bigger than me already, over six foot, but he walks so gracefully I wonder where he got his grace. His mother, I suppose. Same place he got his blond good looks. Me,

I'm built like a wrestler, I move like a wrestler, my hair thick, curly, once black.

"Wicked huge," he says, looking up, and I laugh at the language and he knows that and grins.

"You've been here before, haven't you?"

"*I* can't remember," he says. "Not for years and years I think"—and he smiles his extraordinary smile. Not his polite smile or his happy smile or his ironic grin. This one's like a love gift, not just to me, love gift to the world, and it dissolves the need for questions and answers.

We climb the great staircase, but at the top there's a dead wall that doesn't belong, cutting off the gallery where Breugel's *Harvesters* hung. We wander the labyrinth of rooms until we find it; he likes the color, I tell him I used to lose myself inside that sunlit field. I don't tell him why.

I try not to lecture. We look at young Rembrandt, then old Rembrandt, and I talk changes in brush stroke to avoid talking about the real changes—what life did to Rembrandt, what it's going to do to Peter. I don't want to come on as some middle-aged tragedy soul, because that's not the father he needs me to be. His stepfather, administrator in a small Vermont hospital, is a good guy and reliable, but dreary, bland, and I figure Peter needs a more exciting model. We go from canvas to canvas in the room of Degas pastels, where I can talk upbeat about "vitality" and "experiment."

Now we wander through little rooms of late medieval paintings, and looking up I find he's gone, and I'm uneasy—we made no back-up plans to meet if we got separated. He's a big kid, I'm not worried; still, unease roils in my stomach as I jog through the maze again. It's like fast-forwarding through the history of Western art the way paintings blur past. And there he is, next to El Greco's *View of Toledo*, he's looking at the picture with a girl, older than he is I think, and I see his shining, I wonder if *she* sees it, if other people *get* it, this shining he does, something he *does*, that emanates from him, for me at least, a thing of the eyes, I suppose, but it seems to be generated by the whole of him.

I keep my distance, but he spies me and waves me over.

Waves me over! Used to be, when I drove up to see him in Brattleboro, he wouldn't let me near his friends. "Dad, just pull up here. I'll walk the rest of the way. Okay?" But now—now I come up to him, and he says, "Dad, we were talking about movies. What's that early Scorcese film we saw?"

"*Mean Streets*?"

"Right. *Mean Streets,*" he says to the girl.

"Oh, I *love* that movie," she says. "Well, I love *Scorcese,*" she laughs. I feel the affectation and don't care. I'm taken with her smile. She tosses a wave of blonde hair back from her eyes. The gesture reminds me of Peter's mother when I first knew her. Blonde like Peter, girl with long legs. A pretty girl, and that she seems interested in Peter pleases me. "You go to college in New York?"

"I'm still in *high* school," she says, and her eyes half close with the tedium and embarrassment. "I'm a senior."

"You want to join us for a cappuccino?" I ask her.

"Oh I can't, I'm sorry. Maybe I'll see you. I'm meeting a friend at the restaurant. But thanks. Thank you. Really."

Peter says it was nice talking and when we're alone he stares up at the El Greco. "God. That's some weird city," he says. "A ghost city…Nice!"

"I always liked it." We walk to the restaurant. "So, you dig that girl?"

"Oh, Dad!" Not needing to understand exactly how he's making fun of me, I grin.

There's not much of a line—it's after lunchtime—we sit over cappuccino and biscuit and I remember the bronze boys lifting arcs of water from their penises, circles on the surface of the pool expanding and conjoining. Now it's just columns and white table cloths. "Before we go, I want you to see the American wing."

"Fine. But we want to see the house you grew up in, the school you went to. Right? There's still plenty of time, Dad."

"That makes me feel real good—that you *ask*. It does. But you know—it's nothing special, where I grew up. Nothing special at all.

A third-rate apartment building on a lousy side street. I want to go back up to Columbia, really check it out, maybe you'll apply. I guess I'd be proud. And I want to take you downtown, show you the *real* New York!"

"That's okay, Dad. *Special.* I don't expect anything special. I told you—it's my history I'm after. Okay?"

There's a woman by herself a couple of tables over, my age, mid-forties, new kind of mid-forties. When I was a kid, a woman forty-five was a dreary, pudgy matron, permed hair, dead clothes. This woman pulsates shrewdness and sexual stuff. Her hair, auburn flecked with gray, is cropped pixie-style around her head. Its severity shows off her strong-boned, suntanned face. Her eyes, calm, are the eyes of a woman who knows what she wants.

"Dad, you're staring."

I guess I am. I grin and look down at my cappuccino and eat my biscuit. Odd. Usually, I don't mind if Peter sees me interested in a woman. So long his mom and I have been apart. This time I feel flustered. I keep her face lit up behind my eyes, and as I do, it changes, and now I get it, I get it and look up. "Excuse me, Peter." I stroll over. "Sylvia?"

I can see she doesn't know me. But looking into her face, I'm sure. "I'm sorry?" she says.

"Sylvia. I'm Daniel Rose. We were kids, I used to come over to your house; your father, the doctor, he played in a quartet. Thursday nights, remember?"

"Oh, Daniel—Daniel, for godsakes!" She laughs and stands, a small woman—I'd forgotten that—strong and lean, a runner, I'll bet, wearing a mauve cashmere sweater as if needing the sweater to soften her act. She squeezes both my hands in both of hers. "Oh my God."

"Your father played viola, right? When Joséph Roismann was in town, he'd come by and sit in. Out of friendship."

"That's right. And the cellist was my Uncle Leon."

"He had long hair."

"Oh! Very long, for those days."

"He was a truly terrible cellist." We laugh together. I remember

Uncle Leon's hair wild over his eyes, making him feel, I think, like a passionate, serious musician. "But I loved those nights," I tell her. "I can see your father getting furious, stomping his foot to keep poor Leon in time…"

Peter comes over. "Sylvia, this is my son," I say. "This is Peter, my son. Peter, I knew this woman, I knew Sylvia Gold when I was your age. It's been twenty, twenty-five years since we lost touch."

I go back to our table to get our trays and give them time to meet, and I watch her face, as I always do when I introduce Peter to someone.

We sit together. She says, "Your father and I were good, good friends. *So* long ago…I have a son and daughter," she says to me, "both grown up. My girl is married already."

"And your father?" I ask. "What a sweet man. What a dear man."

She nods. "Dad died three years ago. My mother's moved to Florida. And—*your* father?"

"*Many* years ago. Well…you know he was much older than my mother."

"He did what he could," she says solemnly. "I mean *afterwards*." And I see out of the corner of my eye that Peter's curious. I know without seeing.

"He tried to be a good father," I say mechanically. And the snakes in my belly start their old shameful gyrations. Shameful—I'm ashamed to be at their mercy like this, and I try to give Sylvia a Look, but she doesn't see.

She says, "I remember like it was yesterday."

"Yes…yes. So—are you living in New York—all this time in New York?"

Now she gets the drift, and she changes her tune, begins to tell me about her career as an historian, about her book on nineteenth century women's diaries and photographs. I tell her about my work healing sick companies, growing healthy ones. I tell her about Peter's history project. This lights her up; she wants to ask more.

I exchange glances with Peter, and I tell her, "We've got to go, I'm afraid. Well, you look lovely, Syl."

"Oh. I'm…really sorry," she says. I know what she means. I nod—it's okay, it's okay—and shake her hand and look around for the best way through the tables, we stand, and there's that girl again, the blonde girl we met upstairs, she's looking all around and Sylvia stands and waves her over.

Now we laugh, the four of us, and go through three minutes of a flustered dance. My goddaughter, Sylvia says, Alicia O'Connor. The daughter of my dearest friend, she says, Ruth's daughter…and Peter's grinning and they shake hands, Peter and Alicia, can you imagine, how funny…and now the two of them go off for pastry.

"I *am* sorry," Sylvia says again. "So Peter doesn't know?"

"He knows she's dead."

"I suppose that's enough…"

"I've always thought so. I suppose I intend to tell him someday. But even then—why?"

She nods and stops nodding. Now: "What are you afraid of?"

"Nothing. Nothing, really. But why? What for?"

"Of course I understand. I do understand."

I take that in. "Yes. How wonderful you were to me!"

"Not so wonderful. I felt for you. Daniel? I *felt* for you."

"You were what?—fourteen, fifteen. And we weren't even dating. It's unusual for kids to feel like that for other people."

"Oh, I don't think so. No, I don't find that to be true at all. You were a person with heart. You *were*. And now Peter, too. I'm sure of it. Don't you feel that about him?"

I feel as if I've revealed some defect in my way of seeing, in my heart now. "I'm saying it wasn't…*ordinary*, that's all. I want to say thank you, I've never forgotten, Sylvia. You listened, you didn't try to smooth it over. My father needed me to tell him it was all *okay*."

"Your poor father."

"Poor everyone. Right? Poor goddamn *every*one." We sit there, mourning. Finally I say, "And your husband—what does he do?"

"I'm no longer married. Not for many years. I'm Sylvia Gold again."

The kids come back, Peter's carrying Alicia's tray and they're talking as they come, talking rock groups and sitcoms to check out each other's taste. I tell Sylvia that I, too, have been divorced for a number of years. And right away I find myself playing with the idea of seeing Sylvia again, of starting something—as I do so often when I see an attractive woman. And I think how automatic it is for me and in this case what a riot—because even when we were young she and I never thought of ourselves that way. We talked for hours when we could get away with it, we came here to the Metropolitan, we sneaked into second acts of Broadway shows. I told her things in Village coffee shops.

She must see something in my face, I must have given myself away, because what she says now is so clearly for information, clearly so I won't make a mistake. "You'll have to come over and see me. And meet Alicia's mother. Meet *Ruth*. We *live* together, we have for five years."

"Sylvia's my co-Mom, as well as my godmother," Alicia laughs, and it's obviously a well-used line. Now, maybe embarrassed, she touches Sylvia's arm, and says, "mostly, she's my friend. She's always been."

"Well, you're lucky. I know. She was *my* friend," I say. "In a way, she still is. You still are," I say. "Funny how it is, how nearly all the cells in our bodies change every few years—not to mention marriages and careers and children—and here we are, still the same people. You're still Sylvia. Or I'm the same, I mean I see you the same. More and more this afternoon, your face; it's like a special effect in a movie, the way your face has turned into the face of the girl I knew."

"Will you stop by? There's something I'd love to show you," Sylvia says, putting her hand on mine. I understand the gesture: now that she's told me about Alicia's mother, she can chance it.

"What about tomorrow? We have a show tonight."

"Please. Tomorrow. Come for brunch about eleven. Will you do that?"

I feel a little uneasy walking back across the park now that the sun has slipped behind the rooftops of the grand apartment buildings of Central Park West. Looking back we see the upper stories of the buildings along Fifth Avenue glowing. When I'm in the park, old habit—I keep my eyes open for danger. But it's still bright out, and we're not alone. Strollers. A karate class all in white. Homeless men, strollers loaded with plastic bags. Warm fall day, Peter's feeling expansive. He stops in the middle of the Great Lawn, looks around him 360, and says, "In-*cred*-ible!" And he spins as he used to when he was ten, arms spread, head back, floating, letting Manhattan issue from his fingers.

"So how did you lose touch?" he asks, returning to earth.

"With Sylvia? Oh. She went away to college when I went to Columbia. Then I went away to grad school. Then your mother and I moved away and...we made different lives, that's all. It happens. You'll see."

He laughs. "Dad! I wasn't criticizing you. You're so funny."

I show him the rocks I used to climb; once they seemed like a cliff, now a small granite outcropping. We leave the park and walk up Central Park West and down a side street to the small apartment building where I grew up. The same and not the same. I remember *shabby*: the street littered, the canopy torn, tile of the lobby filthy, the walls faded and soiled, the enamel-metal door of the elevator scored with curses. It's not fancy now but clean, cared for. I don't say any of this to Peter—just tell him, into the tape recorder, "*This is where we played stoop ball. And Chinese handball! A lost art.*"—I describe how the hollow rubber ball had to bounce. I show him the brownstones along the street, nice now, kept up; those days, before they were bought up and refurbished, walkups of the poor.

"So? What was it like, you and your parents?"

I shrug. I point out our windows on the facade. Our building had an elevator, but the line between us and them was too thin. I hear the words, "*You see how he makes me live? You see?*"

What can I do about that now?

And the poor giant roaring in pain, roaring at me out of his pain, poor father I wished dead for her, for both of us. She wanted her real life back. As if there were some Real Life, meant for her in heaven, stolen by Hitler, stolen by my father.

"So your father—" Peter prods "—your father sold dresses."

"Wholesale. He sold for a manufacturer. It was a struggle."

"And your Mom? You never said."

"Mothers didn't usually *do* back then," I explain.

"I know. But wasn't she educated in Vienna?"

"Budapest. Yes. She was a student of literature. She was never a professor, but she said she was. She came from money, she spoke half a dozen languages. Why did she marry my father? He was handsome, he looked like a success. But he was a disappointment. He became her exile. She came over just before the war. Her family was mostly lost in the camps. He was...a handsome disappointment. Now I don't see things the same way, I see him as some kind of broken hero, because every damned day, Peter, six days a week, you understand, he put on his pants, went down on the subway and sold his heart out for a bastard named Meyer, and brought home a paycheck that kept us going."

I can feel it wanting to spill out, and I take Peter's arm and change the subject to tonight's musical comedy as we walk back toward the corner, toward the ornate apartment building in yellow stone that served as one more pretext for my mother's bitterness. My mother and I would walk past on the way home and she'd sigh, "You see? *That's* where we should be living." But in the last years, when I was eleven, twelve, thirteen, before she went silent, what *didn't* serve as image of her condition?

Now, father and son, we walk past those ghosts, mother and son, on our way to the subway. And in the roar of the train coming into the station, rumble and grinding down as we go from station to station, 86th to Columbus Circle, I discover I want to say something over the noise, as if, as if, if I don't, something between us, Peter and me, will be lost. And I'm amazed. I realize I've been holding my breath; now my breath comes deep, like when you make love. Am I really going to do this? I find myself in panic, rehearsing phrases, phrases that begin sentences I can't imagine myself saying.

We walk Central Park South to the St. Moritz, where we're staying, and glancing over at the tape recorder in his hand to make sure it's off, I say, "All right. You want to know about your grandparents."

"I don't mean to push you, Dad. I know it's not your thing."

"It's okay. Well, my old man was a hardworking, old-fashioned guy. Not very smart, Peter. I've told you that. Not smart. He was crude. He used to brag that as a young man he and a buddy would pick up 'faggots' just to beat them up—but at parties he wore lamp shades on his head. You know what I mean? He played handball and stayed away from home as much as he could. My Dad hated everybody in *categories*—not just 'faggots,' 'pansies, 'mamas' boys'—I was a 'mama's boy'—but 'Wops,' 'Micks,' 'Chinks,' 'Spics,' 'Coons'—even 'Kikes.' But with individuals, it was different. He was kind to the men at work—Cadillac pushers they called them—black, Hispanic, guys who rolled those huge racks of clothes around the street. Really kind. They liked him. I could see it. Then he'd talk like that. So…I hated him a lot…he smacked me around. But he meant well. God, he was like a big bear trapped in a zoo instead of off in a woods somewhere."

"He hit you?"

"Ahh, not much…. People make such a big deal out of hitting. Hitting's no good, but that was the least of it. Anyway, that's not what I want to tell you." I glance over at his tape recorder again. He sees me, and he puts it in his book bag. "It's about your grandmother. She suffered a lot. See, she was supposed to have a different life. She'd wander through the house muttering to herself in languages I didn't understand. So she made *him* suffer. When it got too bad, and she couldn't express any other way how terrible, she used to get on her bony knees and stick her head in the oven and turn on the gas."

"She did? She did that?"

"Imagine—a parent doing a thing like that? Dramatizing her suffering like that in front of her child?"

"'Her *child*'? Dad. You make it sound like it's somebody else."

"You see, Peter…Christ…see, I'm as old now as she was then. How long do I have to hold onto it all? You've got to let it go eventually. There's nobody to complain to. How long can you keep a chip on your shoulder against the dead? And she could be so funny and charming…"

"But it must have been so awful."

"She would have loved you. She would have been so proud. My mother. She'd put on a formal dress she hardly ever got the chance to really wear, she'd sit on top of the rented piano, cigarette dangling, legs crossed, and sing to me in a breathy German or French. Café songs. I loved it. Only a long time later I understood she was playing Lotte Lenya or Edith Piaf…

"Well, as I say, partly it was drama. She was always telling the poor guy she was going to leave him. And he'd roar and shove her through the apartment, and this would justify her vision of her life, 'Go back to Europe, you crazy woman, maybe Hitler would take you back.' This was after the war, you understand, there was no Hitler. But there *had been* Hitler; so her eyes would roll up in her head, she'd maybe go into a faint or she'd rush to the medicine cabinet—'Say—which bottle do you think will do the job best?'"

"And then she died of a heart attack."

"Not exactly…I know that's what I told you. No."

Peter waits for more. We pass the pompous architecture of the exclusive New York Athletic Club. More like a palazzo or a bank. No Jews, my mother used to tell me whenever we passed. No Jews.

Horse-drawn hansoms wait at the curb and carry lovers and families amidst the taxis.

"Actually, honey, actually, she killed herself, your grandmother. When I was fourteen. That's what Sylvia was talking about before. Your Mom never told you, did she."

"Dad, how awful." I say nothing; I nod. "Dad? You never, never told me."

"No."

I hear his silence, and it makes me want to smooth things over. He doesn't ask and I don't say: *how*. I pick up the pace, I tell him I've always loved Central Park South. I tell him about Fitzgerald splashing in the fountain in front of the Plaza. Glory Town, Promise Town. "Peter, we're going to do New York up and down tonight. We'll have a snack before the show, but after, we'll take a cab down to Windows on the World and have a spectacular goddamn supper up on top and look out at all the lights."

And we do everything I wanted us to do, and the show is Gershwin and the taxi driver is a flamboyant Lebanese who used to be a trapeze artist, and we get the table I've reserved, at a window, and from a hundred-something stories up, New York looks like the promise of glory I used to think I wanted. But Peter is quiet. He keeps looking me over whenever I'm looking away. It isn't until the taxi ride home he says anything—then it's to ask what's wrong.

"With *me,* Peter? Wrong with *me*?"

"I guess it was telling me—I guess that's it? You've been so different. I don't think of you as ever heavy and sad like this. It's like you're somebody else."

"Oh, honey."

"No. I'm not stupid. I know you get sad, everybody gets sad."

"I didn't know it showed. I don't want it to spoil our weekend."

He looks at me so seriously, so *new*, that my mind falls into a gap; for half an instant I don't know this young man across the table. "Dad, it's all right. You got to be sad thinking about something like that. Your mother."

"Funny—and I thought *you* were the one feeling bad."

"Well, maybe. I guess. Maybe. I mean, it's so weird," he says. "Like all of a sudden you told me I was adopted or something."

"This isn't about *you*, honey."

He stares out of the cab. "It *is*. Sure it is."

"I guess it is. Well? You were the one wanted family history."

"Sure. *History*."

"What do you mean, 'history' like that?"

"People are crazy," he says. "They hurt each other. That's family history. That's you and Mom. That's my history."

"I'm sorry I told you. I'm really sorry."

"*No*. You should have told me before this. How could you not tell me?"

"You think *I'm* crazy, too?"

We sleep late—or Peter sleeps late and I go down to the hotel gym and work out. I saw my father's face in dreams last night, first time in years. But in my dream it was a handsome face, not thick, bulbous-nosed. It was the face she must have loved once. I see it again as I jog the treadmill. It's almost half-past eleven by the time we get to

Sylvia's. Riverside in the eighties, high up over the river, a big, bright apartment just a couple of blocks from where she grew up.

The three women fuss over us a little, and I can see from the foyer the dining room table set with white linen and crystal. It makes me glad. Today, especially, I need all the formality I can get to enter any kind of dance.

Peter's brow is furrowed; I want to touch my fingers to his forehead.

Ruth and Alicia go off for coffee and come back carrying silver trays. The apartment is decorated to my soul's taste, in books and sunlight through plants and a hodgepodge of mahogany from any-old time. The Sunday *Times* is piled in sections by the old couch draped with Turkish kilim. I feel at home with Ruth. She's a doctor, in family practice for an HMO, she's soft, a little heavy, comfortable in her body but firm in her carriage. She doesn't look at all like long, blonde Alicia. Things amuse Ruth; she holds them up for inspection: the muddle of their books by every chair, the talk of the young people about SATs and college applications.

We have coffee, and Sylvia goes off, comes back with a large black leather album embossed in gold. "This is what I wanted to show you." She pats the couch; Peter sits on one side, I on the other. "Look." She turns past pictures of her childhood, her father as I remember him, except that then he seemed old, now young. Her generous mother, who for a time, afterwards, became *my* mother. And then I see myself in black and white, maybe twelve, thirteen, a handsome kid, a little pudgy, no teenaged acne yet, mouth twisted up in tough-guy irony at the camera, and next to me, Sylvia smiling full-face. We're in front of her old apartment house on West End.

"Look, Peter, you see?" I say, though what it is I want him to see I'm not sure. We turn the book around for Ruth and Alicia.

Sylvia turns the page. "*This* one," she says. Sylvia as a young girl, maybe thirteen, wearing a flowered dress, so pretty, her hair long and dark, my parents behind her. I must have taken that one. Vaguely, I remember there were times our parents got together. The next picture is in a park. My mother's all dolled up, she's wearing a broad summer hat, pale linen I think, and a silk dress—I remember the dress, navy blue, silk—perhaps she was trying to impress Sylvia's parents.

But Sylvia sighs, "She was always so stylish, your mother. Do you remember that? And look at that hand on her hip. The *grande dame.*"

Peter's bent over the photograph so I can't see. "Sorry," he says, sitting back. "That's practically the first picture of your mother I've seen. Except for her wedding picture. You know that, Dad?"

"Stylish…" I say. "Look, Syl, look at how false. You and I look like boyfriend and girlfriend here, and they—they look *happy*. Now, I'm sorry, but that's simply not the way it was. My mother?—I told Peter last night," I say, "about my mother's death." I announce this to all of them, as if assuming they've talked about it among themselves, and I see I'm right—there's no surprise. I catch irritation in my voice—as if Sylvia had forced me to tell Peter. As if she had intruded, as if she had a long history of intruding. "No, not so happy."

"I know," she says. "But *look* at her. How proud of you…"

I see what she means. My mother's putting on an act, of course, smiling, face tilted to be charming, but she's got a hand on my shoulder, in possession and pride, I see the look Sylvia means. And instantly I feel heavy, I catch the scent of her powder, I feel smothered. "Well, you're getting a history lesson," I tell Peter. "About the unreliability of photographs."

"Maybe they *were* happy that afternoon," he says quietly, as if it were simply one logical possibility. I hear annoyance.

"I do think so," Sylvia says. "You know, I liked your mother. She was very loving to me."

I don't say anything. I wish we could leave. I look out at the Hudson, that grayest river. Ruth finds a crack on the ceiling to stare at. Alicia and Peter avoid each other's eyes. Peter's been staring at me whenever I look elsewhere. The brunch about to be served feels like an ordeal.

Now one more photograph, this one in color, the color fading.

"This must have been a different afternoon," she says. "She's wearing the same dress but look, there, there's our Mr. Ornstein at the picnic table. You remember?"

I shrug. "No."

"You *don't remember*? He played violin those Thursday nights?"

"No."

"Your mother was very fond of him. *Daniel.* You don't remember?"

"*No*, I don't remember. There must have been a violinist, but I don't remember." *What do you want of me?* The man is in a dark suit. He looks seedy but interesting. His face is long, handsome, hawk-like. He has heavy, black eyebrows. It comes back a little. "I don't remember him exactly, but I think I remember his face." I look more closely at the picture. My mother and father, Sylvia's mother and father, are posing by a tree. The man is seated, he just happens to be in the picture. He's smiling up at them.

"Maybe *I* remember so well," Sylvia says, "because we used to gossip about it. My mother and my father." She glances at Peter, and seeing the look, I puff out my lips, give a toss of my hand, as if to say, *Go on, say what you want—what can it matter?*

"There's nothing to tell."

"She liked him?" I prompt.

"Well, yes. *Yes*. He was a man of culture. A scholar, a musician. He taught at N.Y.U. He spoke I don't know how many languages. She began coming over on Thursday nights to see him—that's how it was that *you* came at first. They spoke German for hours. Your father…didn't like him."

"I bet. I'll bet he called him a 'goddamn refugee.'"

"But *you* did—you liked him very much."

"*Ornstein.*"

"That's right."

I go inside the picture. Ornstein. Now, saying the name, I feel his long hands, long fingers. I remember his heavy breath, or imagine that I do. I look at him looking at her. He wanted to marry her, I wanted him to marry her? …Am I making that up? I don't know.

This memory, the sense of their relationship, holds together like the skin on a pudding, as if, were I to breathe, it would dissolve.

Sylvia says, "My father worried your father felt humiliated."

"You remember one hell of a lot," I say, and Ruth looks over at me; I know she's hearing something in my tone. She nods to Alicia, they go off to set the food on the table. From the kitchen, Alicia calls, "Peter? Will you give us a hand?"

He excuses himself. He doesn't meet my eyes. I close the album and sit back, shading my eyes from the bright day outside, my stomach turning over.

"Remember a lot?" Sylvia repeats, very serious. "I suppose I do. Maybe that's why you stopped returning my calls, stopped writing. Was I too nosy?"

"You went away to college. That's all. Kids lose touch."

"I was home on vacations."

"Who knows after all this time?"

"Your mother stopped coming over," Sylvia says, "after Mr. Ornstein went to the West coast. And wasn't it just a few weeks later…"

"So that was your family's story?"

"Yes."

"I have a different view—I can't remember a time she didn't talk about doing it." I say this flatly, authoritatively, a little bitterly.

"I'm sure we romanticized the situation. I don't mean to argue with you, Daniel. It doesn't matter."

"Maybe it was a catalyst. Ornstein leaving her. I didn't even remember that this Ornstein left, but *maybe*. We never put that together…or maybe my father did. Who knows after all this time? Sylvia, you're still upset with me, aren't you? That I disappeared. You're getting back at me!"

"You know, I suppose I really am." She laughs as if she's surprised. "It's odd, Daniel. It's been bothering me a little all these years…"

I find something funny in this. I take her hand in my two hands. "I'm sorry."

She encloses my hands. "It's so long ago."

We're called in to the dining room, and we spread great, starched white napkins and Ruth sighs, "We do love Sundays. We stitch ourselves together into human beings every Sunday morning."

A Schubert trio is playing. I can't help thinking of my mother: how she would have loved to be here; but how she would have lost everything—the smell of good breads and the music, and the young people Peter and Alicia, and Ruth and Sylvia—by trying to establish herself as The Duchess, by experiencing this Sunday grace merely as what-was-lacking in her own life.

We talk about larger sadnesses. Children who grow up without nourishment of body and soul. The way hope seems to be closing down in America. A meanness that first degrades, then blames and punishes those who are degraded. Like something out of Dickens. Oddly, as we speak of these things, my stomach calms, I rest in our shared sadness.

I think this larger pain is seductive. I think I need its music in order to permit myself to feel my own sorrows—but put them in perspective. Our collective sorrow—feeling it, speaking of it this way—is like a penance for self-indulgence. It comforts.

Only for awhile. As I drift down into the griefs we share, I find my breath heavy and damp, and I see a hotel room not a mile away, cheap hotel, respectable, no flophouse but not the Ritz, God knows. God knows, no place for a Duchess. I turn away to other music, the Schubert trio this Sunday morning floats upon, and I snatch a piece of smoked white fish, my first in years. Now something in the music or in this food, European-Jewish, something in the bookcases full of new and ragged books, something in the dark woods and crystal in an old glass-fronted breakfront I seem to remember from Sylvia's old apartment, something brings me a word: *foreigner*, I hear it in my father's voice, not *refugee* but *foreigner*, and all at once I *see* Mr. Ornstein and I think, *Oh, Mr. Ornstein, that Mr. Ornstein*. . .and of *course* I know Ornstein, and now I see him by the oval sailboat pond in Central Park near Fifth Avenue, I see him pushing off his handmade schooner with a pole tipped like a cane, with rubber.

They're talking, Sylvia and Ruth, about public indifference to children. Peter tells them, "My history teacher says, 'We reap what we sow.' But the thing is, *We* reap what *They* sow. I'm not the one who's indifferent. But I'm going to be the victim of their indifference." I've never heard Peter speak like this. The Peter I knew was a child.

Sylvia fills our cups with coffee, and touching my forehead I say, "Sylvia—I just remembered: Ornstein made a beautiful wooden sailboat; not just a sloop—a schooner. It was his weekend hobby. It was all fitted with brass cleats and winches and white sails. The hull glowed under layers and layers of shellac. Did you ever see it?"

"I don't think so."

"Funny!—now that I can see *it*, I can see *him*." I stop. *Goddamn foreigner,* I hear in my father's voice. Am I inventing? I don't know. "He *gave* me that boat," I say.

"When he left New York?"

"I don't know. Maybe. We used to sail it together, I remember that, I remember the three of us going often to the little pond, he rented a berth for it—you know that brick building by the pond?"

"You and your mother and Ornstein."

"And he *gave* it to me. Where is Ornstein now? Is he still alive?"

"Oh, Daniel, I don't know. We lost touch."

I nod and stay silent and talk drifts away, I take part, oh, but I'm not here now. Alicia and Peter are talking about their futures. I'm remembering my mother and Mr. Ornstein. I remember them sitting on a park bench together by the pond, I remember how proud I was to borrow his pole and sail his boat for him. And I'm wondering—that boat, what could have happened to that beautiful boat? He *gave* it to me, I'm sure of that, and it was precious, I would never have gotten rid of it—then what?

While the others are still lazing over brunch, I go look out the window, it's not polite, but I do, and I watch a big cabin cruiser making a V wake down the Hudson, and I watch the Sunday traffic heading out of the city for family Sundays and I remember family Sundays, the silent drives, and Sylvia stands next to me and touches my arm, and I realize I've been waiting for her.

"You came to the funeral," I say.

"Of course."

"I can't remember much. Can you?"

"No. I remember you."

"They didn't want me to see her, but I did." There's a velvet cushion on the radiator; we both sit there and stare out at the river. Laughter from the dining room. I look into Sylvia's face. "You know, I guess by the time I got to Columbia, I wanted to be somebody else, not that boy you felt sorry for. I suppose that's it. Why I stopped calling."

"I think so, Daniel."

"...Finally, she looked like a Duchess. Lying there in blue silk. I was afraid I was going to laugh and they'd send me to a psychiatrist."

"But you handled things. I mean—not perfectly, but well."

"I did. I made my accommodations."

Now we don't say a lot of things for a long minute. But it feels comfortable. "Isn't Ruth wonderful?" she says finally. She kisses my cheek. "You'll come back and see us?" I take her hand, we walk back to the others.

We have a couple of hours before the train to Boston. "There's a place I need to see, okay?" I ask. "Please. For me. It's just a few blocks away."

Peter shrugs, he humors me, but I feel he's walking by himself. We walk from Riverside over to Amsterdam, up Amsterdam and down a side street to a refurbished hotel on the corner of Columbus, flat gray stone, with new steel-banded windows. I haven't been here for thirty years. At first, I went out of my way to come by after school—maybe to see if I could. Then, never.

There used to be wood-cased sash windows, the hotel name engraved in the glass door was different, and the glass, I remember, was cracked diagonally, corner to corner on the door. "This is the place.... My mother walked out one night, I don't know why, I mean why *then*—a fight, I suppose."

"Maybe this man she liked?"

"That's what Sylvia thinks. I don't know. She took her fancy suitcase. She had this one Louis Vuiton case from Europe. With fleur de lys.... We called all over the city, but my father and I were imagining the Plaza, the Pierre—high drama, you know? Instead, she came here, I don't know, because it was nearby, because, maybe, it expressed her spirit that day? I don't know. Or maybe because of the gas. Those days, residential hotels, some of them, still had gas. I think she figured on that."

"So that's how she killed herself?"

"No. No, I think that's what she imagined, you see? *Gas*. But no. This place had electric kitchens. No. I'm simply guessing she imagined...because she used to talk all the time about gas."

It takes him three or four breaths to ask. "Then—what, Dad?"

"Oh...well, she used a razor blade." I stop.

It's night in my mind. Ambulance and a cop car, whirling red lights. I don't speak about this. My father driving around the neighborhood, hunting, when the call came. I don't tell Peter it was me, I was the one got the call and left him a note and came down here. Columbus Avenue in the night.

And a Police Lieutenant didn't want to let me up, but I started screaming at him, I acted crazy beyond what I was feeling, I watched myself doing it, crazy for effect, or I so thought, and he gave in and put an arm around my shoulder and took me up. He had whiskey on his breath, he needed deodorant. I can feel his hand around my shoulder, I wanted to make a gesture of shrugging it off but I was afraid he'd really take his hand away, and he was all I had.

They'd cleaned up the worst of it, she was lying on a rubber sheet, there was still blood, blood on the floor, handprints of blood on the wallpaper, and the room stank of cigarettes and everything else. There was a bottle of sherry; it was more than half full.

I said, *That's my mother*, the way it was said in the movies. Deadpan. I *felt* deadpan. I think I wanted to make some kind of theatrical display equal to the situation, but I couldn't. The room was bare, the bed was covered in what looked like a brown Army blanket. The shade was up. I could see the throbbing red light of the Police cruiser, I could see Columbus Avenue. I think now she condemned herself to a prison to carry out sentence.

My father came and took me home.

Suddenly, *I know what happened to the boat.* What must have happened: my father. I don't know exactly, but I understand. And I understand that in the turmoil, I decided to pretend to forget about the boat until, after awhile, I really couldn't remember.

We walk down Columbus towards eighty-first. Across the street, the old saloon, plate glass windows still framed in heavy, dark, shellacked wood, where the man with the bloody face got tossed out into the gutter.

Peter says: "Dad? Are you all right, Dad? You want to go somewhere and sit down?"

I stop on the street. My hands are cupped, held up to Peter as if they contained the story. "She went out *without stockings*. I don't think she ever in her whole life…I think she was playing Ophelia—remember?—the mad scene from Hamlet? You know…maybe I *would* like to sit down, Peter."

Peter's hand is planted on my back all the way to a bench on Central Park West. I let it stay. "Afterwards, she was less absent in the house than before; she was always there."

He's frowning in sympathy, I feel cheap for requiring sympathy. I touch the knot between his eyes with my forefinger, and he smiles with irony at my solicitude. But what I'm feeling isn't just solicitude. It's shame. This isn't the father I want to be. I've been the adventurer father. Now I feel my own sad father filling my living bones.

You want family history? Here's family history. My father coming home like a rag and slumping by the stove, cooking hamburgers and homefries, night after night, with canned peas, rye bread from the bakery at the corner, or—when he was just too wiped out—taking me to the deli, roast beef for me, liverwurst for himself because it was cheap. Smell of brine from the pickle barrel. Smell of my father's sweat and dirt after a day dragging samples store to store. Walking home along Columbus after dark, he didn't talk. Sometimes he patted my shoulder—a beat and two half-beats over and over. He had a big belly, his "corporation." It was an effort to carry it home. Still, usually he'd poke me and grin as if he were suggesting an illicit drug—we'd stop for ice cream. Then he'd fall asleep in the big chair, newspaper, over his belly. I'd do my homework. And my mother wouldn't prowl, cigarette in hand, in her old blue housecoat. She wouldn't light *Yortzeit* candles for her family that didn't get away from Hitler. She no longer sat on the toilet gazing into inner space, tapping the ashes from her cigarette between her legs.

I sit on the bench by Central Park patting my son's shoulder. A beat and two half-beats, over and over. "My father needed…reassurance. Now she was gone, he wasn't so angry, he didn't need me as something for them to quarrel about. He needed me to keep him getting up in the morning, going down in the subway to his job. I said he was a kind of hero? See, he kept doing his job, coming home and cooking terrible dinners. My aunt came from Los Angeles, she offered to take me off his hands. He said *no*. You see?"

There's a filthy, chemical cloud soaked in sun just starting to set over Jersey. It's gorgeous—I want him to feel how splendid so *I* can feel it. I want to borrow Being. I want Peter's smile to dissipate what's going on in my heart. I point at the sky, Peter nods, uninterested. He looks serious, looks sad. Backlit by the late sun he himself glows but he doesn't know it.

"She didn't mean to leave me—but she left," I say. "And he didn't want to stay—but he stayed." Now, as I say this—say it to put it away in my pocket with an encapsulating irony—a silence brews underneath the city music. There's no beauty in this silence. Into the silence something thick and grim and dark seeps, and I'm dizzy and can hardly breathe; for an instant I wonder am I having a heart attack. But it's not that—it's what we're neither of us saying. I say it: "Yes. All right. My father stayed, at least he stayed."

Peter looks at me with the new intense look. "You left."

I sit with this. It takes me time to look at him. "I knew you were thinking that. It's not completely fair. I drove hours on weekends to see you. Didn't I? I *had* to leave for my work, I mean Brattleboro, what kind of place for a business consultant was that?"

He doesn't argue.

"Yes. All right, I know there's more, Peter."

He looks away, at the cars and buses that pass on Central Park West.

"I know. The truth is, your mother and I, when we separated, I wanted to be anywhere else. So I went to Boston. I'm sorry, Peter. I am sorry."

"'Sorry' won't cut it. You left. You *did* leave. I never said anything. Did I? I never did. But I guess 'Sorry' won't cut it."

He says this gently, and that makes it worse. "No, it won't. I left. I did leave you. And I know what that feels like, don't I?"

"Oh, I know there's no com*par*ison, Dad." But he says this as if he's angry that it's true.

"I know there *is*," I say.

Now the silence we share grows different; strange; not angry, not peaceful. Oh, there's no radiance, forget about radiance. But it's become something we *do* share, Peter and I, this silence, full of grief, but *ours*—a third party on this park bench. Some of it is purely my own, I know that. I'm the only one sees my mother so ashamed of her life she punishes herself by walking around the house all day in the same housedress streaked with sour cream, her face ravaged, the penciled lines of her eyebrows blurred; and the ash gets so long at the end of her cigarette I wait with a hollow in my stomach for it to crumple into the bowl. The hollow is still there; that's mine. And the fact that it's mine means that Peter can never know what I know, as I can never know what he's gone through.

But in a way this gap is what we share. We sit with it as the families pass by on their way to or from the park, kids rushing ahead, we nurse it between us like our sick child, and once in awhile Peter looks at me or I lift my eyebrows like a gesture in some code I don't know how to translate, until it's almost too late to pick up our things at the hotel and catch the train for Boston.

Originally appeared in Agni, *Spring, 1996*

Glory

This is a story about glory, not mourning, but there'd be no story to tell if Avrom Hirsch didn't lose his best friend, his only close friend, to cancer. Cancer of the everything. Slow, so slow it seems he can barely remember the time before (though it was less than a year) and Avrom lives in terror for Ben, terror of the pain, as he's always feared pain for himself, so it's not just in sympathy but in shame, as if it's Avrom's own physical cowardice that made life choose Ben for the torture.

But the pain is kept down. What happens instead is that over the next six, eight months, more and more of Ben Seigelman's life is closed off. Now he can't walk fast, now can't walk at all. He sits; now he can't sit; he's propped up in bed, and now he has to lie down. He can't write anymore, but he can read, and knowing he's likely to die, he takes to the books that meant the most to him—*Middlemarch*, *The Tempest*, the stories of Chekhov and the poetry of Williams and Yeats and Blake. Ben is a computer scientist, but he studied literature at Reed, and it's always been his passion. Sunday mornings, Avrom and Ben used to go out for bagels, and the two families would brunch together, and afterward, the men would take a walk and often talk about what they were reading. So now, afternoons, Avrom stops over after work to sit by Ben's bedside and read aloud. Until one day Ben shakes his head.

"Ave, the thing is..." (and then a pause; the pauses get longer week by week) "...when you read me a page or when I read a page, it's as clear to me as it ever was, but the page before, I can't remember.... God is finally making me live in the fucking present," he says, and they both laugh. "And how do you follow a novel in the present?" Ben's head floats slowly from side to side in the sea of his cancer. "In a sense, it's a gift. I can read everything I love over and over again like it's the first time."

"Maybe we better stick to poetry," Avrom says.

And now even the poetry won't go down, and he sits, taking turns with Ben's wife Susan holding his friend's hand sometimes for a half hour, and sometimes Ben is awake and sometimes he sleeps, and at night Avrom listens for a call. He even wants the call to come.

Sometimes Kristin visits with Avrom, but more often she leaves Ben to him. Strange for a professional actress, she's always been reserved. Avrom has stopped fighting her about that, stopped demanding that she be expressive. Now her calm, distant grace helps him. She soothes by not soothing too much. Micah soothes by being five years old. At night, so much the best time, leaning over the boy's bed, Avrom kisses him in the middle of his warm smells, his special blanket and special bear—the eyes of the others, wolf and rabbit, watching over; five years old—kisses Micah's cheek, or not exactly kisses but rather keeps lips pressed to his cheek and breathes more deeply than he's breathed all day; best time, warmth and smell of him, almost erotic but that's not it, Avrom considers, it's the other way around; exactly: that sometimes, making love, Kristin and I can get to this sweetness. Avrom looks up the prayer in the Siddur. He prays for Micah and Kristin when he prays for Ben. *May the Holy One, blessed be God, remove from them all sickness, preserve them in health...*

Micah, their small hostage to life: Avrom pictures, when he says the name, not Micah the prophet but flakes of shining stone. But soft. Skin so delicate, and all the mystery of the soft parts inside that have to work just right. I want to keep him like this, this long burrowing into his cheek.

And when the call comes, Avrom lets go and again his breath comes deep, and when he is through, he goes to sit with Susan until Ben's sons get to Boston from Seattle, from Sante Fe. Then all the next night he sits *shiva* with the sons, Steve and Charlie, sits all night with the body of his friend. The younger son, Steve, a practicing Jew, wrapped in his prayer shawl, is the one to say the prayers for the dead. Mostly they three sit in silence, and Avrom keeps thinking, *Nothing will ever be the same.*

When he met Ben, they were in their late twenties, 1970, in a political "affinity group" in Boston. But they became friends one night when, stoned, they admitted that political analysis bored the shit out of them, that sure, the war had to be resisted, but really they preferred Groucho to Karl, as they preferred Brahms to the Stones, George Eliot to Situationist manifestos. Ben was the friend Avrom took long walks with, all these years walked the Esplanade by the Charles across from M. I. T. where Ben taught, skaters passing, sailboats and sculls on the river, and talked about computers and business or, much more, about the new America of deep-structure poverty. Or they agreed to read the same stories by Chekhov or the novels of Nabokov. And they talked about God; not about God's existence—Ben liked to say that was a bullshit question—but about God's presence in a passage of Torah. Even with God Ben was tough. Ben had to be the hard-nosed guy; it was the only way he could talk about God—if he kept the talk tough. But they could both talk about the gap between words and the pulse of life, and agreed that the gap was not necessarily an empty place, might in fact be a place of fullness, the place where God hung out, while all words could ever do was point. The gap between God and the language was one thing; the other was the gap between this world—which both of them took for granted was a broken one—and our longings for God.

Ben hung out on one side of the gap—the world was broken, filled with evil—and Avrom on the other. Their friendship sometimes felt—Ave said this once, and then they kept silence for many minutes, peculiar in two talkative Jews—a memorial to the world it might have been.

When Avrom Hirsch loses Ben Seigelman it is as if the hollow place under the words has grown bigger. He feels pregnant with emptiness. He speaks at the memorial service at M. I. T., makes sure Susan comes to brunch on Sunday and the next Sunday. Avrom fantasizes asking her to move in with them—as if he were some desert patriarch. And Susan, Susan has her work, she's a psychologist, she has her friends—Kristin for one, though she and Susan have never been as close as he and Ben. And she has the boys.

First thing in the morning, when Avrom gets to the office, he turns on his computer and checks his E-Mail; every day he has the same fantasy—of seeing on his screen a message from Ben. Well, it's because Ben is so mixed in his mind with computers—he's been part of their development his whole adult life. Avrom imagines, wills himself to imagine, that in the billions of chips out there are remnants of Ben's consciousness, the synapses of a soul. One morning he closes his eyes to think a Ben that might be reconfigured out of all the connections among those points. Right away he stands up and closes down the machine, furious at himself. You phony bastard! Sugar! Bullshit! Uch! Listen—if all the remnants were recombined so you could store them on a single hard drive, there'd be nothing of Ben.

There are times he forgets and thinks of calling Ben. It's still that way since his mother died last summer. *Mom will appreciate that*.... Is that crazy? That's not so crazy.

The school bus that hit an anti-tank mine is gutted, stripped to twisted black steel; paper is caught by the wind; scraps of clothing, hardly colored at all, as if all the color has been blown away, cling to a twisted chain link fence and, as the camera pans, to branches of a burned tree. The bodies are gone but men and women in dark clothing hover over the ground like birds looking for food.

In China thousands are executed every year. Their organs are harvested for transplants. Connect these two sentences.

The soldier who forced a Bosnian next-door neighbor to drink his grandchild's blood. A mother whose...a father whose...

And so on.

You've got to talk to me, Ave. You have a responsibility to talk.... And then

You have a child. I don't care about me so much. You've got to talk.... And then

It's not the end of the world, Ave.

For a week, the ground, whatever floor he stands on, has been tilting, and a high sound half hum, half siren, faint, far away, comes closer.

Four young men in California, worshipers of Satan, tortured and raped and murdered a sixteen-year-old virgin in order to win entrance to hell.

A man is arraigned in Superior Court for manslaughter. He was anally raping his girlfriend's five-year-old daughter; to keep her from screaming he pressed her face into a pillow.

The Charles River bends and bends again towards Boston Harbor. Ducks and sculls on the steel-gray river. Sometimes Avrom talks to himself; more often he is silent in his head. He wishes he had something to say. He wishes Ben were there to face things so terrible. He wishes he were a Jew, really a Jew, like his grandfather, so he could sit in temple and say Kaddish.

Before the river opens and the sky, before the world breaks apart like a pomegranate to reveal its seeds, he hears cries of gulls, car alarms, drone or whine of planes, fragments of a bewildering music. He listens; it's only noise.

When the sky opens, he's biking the Esplanade looking across the river. Or rather he's stopped, he's leaned his bike against a tree. He wraps his arms around himself and rocks, as if he wore a prayer shawl, like old men davening in temple. He rocks.

And now the sky opens; or is it the air? But that's not it, because the gray river opens as well, and the buildings of Boston University, and downtown, and the grass of early spring and the sounds that were only noise. *Opens.* And his chest, and so the hollowness is exposed to, is contiguous to, the new openness, which rushes in to fill him.

He is aware of the air opening in the middle of the air. It's like one of those pictures which look like a two-dimensional pattern of colored shapes, but if you stare long enough you see the fragments receding and others coming forward and it's a lion or dragon in three dimensions, and everything you saw before is still there but now it's part of a different picture.

For there's nothing new. He's seeing, Avrom is seeing, the ordinary world, or not "seeing" so much as sewn with threads of light into the world, fibre by fibre. But it's nothing like LSD, which he remembers well, there are no flashings and color bleeds, nor is it like being stoned—the *opposite*!—for when he was stoned, things vibrated with such intensity because the frames and edges were dulled, so there was nothing but the one experience, *the loaf of bread on the table*, but now, when the air opens, he sees everything underneath and behind and on all sides, sees in more and more context. The contexts are multiplied and seem to exist in time as well as space.

And seeing, he can step inside, his spiritual metabolism has speeded up, like a fly in human time; slow up the film so that the fly moves in human time and the human hand trying to catch it lumbers, slow as an elephant.

Take that Back Bay house, black fire escape facing the river: the umber stone wall "opens." What does "open" mean? The wall takes on depth, it pulses with its own being, exists not just in space but in time. He can see it inside its time, it vibrates with its existence in time, so that Avrom is aware of the workers who laid the brick and stone in the late nineteenth century after Back Bay was filled and streets formed, and is aware of pain behind the wall, not its precise nature but certainly pain. It doesn't seem projection of his own pain.

Even the atomic structure that makes up the universe is only the temporary shape of something, the form it happens on, no more or less real than a hologram. Bach understood this; and the place between the notes is an indication, a guide.

In slight panic, giddy, he holds the railing of the Esplanade and reassures himself. Oh, the world is out there; it simply isn't what he'd believed it to be. In a song any note is what it is only because you know what went before and what will come after. Without memory and expectation there is no music. He remembers Ben saying you can't read a novel in the pure present. It's the same with all existence. This fragile version of world takes its significance, its being, from context, from time and oh, my God, so many other relations, so that each thing in itself is webbed into a mesh of things, times, people. He was here, walking last year, with Ben. He was here last week with Micah. They're still here, part of things now. Each thing, leaf, tree, house, moment of shimmering river, is a temporary, insanely complex poem that speaks itself in relation to a thousand things inside silence and time.

He is aware now that he is crazy; so perhaps he is not in fact crazy. He is simply aware of the lines of connection. *If I were aware of more, how could I deal with it?* He is sure that there *is* more.

He carries his bike over the footbridge above Storrow Drive, and as he bikes slowly along Commonwealth, he could say he sees ghosts walking on each side of people.

He's from a family of atheists, Jews who were no Jews, though he was named Avrom in honor of his grandfather, who died somewhere in Poland during the war, in a camp or in Warsaw, they heard both stories. He has tried only lately to be a Jew, and then in a clumsy way. He's ashamed he can't even read Hebrew decently; only recently, his finger pointing out the words as if he were six years old again, has he begun to read the prayers in Hebrew. He's studied very little, he's prayed very little. He has no preparation, why should this come to him? But, then, what does the opening of the world into fuller being—what does it have to do with God? Maybe nothing. It's just what is.

Kristin has seen him lately burrowing into himself, squirreling himself away from her, worse and worse, for months now, even before Ben died. Friends call, he won't go out. She has taken to cooking seriously every night she's home; nights when she has rehearsals or student performances or a late meeting, she makes sure their sitter gets the table set with napkins in rings, candles, the curtains drawn against the dismal half-dark of early spring evenings. Indian food, Cajun, West African, Mexican—it dawns on her she's trying all the spicy foods she knows to try to wake his spirit, woo him back to this world. Friday nights, though not a Jew herself, Kristin coaxes Ave to say the Sabbath prayers. *You're not dying. It's not the end of the world. You have a child.*

But he *knows* he has a child. It's his one connection. He holds Micah too often, too tightly.

And this goes on. She, too, loved Ben, God knows. And since his death she talks to Susan one or twice a week. It's something she can't fully express, and it frustrates her, his brooding silence, as if Ave thinks he has a monopoly on grief. When he speaks he half whispers, so you have to say, *What? What, honey?* And then half the time he shrugs and won't say.

She wonders, should she call Harvard Health and make an appointment for him? For now tonight he's come home with a new walk. He's a tall lanky man, gawky sometimes. It's endearing; she noticed it when they first met. She used to tease him with *Abe* or *Honest Abe* instead of Ave. It's odd, after living with a man for fifteen years, to find suddenly, tonight, his walk has changed: he plants / his feet / slowly, he plants *himself* in his red chair. Kristin teaches drama and theater at B. U.—she can't help reading the body, the stories it tells, but this story she doesn't understand. If he were a character in a Chekhov play, which would he be? She's tempted to think, he's in *slow motion*—but that's not it. It's as if tonight he were from another planet and not quite used to our atmosphere.

She sits across from him pretending to read the paper and watches. Worried—and yet, isn't there something strong, the way his arm rests on the arm of that chair? He isn't sad tonight. He's been so full of heavy sighs. *Oh, your gefilte-fish sighs,* she teases; his breath is thick and hot with them. Not tonight.

Micah's been picked up by Stephanie at kindergarten; only a few minutes till they're back. She wants to sit down next to him and touch his hair and say, *I know, I know*. But she can't. "Can I get you a drink? Micah's at the library."

No drink. He looks into her eyes the way he does when they're about to make love. He closes his eyes. "Ben's here," he says. He waves his hand towards the space between them.

Now she's worried. She goes off to the kitchen for a bottle of red wine and pours herself a glass. She asks him what he's seeing.

He looks into her face again and says "I never understood. Now I understand." That's all. He waves his fingers as if touching or pointing. "I mean *about Ben*." And he goes to her, sits on the arm of her chair. "Poor honey, you poor honey."

She lets go; cries and cries without explanation, and he strokes her hair. "You had to keep it to yourself," he says. "You couldn't even mourn him decently, not the way you needed."

"No."

"No."

It was Ben who introduced her to Avrom. Kristin and Ben had been lovers on and off for a few years, since she studied drama at Yale and he'd been finishing his Doctorate there. Kristin sees a borrowed graduate-student apartment, sunny afternoon, movie posters covering cracks in the walls. They'd made love deliberately and tenderly, and now they were dressing as if it were so preoccupying to get dressed they couldn't spare the time to look at one another. Ben waited (so she supposes now) till they were protected by their clothes, and then he took her hand and sat down with her on the mattress that was the only furniture in that room.

"Love," he said, "love, I've met a real good guy. He's doing a degree in economics, but he's a good guy, he loves music, he can talk literature. He's becoming a friend. His name is Avrom Hirsch. I think I want to introduce you."

And she said, grieving, feeling herself like an astronaut cut off from a mother ship, floating nowhere, "So. Are you handing me over?"

"Look into my eyes, Kris. Does it look that way? Do you think I'm just 'handing you over'? Do you think? I've got my sons."

But of course he was handing her over. She's forgiven and not forgiven. Look what came out of it: Avrom, who became dear to her, then Micah.

For three years when she and Ave were first married, she kept apart from Ben except for dinners and walks as families. And then there was a weekend afternoon on the Vineyard when they found themselves alone. And then he called and said he couldn't be without her. Then six months later she was the one to call. And so on.

She burrows into Avrom's chest and he mothers her. Coming up for air, she asks, "What do you mean, you say Ben's here?"

"It's all right," he says.

"Then you knew about me and Ben?"

"I know now."

"It's not been for years, Ave. Not since Micah. *Before*."

"I don't mean 'all right' like that. That, too, Kristin. But I mean that I think *Ben's* all right. I don't know for sure. But I think. I mean we don't have to worry."

She pulls back and looks at him. She's irritated by this otherworldly crap. What role is he performing? She wishes he'd just show he's hurt and angry, get it over with, so they can go on. Did he find an old letter? Did Ben tell him at the end? "How do you know? What do you mean 'seeing'?"

"I mean I see it. In my skin, as if my skin had eyes."

"Ave, stop. Please?"

"He's in this room, but not a ghost. It's good to have him, he's here for both of us. Well, this room is very full," he laughs. "I'm trying to get a handle."

❧

Avrom sits in the rose-velvet old wing-backed chair trying out his new skin, naked to the air. His mother is present in all her caustic elegance, his father, dead fifteen years, in a heavy brooding anger; the living room is very full, full of living, of past lives not past. He takes Kristin's hand. He's told her, *Ben's all right*. Well, Ben *is*. Still—there's something dark and hurt about him.

The seeing doesn't go away. His mother smokes, cigarette between stiffened forefinger and middle finger. It's at the precise moment she has warned him not to marry a *shikse*. A Christian woman. *Oh,* she says, *I can see the attraction: that aristocratic insouciance of hers. But her lips are too thin, my dear.* Then: *Oh, don't mind me,* she says drily, at once both being and imitating a masochist, archly, parodically so that she doesn't have to own the masochism, *if you want to put me in the grave, my dear, why it's perfectly all right. But you must know what they're like?* He remembers laughing, Mom, what about Joan of Arc? *Well, and didn't she dress up in men's clothes?*

When Avrom was a child, he used to lie in bed and stare at the frame of the window against city lights. He learned he could alter the window, make it grow small and smaller, till he became afraid each night that if he kept on it would become untenably small, smaller than he would be able to label a visual trick. And then where would *he* be, would he dissolve out of the shared world?

There are strings of attachment between himself and Ben, between Ben and Kristin. It's as if he could pluck them for their music. He wishes she could have told him—if she had, she could have grieved more completely. He thinks: *a triangle*, thinks it visually—a complete, stable figure—he feels his own point in the figure.

He's never been so full of her. Kristin nestles against him. And he takes comfort; after all, she's not naturally a nestler. If you cut your hand open on a shard of glass—as he did last month—and the wound poured blood, you'd want Kristin there to handle things, to bandage you while keeping Micah calm. She nestles. He wonders: who's comforting whom?

In the morning, it's gone. Avrom wakes to a house full of ordinary life. There's no depth in the air, no matter how he tries to see it, the window is open, it's spring, and there are car noises from Beacon Street, bird songs, but the air is closed, the world has flattened into the present; and no one's present but Kristin, who, still asleep, curls away from his waking. As usual, he thanks God for the morning in Hebrew words he has learned by rote. He looks around him wondering how he can coax the air to open again.

He does his stretches in Micah's room, humming, "Wake up, time to wake up, big boy." Micah wakes slowly, but once awake, he's singing. Loud child, gorgeous in his bravado, he sings, "Some day he'll come along, the man I love…" Like a torch singer, quoting a style a decade gone when Avrom was a child. Look, he thinks, how we poke through the closet and choose an instrument of language, and the past issues through us.

Micah is especially sunny this morning and Avrom sits in the good-night chair and watches him pick out his clothes; for a change he doesn't complain about his jeans or the way his belt feels. Kristin fixes breakfast; she doesn't talk about last night. She's teaching today; she's dressed in a soft wool skirt, heather, and a mauve blouse; years ago, he thinks, she wore only cool clothes, black and white, pants, and her hair, now trim but long, was cut like a boy's. He's known this change without knowing; now, when she's turned away, he stares.

He drives Micah to school in Cambridge, then down to his office around the corner from the State House.

He does what his grandfather did, and his grandfather's grandfather. He buys and he sells. His grandfather bought and sold sheep; Avrom buys and sells—internationally—container-loads of coffee, fruit, electronics, it doesn't matter. It hasn't changed much since the fourteenth century; a merchant fills a ship's hold with goods to sell, then takes on cargo for the return voyage. Avrom doesn't own the ship; he's not even the merchant. He finds space, he finds cargoes. Now it's telephone and fax, it's planes as much as ships, trucks as much as planes, and sometimes it's nothing for days, futile calls to arrange deals that fall through, deals that never had real backing. But sometimes he can spot a potential buy in Egypt and see a way to make it dovetail with a great deal for someone in France. And he sets up the deal. He risks no capital of his own, he produces nothing, owns no companies. He's a trader. He's always felt there was a certain spirit of adventure about the work. A careful flamboyance.

Today, pushing a button in the cherry-paneled elevator, Avrom walks into his office and says hello to Shahid, the young man who assists and is learning from him. Duval called. Shahid had to placate

Fahoud. You want to set up a conference call with Syscom and the Stern brothers?

Avrom sketches out a strategy for the Syscom deal. Shahid leaves, and Avrom is about to sit down to work when, looking out the window at a patch of the Charles, he thinks, *Ben. Oh, Ben....* The grieving rushes through his chest, and in defense he whispers the first phrases of the mourners' *Kaddish.*

But praising God doesn't help. For he's not mourning Ben the way he did yesterday. His eyes are swollen with things he needs to say to him, ask him, hear from him, and there's no one there. He knows that Ben must be here in this office. He knows now that the world is drenched in past, he knows that simple versions of experience are laughable. The world isn't flat. It isn't even round. But Ben is gone. He sits, staring off into the ordinary air.

"Nothing new about Rwanda or Bosnia," Ben said on a walk one day. He could still walk. It was just after he understood what was happening to his body. "Look at Robert of Geneva, butcher for the Pope. Late 1370s. He used Sir John Hawkwood to attack a little Italian city, Cesena or something, and they had the gall, the burghers, to resist. Robert swore an oath—clemency if they laid down their arms. So they did. Exactly like the Peasants Revolt in 1381 in England. Robert ordered the soldiers: kill everybody. Every fucking person. Sacred justice he called it. Some such shit. The soldiers even protested, but finally they closed the gates and slaughtered for two full days. They sold the children and killed the men and raped and killed the women. I mean thousands—seven, eight thousand dead. A small Holocaust. Fuck this life, Ave. We hear about 'post-Holocaust theology,' as if the six million made everything different. It's no different. Generations of African slaves. Whole towns of Jews burned. The Armenians. The Cambodians. The Ukraine: Stalin starved millions—a country—to death. How do you pray past that? I don't get how to pray."

And Avrom remembers saying, "But that's why we pray."

"Look at me," Ben said. "I don't go around killing people. But I'm no saint, Ave. I'm full of hate sometimes. I'm a betrayer."

I didn't get it. A "betrayer." What if Ben could have really said what he meant—maybe we could have invented something, some new form of love—why not?

He mourns, knowing how impossible that would have been. *What about Susan*?

And now, though nothing changes in the world he sees, a strange thing happens. Turning to his desk, he doesn't ponder his strategy for Syscom, doesn't make the list of calls he'd planned. He finds himself picking up the phone, punching in numbers, watching himself from outside. Whom am I calling? At once, surprised, he knows, and gets hold of a client he hasn't dealt with in a year. And it proves just right, the call is timely. A deal starts to take shape, something out of nothing.

Looking up, he half feels, half sees, pools, pockets, billows, of energy. They hover around his computer, around the files and telephone, and as he looks in any direction—say at a file drawer—he becomes aware of filaments of energy pulsing to telephone and computer.

Giddy, he rides the connections. Picking up the phone he knows who he has to call and punches in the number without having to look it up. So by the end of the morning he has a deal arranged for two container-loads of coffee from Nicaragua, a container shared by two electronics firms from Czechoslovakia, another of machine tool parts to Hong Kong. In each case, he doesn't have to think. He sees the deal, he sees consequences and possibilities like a genius chess player on a board the size of the world. He rides the connections.

Yet by noon he's exhausted and in an odd way sad. Why sad? It's not Ben. He lies back in his leather reading chair and closes his eyes, and what he sees is the deals he's made, and they aren't numbers on a computer screen, they're busy with grief, there's sadness emanating from them, they speak to him of lives draining out of the bodies of men and women. Nothing's changed. It's a hundred years ago, it's seven hundred, deals are made and people earn their bread and pay their lives away.

He thinks, *Ben*. This is something he could talk to Ben about. He speaks to him now, a rush of awareness goes out to Ben. But Ben can't reply.

He has put together so many deals, taken upon himself responsibility for so much pain. Oh, life, too. Sure. He has provided livelihood. He knows that. It isn't guilt he feels but his own participation in the dance of pain and life.

The fingers of his heart fumble down inside himself. Eyes shut, he reads himself as braille. As if within him were a Torah. But he's not equipped to read it.

He reads: *Ben.* Ben. He remembers the afternoon, New Haven, he first met Kristin. Ben got them together for lunch and then they visited the Museum of British Art—an exhibit of Pre-Raphaelite painting—and Kristin played docent. There she was, waving her hand like a long-legged sprite, Ariel leading two big Calibans—Ben thick like a football player, he, Ave, long and gawky—through the rooms full of spiritualized beauties. Kristin's hair was chopped short that year. He couldn't take his eyes off her finely sculpted face; he found himself placing her face in the decorative canvases on the walls, she was so much more beautiful to him than the heavy-jawed beauties of Rossetti. But that wasn't it, it was her eyes. He saw truth in her eyes, simple truth, even when she was kidding Ben about his taste—oh, Ben played the boor, he charmed with a kind of parody crudeness—and maybe Ave's sense of her truth was intensified by her contrast to Ben. Truth, "soul," the kind of thing that Ben groaned at and Rossetti or Hunt faked. Even now he sees her eyes in the same way. And that's the funny thing—that professionally, she's an actress, that with him, too, she's been an actress, and yet he knows her—*knows* her—for a woman of truth.

And as that first afternoon went on and they had drinks somewhere and Ben patted them in blessing and went off, Ave gaped at her as if she were a most precious gift.

And that's what this is coming to. He recognizes that she was precisely that: a gift from Ben—he recognizes that even that first afternoon he knew. Something in the bluster of his friend, something in the pauses, the too-fast exchanges of banter, the way they didn't look at one another, was that it?—of *course* he knew they'd been lovers, of *course* he didn't let himself know he knew.

He looks up as Shahid, recent graduate of Wharton, walks in with a stack of mail and a sheaf of faxes. Shahid's hands are full; he nudges the door shut with his hip, squeezes the mail under his arm while he sorts the faxes into piles, then puts the mail down on the desk. Avrom is amazed at what he wouldn't have noticed yesterday. All this *knowing* of the body's mind, not thought-out—like a ballplayer running at the crack of the bat precisely to where the ball would arc. "Thanks, Shahid."

"Some morning, oh, Avrom, some spectacular morning!"

Oh, he knew, knew they were lovers, though not that they became lovers again, but even *that*—there was always something charged between them. He knew. He was willing to take her on any terms offered. He knew; he didn't let himself know he knew.

He is swollen with knowledge. And with the knowledge comes a fullness of anger—his generosity of spirit of last night gone—anger that washes through his chest and neck and face. He's touched a shorted electric wire—*that* potent, *that* unexpected. He could kill him over again. He sucks in breath to cope, and with the breath he enters an altered world. Feelings aren't "feelings"; they're palpable, visible, they surround him as thick lines of attachment, like threads of a monstrous spider, and he can't move. He senses them through his body, senses them blocking the room, barbed filaments joining him to Ben—you betrayer, betrayer—what kind of friend?—he pushes away the entanglements. If anyone came on him then—oh, he's aware of this—they'd see a crazy man pushing his hands through the air. He wants nothing to do with Ben, the son of a bitch, there in the corner. But oh my God he looks so full of grief. *Is that phony? My way to alleviate my pain?*

Maybe. But that's what he senses, Ben grieving in the corner, and he can't help joining him, mourning not for Ben this time but for the lost real impossible life between them, among the three of them. And as he begins to weep, sitting there at his rosewood desk, the strands grow soft and stop constraining him, the room is ordinary again except that Ben is there and the air between them has opened. It's like being inside a Cubist canvas, except it's not flattened, it's like having your molecules suffused with light so that the boundaries are indistinct. What is this world?

He's sitting at his desk and at the same time on Ben's sailboat off Martha's Vineyard catching a look between Ben and Kristin, replaying that look during the morning to interpret it *any other way*, then hiding the look away.

Once: "How are you and Susan? You okay?"

"Okay, sure okay. You know. We fight. We like each other, Susan and me. We get along. We do okay in the sack if that's what you're asking."

"It wasn't."

"And…you and Kris?" Ben asked.

"Good."

"Good. That's good. Nice."

❧

Kristin is released—the tooth is pulled, she fits tongue into hollow. All morning there's been this giddy, anarchic feeling of having nothing to lose. Free fall. But then, taking a few minutes off from her work to straighten Micah's room, she felt in this hollow a pocket of grief. She straightens her study, already tidy, its books categorized, alphabetized; she rests in its neatness. Nothing to lose, no—but so much already lost. And when Avrom comes in unexpectedly after lunch, as she's preparing a theater exercise for her class, she experiences him as the embodiment of all that loss, the life she denied herself. Now there would be years ahead with the false surface of their life together stripped away—and what would be left? Only Micah. And she and Ave would turn into her parents, living separate lives in the same house.

He's standing at the door to her study. She glances his way and away again, not wanting to look at him because then she would have to feel his kindness. And it's his kindness that balks her, that's always balked her—because it made her believe in the value of their life together, it seduced her into pretense.

So when he says, “We need to talk,” she snaps, furious, “It’s too late for talk”—though this *is* the beginning of talk and she knows it. And, still lying, because after all, it’s Ave she’s angry at, she tells him, “I’m furious at myself, Ave.”

“For the deception?”

“Stop being my analyst! For not being with Ben. For not having the courage. I could have had all that life. Instead, I’ve lived a half-life.”

“Have you? I don’t think so. No.” She spies him staring at her, or rather *through* her. He roams the little study, fingering her shelf of Samuel French acting editions. “*No*,” he says finally. “It’s not true.”

“*You* can’t know. If I’d gone off with him.... There were times we talked about it.” And for just a moment, the music of their being together plays in her. And quietly she adds, “He was the love of my life, Ave.”

“You wouldn’t believe how much life we’ve lived, you and I. You wouldn’t believe it—how much life surrounds you now.”

“*Please* don’t give me that mystical crap, Ave!”

“I’m sorry. But it’s not mystical. I see it, as tangibly as I see you.”

“There was this passionate life between us, and I missed it.”

“I wish we’d talked. Kris, love, Kris, maybe we could have invented something. We all did love one another. And the thing is—Kris, I knew.”

“You *didn’t* know. Oh, bullshit you knew.”

“I saw looks, there were moments you were on the phone and suddenly blanched when I walked in. I turned the other way. I knew. I turned the other way. I’m ashamed. I made you take the whole burden.”

She refuses to give him even this. “But *talk*—what would have been the good,” she says. “Charlie and Steve, Susan too, and you and me. There was too much at stake. You see, the thing is,” Kris says, and now she’s coping with tears, “we did the right fucking thing.” She says “fucking,” she recognizes, in Ben’s voice.

“And there’s Micah,” Ave adds.

"*And* Micah. Micah. Micah's why we stopped. Ave? I can't swear who's his father."

Now she waits, getting sick to her stomach through a long silence, before he says, "I am. I'm his father."

"We hardly saw each other by then. You *are.* Oh, but Ave, Ave, I want to go backwards and live the other life. I don't know how we can stay married now." She says this to him because he is, after all, the closest adult in the world to her; furious at Avrom her husband, she says it to Avrom her friend.

"Because we *are* married. We were all so enmeshed. We should have talked."

"I don't know."

"The trouble with the dead, you can talk to them but they can't answer. I want to invent a different spiritual universe."

"Stop! Grow up."

"Ben told me the same. One day I said to Ben, 'Maybe there's something to the reports about the light you move towards as you die.' And he still had the strength to get pissed. 'We can talk about God, okay, but don't give me any of that white light crap! Don't hoke it up, Ave.'"

At this she had to laugh. And she felt the impulse to hold him and soothe Avrom and be soothed, but, afraid it would be seen as begging absolution, she held back. "'Don't hoke it up.' I can hear him say that. He loved to play the tough guy with you, didn't he? Especially because you were the businessman and he was the academic."

Now he sits on the edge of her desk and holds out his palms as if he's waiting beneath a tree to break a child's fall from a high place. She closes her file and shuts down the computer and his hands are still there, fingers stretched out to her. With a sigh of irritation she gives him her hands as if they were foreign objects.

He has this diffuse gaze *into* her—*smarmy*, she thinks—that makes her yank her hands away again. *I won't let you use me this way.*

He says, "For awhile this morning it was gone, but now it's always there. I wish I could bring you into it with me."

"I'll stay where I am, thanks."

"Though there's nowhere to bring you. It's just the ordinary world," he says. "You're already there." He stands up and, in a kind of giddy, spurious victory, tilting up his face, he holds his hands out, fingers spread, first as if he were riding the air, then as if he were connected by each finger to—she didn't know what.

"You're spooking me," Kristin says very quietly. "Please."

"It's not like that. Kris. Come inside. We're so absolutely connected here. It's beautiful if you let it be."

"What are you doing with your eyes like that? Please. Ave? Be careful you don't go too far with this. Please. Oh, Ave." She reaches out to pull his hands to her. "It's been a terrible time, for you. I know. Such a terrible time. Oh, honey…you'll be all right." But what *makes* it all right, suddenly all right, is that his craziness, this crazy way of handling pain, has touched her. For a moment the word, *honey*, releases its sweetness in her. This sweetness, the tenderness she feels, her longing to soothe, makes her think, why, there must be something between them to make her care like this. This dear fool. This complicated, crazy man.

"Are you seeing Ben now?" she asks.

"Here, and here, and here," he gestures, a magician pulling small change out of the air. "But it's more than that, Kris. I'm in touch. It's like being in this other country."

"All right," she says, and she reaches up to touch the fingers of his other hand.

❧

There's no way to take her here, and yet *here* is where she is, Kristin; he isn't even separate from her; they interpenetrate. She breathes him in, he breathes her in. Then how can she not be here with him? He breathes Ben in, he breathes Ben out. The air is also thick with grief that finds its way into Avrom's open skin. Nerve gas, used to murder whole villages of Kurds. Smoke that rose up the chimneys at Buchenwald, still in this air. It must be here.

Ben wanted to feel like a tough guy; he chose to stare down

murder. And so I didn't have to, he did it for me. He did the dying, too. I wish he could have said, *Kristin and me* and I could have said, *I know, I know*. It seems so much less difficult a thing than murder.

I need to speak to him about that.

The study is suffused with Ben and with the loss of Ben. And Kristin—Ave sees Kristin as if meeting her for the first time. He's never known her, known that she's this much music. She's a new love. She's almost a different species, it takes his breath away. And yet he can read the codes of pulse in her wrist. She's a grad student sitting cross-legged on a blanket in the grass, examining his face shrewdly just as they're about to make love the first time, she's the nine-month woman whose belly shone with oil from his fingers, belly that shifted with Micah's hip or elbow, and he pressed his ear to hear the strange heart singing. She's a young woman who knows she can be a great actress and at the same time the teacher who performs in theater around Boston but has never established a career. And she's the old woman he will be living with in twenty years, he sees that possibility in the room, too. And Ben is with them and so is the loss of Ben.

Strands of grief and love connect them all to one another. He doesn't say to her: the boundaries are so blurred. Between me and Ben. Between dead and living. Be with me. I'm all you'll have of him. But Avrom mourns for Ben, mourns in a different way now, the way one mourns for one's own lost possibilities.

But the air is open and full of dreams, the walls and books pulse with their talk and the stained-glass lamp over the desk and the second-hand desk itself and the brass candlestick of her mother's and the worn Turkish carpet, they break open and spill their constitutive dreams, dreams that permeate the almost-visible air. He feels now, right now, he is making something, completing something, doing real work by his openness to the permeable air, *making* the world of wholeness he and Ben mourned for. Is it wishful seeing? The dark greens and reds of the carpet say themselves in waves to his eyes. If I'm crazy it doesn't matter much.

Not to frighten Kristin, he says it only in his heart to Ben, *Talk to me*. And Ben does "talk"—Avrom isn't hearing voices, he's feeling the words from Ben's many presences: friend teaching him to sail, friend who puzzles out a passage from Torah with him, deceiver who tried to tell him. But what Ben can't say is anything new. *Only I can do that, now*, Ave thinks. And so he says it, aloud: "I survived, not you. I have to tell you, I'm glad of it."

"Is that it?" Kristin says. "Is it so terrible to survive?"

He doesn't answer. He says, "Please?" and helps her up from the desk to lead her to her daybed. She says, "How can we do it? How can we stay married?" but she doesn't resist him. He knows very well she thinks she's humoring him, placating, but he knows, too, that in this *other* place in which even the air has depth and the depth gushes out through its secret pores, they are very close, so close that he's a little afraid. He isn't sure he knows where he leaves off and she begins, though she's also an alien creature. They sit cross-legged on the bed together the way they do sometimes before sleep, and he says, "The bed is very crowded."

"*Not* crowded. It's just us. Just us. Please, Ave."

"Well, I suppose beds always are, that's the way it is with beds." Tentatively, he strokes the nape of her neck. Tenderness coats his fingers. And with the touch, his fear subsides.

Originally appeared in The Journal, *Winter, 1997*

Muscles

His father—bull of a man, red-faced and thick of neck, wearing sloppy old pants and worn-out business shirt, the collar frayed—carried the pail of soapy hot water, Ben the sponges and a pail of clear warm water. "C'mon, c'mon, c'mon."

Ben's mother warned as the elevator doors close, "Leo—try to be decent with your son! Oh—and be sure to remember me to your charming brother." Down the elevator and up the street to wherever the car was parked.

This was the 1950s, New York City, West 84th off Columbus, where they'd moved from Jackson Heights.

When he was eight, and still when he was fifteen, Ben promised himself he'd stay home on Sunday and play sick or say he had homework. Why was it he always went along? To show his father he was loyal to the activities of men? Did he really believe that this time he'd scrub the old Chevy without missing bug spots, wouldn't waste the soapy water or the clean?—wouldn't hear his father holler in that operatic baritone—you could hear it a hundred yards off—"If you're gonna slop up the car like that, forget the whole goddamn thing. You just leave soap film."

Some Sundays Ben blew up and stormed off, not looking at his father, cursing to himself. More often, he ended up arms folded, leaning as if bored against a car. Yet secretly he watched his two-hundred pound father, pail in one hand, sponge in the other, scrub that car with every bit of his amazing force, grunting his breath, cursing the son of a bitch Chevy as if it were trying to defeat him by staying dirty.

Now, fifty years later, he thinks of the man in Homeric terms, like a drawing of Achilles by Leonard Baskin, all that crude passionate force expended so purely but so pitifully on such an inadequate object. To be in the presence of that angry power!

Say it's 1955, late spring, Ben is fifteen, and after a humiliating half hour with sponges and pails, he was Silent Cal, driving alongside his father to a pickup softball game in Central Park, and his father, softened now that the car is clean, was trying to appease him with sweet talk. "Ahh, you know me, Ben. I'm a fussy son of a bitch. I know it. We both know it. You don't mind your old broken-down father, do you?"

And Ben said, as he was meant to say, "It's okay, you just get excited. You've got your ways you want things done."

"That's just it exactly. You know I'm nuts about you."

They parked on Central Park West. It was the first Sunday they were trying this pickup game, so Leo Kagan was nervous, clearing his throat a lot and spitting it out on the grass, pounding fist into glove, saying, "Hey, straighten up, Ben. Look like a ballplayer. You want to get picked, don't you?"

This was the year Ben grew almost an inch a month. He used to be pudgy; now he was skinny. But fat or skinny, he couldn't play softball, not well enough to be here. He stood in the clump of men and older teenagers getting looked over by the captains.

Leo Kagan was in his early sixties, gray-haired and heavy-gutted, and nobody here knew him. He banged his fist into Ben's side at each pick, as if saying, *Good pick, good pick*—or else, *What? That schmuck? Looks like a pansy.* Ben knew which by the rhythm of the poke.

Ben got chosen with only a few players left standing, his father on the very last round. Only a few young kids left at the end.

"Hey, Pops, you want right field? Or can you maybe pitch?" Slow-pitch softball—they figured maybe he'd be a steady slow-ball pitching machine, but Leo said, "How about first base? That's my position."

And because he was an old guy and they didn't want to insult him, somebody shrugged, "Let's try you out. A little pepper." And they tossed the ball around and made Leo reach, and he pulled them in from goddamn all over, even jumping, even down in the dirt. "Okay, Pops, you've got first."

Ben was on the other team and didn't get up in the first inning. In right field he stood rocking. Second inning he popped up; his father said, "Good piece of the ball, Ben. Next time!"

His father got up bottom of the second, middle of a rally, two on, one out, and slammed the first pitch way over the head of the left fielder. Way the hell out, over any fence they could have put in that field, but there was no fence, and the left fielder took off after the ball, and Leo, slow as he was, trudging heavy around the bases, puffed home.

And so it went. Ben got a single in the eighth, a fluke off the tip of the bat. And his father played perfect first base, hit three home runs, though the fielders play him further and further back; and the center fielder barely got his glove on another. They slapped his father on the back, asked him to come back, and he was red-faced and grinning.

Only when they were heading back to the car did Ben start to feel his own failure. At first his father was in too good a mood to care. "You see me smack that son of a bitch? They didn't know who the hell they were dealing with. You see me smack that third one? Your old dad ain't got no legs. But can I belt that son of a bitch?"

"That was something. I guess next time they won't wait to pick you."

"They can kiss my ass, Ben. Next time, it's me picking them."

"Great! Well, you're a ringer, you were semi-pro."

"That's right.... So how is it *you* can't hit worth a damn? The thing is, you got to watch me, the way I keep my eye on the ball all the way in, the way I get my shoulders into it. Vooomh! Maybe we'll go out this week and practice. If I can get off a little early? What do you think? You game?"

"You're the ball player in the family, Dad."

"Well, we're different, right? But don't think I'm not proud of you, Ben. When they handed out the brains, you and my brother got all they had to go around."

Leo Kagan was in high spirits all through the park, but when he saw his clean black car, his real life came back to him, and his eyes dulled, his face seemed to lose definition.

"You think we ought to go home and change?" Ben asked, trying to bring him back.

"Nah. Cy says, your uncle says, 'Come as you are.' He says, 'Don't stand on no ceremony with me.' Anyway, there's no time. The big guy's leaving to play golf at one o'clock. I brought us a couple of clean shirts and pants and a comb. We can change in the car." He took out a handkerchief and mopped his own face, then used the sweat to wash the dirt off Ben's.

"I thought you were supposed to be getting a haircut," Leo Kagan said as he jammed the car through its changes. "Look at your hair! I can't trust your mother to keep her word.... Goddamn traffic for a Sunday! And they don't know how to drive. This city is getting to be unlivable. We'll cut across town at fifty-sixth."

Uncle Cy, recently divorced, was staying temporarily at the Warwick; his wife had "kicked him out on his ear," Ben's mother said, "because he *wasn't a real man with her*, you understand me, Ben?"

Ben didn't understand. Who could be more powerful than Uncle Cy? Ben saw his father as a clumsy giant of some strange race. But his uncle!—Uncle Cy, though no athlete, was taller than his older brother Leo, more handsome, with a Dick Tracy chin he carried high and beautiful silver hair usually covered by a Stetson. He strode through the sonofabitch city like the cattle baron in westerns, though he grew up in Chicago, an immigrant kid, and the only West he'd seen was once on the train to Los Angeles. A poor Jewish kid from Chicago who happened to be smart, he learned to be a courtroom stenographer at fourteen, became an officer during the First World War directly out of civilian life, landing a job in Washington as secretary to a general.

This general must have given him a smattering of style—after all, what could a kid like that, his father a cigar roller, his mother a boardinghouse keeper, know about clothes, about food, about business talks and deals? Yet by 1926 Cy was working for himself, building a tire sales operation, starting on not much more than a phony slogan—"World's Largest Distributor"—and by the time Ben was born, Cy was a millionaire owning half a city block in the West forties. No longer a Jew—his name Colburn now—he had made himself into the American *Sport* of his youth, dapper but street-smart. He blended his own whiskey from unblended imports, spent a part of the racing season at Saratoga. But none of that expressed the power he gave off, power that made Ben—in spite of himself, in spite of the loyalty he felt to his mother ("That uncle of yours has ruined my life")—feel more alive just to be in his uncle's presence.

"Mr. Colburn is expecting you." In the gilt-framed mirrors at the Warwick he saw himself reflected as if he were another boy. His father had spit on the comb and wet down his hair, a severe part too near the middle. Now Leo stopped and looked Ben over. Ben stepped outside his body to see himself with his father's eyes. But in turn, his father was seeing Ben with not with his own eyes but with the eyes of his brother, Ben's uncle. So he and his father both disappeared, and the only eyes between them belonged to the uncle/brother they imagined.

While they waited for the elevator, Leo Kagan kept talking. "If the Big Guy asks, you tell him how good you're doing in school. Tell him math, tell him history. He don't believe in literature if you get me. Frankly, Ben, he's grooming you."

In the elevator Leo squirmed inside his clothes, stuck two

fingers into his collar. *My poor father, my poor, big father*. Ben watched the little light rising through the glass numbers.

"Come on in, this here's the President's office and I'm the goddamn President, so what're you waiting for?"

Cy sat at the window, leg crossed at the knee, in a crisp blue cotton knit shirt, pale beige linen pants, brown and white golf shoes. The King of Fifth Avenue. Ben knew he'd just set himself into that pose to seem relaxed and in charge—but knowing, still he was charmed.

It was the room of a transient. There were file boxes and suitcases piled up in the corners. On two open card tables were stacks of papers. The furniture was just expensive, pompous hotel furniture. Still, this was the real world. Ben bathed in it.

"Don't an uncle get a handshake, Ben?"

And Ben, about to plant a nephew's kiss on his uncle's fresh-shaved cheek, stuck out a hand. *Don't an uncle get....* It was Chicago street talk, held onto the way a Frenchman may hold on to a charming accent. The bad grammar was his uncle coming on tough and American, buddy to gangsters, no Jew. And his father copied it. Once, Ben tested his uncle. He said about a second-rate pitcher, "He ain't nothin'." And Cy said, "Christ, haven't they taught you better English than *that*?"

The funny thing was, Uncle Cy wanted *him* to be cultivated. He wanted Ben to attend an Ivy League school and turn into the kind of person both brothers made fun of. His father truly wanted a jock for a son. Cy wanted a nephew who was going to "become something."

"We've just been playing softball, the kid and me," his father said. "Tell your uncle."

"Dad was fantastic. He hit three home runs."

"Wellll, I'll tell you," Cy sighed, a philosophical sigh, a profound sigh. "After you grow up, who gives a good goddamn if you can hit a home run? See what I'm saying?"

"That's what I tell the kid," Leo said. "He feels bad he can't play like his old Dad, but look where the hell that got me." Ben saw his father waiting for a grin. It didn't come. His father picked at the dirt under his nails.

Deadpan, Uncle Cy stood up and picked at the things on his desk. Taking up a file, he began filing his nails. Imagine, underneath the rest of this conversation, the rasp of a file. "What's the matter, Leo? You saying you don't appreciate your job?"

"Sure, I appreciate my job, I like my job, I do a good job for you, Cy."

"Because if that wife of yours is dissatisfied, you just tell me and we can call it quits anytime, no hard feelings."

"She's got nothing to do with it. She doesn't say a goddamn thing. I wouldn't let her."

"You know," Cy said, "you're my brother, and I'd love to come over to the house more...."

"Cy, the boy here—"

"What's he—some little kid that he can't hear what's going on? You and I were out in the real world we were his age. We were supporting Mom and Dad."

"Exactly. That was another generation entirely."

"I'm not saying he shouldn't get an education. Who the hell's sending him through private school?"

"You are, Cy."

"I'm saying, let him know that his wonderful mother—who he should be loyal to, I'm not saying he shouldn't—can sometimes be one royal pain in the anatomy with her fantasies about what I owe you."

"You don't owe me a thing."

"Hey. Do you think I owe you, Leo?"

"You do okay by me. You're my brother."

"You bet I'm your brother. You think otherwise I'd put up with you?—only kidding, Ben. Your pop is some salesman, he's some manager, no kidding. But listen—you guys got here too late for lunch. I got to play golf with some hoity-toity sonofabitches. I hate to hurry you out of here. Leo, do me a favor, can you drive out to Great Neck and pick up a signed contract for me from old man Lipman?"

"Sure, but it's Sunday, Cy. I figured me and the boy—"

Cy didn't say anything. He put away his nail file, picked up his attaché case and got his golf clubs out of the closet. He checked his watch.

"Well," Ben's father said, "how about a little later on, maybe four, four-thirty? Ben and me can go out to LaGuardia on the way, watch the planes come in. Or—I c'd go over earlier—"

"You just bring me the contract early tonight so I can get started on it. Okay, Leo? You remember how to get to Lipman's?"

"Sure I do."

"Your father, Ben, is one loyal brother. I dragged him to New York from Chicago when I started this operation. If I hadn't, you know where you'd'a grown up? In some triple-decker in Chicago, the son of a shoe salesman. Hell, nothing wrong with that. But I knew I needed somebody I could trust. You get me?" And beaming, he put his arm around his older brother's shoulder. To Ben it looked as if his father—grinning, melting under Cy's touch—constricted physically. Shrank.

Then they were out the door, his father behind him, one hand on Ben's shoulder, patting.

"He knows he can rely on me for little things, Ben. So he can rely on me for the big ones. You get me?"

Cold as stone, Ben watched the gold arrow above the elevator fall.

"Ben? What's the matter? You angry because I said you just played 'okay'?"

Ben shook his head. All the way down in the elevator he didn't look at his father. In the lobby his father grabbed onto him. "Hey, in fact, in fact you're getting to be one sweet little ballplayer. Your fielding's a hundred times better than last year."

"So? You think I care? Somebody hits a round object with a wooden stick? You think I care?"

"What kind of crap are you talking?"

"Why does my uncle hate you so much? Why do you let him get away with that shit?"

"You watch your mouth. You been listening to your mother?"

Ben guffawed. He took off through the lobby. Leo followed. Ben thought about losing his father—split for Columbus circle and take the subway home. But why *now*, why was he so angry *now*? After all—the poor bastard! Ben felt lousy, heartless. Fishing down into himself he felt a nibble—something—what? Slowing, he let his father catch up.

"You gone crazy? Tell me. You gone nuts or something? My brother barks a little, I know how he can get on his high horse, what do you take him so seriously?"

"That phony!" Ben yelled at the corner of Sixth and fifty-fifth.

"Shh!" Leo took Ben by the elbow and spoke confidentially. "Sure. Phony is right. I'm glad you spotted that. You take for instance his pansy clothes. Yellow pants? Imagine wearing prissy clothes like that. That guy makes believe he's tough. Back in Chicago I had to protect him. He couldn't walk to school without his big brother. He was something of a candy-ass, your uncle. But the kids stayed clear. They knew—I hit 'em, they stay down. Right? Am I right?" He laughed and chucked Ben under the jaw.

"Well," Ben said, "*it's not that way now.*"

"What the hell you know about it?"

"Muscles. You've got big muscles. So what? You still got a lousy old car and you scrub and scrub till the paint's half off and your phony brother tells you what to do on a Sunday."

His father didn't get red in the face and yell. He held his lower lip in his fingers. It took him awhile to find his keys, and awhile for him to open the door. Leaning, he opened the passenger side.

They were silent all the way out to LaGuardia. Ben wished he could unsay it; still, he had a right! It was true! He felt the tingling of victory in the long war with his father. It wasn't until Leo Kagan put a dime in the turnstile to the spectator's deck and, as always, slipped Ben in for free on the same turn, not until they stood watching the big DC-8's and Constellations taking off in the vibrating air, that Ben saw what was *new*, saw why beneath everything, he felt so terrible:

Uncle Cy had done it as a piece of *theater*—for Ben. Ben was the intended audience for his uncle's power and his father's shame. That was new.

His uncle was saying, Look how leaky that vessel is. Well, it was tempting—to see his uncle fighting on his side against his cloddish tub of a father. Abandon ship.

But as the shining planes rose through their powerful guttural growl and whine, he felt himself sink, as if he, too, were leaky and his substance were seeping away through the cracks. Victorious, he felt diminished.

His father, leaning his bulk on the rail, was watching men in mechanics' zip-up suits load luggage from cart to the belly of a Constellation. Ben leaned down to watch with him, and his father, sensing he could say something, knowing that sooner or later he *had* to say something, pointed, "Look at that—they do one hell of a job, those guys."

"Like the tire changers down at work."

"Sure."

A plane touched down; they watched it glide away from them. "I want to say, I'm sorry, Dad. What I said before. It's no big deal you let him get away with stuff. It's just because…you're *loyal* to him. He's your brother," Ben said, dusting off the words his father used when Ben's mother snapped at him for "*letting that brother of yours walk all over you.*"

But today, looking not at Ben but at the planes, he opened his palms and said, "No, you're right. When you're right you're right. I let him get away with murder. He's no goddamn good, my brother. I wasn't so scared, I'd've walked out on him. But I got a family."

"What about this Jimmy MacMillan you could go work with?"

"Your mother's dreaming. Look, Ben, your mother's a goddamn wonderful woman. She's worth ten of my brother. Don't you think I know that? But Jimmy MacMillan, that was years ago. 1946. I'm no kid, Ben. Who wants a new man sixty-three years old? You get me?"

"Sure."

"You're a smart boy. You don't ever let him get his hands on you."

"Don't worry…. I'm sorry what I said. About muscles."

"S'okay. We'll play softball next Sunday, okay? I'll get you on my team. Hey—but you look at this old car," he said, patting the 1946 Chevy. "What's wrong for an old car?"

"Sure. You really keep it up."

"On the way to old man Lipman's, you want, we can stop for a soda."

But on the way to Lipman's house, Leo forgot the soda; he brooded. Getting back to the city, in heavy traffic on the Triborough, Leo hunched in a rage against the stupid drivers. By the time he got off at 96th and headed west, he was honking and cursing. And when the guy in the big Chrysler in front of him dawdled and cost them both the light, Leo held his hand down on the horn and his face got red.

Then the other driver did a dumb thing—he gave Leo an upraised middle finger. You didn't do that to Leo Kagan. He stepped out of his car, put his big body against the Chrysler and rocked the car, and when the driver, in gray suit and fedora, pushed down the lock, Leo pounded on the side window and the windshield, yelling, "You come out of there, I'm going to beat the living crap out of you!" Not an invitation any sane New Yorker was likely to accept. Ben had seen the same thing five, ten times, and never had anyone come out—nor even looked his father's way.

At the green light, the Chrysler took off, throwing Leo back a little. Cars behind started honking. Leo got in and chased the Chrysler up the block, but when it turned south on Park, he gave up the chase with a laugh. "I scared the jerk off." He sat back, cleared his throat, growled. "It's lucky for that guy he didn't start something."

Ben didn't say anything. His father stopped for cold cuts on the way home. A block from the house miraculously Leo found a space good for Monday, and he pulled in. Ben saw his new fielder's mitt on the back seat. Quick, he shoved it under the front seat; to disguise what he was doing, he collected the pails and brushes and sponges. His father, baseball clothes over his arm, wanted to get back to the *Journal American*, to Sunday cold cuts, to Walter Winchell and Jack Benny. Ben trudged after him up the street, staring at the shiny cloth on the seat of his pants.

Son of a shoe salesman, he thought. He'd always known his father had sold shoes, but something about the way his uncle put it made him think about shoes. How his father cared so much that Ben's shoes were tied just so. And until he was a big kid, maybe seven or eight, much too old, his father would grump, "Let me tie your shoes *right*," and Ben would have to sit on the edge of the bed and his father would bend a little and, sweating with the effort, take the boy's right shoe into his own crotch and tie it firmly; and then the left, tie it firmly. It was an expression of tenderness and professional competence.

He wished his father had stayed in Chicago. What was so wrong with being a shoe salesman?

It was his father who traditionally bought and laid out the cold cuts on a Sunday evening. "Look at that roast beef," he'd sing out as he slapped the meat onto the blue willow platter and spread out the slices to look more impressive. "Is that some roast beef? Fit for a king. At least one time a week I get the kind of rye bread I can eat."

Not tonight. Tonight, he was quiet. He left the waxed paper under the meats and made no claims.

At dinner, Ben's mother, chain smoking, looking ravaged for a Sunday spent with the papers, asked him, "Well? How did it go with your big shot brother? Did he serve you a nice lunch? I suppose he asked graciously about me?"

"Never mind about my brother. He's my problem."

"Oh, no, my dear. He's very much *my* problem, don't you think? That man—why, he isn't fit to kiss my foot." And then her uplifted chin—a breakwater against the indignities of living a mediocre life, of being forced to keep track of every dollar—fell to her chest. She looked as if she were praying; Ben knew she was wrapping herself in her griefs.

"Listen, you—" Leo growled—"He knows what you are, my brother. All you're interested in are the material things you can't have."

Even at fifteen, Ben knew these were not Leo's own words. Fifty years later, Ben knows, too, how *inaccurate* those words were. What his mother hungered for wasn't really material at all.

Fed up, this night in 1955, with her life, she ground out her cigarette in the food he'd provided and she couldn't eat. She sat nodding, nodding, nodding, like a crazy person. "Say, I'll tell you what," she said hoarsely. "Why don't you and your brother cut me up and eat me? No, really. 'Rahlly,' as Bette Davis says. Then he can cut your salary."

Ben knew the next line—*You're so goddamn jealous.* Something like that. But his father didn't say it. His face didn't get hot and red, he didn't yell. Instead, he cleared his throat, as if a truck engine were revving up, cleared his throat and stood, heavily, brushing the crumbs off his shirt front, as if he were about to make an after-dinner speech. A big man filling the kitchen.

They sat there and looked at him. Now, a little as if he were on stage, Leo walked into the livingroom and picked up the phone. Usually, from anywhere in the house you could hear everything Leo Kagan said on the phone. Not tonight. Tonight the words were quiet. Then Leo came back and said nothing and sat down.

"Well, my dear," Ben's mother said, "well my dear, and did you tell your brother how terrible I am?"

"You?" he said quietly. "It had nothing to do with you. I told him I couldn't get out tonight. I said to him, 'Cy, I got you your contract. You want to look it over, you're gonna have to stop by.'"

"You *said* that?" Ben asked.

And now, fifty years later, Ben holds his breath remembering, though at the time he didn't know that he knew how extraordinary it was, that moment of quiet in the kitchen.

"Sure, that's what I told him. Cy said, *Okay bring it to work in the morning.* He wasn't too happy."

"Dad. You told him *that*?"

Leo snapped—"Yeah. What's the big deal, Ben? I'm *tired.* I played hard today. Did you tell your mother about the game I played? Anyway, this is none of your business."

With the Yiddish intonations that indicated she was offering communal truth, truth of all mothers, she asked, "So why can't you be decent to your only son?"

That did it. The quiet in the kitchen was over. "I don't want another goddamn word out of you," Leo yelled at her. He shoved away his plate. He cracked his finger joints and stood, big-boned man ready for the usual fight.

Ben shoved meat between two slices of rye and took the plate back to his room. A magazine reproduction of *Starry Night* had come lose from the wall at one corner; he pressed the tape. The walls needed painting. Maybe he could cover them with movie posters? He put on his radio, the classical station he'd begun to listen to, and played it loud enough to blur the voices, not quite loud enough to make his father bang on the door and crack the paint some more.

She'd left his laundry, folded, on the bed. She'd sewn his pants with fine stitches that couldn't have mattered less to him. But he ran his fingers over her work. Voices! He turned up the music.

The voices, they seeped in. He lay on his bed and took up a history book, but the words wouldn't stay together. The room was carrying him through space—dizzying!—this rickety boat he'd nailed and glued. It was all he had; it could carry him only so far. He chewed his sandwich of meat and grief; with the clenching of the muscles of his jaw, his will coalesced and knotted. Outside, waves of anguish—door slammings, shouts, guttural threats—smashed at the leaky walls.

Time Exposure

Now, half a century later, he's been thinking what it must have cost her, her transformation from little Jewish girl in Kishnieff in the early years of the century to a modern American woman—a career woman in New York—and then to fade, like a shooting star burning out, into marriage with "your poor fool of a father."

The staircase to his study is lined on both walls with family photographs. One side of the family on each side of the stairs—his father's side, his mother's. Facing each other now: his father in shirt sleeves, an idealistic-looking boy; and his younger brother with tough, cynical grin—against a brick wall in Chicago—and with them their father in short hair and moustache, dapper little man, his hands on the shoulders of his sons. And across the stairway, Ben's mother, black hair in ringlets, older brothers and sisters surrounding her, she the youngest, the pet. Her father, in skullcap, with heavy beard and intense, wise eyes. Her mother looks thick like a peasant; hard work shows on her face even in this studio portrait. His father's family looks American; his mother's, like immigrant Jews. Black coats, heavy silk dresses. For his mother to turn herself into a bright, gay woman of the late twenties, a successful fashion buyer, must have been like skipping a century. To love and marry and relapse into her mother's role must have been a relief as well as a failure.

Now he understands; it's like replaying a dialogue secretly taped and then replayed, and this time you *get* it: the way she'd hear swing music on the old Victrola radio, mahogany case like a miniature gothic church, and dance in circles on the kitchen linoleum, flirting with an elegant, invisible partner, singing in her throaty cigarette voice and smiling a public smile. "You think your mother is old fashioned, don't you? You don't think I'm a modern woman?"

Her only audience, Ben waited—amused, critical, understanding the pretenses but not the need for those pretenses.

"God grant me long life as true as I'm standing here I was in Flo Ziegfield's apartment—some apartment, let me tell you—over the theater, and he said to me, 'Myra, you're something special. You know what's going on. Where did your family come from?'

"'From Russia, Mr. Ziegfield,' I told him. 'I was born in Kishnieff.' Well, the whole world knew Kishnieff because of the terrible pogrom. Before I was born.

"'No!' he said. I said, 'Yes, Mr. Ziegfield. From Russia. I came to America when I was five.' 'My God,' he said, 'and you are every bit an American girl.'"

This was like getting a PhD in American Girliana. Did Ziegfield really say that? It doesn't matter; it's her imagination of herself that matters.

"'Myra,' Flo Ziegfield said to me, 'if you ever want to come to work for me'—he meant in the Follies—'you just come to see me.' Of course, he was joking—would your mother ever do such a thing? But I charmed him. *Well*? You don't think so?"

She waited for her son to dare laugh at her.

"What? You don't think your mother used to be beautiful? You think I was always a *hausfrau* and a frump?" She'd find a couple of quarters in the pocket of her house dress (tips for the delivery boys) and place one between her knees, one between her calves. "You see? This is how Ziegfield made his girls stand. To test their legs, *ferstaste*?"

Once, she sighed, once she sailed first class on the *France* to France and ate at the Captain's table. A Rothschild fell in love with her. And now look—look how she'd come down in the world. "Your poor father. A slave to his brother. But a better man God never made. He can't help being what he is. I can't help being what I am. I fell in love. Do me something—your mother fell in love."

And so now, because of love, they lived in Jackson Heights, Long Island—in a dismal, red-brick apartment building on a street of red-brick apartment buildings. The wrong side of the East River, Manhattan a short but shameful ride away.

"He means well, the poor fool. Can he help being what he is?"

"And now!" she'd sing out. "*Voila*! Isn't your mother a stunning woman?" Hands lifted: a statue. Her one good black linen outfit, a blue silk scarf at her throat.

"It's true, Ben," his father would roar. "She's a goddamn stunning woman and look what a bum she married."

He called in reservations at the Sea Fare in the name of "Judge Kagan." They drove the 1940 Pontiac, obsessively polished, into Manhattan over the Queensboro Bridge. From the bridge, the downtown lights flashed like jewels his mother wasn't wearing.

He was an actor, not a patron, at the Sea Fare: Leo Kagan as "Judge" Kagan. Ben was fearful lest the headwaiter unmask him—"You, a judge? Don't you know it's against the law to impersonate a judge?" But no, it was always, "Follow me. Please, Judge." The judge winked his way.

Five times at least during the meal his father computed, recomputed, the waiter's tip. "We're getting pretty decent service, right, Ben?" Or else, he'd flash the fancy racetrack watch his uncle Cy gave him for his birthday. "You see how slow he is with the bread and butter? I can predict what kind of tip that schmuck is going to wind up with."

And, cupping his hand so his mother could pretend not to hear, he'd whisper, "I wouldn't give that schmuck the sweat off my balls."

Partly, it was spending the money; partly, it was having to

be on his best behavior in front of his wife. But always, on the way home, things fell apart. Some driver would pass him or squeeze him over. Leo Kagan would pull alongside and yell out the window, "Who gave you a goddamned license? You faggot! You ought to have your head examined."

Now his wife would refuse to recognize his existence, and that would drive him wild. He'd thump the dash, explain and explain, "That sonofabitch—did you see him cut me off?"

She'd sigh, in her cultured, near-British voice, "Well, and *isn't* it nice weather, Ben? D'you think it's likely to rain tomorrow?"

Louder, louder, he'd explain. Finally, "Goddamned woman! Goddamn you!" It was a war. Only now Ben understands: In this roundabout way he played out the drama of his own worthlessness. He needed to goad her into despising him—so that then he could hate her for despising him and not have to hate himself so much? Wasn't that it? And she used *him* to excuse her retreat from complicated modern America. So that both of them could be justified in how they imagined their lives.

Next morning, she'd be her most charming, regal self, telling stories.

"You think I'm your ordinary housewife?" she'd say over breakfast. "Listen: when you were born, Old Man Bonwit, God rest his soul, called me up to see him. I'd been away from the business for three, four years. Well. I dressed in my smartest suit—you'll laugh, darling, there was a moth hole in the collar; I wore a brooch to hide it, and I took a cab down to Bonwit's. When I came in, his secretary announced me, and I could hear his voice over the intercom, 'Myra Bresloff? Send her in, send her in.' Well. So I went in, he stood up from his desk and took both my hands. 'Myra Bresloff. Myra Bresloff.' I can see him to this day. A little man growing bald—but *smart.* 'I'm Myra Kagan now, Mr. Bonwit,' I told him. 'Myra, you can name your price.' 'How sweet you are,' I told Old Man Bonwit, 'but I have a little boy, my dear, and I believe a woman belongs with her family.' 'Is there nothing I can do to change your mind?' 'If anyone could, you could,' I told him. 'But my *family.*' 'And I admire that, Myra. Every woman should take lessons from you.' So—that was that, you understand. *You* came first. But when I got home that afternoon, there was a bouquet of flowers waiting. *That* was a big man. Well—so you came first. You see? Now, what kind of mother do you have?"

"A bitter mother."

"Nonsense. Bitter? I'm a happy wife and mother."

When she was just twenty-three, twenty-four, Old Man Bonwit sent her to Paris for the first time; then he sent her every spring to preview the fall lines. She stayed at the *Georges Cinq*. Rich men danced with her; coming back to the hotel, she would find a dozen roses and no card and not know which of a half-dozen men to thank. But she married "your poor father" and expected he'd be rich someday. Only it turned out—"funny how things turn out"—he was just a slave to his younger brother. "An unsung hero," she'd praise him when she wasn't feeling bitter. "That *grubyom,* that peasant!" she'd snap when she was. "My poor father wouldn't sleep in his grave. Did you know he brought me up like a son? To read Hebrew, to say the prayers. He had a great, long beard—well, in those days, you understand. He held me on his lap, I can see him as clearly as I can see you, and he loved me; oh, how he loved me. Well. I was his youngest, he was an old man by the time I was born. May his soul rest in peace, he was some man. In Russia, he owned land, he kept lambs. In Russia. A Jew couldn't own land, but my father had special rights. The Jews in the town, even the Gentiles, they worshiped him. Anytime there was a problem, a husband and wife, two men squabble over a cow, they came to my father. He was like a judge. So. You see where your roots are. He didn't come to this country in steerage."

And a Yiddish lilt crept into her voice, and her eyes grew soft as they saw the past, as if the past were in soft focus, as in a romantic film from the thirties.

She crushed out her cigarette. "And now, look at me. To live in Jackson Lice, Long Island. My father would turn over in his grave."

They'd wooed her together, a team, Ben's father and his Uncle Cy. It was Leo Kagan she fell in love with, but it was Cy Kagan who'd made the money, who convinced my mother she was marrying into a "family of Somebodies." She didn't understand that Leo was nothing but Cy's frightened servant. And so she gave up her career.

Frightened servant: how much that leaves out. Trying to tote it all up now, half a century later, he knows his father was more than that: a powerful man, a tender man when he wasn't frightened, a man well loved by the taxi drivers, the fleet owners, the cops, the tire changers he worked with every day. But he couldn't stand up for himself, and when his own father became sick, Cy sent him to California—again and again—to nurse the old man. Leo didn't know how to refuse.

And maybe he didn't *want* to. Did he flee from her, using his brother's orders as an excuse? He stayed in California four months, then a year later for nine months, again, six months. Without Leo around to curse for her lot in life, she grew more inward and strange, saw no one, surrendered. Ben was her "reason for living." At night she prowled the house, smoking. He would wake to find her standing in the doorway, watching him sleep.

Last month Ben found this letter among her papers. Not a carbon. His father must have brought it back with him from California. *If* she ever sent it.

> June 10, 1949
> Dearest Leo,
>
> Your Thursday letter came today. With the snapshots. Your face looks good, and you don't look too heavy. But your pants need pressing, and don't they wear ties in California?
>
> Please, Leo, don't say to me, "please be sweet." I have been sweet too long. It is now into the sixth month since you went away. That's nice, isn't it? I don't say you went there out of choice, but after all, you are not a dummy, and if you are a human being, you could have said the second month you were there, "I am going home to my wife and child." Well, you are as you are, and I will never change you, Leo.

> Enclosed you will find a short letter from Ben. Why he loves you is more than I can say. He is deserving of a devoted father not a dummy who is shoved around by his brother.
>
> I will have to pay Hoover $14.65 for repair Thursday. Remember, Leo, I have been a good wife, and a girl a man doesn't have to be ashamed of. And I have given you all my love, Leo dear. But your staying away has disgusted me beyond repair.
>
> Love,
> Myra

When it grew too terrible for her—and by the time Ben was eight it grew too terrible nearly every day—she would stagger to her late afternoon, bitter nap, seasick grope to bed, holding herself straight by fingering the walls. She slept, then, and woke transformed—back centuries, an ancient Jewish crone. If Leo Kagan was away in California, she stood in the doorway to Ben's room and mumbled curses in Yiddish.

"Mom? What is it?"

She nodded her head rhythmically as if to offer assent, an audience of one, to her own propositions of suffering. She thumped her breast and rocked. Ben wanted him to come home and do something with her, for her. "As God is my judge," she'd say. "You see what my life is?" she'd say—but then she was past rational saying. *Mein lieb ist schwartz,* black is my life, black is my blood, *schwartz, schwartz,* my life is black, my blood is black," Yiddish, English, as she rocked. Until she could raise the pitch of pain enough to thump her breast through her nightgown, score bloody claw tracks deep in the skin of her arm, always nails of her left hand into skin of her right arm, and blood would lift in the old places to the surface of her skin.

But it was Ben's father she needed.

When he was back from California, often she'd still be asleep when he came home at night, her late afternoon, early evening stupor.

He'd come home and scrub the walls she'd stained with her fingers, or he'd sit at his desk, back turned. There he was, paying a pile of bills, the whole weight of his enormous back and shoulders protesting what she was costing him. She'd wake. She'd stand behind him, holding onto the doorjamb, rocking.

"Sonofabitch, you sonofabitch, oh, you sonofabitch. A Man, some man I married," and Leo's neck thickened and he went down deeper into himself, all that flesh and muscle thickened, hunched against her words.

Until—"GODDAMN you!"—he'd jerk to his feet, maybe knocking over the red velvet bench and making the floor lamp wobble, and that chaos would let him release his rage and he'd bellow, his face flaming, "I've had plenty from you!"

Now she'd have her claws out, pawing the air before her eyes, and the wild old *shtetl* crone look on her face, lower lip folded down, teeth bared. "Come on, you!" she'd hiss, old Russian Jew Medusa; and, clumsy bear, he'd come at her, she'd scratch out, he'd grab and slap, push her towards the bedroom and sometimes she'd let him, sometimes she'd moan and go down, crumple to the carpet, tragedy-queen poisoned, eyes rolled back—too slow and too graceful to be completely real.

"Your mother's a crazy woman—I hardly touched her. Get water, Ben."

Or say he yelled at her and didn't touch her, just yelled in his amazing Army Sergeant voice Ben blocked out with fingers in his ears—then she would forget her original curses, would rush from window to window, shutting, shutting, "so the neighbors shouldn't hear," and so he'd bellow louder, he'd open the goddamn windows after her and *really* yell.

"And *you*! You goddamned mama's boy, you, you spoiled little mama's boy, you're the cause of half the goddamned fights in this house. Money! You think I'm made of money?"—because most of the fights began over money, day after day of one continuous battle about buying and not buying. Battle over his inadequacy to justify her life, her renunciation of the amazing career she'd built for herself, justify becoming a Good Jewish Wife.

Now, when he turned on Ben, she'd stop cursing, smile all of a sudden—"*I'll* tell you what!—" as if she'd just had *such* a clever and amusing idea, smile politely, and rush to the oven, turn on the gas without lighting it and, crawling on her knees, stick her head inside. Then Ben's father would yank her away, shut off the stove, open the window and wave a dishrag. "You want to blow us all up, you crazy woman?" Or else she'd run to the bathroom and pull open the door to the medicine cabinet, stand deciding which bottle would do the job on her. He'd grab her away. And she'd weep. And he'd lead her, gently, lovingly, to the bedroom, rubbing and patting her bent back, and put her to bed.

When Ben was bar mitzvahed, the fights intensified—she wanted a catered affair at the Pierre. This was, of course, impossible. Half a year's salary. More. Leo put his foot down—if there had to be a bar mitzvah, let it be a simple party upstairs in the social hall of the damned synagogue. She had to settle for that, but it led to the one time she did more than weep or curse or threaten.

She left him.

First, the usual shouting, then theatrical laughter. "I'll tell you what!" Another gesture of suicide? But no—she rushed, hands in front of her as if through a fog, into the bedroom. He went back to his *Journal American*, unfolding it with a furious shake. Half an hour later, snazzy in her one good black dress and old Persian lamb coat, suitcase in hand, she came into Ben's room. "Ben, dearest—I'll call you when I'm settled."

"What are you talking about?"

"You see how it is, my dear."

"Mom! Really?"

"Tell that man goodbye."

That man stood in the doorway, arms folded over his chest. "What the hell d'you think you're doing?"

"Nice weather, isn't it? I'll call you when I'm settled."

"You can go to hell for all I care."

"Sweet," she said. Taking up her suitcase, she walked out the front door.

"She'll be back," he said. "Where's she gonna find a cab at this hour?"

"I'll follow her."

"You will not follow her. She'll be back in five minutes if you don't make a big fuss. Crazy person. Where's she gonna go?"

He went back to his paper. Ben listened for the elevator but hoped he wouldn't hear it. He felt giddy with this gesture, its possibilities.

"What's she doing, goddamn woman," he said after a few minutes. "Walking the streets!" He folded his glasses neatly into their case, put on his coat and trudged out—stay put in case she calls. She's probably—you know where?—standing right downstairs."

But he didn't come back—half an hour he didn't come back. Then the telephone rang.

"Hello, my darling son."

"Where *are* you?"

"Is he there?"

"He's out looking for you."

"The poor fool. I'm registered at the Plaza."

"The Plaza? The Plaza on 59th?"

"There's only one Plaza, my dear."

"Well, what are you doing at the Plaza?"

"I'm not quite sure," she said after a moment. "Perhaps I'm teaching him a lesson."

"Maybe," Ben said, "you ought to stay away for awhile. Maybe—Mom?—you ought to get back into business? Mom? Why not get back into business, call Mr. Bonwit. Why not?"

"You think I couldn't?"

"I didn't say you couldn't. Maybe you'd be better off is what I said. Maybe you'd be much better off, Mom."

"What would your poor father do without me?"

Ben listened to the hiss of the wires. He listened to his mother breathing. Neither of them spoke for a long time. "Mom? You want him to call you?"

"Let him worry," she said. "But tomorrow, if *you* wish to visit your mother…"

How could he keep it a secret? She must have known, he thinks now, fifty years after that night. After they hung up, he left a note for his father and went downstairs after him. But he was nowhere—not the drugstore on the corner, the subway station. He must be out hunting her in the car.

A taxi swung around the corner. If it happened along, he would have gone back home to wait, but, without thinking, he flagged it down. "To the Plaza Hotel," he said, and felt in the name the magic she felt.

As they crossed the East River, he ignored the lights of the city, kept his eye on the meter and fingered the loose bills and change—pay and tips from delivering for the drug store. It was just fifteen minutes to the hotel, grand chateau with its green mansard roof lit up, and inside, mirrors and candelabra brilliant after the dark ride.

"Mrs. Kagan?" I asked at the desk. "She's my mother—she just registered."

There was no Mrs. Kagan. Panic caved him in, what was he doing at the Plaza Hotel in the middle of the night? Didn't he know better than to believe her? But then he asked, "What about Bresloff? Myra Bresloff?"

The desk clerk nodded, finger over some list. "Miss Bresloff? Room 414."

"In case anybody calls," Ben said, "it's the same person. Miss Bresloff, Mrs. Kagan. Bresloff is her business name. It's the same person."

Her room faced the park—nothing but the best. She was still in her black dress. "Well, isn't this a surprise." Ben looked around. The windows looked out on the lamps of Central Park. Dirty windows and paint peeling from the corner moldings and the carpets were sad, for the Plaza hadn't yet been restored.

"It's come down in the world," she said. "But it's a little bit of all right. It's still the Plaza." She looked her son over. "Couldn't you dress up a little? That old shirt of yours—"

"Who *cares*? Mom, what are you doing? Are you really leaving him?"

"Don't I deserve a vacation?"

"You deserve. Oh, *sure* you deserve…" Taking in everything, he noticed her beautiful suitcase from the old days, with its brass fittings and fine linen sides covered by pale fleur-de-lis. It sat on a luggage rack for the maid to admire.

"That's some workmanship, isn't it?" she said. "You see the workmanship? You should have heard me *hondel* with the salesman. This was many years ago of course. When do I go anywhere these days?" she sighed. "This is for your wife someday, after I'm gone."

She watched him looking at the high filigree ceiling.

"Long before you were born—this is as true as I'm standing here—I was at a party for Al Jolson at the Plaza. Naturally, it was the finest suite in the hotel. Everybody in New York was there—"

"*That*," Ben said, "must have been some suite."

"Smart. Jolson and I talked about family. At heart what was he, after all, but a good, simple, Jewish boy?"

The telephone. My father. She listened.

"*No*, my dear," she said finally. "I'm not *coming* home." Hanging up on him, she turned to me. "He won't let me alone. Well, naturally…. Would you like anything from Room Service?"

"Where did you get the money?" Ben asked.

"Well, and shouldn't a woman keep a little money in her own name?"

"I'm not *blaming* you, Mom." Ben stared out at the lights of cars cruising the perimeter road in Central Park.

"If you were a little older, I could tell you a few things."

A light tap at the door. Suddenly, Ben understood: his call must have come not from home but from downstairs. And she must have known this already, but she went to the door as if curious.

"Myra."

"Hmmm," she said, hand on her hip. "You've had enough?"

"Listen, you've been crazy enough for one night. Would you get your bag?"

"My dear—"

"Oh, don't give me that phony voice, Myra. For godsakes."

"Isn't he elegant, Ben?" And then, all of a sudden, like turning off an electric light, her face dissolved, the gracious lady dissolved, she grimaced as if pain had caught her heart, as if she were choking, and she shook her head. "Yah. Yah. Yah. Nice. Elegant. You think this is a joke? It's no joke. My life isn't a joke. Understand?"

She sank into a big armchair, and he, not asking nor being prevented, collected her things and snapped the fancy suitcase shut. Then, not speaking to her, he lifted her, unresisting, half limp, from the chair. "Come on. We're going home. Ben, take her coat."

They hardly talked on the way. Home, still she didn't talk. Except to moan, "This is some life. Look at this life. Jackson Lice." And he said, "Leave us alone for awhile, will you, Ben?" From the closed bedroom there was no shouting—just thick, guttural whispers.

Ben tried finishing his homework, but as his eyes read, his ears listened. Whispers answering whispers. "Then we can move," he heard his father say aloud. Then whispers. Waiting for it to be over, Ben brewed a cup of tea and sat in the kitchen, remains of a pot roast still in the platter, cold grease caked around the brown meat. Then weeping. He drank his tea. When the door opened and footsteps came and went, he stood at the end of the hall and looked into the bedroom. She was sitting beside him, rubbing his back, and *he* was the one crying, his big father crying, and she was saying, "You are what you are, my dear." Then, to Ben—"You know how I love your father."

This love, that seemed to take away her life. Ben never understood this love, as years later, when he was himself married, he couldn't understand her telephone call.

"My *son*?"

It was the vibrato in her voice that let him know his father was dead. "It's Dad?"

"One hour ago. A heart attack—you know what his heart was like. I had to collect myself to call you. 'Myra,' he said to me as if he had a joke to tell. Then he took a step towards me and he fell like a tree. Like a tree. Poor soul. Poor simple soul."

"I'm very sorry, Mom."

"God grants some special people very gentle deaths. He was dead, your father, before he touched the floor, so he wouldn't feel the hurt from the fall. I turned him onto his back myself—he was light as a feather. You know the weight he lost. So. So. So. It's done. It's finished. *Fertig*. A life. You understand me? No. How can you? That man—he was as good as gold to me."

"Good to you?"

"A better man God never made."

"Mom. I'll be down in the morning. You'll be all right tonight?"

"Listen, my dear—you have a decent suit?"

The photographs on Ben's staircase walls were culled out of the boxes his mother left when she died. Whatever happened to her suitcase with the fleur-de-lis? Was it stolen along with the blue willow? At least there were these photographs going back, back through the forties, the thirties, the twenties, the War, to Russia. His father, born in Odessa, Ukraine, then Russia, 1894; his mother in Kishnieff, Bessarabia, then Russia, 1904. His mother, his father, coming so far from Russia to marry in New York, coming all that way as if God had laid out a plan, a mystical conjunction, so that they could live with one another in love and misery.

Highest up the stairs is a photo of his mother in the late twenties, her own mid-twenties, another world, before she married. Fur wrap over wool suit, she stands on a deck of a ship—porthole, brass fittings, polished wood—with a friend, "*with the wonderful actress Joyce Bancroft*" written floridly at the bottom of the photograph. Both of them hamming it up for the camera. Playing elegant. He remembers the posture. So young they seem. He could be their father. He could offer her advice. Knowing that in just a few years she will meet the man on the other side of the stairs, that good looking, overweight man posing with baseball bat as if waiting for a pitch, grinning with all his powerful good nature for the camera. A man with drinking buddies. Scared of women. Loyal to his parents. Scared of taking chances. He will do well enough early through his charm, then pale, fade, work in fear and loyalty and trust for his brother, love a woman who was too much for him, too complicated, too smart, too full of the need to be grand, love a woman he had nothing in common with *except* love, then retire to grumpiness and heart attack.

But there he is, pretending confidence, waiting for the pitch, and across the stairs, she has her eye on him.

Originally appeared in Tri-Quarterly, *Spring, 1985*

Open-Heart Surgery

On the operating table, as the cocktail of anesthetics took effect, Ned Koenig felt paralyzed before he was unconscious. He was not breathing but being breathed. He wasn't really *there* anymore—a machine functioned in his place, and he was attached to this machine, *being lived*.

This wasn't a totally unfamiliar experience.

His heart must have known the pain of having to live another day and another, year after year of having to perform for others—for *an* other, who was himself—until one day, it balked like a horse at its thousandth jump. Flying back to Boston from L.A. , he grew weak, then dizzy, and lugging his overnight bag to a taxi wondered was it down his arm, was it in his chest, those pains? He was sweating in the tunnel, maybe from embarrassment that he was going to have to ask the driver to take him to Emergency at Mass General.

Leaning into the car to take his change, he must have passed out, for he found himself splayed on the sidewalk with money in his hand and the driver (shouting, shrill, frantic, in Hindi or Persian) hurrying out of the cab. But he rested a moment and was up, attaché case in hand, followed by the cabdriver with his suitcase. He didn't let himself crumple until he'd reached the desk and gotten his Blue Cross card out of his wallet.

This was characteristic of Koenig. It was his greatest satisfaction, to complete a project. He was a well-respected consultant in direct mail and telemarketing, highly paid—so outlandishly paid that his income surpassed that of most of the CEOs he dealt with. He *got the work done*—that's what mattered to him. It disturbed him to talk to people whose deepest satisfaction lay in exhibiting themselves, in getting petted, in telling you how powerful they were, in scoring, in shining. Koenig was interested in the work, that six-in-the-morning he could be up with coffee in front of his terminal, captain of the ship—with Margaret (if she happened to be home, for they both traveled) still asleep, the dog asleep, a Haydn trio coming in over his headphones—creating the shape of the program that might turn around sales for another company:

- Methodically dividing the problem into its parts as company thinking conceived it;
- Making an imaginative leap that bypassed the original blockage, the stuck-place, because if there was a solution (and sometimes there was none except to dissolve the company), there was always something stuck in the company's thinking.

Once he found the stuck-place, he could feel his own thinking open itself to light and his words be moved by that light into the shape of the report. He'd wait until they had accepted the report, and then he'd fly back to Dallas or Atlanta or Los Angeles to show them how to implement the plan of action.

His body, after the attack, he saw as a company in trouble. This time, he was the one who had to call in a consultant.

Acute myocardial infarction. He rested a week; the company could function again. But the consultants made it clear: he would need a double coronary bypass.

Koenig was sensible, always. Facing a problem, he grew calm. If you needed a team to blow up a bridge, you'd want Koenig. It was a trick, his calm strength, a trick of deliberate detachment, deliberate slowing down. He knew he had none of the inner strength he was given credit for. What was inner strength? He'd learned at least that no one could know what was really going on inside; all he had to do was to speak carefully, to smile an assured smile, and other people entered his calm and felt it as strength and took strength from it. That, he supposed, was strength enough.

And so, he let himself be scheduled for surgery. Wanting to avoid what they called "complications," he had his own blood drawn for autologous donation; let his wife, Margaret, take care of things or, when she had to be away, hire someone to take care of things. He limited his hours at the computer and on the phone; until surgery, he let his equipment rest.

Then he gave it into the hands of professionals, and they wheeled it down corridors, while Koenig watched the ceiling turn at right angles and wondered if he might be about to die. He was only in his late fifties—the percentages were with him—but just in case, his papers were in order, a checklist drawn up on his desk. His son and daughter from his first marriage were grown up, Pete, Lisa; his will provided for them and provided for Margaret, though none of them really needed provision.

The tranquilizer was taking over, and it was nice to let his body go, not to make it get on planes and get off planes, not to chastize it for soreness or flu when he needed it working well if the job was going to get done. He felt a little giddy with relief from all that. Separation from the machine was familiar enough, but this time he could—he had no choice—not *make* it go but let it go its own way. And then the slow workings of the anesthetic, and then the complete loss of his responsibility for the distant body, and then the surge of his own breath, his own heart thumping in his ears, and pain, pain, just under the medication.

After all, they'd split him in half like a broiler, sawed through his ribs and come inside. They'd removed a vein from his thigh, and from beneath his nipple plucked that strange female anomaly in a man, his internal mammary artery, and had somehow spliced them both in, in place of the occluded passages. It was amazing to him that a day later they had him out of bed and walking a little. In just over a week he was home and the children could fly back to their lives and Margaret fly off to a business meeting, though she was home the next day to take walks with him around the yard, then down the street and back.

"I think you enjoy me helpless," he kidded her.

"When else do I have a chance to take care of you?"

It was a good second marriage. She chose him, he suspected, partly because he let her rest from her competence. Sometimes she liked—this intense woman of business—to pretend to be frail and frivolous and let him be the *doer*. Now, he rested, and she *did*.

It was in his music he found the first strangeness.

Leaning back on his pillows, skimming the *Globe*, only half listening to whatever cassette he'd inserted in the Walkman, he realized that he was suffused with the music, that he was taking it in through his heart, as if it were an organ of perception instead of a muscle. This wasn't his metaphorical heart but something at his chest that was taking the music inside and diffusing it through his body in waves of—not exactly color, but something very like. Even becoming conscious didn't stop the process, though it did stop the instant he tried to hear the music, a quartet by Brahms. To hear the old way: *through his ears*. Then he wanted to hear in the new way and for a moment panicked—he'd forgotten *how*! But oh, there it was again, absorbed into his chest and vibrating. The sound, of course, entered his ears still, but the *music* came in at the chest. His whole body was weak with music, like after making love.

When he listened, turning his eyes up to hear better, it dissolved; there was in fact new clarity of attention when he listened with his ears, but not—as when he dropped his eyes and opened his chest—this music at the heart that was making his face wet with tears. *The medications*, he thought, but there was only a painkiller at night, and when he felt the need, a low dose of tranquilizer, nothing he hadn't taken before. In mind's eye he opened his chest as if the ribs, having been split open, knew the way now to peel themselves back, and let the music in.

Fearing to lose it, he didn't tell Margaret. Evenings, he sat with her while she worked on a report, and he listened. It was like having in the music a secret lover. But at the same time, it brought him closer to her.

He'd met Margaret through music, was charmed by her first because of the way she looked playing violin in a string quartet, serious amateur group she still played with, though less and less as each of the players grew more successful, more immersed in their careers. His early weekends with Margaret were built around concerts; the summer they married, they took a place near Marlboro, Vermont during the chamber music festival. And still, once in a while, they went to concerts together. But most of the time, now, they kept each to themselves, he working in his study, she in hers. Fewer evenings, now, they sat with sherry and listened together in their livingroom.

It was a high-ceilinged room, warm, with ornate moldings and built-in bookcases (but who had time to read?), a soft taupe wall-to-wall carpet and lush fabrics, afghans and cashmere throws draped over the velvet arms of sofa and chairs and antimacassars. Margaret filled it with flowers that wilted when they were away. The room made his son, Pete, laugh—it was so Viennese, so, well, *uncool.* Koenig didn't care. And they weren't ashamed to have it full of photos. Margaret was kind to his photos from before they met. He was kind to her old books. He and Margaret would tell each other over the phone (he in San Diego, she in Denver) *We really ought to spend more time in the living room together just listening.*

They made it a point. Last year, her fiftieth birthday, he'd given her a fine violin from the early nineteenth century, a Gabriel Lennbock, and she'd cried and held it to her breast like a living creature—though rarely did she have time to practice. But when they sat together in the evening, she'd take it out and play an old piece for him, something she'd worked up for a recital thirty-five years ago. He wondered whether she always heard as he was hearing now, with her heart. He was embarrassed to ask.

So it wasn't that he had never loved music—for he had, always.

But now he went back to his CDS and cassettes with his mouth open and jolts of anxiety at his diaphragm in anticipation of what would happen to him as the old music entered his new organ.

Nothing to worry about, certainly nothing to talk to Dr. Cogswell about. Still, he wondered: was it just the new lease on life and all this untoward rest—or was it some peculiarity of the operation? He imagined someone deaf to all but middle frequencies his entire life who then had an operation changing that—to hear so much, to hear music fully, must be dizzying. *This* was dizzying.

He was back at work, first at home, soon at a company in New Hampshire—he could drive up and back. And then one morning, after less than two months, he was flying to Los Angeles again. He could have found a direct flight but wanted a stopover at O'Hare to see his son.

These past few years, it was mostly at airports that he saw Pete (Chicago) and Lisa (San Francisco). Five, six times a year, Koenig, a little ragged, but cheerful, waving, came into the peculiar combination of fluorescence and sunlight of an airport waiting room, and he and Pete ceremonially hugged and patted, or he and Lisa hugged and didn't pat, and Pete took up his overnight bag or Lisa his attaché case, and they walked to the airline club for lunch or a drink. It was just enough time to catch up and not enough for silences to brew. They showed each other photos, they recited successes. Pete was doing corporate law, Lisa was assistant curator at a museum and finishing a doctorate in art history at Berkeley. She was engaged, Pete was "seeing people." Koenig was pleased with both his children. He loved them, would have died for them. But as the years passed, he knew them less and less; maybe he knew his tennis partners better. It was sad, it was what happened to parents and children. Yet they flew to be with him for his surgery. And after, embracing him clumsily, they were haggard, they had cried. Their outpouring of plans and memories seemed foreign to him.

Maybe it was that. Still, he hadn't anticipated this meeting, not even as he waved to Pete at O'Hare. This time, Koenig wasn't smiling as he came up the dark tube into the airport waiting room. He was frightened and didn't know whether he ought to tell Pete, *Something happened in the plane to me…*

In the plane:

It might have been the five milligrams of Valium or anxiety about getting back to his life. But he suspected it was something that went wrong in the operation, a mis-wiring; maybe too much blood was flowing, and his brain couldn't handle it.

He'd settled himself, headphones on, to let his heart apprehend a quartet by Beethoven. He sat, eyes half-shut, through the takeoff and climb; then, at cruising altitude he looked out at the quilted farmland and woodland and the little towns of Western Massachusetts, and found himself *seeing* with his heart.

Oh my God, he whispered through the music. At this great distance, five miles high, it wasn't frightening. He was scarcely in a plane at all. He let the land below flow into his open chest and dissipate through his blood to make his feet and fingers hum. The light was, of course, still entering at his eyes; it was, he supposed, just a diffused form of seeing, that let him absorb all at once the web of relations—texture, color, shape. (He'd call Dr. Cogswell as soon as he was back.)

Then, filled with the land below, he rubbed his eyes and turned to the interior of the plane. He started up the aisle towards the bathroom at the rear, and suddenly, looking at the passengers, he was taken up, the way it must be in labor, the first strong contractions carrying a woman with them past control. There was no control. He was invaded, and it wasn't like music, it wasn't like landscape. *Cogswell had done this*! There were all these lives entering his chest, faces of desire mixing inside him, and he grew frantic and turned back to his seat, shrank back with his eyes closed to feel his heart's new beat. And he knew his calm had been a way of keeping things out, keeping the other in its own separate place, keeping it for his use, and nothing could do that now.

What was so terrible? Eyes closed, he thought, *I'm simply not used to it. Relax. It's just people's lives, or my own feelings I'm putting on them*. But he didn't have the courage to look again, and when the plane landed in Chicago, he kept his eyes lowered. His heart was open to the energy of legs and hands, briefcases of money-hunger, dark-blue business suits of aggression. He felt erotic tumult like the time he'd taken a nephew to a water slide and got shamed into going along, got water up his nose and a stiff neck trying to fight the slide, and still the only way was to let go; then it was almost all right, he gave himself to the fall and sank and sank, rising to his nephew's laughter.

And then he saw Pete in the waiting room, something to hold onto in all this, and he waved. Pete took his case and said, "Should you be carrying something that heavy? Jesus—what've you got in here? Good to see you up again, Dad."

"Something's been happening to me," Koenig began, and then he looked Pete in the eyes and couldn't keep him out, his heart saw, and his heart was open-mouthed and voracious, his heart couldn't keep decent boundaries, and Ned Koenig began to sob, and Pete was saying, "Come on, we'll get to the TWA clubroom, it's okay, you've been through something." And Ned Koenig tried to say to his son, "No, it's *now* I'm going through something," but his son was patting his shoulder, telling stories, covering over, saying, "You hungry, Dad? What's your food trip post-op? Low cholesterol and what else?" But Ned was without defenses: he was taking in this son he loved so much, infant he'd snuggled naked and little boy he'd held against rough waves how many summers, youth he'd shored up and backed away from and pushed out as surely as if he were birthing him a second time, then mourned his loss, only he wasn't lost, he was impossibly, unbearably present, flesh of his flesh. Now, seeing Pete through tears, Ned felt Pete's own loss, that Pete had become like his father, had learned his father's tricks, and while Ned wished he could use those tricks again, he felt the sham, and couldn't stand it when he felt this close to this son and knew his son was using them.

Pete was ordering for both of them; he was asking about the consultation in L.A., about Margaret, about the stitches, finally about these peculiar feelings his Dad was having and "Have you…seen somebody, a doctor, maybe some short-term therapy—Dad, everyone is looking."

Ned reached out to touch his son's face, but this was much worse than sound or sight—touch knocking at his heart. He drew back his fingers; he could see Pete withdraw his eyes until they were camera lenses, not eyes anymore.

"*Please, Dad*!"

Ned was weeping for both of them.

And then he was running up an incline towards the terminal, running from his son. "Dad," Pete called in pursuit over boarding announcement, howling child, "all I said was, you ought to think about checking into a hospital. You're not ready for business, not like this."

But Ned Koenig was running, overnight bag in one hand, attaché case in the other, and Pete was running after. Arriving passengers flooding from a gate got between them.

"Dad! You can't run like that. You *can't*."

Koenig stopped and called back, "Then don't run after me, Pete. You don't run, I won't run."

"Okay. Okay. Please. I'm not moving, Dad."

"Here. I'm leaving the bag." The terminal's great fluorescent space swallowed his voice; they were only twenty yards, a scattering of people, apart, but he had to shout. "I'm buying a ticket home." He left his heavy bag and slipped into the crowd.

First class, he took the next flight back to Boston; Margaret was at Logan to meet him—he knew what that must have cost her, busy as she was. He wanted to comfort her but was afraid what might happen should he touch her hand or look her in the face. He was in disarray, hand-tailored Italian suit crumpled and Mark Cross necktie slack. It must look as if he were a lush and his elegant wife was picking up the pieces.

"I made an appointment with Dr. Cogswell. Pete says you think they made a *mistake* in the operation. A mistake? Why don't you look at me, Ned? Ned? What kind of mistake?"

He looked at her, and with no chest to protect him how could he keep her out? She wasn't the handsome, ironic woman who'd attended concerts with him, who shared with him the same financial planner; the woman who, when they both happened to be in Boston, made love with him in the dark before sleep, then laughed and kissed his nose, his chin, his cheek. She entered him now as flame without heat, there was nothing else but this fire. The terror wasn't that she was someone strange, a foreign body, but that, entering at the heart this way and filling him, she wouldn't leave any room for *him.*

He wrapped himself in his own arms and turned from her, like the Virgin from the Angel, terrified to bear this annunciation. But she had her arm around him, and her touch rushed through him like a hot wind.

"It's all right, Ned. I'll get you home. We'll see the doctor."

She was soothing him, afraid for him. He wanted to say, "Cogswell has to fix this," but now he knew there was no repair. His body wasn't separate from himself, a set of problems to solve. Even though his mouth was agape with terror, his heart, full of world, was unwilling to return to its safe separation. Willing himself not to fight, he took both her hands and then his heart was suffused with light that lived through him. He was only a vehicle being lived by the light, until, tossed by the tumult, he was flooded at the heart with light that was almost pain. Light was all there was and all there would ever be.

Originally appeared in Georgia Review, *Summer, 1991*

Dance to the Old Words

Only one year of separation, but look how much his children had already taught him. For the first six months, Eli, five years old, then six, would cry at night, middle of *every* night, and Jake would have to lie down with him, pressed firmly against his back like a lover. Next morning, Eli didn't remember. And not just that he didn't remember: you couldn't believe this was the same creature who'd wept so hard, who was barely in the shared world, barely aware of his father's comfort. Often, those first months Jake held him the way he had when Eli was two.

It was getting better for Eli now. Jake loved the brave way Eli would hold up his skinny frame, like a knight, and breathe to fill his chest with grown-up-ness. But Sebastian, at eleven, was still often furious and unforgiving. When he wasn't storming, he was sullen, storing up grievances. Jake learned to respect Sebastian's silences but to hold firm.

This morning, as he caught one of Sebastian's sour looks—they were hustling to get him to his soccer game—Jake held Sebastian by the shoulders. "Look—we've done you damage, and it's lousy, it's not fair, and that's what you're saying with those crappy looks of yours. Right?"

"No, it's not. But it stinks, it *does stink*, if you want to know."

"All right, so it stinks. But I won't be guilt-tripped. You can yell at me or punch a pillow, that's okay, Sebastian, but when you're finished, you've still got to set the table and keep your things in order and get to bed at a reasonable hour and be ready on time in the morning."

All the mad precision of scheduling to keep the children on an even keel while they lived in one house for a week, then the other for a week—was absolutely required to turn a mess into a reasonable life. It was fucking exhausting. But there was no good option. Children were conservative creatures, nurtured best in habit and ritual; even predictable oppression was better than chaos. Chaos was the alternative, the enemy, chaos was the real devil. "Let's get out to the field," Jake said. "You want hot cereal?"

Sebastian's eyes softened. "Eggs. Okay?" He had such deep, soulful eyes, Jake thought; he imagined him as a young man looking into the eyes of a friend. Grateful for the softening, he found his own eyes welling up.

"Sunny-side, coming up," he said in his short-order voice.

"This has been a tough time for husbands and fathers," Jake began one of his articles. "They're seen as large, clumsy beasts that need to be domesticated. Valuable for fixing electric wiring but resented for somehow keeping a monopoly on such knowledge. Resented for keeping emotionally distant from their family; resented, too, for emotionally intruding. They're seen as dangerous to women and children."

Jake, on the other hand, believed in a child's need for a father who could help establish the moral parameters, the ground rules, who gave a child a firm structure to push off against. Not that he saw himself as this model father; but he felt he knew what was at stake.

At gentle heat he cooked up eggs for the three of them. Hell with my cholesterol. Toast from his own baked bread. Sebastian had settled down. He laced up his cleats and told them how fast and slippery the Cambodian center on the other team was rumored to be.

Jake sat high above the field in the wooden bleachers. All the fathers, a couple of mothers, hunched up in parkas on this cold, gray Saturday. Jake had his eye on one of the mothers, a single mom he'd spoken to a couple of times. Thickening in torso, curly hair turning gray, Jake saw himself as still a handsome man, maybe on the rough side but handsome; he never had a problem getting women to want him. The problem was how to fit new women into his life with work and kids. Or was that just a cover. On second thought, he gave up this new woman as a bad idea right now.

Sebastian took the ball down on wing; Eli hunkered against his father, yelling, "Come on, Sebi! Sebi! Yes!"

A whistle for the half. No score.

Now a strange thing: a man by the players' bench waved at Sebastian, and Sebastian waved back. Eli poked Jake. "Dad! Daddy! "That man there, it's *Carl*, Mom said not to talk to him. *Can* I talk to him?" He ran down the stands between the fathers. "Carl, Carl!"

A couple of months ago, Jake would have been pissed. This guy invading my turf! Confusing my kids. Screw him! It was different now. Christine had dumped Carl, too. Just as with Jake himself—no warning, she made the decision, that was that. "Ha! Y'see?" Jake gloated. "She dumps everybody."

So when Carl climbed the stands, Eli trailing, Jake grinned at him as if they shared a joke. Carl looked uneasy, wanting permission. "You're Jake Peretz. Sebastian and Eli's father—I've seen your picture. I'm Carl Degler. I've been wanting to meet you." Lean, nice-looking, red-haired, Degler was dressed in an elegant suede belted jacket and suede boots and fine corduroy slacks—casual clothes that must have cost near a thousand bucks. He was a few years younger and looked younger still. Jake held out his hand. "Have some coffee?" Jake found a styrofoam cup and poured.

Jake is a Jew. He hears a name like Carl Degler? Probably an anti-Semite. His kids brought up by an anti-Semite! Country house and BMW he knew about; the rest he made up. Christine told him that Degler bought software and medical technology in Eastern Europe. Jake turned him into a ruthless business type, maybe trading in weapons, maybe hiring nuclear scientists for Iran.

So now he was giggling because that sinister Nazi wheeler-dealer in the BMW had turned into a prep-school type who spoke in complete sentences, precisely, with no expressive edge. "I've read quite a number of your articles in *The Nation*," Degler said. Jake was always listening for language. He was aware that, talking to Degler, he himself was speaking *Brooklyn*, the Brooklyn of his childhood, exploding the stressed syllables, hitting the dentals hard, pumping up the city beat of his sentences. Hostile?—ie., street-smart, populist, hip, against Connecticut prep-school *politesse*? Yeah, maybe hostile—but expressive, too, of male comradery. One-on-one.

Maybe the mix of his father and his mother's ex-boyfriend confused Eli. "Dad, I'm going down to the field, okay, Dad?"

As Eli danced off, Degler said, "They always talked about you. You were always there with us."

Jake shrugged off the gift. "Yeah. Well, I'm not letting go. I'll hang on with my teeth like a fucking pit bull."

"I came here to say goodbye," Degler said. "Christine won't let me near them."

"I know. She told me." Jake guffawed—but shook his head in sympathy.

After the game—someone on Sebastian's team ricocheted a last-minute goal off someone's shins—the two teams lined up and passed one another, shaking hands. Jake had an idea. "Hey, Carl—why don't you come back with us, have cold cuts back at my place? Yeah, yeah, it's all right. It's *my place*. You ought to be able to say goodbye, for chrissakes. It's only right."

The boys walked together in front. Jake caught a glimpse of Sebastian's solemn face and could read his subdued excitement. "That Cambodian kid was good, but you guys, ha!—you took them to the cleaners," Jake called out, and Sebastian turned and grinned. Eli was blabbing, high-pitched, dramatic; he danced a soccer ball down the path to the cars.

Digging through the refrigerator, he called out, "Sebastian, Eli, I want you guys to go pack, and straighten up your rooms, you're leaving at five. I'll get lunch on the table. Check lists are on your desks."

He opened bags of cold cuts. He saw Degler look the place over as if trying to find something nice to say.

It was a beat-up old kitchen, nothing like the new kitchen in the house he'd had to leave a year ago. He did the work himself to keep costs down—took a sledge hammer to the old plaster walls and in rage and pleasure pulled the lathing until all his muscles ached and his throat was full of dust. He only griped once in awhile, but he had to admit it was a come-down to this rented place. Here he was, still paying half the mortgage for that beautiful old Newton house while he had to live here like a student.

The furniture he took was the old stuff that came to him from his parents or from his first marriage. Old sofa that had weathered two marriages—the new sofa, Christine held on to. Well, he didn't want to change the home the boys were used to. So for himself he bought used tables and chairs. The scratched, white enameled kitchen table was just like one his mother had stored away when he was a kid. It embarrassed him a little, bringing Degler to a place like this. But he loved sticking it to Christine. It would bust her balls!

With the boys away getting packed, Jake and Carl fell silent. "I get you a beer? You probably think this is typical—cold cuts, I mean," Jake said. "I don't know what she told you."

"Actually, she said you were a good cook."

"I *like* cooking, anyway. Last night I made 'Adventurers Stew'—that's actually *boeuf Bourguignon* but don't tell the kids. And you?" Jake asked Degler. "You have any children?"

"No. I was married to a businesswoman," he said, as if that explained something. Then Degler wandered off. And after awhile Jake, making up a pitcher of lemonade at the sink, overheard him talking to Sebastian and Eli. "Just so you understand—I want you to understand. I've really cared about you both. I'll always feel love for you, for both of you. Just so you know…I regret so much the way things worked out. Just so you know…"

"Sure. Thanks," Sebastian said. "Mom gets real mad sometimes."

That was when Jake's heart opened. Until that moment, Carl Degler had been a decent, if white-bread, guy, and the meeting had been a joke on Christine. A *men's* joke. The Guys, teamed up against Women for an afternoon. A confirmation of blamelessness—ahh, who could figure that bitch? But standing at the old, stained white porcelain sink, squeezing lemon halves into a pitcher, even with the water running Jake could hear Carl's stammering pain, and instantly, the situation became something else, something sadder.

Now, without asking again, Jake opened a beer for Carl and carried it in and handed it to him. Without a word Carl followed him back into the kitchen. Jake laid out the cold cuts on a platter. "A real kick in the stomach for you, huh?"

Carl didn't pretend not to understand. "A *real* kick in the stomach. I didn't expect it. You read about men, they get so obsessed with a woman they go to restaurants on the off-chance she'll be there. They haunt the neighborhood. But you see, ordinarily, I'm a pretty conservative person. I never imagined."

"I didn't know—I mean, that it was that bad."

"She actually took out a restraining order."

"I didn't know."

"I'm embarrassed, to be so foolish. And—well, I'm not the type to hurt anyone," Carl said, palms out, grinning. "But I can imagine it looked bad, my hanging around. I couldn't think of anything else to do. Then I wanted at least to say goodbye to the boys."

"I'm sorry. Sebastian's right. She's one angry woman."

"Sure. Christine's angry, it's true," Carl said. "*Oh. But.* She can be a wonderful, generous woman, too," Carl said. "I know it's a funny thing to say—I never met a woman so splendid."

Jake laughed. "*Splendid*, sure. Splendid I won't deny. I remember a few summers back, a cocktail party in Wellfleet, I look up to see Christine in a long white summer dress, her skin all tan and her hair loose, lightened gorgeous by the sun, and all around her a circle of these big shots in thrall—professors and analysts and CEOs—she shone like some kind of goddess. It made me hold my goddamned breath. '*I'm* married to *her*?' I said. Soon I wasn't."

"It's funny," Carl said. "She used to tell me how *different* I was from you—I knew her better in a few months than you in ten years. I looked at your picture over Sebastian's bed. I looked up your articles in different magazines. I felt good, being able to take care of her better than you. By the summer, she said I was just like you after all. 'Another arrogant male. Selfish, inconsiderate, controlling.'"

"What is it about Christine?" Jake said. He meant it rhetorically, like, *What's* with *that woman*? But Carl Degler took it as a straight question.

"I think I know," Carl said, "what Christine had for *me*. A long time now, I've been a success in my work, and *in* my work I've felt expansive—you know? I don't put limits on myself. But in my emotional life—a lot of the time I live in a box under brown glass."

"She helped you feel free?"

"She gave me the sense that I *built* the box. I screwed the thing together, you understand? So then maybe, *maybe,* I can dismantle it and walk away."

"But not without Christine, am I right?"

Degler didn't answer. He sipped his beer. The two of them sat at the kitchen table, and Jake began to see something peculiar: to see middle age peel away from Carl Degler, began to see him the way he must have been twenty years ago. He stared. He didn't want to be rude, but there was something—and he said, "I think I know you. I know you from somewhere."

"You know me?...Have you done any articles on the Young Presidents Organization?"

"Who? Me? Are you kidding? No, no—*long ago.* It's something personal. Wait a minute—*you have a sister*—am I right?"

"You know Jenny?"

"*Jenny*. That's right, *Jenny.* But...not Jenny Degler."

"No. She's a half-sister. Jennifer Corcoran."

"Jenny Corcoran! Sure, I was *with* her for awhile. A few months. You used to visit sometimes. That's it."

"The farm! The commune in Vermont."

"Half-acre Farm. It was a joke, the name. Remember? I lived up there. We lived up there."

"Oh, my God—of course. *Jake*. You lived with Jenny. You played guitar. Right? I'm not sure I ever knew your last name. *Jake*. Sure."

"You came up on weekends."

"You played folk guitar."

From the other room, noises of Nintendo violence. Ordinarily Jake would have stopped daytime TV and especially video games of male violence and especially when the boys were supposed to be packing. But now he sat grinning at Carl Degler. And Carl smiled back. And then they were laughing and a little too shy to look at one another, and it was like the old days, being stoned and knowing more than you usually let on you know, not censoring it out. Laughing—and finally it was Jake who said it. "Okay, okay. You slept with my wife, I slept with your sister. So—how *is* she, your sister? Hey—I really *liked* her."

"She's good. Married. She has a boy and a girl. She's a lawyer in Denver."

"I'm glad. See? I should have stuck with her." Jake grunted. "But should she have stuck with me? That's a whole other question. And the answer is, Fuck, no. I was a wild-ass punk, acting out like crazy."

"Well, it was the times, Jake."

"Naw. I refuse to get off the hook that easy." Jake sighed. "The times just let us be the arrogant pricks we wanted to be."

"But Jenny, too," Carl said. "Her first marriage, she wound up in a terrible depression.... Jenny's been through things."

"I'm sorry. She was really fine." Now, as Jake walked into the livingroom, he remembered her red hair, like her brother's, only so long!—remembered it loose—like sea wrack, he thought, under him in bed, and he imagined a whole other life he hadn't had with Jenny. He couldn't even remember why they stopped being together.

Now, back in the world he was actually living, he shrugged at the boys, palms up (like Carl, he thought)—like saying, What's this daytime Nintendo crap? "Lunch, you guys." Sebastian shrugged back, got out of the game and called "Eli?" and they came into the kitchen.

And while the boys set the table, Jake poked through his old records and pulled out *American Beauty* by the Grateful Dead. He switched on the small kitchen speakers he'd wired up. It was music he hadn't played for a long, long time. But he was certain that when he sat down at the table, Carl would be nodding to the rhythm of the Dead. And Carl *was.*

Jake thumbed at the music. "I never listen to that stuff anymore."

"That was my music."

"Sure. That was *our* music. I never listen anymore."

Jake honed in on Carl's face, his sad eyes. The old face was there, more and more, but it had developed distinction during the past twenty years. He was the kind of guy who looked like a wimp in high school, Jake thought, but now at reunions he looked youthful and handsome while the others had gone to pot. For a moment Jake thought he saw Jenny's eyes in him.

Now over the music, Carl, spreading mustard on his pastrami, said something something, Bob Dylan…and Jake said something something Herbert Marcuse, and Carl said, Cambodia incursion, March on Washington…Woodstock…Norman O. Brown. It was like a dance to the old words.

Eli looked over at Sebastian, who, not wanting to admit he didn't understand, wouldn't look his brother's way. But Sebastian drummed his fingers to the rhythm of the Grateful Dead.

Jake realized he himself wasn't speaking Brooklyn anymore and maybe Carl, too, wasn't speaking in the same way. And so deeper losses—or if not deeper, *communal*—entered the kitchen. It was as if the music of a shared history were vibrating like invisible guy wires supporting this platform in space and time and feeling, two men in a fluorescent-lit, rented kitchen.

"I helped manage the alternative news service," Carl said. You remember?"

"Freedom News."

"Freedom News. Right. I think—often I think—that was my best time," Carl said. "Those days, you worked with Jonas, right?"

"Jonas Segal."

"Jonas Segal. Brilliant hyper kid who killed himself." Jake said this not to remind Carl but to memorialize. Everything came back: the old Volkswagen on the hill, vacuum cleaner pipe from the exhaust into the window. *I retrieved the paper from his pocket, where his will, his money, were to be found. The list of jobs that needed to be done at the farm.* Jonas died on a sunny day on a hilltop reading the *New York Times.*

"That was terrible," Carl said, "Maybe the beginning of the end."

Jake thought a minute. He got ice cream and handed the scoop to Sebastian. "So that's the thing in you, the thing Christine woke up again?"

"Something like that." The boys kept their eyes on their bowls. Jake realized once again what a loudmouth he was. He shut up; they sat, silent.

"We'll take our ice cream into the bedroom, okay?" Sebastian asked.

Sure. Jake was glad. "This once. Finish your packing and straightening up. Just be careful with the ice cream, okay?"

Sebastian rolled his eyes and looked glum.

Gently, Jake called him on the eye rolling. "Okay. What's that supposed to mean, Sebastian?"

"Why are you coming down so heavy?"

"What *heavy*? I just said, 'Be careful.' Is that so terrible?"

"Dad. In your house, we *can't* eat in the bedroom but we *can* eat in the living room. In Mom's, we can't eat in the living room but we can in the bedroom."

"I'll *talk* to her."

After they were gone, Jake sang to the Grateful Dead, "…and if I knew the way, I would take you home." He shook his head and thought again about the commune. "Well, it was my time, too," he told Carl. "Narcissism and vanity. Masked by ideology," he added. "We were full of experiments. On ourselves, on our children. A professor I knew at UCAL Santa Cruz, he believed in giving his three and four year-old kids acid on weekends. I often wonder what happened to those kids…." But that wasn't what he really wanted to say…. "I know about my *own* kid." *That* was it.

"You don't mean Sebastian and Eli. You mean your daughter."

"Christine must have told you? My daughter, my first marriage. Look at her now, Ellie's almost twenty-five, in and out of jobs, in and out of school, hospitals, relationships. Hah—relationships! …And drugs. Christine told you that, too?"

Carl nodded.

"When we divorced, her mother and me, twenty years ago, we were freeing ourselves from boxes. Same way you were talking. And what about our little kid? Well, of *course* a child would be happier after a separation, right?—because her mother and father would be truer to their *authentic selves*…makes me sick. Makes me sick to think."

"You think you wrecked your daughter?"

"See, the times—the times were full of chaos, I grant you. They still are. Worse, now, because it's without hope. But that's all the more reason I needed to watch over her. It was up to us to make up for what the community couldn't give."

"So do you see her? Your daughter?"

"In my mind's eye."

"I'm sorry," Carl said. They sat in silence. The music ended. They heard Eli and Sebastian clomp outside to throw a football around. Then Carl said, "Still, I believe in our old life, those days. The old hopes. I was this really straight kid. Maybe I wasn't free, but I believed in the possibility of becoming free. Like Jenny. The same. I still believe in *having believed*, caring enough to believe *some*thing. What can you give a child, Jake, you don't bring that?"

"I see what you're saying," Jake admitted. "All right. I grant you. I grant you. Maybe something good got lost. Maybe it wasn't all vanity and narcissism. You know what I think?" Jake said. "We were *right* back then. We knew it wasn't just politics. It wasn't just *out there* we had to fight. *We had to turn ourselves inside out.* We just didn't know how fucking hard that would be. We're half crazy, cripples, all of us. Christine. You. Me, too, sure. Me, too."

"I would have been a good stepfather."

"You *would* have been. I sympathize. You wanted a ready-made family. Well, why not? You seem like a really good man. No—you *do*. You *do*." Jake waved a hand at the air, as if getting rid of a bug or a bad smell. Enough. He let his eyes close. He felt the afternoon growing sour…. *Christine*: I say her name, Jake thought, and all this freight attaches to my heart. *Enough.* He looked at the ceiling where the landlord still hadn't fixed the cracks, and he sank down deep inside himself and wished Carl would go home.

The boys came in, laughing at something, and Carl motioned towards them with his head and smiled. "Thanks for this afternoon," he said.

The kindness of the remark made Jake look at him and soften. Softening, he wondered how gentle a man had to be to get Christine's approval. "You know," Jake said, a hand on Carl's arm, "There's something I've been wanting to say. There's something about this talk between you and me makes it feel like an *absolute* moment. Like one of those times late at night, you're drunk or stoned—especially stoned, especially years ago, stoned—and get to talking about your lives. I remember back then talking like this with a friend all night long. You lift above the selves you pretend to be everyday, and it's not that you won't be the same tomorrow, it's not that the talk changes any goddamn thing, but you feel like you've stepped outside your lives and you can look at them. I feel that with you." Not wanting to force Carl to confirm the feeling, he said, "I'm glad it worked out."

"Me, too." Carl got up, went into the livingroom. "Eli? Sebastian? I'm going now." He reached out his arms, and Eli ran into them while Sebastian hung back. But after Eli, Sebastian came up and hugged Carl.

"If either of you ever need me for anything…you understand?"

Jake put a hand on his arm and led him to the door. "Remember me to your sister…. Look—maybe—what d'you think?—maybe we can get together, play some tennis—you do play tennis, right? You look like a tennis player. I'll give you a call, okay?" They shook hands and Carl Degler walked down the front stoop and the boys waved and Jake felt he'd known him a million years and wondered, would they get to be friends—or maybe not see each other for another twenty years?

And he was thinking about this and about his date for tonight—her hair was also red, auburn—and puttering around the kitchen, when he heard a car door slam in the driveway and looked through the glass of the kitchen door to see Christine in her usual violet Lycra stretch pants and runner's sleeveless shirt coming along the flagstone to the back deck and right away knew she was pissed and knew why. He couldn't help particularly liking the way she walked when she was mad—long, strong hippy strides, blonde hair wild.

So the boys wouldn't see Christine, wouldn't have to hear the brawl he knew was coming, he went out onto the deck to meet her.

She waited till she was up the stairs, level with him—taller than Jake by an inch or two—and, arms akimbo, spoke huskily and precisely, as she always did when she wanted to make a really intense statement. "I am simply furious. I resent this terribly. God, I can't trust you for a minute. And you—you think it's funny? You're so smug!"

"What happened? You were driving by?"

"I wasn't snooping, if that's what you're implying. I was on my way home, I thought maybe the boys would be ready early. We're going to Connecticut, I wanted to get an early start."

"Sorry. Fuck you. You get them at five on the dot."

"I couldn't *believe* it, I saw his car, I couldn't believe it. What *right* do you have? To undercut me that way? How dare you let him near my children? Do you know what I've gone through?"

Leaning against the deck rail to suggest calm, Jake said, "He came by the game. I'm not saying the guy has rights, but he's got a lot of heart invested in those boys. I felt bad for him."

"YOU!" she said, as if the word were a curse. "You love this, don't you! You don't know the first thing about him. Heart! You don't know what he was like with me. Well, do you? You can't judge, Jake. One week Mr. Sweetness, next a cranky, depressed bastard. Do you know what he did after I told him to stay away? He sneaked into the house when the sitter was there. Only by pure chance, I came home and caught him."

"Maybe he wanted to say goodbye. And maybe he still wants you."

"He sneaked into *my house*! Frankly, I was scared. Wants me! How can I trust him after that? I had to get a restraining order."

"Ahh, he's no abuser, Christine. He's a kind man. He'd be good for you. In fact—maybe you should marry the guy."

"Don't you dare tell me who to marry! Don't you dare! I'd rather bring up the boys alone."

"Alone, huh?"

"Oh—I don't mean without your help. I mean I don't need to lock myself up inside some businessman's fantasy of a nineteenth century marriage. *His* friends. *His* house. *His* career."

"Oh, come on, Christie. He's a decent guy, a sad guy."

"You're all just 'sad guys.' He just likes to come off like a sensitive man. Men, nowadays, they want the old prerogatives *plus* a stamp of the new sensitivity."

"Then why go out with men? If we're all such low-lifes."

"I didn't say *all.* And then—it gets hard, it gets lonely—*listen*, you've been sleeping with dozens of women for every man I've seen. I don't have a thing to explain to you."

"Dozens! Look, baby: the problem is, you're bringing up my sons. And they're going to be *men*."

"*Good* ones. Decent ones."

"Not like their father?"

"*That goes without saying*." But she said it—through half-clenched teeth.

"Me and Carl, we were discussing ideology," Jake said. "You, Chrstine, you use ideology to cover your anger. 'Men's selfishness, men's arrogance.'"

"And you *weren't* selfish? You *weren't* arrogant?"

"Maybe. Yeah, I'm a handful. But you—you wanted and wanted. You were hungry and nobody could feed you. You think I wanted to push you around? I wanted to live a decent life with you. I was twelve years older. I figured I knew what was up. 'Stick with me,' I said. 'Stick with me and maybe we can get through this life in one piece.'"

"You mean you wanted me to shut up and let you drive. That's ideology too. The ideology of men in power keeping women in their place."

"Yeah, *you* lecture *me* on politics!"

"And that's another thing. You think you're so full of political virtue. The great healer. At $1,500 an article. It gets tiresome, sweetie, you can't imagine. But we were discussing you and Carl," Christine said. "You just make sure you never—"

"Hey, it's my house, my kids, sorry, baby."

"And you may not know it," she said, "but your swaggering 'MY' and that 'Baby'—that's ideology, too."

"I was saying to Carl, we're all cripples. We are," he sighed. "We are. Come *on*, Christie. Please. Carl was just saying goodbye. He'll leave the boys alone now. You ought to thank me. He said goodbye and finished something and you didn't have to be involved. See what I mean?"

She saw. She let out a huge breath and closed her eyes. Sitting on the edge of the old wooden table they'd once had in their basement playroom, she said quietly, "You make me so mad."

"Well, it must have been a shock. Like we were ganging up. He's still in love with you, you know."

"Stop that. Yes. Yes, I know."

For the first time in months, Jake felt a sexual warmth around Christine. Must be from the fighting, he thought. In his mind's eye he saw an image, quick, incomplete—must have been their bedroom, scene invented or remembered, books and clothes scattered in their joint mess, hot water bottle from the time she wrenched her back in modern dance class. He saw a tennis racket, a crumpled leotard, a pyramid of paperbacks with half-glasses on the top. The debris of married life. The weary debates halfway to morning, nobody giving an inch. Or sometimes the surprise of laughter and surrender, your own or hers, and lovemaking that seemed like the satisfying last piece of a puzzle.

"You got to be an angel," Jake said. "A complete angel. I mean, to be married. Especially in our times."

"Sometimes," she said, quietly, so quietly he almost missed it, "we *were*."

Now that they were quiet, Sebastian and Eli came out onto the deck, and Jake realized that they must have heard the rumble of a fight and waited. It was sad—how politically adroit children had to become after a divorce.

"Hi, guys," Christine said breezily. She opened her arms.

Jake said, "Sebastian, Eli, please get your things ready. Your mom's going to take you a little early. You're going off to Connecticut, remember?"

Christine looked at him in surprise. "Thank you."

But suddenly, the children stopped being all that politic. Sebastian hunkered down over folded arms as if battered by a cold wind. "You see what I mean? You see? The way you jerk us around?"

"Come on now," Jake said. "A couple of hours, what's the big deal."

"It *is* a big deal. And I can tell you why."

Sebastian waited for the go-ahead, and Jake found himself irritated but at the same time goddamned pleased, proud, that Sebastian was bucking them like this. "Okay. Why?"

"You don't even ask us anything. You just push us and pull us and we're supposed to do—whatever whatever whatever!"

"I'm sorry, I'm sorry, I'm sorry," Christine said. She heaved one of her dramatic great breaths. "But I am really ex*haust*ed," she said, her voice rising in pitch with each word. As if somehow this formulation did something good for her, she said it again, "I am really exhausted. I try to make a pleasant weekend for us, and you know all the work I've got!—and I don't need all this..."

...*crap*, Jake finished in his head. "Boys," he said calmly, hands upraised like a Pentacostal preacher offering blessing, "boys, please, help your mother out."

Christine shut her eyes and, her fingers fluttering like a drowning swimmer stretching for a hand, she waved at the boys to *come, just* come, *for godsakes,* and now Eli—this amazed Jake—got into the act, and he yelled "No way!" and for support hugged his brother around the waist, and there stood Jake and Christine on the deck facing off against Eli and Sebastian, and now Jake began to laugh at the stalemate, he couldn't help it, and Christine said, "I don't see anything so funny," but soon she was giggling and Jake crumpled in laughter on the deck, legs crossed yogi-style, and maybe the laughter was half fake, pumped-up to help smooth things over, but it was half real, too.

Then Sebastian was smiling and shrugging, and Jake went up

to him and kissed him hard on both cheeks, and he turned and went inside for the bags. Christine was hugging Eli.

And soon she and the boys were gone, hugs and goodbye and gone, waving, into her Volvo station wagon and back down the driveway. Jake felt his laughter dry up, like nothing would ever be funny again, like his mouth, his heart, were full of sand. He straightened up the boys' rooms, and laying back on his battered two-marriage sofa, called his current woman friend to see if she maybe wanted to get together a little early.

Originally appeared in Virginia Quarterly Review,
Autumn, 1995

The Man Who Could See Radiance

Before he saw radiance, he saw the way we all see. He saw his wife Rachel as threatening or contributing to his equilibrium; an irritation or, sometimes, someone he loved so that touching her was like touching the source of all metaphor, making his mind gasp and his mouth open. It's not something he ever put into words, what that was all about. Usually, she was someone to eat dinner with, someone to tell stories—he met lots of people, he told her stories. And all other women he saw as, first of all, more beautiful or less beautiful than Rachel, older, younger, could-be wives or lovers or godforbid-to-be-married-to-that-one. Or he saw them as Rachel's friends, taking her away from his life or maybe giving them someplace to go on a Saturday night. Then there were the old, he felt sorry for, and the young, he felt tenderness for, the young who made him remember the failures of his life.

Of course, his own children were different, they still made him glow, eyes fill so he had to turn his head away. Out of the house now, Jennifer in law school, Noah in his senior year at college, and he worried when they flew home, worried when they went off on ski weekends.

At work he saw guys he liked or didn't like, men and women the same, good to work with or hard to do business with, dumb son of a bitch. McAndrews knew how to smooth over tensions at a meeting; Myers stepped on his lines.

And he saw time as his enemy, keeping him from ever getting everything done, and energy he saw as something he held in a psychic bank and had to replenish if he spent, and never could he keep the account fat for very long.

So he saw and saw and went through Boston seeing and that's the way it was. He saw the world fabricated from his needs, the world pleasant or unpleasant, curious or dull, never beyond his fabrication, though he didn't see the fabrication.

Peter Weintraub was past mid-life, no crisis in sight; all the crises he could handle, he'd handled—doubt about his work, a beautiful woman who came along at the right time—and then Rachel, too, turned out to be having an affair with the Headmaster at the prep school where she taught history. A hard couple of years, but somehow they lasted and knew each other now, they said that in bed sometimes when they were about to make love, we know each other now. Fondness of the extra flesh at hip or belly as if to touch that flesh were also to know, with compassion, *limits*, this is it, my particular life, and it isn't bad or dull.

This should be the end of a story; trailing into flashes of erotic glory, or a moment awash with tenderness, or joy of the capture of new markets for the software his company sold, vacation trips (Florence, Aruba), losses, sorrows, death, please God the lives of children continuing, history complicating or exploding everything, maybe the planet. Otherwise, Friday evening concerts in Symphony Hall.

But one day at the end of grimy winter, riding the MTA from Newton into downtown Boston, he looked into the eyes—maybe they were temporarily unprotected, they must have been unprotected—of another middle-aged man (lap-top computer, London Fog raincoat) sitting across the aisle. The trolley went underground at Church

Street and as Weintraub glanced up, the legs and bookbags in the aisle shifted and he felt this man's eyes, felt oh, my God, the *damage* and, instantly, saw the minor panic of this man putting up eyes in front of eyes like an alien discovering his humanoid mask wasn't right. Yet Peter felt it *more* now, the damage, heard this man not-saying *I'm afraid of your eyes seeing me, making me pull too hard at the guy wires that keep me from breaking apart in this terrible wind.* Trolley shivering and howling in the tunnel. Then overcoats and briefcases between them. When Peter was able to see again, the man was gone.

Weintraub shuddered and, his own eyes closed, he saw again the panic in the gone eyes and, under the eyes, the pain. Maybe the poor son of a bitch was cracking up. Just, aaach, just some poor son of a bitch. But he couldn't account for his own turbulence, as if a door had just opened into hell. And here was the worst of it: he suspected that he'd seen this way before. Not once. *Always.* He'd kept himself from knowing. But he'd never *not* seen this way.

At work, he forgot. March 1: he had a report to get out for a meeting with management, and he played with the stats and graphics, altering the units of measurement so a fairly flat curve looked pregnant. The report went to the laser printer and Jean Collis had eight bound copies on his desk ten minutes before the meeting, and he smiled up at her—and with a terrible rush felt *her life, her life,* and had to close his eyes to keep the knowledge off. Pain again, though not the same as on the trolley; then was it his own pain he was seeing? But no, he was sure it belonged to Ms. Collis, brittle Ms. Collis who had a well-publicized secret life he'd always known, you could see the posters over her desk, soft-focus landscapes with New Age aphorisms about the soul, but what he saw now was a life intended to stay secret, even from herself, and it was so open to him, the balance sheet of humiliations she kept, he couldn't breathe. He pushed back from his desk, hand over his heart. "Thank you so much. Thank you, such a good job, thank you."

"We forgot to single-space the indents."

"But it's beautiful."

Weintraub stumbled through the meeting. He was afraid to look anyone in the face; he was afraid to breathe too deeply, as if it were *breath* that was taking in the pain, like the summer in college when he worked in a State hospital and there were certain wards where it was best to take a deep breath and hold it until you walked out.

He tried to explain to Rachel.

"Well, as for Ms. Collis, what do you expect?" she said. "Your Ms. Collis is a sour bitch. I can't stand Jean Collis." She poured their wine. "Don't get me started."

Now he was afraid to look into Rachel's eyes, but it didn't matter, he was *anyway* flooded by her life, nothing she *said*, her life naming itself secretly in her voice so that he found hot tears coming as he tried to answer, thinking *I didn't know, I didn't know*—knowing it had nothing to do with Jean Collis, whom she'd met maybe twice. What then? He couldn't say, but he held her hand against his chest and stroked, mothering them both.

I'm just having problems about boundaries, he thought, thought over and over; fusing, confusing. This has to stop.

Then a week without trouble except at night, dreams of hard travel through a half-strange city, the bus not coming, subway station the other side of an impossible highway, maps he couldn't read without glasses, and along the way irritating helpers who put him on the wrong elevator, tumbling him into the morning radio news, cranky and fatigued. Then the next night, the same confusing city and so much to carry, clumsy not heavy, and the overcoat he had to go back for probably lost.

I need a spring vacation, he said to Rachel. You and me both, she said.

The first seeing came almost as relief, like rain pouring down to break a heat wave and finally you could breathe, worth it even if you'd left the cushions out on the deck chairs. This time, it was a friend. Aaron and Beth Michaels came for dinner and Weintraub had nothing to say and longed for them to be gone, longed for sleep, held a glass of good wine that tasted sour.

He felt hot, itching—soon he'd learn to recognize that itching in his chest—he looked up to see Beth, who'd been talking about their daughter's suffering in marriage, to see Beth's own suffering, her life suddenly visible. He half stood to reach out to her and fold his arms around her but that wasn't possible. But he wanted to, and it was his having to sit there and listen quietly to Beth's story that sent him over into seeing the radiance that first time.

It shone from her eyes, something to do with her eyes, but it was centered at her chest, pulsing out like the Northern lights he once saw, visible, not visible, a trick of the light?—oh, no, she glowed, out of the suffering something radiated. *I can turn this off*, he thought. I can examine it critically and get rid of this golden light.

But he'd always liked her, and all at once he was breathing so fully again after suffocating weeks that he didn't have the heart to try. *I know you, know you.* He drank his wine and felt vaguely adulterous—and hoped they couldn't see. He changed from Handel to Brahms, a trio, and checked the casserole. When he came back to the couch, he was afraid it wouldn't be there, but it was. Everything else went on according to the rules of the dance.

The Brahms that everyone else seemed to tune out was almost too much for him to bear, with this light pulsing around Beth in the wing-backed armchair. A trick of sight, a trick of hearing as well, for the cello pulsed within his body. A trick of the heart. *I wish I could talk about this to Rachel.* But he was afraid it might never come back. And then…she'd think things.

"Anybody for more wine?"

Maybe if he saw truly, Weintraub thought, this is how he'd see everyone. Every human creature in the radiance that made him tremble, made him—terrible dinner companion—gawk at Beth all evening. And Rachel *did* think things. Getting ready for bed, she wouldn't talk. "Rachel?" he said. "Please?"

"You were staring at that woman all night. I wouldn't care but it was humiliating. Everyone must have noticed."

He couldn't see the light pulsing from Rachel. He even dimmed the bedroom hoping to see. I mean, imagine—to live in the presence of that radiance!

She turned the lights up again. "You're *not* all of a sudden getting romantic with me—not after staring at someone else all night?"

"*No*. Listen, Rachel, it's just that I *noticed* something about her. Like her *soul* for godsakes."

"What a peculiar animal I married." Rachel started giggling the way she used to years and years ago, until the giggles emptied out, then brimmed up in her again and bubbled over so that she had to lean against the bed and dry her eyes. "Her soul! Tell me another. Oh, you dumb bird!" Stepping out of her skirt, she went to the closet for her shorty nightgown. "Peter? I think I'm changing my mind about romance. You can make love to my soul."

About Beth, at least he could understand. Wasn't it true he'd always imagined taking her to bed? Her soul? Rachel was right to laugh. But what about Jack Myers, Vice-President in charge of Sales and Being a Prick? They couldn't be in the same meeting without putting each other down. Just the hint that one of them supported a plan was enough to get the other suspicious. Myers! The guy had a big mouth for (1) swallowing the world and (2) emitting hot air. But the next Monday morning at the weekly marketing meeting, Peter Weintraub looked up and there was the narcissistic son of a bitch glowing, pulsing. He could hardly bear to see, it was so rich, the light. The son of a bitch, so *precious*—why was he so precious?

Myers laid out a campaign for sales to large corporations. Weintraub had a hard time listening. So precious! He got up and sat next to Myers—"Mind if I look over your shoulder?"

Myers kept talking. Weintraub conducted an experiment; casually straightening papers, he let his fingers get close to Myers' chest: *What did the light feel like*?

Myers gave him a Look.

"Mmm, nice plan," Weintraub said.

Now McAndrews, the guy who made everything move in the company, McAndrews also gave him a Look, and Ferris, the aging golden boy who'd developed the original software concepts, said, "Well! It must be one *hell* of a plan." And Weintraub, thinking fast, said, "Myers, you're finally coming around to what I said a year ago."

Now, for the time being, it was okay. Everyone laughed except Myers.

He could feel the light or feel something at the borders of his own body, not see, but feel in fingers and cheeks and chest a humming like when he stood at night outside a Con Edison plant—a kid, summertime, doors open and the turbines humming like a giant chorus in all registers, and it seemed they were producing the energy that made the earth turn and the trees grow. Whose energy was this? Myers'? His own? No saying.

At work, colleagues had always seen Weintraub as a little peculiar, but—he knew—they were fond of his strangeness. So there were times you could walk into his office and find him checking proofs on a catalogue, headphones on, arms conducting a silent Mahler. He knew they accepted that. It made them feel that the workplace wasn't a concentration camp. They *used* his freedom as symbols of their own. But now they began looking at him after he passed down the hall; he caught reflections in glass doors. People spoke to him carefully and slowly. Sometimes that was when he was staring into their radiance, sometimes not. And then Rachel sat him down one day and said, "Peter? Peter, I got a call from Joe Ferris. He wonders…"

"I'm *not* going to do therapy. Isn't that what you're asking?"

"Do you want to go off somewhere? You said…"

"Actually," he said, "*I don't want to lose this.*"

"Lose what?"

He was afraid to kill it by saying. "It's too good to talk about."

It was so good that he had to wonder. Look. He was no saint. *Especially* now. Sometimes five minutes after he saw radiance, he felt rage. And it was worse when he tried to live an ordinary life. One night, he had a fight with the young jerk behind the checkout at the video store. The kid mixed him up with someone who'd tossed late tapes on the counter. He called out to Weintraub, "Hey! You owe $6.50 on these."

"Me? Those? No—they're not my tapes."

"Hey! Don't bullshit me."

"You got the wrong guy."

"Hey! You can just stop looking—you're not taking out any more tapes until you pay."

"And I told you, you moron, they're not mine."

"Yeah? Let's see your card, then. Hey!"

"YOU! YOU!—shut the hell up! Close that mouth, you understand?" And Weintraub discovered he was suddenly raging, shouting, and the other browsers were staring. "I said they're not mine, prick! You'll see my card when I'm goddamn ready. Now—not another word out of you! Not another word!"

"Hey! I said show me your card if it's not you." Now the kid wasn't sure. "Who are you then?"

Weintraub, affronted, righteous, trembling, hot, hot in the face, took his time, picked out a movie and slapped the cover on the counter—along with his membership card.

"Yeah, well, okay—you could've showed me this and saved the hassle."

There were twenty, thirty tapes piled up on the counter. Weintraub swept them off with the sickle of his arm, and they scattered against the metal shelves and Weintraub stomped out, neck tight, victorious—victorious over a child. All that rage! The kid had him by twenty pounds and twenty years but wouldn't have stood a chance (Weintraub was sure) against his battle fury. He could imagine a bloody fistfight in the video store, all the Newton lawyers and doctors waiting for their professional services to be required.

And that he should be the one to see radiance! It made him squirm. Maybe I *do* need therapy. He drove around awhile. Then, sitting in the silence of his garage with the engine off, he wondered if it wasn't wishful seeing, pretending the world secretly expressed *love*. When it didn't.

Calmed, he could still feel his own blood, and, at the borders between his body and the world, the humming that was always with him now. Peter had never been a fighter, hadn't fought since grade school. *I wanted to kill that boy.* He tilted the rear view mirror to look at himself, expecting to see a terrible radiance, green or red ugly light pulsing around his head. But all he saw was his ordinary face; the eyes, at being questioned, questioning.

"I'm home!" he sang out, entering.

"I'm in the family room. Come have a drink."

From her voice he knew she knew.

She poured him a sherry and sat beside him, capturing his hand. "The store called. The owner: he was very, very upset."

"*I* was very upset."

"Not the young man. The *owner*. He's cancelled your membership. He says, if we make trouble, he'll sue."

"I couldn't care less."

"And…Nancy Pollock called."

"Christ—was *she* there? Well, to hell with the Pollocks."

"No—Nancy was being kind, she was terribly worried. I said you'd been under some strain." She stroked his hand. "Poor Peter."

Now came the strain: he worked hard to do the work of the world. He tried to avoid being peculiar, even in the old ways. Goodbye to his Walkman and headphones and waving his arms to *Lied von der Erde*. He never loosened his tie. It would take time, he knew, to regain his position of normality in his company, but soon, at least, sooner than he'd expected, they had stopped talking slowly and carefully to him. Ferris brushed invisible dust off Weintraub's Italian suit and congratulated him on a report—really on reentering the world. Weintraub knew he was really staying outside, outside other people's hearts and safe from radiance and rage. He could tame the eyes of colleagues if he looked *at*, not *into* them. Sometimes he wondered whether they knew what he knew and had taught themselves to see only just enough to get by on—then to forget they'd done it.

No radiance, but the cost: the world stopped glowing, and then stopped mattering. It was *only* matter. He imagined it was like being an alcoholic or say a heroin addict, who'd felt the rich fabric of life through his drug, and then, his blood neutralized, felt nothing.

But then, he began to be aware, dimly, unsure, out of the

corner of his eye, but soon intensely—of a visible dissonance; shock waves. Always.

He saw them first faintly in the street on his way to work. Twice, he saw them in the supermarket, but they were just jangling, just irritating, they weren't terrible—not until the regular Monday morning meeting.

The meeting hadn't got started, people wandered in, coffee mugs full, talked football scores. Laughter. Of *course* it was a little phony, a pretense at relaxed congeniality, but so what? That, Peter knew, was how business got accomplished—people put on underwear and shoes and combed their hair and made up their faces and worried about their own projects, their own places in the company, about their children, about their health, and wasn't there something noble about the false good humor that gave them, temporarily, a common speech, a key in which to sing all their different notes? And then work got done.

But this Monday morning he saw not radiance but only forms of brittle energy surrounding, bounding everyone, like the concentric circles around a rock dropped in a pool, fending off the circles around other rocks. But *these* shock waves weren't concentric; they were crazy-irregular. No angel would wear such a thing as nimbus. Ugly, jagged, the waves of air jarred against each other, distorting, and Peter sank back in his conference chair to keep out of the way.

The squawk! As if every man and woman was a miniature broadcasting tower sending out these waves, jamming each other's broadcasts. Worse: the lines of force—though nothing, though air or a trick of seeing—had nasty, sharp, staccato edges—watch out!—like concertina wire strung up to keep off thieves. Peter dug in as if his chair were a trench. It was war. He gaped.

Then the meeting settled down, and he saw these protective waves settle back close to their owners, condense, intensify. Then Ferris' voice, getting things underway, warm and cheerful: all the barbed lines of force opened slightly like lips to let his voice enter, but the force felt it as invasion. He could see how his colleagues handled the alien force that they had to let in: prepared, they shaped it, surrounded it, until it became part of their own force. But when he looked at the room, he understood why Ferris was so successful with personnel. Gradually, the lines of force grew less staccato, smoother, and the edges less fierce. It was like wild beasts under the sway of a tamer. Oh, but he knew how temporary. No hope! No hope! No hope!

Less afraid, now that the individual boundaries had grown less jagged, he had time to mourn. Behind his hand, he wept for all of them. This wasn't smart! Thank God he had a tissue in his pocket, he could blow his nose—a spring cold—but what did it matter, the hopelessness was so much more terrible than his individual embarrassment. So, his weeping unprotected by tissue, he collected his papers and went back to his office.

"Jean, I'm not feeling well. I don't think...I think I'm—"

But the barbed lines of air around Ms. Collis were fierce, and he rushed past her, down the elevator and into a gray spring day, downtown Boston, but it was like entering Beirut in civil war or the hell where city gang fighters go when they die. Burrowing down inside himself, he walked fast towards the subway at Government Center, then broke into a run, but there was nowhere to run, all around him on the open plaza in front of City Hall were indifferent people with fields of force that weren't indifferent at all. So many people—each surrounded by a jagged perimeter of defense, and the lines jarring silently against each other, a giant interwoven beast or bitter maze that shifted to let him through. He himself was without protection. Worst, he was without protection from his vision. So this was it!

He flagged a taxi just empty and ran to its open door.

For the first three days Peter lay on the beach and didn't look at people, kept his eyes to himself like a shy child. He let Rachel decide where they would eat, when they would sleep. Did he really sleep? He couldn't tell. Ashamed, he clung, big man, wrestler in college, close to her warmth against the crisp white hotel sheets, and, tense until her breathing deepened, then he sank into a flowing dark inside the dark; it was like, by day, letting the Caribbean mild tides carry him as he floated, breathing through the snorkeling tube and letting his eyes fill with gentle, glowing fish, the colors leading him down under giant coral and through the reef passage, where he would breathe deep and plunge, a sudden drop of fifteen feet, into darker water of the bigger fish until he couldn't take the pressure. Then he'd surface, clear the tube, and drift back through the passage.

He couldn't read. What did he do? He lay on the beach.

"You're healing, don't worry," Rachel said.

On the third night, they made love again, and it was gentle as the fish. For three days, he hadn't looked at her, not looked all the way down, but while he was inside her he opened his eyes and her eyes were open, and moving slowly inside her he saw at the perimeter of his seeing a dim glowing that might have been him or might have been her or both, like a pattern impressed into the dark, angel-in-the-snow they made an angel in darkness. The radiance had come back to him. He was afraid to ask, *Do you see it*? He closed his eyes; coming, he drifted into the radiance.

It was after two when he awoke and went to the balcony to look at the ocean. No moon. He felt his blood rising into fingers and put up his humming palms as if they pressed against a window of darkness and for the first time he could see his own radiance, faint, glowing. *I'm all this*, he said to himself. *This is who I am! This is who I am!* Turning, he saw Rachel with her hair spread out on the pillow, and it seemed to him that faintly, from the dark of her hair a light hovered around her. And in that light he could read her sorrows—miscarriages and work she'd grown tired of, failure as a musician and compromises in loving him and fear that Jennifer didn't love her. Saw. As he looked, her radiance flamed.

I can never be the same, never... he whispered and whispered again, longing for it to be true.

They held hands on the flight home. He could look again, though it frightened him to see the jagged perimeters of strangers, but his vision protected him, his *knowing*. He walked safe inside his own space of knowing.

At Aaron and Beth's house he took a chance on coming back into his old world.

Candles on the coffee table, old friends as in a beer commercial. Beth and Aaron laid out a platter of artichoke hearts and calamata olives, scallions and red peppers—an antipasto. But the shocks of air, the brittle, jagged energy protected Aaron. Protected from what? *From me? What am I doing?* He smiled across at Aaron as if to say, *Hey, no need, no need—it's all right.* But though Aaron smiled, humoring, Aaron's fierce shock of air intensified. Peter wondered, *Can I feed him from my own radiance*? But that was the moment, lifting his hands as if to pass on a blessing, he saw for the first time his *own* barbed field of force, it grew out from his hands and through his jacket and surr-ounded him, and as he grew afraid it grew uglier until it seemed to wrap around him like a stockade. And murderous—it wanted death for Aaron, wanted absolute exclusion of other life. "Oh, please…I want to get out," he said, in a small voice, meaning this prison of his own making. "It's not like I thought. Nothing's like I thought."

"Rachel—you want me to get your coats?" Beth said, and her voice implied long conversations about him on the phone.

"No—that's not it—" Peter started to explain, but stopped, because in this moment of emergency everyone had come temporarily together, maybe it was that, and that his own need was so great to get past himself, and he *saw* as if all the cells or atoms of each of them were pointilistically vibrating in golden space and each desperately holding separate being together but he could see that boundaries were almost arbitrary. And all the defensive fields, too, were not separate but intermeshed. Aaron's field depended on his and his on Aaron's. If he looked too long, all the boundaries, the visible forms, would disappear. Like a computer engineer getting underneath the software, underneath the hidden codes, underneath the program and even the machine language to the essential on-and-offs that you couldn't see. And he tried to explain, and Beth said, "Can I get you a scotch, Peter?" and he knew it wasn't possible and bent his head and stayed silent and made his heart stay silent. "Pass the wine," he'd say. "Pass the steak. How's work, Aaron?" They were all relieved.

He stayed mostly silent all the next day, a Sunday, and Rachel let him be. He listened to music. When he heard her getting dinner started, he came down and helped her cut up vegetables, because *that's what you do*, you cut up vegetables and sauté them in oil and add cumin and coriander. You say to your wife, "I'm feeling okay," and take her kiss and say, "You get your lesson plans finished?"

And slowly, because it was necessary, the vision faded. He wept at odd times and for no reason. The vision came to him less and less the next few months, finally not at all. And sometimes he thought, *It was just chemistry.* And sometimes he thought, *I know what's under there.* He took up his work again and was careful what he said. So after a while he was able to wave his arms while listening over the headphones to Mahler, and the others shook their heads and grinned, relieved: Weintraub was back. And he was able to fight with Jack Myers and when he talked with Joe Ferris didn't see more than Ferris wanted him to see, didn't see with his heart. He saved his heart in a safe deposit vault and brought out small sums when he could, especially for Rachel, for Rachel and for their children.

Originally appeared in Agni, *Spring, 1990*

Old Friends

"We couldn't put you up in your usual rooms," Wink says. "Actually, I'm camping out there myself while Nan gets better. But we'll try to make you comfortable.... You'll recognize the furniture," he adds, smiling under his bushy eyebrows that have turned gray and wild.

Pete erases the air with his open hands. "Christ, Wink, I'm here to help you guys out, you and Nan. That's what I'm here for."

"Well, you must know what a relief it is for me." Wink shrugs his big shoulders and Pete loves him for his gentle humility; Wink seems to him a man who seldom needs you to notice his strength.

Now Pete is left alone in the guest room with furniture left over from earlier, simpler times of their lives. Pete remembers the Victorian dresser from a flat in Pimlico in the mid-fifties—the first time Wink and Nan had money to go down to Portobello Road and find pieces they liked. *I helped them lug it home*, Pete thinks. And that tapestried wing-back chair. *We carried it through the street and took turns sitting on it as if a London sidewalk were our parlor.*

Not jet lag but just being in his friends' house has wiped

him out. Funny. He's past the shock of it. But it's still something he can't take in. He keeps saying to himself, *Anyone can have a stroke.* Then—*But Nan*!

For weeks, Pete listened to his friend weeping in the middle of trans-Atlantic silence. A guttural, baritone weeping, it shocked him. Pete remembered when they first knew one another, in the fifties, and were poor, and calls were so expensive, when they respected a trans-Atlantic call like a telegram. The hiss of long-distance silence would have scared them. Now, not. "Oh, Wink, ah Jesus Christ, man," he'd say, and then silence, silence, and Wink blowing his nose. And then, gradually over the weeks, Wink began telling him that, thank God, *something* was left, some fragments of memory, he meant, Nan was beginning to remember things. "Well, thank God, Wink."

Pete said to Betsy, "I should fly over and see Wink."

"Of course you should."

Every day he said, "I should go over."

"But why *don't* you go?" Betsy said. "You'd be such a help to Wink. I can't, you know I can't—Jennifer will be having the baby any day now. But *you* can."

"Oh, Betsy, it feels so sad. I keep seeing the four of us swimming from that motorboat off the coast of Malta. Remember? We have a snapshot somewhere?—Wink mugging a dive? We were all so beautiful."

"Well, it *is* sad. Naturally." Betsy noticed that the mirror was spotted; she found Windex in the bathroom and went to work.

"I'll tell you how it feels," he said, sitting on the bed. "Not like dying. That's not what I'm afraid of. It's entering the time when things start to happen that can't be fixed. When the specialists take charge—that's what scares me. And then…"

"And then?"

"Well, and then—and then, it's the end of something we were."

Betsy just looked hard at him, as if measuring the strength of a companion on a hard climb. Always the firm one, she didn't have to say a thing.

"All *right*," he said. "All right, all right."

"Oh, Pete. What are you so afraid of?"

"I *said* 'all right.'"

He left a message on Wink's answering machine, and took an evening flight to Heathrow. It was late March, a month since Nan's stroke.

Miles' *Kind of Blue* plays muted in the muted sitting room. Playing this, Pete thinks, is meant to be understood as a quote, as Wink's homage to what they used to be. Wink sits listening, big hands hung between his thighs. Pete watches him: big galoomph of a face, craggy monument of a face, above the heavy slumped shoulders. Nan sleeps upstairs in their eighteenth century town house that fronts on a little gated park. They're alone in the house, the three of them, as they were alone so often in the fifties, before Betsy made them a foursome. The cleaning lady has gone home, the community nurse has stopped by to check Nan out, the physiotherapist to help her begin the long climb back. But Wink has been her real nurse. Their daughter, Alice, flew out from California, but she could stay only a week; she has her family to take care of. God knows Wink could have hired a full-time nurse, but this—nursing Nan—is what he wanted. He's dropped everything else—the banking, even the steering of his own portfolio. Everything.

Waking, Nan buzzes, and the buzzer rouses Wink; he calls up, "Coming, I'm coming." It's so odd to see Wink with his great head and groomed, somewhat mane-like graying hair, an important man, Wink in an apron, fixing tea—herbal tea—and carrying it up to her, the pot and cup and miniature spoon and folded linen napkin so small on the large, filigreed silver tray. Walking up behind his big friend, Pete notices how Wink has spread out some in the beam, and somehow this makes him feel intense, bizarre affection for him.

Nan looks small in the great four-poster. *Does she know me? Does she even know Wink*? Wink puffs up her pillows, white pillows, white coverlet, and the two big men sit at the side of her bed. Wink says, "Nan, it's Pete. It's Pete Hayes, Pete and Betsy, it's Pete." Nan tries to articulate speech. The words come out as if she were a new speaker of English who didn't quite get the rules of syntax. She's able to smile on one side and say, throaty and thick, "Pete...Pete it *is*."

"You look fine," Pete says. It's a lie but not a lie. Her mouth twists down at one corner. Her hair seems to have whitened even since last summer, when they all met at the Montreux Jazz festival. She looks ashen, dim. Still, it's good to see her. Five minutes by her bedside and she's just Nan again. Maybe floating on whatever drugs, maybe it was that—but she seems younger somehow, the architecture of defenses gone from her face; a girl with white hair.

Nan has always been the poet among them, the one to collect wild flowers and grasses for table bouquets. She wears Russian capes and loose, flowing silk dresses, collects antique rings and often wears one on every finger. She depends on Betsy for recipes; throwing an important party, Nan would call Betsy, London to Connecticut, to ask whom she should place next to whom. Always, Nan has flung herself on the sweetness of the world, and until now, the world has held her gently.

Clear-eyed Betsy skis with precision and control; after all these years every November she still trains on Nautilus machines and takes master classes when she starts a ski week. Nan is a graceful, spontaneous skier. She makes it look as if all you have to do is fall, and as if falling is splendid. Skiing behind her, Betsy, Wink, Pete used to laugh at the way she'd lift her poles outspread like wings and sing, sing opera, conducting with her wings, as she floated down. Once, not seeing a patch of ice, she tumbled hard into a tree, and then refused to wait for the ski patrol. Wink splinted her leg with broken poles and scarves, and Pete on one side, Wink on the other, they skied her down the mountain, Nan crying and shaking and laughing at herself.

Now she shakes her head and smiles as if apologizing for her stupid speech, or as if, *not* apologizing, she were making fun of herself as she often did, the impractical one—just look what I've done *now*.

"She's doing so much better, my girl," Wink says. "Sometimes she says 'glass' when she means 'book,' or she can't think how to begin a sentence, but then once she gets cranking, it comes, it comes. And you *are* remembering things, aren't you?"

"My mother, voice, sing she did…me." Nan smiles. A victory. The two men lean forward, as if the leaning might make it easier for her, for Nan's voice is soft and slurred and takes a long time. And now they sit back, Peter fatigued from the flight and the sadness, from having to smile at Nan.

"Beginning to remember. Like finding a piece here and there in a jigsaw puzzle. The more she finds, the more she's got to attach new pieces to. Little victories, isn't that right, my girl?"

Nan nods. Her eyes are a little vague, but then, they've always been a little vague. It's part of her charm. Pete takes her hand. "It's so good to see you, lady."

"Tea?" Nan says and points with her eyes.

Wink understands. "We're all right. Had ours. This tea's for you."

She hoists herself up and sips, one hand holding the other holding the cup.

"She's begun therapy, did I tell you? Every morning, exercises. Next week we go to hospital, to the fancy machines."

Nan throws her eyes up to the heavens. Pete and Wink laugh, and Wink says, "Plenty of excitement, love. Now you rest awhile."

"It's looking good," Wink says on the way downstairs. "She won't be fully paralyzed on the bad side, and I think she'll remember more, get more language back. But it could happen again, Pete."

"There's the drugs to keep down her blood pressure."

"Sure. Still..."

Now it's evening. They've foraged for dinner. Pete remembers the whiskey, not what they ate. Wink said, "There are all these spice bottles with no labels. Nan just *knew*, you see. I could ask her what's what, but you think I'm going to learn to cook?"

"You'll need a housekeeper."

"I know. I'll have to get a housekeeper. But that makes it feel so final, Pete."

"You think it *is* final?"

Wink strokes the leather of his armchair as if it were a cat. "Well. That part. The cooking. Her right hand barely functions."

"The skiing."

"The skiing. The skiing. Can I get you another drink?"

"You drink," Pete says. "Go ahead and tie one on. Like we used to. I'll stand watch. I'll be Designated Nurse."

"She'll need her pills at midnight."

"All right."

"The two containers nearest to the bed. Not the others...but I'll probably be fine. All right. Let's drink to what we were," Wink says, and laughs at himself and pours himself a large scotch, a short one for Pete. "Well—not maybe all that grand."

"Sure we were grand."

"Well, we thought so, and maybe that's all it takes," Wink says. He raises his glass and drinks a ritual drink, then leans back in the big leather chair. "We fooled the bastards, didn't we?"

Pete understands and grins as he's meant to grin. He looks around this lovely, elegant room—old ship's clock in well-oiled cherry, the small original watercolor by John Singer Sargent, an inlaid eighteenth century table. Behind built-in walnut cabinetry, the stereo system playing Coltrane must have cost thousands of pounds. All to be taken with irony. *We fooled the bastards*. As if all this didn't *define* the four of them.

There's always been this con. Winthrop Thompson—Wink—had risen to be head of the London branch of an American bank. His wife Nan contributed her services as a member of the Board of Directors of Oxfam. But through all these years Wink claimed to feel like a spy, a successful fraud, secret 50's hipster in Bond Street suits. What they loved, Wink and Nan, was to wear the trappings of success (they were on one of the lists at Buckingham Palace) with the special grace cast by irony.

It was a shared comic irony—shared since the time of HUAC and the loyalty oaths. If, all these years, Pete and Betsy Hayes, Wink and Nan Thompson, would meet in Interlocken for skiing or share a villa on Ibezia or in Provence, always they did it with irony. It was partly their love for the outdoors that let them feel superior to the business people they worked with. They hiked in the Alps; once in the Himalayas. It was a sign of their secret personal anarchism. It was as if most of the year they were in costume, the four of them, and since it was the costume everyone else wore as *clothing*, only they knew it. It was their secret, not even spoken among themselves, but somehow sustaining them, helping, certainly, to sustain their friendship for over four decades.

Now he wants to tell Wink: all we've fooled is ourselves. The operative irony actually belongs to our class and our culture. And those are laughing at us: *You think you can escape being defined by class? Escape through style? Through hipness? Through sexual elan? Through political cynicism? That's our little joke. You belong to us.*

But of course he doesn't say this. "We've had a hell of a good run for it," he says.

"Nobody's been young like us," Wink says.

"Sure. Nobody."

"I'm glad you're here, Pete. I feel I can let go and bullshit a little. Who can I talk to this way? You, hell, you probably know me better than anyone does."

"Except Nan."

"Sure, oh, sure…"

Pete understands: Wink isn't sure *what* Nan knows. Pete says, "I *should* know you. You saved my life. You held me with your hands—" and he mimes Wink holding the rope when the piton gave way.

"God made me a fullback," Wink laughs.

"Without those arms and shoulders of yours, there'd be no Steven, there'd be no Jennifer—I mean it was before my kids were born."

"Well, I couldn't do it today." Wink laughs. He's more cheerful. "Christ, we couldn't do that *climb* today. Some men in their sixties could, but we're out of shape. At least I am."

"No. No. Have another drink," Pete says, and pours.

Wink goes to bed a little drunk, but not too drunk to wake Nan for her midnight pills. Pete, swaying a little, stands by the door as Wink hovers over her bed and murmurs something and a husky voice fumbles a reply.

Now Pete settles down for the night. Naked in the full-length mirror, he sees himself still lean, but beginning to droop; sees the start of a turkey wattle, sees legs sturdy from tennis but lumpy, full of lumps and bumps, as if a sculptor had patched an old statue to add support.

"Well, we *were* grand," he says to himself, "grand as…grand." He remembers—sees in his mind's eye sunlight and a boat—one all-day sail to Nantucket a summer the Thompsons visited. The air so clear. Boats and islands were delineated precisely. And in this sweet light, that's how he remembers the families: *delineated*, etched against blue sky as if they were ritual dancers miming gestures of certain gods.

Alice Thompson must have been ten or eleven that summer, because she was having her first period. There were whisperings and brooding and deep silences, and Nan keeping a wing over her. Pete had always delighted in Alice, and it hurt that she wouldn't soften to him as she usually did. Secrets, secrets. His own daughter, Jennifer, seven that year, was bewildered—she always looked up to Alice. *She still does.* Steven was an infant—Betsy lay on the deck with Steven at her breast. Nan sat at the prow with Alice, caressing her and singing. Nan's long auburn hair was blowing out of its scarf around her face. Pete remembers her smile.

All this ordinary, astonishing young life going on one afternoon on a twenty-six foot sailboat, while he and Wink took turns at the helm and the boat leaned against the wind. Now Alice and Jennifer and Steven each have children of their own, days of their own like that day.

Of course there are the things he chooses not to reimagine about that luminous afternoon. The complexities. He can sense himself stuffing the complexities away in the pouch he always stows somewhere on his person. But never mind. That sail! He takes it to bed with him tonight, remembers, back of his eyes, the light, like a talisman to defend himself against the image of a darkened room, silhouette of a big man hovering over the dim shape of a bed.

Pete wakes to the smell of bacon frying. It's been a long time, fifty points of cholesterol, since he last had bacon for breakfast. He's touched; he knows Wink has done this for his fellow-American. He shaves and comes downstairs to coffee and scrambled eggs and bacon, thick-sliced. He remembers the four of them hiking in Cornwall. The eggs every morning—they made you say, *Oh, this is what eggs are supposed to be—I never ate eggs before*. So this breakfast feels celebratory, like last night's whiskey. But after, Wink fumbles with the silver, shrugs, starts to speak, just asks, "Want more coffee?"

Always, Pete has thought of Wink as a great bear. Even to the grunts—he grunts when he's trying to say something and having a hard time. Now Wink straightens. "Look here: you don't mind keeping guard a few hours? A meeting I decided to sit in on. Pretty important. When I heard you were coming…"

"Of course. Wink. Christ—"

"You can read to Nan. She likes that, especially the poets, poets she knows well, Keats, Whitman, Shakespeare sonnets. It's the music, you know what I mean?"

"Does she understand?"

"God only knows. You get hints and clues, but if she could say, 'Here's what I understand, here's what I remember, here's what I don't,' then she wouldn't have the problem, would she? Sometimes I see her grope for a word. It's hard on her. She gets down, way the hell down, defeated. Imagine Nan defeated? *Nan*?"

Pete can't.

"I'm the fullback, I always have been, Pete. I get the job done, pick up the yardage, but she's the quarterback, she calls the plays. I'll bet you never knew that. I'm not putting myself down—I'm as smart as I need to be, and a lot more worldly-wise than Nan. But she's the one, you know?"

"You love her a lot. Anyone can see."

Wink hunches forward over the table, grunts a couple of times, talks low though there's no need. "I wouldn't say this to a soul but you, Pete. Nan and I—it hasn't been the marriage it looked like. Even when you first met us. Even before Alice. I'll tell you a funny thing. Nan's such a romantic bird—*you* used to call her that, remember?—'bird of bright feathers.' And me—well, you know me. But the funny thing is, *I'm* the closet romantic. I wanted a great romance in my life. And what it *has* been—well, it's been a team, we're teammates. We're partners. It's been Alice, of course. And grandchildren. It's investment portfolios and trust arrangements. It's *getting on*." He grunts low in his chest and fingers the table. "But the past few years—just the past *couple* of years—we've become more—I don't know how to put it—*interesting* to one another. So..."

"Makes it all the harder."

"Makes it all the harder. Now I'm totally with her, Pete. We've begun to take walks around the room. I pretend it's the Alhambra or Vence. I point out the sights, and she laughs. Doesn't sound much like me, does it?"

"Does Nan remember Vence? Do you think?"

Wink shrugs his big shoulders.

When Wink leaves, Nan is working with the physiotherapist. Pete thinks about what Wink said last night. *Nobody's been young like us.* So much falsity, he thinks. We were so grand for God's camera. But you got no points from God or whoever was keeping score for acting exactly as you were expected to act and pretending it was a put-on. And their insistence on youth. When they were forty, it wasn't the way the others were forty; when fifty, why, they, they were young, while the others were old and sexless.

And now look: that beautiful woman upstairs. Look.

When Pete began to understand this four or five years ago, he cut his hair short, almost like a monk. He'd always traded on being a handsome man. Well, he stopped. He took long walks and didn't think. Well, he didn't *have* to think, he was weaning himself into retirement. For awhile, he was almost unbearably sad; hell, *still*—he's still sad. But he felt that for the first time, he really inhabited, for better or worse, his life.

He didn't speak about it to Betsy. He didn't speak about it to Wink or Nan. Now he has to simulate the irony he once believed separated them out into a caste of their own. But it's as if he looked at them all, himself included, from the other side of a stroke, other side of the grave—their real beauty, their vanities. Everything seems tainted by vanity.

Still, he knows, there are things he's not ready to give up.

After the therapist goes and before the nurse arrives, he takes tea up to Nan on the same silver tray. He helps her sit up in bed and take her pills with water. They play at being cheerful.

She wears an off-white satin bed jacket. Wink or the therapist must have helped her put it on. Her hair, the auburn it's always been but graying at the roots, is brushed and tied back. The softness of her face surprises him again. With her left hand she lifts her right hand out of her way. He probes her eyes, avoiding notice of the discrepancy between her eyes. "So," he starts. "So. We have so much history between us—among the four of us. Now our children carry it on. Austin and Jennifer send their love. They've spoken to Alice. *So* much history."

"Skiing," she says. Just the one word.

"Yes." He pulls his chair closer. "*Skiing*. You do remember?"

As if communication has to travel through great distances to reach her, there's a long silence before she says, "I remember."

"And you remember, oh…remember swimming off the rocks near Bandol? We were in our twenties, the three of us, it was before I met Betsy. You remember the afternoon I mean?"

It's too much for her to process. He watches her mouth, drooping clown-like to one side, form but not say words, and he feels ashamed, making her work this hard. He simplifies: "Bandol? *Bandol*, Nan?"

"I remember."

"What do you remember, Nan?"

"I remember…" and now sounds spill out, maybe words, and her eyes close in frustration and she takes a breath and says, "everything. I remember *everything*. I even worry…"

"What about? You *worry*," he prompts, as if she might lose the thread.

"At night…my sleep…I may talk in sleep…. Talk things…. Wink hear. Remember? I remember everything." She sinks back into her pillow.

Now they inhabit the same silence.

"I'm sorry, I had to ask. Forty years, Nan. Dear God. I had to know. I was scared I was alone in all that remembering. Then it would be as if it had never happened."

"Remember…Venice?"

"Yes. I remember, I remember," Pete says, breathy, almost like singing the words, but he's uneasy. He wonders, when she remembers "everything," what *everything* does she remember? *He* sees white sheets, French doors opening on a little balcony, he can feel Nan's soft body at his fingers and smell the warm, furry scent of her body after making love. And Nan?

"Remember...what?" she asks.

And now he stops, surprised, as if he's found his way into a strange room. Maybe Nan remembers other things, wants *him* to remember other things. Maybe *his* is the flawed memory.

And at once, in mind's eye, he sees Nan's look sometime late that afternoon—if it *was* that afternoon. Was it? A bleak look at the white wall. All the complexities. Where they'd come to.

"Remember love," he says simply.

And it's enough for her. Still, she's struggling to speak. "You came to see...if I remember? That...because...why...you came."

"I came to be with you. *And* with Wink. I love Wink." Now he was sitting at the edge of the bed, stroking her hand on the hurt side, though she probably couldn't feel it. "But mostly—well, to *know*. If you didn't remember, it would be like being the last survivor of a world."

She presses his hand with her good hand. He feels, as he has always felt, at least these past thirty years, since they both knew that nothing would ever change in their situation, feels intensely real in her presence and at the same time feels as if he's play-acting, false not just to Wink and Betsy but to himself. He doesn't fully understand this feeling. It's grown these past five years. It has to do with how he's exploited a real love—real, yes, no doubt about it—for forty years, keeping it in his pocket like a secret piece of himself, as one in exile might finger a secret seal to remember he was royal. In this way he exploited their love and turned it into theater for an audience of one. This he can't say to Nan, he could never say. In this knowledge he's always been alone.

He strokes her cheeks with his fingertips, wanting her to know he isn't unnerved by her changes. She leans toward him and closes her eyes and he closes his. This is what they have, they have what they have. He doesn't talk about history, she doesn't talk about love.

Wink's home, Wink's up there with Nan. Pete can sometimes think, it's like a strange marriage of the four of them. But of course they don't all know that, so it's not. Often, he wishes he could tell Wink all, or part. Maybe, he thinks, when the eros is really gone. But if that hasn't happened now—if he's still roused by her, soaked in her, not like when they were thirty, rushing to little hotels in back streets in London or New York, but *still, still,* as surely as he was last year at Montreux, when she went "shopping" and he went "fishing" on the lake knowing Wink hated fishing—if not now, when will it happen? And even if it did—he knows he lacks the courage. It's not that he fears Wink would turn away from him—though perhaps he would—but that it would make *Wink* feel the sole inhabitant of a world. What would the guy have left?

He'd have Nan, you fool. That's what he'd have. Pete laughs at the grand joke and feels suddenly desolate. At this moment, while upstairs Wink gives her comfort, while maybe they walk around a room that has become a crowded, remembered market in Cairo, while they share something that's grown between them privately all these years, Pete feels as if he's already inhabiting a world of one. As if he's always lived there. Courage—it's not just that he lacks the courage to speak to Wink. It's that he loves holding the secret *secret.* His last vanity. In this endless love affair, maybe he hasn't loved Nan as much as he's loved their *affair.*

From his room, lonely, he calls home. The machine answers—his own voice—though this was the time, late morning in Connecticut, they'd planned to talk. But now Betsy picks up and stops the recording.

Nan's better, Peter reports. And he invents, "She sends her love to you."

"Tell her: I want to talk to her as soon as she feels able."

"Of course. Of course. I'll let you know. Not yet, honey."

"How bad is it, Pete? Is it very bad?"

"She's cleaved in two, but with therapy a lot will improve. So Wink says. There's loss of memory, but her memory is coming back to her. I guess she'll be nearly all right."

"And *does* she remember?" Betsy asks.

"She remembers us. She remembers you and me."

"Pete. *No*, Pete. I *mean*," Betsy says, "I'm asking, does she remember *you*? Remember the two of you?"

There's a long trans-Atlantic silence, hiss of the wires. And from within the white noise, Pete can see Betsy sitting in the conservatory they added on last year; the air warm, golden and green. It's late morning; she's wearing her old gardening pants with its many pockets; he imagines her sitting with a cup of coffee and staring at the trays of seedlings she'd started last week. And for a moment he's there with her; then, trick of the heart, she's there alone, it's like a movie tracking shot, from close up to long shot, until he's seeing her through glass and the bare branches of March trees in Connecticut. And then there's just this black phone and old furniture and they're thousands of miles apart.

"She remembers."

"Well, that's *good*," Betsy says. "I'm glad. I am glad."

After they say goodbye, as Pete stands at the window staring out at the little railed park, Wink calls through the door, "Pete? Can you come have tea with us? With Nan and me?"

And he collects himself and combs his fingers through his short-cropped hair and goes upstairs to take tea.

First appeared as "Secret Lives" in Fiction, *Spring, 1997*

The Builder

So, God is there. Simply *there*. Nothing fancy for Michael, no choral music, no auras or penumbras. No mescaline tricks. Just God. For *me*—the word catches me in the chest and makes my breath pulse, blood thump in my temple. For *me* it's almost erotic. I feel the danger of the word. But for Michael at that moment, it's ordinary, always there, he just hadn't known how ordinary.

Later, on the drive home past fields flooded with rain and melted snow, foothills of the Berkshires, Michael asks himself, *What was it like*? It was like breath. He breathed in—all right, that was God. He breathed out, and his (impure, exhausted) breath became a part of a perfect God. Odd, it was so simple. It was Saturday morning service, the synagogue suffused with sun through the stained glass of what was once a Congregational Church. Being wrapped in the *tallith* was like being wrapped in God. The knots of the fringes of a prayer shawl symbolize the *mitzvot*, the commandments for a Jew, but that had nothing to do with what he felt. Rather it was like being held, held *up*, by hands in a sea.

There was a *Bat Mitzvah* in the synagogue that morning. As he'd looked around, he knew that except for the family of the girl and a few others, he was alone. He wanted to call out, "God is here with us now!" Instead, he closed his eyes, trying to ignore the family friends dressed up for the Bat Mitzvah, their eyes wandering, waiting for the service to end and get down to the congratulating.

The girl herself was unusually competent in Torah, and she was surrounded by a family of devout Jews he knew slightly, and he wondered if they had brought God here. He didn't think so. He said, *Dear One, I know you're also with me in the car, in the woods when I ski, in meetings with clients.* He tried—as I am trying now, dancing on a wire in these words that feel so unfamiliar—not to ask questions, afraid to dislodge the connection, but it's like telling yourself not to think about your breathing. He tried to hold the awareness as he drove home, but it was already gone—

—leaving him not refreshed, open to life, but ragged, tired, brooding, wanting to be alone, away from Jeremy's piano and Karen's worries—*Would there be appetizers enough for the party?—There's* something to worry about! He knows it's only Karen's way of expressing stress. But he tightens against her. And heavy in his chest is the work he's supposed to forget on the Sabbath. Not just the ordinary pressures of his business, but Azakarian, George Azakarian, who thickens his lungs, forcing long, turgid breaths.

These days, Michael can't keep things out. He has no skin. Most of the time, I think, we walk around in an extra skin manufactured by a processing plant in Texas or Minnesota. Now he walks through Stop and Shop with just his clothes, and, drained by fatigue and contempt, sees people living in a world not only invented—of *course* invented—but boring, a boring invention, a bad animated cartoon world. Unconvincing. If he could see truly, he could make this supermarket into a sacred space. He can't. The neon, the color on the packages, seems to press upon his sinuses. God's world is blotted out by words and fancy logos. He wants to leave his cart and run. But he needs to bring home appetizers.

Down the next aisle a child howls like an animal. A mother

yells, "I already *told* you, *No!* And No means no means no!" over the selling-music.

It's humiliating that after this morning he has this little peace. Look how I am screwing up God's holy instrument—like leaving a violin out in the rain.

As he serves drinks to his friends, he feels he's the only one who has visited, just for a moment, the real world. Four couples: he wants to care about what they say. He's ashamed by his own arrogance. But in the middle of the party, between drinks and dinner, he slips away, sits cross-legged on the floor of his walk-in closet. He says, over and over, *Praise God who has brought the world into Being.* Nothing happens except for stiffness in his hips. Besides, is this how a Jew should act? His place is downstairs. Tell them about Azakarian and the children. Or comfort Stephen, whose mother is dying; Michael remembers what it was like, to lose his mother.

"Michael? *Dinner*, Michael!" He hears Karen's impatience.

At dinner he tells his friends about George Azakarian and the shelter for children: how this non-profit—Aid for Children in Transition, A.C.T.—found a big Victorian house in a wealthy neighborhood in Springdale for a group home, but the neighbors wouldn't have it. An old story. *This,* they said, *is one of the only decent neighborhoods left in Springdale.* "We're talking about a shelter for little kids," Michael told his friends, "children five through twelve. Not disturbed teenagers—little kids taken from families where they're beaten or raped. The neighbors hired a lawyer. Hell, these are the rich and powerful. A.C.T. had the law on its side—could have won a court fight—but these rich bastards would have gotten the legislature to put the squeeze on funding. So, A.C.T. had to back off. And we got called in, Peter and me."

"Tell them why it was you," Karen prompted.

"Because of our work in rehab housing."

"Michael and Peter have a great reputation."

"Anyway, A.C.T.'s going to have to stay where it is. In a semi-slum in Springdale. They want to build an addition. But they haven't got the money. I mean, not even close. And this guy Azakarian—he wants the impossible."

His friends sympathize, then pass on to other things, but Michael doesn't follow them. He remembers Azakarian's photographs: two smiling children, one seven, one four. Next, the little one lying crumpled like a rag, a police photo. *His brother lives with us now; his mother is wasted on drugs, his stepfather is awaiting trial.* Michael picks at his roast and for comfort rocks slightly, like an old Jew in synagogue, not so anyone can see.

But Karen has seen. And later—"Do you think it's a pleasure to live with you in these moods?"

"It's not something I want to talk about. Something good happened. In synagogue today—"

"*Today*! Michael, you've been this way for months. Maybe a year. You're getting so peculiar. Michael, look at you, look in the mirror. 'Something good'?—It's like you're in mourning. For whom? Who died?"

He could tell her, but he doesn't; he takes his pillow and once again sleeps wrapped in self-righteousness in the study.

Monday morning begins with the usual planning meeting, Michael Kahn and Peter Malley. They've got an architectural design firm just outside Green River. House Smiths is more than a design firm; it's a company that designs and builds houses—prefabs a lot of the components themselves in a big steel building they were able to pick up for a song when businesses were dropping like flies, 1990, rode out the recession and now they're squeezed for space.

Michael's the front man, he shmoozes with architects and clients. I conjure him to be good looking, lean; thick hair still black; he has tender eyes that really look at you and a kind smile, though he hasn't been smiling lately. Peter, powerful, balding, he's the money man, positioning the business for sale in a few years so they can both retire, if they feel inclined, just past fifty—not bad for a couple of leftist carpenters, hippie carpenters, who met on a commune in Vermont, early seventies. Peter's father was an inventor, a tinkerer, a genius with tools. Peter built his own dresser, with his father's help, at age seven. But Michael grew up in Boston, son of a research psychologist father and a sociologist mother, and hardly used a hammer until he needed a summer job in college. For him, doing carpentry was partly carrying on the quarrel with his father.

As was being a Jew.

For to be a practicing Jew was to slip back out of the modern world, to be like his grandfather, his father's father. His mother wouldn't have minded—she was tender with the old man. His father would have rolled his eyes.

His grandfather lived in the third-floor apartment they fixed up in the big Edwardian house in Brookline, Mass. Michael's mother used to walk him to shul. Later, when Michael was eight, nine, ten, he was the one who walked with his grandfather Saturday mornings, and the old man would hum synagogue melodies in anticipation. That was Michael's Jewish education. If his grandfather had lived a little longer, Michael might have been Bar Mitzvahed. After his grandfather's death, when Michael had time to himself, he would climb the servant stairway to the third floor and knock. "Grandpa? *Zeide*?" It was a word between the two of them, *zeide*, for when he forgot and called his grandfather *zeide* at dinner, his father would lift his eyebrows, and Michael would correct himself—"Grandpa."

There was a different smell to the third floor. Old-man smell, smoked fish on his breath, dusty upholstery of cast-off furniture, gaberdine that never went to the cleaners. Michael liked to breathe in the smell, though it was sour, strange, and half of what his grandfather talked about he didn't understand. I mean, not at all. Yiddish, Hebrew. Stories about the long dead. Later, when he was a teenager and his *zeide* was dead, he'd sometimes take a book up to the third floor, by then shut up, dim, storerooms really, and sit on the sagging red velvet sofa to read.

"Your grandfather is from another century," his father would say. "He still lives in Odessa." And Michael believed this. His father played his collection of jazz records and felt they somehow made him part of modern America. Upstairs, Jacob Kahn sang in Yiddish or chanted in Hebrew; he had a quavering but rich voice and it wasn't until Michael was seven or eight that he stopped acting as part-time cantor. So then it was only Michael who listened. When his father overheard, he would roll his eyes. He permitted the old man to say a blessing at table, while he—Ira—busied himself salting his food. So now, being a practicing Jew has been like undergoing conversion. He inherited his grandfather's prayer shawl, and now, when he wraps himself in the shawl, he imagines his grandfather within his flesh.

My own grandfather, also Jacob, was dead before I was born. I wish he'd lived upstairs. He's the old man whose photos hang on the wall of my study, heavy beard and the wide-brimmed black hat and long black coat, grandfather with my grandmother and seven children, two almost grown, my mother the youngest, a studio portrait taken just after they arrived in America, 1906, after the pogrom in Kishnief.

Why do I need this other grandfather and this "Michael" between us—between you and me? Michael is a word fumbling towards becoming a person. That's always true of a character in a story. But *Michael himself* feels like a character. Before anyone else was awake this morning, he looked in the mirror and was unfamiliar to himself. He didn't dislike the man he saw, but who was it, anyway? The only person with whom he felt at home was the one aware of the incongruity, asking question with his eyes.

I know what that's like. Sometimes I read one of my old stories and wonder who wrote it. Michael feels like the author of his life; but that means his life is...just a story—and in a sense, not even *his*. For several seconds this morning he stood outside the company entrance trying to inhabit the body of the lean, middle-aged man in clean jeans and expensive Shetland wool sweater so he could walk in the building without feeling like an imposter. He didn't mind borrowing this particular person to live within; he had nothing against him. But it was a borrowing.

This Monday morning, he and Peter go through current projects and prospects, pull in their three project managers for briefings, cope with schedules, problems, ruffled feelings. It's spring, peak season for them. Peter—recently remarried—groans, his way of bragging, that he's recovering from an all-day Sunday love session. Michael pats his shoulder and grins as he's meant to. They *don't* talk about the group home. Alone in his office, whine of the mill, factory noises, mostly insulated out, he puts *yarmulka*, skullcap, on his head, wraps himself in his grandfather's *tallith* and says the morning *Shema*.

On his walls are pictures of completed buildings—a co-housing development he's particularly proud of, a whole street of rehab apartments, the rest subdivision houses, modular but each unique and strong. He likes what this "Michael" does. But from the quiet of his prayers he sees Michael's life a complicated fabrication, substantial and invented as architecture. He feels he might tiptoe out of Michael's body and let it go on doing. Then he could slip out of the invented world into the world God made.

God isn't here this morning, not like in synagogue the other day. But the world out the window, the parking lot, the orchard across the road, the hillside beginning to green, hum with living silence.

Peter raps and enters, already talking about a bid he's preparing for Smith College, and Michael has to reenter the invented world. He folds the prayer shawl away, feels like a high school kid caught with a cigarette. Peter squints, taps the crown of his own head. "That thing, what d'you call it?"

"This? A *yarmulka*." Michael covers it with his palm as if protecting.

"Yeah. So. You gonna wear that 'yamuka' with clients around?"

Michael pulls out a file and ignores him. Peter opens his arms and raises his palms, accepting the burden of this craziness. "Hey. It's okay with me you get a little nuts." But he doesn't leave.

"*What?*"

"You're *not* gonna wear that…*shawl* thing?"

"Not with clients. It's for prayer."

"Well Ah'm fuckin' relieved."

Michael hears Peter pretending to be crude, playing the role of tough ignoramus as a way of putting himself into a comic posture, and Michael, aware of the subtle delicacy, the kindness under the toughness, smiles at him tenderly.

Peter squinches up his face, refusing the generous eyes. He hates bullshit and looks it. He's a thick man, built like a wrestler—*a Sumo wrestler*, he jokes sometimes, rubbing his balding head and thrusting out his belly, pouting his lips. "I realize we didn't talk about the group home. Later, okay? Now *there's* a can of worms."

Michael gets on the phone to clients. He drives out to oversee the million-dollar showplace he's building for Mr. Gianapoulos in the hills above the Connecticut Valley. The land is being cleared. Gianapoulos is poking around today, so Michael has to stand with him admiring the view, as if Gianapoulos had made the valley he sweeps with his hand.

When he gets back, George Azakarian is waiting for him. A bloated man in his forties, man with a thick nose and thinning hair, Azakarian has apparently just finished a bag lunch in the waiting room; there are crumbs on the rug, stains and cigarette ash on the shapeless sports jacket he always wears and on his tie. Azakarian may be the last man on earth, surely in the Connecticut Valley, to wear a bow tie. Which he ties himself. Badly. His shirt is missing a button; it's a cotton shirt that needs ironing and isn't ironed. All this is disarming. You feel comfortable with the slob, and then he puts the squeeze on.

Azakarian brushes himself off and follows Michael into his office. He smells of cigarette smoke. "I don't mean to badger you," he says, "but what's this message you left on my machine? I don't understand, Mr. Kahn. *Michael.* I thought we had an arrangement, Michael. I've put a lot of time into this."

"Sit down. Please. Look—you guys are a hundred thousand under-budgeted. A lot of the problem is disability access, sprinklers, all that crap. It's State requirements, I know, but whoever you work with, nobody can do it for the price you're talking."

"With you. We're working with you."

Michael closes his eyes.

"There are six children in the house; too many as it is. And we need space for twelve more. The good people of Springdale decided that their property values—"

"I know, I know that. It was in the papers. My partner…"

"I'm not dealing with your partner."

"Every agency guilt-trips the builder, Mr. Azakarian. Everytime we do a rehab or co-housing—they want a benefit performance. Tell me—do you take a cut in your salary?"

Azakarian laughs. "*My* salary?"

"Okay. I get it. But look: this is our *business*. We wouldn't be here if we didn't make a profit."

"Did I ask you for charity?"

"Essentially—yes."

"You remember the photographs I showed you? I ask you to think hard about those children," Azakarian says on his way out. And as if in after thought: "You have children, Mr. Kahn?"

Michael asks back: "Do *you*?"

"All-told, resident and non-resident, forty-three of them, Mr. Kahn."

Their usual cost-plus contract gives them a ten percent edge. "Suppose we drop my part of the profit," he says to Peter. "Cut it to five percent."

"It's not just profit, Michael, it's money for the business."

"You can take it out of my bonus the end of the year."

"Oh for chrissakes. Don't fuckin' insult me. Sometimes you can get so goddamn smug," Peter says. He sits on Michael's desk. "You really think it's the five percent? Don't insult me. It's spreading ourselves too thin. We take on this, we can't concentrate on that—and *that*, m'man, is work for Smith College. *Money*. Eight hundred thousand. You take on a little project for A.C.T., it'll eat up the same effort. Am I wrong?"

"You're not wrong. And as it is, they don't have the money."

"We're not a charity."

"We're not. That's what I told him."

"Tell him you'll cut him a check, give them a couple hundred. Okay?"

For a while he can keep the two of him going at once. God is not at his beck and call; but there are times. There get to be times in an ordinary day when he has to stop the car on the way home, because everything he sees is suffused with the same single life, the same being, and it's not a world of *things*; or it is and it isn't, for there are certainly "things" but they are all conjoined. Praise God who has brought the world into Being. This is Being.

And so he tells Mr. Gianopoulos, for whom he's building a 1.2 million dollar house on that beautiful piece of land overlooking the valley, Mr. Gianopoulos, who's a haggler, a cranky, pompous sonofabitch who owns a trio of gas stations, that if the house they're building for him were turned thirty degrees, oriented so that the morning light could enter *there,* it would invite God in. "This way, you see?" Michael says pointing to the screen, turning the computer model in relation to a computer sun, "God will be there. Well," he laughs, "God is always there, but this way you'd feel it, you'd feel it. Every morning—imagine!—you'll feel God's light like breath through your house."

They don't lose the account, but Peter has to take it over. "I'm sorry," Michael says. "I got carried away."

"Suppose Gianopoulos doesn't believe in God."

"Belief is beside the point, Pete. I'm not interested in a God you 'believe' in—or don't 'believe' in. Belief's got nothing to do with it."

"Well, hear me—I'm not interested in what you fuckin' *feel*, if we're talking feeling. Okay?"

This time, no kind comic posture.

Azakarian stops by just as Michael is to leave for the day. He stands and brushes himself off; always he's got something *to* brush off, in this case, crumbs from tortilla chips. "Don't think I want to badger you—"

"Of course you want to badger me."

"Look, Mr. Kahn: the situations we face are getting worse and worse. We talk about making transitions for children to go back to their families. But there *are* no families. The children have always had multiple problems, but the problems have gotten worse, and money is being cut back. We've run out of possibilities, Michael." He opens his hands to show there's nothing up his sleeve.

"So that's my responsibility?"

"You ought to come for a visit."

Michael drives from Green River down to Springdale. Springdale is a defeated mill city, maybe sixty percent on public assistance. He's got work to do—supervising the rehab-ing of new apartments in six adjoining tenement buildings in the poorest section of town.

As he drives, he chants the *Amidah.*

He irritates me, this Michael. It's not hard to love God-in-the-world through the window of a Volvo as you pass cows pastured under a hillside. What about in Springdale?

In Springdale, he passes boarded-up stores, whole streets the City has taken in default of taxes and covered the windows with plywood so that the buildings look like frightening dead things. Can he tell those two overweight young women pushing babies in strollers that there is available to them a world in which God is present? The children will go to a firetrap school—he's been there to consult on renovations—where the money goes for boiler repairs and heat that escapes through cracks in the old brick, cracks you can see through, and the teachers have thirty-five kids, including kids with special problems, some with hardly any English, instead of the fifteen in Jeremy's class. In a world this crippled, what does it mean to bless? To put it plainly—does the blessing make him an accomplice in the crippling? Michael tells himself, *Oh, but this crippled world, that's not* God's *world; it's the world people invented, it's Babylon—where the poor are, with a shrug, shoved out of sight into their poverty.* And isn't he doing something to unmake Babylon?

He and Peter make a very good guaranteed profit on rehab housing.

On his way to the job, he drives a few blocks out of his way to see group home. A.C.T. runs a facility in an old two-family house on a dead-end street. It's nothing fancy, but it's clean. The kids seem okay. Three running around or climbing, one standing, rocking himself against a chain-fence. They're dressed warm, there's some woman watching out for them. He looks into a window. Drab but not filthy. Still, he thinks about Jeremy living in a place this bleak. Out of sight of the kids, he prays to try to get sadness out of his chest. He doesn't go inside.

It's Friday evening; he tries to find refuge in the Sabbath. He has to shop again; home, he unloads his bags and his heart, sits down with Karen and Jeremy to light the *shabbat* candles and say the prayers. Karen goes along with this for his sake. Jeremy likes the ritual; he's the one to light the candles as Michael says the prayers in Hebrew and English. In the silence afterwards, Michael finds his hands, eyes, mouth, lungs, opening; everything will work out. The children, this marriage, our common life. He is so open he has to catch his breath. "God," he announces, "is here. Now. Is here with us tonight."

Karen scrunches up her eyes. He knows that tilt of her head to one side: she doesn't know how to take him. She reaches under the table to take hold of Jeremy's hand. Michael understands the gesture as part of an ongoing dialogue from which he's been excluded.

He reassures her. "The world that God has created: look: it's simple: it's here, *we're* here *in* it." He opens his hands as if catching rain, and combs his finger through the charged air.

"I'm glad for you," she says. She doesn't look glad. "Michael? Are you here at the table, Michael? We're having dinner, all right? Look. I made *coq au vin* instead of roast chicken. And I bought a *challah* for you."

Jeremy seems to understand that his father is not speaking in metaphor. He won't let go with his eyes. Michael wants to reassure. But what can he say? *I love coq au vin*?

God no longer seems to be with them.

To write about a man experiencing the world-God-made, the world of Being, it's as if I am wearing a fish-smelling beard in Western Massachusetts. Michael becomes a fool; these words make me a fool. They don't work anymore. I'm supposed to speak the language of the invented world. But it's so clumsy for expressing the world of Being. How do I talk about the world that God makes and makes and continues making? Michael invites God into the world; I invite God into a "realistic" story. The form is strained; it wants to see Michael as "disturbed."

Well, and isn't he disturbed? God knows he is. God-crazed, his eyes inappropriate for overseeing construction, he walks out on a scaffolding over a two-story living room in his father's old fedora coated in sheet-rock dust, and pretends not to notice the carpenters grin at one another. Even at synagogue he feels that people are looking at him curiously. He makes an appointment to speak to the rabbi.

Rabbi Singer is in his early thirties. Michael likes him but wishes he were at least seventy, with labored breath and deep-set eyes. He doesn't tell him God appeared to him in synagogue. He says, *I can't walk through the mall without tears coming to my eyes. I can't look at the* New York Times.

"Well, the *newspaper*, of course, of course."

"There's a story about Tutsi women raped by Hutus, and now the women are outcast, the women and their children, and terrorized as well. Or I read about the great famine in China in the early sixties—as many as thirty million died. That's five Holocausts."

"There's no comparison—" the rabbi begins.

"That's not my point, Rabbi. It's that on the next page there are recipes for peppering foods, there are sexy men and women in jeans. Furs are 'in.' There's fabulous new architecture in New Zealand. This is nothing new, I understand. An old story, Rabbi."

"Of course. Terrible ironies. Cognitive dissonance."

"It's dissonance—but not 'cognitive.' I sit at the kitchen table and weep. And then there's God's world, it's here and we can't live in it. It's dissonance of the heart, and how do you live with that?"

The rabbi nods his head. "I think you're seeing accurately, Mr. Kahn, you're certainly seeing what's there. But the *weeping*..." Haltingly, he suggests that Michael "seek help." He means not divine guidance but a psychotherapist.

At night he is afraid to go to sleep, because lately dreams have been engulfing him like a deadly sea; in the morning he feels exhausted by the struggle. People turn to God to give them stability. Michael *used* to be stable; God has destablized him.

As he dresses, mornings, he becomes aware that he has been inhabited by his grandfather. It slows down his walk. Odessa has come to Western Massachusetts. Michael remembers when he was a little boy and his grandfather went around their house humming synagogue melodies, murmuring the Hebrew with its heavy *ch* sounds that relieve the heart. His breathing was so thick and labored that sometimes Michael was afraid to stand near someone whose bronchia were constantly singing of death. Yet now, he can't do without him.

Inhabiting his grandfather, he is astonished by the microwave, the VCR, the pastures and hills appearing and disappearing with magic speed as Michael drives to work. To make his grandfather feel at home, he stops shaving. It isn't a decision exactly; one day he forgets to shave, and Karen goes off for a weekend workshop, so he doesn't have to shave, and when she comes back he has the beginning of a beard. He has a picture of his *zeide* in a photographer's studio. The old man is trying to be American; in this picture he is not wearing his black hat. Michael, brought up American, needs to become a greenhorn.

So he stops shaving, he grows his sideburns and twists the ends into the beginnings of ear locks. He doesn't wear a skull cap but the old fedora. A fedora doesn't go with a zip-up windbreaker. It's as if he has to recreate his grandfather's condition, make himself a mourner and a pariah—he is making himself a pariah fast—in order to have the privilege of loving God as his grandfather did.

Karen says, "If I wanted to marry your marvelous grandfather, I'd have gone to the Lubavitcher in Brooklyn."

Peter takes him to lunch and talks about buying him out.

For school vacation, Karen takes Jeremy to her parents—just half an hour away. "At a time like this, I don't want to leave you alone, Michael—no, really, I don't—but I worry what this is doing to Jeremy. The way you look. And it's not just the way you look. It's all right that you pray, but I catch you standing at the window and rocking, *davening*. This isn't a synagogue. Michael? Even the way you *breathe*, so heavy…"

"I can shave. You want me to shave?" And when she doesn't answer, he asks, "Are you coming back?"

Karen shrugs. "It's not been so great lately, Michael."

Michael sits with Jeremy in his bedroom the night before they leave. He puts his arm around him and feels him stiffen. "It's all right, honey. I've got a beard, but I'm not crazy."

Suddenly, Jeremy hugs him back, furiously.

Alone, he eats tuna out of cans, doesn't change his underwear. He prays, he's a prayer junkie, waking early to pray, getting to work late, sneaking prayers at his desk, not taking home bids to work over but reading Torah. The required three times a day he prays, and then he stops the car and walks in the woods to talk to God. Prayers that always seemed empty, circular—*Praise God, who is to be praised* (vainglorious, as if God were a sports hero, as if this were a celebrity God who needed praise, basked in it)—now, at the good times, they seem so clear: instructions to attune yourself (like adjusting the dial) to what hums beneath things, divesting yourself of glories customarily praised: the meretricious. False gods. It doesn't matter if I can retire at fifty with an income. It doesn't matter if Karen wins High School Teacher of the Year. All he wants is to live in the part of himself that's holy because it's permeated with God.

As I, too, want to enter the original world. These words, a prayer. I use words to get beyond words, hammer and nail this strange space. But then I'm shut off inside the words I make. I hardly know what it's like outside—I mean this earth, the sun, squirrels trekking across my deck rail. I sit typing these words and forget what's outside the window and the people who can't say where their next meal is coming from or how to pay the doctor. The words are a clumsy prayer, but the words keep me outside the only world God can find to inhabit. It's an occupational hazard.

After the week's vacation, Karen begins to commute to school—temporarily, she says—from her parents' house instead of returning home. Michael broods about Jeremy and is reminded of the *Akeda*—Abraham's willingness to sacrifice Isaac before God's release of them both. Yes, God's release—but think of the trauma, *the walk home, father and son*! Is he, Michael, sacrificing Jeremy? He thinks about the children at Azakarian's shelter. He's made Jeremy one step closer to their condition. To be in God's world, does that make him complicitous in injury, like Abraham?

He wants his family back. He know he needs to stop this.

He asks Peter to meet him in the conference room. He can see himself in Peter's eyes. "So I look that bad?"

"That old dirty hat on your head, your dirty beard—they think you're crazy, the guys. D'you know that? *Are* you crazy? You want to take a crazy leave?"

And Michael doesn't argue. It's like he's *using* Pete's anger the way the *Penitente* used whips to scourge themselves.

"We've got something going here, you fuck it up you're doing it to both of us. Man, you've got to pull your weight. I'd sue your ass, I'd find a clause, but we're supposed to be friends." He turns away.

"Peter? I'm thinking maybe I should build for Azakarian. For A.C.T.. A home for the children."

Peter sighs. Michael can see his friend and partner leafing mentally through the company's medical insurance policy. "I thought we decided we're not a charity, Mike."

"I'm not talking charity. I want…to make a home for God."

This is too much. Peter picks up his sheaf of papers.

"'Let them make me a sanctuary that I may dwell among them.' God says that in *Exodus*. The passage is talking about a tabernacle, but why limit it? Please. A month, a couple of months. But only part-time, Pete. Pete, I'll keep on with other projects. And look—I'll pay us back, hour for hour."

"You can't separate it out like that. You're needed full-time. And the thing is, it's not *you* that's needed. It's the guy you've always been." He's quiet for a minute, pokes at his papers. "I need him," he says quietly.

"*Call* it crazy leave, if you want."

"Oh, Michael. We've been together twenty years. What the fuck." Peter turns and puts his two big hands on Michael's hairy cheeks. "Please be okay."

Azakarian's phone rings and rings; no message machine picks up. He wants to settle this tonight before he changes his mind, so he drives down to Green River to drop off a note. Azakarian lives in one part of a small two-family house on a street of two-family houses. A street of workers' houses from a time when Green River was a booming industrial town. It's drizzling. Under the street lamp, one side of the lawn is cluttered with toys—a plastic car, a soccer ball, a refrigerator carton with windows and doors cut out of the wet cardboard. On Azakarian's side, nothing.

Michael stands on the sagging porch and tries to see inside. Lights upstairs give him a dim view. The livingroom is pure Azakarian—shabby, papers piled everywhere, a vinyl couch that looks like it was borrowed from a dying motel. No, Azakarian's not married. He hears voices, music, faint, tinny, from upstairs: a TV. So he rings.

No answer…no answer—he's about to put the note into the mailbox next to the buzzer when the stairwell light comes on, the television gets louder. Heavy thump of Azakarian on the stairs.

For a few seconds, Azakarian doesn't seem to know him. Michael is instantly sorry he came. Beer on his breath. He's been sleeping or drunk; his hair, what there is of it, has come down in all directions. Sure, drunk. He's wearing no belt, the top button of his pants is undone.

"Is this a bad time?"

"No, no. It's okay."

"We can talk tomorrow," Michael says. But he comes in.

The bitter smell of old cigarette smoke mixed with dried sweat from unwashed clothes; that, he expected. The sour smell of beer is a surprise, the books are a surprise. What looked like papers through the window turn out to be books and magazines spilled out onto the floor, onto the couch, onto the varnished spool for electric line that serves as coffee table. He can't find a place to sit.

"All these books…"

"It's my hobby. I read history. Let me get you a drink. Here—" Azakarian clears the sofa with a sweep of his arm and goes upstairs to turn off the TV. Michael tilts his head to look at the titles. History? No history he could see. Detective fiction, soft porn magazines. Azakarian comes back with two cans of beer, two dirty glasses. "I unplug the phone at night when I'm not on call." Now he stops, scrunches up his eyes, bleary eyes. "What's happened to you? Since I saw you last? A beard, of course. You grew yourself a beard. What's the matter? You sick?"

Michael feels the comedy of this. A couple of ragged guys each seeing the other as ragged and peculiar. He doesn't want to talk about it, it gets to him. But then he laughs at the two of them. If, in his half-stupor, Azakarian's shocked, I must really look like something! He takes off his fedora and leans forward. "All right. Forget what I look like. Here's what I'm willing to do." He stops. "Tell me. Are you okay enough to understand what I'm saying?"

"*Sure*. Sure. Just a couple of beers."

"I'll organize the construction for you. On my own. Weekends, evenings. I'll do the hiring, I'll handle the project, and I'll charge nothing except what I have to lay out for labor and materials."

"That's reasonable."

"Reasonable!" He laughs but lets it slide. "Even so, it'll come in over budget—but...maybe we can handle it. Now, Mr. Azakarian, will you work with me? Because listen—you keep trying to guilt-trip me, you ask for more and more, and I'll walk away."

"Of course, of course."

Of course, of course, but inside his belly Michael feels a moan wanting to float up: it's Azakarian's mess rising up in him. It's as if he could feel Azakarian's life from inside; the attempt makes him thick, blurred. "The house in Springdale looks pretty nice—"

"—Good! You went to look."

"—But *you*—you don't look so good. I worry when I look at you. Let me tell you plainly, I worry. Can you handle it?"

Azakarian doesn't answer. He walks around the room collecting beer cans, straightening books, clearing a leather chair with a gash in the seat. "Daytimes, I can."

"I see."

Azakarian says, "So we better talk in the daytime." He grunts. "Tomorrow. Tomorrow I won't look like this.... You let yourself out." And he climbs the stairs, not looking back.

"I"m sorry," Michael calls after him. "Hey. Don't *worry*."

"You don't look so good yourself, you know."

A door shuts. Michael is left in this room strewn with papers. He prowls. The kitchen sink is as he expects. The fridge is full of moldy food, the freezer compartment thick with nothing but frost—you couldn't squeeze in a box of frozen peas. Underneath the vegetable bin is a pool of water growing mold. How can this damaged man provide a home for damaged children?

He should go home, he should sleep, but he sits and sits, squashed by the chaos.

So he begins by finding a pail and a utility sponge in the kitchen closet. At first the idea is to suggest to Azakarian that he should clean up his act. But that idea dissolves the first few minutes, and he doesn't know why he's getting rid of the pool of scum at the bottom of the fridge, the old containers of mold or dried-up soup that had separated from the plastic. It starts with the scum, but then he realizes he has to defrost or the freezing compartment will drip a new pool. So he boils two big pots of water, and while he cleans the kitchen, he lets one pot sit in the freezing compartment, then the other, until he can pop the solid ice with a screwdriver and sponge the mess into a pail. And then it's the racks, so he can get to the mildew on the ceramic walls, until the fridge is immaculate and bare except for a bottle of milk and a six pack.

That feels good—until he notices the mildew on the walls, finds Clorox and detergent and goes to work, while the dishwasher cleans the dishes.

He still has energy. Energy or anxiety, he can't sleep, what the hell, so he turns to the living room. He thinks of stories of fairy godmothers, and giggles, imagining Azakarian waking up. But nothing, not even dumping cans in a green garbage bag, wakes Azakarian. The magazines—none of his business—he piles in a corner, the books on the coffee table. He straightens the chairs and gets rid of the diagonal bump in the rug.

He listens. Okay. Even if he *vacuums*, Azakarian will sleep! Michael goes to work with an old Electrolux, feeling pleasure when bits of dried cracker and chips, sand carried in from the winter, ancient nuts and raisins, ting, ting up the nozzle. Until the living room rug is without obvious dirt—though now the stains show up even worse.

It clears his own head. Stopping, he combs the air with open fingers, inviting God in.

It's after one in the morning when he finally slips out, drives home, and even then not to sleep right away. He sits down at his desk to make lists of jobs. He goes through the names of members of the synagogue and culls out the lawyers, the owner of a building supply company, a banker. Then there is his own money. He's got savings for retirement, for Jeremy's college. He doesn't touch his IRA's but makes a note to himself to withdraw twenty thousand from his cash reserves and open a special account. Not something to tell Azakarian, but it'll be there.

Before going to bed, he looks at himself in the bathroom mirror—Be honest—can he *schnorr* money with a beard like this? Regretfully, as he's known he must, he shaves; regretfully, he throws the fedora in the garbage. Well, by now it's gray with sawdust and stained with machine oil. He slicks down his hair. Like a zoo creature, he wanders the empty house, every few minutes stopping to look at his face in a mirror. He doesn't feel close to this person; a competent professional. Clean-cut and feeling efficient again, he finds it harder to pray tonight. He says the *Shema*, but the words seem to go nowhere. And tomorrow—a haircut.

Karen and Jeremy are home again, Karen a little too solicitous. Oh, it's *Peter*, Michael is sure—Peter, worried, must have got on the phone to her. She's relieved to see him looking normal. *Looking yourself*, she says. They're polite to one another, kind even, as they cut up vegetables and put out plates. They're not lovers yet, but at night she holds his hand and once takes his head to her breast.

Peter is equally relieved, and, to show it, has become conspicuously generous to the project, pulling off workers from other jobs, offering free use of forms for pouring the foundation, costing-out parts of the job because he's better at it than Michael.

It's a Saturday morning, more than a month after the cleaning of Azakarian's. He's never been back there, and Azakarian never spoke about it, but there's less bullshit between them now, less "Have you considered the children, Mr. Kahn?" Sometimes Azakarian stops by to go over plans. Once they went out for coffee and talked about finishing materials. Azakarian's okay during the day, and Michael doesn't ask about nights. It's a tough job, human services, what the hell.

The foundation's done, exterior walls are framed and sheathed. On this Saturday morning Jeremy wanted to see the work, maybe help, or just be with his father, so Michael drives down with him to

Springdale. He's there instead of synagogue because on Monday the electricians are coming to rough-in the wiring, and he needs to make sure they'll be ready. But once he's there, he goes to work. One guy's framing interior walls, one putting up sheet rock. A table saw whines. He shows Jeremy how to nail up sheet rock and he takes over the cutting, getting the pieces ready for Jeremy.

It's like praying with his hands, he thinks. It's okay to be here on the Sabbath. He wants, fervently, to believe this, to believe that he's helping to rebuild God's world. His hands and clothes are filled, as in the old days, with sawdust. God's world smells of machine oil and sawdust.

Still, he misses something, and there's no one he can tell. He misses the Original world. It's God's presence he misses, it's God he feels he's had to say goodbye to: like saying goodbye to a lover at a rendezvous and having to face the dreariness of all the rest of your life without her.

He takes charge of the framing. The ring of the nail gun thrums through his chest. Country music from a boom box keeps the work moving. He wants to feel himself part of a congregation. As he cuts wood or slams in the nails, he tries to imagine that he is building a world for God to inhabit.

It's a warm day; kids are out back on the playground's climbing structure. Two boys want to be in on it; they stand in the doorway looking cool. "It's okay with me," Michael says, "if you help Jeremy with the sheet rock. It needs to be held in place." One, a boy about Jeremy's age, gets into it.

The work takes on a rhythm, it's like a dance, the three men, Jeremy and this boy. And both the work and these words with which I shape the work, shape Michael's sad peace this morning—both become a prayer, the same prayer in two languages.

Wrestling with Angels (2007)

The Contract

My wife thinks I'm depressed. Certainly I'm depressed. Why shouldn't I be? But when she complains about my study of the holy books, she doesn't know. "Your practice is going to hell," she says. "You're too young to retire." I'm an estate lawyer, part of a small firm in Boston—maybe I have less push these days. I am conscientious in behalf of my clients. It's just that I don't work hard to replace them when they leave this world and their affairs are straightened out. "What are you *doing* with your time?" she says.

"What? I'm reading Talmud. I'm reading Midrash. This is not unheard of in our tradition."

"I look in the morning," she says, "and you've got a pile of volumes. Very impressive. I look in the evening, the books haven't moved one inch. But now there are more volumes."

"You should have been Sherlock's sidekick Shirley," I say.

"Go wrestle with angels, big shot."

I laugh and pat her hand. I'm gentle with Natalie these days. Once upon a life I was an unholy terror as a husband. Now, no. Natalie gets tired. She's lost weight, she's lost hair, she covers it with one of a number of lovely silk scarves—paisley, mauve, and her eyebrows she pencils in like a film star from the thirties. She has a whole new set of clothes, which she says she won't ever outwear. A pharmacy of pills is lined up by her bedside. It's understandable she gets upset. She wakes up, nauseated, in the middle of the night, trying not to disturb my sleep, so I lie there and pretend for her sake.

I'll tell you what I do with the books. I'm investigating, I'm trying to figure out. I am, after all, a lawyer. So if I get stuck in a line of reasoning, I follow a thread back through Maimonides; sometimes it takes me to the library at Hebrew College in Newton where I examine records of rabbinical courts, or *responsa,* opinions of the great rabbis.

"You think that's going to get you anywhere?" she scoffs.

"No, sweetheart. Frankly, no. But there's a little comfort knowing great men have also tried to understand."

"There is nothing to understand," she says.

"That's your opinion."

"It's like a tornado. It just happens. You want to say God did it? *Say* God. Then say God when your shoe squashes a bug."

"I do."

She rolls her eyes. Same eyes when we met at Jewish summer camp 40 years ago. I was afraid of them then, too. Natalie can be ferocious. She's a very critical person when she wants to be. Until this year she was a high-school teacher of English, and I used to kid her, "God protect those children from your wrath." Often, say when I was soothing her, praising her the way we do every Friday night with the passage from Proverbs, "An accomplished woman who can find? Far beyond pearls is her value," that's when she'd go on the attack: "Beyond pearls, sure. You know what it's like to be a Jewish woman beyond pearls? With God a male—King, Father, Lord of hosts?" But nobody else better say one word, and you should have seen her searching for the crumbs of leavened food just before Passover. Again, ferocious. So she thinks she's earned the right.

"You're looking good today," I say. "Anything could happen."

"Three strikes and you're out," she says. Like: no palliatives, thank you very much.

Her speech has begun to be a little slurred.

I carry her up the stairs; unfortunately, it's not hard. She was always wiry, lithe, a gymnast when she was at Sarah Lawrence; but now the wire has gone soft.

I think about Moses, Moses having to carry the children of Israel, a terrible burden, as the Holy One carries the Universe. At the burning bush Moses said: please, go choose someone else. Was he afraid? Who wouldn't be? And humble—I'm not worthy. Well, who is? And also, I think, exhausted in advance, given the knowledge of what was coming. Because he must have known those Israelites in his heart—a willful, spoiled people, wanting easy victories and a varied diet, not particularly interested in being a nation of priests. *What's wrong with these people? Every day, food falls from the sky! When will they stop complaining?*

But maybe that's not the issue—the burden. Maybe Moses looked into the burning bush or the fire on the mountain and saw in advance the black smoke rising. *Am I willing to subject to such suffering the future children of our exile, children of children of children?* He knew—he warned them, didn't he, before he died? Maybe, at Sinai, that's what kept him up there on the mountain so long. *A land of milk and honey? Dear God: We both know what's coming. What kind of contract is this?*

What kind of contract? I wonder myself sometimes. I mean about my own two boys, their children, *their* children. Born and unborn, what have I gotten them into? It's not just (God forbid) future Holocausts. It's everybody's life—everybody's ordinary suffering, everybody's death. Losses.

I'm imagining myself in the desert. That's not so unreasonable, I'll tell you. Some nights, it feels that way. But I mean the desert at Sinai. Suppose I was a little child in the desert when the Lord appeared to Moses at Sinai, and now that whole generation is dead, my mother, my father, even Moses; we've crossed the Jordan and taken cities, and I've got grandchildren of my own. And as a child of the sojourning I wonder: was it worth it? Not being a prophet, I don't even know what's coming—exile in Babylon, imperial rule, the temple, its ruin and then its ruin again until we are all cast out. I don't know the tearing of flesh and the burnings to come, the humiliations, so many. But already I'm uneasy. *Is it worth it?*

Quietly as I can, I dress in the dark weekdays to go attend a morning service. There are always barely enough to make up a minyan, a quorum, so I feel bad if I would have been the tenth and I don't get there. She sits up, and in the dark her silhouette is of a preadolescent child. "I'll get your tea warmed up," I tell her. It's a brew of Chinese herbs she swears by.

"I can do it," she says. "Better go pray. What are you praying for this morning?"

I don't say.

"I'll tell you something. It makes me hurt more," she says, hacking up morning phlegm, "to see you praying. *'Hashem echad?'* God is one? Is that what you say? All right. The same force that organized the stars is at work in my body."

"Please. Natalie. Please." I go downstairs for her tea. Why be bitter, I think, make it all lousy, because you go through this a few years before I do? I'm as good as dead myself. What's a few years? All day I talk to her in my head. And what about the boys? Hasn't it been worth it? One son at Berkeley in physics, the other working for a trading consortium in Paris. She'd say she wanted to see them married, to know their children. And you and me?—I want to say—haven't there been good times?

She's right, of course—it's all one. I acknowledge this as I pray. Love and cancer. So does that mean there's merely amoral power in the universe and *we're* the ones who invented compassion, invented goodness, out of whole cloth because we couldn't stand it that our Source has no soul to care with, is careless, couldn't care less if we live or die? And so we had to teach God how and what to be, and *that* is the meaning of our prayers?

It's hard for me even to say such words.

For, at times, I do feel held. At times, I feel, impossibly, it's all right, dear God, all of it. Maybe the division between love and cancer only exists in our narrow vision and it's *all* charged with love—and how can such love be a human invention? For look how incapacitated we are, how crippled. Look at the way we waste life—I mean, to get down to cases, Natalie and me, the way we've wasted our life. Take the time we're climbing a switchback on the Appalachian Trail and my elder boy, Michael, calls out he forgot his canteen a half-day back at the shelter where we slept, and I grouch at him, and his mother defends, and Peter, our younger, makes fun of the three of us; my jaw hardens, my eyes thicken with anger and headache and I stomp on ahead. And all this time there's mist breaking and through the trees a steep drop to a green valley and, beyond, high peaks of the Presidential Range, and we hardly know it's there.

The boys are frantic. Michael e-mails every day, passing along Internet sites he's discovered—experimental treatments for recurrent estrogen-negative breast cancers. Well, he's a scientist. Natalie deletes. And Peter calls from Paris, furious at the doctors for not catching it sooner. "Should I fly home this weekend?" he asks. "Don't even think about it," she says. "They're not putting me in the ground just yet. It's not time to say goodbye. Anyway, I don't want goodbyes." Then, hanging up, she reconsiders, calls him back. "Honey? *I do* want goodbyes. But not yet."

"There must be something they can do," Michael says, almost yelling at me over the phone. Neither son gets it yet. They think battle, strategy; they think, handling problems through human intelligence.

Me, I think: life. Its terms. My friends, who know I'm religious and see it as a peculiarity they don't discuss, now ask me, "Are you praying? I suppose you're praying." I'm praying. Every day in the *amidah,* the standing prayer, we say, "Heal us, Lord, and we shall be healed." And we can name those in need of healing, so I name "Natalie, daughter of Ruth"; then with her Hebrew name, *"Naomi bat Rut."* And at odd times I stop and say what Moses said when his sister Miriam became leprous: *"El na, refa-na lah"*—O God, please, heal her, please.

But Moses was Moses. The only healing I feel I have a right to pray for is of her spirit. Still, at odd times, I close my eyes and see the lumps dissolve, blood and lymphatic fluid carrying only pure cells to strengthen her. Or I talk to God, as if God were a difficult friend. Look, I say. Look. I admit we threw away Your gifts—all right, a lot, a lot! We didn't see what there was to see, didn't bless what there was to bless. We were small potatoes with each other, quarrelsome, self-righteous, petty in exactly the same way day after day. Please, I say, I'll pay attention. But heal her.

I don't tell my friends. People think it's primitive to speak to God as if God were a person. They may say, like Natalie, yes, there's an energy, constrained by law, an energy that sustains us at every moment—without it, there'd be no dance of quarks and electrons, no blueprint for molecules; it would all collapse into aboriginal soup, hot or cold. But why presume to *talk* to this energy?

I disagree. How many of us, really, can love an impersonal cosmic dance? I need to whisper to God, to feel God hears. I admit this presents an old problem. If God hears, what would it take for Him to change things a little? Job was cowed by God's power. But it's that divine power that makes us expect better in the first place. If you're hanging by your fingertips from a bridge, and a muscular friend comes along and you call out, *please, please*—wouldn't you expect a hand up?

"El na, refa-na lah."

Meantime, I prepare a cocktail of pills, cook food that's like baby food but that she can hardly eat anyway; I run errands, read my books while she reads hers.

"This is happening because I refused to wear a *sheytl,"* she says to me a couple of days ago: the wig an Orthodox woman is supposed to wear after she marries. We've never kept a strictly kosher house, never been as strict as I'd like to be about keeping the Sabbath. But now she pulls a box out of a big shopping bag and says, "Don't look." Then: "All right, turn around." She's wearing a wig, light brown, a little stiff; she's bought it to cover her lost hair. "So? You think God will be pleased?"

"Oh, Natalie, this is not a punishment situation. Even as a joke." I look some more. "But I have to tell you, frankly, the wig doesn't look bad."

She laughs, harsh and quick like a cap gun exploding.

At times, afternoons, I play with her. We were never good at playing.

At *being*. For example. Most winters Natalie and I went to the Caribbean for a week, with the boys while they were kids, then, empty-nesters, without. Frankly, I wasn't the greatest companion. "Do you know how much we're paying to drink this watery margarita? Including air fare?" "If I want to see fish, I can go to the aquarium in Boston." "Michael decides to scuba, so now I've got to shell out for *two* dive packages."

This December, I stop in at a building-supply place for two-by-fours and lag bolts, at an import store for bamboo screens, at a garden store for big tropical plants, and when Natalie goes down for her nap, laughing to myself, I slip downstairs to the unused floor of our split-level house. The boys grew up here. It's not a big house, but huge for just the two of us, so we keep the lower level for their visits. But now I remake the family room.

This takes two afternoons. I push back the living-room furniture we left down there when we could afford a new set for upstairs. I move the exercise bike, the television, and build the frame of an inner make-believe room, hang colored lights across the top and a heat lamp glowing down for the tropical sun. I make the bamboo screens into the walls of a beach shack. To one of the screens I attach a framed travel poster: a beach, blue water. I'd considered a bag or two of sandbox sand, but no—that's *really* crazy. But a foam mattress I cover with summer bedspreads as a beach blanket. I lower the ordinary lights, put reggae on the stereo, prepare fruit-and-ice drinks we can sip through straws. No pineapple—the sores in her mouth would burn; even apple juice I need to dilute. Final touch: I switch on the little rock fountain in a bowl to add the sound of moving water. Now, in swim trunks and a robe, I go get her. "Natalie? Natalie? Are you awake? There's something I want to show you."

She drags herself downstairs. And, praise God, she laughs. She giggles. "Max! A movie set."

"Lie down. Here." I give her a backrub with left-over suntan lotion so the smell will be right. At this, even Natalie grins. I lie back, margarita on my chest. And then what? I look up at the little lights and don't know what else to do. I sigh, take Natalie's hand, smell the smells, listen to music and gurgling water, pretend. "For once," she says, "I don't have to listen to you complain about overpriced restaurants." This means she's pleased with her personal theme park. Pleased I created a world for her. It's a world without dying in it. Not God's world. I made it myself.

"Close your eyes and get your expensive tan. Later on, we'll put on our masks and snorkel over to the reef to watch the Technicolor fish."

I look over and see you shaking your head. Laughing at my foolishness? But no, you're crying, and you won't talk about it. I avert my eyes.

I imagine my ancestor in the Promised Land. He must have had a wife, and let's say they quarreled even crossing the Jordan, and now she's dying. And he feeds her dates and figs from their own trees, and she complains. "Why didn't you do this before—when I could enjoy it?" "I was too busy getting us here," he says. But privately, he has his reservations—the covenant, the journey, building the Promised Land. It's not all been milk-and-honey.

We followed Moses, my Israelite says to his wife. We were too afraid to face the Lord of Hosts ourselves. That cloud of fire, that terrifying voice. The ordinary cracked open to reveal the extraordinary. And the *shekhinah,* the Holy Presence—even me, a child, I "saw" it. But we begged Moses to do our *listening* for us, and I wonder whether he heard all there was to hear.

"Let me know Your ways, that I may know You," Moses asks the Holy One. Was there a secret Torah that made it all add up but that he couldn't transcribe—maybe couldn't even hear? I want to understand—as a lawyer—the contract. I imagine there was no room to negotiate. But maybe he was given to understand, in the *music,* that by the terms of this secret Torah, we would be held in God's hands, even if it doesn't seem that way.

These speculations don't impress my wife. She gets tired. She gets so tired.

"Do you want to fly downstairs, to Aruba? You can rest, I'll give you a massage."

"No, thank you!" She bristles. "Enough massages." She refuses again the next morning, Friday. "Soon, I'll get plenty of rest." I go off to work but I have no heart in it and come home to make her a lunch she won't eat. "You think this solves something, makes up for something? Why do you feel so guilty?" she asks. "What did you do so bad?"

"Who says guilt?"

"What did you do so terrible you have to expiate with big tropical productions?"

"It was supposed to be amusing—a way of helping."

"Oh, I know you."

"You should."

"I was at least as rotten to *you,*" she says. "You remember how mean I was at Cindy's party on Block Island?"

"No. You were…unusually mean?"

Now her hard laugh. "I like the 'unusually.' Can I take you up on that massage?" So we go downstairs. She holds on to my hand, only half as a crutch. "But listen," she says. "Please. No more reggae. How about Mozart?"

For years we've been saying, we should take time to listen to music, but we never do. Today, we just listen. Mozart, then Schubert. Natalie says, "I'm not so sick I can't give you a massage back." And that's how it is. I massage, she massages. Her fingers are weak, so weak. This beach resort, this land of milk and honey—so fragile.

It's almost the Sabbath. I run upstairs for candles and wine and the challah we froze last Friday because she became sick to her stomach. She lights the candles, we say the blessings, thanking God for the Sabbath. I recite, "An accomplished woman, who can find?—far beyond pearls is her value," and tonight she doesn't have any smart remarks. She closes her eyes. I drink the wine. She drinks her herbal tea. The endless heat-lamp sun, set on a timer to shut off when we sleep, shineth down.

This is my land of milk and honey. I'm the proprietor, forgive the shabbiness. Fragile, but the best I can offer. Even now, to say these words gives me goosebumps, as if I'm usurping sacred prerogatives, as if I'm saying, dear God, why can't You do something about that world of Yours? Of course, I'm only a subcontractor, borrowing the materials and the relations among atoms that we call Your laws of physics. I'm not starting from scratch. But in my world, thank God, there's warmth and no bugs. You're practically guaranteed not to get electrocuted; only the suffering that Natalie brings here comes from that other world.

You and me, Natalie, we signed *a ketubah—our* marriage contract—and God knows I can get annoying, just like you, I can get grumpy, just like you, but I'm going to comfort you, I'm going to carry you to bed, to wash you, to read to you if you're tired, I'm going to say kaddish for you if things don't turn out. In this world: Mozart, Schubert. In this world, possibilities bloom out of our imaginings.

All right, all right. I'm *trying* to be humble.

The next afternoon, Saturday, both boys show up at the door together. This must have taken no small arranging: from Paris, from San Francisco. Telephone calls, e-mails. Michael caught the red-eye from California, napped at a friend's apartment before meeting up with Peter. Peter, who has plenty of frequent-flyer miles, flew business class from Paris.

Hearing laughter, Natalie calls from downstairs, "Who is it? Who's there, Max?"

"Friends of ours," I call back. I put my finger to my lips. "Boys, this will sound peculiar, but have you packed bathing suits? Of course not. All right. Tiptoe upstairs to my bureau, bottom drawer, get into swim trunks, don't ask questions, and come downstairs to the family room. Please? Just do it."

"Max?" she calls up from Aruba.

"Just a minute, just a minute, sweetheart. We're coming."

They look at each other and back at me, and I raise a lecturing finger they well remember. Off they go, and back they come in swim trunks—*baggy,* I grant—with towels across their shoulders. They're both big guys with small waists. Michael is chunky, takes after me, a wrestler in high school. I look at him, I see myself as a young man. Peter is, I suppose, more handsome. He looks like Natalie, blue eyes, high cheekbones. He's wiry, lean, a runner. Big, both of them. I forget when they're gone for a couple of months that these aren't children anymore. They were our chief project, and praise God, they've turned out fine young men. Except for High Holy Days and Passover, they're not so observant, but I think that when they marry....

Peter says, "Has Mom...has something happened mentally? What's *going* on?"

"Not to Mom. To *me,* if you must know. Boys, we're *going* to Aruba. No, really—I've made Aruba in the family room. It's a joke—but not just a joke."

And they look at each other and follow me to the now unused, once-jumbled-with-life lower floor of the split-level. Natalie sits up and immediately sinks back onto the beach blanket in tears, and they hug and kiss her. I say, "Gently, boys...gently," and they're laughing. "Your father!" she says. "The big shot. He thinks he's Jacob. Wrestling with angels."

And I think, I'm not acting in the place of God. This is it—this is how God operates. Through us.

We sit cross-legged on the beach blanket, I get fruit drinks. Now it's Natalie who improvises. "Isn't this beach nice? You see? Not in the least crowded. And wait till you see the luxury accommodations." It tires her out. She lies down again and from the way she's moving her tongue in her cheek, I know it's time to get her Nystatin to soothe her mouth. Michael is holding her hand and admiring the tropical decor and the view. Peter is in a different script—he's banging his fist on the mattress. He thinks she doesn't know, but he's wrong, she knows, and I put my hand over his fist and hold on.

"I don't have the heart for this," he whispers.

I tell him, "You do."

Michael tells her about Sophie and Aaron. "Getting married. And Arnie's getting married. And Saul."

"Who's Saul?"

"Saul Kaminsky."

"Oh, you mean Jessie's friend. Saul's getting married. Unbelievable. And you?"

"Not yet. But Mom, I've got news," Michael says. "A post-doc. I'll be working with George Singer next year. It's perfect. And Pete—he's got good news too, Mom." And Peter says, "Just that Chase is courting me. Maybe for London, more likely for New York. I'll be able to get up to see you a lot."

She scowls. "Make sure you're not doing it for me. I'll get furious if I think you're doing it for me."

Peter broods. Michael tells Natalie about new medical research: a few studies show that people who get prayed for—even when they don't know it, even when they don't know the people doing the praying—are more likely to get better than other people. Natalie, wanting to comfort Michael, nods—but she sends me a look. I try to liven things up. "So—how does this compare to Aruba?" The three of them are silent. I get nostalgic. "Remember that beautiful empty beach? Remember snorkeling by the reef?" Silence. I'd brought downstairs an album of family pictures but I figure, this isn't the time. Everyone looks around at this Aruba of mine. I become defensive. "Well, if you'd rather, we can go upstairs."

Peter says, "I remember Aruba."

"Can't forget it," Michael says.

Natalie sighs. "Max, they mean that terrible fight we had."

"We had a terrible fight?"

"Don't you remember? We stayed on one end of the beach not talking to each other, and the boys stayed on the other end of the beach as far away as they could get."

"They did? What was it about? I honestly can't remember. Anyway, does it matter? In my Aruba we're *going* to get it right."

"Max."

But now I remember the fight and fall silent myself, because there are still things we can't say in front of our grown sons, private things. Shameful things. And I'm annoyed with the three of them for bringing ugliness into Aruba on a Sabbath. The Sabbath is supposed to be a foretaste of paradise. Especially now.

Peter lightly punches Michael on the arm. *"You,"* he says. "I was maybe twelve. I think it was the January before my bar mitzvah. You, Mike, the big brother who knew everything, telling me—the little twerp—it was all my fault, I started it, their fight, they'd never fight if it weren't for me."

"I don't remember that," Michael says. "Well. Not nice. Sorry." Silence.

They're in their late twenties, the difference in age between them now inconsequential. They've each started good careers, they're grown up, they're not *going* to start punching and wrestling, throwing sand in eyes, cursing one another the way they once did, God forbid. Last summer they went sailing together off the coast of Maine. Friends. For the most part. Now, it's subtle; once in a while one says something that only the other will recognize as a dig.

Natalie gives me a signal with her eyes; I check my watch, open a container, hand her her pills and a glass of water. There's Peter, watching, furious again, squeezing the corner of the bedspread in his fist. I say, "I think we should say a blessing together."

"*A blessing*?" Peter says. Natalie would say the same, in exactly the same sardonic tone, but she's occupied with trying to keep her medicine down.

I almost rise to the bait and preach: we are to say a blessing for suffering as well as for happiness, having faith that they both come from the same source and that that source is loving, ultimately loving. But I don't, I say something easier. "A blessing that we're here together, a blessing for your lives, Michael, Peter, what a gift you are to us. And also—a blessing that with a little imagination we can make the old family room into Aruba."

But Michael hulks down, brooding. Peter looks through the album of family pictures. What blessing? I should never have mentioned Aruba. So let's call it Martinique, St. John, Jamaica. But it's getting too warm in my tropics. I've got the thermostat jacked up for the sake of my skinny little wife, and with the heat-lamp sun it's maybe too much. It's the Sabbath, I can't switch off the bulb till after sun-down, but I can lower the sun behind the tropical plants so it glows through the leaves. Anyway, the day is almost gone. The real sun is down outside, what sun there was, and through the window, past the frozen lawn, the houses across the street are growing dim.

I'm *trying* to keep up my spirits.

My world all of a sudden doesn't seem all that beautiful.

"My three big men," Natalie says. And then she surprises me. It's hard for her to talk. Everything's hard. But she sits up. "Your lives *are* a blessing to us," she says. "Your father's right. And look—forget Aruba. This is our island. It's another blessing."

This takes a big load off my mind. But Natalie using the word *blessing,* even as metaphor?—I don't know what to say. Anyway, we sit for a while, I fix pina coladas for the boys. We drink, we look at pictures, and some of them actually remind us of happy times. It was foolish of me to worry that I was playing creator, implicitly critical of what God had provided. What a joke—we shlepp the same old creatures we are into this new world.

It's getting dark outside. Can we see three stars in the sky, a sign that the week has begun? Not yet. Only the little lights strung above my beach shack. But soon. Time to get dressed, go up to the kitchen table and mark the end of Sabbath, the beginning of ordinary time. "Boys," I say, "you want to make a sling out of your hands, carry your mother upstairs? Remember how you did that when you were teenagers? I'm afraid it's even easier now."

"Max, this was very sweet," she says.

They carry her, perfect teamwork, upstairs. Words from somewhere in the Bible come to me, *How good and how pleasant when brothers dwell together—like fine oil on the head running down onto the beard.* Peter is singing some pop song from ten years back, and Michael joins in.

I'm lumbering up the stairs behind the music. I'm glad to let them do the carrying tonight. Natalie smiles down at me, an arm around Peter, around Michael. And that's when I get it, the nature of the gift. Oh, I think, the real gift—not mine to her of Aruba, but hers to me. For her to accept my island *as a* gift—today, when she's bedraggled, nauseated, angry; when breathing comes hard, when smiling comes hard, that's the gift. This is how God speaks to us.

Is it enough? I'm filled with love for her, but the lawyer in me wants another look at that contract. The blessing and the curse. "I have put before you life and death, blessing and curse." My ancestor who heard Moses explain the contractual obligations, explain the penalty clause—even with all the faith in the world, he must have been bewildered.

Maybe, he thought, Moses himself can't put it into words, the way it works. The blessing—we enact. The curse—that, too. And then…there's cancer.

Maybe, if Moses were here, he could explain.

At the top of the stairs Natalie snaps, "Enough! I'm not totally helpless yet! That's next week." She's trying to get them to laugh at her tough-guy voice. They don't laugh, but they set her down. Michael on one side, Peter on the other, they help her to the kitchen, where I've got an easy chair set up at the table. A queen's throne, but so big around her it's like Alice in the queen's chair, or as if the queen had shrunk into Alice.

She sits up, arms folded. "Peter, please, I'll make a deal with you. You stop looking at me like that and I'll buy you a beautiful silk shirt for your birthday."

My boys look at each other. Michael sits beside her and squeezes her arm.

"And Michael, you, too. Cut that out. Stop evaluating my muscle tone."

"I'll start dinner," I say, "right after we make *havdalah.*" I get yarmulkes and the little prayer books we've always used. Silver spice box for scent, kiddush cup for wine, colored candles twisted into a single candle for fire: we praise the gift of the sensuous world, the world that will die.

Soon, I think, as I pour the wine, soon I'll be alone in this house, too big for me the way the easy chair seems outsized for Natalie. Sure. But the gift has been given and the gift has been received, the contract passed on. And these young men will go on, God willing, to be fruitful and multiply, like the stars in the sea and the fish in the sky.

Originally appeared in Commentary, *February 2003*

Adult Fiction

Frankly, I don't see much difference between what sits on the fiction shelves of my bookstore and what walks in the door. In a vacation town way out on the Cape, you expect ragged, you expect half-dressed—and hey, there is that: baggy bathing suit holding hands with skimpy bathing suit, psychoanalyst on vacation wearing a Viagra tee shirt for a gag. Beat up and informal, my customers, like some books I've got, well-wrecked, covers lost, illustrations and layouts that seemed fresh and hip back in the sixties. But ragged and out of date isn't what I mean. I'm thinking of how people walk around the store as if they were inhabitants of the novels and plays I sell. You can see it in the elegant ways they mispronounce *Baudrillard* or *raise en scene* or *gemeinschaft,* the trill or growl of an *r,* the nasal vowel, little signs to indicate how at home they are in my United Nations of literature. And even more so in their swaggers and slumps, the way a simple question can open a whole address book of miserable relationships.

Or the things they say to the lover or husband or child they come in with. Say it's a gray day, which is when I do my best business, and here they are, paying $2,000 a week for sun and sunsets, and my shop has become a device of desperation between an overpriced lunch and the galleries of seascape art. So they come in, wet, their eyes glancing everywhere, loathing the store, looking at everything with hunger and disgust, and the drama begins.

"Haven't you brought enough books already?" he says, or she says, drawing out the gruff *"ough,"* knowing the answer. Saying: I despise you for wandering around killing time till dinner, making me aware of my own emptiness; this was supposed to be a vacation. Me, I keep my eyes lowered, I'm not listening. I picture them in bed, each with a book and a pencil and a reading light, counting the nights since they made love and checking their inner clocks and deciding yes, and then one turns to the other and cocks an eyebrow and the other puffs out the lip as if in deliberation—and nods. But today they cannot stand one another, at least until each of them lights upon a soothing shelf, old cookbooks or books of sailing instruction or a giant book of Renaissance art, and sits down on one of the simple Shaker chairs I've scattered around, nice to look at but not so cozy that you'd want to sit all afternoon.

Or a young woman with unkempt black hair twisted into yarn by salt and rain comes in and wants something on raising a Jewish child, maybe she's heard I've got a nice Judaica department, and I see the swell of her belly and right then and there I love her very much and want to give her a comfortable chair, a cushion, and I run around looking for books for her, basically *feed* her, you know? And I love the child she's going to have, and she tells me about her husband, who's an intern at Lenox Hill hospital in New York, and we laugh: how busy the two of them will be in a couple of months. And here's a nice book, almost new, on being a Jewish parent, and I take a couple of dollars off the price. And as long as she's here, I write down the names of other books I know, and I talk to her about Abraham Joshua Heschel.

Nice! I feel my blessing go out to this young family, and because she feels it, too, and because I seem avuncular (well, I'm almost fifty), she tells me about her prune of a mother-in-law, nothing's ever good enough, and how badly she wants to do everything right. And I know she won't, and I tell her she will. Easy to feel openhearted talking to this young person with the beautiful stringy hair; less easy when I come home and the two of us, Ruth and me, we go at it. But that's neither here nor there. In the meantime, a couple of months, we laugh, how busy they'll be.... A couple of months? A couple of months later is the middle of September 2001, and all the hospitals in New York are on 24-hour alert.

But as I was saying, it's always amazing to me how life displays itself there in my shop. Like one particular morning, August 2001, I'm behind the counter checking lists on the Internet from used-book consortiums, and this man, a little younger than I am, thinner, nice-looking, comes in, no suntan, city pants, a cap with a long peak but no logo, and as he browses I feel sadness cloaking him like an emanation. It's no surprise to me that he's looking for the Judaica section, and when he finds it and tilts his head to scan the titles I go up to him. "This is my specialty. Can I help?"

"I'm looking," he says, "for Jewish books on mourning."

I'm dying to say, That's something you have to learn? But I keep my mouth shut. I know what he means, pull out Wieseltier's *Kaddish,* find him others on ritual practice, and he chooses one and follows me to the counter.

"If you don't mind my asking—?"

"My mother. She was in a nursing home in New Jersey."

"I'm sorry. May you be comforted."

He puts his hands to his cheeks and starts to rock—not big, the way some Jews do when they pray, but little, so you have to look closely to see. This goes right to my heart. How many people can express themselves so directly? "How old was your mother?"

"Old. Not so old: going on eighty. But for a few years she was more and more...somewhere else. Sometimes she remembered my name."

"So, you sat shiva?"

"Last week. Then—well, we had this vacation place paid for, so we came. God knows why. Not much of a vacation. And I can't say kaddish."

This, I was waiting for. "You've come to the right place."

"They told me."

"Ah." It's not a big town, everybody knows Lenny Lensky. In a way, I'm the town Jew. Sure, there are a lot of Jews on the Cape, but they come and go. To *daven* in a traditional way, you've got to go all the way to Hyannis. And you need ten adult Jews if you want to say kaddish. That's the way it is. And it makes sense, because, remember, the kaddish is a prayer by the community, it's really just a congregation praising God; it doesn't even mention death. In the midst of loss, we praise the Holy One.

But, okay, you need ten Jews, a minyan. So here's what I do. Somebody comes in who needs to say kaddish, I make a couple of calls, I go out on the street—we're right on the main drag—and I've got this signboard, two signboards connected by a chain back to back, it makes a tall isosceles triangle, and on each board I pin a giant sign in Magic Marker:

> JEWS! MOURNER NEEDS MINYAN TO SAY KADDISH! PLEASE COME IN!

"So you think it's really possible?"

"Certainly it's possible. *Please.* What's your name? I'm Lenny."

"Howard Rose."

"Lenny Lensky. I'll make a couple of calls. You watch. It's interesting." And it is. So I make my calls and check the passersby. Every couple of minutes I spot a Jew, or a Jewish family, or a young man I'm almost sure about, or a young woman in a bathing suit. For some mourners, a woman doesn't count for making up a minyan. Others aren't particular. As far as I'm concerned, man, woman, a Jew is a Jew. But it's up to the mourner. For Howard, it's got to be men.

"Watch," I say, as a big athletic guy reads the sign. He's pushing a stroller. He reads and turns away, eyeing the other side of the street. Like: *Who, me?* If I see the shoulders getting guilty—I'm fluent in the language of shoulders—I'm not above calling out, "Hey! Excuse me, do you happen to be Jewish?"

A direct question like that, they have to say yes, and I go, "Can you come in just for ten minutes?" And often they do. Maybe I'm fibbing when I say ten minutes, but it's not too much more than fifteen.

I let this young father off the hook because my regulars haven't arrived. In another five, ten minutes, here they are—Rudy, Jack, Stan, each in his own car. That's five of us already. Then a kid off the street, eager, and a gay couple, that's eight, and now I put the RELIGIOUS SERVICE GOING ON—I'LL OPEN IN A FEW MINUTES sign on the door, and David Samuels arrives, beautifully dressed, a jeweler, pretty rich. We pull the chairs up against a cupboard at the back that's covered with a red velvet cloth. Here's the small Torah scroll I own. For some people, nine Jews plus a Torah is sufficient. For others, no. For Howard, no. But I'm positive we'll get another—and sure enough, we're mumbling through *ashrei* when another Jew arrives, a tourist in shorts, sunburned, florid, floods of white hair in a pony tail. "Shalom."

I hand out yarmulkes and prayer books, and we *daven* among the books. Howard gets to say kaddish; also Jack Schwartz, for his brother. I open a bottle of schnapps, pour a little for each of us. *L'hayyim.* Now, as long as the store is still closed, a little before noon, I take in my signboards, put the CLOSED FOR LUNCH sign on the door, and say, "Howard? How about some Chinese food? Almost kosher."

The Chinese restaurant I lead him to used to be a pizza parlor; it's just down the street, past a couple of tchotchke shops and a store for women's beachwear. I don't know why I asked for Howard's company. Maybe I figure he needs some human contact. I ask about children. No, he says, it looks like they won't be blessed. They've thought of adopting. "But we're not so young anymore."

"Younger than me," I say. The restaurant is muggy with damp and with cooking oils.

I'm grinning inside. I enjoy inflicting surprises. Not that the food is a surprise—it's a B-plus—but ah, the fortune cookie! He breaks it open without glancing. "So? What does it say?" I ask.

The place is getting crowded with vacationers depressed over the weather. Howard looks at the slip, does a classic double-take—Abbot and Costello couldn't have done it better. He reads: "May you be comforted among the mourners of Zion and Jerusalem." He looks up at me. Now, he laughs. Other patrons turn around. It's good to see: a nice laugh, his whole long face seems to expand, the eyes get into it. He breathes and the shoulders heave.

I hold up my hands in surrender, "okay, okay," and I call out, "Jack?" From the restaurant kitchen, wrapped in a stained white cooking apron, comes our other mourner, Jack Schwartz, laughing. He's been waiting to make his appearance. "What is it? You find something wrong with the food?"

Howard sticks his hand out; Jack wipes his hand on his apron and shakes. "May you also be comforted," Howard says.

So I can see he's a mentsch. He's okay. I imagine his repressor wife at the house, complaining he's down in the dumps; you can go stir crazy in a rental in lousy weather. I hear her saying, "Why did your mother have to die just before we were supposed to go on vacation? It was just like her." A time like this, a mourner shouldn't be left alone to brood. He should be in a community. I say, "Howard, I've got to get back. You and your wife, you want to join us for a simple mid-week dinner.

This maybe wasn't such a good idea. "What are you doing inviting people off the street?" Ruth says over the phone.

"A mourner."

"Len, think how many mourners there are on the Cape. Why don't you just invite them all?"

"From Brooklyn. A Jew."

"I'm supposed to entertain people from Brooklyn I don't even know?"

She makes Brooklyn sound like milk gone sour. I tell her, *"I'm* from Brooklyn."

"Yes," she says snidely, "I know," and hangs up.

Ruth is all right. She can't help it. She came from the wrong side of the river. I'm kidding. But you see, we take turns. Sometimes she's the compassionate one and I'm the tough guy, especially when it comes to her women friends. Today, she's the begrudging one. It may mean she had a bad morning. She writes young-adult fiction, pretty successful: I've got a Ruth Stern-Lensky shelf in the store for her remainders. She also writes adult fiction, but so bleak no publisher will go near it.

Late in the afternoon, she picks up Gabe from the day-camp bus. I'm hoping that by the time I arrive home, fish and vegetables in hand and a bottle of good white wine to sweeten her disposition, it won't need sweetening. But coming in I see right away there's trouble. Marriage! Worlds upon worlds, such a mystery—no one has ever been able to name it. I come in the back door and see she's got the table set in our big farm kitchen and she's peeling a cucumber, itself a Sign.

Of what? It could mean she wants to share in the evening. But no, she knows I'll be doing the cooking. What she wants is to be able to say later on, You see? This was an imposition.

She starts in on Gabe. "Gabe, sweetie...." Oh, I hate that sweetie business. "Gabe, sweetie, you haven't finished your practicing. Don't let your father distract you."

How do people ever get past this? At times we do. It's like being in a city full of chemical odors, exhausts, ozone, cooking smells, and suddenly lifted by a giant seagull to the top of a dune on the Cape, clear night air, the sea you can hardly see, just points of light below. It happens. Moments of clarity, Ruthie and me, the hum of the blood, everything alive and One and all the bad stuff is foolish and unreal, we brew it in the hot vat of our psyches.

Not tonight. She looks at me. "Are you going to wear that shirt?"

Oh, my God. One of those nights. I look in the dining-room mirror. I sigh. She's right, the shirt is halfway out of my pants, it's stained from book jackets, a button's gone. I'm not a movie star, I have to tell you. A little overweight, a little random you might say, as if the parts of my face, like my nose, were kind of stuck on. A little soft, a little casual—all right, sloppy, let's get down to it. I've had success with women—not since my marriage to Ruthie, you understand, God forbid. But I'm not totally disgusting.

Ruth is ten years younger, neat as a pin, runs two miles a day, wears two-piece bathing suits. God knows she's pretty. And Gabe takes after her. Another blessing, our major blessing, our major accomplishment these twelve years.

So I change my shirt, and then she makes me put on an apron. I listen to Gabe playing a little piece from the Anna Magdalena Bach notebook, and then I let him help do the cooking on the gas grill out on the brick terrace. "We can have drinks outside," she says, looking up at the sky. Weather's blown out to sea; we may even get a sunset. Ruth puts the wine in an ice bucket, sets out appetizers, so I know she's been shopping as a supplement. The appetizers say, You see?

"That was very thoughtful of you," I say. "Fixing things up so nice." But she isn't buying my soft soap. She spreads Saran Wrap over the plate to keep off the bugs and Gabe. "The man's name is Howard," I say.

"What does he do…in Brooklyn?"

"I forgot to ask. I don't know that he works in Brooklyn. Maybe he works in Manhattan. When someone's in mourning…."

She checks her watch. She doesn't particularly want the mourner and his wife, but she wants to ascertain if they're late so she can get critical.

But they're not late, or only a few minutes. I'm relieved (because of Ruthie) that they're not in shorts or tourist shirts. Both are dressed for an evening out, nice slacks, nice shirt, and she's wearing a white linen skirt, long, over pretty sandals, not beach shoes. She's in sun glasses, takes them off when she shakes my hand, puts them on again. I can see she's a kind person, not like my fantasy of the grim repressor. Her name's Louisa. Remember what I said about the young mother-to-be, how I fell instantly in love, took her and her family-to-be into my heart? Not Louisa. This is a grown-up, plain-looking, nothing to delude myself about. She has a job, maybe she's an accountant? She has a hobby, maybe birding? I'm not impressed.

We walk out on the terrace, and I'm wondering, was I crazy? Why did I want to make a big production for these strangers? But the late sunlight could almost take your breath away as it hits the garden, steam rising as the evening dries.

"Howard *Rose*?" Ruth says when I introduce them. We all sit down around the wrought-iron table. She can't keep her eyes off him—it's getting slightly embarrassing. *"Howard Rose?* You didn't grow up in New York, on the West Side? Near the Museum of Natural History?"

"I did. Yes. Right. We live in Brooklyn Heights now. From upstairs we have a marvelous view of lower Manhattan."

"You don't remember me? Ruth *Stern*?"

He does another double-take. "Oh, my. Of course I remember you. Ruth Stern!"

And he does. They went to the same private school. They went out together in their teens. "Remember the place we used to go to down in the Village?"

"Bruno's. Of course."

"Your family and my family—we were both at the Jewish Center on 86th Street." And suddenly she's silent, her face freezes. "Oh, Howard—and so it's your mother? Mrs. Rose? Rebecca Rose? Oh, I loved your mother. She was so wonderful to me."

And my Ruth is in tears, and Howard is in tears, and Howard's wife, Louisa, and I, we look at each other and don't know what to say. You see what I mean I don't find much difference between what's on my shelves and what walks in the door? Here's a coincidence right out of a 19th-century novel. Those guys loved coincidence. "Here," I say, pouring wine, "we should drink to the memory of Howard's mother."

They don't even hear. But Louisa and I tap glasses, and at the tapping, Ruth and Howard, turn, take up their glasses, drink—and turn right back to talking.

"I'm a literary agent," Howard says.

"An agent," she says. "I've been thinking about changing agents." And they're off again, remembering, or flirting, or negotiating; checking each other out. Gabe comes in, and his mother is the one to introduce him. She holds Gabe between her knees and says, "This is a man I knew when I was just a little older than you. Our families belonged to the same *shul.* We went to high school together. Oh, Howard, your mom…."

I check the salmon on the grill. I go back to the kitchen to warm the rice in the microwave; when I walk outside again and they're still reminiscing, I see I'll have to talk to Howard's wife. "So," I begin, "and what do *you* do?"

"I'm a neurologist," she says. "I teach post-docs at Rockefeller."

"I see," I say, abashed.

"And you're a book dealer? That was very kind of you this morning."

And Ruthie's saying, "This man's mom used to make cookies for me, Gabe. Chocolate chip. You know the recipe I make for you sometimes? That's her recipe. Oh, Howard, and she was so *funny.* So… droll. I remember walking down Broadway, the three of us, and she kept up a narrative, a patter, describing all the characters. We rolled our eyes at her *shtick*—but we laughed. She took me on an anti-war march. On Broadway. My own mother was furious."

I bring the fish and vegetables from the grill. Louisa and I talk about our view of the bay; a tall sloop heads out to sea. But I'm listening. "That's my mother," Howard says. "I mean, you see, *that's* the mother I'm mourning. Louisa never knew her. The woman my wife knew, these past eight years"—now, as if it dawns on him, *Ach, my wife is right here,* he calls to her, "Louisa, it's just the way it is, she was incontinent and senile and took a lot of my attention. It's hard to mourn for that Rebecca Rose. This is amazing for me, you being here to remember with me."

They're nodding together. Ruthie's not a weeper; but she's got tears in her eyes. They both do.

Louisa leans over, places her hand on Howard's hand. She pats, she pats. Then, leaving them alone again, she says to me, as if they were somewhere else, "I do get it, I get what Howard's going through. I never knew her, but I know Howard." And me, I think about my own mother, gone fifteen years now. And I want to go call my father in Florida.

Instead I call everybody together for dinner. We take our wine glasses and move inside. "A wonderful house," Louisa says.

We all talk together during dinner. He thanks me again. I say, "Making a minyan, Howard, you've got to understand—I do it for me. The Cape is beautiful, but it's a kind of exile."

After dinner, we move to the living room, what in the 18th

century was the kitchen, broad pine flooring and paneled walls. Howard and Ruth sit on the hearthstone of the gigantic fireplace we never use. Their knees are almost touching, and they're talking non-stop. Even with my big sonar ears straining, I can't hear what they're saying, so I talk to Louisa about recipes for fish, about their congregation in Brooklyn.

Why am I straining? Because, frankly, I usually don't see Ruthie this way. Look at her! Wistful. Vulnerable. She saves wistful and vulnerable for her young-adult fiction. If you want to go on a ten-mile, heavy-breathing hike up a mountain in a cold drizzle, take Ruthie along. No complaints from my wife. But she's sitting with Howard and holding on to Gabe tonight, holding his hand for dear life. Holding her child self? I don't know this woman. I wish I did. I see how soft and pretty this little girl was. Losses? Well, me, too. I remember as a kid in Brooklyn going with my father to services Saturday morning, then shmoozing with the neighbors, door to door, eating cookies in honor of the Sabbath. Me as a child; Ruthie.

Finally I catch a word and, faking a laugh, pick it up, run with it over to their side of the room. Louisa has no choice; she follows. "It's really something," I say, "your meeting again like this. Howard, here's what the Chinese fortune cookie should have said: 'You'll meet someone from your past who can comfort you the way no minyan of strangers can.'"

He smiles. "No, no. It's a different thing. Ruth was practically a cousin."

A cousin, huh? I feel like telling him, You know, Mister, this is not so polite of you. I pull together a minyan, I bring a guy home, it's not nice to play kneesies with my wife. Worse: to change her face this way. There's a long history of guys messing around with the rules of guest and host. Look at what Menelaus did when Paris took off with Helen. The result? A ten-year war and a great poem.

But that was an epic, I remind myself; this is a not-so-hot novel straight from my shelves.

And we talk some more, and the long looks seem to stop between them. It grows dark on the bay, lights from fishing boats, lights marking the long curve of Cape Cod, the glimmering from

P-town. And Louisa says, "Why don't you drop in on us when you're in New York?" And Howard says, "Please come see us." Oh, we will, I tell them. He thanks me again for the minyan, and I notice he doesn't ask about making another one for him while he's on the Cape. I figure that's the end of it, goodbye.

But after that night things will never be the same. I look at my wife; Ruthie's face seems sadder. I come in one day, she's on the phone, and from the abrupt way she puts down the receiver, I know, I don't even have to check caller ID when she goes for a shower. But I do.

The rest of the summer she's walking around inside a story. Here's the story: Someone from my youth, he can help me reclaim the Ruth that got lost. So just after Labor Day, the Cape quiet, most of the tourists gone, she tells me, "Len, do you mind if I go down to New York for a few days? I'd like to get back to—God, you know—civilization. Go to a couple of museums, maybe see my agent."

Why not?

"You don't mind? You and Gabe will be all right?"

Oh, sure. Sure.

So she makes her plans, and I could tell you word for word the story she's in, I could pull it off the shelf. She's walking around in a daydream, eyes soft-focus, and she tells me twice which hotel—the Gramercy Park—but not when she'll be back. Live and let live, my mother used to say to me. She told me at times about her loving father Ezra, may his memory be for a blessing. One time Ezra's younger brother, this is back in Bessarabia, now Moldova, was looking out for my grandfather's sheep. My grandfather was rich. You can imagine, a Jew in Bessarabia owning land and sheep! So one day Ezra's brother fell asleep under a tree and the sheep followed one behind the next into a river, and a thousand sheep were drowned. My mother raised her teaching finger to me: "My father, may he rest in peace, you think he groaned and yelled? He didn't even raise his voice. He knew how bad his brother felt and he didn't raise his voice."

Me, I'm not that much of a holy man. A catastrophe comes my way, I have been known to yell. But in the case of love, what good is it? No good. "So long, Ruthie. Have yourself a nice time," I say. Maybe I'm sad, but I mean it. Get it out of your system, it's not the end of the world. And I know she knows I know. Which is, frankly, a little embarrassing. She gives Gabe and me big hugs on the way out the door that Saturday morning.

On Sunday she calls, tells me about the play she saw the night before. She'll stay a couple of more days; there's something at the Brooklyn Museum, or there's a gallery, and oh, she had a terrible fight with her long-time agent Sandra. This I could have put in a fortune cookie: You will have a convenient altercation with your agent.

So she'll be home Wednesday bringing bagels.

But then it's Tuesday, September 11, and all bets are off. Gabe's at school; I pick him up at noon and we sit in front of the tube and watch the planes flying into the towers over and over, the towers coming down over and over. And we wait for a call, and we wait. No call. And I know where this Howard lives—on the other side of the Brooklyn Bridge—and I can imagine scenarios. I can't get through to the hotel. Then I reach the hotel, but she's out. I don't call Howard. And finally Ruthie gets through, she's hard to understand, a rush of story spills out, and Gabe keeps saying, *"What,* Mom?"

She starts crying, tells, cries. She was having breakfast just north of the Village, she heard the engines of the plane coming downtown and everybody went out into the street. But they couldn't see anything. She couldn't hear the explosion, but something changed in the sky. And the guy behind the counter turned on the radio for all of them, and the reports started, then stories from people coming in the restaurant. Later, she saw the darkness, though the sky above her was a beautiful blue. By then she was running uptown. She couldn't get through on a phone—now she's on a borrowed cell. And she's crying, she's afraid to go to the hotel, she wants to be home. "Is Gabe okay?"

"Sure Gabe is okay. Are *you* okay?"

All she wants is to be home. But she can't get home, can't get a train or bus that day, and in the middle of the night she calls from the hotel, says, "I've been trying to get through. Tell Gabe I'm okay. I'm safe, tell him. Listen. Lenny. Lenny, can you bring me home? I can get up to the Bronx."

I leave Gabe with his best friend, drive down first thing in the morning. Ruthie leaves her bags at the hotel and walks—luckily, she's used to long hikes—walks and then gets a bus and walks some more and winds up in Riverdale at the Hebrew Home for the Aged, where her mother died. And when I see her there, sitting on the lawn by the driveway, she hugs me and gets in without a word.

I can smell the bitter dust in her clothes. It feels as if we're living together in sacred time. We don't discuss it. We don't discuss anything. I get her home and make dinner.

For a month she squirrels in right here on the Cape. We're very polite, Ruthie and me. Some beautiful fall. All the cars sport ragged American flags. For a while we aren't inside a novel; maybe we're incidental characters in an epic. Epics, I keep in the dusty back room of the store. Ruth is somber and shaky, she goes off into crying jags and Gabe massages her shoulders.

We live, all three of us that fall, under a thick weight of communal darkness that lifts as the months go by. As for the personal love that might put your lost self back together? For better or for worse it seems like a small, quaint yesterday thing next to our communal losses. Or simply as unlikely as those towers rebuilding themselves, the collapse playing backward to wholeness. Whatever accounts for it, I don't say anything, she doesn't say anything; we're more each other's comfort than each other's accuser.

A couple of times I call together the folks from our minyan. Jack and his wife; Rudy—he's a widower; Stan and his lady friend and her kids; a nice young couple I haven't mentioned; and Ruth, Gabe, me. We have a potluck. And then men and women, Jews, non-Jews, we hold a kind of evening service. Maybe it's not exactly kosher, but we all stand up to say kaddish.

Soon enough, things get to seem again like the remainders on my shelves. One day, Ruthie says to me, "Lenny…." That's all. It's the breathy way she says my name, I guess I've gotten used to her various songs, like recognizing birds from their calls, and I know she's recuperated enough to walk out.

The rest of the story you could write yourself. Gabe with me for a month, just the two of us, and then she wants him with her, and I'm not about to pull the kid apart. How can you make joint custody work, New York to Cape Cod? I say, okay, if I can see him a lot. "What makes you think I'd be mean to you?" she says. Her way of saying, Sure. And, of course, in less than six months she and Howard break up, romance gone awry. He goes back to Louisa, and Ruthie, she stays in the city, takes a job in publishing, finds a therapist, moves in with her divorced sister. I call Gabe on the phone a lot. I visit, he visits.

Maybe I'll move back to New York.

Summers, thank God, I'm busy. Off-season, a lot of the time, I'm at the store, ordering, reshelving, selling. It's quiet; I sit reading Dickens and wondering how he might have put it into a story. *It was the worst of times, it was the worst of times.*

Originally appeared in Commentary, *May, 2003*

I'm Here, You're There

After my brother died, I tried to reach him in the World-to-Come. In a way this was his idea. You can't reach across worlds is what I always told David; he agreed, but said, said with a grin but he wasn't kidding—this was at the end, when we both knew what was up—"Exactly, Bernie—so you've got to *travel* there." So to get closer after the cancer took him, I performed certain spiritual exercises. And here's the thing: ordinarily it was David, not me—*he'd* be the one to sit cross-legged on a prayer cushion for hours lifting kundalini energy or chi or the holy spirit up his chakras or meditate on the impulse of Loving-Kindness. Or drag me to shul, daven and rock, rock and daven. Or—democrat of the realms of spirit—sit almost naked in a closed-up sweat lodge, frame of willow branches arched overhead, blankets and old sleeping bags, animal skins, whatever, keeping the heat in; glowing stones the Indian teacher splashes with water till the body doesn't know where skin ends and steam begins. I know because he took me once. The sweating was okay, the chanting too weird. Not my thing, I told him; *and—hey—not yours*. What's a Jew doing in a place like this? Which led to interesting disputes.

Not to say *arguments*. No. I'd tell him, "You don't know what you're talking about." But as a matter of fact, I loved the talking. We both did. There was a kind of talk we could have with each other that he couldn't have with Carolyn, much as he loved her. That's a lot of what I missed when the cancer took him. The half-yelling over the phone, "Listen, *listen*..." Who else is there to talk to the way *we* talked?—me in Boston to David in a little town in Vermont, way up, where he lived the last ten years, my baby brother.

I was hurt when he left Boston, annoyed he left me with the business and stayed up there in the boonies; but outraged when he began to die. My baby brother? After he'd lived the healthiest life anybody could live!—oh, *pure*, you know?—organic everything, no pollutants, no alcohol—and then *he's* the one to develop pancreatic cancer! God knows why.

But getting back to when he moved up there—left the business, Dad's business, *our* business, import-export—shlepped his family into a desert; or, more precisely, the wooded hills of Vermont. What for? It's one thing for a bachelor—but with wife and child? And what's Carolyn going to do in a place like that? An educated woman? They have a phone, they have telephone, electricity, but it's otherwise primitive. A wood stove for heat. Off a dirt road off a tertiary road. You have to lug water from a spring two hundred yards away.

And Carolyn, she was *with* me on this—at first. But later, she took to it. And when my beautiful baby brother was gone, I begged her "Let me help, please—I'll get you moved back to Boston, set you up in a nice apartment and stake you till you're on your feet"—because you can imagine the great wealth my brother left!

Not a chance. This is her home. This is her life, their life.

Carolyn can be a stubborn woman.

"But think about Gabe. Where's he gonna go?—some lousy regional high school in the sticks? He's so smart, your Gabe. Let me put him through school. I'd be *happy* to put him through school. Andover, Groton, St. Paul's. I've got connections."

She wouldn't hear of it. Up till now, they'd home-schooled the boy. He was going on fourteen. Alone, what would she do? And I was alone in Boston. My ex-wife and I are kind of friends. I've got guys to talk to, friends from business and a few people who love music the way I do, we attend symphony together, go listen to chamber music. Sometimes a woman, nothing serious. I go down to the Caribbean with a woman friend, look at the little fishes. And sometimes I go to my synagogue on a Friday night and stay for the Kiddush to shmooze. I tell you this so you won't think it's ordinary loneliness I'm talking about. But David...my brother, I changed the guy's diapers—you understand?

Okay, not often—the diapers. But Dad wasn't around a lot, and I was ten years older. So I was the one to teach him to ride a bike and bandage his knees when he fell off. I showed him his Hebrew letters! When I was at Wesleyan he spent weekends at my dorm; once we went winter camping, and while the other guys were toking joints or drinking six-packs, I took care of the kid, tucked him into his sleeping bag, read him *Lord of the Rings.*

Now there was more to separate us than the ten years. A *wall*: this world/elsewhere. He was right, my brother: from my narrow place, from Mitzrayim (which was what the Israelites called *Egypt* but really means *a tough, narrow place),* from the old ego, looking out, how could I reach him? I'd have to travel. So? Is that so impossible? Is the gap between worlds unbridgeable? Astronomers listen out into space to go back in time. Go far enough out in the universe, listen to the hum, and you're recording light energy or radiation from a thousand years ago, a million, fifteen *billion*, all the way back to almost the beginning. Music of the spheres. Then can't I get to someplace where the difference between my form of energy and my brother's is insignificant, miniscule, the difference between my *being* alive and my brother *having just-been-*alive wiped clear away like a statistical blip, and in that place we can be together?

He was much nicer than me, he was my best soul, and he could live that way most of the time. I honestly believe this: he never put me down for what I did, not just the business but for myself buying, selling, buying expensive wines by the case, driving my Porsche. I'd drive up in the Porsche, which I gave myself as a divorce present, drive up to see him over his rocks and potholes, annoyed at the streaks of mud and tiny scratches in the red paint, and he'd be waving to me from the end of his long, twisty driveway that skirted old trees he refused to take down. He'd be grinning, his tenderness embarrassing me right away because I came from such a different place and couldn't live up to such feelings. I was dressed in cashmere sweater, say, and weekend tweeds, as "country" as I knew how to get. It felt like a costume. I'd get out, we'd hug, I'd smell the wood-stove funk in his raw-wool sweater, and under that the specific scent of my brother, and he'd laugh, I'd laugh, I don't know at what, maybe the differences, maybe just that we were glad to see each other, and I'd brush the sawdust off my cashmere, he'd drive the Porsche slowly up the hill, avoiding bumps, like a harbor pilot bringing a fancy ship into dock.

Carolyn would be standing at the door, maybe holding Gabe's hand, her hair long, as if she were still in college, black ringlets, a little gray she doesn't color. No makeup, hand to her cheek, smiling an amused, ironic smile that meant—what? Whatever—it never put me off. She liked having me around. Liked shocking me, if nothing else, an audience for the way they'd done the *déclassé* bit so elegantly. Say it was September. She'd be canning, Mason jars lined up on the end-grain oak counter, restaurant-sized pot with water boiling. Out the kitchen window by the quarter-acre garden, clothes flapped on a line strung between trees, flags of their private nation, their *folie à deux*—or *à trois,* as Gabe grew older.

"You see, it's all a question of energy," David said to me a couple of years back.

He had a habit of looking at you like an angel. It's the blond hair, curly, but also the steady gaze, big eyes, steady smile. He says *energy,* he makes it sound like some kind of spiritual wisdom, but I figured really he must mean natural resources, the environment, electric power. "What? You want us to be responsible? You think not using a dryer is going to mean a damn thing? Oh David, David, a drop in the bucket."

"That's not what I'm talking about. I mean we're responsible for the energy that passes through us. It's all energy."

"What's 'all energy'?" I parodied in the voice of a Blavatsky spiritualist type. "God, you can be a royal pain in the butt."

"Think of it this way, Bern. This energy was around at creation.

We're a temporary form of it. It keeps getting recycled, reconfigured. When other forms pass through us—say breath, say light, or words, or the body chemicals that make us dance, or, say, even money—we're responsible for using them beautifully. While they're in our keeping. See Bernie? It's a treasure. So it's one thing to take this energy and raise tomatoes and corn and make dinner out of them, or even bring up a child—with a child, you help compose a new manifestation of this energy. Sure, the child is from the Source, but you've taken part in creation. It's another thing to *waste* the energy."

"Waste?"

"Say you watch big men batter each other at a football game, and you yell, use up your energy and pump adrenaline and God-knows-what through your body and out."

David knew I loved to sit with a beer and watch pro football and holler. Now that I think about it, I take it back there was no put-down involved. But always it was kindhearted, loving, a loving kind of put-down. Always, the subtext, and not all that *sub*, was that he knew me all the way down to where I was a good person. Not the view of most people. Not the view of people I deal with in business. I can be a tough-ass.

"Or," he went on, "say you make a million dollars. That represents another kind of energy. Now, it's what you *do* with it. You see?" And he's spread out his hands as if he'd *said* something, which, frankly, I don't think he had. Except maybe that a Porsche wasn't such a hot idea.

But who cares about ideas? I don't really care about ideas. I wanted my brother and Carolyn and Gabe within bagel-and-lox reach. I sit in my apartment overlooking Boston Gardens, the pond, the swan boats, the summer flower beds, and uneasiness swells in my belly like a baby. I always have my work to keep me busy; and the work is more satisfying than schmoozing with people. All right. I lied when I said I wasn't lonely. But not hungry for a lot of people. Just for *David.* And for *Carolyn*. For *Gabe*, too. He's to me like my own kid.

And David needed me, too. I know my way around. He could thaw pipes if they froze, replace them if they cracked. I know how to shuffle mortgages, how to bankroll equity into investments. Not that he was an unworldly hippie. He was our father's son as much as me. He'd made the decision to work less, work for dot.coms out of the house, and the guys whose marketing systems he analyzed didn't have to know he cut and split six cords of wood for his heat and drove a beat-up old Jeep Cherokee. When he went on the road, the road was the air and when he landed, a rental car. He could look pretty *distingué*, my little brother. He kept his fancy clothes in plastic so the wood dust wouldn't get at them.

Like me, David had a trust from Dad. Not a whole lot. It all went the last year, because, self-employed, he had lousy medical insurance. He died owing. I had to negotiate away $300,000 in hospital and medical bills. So there they were, Carolyn, Gabe, out in the boonies, no money, not wanting to take from me, and she goes to work for the local newspaper—she'd been writing freelance for them for almost the whole ten years—and goodbye to home-schooling: now Gabe walked to the tertiary road and took the bus to the regional junior high. Where he didn't belong.

"Please, Carolyn," I said. "Let me help."

"Oh, Bernie."

"Bernie, what? Bernie leave me alone?"

"Bernie, come for a visit."

Sure, I said. *When*?

By now, it was three months he was gone. I was saying Kaddish almost every day, mornings, before work. A basement room in a synagogue. But at night, those spiritual exercises I mentioned, not particularly Jewish. Not particularly sane.

It's as if I tried to be an astronomer of the spirit, with no instruments but my own soul—listen out and out, back and back, to the source of creation, before God cooked the soup that composed the stars and my brother and me. To the infinitely small point of latent energy from which all matter derives, energy to which God whispered the laws of its unfolding. We say the Torah precedes creation—Torah is a blueprint for the world—and that makes sense if you think of Torah broadly. Because, look—the dance needs to be choreographed. How will energy radiate from that ancient oneness, how will it manifest itself as matter? What are the rules by which galaxies spun out and the worlds hold together? Back and back, fifteen and a half billion (or five thousand seven hundred sixty) years back: if I could imagine myself from that vantage point, I could be so close to David I could breathe the garlic of his breath again.

Here's how it came to me: I'm driving through Brookline one morning on my way to shul to say Kaddish, and I pass another car, old black Ford Mustang, I pass a lot of cars but this is the one I notice, and for just a moment, I imagine myself as I'm being seen by the other driver, a young man, and as this young man I wonder about the slightly bald, middle-aged guy I'm passing, business-suited guy in green Porsche (me!) but only for a moment, because now the young man spots a cab making a U-turn and has to concentrate, so me in my Porsche, I disappear for him, I'm just gone. And playing this mind game, I disappear for *me*. My hands still hold the steering wheel, I'm driving along Beacon watching out for other cars, for kids crossing at Coolidge Corner. I know what's what. But I'm not aware of me doing the knowing.

Which would be okay, except that I can't reside in that young man's awareness either, because who *is* he, after all? A Fig Newton of my imagination. He's gone, too. So I get pangs of dissolution. I'm as here as I ever was, but not to myself.

Not to my *what*?

At first—oh, great unease. Dislocation. Sure. Pangs guttural, a dark electric current in my belly; I wanted to locate myself again, and quick, quick, but I fought that, or *some*one fought that, you see?—and I let go, felt beneath me, what was holding me up? Because *when* I let go, stopped grabbing for the *me*, I found I *was* being held, held *up*, as in *sustained*.

Who was? By what?

It's as if I'm present not to myself but to something aware of my Being. Here's the experience: of being seen, of being held, of being known, and more. Yes. Of being continually generated from elsewhere—from a Source elsewhere.

That's how I got to thinking of the Big Bang. I am, after all, composed from the dust of stars, or the hot gas that gave birth to stars, into this fabulous organization. It's not nothing, driving a car this morning on my way to shul, not nothing to be moving my fingers like this tonight at the keyboard and seeing the pixels form meaning. Breathtaking, breath-*giving*. All began with a single point, it's said—the point of God's wisdom: *hochma*. The wisdom of God fills all things. Each thing in the universe is the emanation of that Wisdom, like a pure white light coloring green with green, blue with blue. If I reach back and back, I feel something at my source, bubbling up in me, energy I haven't made. All the food, the exercise, the lifeblood itself, even the genetic pool from which I issued forth, none of it is mine, I'm just doing the jig, the sarabande, the gavotte according to a holy choreography.

Look: we can see so little. Literally. And what we see is made mostly of nothing. And within us, the matter within us, is nothing, or mostly nothing, the distances *between* atoms, the distances *within* atoms, they're of the order of magnitude of distances between stars. Trembling through it all a background radiation comes to us from a mere five hundred thousand years after the Big Bang, and pulsing through that background radiation are gravitational quivers from the very first moments of Being, and it takes some ears to hear it! It ripples through space-time, waves of this energy. From the same source that organized me. I'm not saying that you've got to go back and back, behind separation, to reach God. That's not where God hangs out—because, though God is One, *Echad*, yet "*God descends into the world by the letters of Torah*." Into the world of our language, of distinctions, separations—*here/there,* for instance. But, I thought, if I could go back and back, I could be with David—at least inside my soul.

And so that night I was listening to a Schubert sonata (D 958), and when the music stopped, the silence went on, and sitting cross-legged the way David used to do, I felt myself lift up through inner space to get closer to that source, until looking down I was aware of myself in my leather easy chair, breath lifting belly and chest, then falling again. It's not the way my sweet David left his body, but the best I could manage. And even imagining like this, I felt afraid: it's silent and remote out there…so cold.

But seen from that distant point, David and I were more or

less in the same spot, give or take. Give or take. And I saw his face behind my closed lids, and the tears came the way they did from time to time every day. So he was with me in love.

And what about that distant source? That impulse of creation, those laws of the dance—"Kadosh, Kadosh, Kadosh…the whole world is filled with His glory." All right. Glory, sure—but what does that Glory have to do with love? Energy pulsing out of the heart of life, continuing to pulse out moment to moment to moment or it would all dissolve. But the heart of life, does it have a heart? At shul before the Shema, the chazzan chants, "You have loved us with a great love." Sometimes this is hard to feel.

After a few nights like this I went to the phone and called Carolyn. "How about I come up this weekend?"

I drove up on a spectacular day in early winter, sunny and cold, already a couple of feet of snow on the ground as I head north on 89. It was a day almost made me want to ski again. That was something else I taught David, and he got pretty good—but gave up downhill for cross-country—right out his back door into the woods. Friday afternoon: roads clear of snow all the way. No traffic. I could listen to Bach. So who could mind the driving time? In the back, a bag of bagels, a challah from the bakery on Harvard Ave, for Carolyn a down comforter, a backpacking tent for Gabe.

When I'm nearly there, I give a call to Carolyn on the car phone, and as I bump up the dirt road to their driveway, I see her at the bottom in the pale, almost-Shabbos light, waving, and it's Carolyn who gives me a hug but won't rest against my chest, then drives the Porsche up the snowy driveway to the house. Gabe, back from school, is splitting firewood. I yell, "Hey, want some help?" I drop my bags inside.

"Bernie, you don't have to do that."

"But I want to." It's been a long time, but the old swing comes back. The kick of the fierce thrust, the thunk of the split log, it's sweet. I'm pleased. Hey. I do it again. Nice, dry wood, it's easy. I do it again. I think, *David*; I think, *Trying to play David in front of Gabe*?

Gabe, who'd be already a Bar Mitzvah if they lived like sensible

Jews anywhere near a synagogue, stands back and watches. Then he takes his turn. It was Dad taught me, as I taught David. And Gabe has learned from David, so it's as if my Dad is still present in the swing of his grandson's arms.

"So how's school?" I ask, setting up the next log. "I mean *really*, not politely, you know what I mean?"

He shrugs.

"As bad as that?"

"Almost." Finally, he gives me a grin—a gift.

Gabe has been using the axe. I pick up the splitting maul. I'm a big guy, over six foot, thick in the neck, in the shoulders, with big arms, and reaching overhead I can swing the maul down hard. Too heavy for Gabe, but he has to compete, and by torquing his whole body, like a little guy doing a jujitsu throw on a big guy, he can just manage. We take turns, and by now it's nearly time to light the candles, so we go in to wash up.

Leaning outside the mud room, David's old snowshoes.

I'm no fanatic when it comes to candle-lighting times, but I like to make Shabbos. Carolyn could care less, but she humors me. She's got the challah covered with a pretty cloth laid out on the deal table David built a few years ago. The table is oiled; the soft wood shines in the lamplight. The scarred, oiled table, the yellow pine flooring and old barn-board paneling makes the light real warm, like in an old varnished genre painting. It *smells* warm. It smells of wood—not just the sweet tang of wood smoke from the cast-iron stove, but the wood itself, the oils in the wood. And now she lights the candles—one for each of us and one for David—and we say the blessing and draw the light toward us with our hands, Sabbath peace, and I fumble through the Friday night Kiddush over the wine—no sugary Kosher Concord, of course, but a good Bordeaux. No one sits in David's usual place; Gabe has put a sprig of sage there. I try to keep afloat—it's Shabbos, we're supposed to be joyful, it's a commandment, for godsakes.

Carolyn has gotten a little dressed up for tonight. "Dressed up" just means she's wearing a patchwork skirt she sewed herself and a white cotton blouse. Have I said she's a pretty woman? I always liked her twisty black hair. The little bit of gray is nice. She has warm brown eyes but they look at you shrewdly. A little eye-liner would do wonders. She has a long face, a high, smart forehead, and the thing that's nicest is her mouth, *strong* mouth, teeth prominent, not corseted in by some orthodontist. My God, I think, she'll turn forty soon. I can't believe it. I remember when they got married. Dad was still alive. Barely. Well, that's why they married when they did. The wedding up at our cousin's place in Camden, Maine, big house, grand lawn full of thyme, right to the rocky shore. I remember everything. From where I was sitting, the sun back-lit them, turned my brother's curly blond hair into a halo, almost corny, like on a Medieval angel, and Carolyn still wore her black hair long, latter-day hippie. It was nice with her white dress. My then-wife kept poking me to see how beautiful they were.

I look at Gabe. He's got her hair; he's got my brother's eyes. That's hard to describe. *Contemplative* eyes, and on a kid, that's unusual. Or maybe not. What do I know?

Carolyn's made a stew. I compliment the hell out of it. We say, to get it over with, *David should be here*. And then we say, *David is here*. But he's not. His guitar is here, leaning against a chair. Mountain sage at his place at table, that's all. Carolyn tells me she saw an eagle, an immature bald eagle, swoop low over the trees this afternoon…and the way David loved them, whenever she sees the eagle, or the huge barred owl that sometimes flies over, she just wonders. Gabe says, "That's not how it works. I don't believe that." He says it flatly, grimly. I'm sad for him but I like it that he's honest. I put my big uncle-hand on his. He doesn't move his away. So I feel somehow I have to bring us down to earth, and I ask about the estate. When I say *estate*, Carolyn laughs: a harsh laugh.

I'd offered to be executor, but she said no. She says no and no and no to everything.

"All that's left," she says, "is this house. That they can't take away."

"Well, and the land, don't forget. That's going to be worth something. And at least you won't be getting bugged by more bills."

"No. You saw to that." She heaves a big breath. I can't tell if she's thanking me or expressing annoyance that I made the deal. Why do people have to be so damned independent? "Can we talk about something else? Bernie, are you going to take your week in the Caribbean?"

"Frankly, I haven't the heart this year."

We're silent. Gabe gets up to put a Keith Jarrett CD on the stereo. And quickly, I say, "Please, Carolyn. *Please* let me help. At least with Gabe," I say quietly.

She leans forward and looks me in the face. "You're so patronizing, Bernie. What makes you think I need rescuing?"

"Well, you need comforting."

"That's something else."

"And this kid—I want him to go to a great school so he can go to a great college. He shouldn't grow up to be a country hick."

A *country hick*! Oh! This really pisses her off. Good! I wanted to piss her off. Now Gabe returns to the table. He feels it: it's thick, the silence. He says, "Uncle Bernie, maybe next year, if we feel okay, we could all go down to the Caribbean, you could teach me to scuba?"

"The pipes would freeze," Carolyn says. "And I'd be fired."

We get to bed early, as usual, bank the fire so it lasts the night, and it gets pretty cold in my room. I put on a sweater. I put on a down jacket. Now I'm warm enough but don't feel the least sleepy. So I go back to the living room with a book, I stoke the fire and sit in the leather easy chair I got them a couple of years ago. But I can't read. I see David's books on the shelves. Books on gardening, on carpentry, books on the environment, on the living being of the earth—the Gaia hypothesis. A shelf of books on animals—veterinarian science: about five years ago, David got himself trained and certified to take in wounded wild animals. He's had skunk babies in his shelter in the barn. People bring him skunks to get rid of them, tell him the mother's been run over. He tries to put them back where the mother can find them. Or takes care of them until he can release them in the woods. He's had juvenile hawks in his chicken-wire aviary, and right now a young fox that came with a gash in his leg when David was sick, a fox Gabe has inherited.

I close my eyes, I try to reach my brother. Pressing closed eyes with fingers, I am in a dark sky with a growing nebula of light. It takes flower-form: a central glow surrounded by light. My blood sings in my ears, and I gather myself up to hover in the light, as if this were the light created on the first day, before sun and stars (which were made on the fourth day), and look down to these souls below, my own, David's. I imagine all our souls held in God's hand.

It's no use. Please! I can't travel to his world. It's all fake! My eyes are full of tears, not light. I loved this guy, loved him more by a long shot than I love my beat-up self. When David was on the hospital bed at Mary Hitchcock in Hanover, God, I'd have traded places in a heartbeat. So what? Some generous offer. No use. I thump knuckles on my breastbone.

And now, first thing I see when I open my eyes: David's old floppy bush hat that ties under the chin. Brown, stained—but that I remember, I don't see. The hat's half in shadow on the other side of the room, hanging where he left it from a peg by the door. Vertical barn board paneling looks in the dark like his own lean body, but it fools me only a second.

He's also here in a framed photograph on the table, a young David, bat in hand, grinning. I think it was my then-wife Rebecca took the picture. His twenty-fifth birthday—he wanted a real baseball game for all his friends, so we signed up for a playing field with the MDC and pulled together a baseball minyan—about twenty friends, mostly men. It was just before he met Carolyn. Rebecca sketched, took pictures. We grilled hot dogs and drank Cokes.

He was one happy guy that day. We went back to the house of a friend and sang a lot. So I was happy, too. I felt we'd done it—Mom, Dad, me—look what a good person we'd helped him become. My marriage was already bruised. But this guy, he was going to be happy.

And he *was*. And good? Here was a guy could have been making real money back in Boston with me; instead, monthly, he was guiding busloads of local senior citizens across the border into Canada so they could buy prescription drugs at a reasonable price. It saved them money—and made a political point.

I hear footsteps. Carolyn is awake, wrapped in a housecoat, and she takes a look at me and says "Oh, Bernie." She wipes my eyes with the cuff of her sleeve. She holds my head against her. I'm ashamed. "I'm okay."

"I know." She sits in the big chair with me, and now I'm more ashamed, because of what I feel, the sexual heat I feel all of a sudden—and well, frankly, not so all of a sudden. Always. This nuance of sexual connection. And then I think, Well, why not? I feel like there's this big taboo, I feel like I'm wanting what was his. All right—I'm ashamed.

I can feel it—I'm going to say it. No! Am I actually going to say it? "Carolyn? You know, in Torah," I say, as if I were considering some question of historical interest, "there's this thing called Levirate marriage. Of course, it's not done anymore. For the most part.... By most Jews."

She shakes her head, raises her brows; the light sculpts beautiful planes in her face. You should see.

"Levirate marriage—it's the obligation, a brother dies, to marry his widow. In Bible times. Of course, that's only if the brother dies childless, if I remember right" (and of course I remember, because I just looked it up). "But what I mean is, it's not absolutely unheard of. Well, anyway, it's not done anymore. For the most part."

She runs her fingers through my thinning hair. "Bernie." She laughs. The laughter closes her eyes.

"What? You think I'm being stupid?"

"You can't get David back that way."

"You think that's the only point?"

This she considers. "No, I don't." She's smiling. That's something.

"All right. All right, then."

"I'm here, you're there, Bern. But you can come visit."

I bang my fist on the table and make the picture shake. "Don't marry me. Who cares! But let me help take care of you, for godsakes. David made me promise. In the hospital. At the end." All right, I was kind of lying. And she knew. At the end, David said nothing. Groaned, slipped into a coma. No—they induced a coma. I held his hand; Carolyn came, she held his hand. "To help out with Gabe at least? Is that asking so much?"

"Shhh. Shhh."

We didn't speak of this again. Waste of energy. I kept in touch with Gabe by email every day, came up a couple of weekends when I could get away. But the driving—over three hours from Boston—got to me. And so in early spring, when the chance came to sell the business, terrific opportunity, I went for it. And I played with the notion that David had a hand in this—some pattern laid out from above found the buyer for me. While I was negotiating the sale, I'd come up weekends and hunt for land. A pretty area. I like walking in the woods, walking in a place he walked, my brother's place. Right away, it became obvious—a Porsche makes absolutely no sense up here in Vermont. I traded for a huge Toyota Land Cruiser (I could hear David groaning about the lousy gas mileage). This way I can carry a couple of kayaks, pick up a week's groceries and put the stuff away before they get home on a Friday. Of course, when she's back, I get a lecture. Poor woman's going to develop a sore neck, I tell her, she stands around shaking her head so much. I have to laugh.

Groceries, and of course books for Gabe, classical CDs for Gabe. What kind of home schooling, he doesn't know Schubert? The beginnings of a library so he has a chance to grow. What's he going to get at the regional high school? God bless her for the life they've given him. I know how good it is. Sure. She and David have given him the earth, animals, wood craft, the kind of independence that if he had to survive on his own in the woods, he could do it. I watch him clean out the wound of the fox, his concentration, his serious precision. It's wonderful, truly, but why does it have to be exclusively a country life?

"Bernie, really, this has to stop," she said, almost in a whisper, while we took care of the dishes one Friday evening.

"Did I tell you about the concert Sunday afternoon?"

"You've started wearing the same wool shirts David wore."

"You want me to leave?"

She's scrubbing at a pot and furiously not answering. I notice her hands, raw with hard work, the blue veins beautiful against the pink. I wish I were a painter. We don't say anything.

Even half turning me out, she was beautiful to me. She's always been that. I suppose it's the way her hair tumbles and just before it dishevels, becoming total confusion, she's swept it up and pinned it. But that's nothing. It's her eyes. They're beautiful with truth, with integrity. How can you cram such abstractions—truth, integrity—into a person's eyes? I'm being foolish. I remember the day we met. David brought Carolyn to see what we thought of her, of them. It was already serious. Rebecca and I took them out on the Daysailer in Cape Cod Bay—we had it moored in Orleans. When we got up some speed, hull hissing through the water, David sat far up on the fore deck to keep the bow down, his legs crossed, hair blowing, a human bowsprit. I turned to check something; there was Carolyn, looking at David, her eyes shining from the wind. I remember thinking, Here's a moment I want to put in my pocket.

All right, I can be a pain in the butt. But what's so bad, I bring a couple of prep school catalogues? Next morning I find them in my back pack. I take a look at their Jeep. It's falling apart, and when I run down to the store with Gabe, giving him the chance to drive by himself a dirt road across a farmer's field, I wince at the clunk and grind. It's beginning to die, the heater's completely dead. Now that wasn't a problem—but next winter? So one Saturday I went to the Jeep dealer in Hanover. "How about telling Mrs. Levitt it's a recall? I pay the bill, you overhaul the engine and transmission." But the guy just looked at me funny and drew a long breath.

"What I will do," he said, "I'll tell her there's a man willing to fix her car up."

"Hey—that I could tell her myself," I said. And maybe I did, I can't remember, but what's the use? So she drove the miserable old machine to work every day.

By May I'd found some land—just down the road. A nice piece; I could build up on the ridge, squirrel the house in against the hill on the north and face south with a lot of glass. From upstairs you could see the roof of their house. As a college student, I worked summers in construction. No fancy woodworking, far too klutzy for that, but I can do rough carpentry from the foundation all the way up. An architect in Hanover drew up simple plans, little house, fifteen hundred square feet; I hired a carpenter to help, Manolo, guy everyone recommended. July, I left Boston for the month; we went to work. Gabe I put to work too, three bucks above minimum wage. It was helping out Carolyn—she was busy on an article about the free clinic David helped organize. And I could teach Gabe.

Not just carpentry. While we'd lug sheets of plywood, I'd talk to him about Mozart or the Beatles or Thomas More and the English Renaissance, and at lunch we'd listen on a boom box to *The Marriage of Figaro* or read our way through *Henry the Fourth*, me belting out an overblown Falstaff. Manolo was much amused, even took part a couple of times.

Late in the day, home tired from work, Carolyn would stop to pick up Gabe. We were all beat. We'd go out for a pizza sometimes, but the hotter it got, the further along the house, the cooler my sister-in-law.

And I think that's what I was brooding on one afternoon. Or maybe it was the tough talk with Gabe. I had brought school catalogues. He said—this was over sandwiches—"You're really great to me and everything, but I'm not going anywhere, Uncle Bernie. Especially not to some school for rich kids. And leave Mom alone? No way. Sometimes—sometimes you can be a snob." Sure, I said. Sure, okay.

Three-thirty—a tough hour for a carpenter, especially a carpenter used to sitting at a computer console running the numbers. Bones aching. By four o'clock you can see the end of the day and this gives you a little juice. But here I was, three-thirty, neck aching, annoyed by the heavy-metal twang and howl from Manolo's radio—I didn't have the heart to tell him, and after all, sometimes he put up with Mahler. The rock oldie fighting the whine of his radial arm saw was like music from hell, music for thinking about David, about Carolyn…and I guess the ladder was too straight up and down, and when Gabe handed me the two-by-four I was off balance, and the ladder floated back slow motion, then flipped me away and down all in a rush, and I landed on the plywood sub-flooring flat on my back, then snap, my head I guess—at this point all I can do is guess—and came-to with the music off and Manolo and Gabe kneeling on each side like I'm the Virgin in a Renaissance altar piece.

I'm hurting, I'm bruised, my head is humming. But no big deal until I try to sit up, and now everything, everything, aches, and I flop down again. "How many fingers?" Gabe says, kidding. No problem. "Three."

"What's my name?" Manolo asks, not kidding. Well, I always have a hard time with names at the best of times. I get tense about it and blank. I pretend I'm too fuzzy to think straight, and then I realize—I *am*. I'm a blank. And Gabe—I know he's "Gabe," but who's Gabe? Is he my son? No. Maybe? And what spooks me out is the shadow, *Is David dead?* Right away I feel ashamed for thinking such a thing about my brother, like chastise my unconscious. But now I see a grave, newly dug, a funeral service, a coffin, prayers in Hebrew—who were they for?

And I know David really *is* dead, and I start to cry, as if he died all over again. Manolo's off somewhere with his cell phone, Gabe's sitting by my head, and he whispers, "Uncle Bernie?"

"I'm okay." It's like when I got knocked out boxing in college; in fact I remember the name of the guy who slugged me, but when Gabe asks the name of the President, I say,"Clinton? Bush? Al Gore? Isn't an election coming up?" Now I start to laugh at my own condition. "We should put this on tape. It's funny."

Manolo's back. "You think you can move? I'll take you down to Hanover for tests."

"No way. I'm fine. I just don't remember things."

"What's today?" he says.

"Frankly, I have no clue."

"Really? What's the year?"

"I'm laughing. "I don't know! I could make a wild guess. 1999?"

"It's 2001," they tell me, and I guffaw, and they ask me more questions, and then the year again, and again I've forgotten. But I'm standing now.

And now...I'm not. And now it's later on, and Carolyn's where Manolo was. "You know my name?" she asks.

"Carolyn." Easy.

"And what's your name?"

And I know perfectly well. But I think, Aha!—I *could* say "David." I could pretend! But—"Bernie," I say. And I start laughing at the trick I didn't play.

Now I start to sweat. Well, it's a warm day, but what comes to me is this: Suppose I've got it all mixed up, and I *am* David. At whose funeral service did I say the Kaddish and *El Malei Rachamim*? "Carolyn," I say, imitating a patient in shock so as not to be questioned, but discover my talk is slurred without faking, "Lend me your pocket mirror. Something I want to see."

She has no pocket mirror. Well, of course not. I get myself up, she helps me to her busted Jeep and drives me down the road. As soon as I get inside, I go to the bathroom. Why? To look at my face. I know, I know, but I want to make absolutely sure.

It's Bernie Levitt, no doubt about it. A little overweight, big frame, looking like something the cat dragged in. I comb my hair with my fingers. It doesn't help. Sawdust snows down on my shoulders. It's me all right. Bernie.

I feel a tinge of disappointment.

"Bernie? Are you all right in there?"

"Oh, sure."

Slowly, the next hour, my brains come back to me. I sip Carolyn's tea and get the President straight and everyone has the right birthday. I know where David is lying in the ground and for how long. But the synapses are working slow. Brain takes its sweet time. The answers are there, but I have to reach way down in myself to come up with them. I know much better now how fragile is this place, our place, of agreed-on order, place you mark birthdays and *Yortzeits*. Don't go to sleep, Carolyn says. But oh, I'm pretty looped from the shock and the heavy meds left over from David's dying. Maybe they're like a truth serum—because whatever goes through my brains wants to slip out the barn door of my mouth. I babble, I babble. And she's taking care of me.

Gabe is feeling bad for how he handed me the two-by-four. "Come on, come on," I say. "It was my own klutzy fault with the ladder." I lie back on the old couch and close my eyes. Who cares whose fault? I'm half-dreaming David's face. Oh….I get this eerie feeling I'm closer to David now—something has happened. The place I was in, when I wasn't here, wherever it was, maybe I was there with David. Or even *was* David. As good-as being David. That's how it feels. It feels…peculiar…like I've traveled there. Where is there? It's some place you don't know the President's name, don't know what's up…or what's down—place before God divided: earth from seas, light from darkness. I dream backward, out and out of this world we share to the moment (if we can talk about moments when moments hadn't been invented) before the cosmos, suffused by order, by Torah, was released into being. But maybe that place isn't once-before-a-time; it's now, just on the other side of the mind, the mind needing only the jarring from an eight-foot fall to get there.

I call out, "I'll be getting home now."

Carolyn says, "Certainly not. You most certainly won't." The two of them do this dance of busy-ness around my sick-couch, putting on music I like, asking me questions, bringing cookies, and I get it—God help me, we're reenacting the year of bad cancer, the months David couldn't climb the stairs and they made up this couch for him. I feel how easy it would be to fall into those roles, seductive for me, for them, too. I'm liking this couch too much.

I get my aching bones off the couch and straighten up.

"Let Gabe help you," she says. I wave her off. She's mad. "Does help have to be a one-way street, Bernie? You've got to be the one in charge of giving?"

"I'll be fine in the morning," I say. But in the morning, dear God, I can hardly make it out of bed. Not just bruised places: all the muscles, every bone and joint. I take another of David's leftover pills and go back to bed to wait for it to work. She brings me a pot of tea. I don't even drink tea. Sure, I get the picture. She's slipped back into who she was those months of worrying and caring. It's like having him back. And it lays itself out for me, a pattern behind my eyes, almost visible: how we could come together around this. I could be the dying David for her. To be the dying David—who wants that? Well, maybe I do. But Godforbid.

I make her go to work, I drag my collection of bruises and aching muscles to Mary Hitchcock, to the doctor, to radiology. It's a place I know too well, big white medical center with welcoming wings, the radiology unit, all the corridors with machines waiting to be transported to the next patient, the non-denominational chapel, the very space between banks of elevators where we held hands in a circle and meditated on a healing light that would suffuse his poor body.

Nothing broken visible on x-ray.

Carolyn is home when I get back. She has my bed made, a pitcher of iced tea on my bedside table. But loosened up, doped up, I'm not so sore now. I pour us both a glass, sit with her in the cool green-painted enclosed porch out back, looking out on the little barn where the sick animals get sent and some herb-and-flower beds.

She's wearing business clothes; in Vermont that means khakis and a summer shirt.

And we have nothing to say to each other. We sit. Her fingers are stained with ink. Old married couple. I imagine us in ten, twenty years, when it could seem perfectly normal, Carolyn and I together on a porch, and sometimes we'll think of David, talk of him with love. I close my eyes, send my mind out like a seed into inner space, back and back to that place without distinctions, vantage point from which the gaps are almost non-existent, David from me, me from Carolyn. And maybe it's the meds, but David, David is right away there inside me, his glow, but no words come, and my eyes are wet.

All this time Carolyn and I must have been having a silent conversation—because now she takes my hand and holds it to her face; it's wet, too. I remember hiking somewhere in the Green Mountains, nice narrow ridge trail, my long heavy strides, David's light, springy ones. Have I said that?—how graceful he was? I can't imagine David making a dumb move like keeling backwards on a ladder. That light heart of his. Carolyn asks, as if at the close of this conversation we never had, "So—are you going to finish the house, Bernie?"

And I say what I'm meant to say. "Oh, sure. Manolo can take charge. It'll be a nice place to spend time in the summer. Winter, too."

So she sits on the cane rocker, hands cradling her head, as if we were old friends just lazing away a summer day. "Nice. So you'll tell Gabe?"

"I want him to come visit me in Boston."

"Sure, he will. I promise."

"And please—I want to give him…whatever you think he needs. You tell me."

Carolyn comes to sit on the ottoman in front of my chair. She reaches out, and we hold each other, keeping our bodies apart. I smell her soap, I smell garden, something from the garden, I feel her heart, or my heart, going. David is there between us.

"Past couple of months," I say, "you know, we hardly say a word about David?" My eyes are closed. "I'm seeing the baseball game for his twenty-fifth birthday. I see him at shortstop. He was a great infielder. Couldn't hit worth a damn, but he laughed that off. And light?—light on his feet?—and fast and so good with the glove! I see him leaping for a line drive."

She kisses my cheek and leaves, I stay quiet. I can see David's smile. Great smile. I can feel the glow warm me. People loved hanging around him for that glow. See, the thing is, he believed in people. We were maybe crippled and weird, he knew that, but he made you feel he could see down to where you were just your pure soul. Under your patched-together defenses, under your striving, your success, your failure. He saw and discounted the posturings. How you were wounded by your father and covered up the damage—all that, it wasn't essential. He could cut that stuff away and be with you.

So even now, David dead nine months, can't I be with him? A little dopey from the pills, I close my eyes, send my soul out of this aching body, out and out. There's a story about these two Hasidic friends who promise, whoever dies first will communicate with the other. By dreams. But when Reb Yitzhak dies, his friend, Reb Menahem, waits and waits and nothing happens. So he makes a supreme effort, meditating on the letters of the Divine Name, and lifts his soul up out of his body to travel through all the chambers of Paradise, and in each he sees traces of his friend, but his friend's soul has passed through. Finally, he comes to the border, and just outside the border of Paradise, on a great salt sea, is a little boat, and in the boat is his friend. "What are you doing here?" he asks. "This sea," Reb Yitzhak says, "is made up of human tears. When I found it, I said to the Holy One (Baruch Hu), 'Here is where I sit until all these tears have dried.'"

But me, I'm no mystical explorer. I'm not able to send my soul up to find David. And besides—that's not where I'd find him. I'd find him with his floppy hat shading his eyes, crouched down, splinting a bird's wing, the way I found him once, a crow, a young crow. If he found such a sea, right away he'd work to dry it up. And he'd tell me, Sell the salt!

I just miss the guy. Last night I had a dream. David is dead, I know it in the dream, but he's in a home movie someone shows me. It's in color. He's about eighteen, playing the guitar and singing, talking, such sweetness suffusing his face that inside the dream I'm howling in grief and twisted up the way I was when Carolyn called from the hospital with the word that David had just died. I curl into myself and squeeze all the muscles of my chest so I can bear it. I woke in pain—the fall, of course, but it felt like dream residue.

I'm still in pain, but I seem to be in one piece; my brains are back, more or less. I'll stay a day or two. Now I take myself downstairs, go out to the barn David built. There used to be a mare and a pony, Gabe's pony, and chickens. But the animals had to go when David became so sick. There's just the young fox, low-slung, hair red, rust-red, the red of dried blood. It's in good shape; soon Gabe will release him back into the woods. I stay on my side of its hardware-cloth pen.

Originally appeared in Agni, *Spring-Summer 2002*

The Company You Keep

Liebowitz comes into my office again. He knocks, though why bother, since he enters at the same exact instant, waves at me in disgust—as if fanning a putrid fire—and sits his fat behind on the ribs of the old-fashioned radiator. It's been painted and painted, this radiator, until it's become a layered sculpture. the painted iron ribs must be uncomfortable as hell. "Myron, please sit like a regular person. Here's a chair." I get up and pull the chair from the side of my desk. Then I realize—Liebowitz' hips don't come close to fitting between the armrests of a little chair like that. I feel bad I might have shamed him, but he hasn't noticed.

"I thought you were coming to our morning minyan." He raises ragged eyebrows.

"I got to bed late last night," I say.

"Please." He adjusts the knotted strings at the corners of the little fringed garment an observant Jew wears under his shirt. The knotted strings dangle down the outside of his pants to remind him of the 613 mitzvot, the opportunities God has given him to perform

His commandments. "If you got there," he sighs, "you would have been the tenth man. We would have had a quorum."

"Thanks, Myron."

"Look, you think I'm demeaning you? God forbid! I want you to see how important you are." He widens his bulbous eyes and holds his hands open, cradling my importance like an infant. "But that's not what I came for."

"Then what?"

"It's Friedman, the anti-Semite."

"Now Friedman's an anti-Semite? Friedman's Jewish."

"I'm telling you, Peter, the son of a bitch is going to fire me in the next downsizing."

"He can't fire you. Your work is too important."

"No? He looks at me and what does he see? A slob? No, worse. He looks at me and sees..." he raises a lecturing forefinger, "an embarrassment. Am I wrong? Tell me. If I'm a Jew and he's a Jew, then maybe people will judge him by me. *Farshtayst*?"

"You want me to talk to him?"

Liebowitz closes his eyes and spreads his arms like wings, his fingers feathers, as if to say, it's as God wills. I want to say to him, You *are* a slob. Your black pants are grease-stained. And that shirt? Ring around the sleeves, not just the collar. But we'd get into: Aha!—Why are *you* so uneasy just because a Jew wears a traditional black coat and a yarmulke? Don't I do valuable work for the company? And all of a sudden the question would be turned around: Why do you need to assimilate so totally? Are you ashamed of your own people? In the meantime, look what's happening to your son!

He's got me there, even without saying a thing. He knows how I feel. But all he says to me, eyebrow cocked, is, "You've got a good Jewish heart. And don't worry too much about David."

I do worry. My son David attends a private school in Cambridge. That's maybe my first mistake. Why didn't I send him to a Jewish day school? Well, for one thing, his mother wouldn't put up with it. But to be honest, it was me, too. And now it's too late.

Here's a snapshot: David and me last Saturday morning, me asking him, "Why don't you come with me to services? Come on."

My son lifts his eyes from the television to heaven: "Da-ad." This is whined rather than spoken. "I got my bar mitzvah, didn't I? And it's like, I get so bored there, and anyway I have soccer later."

V'shinantam l'vanecha: "Teach them diligently to your children." But what can I say to the boy? My son, you're fourteen. Maybe when you grow up you'll change your mind? Me, I changed my mind considerably. As a kid I was sour on prayer, too. I'd become a socialist. This was in the early seventies, long ago: black and white, rich and poor, Vietnam. At BU, while ostensibly majoring in Poli Sci, I got deeper and deeper into protest.

Look, I still feel it wasn't foolish, the longing for a new society. But it was also a con—because, frankly, I became a bum. Always there was a meeting, always there were girls, and afterward they believed they were contributing to the revolution if they came up to the apartment I shared in Brighton. I pretended my anarchic individualism was an antidote to the injustices of bourgeois America, when it was only a parody—bourgeois America all over again. Me, me, me. Liberation in front of a mirror.

I married and divorced, no children. Eventually, in loneliness and earned shame, I married again—Karen, my woman of valor, her value far beyond pearls. Well. At times. Two children—my boy, David, now fourteen, and Shira, she's ten. It was after David was born that I came back to the synagogue: Conservative, not Orthodox. I've learned to say the prayers, to understand a little Hebrew, to love the Sabbath. I admit it sometimes feels like something I've put on, a costume. I'm part of a generation of the lost, and here we are trying to transmit to our children a culture that doesn't live in our bones.

My mother, who was brought up Orthodox, used to tell me about the fathers in Yiddish plays, grieving over sons who'd abandoned their traditions. That's not what it's like. The traditions, they were lost a long time ago. I'm thinking of those Canadian geese that are bred by the Department of Fish and Wildlife to replenish the stock for hunters; without parents to teach them, they lose the ancient lessons of migration. There are lots of these Canadian geese, lots: they fly here, they fly there, they eat well, they drive around in BMWs and drink good chardonnay.

Liebowitz shrugs his way out of my office with a "shalom," neglecting to shut the door. Did I say he weighs more than 275 pounds? It's painful to watch him waddle off, lugging that behind. But he's one smart guy. At MIT he took a BA in math, an MA in linguistics. One day he tells me about his analysis of Shakespeare's English, how the beauty of the language arises from its mixed origins. He published a paper about it. Raising a lecture-finger, he announces, "Don't stereotype me. I'm not a peasant. Did you know I played Falstaff a couple of years ago in community theater? You see? You're surprised, aren't you?"

This he loves. But nothing surprises me about Liebowitz. He's our house genius: he does linguistic encoding for our main software product, a program that uses a search engine to find audio and visual signals on selected topics. Say, investment in Indonesia. Say, oil exploration in the Arctic. The program scans the web for video clips stored in cyberspace: board meetings, news stories, university lectures. Liebowitz's job is to figure out ways to name the bits of language, the patterns, that the search program goes after. It's tricky. But perfect for a student of Talmud who also happens to be a linguist and a smart programmer.

My job is to sell this program, which is still in development, and to find more seed money. I'm good at what I do. But if anyone's expendable, it's me, not Liebowitz. Near lunchtime I walk upstairs in the remodeled Cambridge townhouse and knock on Friedman's door.

These days, Jon Friedman, our illustrious founder and president, is mainly a communication link between the corporation that's bought us up and the folks who do the work. He shines with charisma and credentials, teaching a course a year and working with graduate students at MIT. Here he's supposedly in charge of "the big picture"—facilitating research, making sure the separate design tracks meld properly, staying in touch with clients. So he's always busy but does nothing concrete, though at a high comfort level. I should make such a living.

"Come in, my man," he says, and strides toward me across his big, woody, corner office, the old Cambridge bay window facing east and bringing in beautiful autumn light. He captures my hand in both of his and squeezes. "Sit down, sit down, you're just the man I want to talk to."

So the agenda becomes his. I sit, he sits. Sunlight on leather is soothing. He crosses one leg over the other. "I just got off the phone with corporate. Joe Welch. We've got six months."

"What? They're going to kill us off in six months?"

"Not really. You know, they like timetables. But it's produce or perish. So what do you think?"

"It's reasonable. I'll talk to the team…I just talked to Liebowitz."

"Uch. Liebowitz."

"That's what I came to see you about. He thinks you've got something against him."

Friedman laughs. "Peter, Peter, don't be such a softy. From this chair I see a guy who's costing everybody in health insurance. Costing you, costing me, costing Martha the cleaning lady."

"But look at what he does."

"Don't worry, his job is secure while the project's up. Just keep him out of the way when Joe Welch comes through. All he needs is to see a fat slob in a black yarmulke."

"And then?"

"M'man?" He pretends to whisper: "When the project's up and running, I can get us a graduate student."

I'm remembering my poor Aunt Ceil on my mother's side. Same story. She was a fashion designer, and for a season, maybe two, she'd be hired to design a line of dresses until the manufacturer dumped her and let somebody just out of the Fashion Institute copy her ideas at half the cost. I remember her after her stroke, an enraged old lady in the Hebrew Home for the Aged. What I want right now, I want to reach across the desk, take Friedman by his Hermes tie and slam his handsome face against his teak desk.

Do I? No. But what I say doesn't make him so happy. "I think you should reconsider. Get sued under the Americans with Disabilities Act, it would cost the corporation a lot more."

"Peter? We're just talking hypothetically, man."

"Right. I know." I settle down and remember my own mantra: *tuition, tuition.* David's education at Stone Hill doesn't come cheap. I give Jon Friedman my warmest boyish smile, the smile that's protected me since childhood.

Anyway, why should I defend Liebowitz? People make choices. Liebowitz isn't stupid. He's particularly smart when it comes to code; so he's made himself into a code for others to read. His black coat, his yarmulke and beard—you could say they encode a 4,000-year-old tradition, or at least the life of a Jew in a shtetl of Eastern Europe, or, maybe, the simplified myth of that life, now gone in Europe and reimagined. The rabbis are said to have built a fence around the Torah, the ten thousand distinctions—kashering your kitchen, standing up to honor the Torah—that can preserve holiness, be bridges to holiness. But they can also be debased into marks of a club, a club that separates us from each other and from God. How to tell the difference?

There are ten of us working in this old, narrow house with bay windows on every floor. I think it's funny, the chipped plaster moldings and mahogany banisters, the flowered wallpaper and high ceilings—all the old charm set against the slim screens, fat cables snaking through walls and along the floor, computers with 64-bit technology stacked in a corner that once held a piano. It's a peculiar office; people schmooze a lot. They laugh, they laugh, and the work progresses. Or they retreat to their desks and work listening to music over headphones, the whole place silent except for Liebowitz scratching hieroglyphs on one of his blackboards.

I pass through the main room, formerly the parlor, at lunchtime; Liebowitz is studying a volume of Talmud. Lunch takes him five minutes, the blessings another five, and the rest of the hour is devoted to a single page of Talmud, maybe less if the going is rough. This is a passive-aggressive act of protest, a way of demanding the office he was promised but hasn't received. Why hasn't Friedman delivered? The house is big enough, and there's a nice room on the third floor that's now used for storage. So there's passive aggression on both sides.

For traditional Jews, Talmud has the sanctity of Torah—it is Torah. In what was once the parlor, Liebowitz rocks and mumbles, chanting the text in singsong. The other employees don't mind—they smile at this fat, passionate, mumbling man. But if you didn't know this was the proper way to study, you'd think it was a little *meshugeh,* crazy. Which is what Joséph Welch must be thinking when he walks through the office one day with Jon Friedman.

They don't stop and stare. They just walk through. But as soon as Welch has gone, out comes Friedman. "Where's Liebowitz?" he asks quietly. The two of them go back to Friedman's office. You hear a voice in angry tenor, lifting toward alto as it lists offenses; you hear a laconic baritone. Tenor. Baritone. The rest of us retreat to our offices, our desks. My stomach's turning over. God keep me from having to make choices.

I'm seriously irritated at Liebowitz for giving me trouble. Why does he have to put on such a display? But then I ask, why does he have to hide? Besides, it's his own time. And where's the private office he was promised? Anyway, who's he bothering?

Ten minutes Liebowitz and Friedman talk. I keep my door half-open. Then they go to Liebowitz's cubicle, and in a few minutes out comes Liebowitz with a big carton that once held a monitor and is now full of his personal supplies, laptop, books, pretzels. A framed picture of his parents sits on top. Friedman, hands in pockets, is escorting him, as they say, "from the premises." Liebowitz looks ridiculous, leaning back, carton propped against his belly. But he gives me a look, like, *You see?* And that's the moment I make the jump.

I'm just as surprised as Friedman, as if the words weren't mine. "Myron, you need help with that box?" He shrugs. I leave my office, follow the two of them down the hall. When Friedman turns on his heels at the front door, I ask Myron, loud enough so the folks in the main office can hear, "Can you come to dinner by us tonight?" "By us" is a Yiddish locution, and I'm speaking with a subtle lilt that I've borrowed for the occasion. Has Friedman heard? I'm sure. But I don't look back at him. My heart's thumping in my temples, I think *tuition, tuition.* But I keep going. "About six? Okay?" As if it were an ordinary event.

"Thank you," he says. "You're a real mensch."

All the whiz kids out in the common workspace look my way, Jeanne, Mel, Gareth, the whole crew exchanging shrugs, grimaces, eye-rollings, grins. I smile back, feeling they're on my side. My blood is up, fingers tingling—what a rush! I haven't taken a risky position in thirty years, maybe not since the day, in college, I lay down in front of Army trucks and wasn't 100-percent certain they'd stop.

By the time I get home I'm more uneasy, less heroic. As if she were my doctor, Karen listens to the story and shakes her head. "If anything happens, God forbid, you'll get another job. But why stick your neck out for one of these black-hatters. *Mad* hatters, my father used to call them. He wanted nothing to do with them."

"I don't mean to disparage the wisdom of your father, but the color of Myron's hat is not the issue, honey. His being a fellow Jew is not the issue. Fair is fair, that's all."

"Fair is fair, but look at the rotten position he puts you in."

Too tired to argue, I go to pick up David from soccer practice at Stone Hill, and on the way home, in rush-hour traffic, stuck at a light, I tell him the story, looking for a second opinion. You don't have to ask twice to get an opinion from David: "That's completely lousy and disgusting."

"He'd been warned, Liebowitz. No Talmud on company time. But it was his lunchtime."

"What a stinking bastard, that Friedman."

"Watch the language. Well, Friedman was embarrassed. But I guess you're right. So. I invited Myron Liebowitz home for dinner, David. I figured he'd want to talk." All of a sudden I realize— wait!— the guy has a family. Four kids, a wife, and I invited just him. And what about the meal? In my house we don't mix meat and milk or eat forbidden foods, but we also don't keep separate dishes, and the kitchen hasn't been kashered. On the way home I buy a bottle of kosher wine and a new set of wine glasses.

This brings me home a few minutes after six. I'm sure Myron

will be late. But he's not, he's there before me. Nor is he alone. Nor is food going to be an insignificant part of the evening. I hear kids' voices laughing as I open the door. I hear women's voices. Karen comes to the door and gives me a look. She's been smiling, but for me her face turns grim. I mouth, *I had no idea.*

"Come," she says, with a pleasantness I'm supposed to read as phony, "meet Zahava Liebowitz. *And* Eli *and* Uri...*and* Leah. Plus the baby. And here's Myron I know you know." I hide under my shoulders and hand her the bottle of wine. "Good," she says. "How nice you could join us."

"*You* should have driven home in that traffic," I manage, wishing it on her. "Hello, Myron." I nod at the whole crew, a plump, pretty young woman holding a baby, kids frozen for an instant, then running. I catch Karen's eye, she follows me to the closet where I hang up my jacket. I whisper, "What are we going to feed these people?"

Now she laughs. "Oh, that you don't have to worry about. Go look in the kitchen."

Two little kids run past, almost tripping me. On the kitchen table is the same huge carton that Myron used to carry his personal stuff away from the company. It's covered with a tablecloth. Peeking in, I see a stainless steel canning pot with its cover duct-taped down. Even with the lid on, I can smell the soup, and along with the soup they've brought bread wrapped in foil, bowls of many kinds and colors, knives, soup spoons, a big bottle of juice, a bottle of wine, a package of plastic cups. So I'm laughing, "Myron, we invited you, and *you* bring the dinner? I should invite you more often."

"We're used to this if we visit a non-kosher family." He smiles broadly; it comes to me that he's decided to make this a celebration, not a funeral. His smile fills the kitchen; he seems to have relaxed outward, expanded magically beyond even his usual breadth, and he stretches out his arms, fat palms up like a scroungy Atlas holding up the world. "Peter, Peter, what a great thing you did today. Zahava, what did I say?"

"A great thing," she echoes.

I shake my head, I laugh, but this is the story and I'm trapped in it, especially since my David is grinning at me, actually proud of me, my son. I'm a rebel again, I'm lying in the street blocking trucks. And since David's at an age when he orders me to drop him across the street from school so I won't be seen by his friends, I like it. I inhabit Liebowitz's story. I lift my hands in surrender; I must be blushing. I can feel my gestures taking on Myron's *Paddishkeit* by the minute.

We open the Liebowitz bottle of sweet kosher cough syrup and Myron offers a special blessing since this is the first time his family has shared a glass of wine with us, and then a blessing over the wine, and I'm giddy with the feeling that I'm acting in a play—but all right, it's a beautiful Jewish play. And at the same time I'm full of heart, irony having been left behind at the office.

"David can have a little bit of wine, can't he? He's already a bar mitzvah."

"A very little." I hold thumb and forefinger millimeters apart.

We have a big old kitchen, it's the one room of the Somerville house we left untouched: lots of light, big pine cabinets. With chairs dragged in from the living room, there's space for all of us to sit around the table. Zahava hands the baby to Liebowitz and spreads out the table cloth. She's such a contrast to her husband—neat as a pin, her marriage wig covered by a white kerchief. Perhaps she thinks she's doubly protected against the looks of men, but I have to admit, I'm looking. She couldn't be more than thirty. Her face is so placid. Under the kerchief it reminds me of the oval faces in Vermeer's paintings, big eyes and soft skin. My heart opens. What is it like for her to be with a wild expressive force like Liebowitz? What's it like on a Friday night, to be weighed down by such a massive creature?

Now Myron invites us to wash our hands. David asks, "How come? My hands aren't dirty." But it's a ritual washing, a purification, and afterwards Myron puts a finger over his lips and closes his eyes, says the blessing over the bread, a homemadeloaf of rye with caraway seeds. Everyone hushes till the bread is cut and passed, and now the talk spills out. Karen serves the soup; it's room temperature, because Zahava won't heat things up on our stove. But good. Myron's two boys are having a playful kicking match under the table. Our daughter Shira is of an age with Leah, and they're in a separate conversation.

Liebowitz settles into the biggest chair I've got. I'm seeing him differently here in his black coat and stained white shirt, beard and hat tilted back. It's as if his corpulence has become an expression of character, as if the fat were power instead of an uphill battle for the blood, as if the beard were lines of electric energy. Sighing over his soup, he puts a hand on David's shoulder. "Tell me, David, do you know the argument between the house of Hillel and the house of Shammai about the blessing over the bread?"

"*Whose* houses?"

"David, you're joking. You don't know any Talmud?"

And now out comes something so shocking my eyes bulge and I stop breathing for a couple of seconds. Looking down at his plate, David replies, "Talmud? They told us something in Hebrew school but…but I've always wanted to learn about it."

David?

Myron Liebowitz turns to me. "It would be my great honor," he chants, hand over heart, "to teach your son Talmud. You could say that our friend Friedman has given me a stipend for that purpose."

"A stipend?"

"As I told your lovely wife before you came home, Friedman gave me a choice. If I fight him, he'll fire me 'for cause.' Then what happens? I get *bubkes.* What do we live on? No unemployment compensation. But if I don't make a stink, I'll get a severance package. It's like a stipend for me to study Talmud—and teach David."

Now David begins to squirm. Sure. It's easy to say, "I've always wanted," but when push comes to shove…. "Mr. Liebowitz? I'm too busy to do much more homework."

"What homework? If we do a page of Talmud, that's a great mitzvah. Better you don't read in advance. We'll look at it together."

Do I really want this?

Dinner finished, David excuses himself, but Myron raises his hands like a wall. "Wait. You forgot the blessing."

David looks at me. I say, "*Birkat hamazon,* David. Remember? Sit a minute." But the minute turns into five, ten, as God is praised for the food and the land, for His mercy and compassion and our sustenance. And David says, "Okay, now?" I nod; he's off. Shira takes Leah up to her room, the boys go looking for a TV, and only the adults remain.

Liebowitz sighs. "I want you to understand, Peter: I know what a fool I am. You were very kind to me. A real Jew. A fellow-Jew." He thumps his chest and tears well up.

"Not the point, not the point, Myron."

"I goaded him, all right? I get like that. Listen. In our own shul they think I'm a little *meshugeh.* Please. It's true. We have zero friends because of me. I say this in front of my own wife. I don't want her to be ashamed of me." He closes his eyes and rocks.

I feel that this is not the first time she's heard all this. Zahava puts a little hand on Liebowitz's giant hand, and in that second I go through a whole alternative life. I'm married to this sweet, pretty woman with a baby in her arms and we're living a deeply observant life together, the kind that Karen would resist with the force of an upraised eyebrow, and we have ten children to mess and enrich our kosher home, and we get old and beautiful together and grandchildren—seventeen, eighteen, nineteen grandchildren—are born to the family; you can imagine what seders! And maybe, erasing, erasing, back in 1980 I didn't get an MBA; no, I became a rabbi, I'm Reb Peter, no I'm Reb Shmuel, and on Friday nights our lovemaking is dedicated to the Holy One, blessed be He.

And Myron Liebowitz says *he's a* fool?

He has tears in his eyes. He puts his hand on my sleeve. "With you, I can talk," he says.

So it's settled. During the next couple of weeks, I come home a few times to hear a talmudic singsong and find Myron Liebowitz sitting at the kitchen table with David. Liebowitz's black hat is tilted way back like a cowboy's; David is wearing a yarmulke. Nice. I wish I had a picture. But Karen, writing a grant application for her clinic at the dining-room table, looks at me through the open door with those eyebrows, one up, one down, her semaphore signal of displeasure: why do I have to listen to this *meshugas*? And the deeper message, which I'm able to figure out because it's making dots and dashes inside my own head, too: how would you like David to dress in a long black coat and fedora and end up in a hasidic yeshiva?

A couple of times, on his way out to his car in the twilight, Myron stops, holds me by the shoulder with his immense hand, looks into my eyes, and nods. This kind of intimacy isn't comfortable for me.

I say, as if to a buddy, "Want a beer before you head off?" He strokes his beard and says, "Peter, I've been looking all over for decent work. Work where I can use my intelligence. Why do I go shoot myself in my big foot? Tell me why? *Moshe rabbeynu,* Moses our teacher, was called 'the most humble man.' So what business do I have acting like such a big shot?"

I shake my head. I've made a few calls. But high-level jobs in information technology are scarce, even for geniuses. And, frankly, I get queasy trumpeting Liebowitz to friends of mine. With a job market like today's, would he make it past an interview? So I sympathize, I walk him out to his car, a Chevy van rusting at the seams, big, but still he takes up the driver's seat and half the passenger seat. "Goodbye, *landsman,*" he says, and drives off in the dark.

Then Jon Friedman calls one evening—another first. "M'man," he drawls, as if he were—what?—a black jazz musician from the fifties. "Suppose I pop over to that big Somerville estate of yours with a nice bottle of Margaux I've acquired. You think we could have ourselves a little drink together?" Big estate, little drink, nice Margaux: I try to puzzle out the significance of these adjectives. You can feel him trying to charm, to disarm. My hackles stiffen, but I say, "Sure, Jon. We're not all that busy at the Somerville end," getting my aggression out. "Fine, fine," he says, ignoring me. "Something to share with you, m'man."

Half an hour later he's ringing the bell. I've warned Karen and the kids; they've disappeared, though Karen says, "I've always liked Margaux. Save me a little?" In comes Friedman, dressed in a hooded maroon sweatshirt with a logo, pulling it off to reveal a blue silk shirt underneath. He's threaded his belt through the leather patch of his jeans to show the Versace logo. It's a peculiar signal: I'm an ordinary guy...but so cool.

We open the wine and sit in the study among my clutter of books. "It's about our friend Myron Liebowitz." He sighs, clinks glasses, sits back in a leather club chair, sips. Each sip, I figure wildly, must cost at least five dollars. He sips, I sip. "Look. Pete, we're in the days of awe, am I right? You're a *landsman,* Pete, a kinsman. So you know what I'm talking about. Days of atonement, days of making amends. Rabbi talked about it. See, eve of Rosh Hashanah, eve of Yom Kippur, I touch base with my roots, Ruthie and I get dressed up, go to temple."

"So you think you should make amends to Myron Liebowitz?"

"Yes and no. What do you think?"

I swing my desk chair around to face him, wheel myself closer. I sip another five bucks' worth and say, "Jon, what I think is that you've not been able to replace our *landsman* Myron. That's what I think." I take another drink. One thing about good wine—the more you sip, the better it gets.

"There's that, too. It's true. I've been looking all over." His face droops.

"So you can give the guy a call, Jon."

"I can't. *I can't.* You know what'll happen. He'll get on his high horse and I'll get on my high horse and we'll joust and fall off our horses. There's absolutely no point. But you can talk to him. What do you think? I apologize, you think he'll come back?"

"It's possible. But it's not likely. Which I hate to say, Jon, because in fact we need the guy. We need him if we want 3.0 to be up and running on schedule."

"So why not likely?"

I chew this over, sipping, and lie a little. "I happen to know he had a job lined up before he left us. In D.C. A lot more money. Something to do with government-funded research."

"Ah, shit. How much more?"

"That I don't know. But"—I consider this at length—"I hear his wife wants to stay here in Boston, so we may have a chance."

"Call him, call the son of a bitch, offer him whatever. See if he can be there first thing in the morning. If that's no good, well, anytime tomorrow. For the good of the company, I'll eat crow."

I can see what's happening with this wine, so I get on the phone and call Karen's line upstairs. "Honey? Better get on down here." I tell Friedman, "Karen's busy, but a nice little wine like this, she's got to have a drink with us. Don't you think?"

"Right, right."

So she does. And as soon as Jon's off, we share a laugh over the empty bottle and, feeling pretty good, I head for the phone. Zahava and I have a little talk. Liebowitz gets on and yells at me because I'm all he has to yell at and he can feel he's done his sacred duty. The mitzvah of yelling. Hanging up, I'm discouraged, but in a few minutes the guy calls back. "Zahava convinced me," he says. "Where am I going to get another good job with the economy the way it is? A Jew has a family to support. Maimonides tells us...."

I'm in the office early next morning, one eye on the plants hanging in Friedman's bay window, sort of holding Friedman's hand. He spews out worries. The economy, the corporation, the bottom line. Copyright infringements. Have I been suggesting Friedman's a fool? He's smart, not just a bureaucrat. The software concept was his in the first place. It's emotionally that he's a fool; vanity, the great fool-maker.

Just after nine, a knock at the door, Friedman is beaming a prize-winning smile—the one that must have melted the hearts of his audience when he won the Promising Technology Researcher award some years back—when he sees what's up. In comes Myron Liebowitz in basic black, thick as a Jewish Santa Claus. I see Friedman shut his eyes for an instant—against his own revulsion, I think.

This disturbs me. Is that my son David in twenty-five, thirty years, separating himself from other Jews, a new generation of the lost?

He's shifting papers on his desk, Friedman. "Real glad you could come in, Myron."

"God willing, we can work out our differences," Liebowitz says. "It's a very great thing," he raises his lecture-finger, "peace among Jews."

I see he means this; when Liebowitz gets emotional his eyes fog up, his deep voice quavers, and he sucks in half the air in a room.

"Jews?" Friedman says, and he emits a dismissive bark. He's amused. Oh, no he's not: he's playing amused, he's signifying amusement. "Jews ain't the point, kid. Look, if you want to wear black and so on and so on, you go right ahead. That's your business. I'll try to be decent with you. Okay? I didn't mean to put you down. Or—anyway, I had no right. But we've got to be professionals if we're going to work together. I expect professional demeanor: no chanting, no slovenliness. Okay? Think we can come to an understanding?"

Friedman's unstated aggression is eating at Liebowitz. I can see it. I sit down with a noisy sigh, I rattle papers, I say, "We need to bring Myron up to speed on new client needs at Yale."

Too late. Liebowitz hovers hugely over Friedman's desk. Friedman starts to get up, but this puts him inches from Liebowitz's beard. He sits back down; there's safety in teak. He's slight, Friedman. Liebowitz has him by 125 pounds and a good six inches. I'm half-imagining Liebowitz intends to pound him with his fist, hammer him down through his chair. He's pointing a big forefinger. He leans over the desk, arms straight, palms on the teak, and says, "Before we talk about software, I want you to understand, Jon Friedman. I'm here *nicely* this time, but I'm not forgetting. You let your Jew-hating loose again, next time I come in here, it's with a minyan—ten at least—everybody in beards and black hats, we'll be praying when the corporate boys are here. Or we'll study Talmud in the parlor, you should hear how loud!"

I don't know if Friedman has registered the threat of a sit-in minyan, but what he explodes at is "Jew-hating." I'm surrounded by rage, and me, I'm furious at both of them. Friedman shrieks something like, "How dare you, you fat slob, how dare you? I'm as much of a Jew as you are." I hear stirrings—whiz kids in the main room. "Liebowitz," I shout over both their voices, "you call this nicely? This is a rotten betrayal."

"Betrayal. Exactly," he answers. I meant Liebowitz; Liebowitz means Friedman—and me.

"He's been trying to apologize, you shmuck! How can you do this to us?"

"Aha!" Liebowitz yells. "Us. Now we see where *you* stand." And he storms out of Friedman's office. The whiz kids scatter, pretend they've been busy.

"I'll have to change the locks," Friedman says, mournfully.

I figure, that's it—the end for Liebowitz, and maybe the beginning of the end for me, too. Look how silent Friedman becomes around me, though sugary sweet to everyone else this afternoon. Needless to say, I don't want Liebowitz anywhere near me—or near David. When he calls that night, I hang up on him. Karen says, "You see? Black hatters!" I give her a sullen look. "Neither of them came off well this morning. Friedman, Liebowitz, they can both go to hell." I go sit in my study. He accused me of betrayal? The fool. I replay and replay the scene. Sure, I did say, "How can you do this to us?" But meaning what? I meant us good guys, accomplices in getting him his job back, him and me. At least I think I did.

This means more to me than you'd think. I flash back to a line of protesters, the Boston Common, 1971, facing a line of police, and all around me guys heckling the cops, "You f—ing pigs, you lousy f—ing pigs," "Oink, oink, you bastards," and I'm trying to shush them. "What good will that do?" I yell. "Stop. They're not your real enemy, those guys."

And bang, I'm slammed in the back by somebody's fist. Hard. Lucky I'm wearing an Army-surplus leather flak jacket. "*You're* the real enemy," the guy yells. "Maybe you're a pig, too. Informant! Anybody know this guy? This guy a stoolie? Hey, stoolie, keep your f—ing mouth shut." And I did. I slipped away, walked to the rear and down a side street just before the cops came down with clubs. And that night I watched it on local TV—the "riot," the guys being hauled away by ambulance. I didn't know where I stood. I didn't stand anywhere.

Next night, I come home late. Zahava, baby on her hip, is sitting with Karen at the kitchen table. David, too. He's home from school, they're all sitting, and Karen is holding Zahava's hand. This is beyond me. Zahava has brought a bottle of water, Karen has a cup of tea; they're buddies. The baby, Shlomo, begins to cry, and Zahava rocks, rocks.

David tries to distract the baby with jangling keys. And Karen, my wife, she says, "What this beautiful young woman goes through!"

Karen's eyes are wet. Zahava's eyes are wet. "Myron is so ashamed. That's how he gets. He feels so terrible what he did to you. He's got a big mouth. And too much pride."

I close my eyes. "He threatened Friedman he was coming back with a bunch of—"

"Oh, listen, I know, I know, I heard what he said. He told me, he was so ashamed. You don't know what a joke this is! Who would go do such a thing? Who from our community would do such a thing—embarrass your Mr. Friedman? For my Myron? They think Myron's a little *meshugeh.* But he's not crazy-crazy—he just goes overboard. At Chabad House he tells them, 'What do you know? Maybe you know Talmud, but you don't know a thing about Western culture, you don't know Goethe or Kafka or Joyce.' He says, 'Even Shakespeare you don't know. My beautiful Shakespeare,' he says. 'How can I talk to *a grobyan* like you?' You see? My poor Myron, he's so alone."

Karen is squeezing her hand, wiping the tears from her cheek. David takes the baby on his lap. "You've got to help this sweet little family," Karen says quietly, as if suddenly I'm the one who needs convincing.

Listen, I'm convinced enough. She must love him, that fat brilliant fool. And my little erotic fantasy? It dissolves, I have to tell you—I'm looking at Zahava in her long skirt and soft skin as someone to protect, a grown child, my own daughter. I want to lay my hand on her *shaytl* and offer a blessing, but you can't touch an Orthodox woman, and anyway I'm afraid Karen will think I'm peculiar, too. I say, "I'm not the one Myron needs to apologize to."

"No," Karen says to me. "And he *will* speak to Friedman," and Zahava nods, nods, nods, of course, of course. "But—" my Karen says, "maybe you can soften Friedman up just a little, honey? Kind of buffer the apology?" All of a sudden I'm "honey." Will wonders never cease, as my mother used to say with no question mark.

Frankly, I'm a little nervous. No, I'm scared. It's hard to be brave when I remember my mortgage. I see myself out on the job market in this terrible winter, depending just on Karen's salary from the clinic. I see myself managing some retail outlet. I see myself selling laptops. Still, after Zahava leaves and after we've had dinner, I call Friedman and I say, "Jon, it's me. Can I stop by for a few minutes, m'man? With a nice bottle of wine?" And I drive out to Concord with a bottle of vintage Manischewitz. I'm hoping Friedman sees the joke.

And I guess he does. I mean, I don't get fired after all, though who knows what could happen next month; and after a lot of talking I won't bore you with, Liebowitz is back with us. Yes! Liebowitz is back.

It's a sunny day, and don't tell me that has nothing to do with it. Trees on the Cambridge side street in full autumn color, and Liebowitz says a blessing for the beauty, and what can Friedman say? So he says, "Right, amen." And I sit between them, middleman that I am, and Liebowitz says this and this and this to me, and I turn and translate into that and that and that. And Friedman says into the air, Well, blah, blah, blah, and I translate as Generosity, Rationality, Teamwork. And we talk about the software; because that's a language we have in common. And by the end of the half-hour, Liebowitz doesn't love Friedman and Friedman doesn't love Liebowitz and both of them probably—no, definitely—think I'm suspect, a trimmer and a weasel. Maybe I am. Nevertheless, Liebowitz winds up with that nice office on the third floor and a lot more money, and after this, you can't hear his lunchtime chanting.

But if at lunchtime you go upstairs and stand outside his office door—*Myron Liebowitz, Linguistic Programming*—you can hear the rise and fall of his Aramaic.

He's sitting on the window seat of the big bay window with the leather-bound volume in his lap. "Stay a few minutes—we can study a few lines of *Berakhot.* Peter, do you know, from this window I can catch a glimpse of the Fogg. I'll tell you—this is some office." He opens the window to a blast of cold air and leans so far out he has to lift his feet from the floor, and I imagine all that weight crunching through the sidewalk.

"Myron, be careful leaning out."

"Oh, sure, sure." He comes inside, shuts the window and sighs a sigh of pleasure.

It's a swell office, with its old, fancy architectural details, the ceiling sporting an oval garland of flowers in plaster. Of course that's not the first thing you see. Papers everywhere, and Myron's three monitors, fat cables strapped down with gaffer's tape, a blackboard smeared with symbols and erasures. On one wall, a portrait of the Rebbe, Menachem Mendel Schneerson; facing him, the famous portrait of Beethoven. Liebowitz spreads his hands. "We should say a blessing—it's the first time you've visited me up here. And it's thanks to you I'm here." His eyes are shining. "You think I don't understand?" He closes them.

A couple of times since, I've gone up there to read a page, in English translation, from one of the tractates, and he's explained the context. If somebody doesn't clarify what's at stake, you get nothing out of Talmud, it sounds like nonsense. You need a teacher. I guess Liebowitz is my teacher. He rubs his beard, I rub my cheek; we puzzle over the argument about the proper frame of mind in which to pray. The thing about Talmud, it's high drama. People think the Talmud is God's opinion; if so, God's got contradictory opinions. This rabbi says this, that rabbi says that.

A couple of times he's come to the house and studied a page with David, and I've sat in.

See, we've kind of taken them on, the whole family. He tells me, "You're the only one I can speak to." But he's the same fat fool. Frankly, I still prefer his wife. She's the one who'll save him, not me. You should hear him get on his high horse about the patriarchs and the Holy Land and Moses. They say that at the end of days all Jews will be back in the Holy Land as they were at Sinai, and I think Liebowitz has a secret ambition to be resurrected as Moses. And like Moses chastising the people, he chastises me, shaking his head, thundering in his fat-man basso about what a disgrace it is to pretend I'm not a Jew.

I let him talk. I remember what Zahava said about his love for Shakespeare. And look at what's happening to the guy! Talk about assimilation. Subtly, over a couple of months, through a stormy, brutal winter, some of his white shirts, they're becoming button-down. The tzitzit still hang out but the pants are clean.

I can't ask what's up, for fear of pushing him back on his high horse. These changes: are they due to Zahava, or to Liebowitz? He's even trimmed his wild prophet's beard, until by now, in spring, it's not so bushy—a neat shadow of its former self. And the whole family comes to our house. Or we go there. I suppose you could say we've become friends. Lately, I spend an hour, one morning a week, at his little shul a half-hour drive the other side of the Charles. We wrap ourselves in talleisim, we strap on tefillin, we pray.

Karen laughs at me. One day, she says, I'll come home in black with tzitzit hanging outside my black pants. "Worse," I tell her. "I'll take to wearing one side out, one tucked in. I'll wear one black pant leg, one beige. A beard and earlocks on the left side of my face, the other side clean-shaven. On top of my head—maybe a Red Sox cap. A fool in motley."

"You're halfway there," she says. "All you need is the motley."

Originally appeared in Commentary, *April, 2004*

Fables of the Erotic Other

In a third-rate motel in Venice, California, Jacob Gershom is being nudged out of afternoon sleep. How can he mind? Marya (rhymes with *aria)* sweeps her long golden hair over his chest. And again. And again. Some whipping.

He's been with few women, certainly none like Marya. He's never been a wild boy, never had a girlfriend he couldn't bring home to his religious parents. Jacob is at Columbia Law now, so what's he doing, a week before spring semester, chasing this wild Marya out to L.A.? Warm afternoon in California, while in what he snobbishly calls the "real world"—New York, Boston, the East coast— it's drear winter. Lying around with her, middle of the week, he keeps his eyes closed so she won't stop. He's damp with sweat, laughing in his belly; a warm breath blows across his nipples and makes him shiver.

"Come on," she half-whispers, half-hums a little made-up rinky-dink tune. "Won't you wake up for me, baby?" Jacob laughs, stretches, presses against her. Yes, he wants her again.

Is it Marya he wants—or the wildness?

She plays at shock: "Oh, well, all right then, if you insist. I mean, what can we do? Jacob? We're just dissolute, aren't we? In*cor*-*r*igible." She whispers the word, lips against cheek, so that the long *ore* will warm his ear.

"This isn't what I think of as dissolute," Jacob says, suddenly somber. "Last night—when I came in and found you—*that's* what I'd call dissolute."

He means her weeping, when he'd finally tracked her down through charges to his Master-Card and found her high on something and low on everything else, ashamed and clinging. Where's *that* Marya? Oh, she clung all right. Room stinking of cigarette smoke and sausage smells from a stand by the beach, stained floral carpet, Monet print faded by years of sunlight, the works. She said, "Hold onto me, Jacob. If you hadn't come, I don't know what I would have done. Yes, I do. It was going to be tonight. I know it."

Trashy, phony suicide script, but those are real scars at her wrists. *You think I'm playing?* No, but maybe getting high on risk: the way she feeds off that story she keeps telling, first one way, then another: an abusive stepfather, the illegal stuff he forced her into. The story makes her high, or at least keeps her from crashing.

"You say take care of me. Then you run away. How can I take care of you?"

"I'm Rapunzel, I'm Snow White, I'm some goddamn princess under a spell. Jacob? You're my saving grace. Please."

A little girl begging for ice cream. He was so fetched by this begging look, he could hardly stick to the argument. Was she putting him on? There are times when she parodies innocence, plays at being a child, as if to say, *Isn't this what you want me to be? Does it turn you on?* Then there are times when her whole system crashes, and all she has left is a shell, a sign across her eyes: nobody home. But last night, with her eyes so open, so full of longing, the word "tragic" came to him. *Help me.*

"But you run away from me," he says again.

Last night, a little stoned, a little foggy, she shrugged off questions and melded with him. Later, bodies damp, still pulsing, half-dozing, she tapped him and said, "But *I had* to run, baby. His friends wouldn't trust me to keep my mouth shut. He must have told them, finish her. Because," Marya whispered, "see, I just won't do it anymore. I'd rather finish myself." Tears collecting, falling.

"Won't do what? What won't you do? Act as a courier?"

"As a mule," she said. His fingertips ran down her spine, the valley and peak of her hip, as if reading Braille. "That was his word, no joke: mule."

"Carrying what?"

"Currency, diamonds, maybe drugs. I don't know. I think drugs. I don't know, but I'm sure to be spotted. DEA, Treasury, they see a pattern, they're not stupid. Can you imagine me in prison with a lot of lowlifes?" She put her fingers to his lips. "I know. It's not just prison, it's what that life does do to you. You've taught me a lot about my soul. You have, sweetie."

"Your soul!" He grins. "What about my credit card?"

"I'll get you your damned card. You know I'll pay you back. Didn't I last time?" She got out of bed naked and went for her purse. In the sick lights from the motel's neon sign and the street lamps outside he watched her, hungry and depressed, and knew she knew he was watching; as upset as she was, she didn't forget to straighten and sway, shoulders back, hips forward and rolling, palms open, offering herself. That's it, he thought, she lives in my watching and gives her eyes away to me, to everyone.

The credit card was tossed onto the bed. Jacob sat up cross-legged and bent it back and forth until it cracked. "No good anyway. I stopped it. You really went to town."

"I went to town? I was desperate."

"At Saks?"

"I needed things."

"I don't get it, Marya. If you're threatening to kill yourself, why do you need to run? If you need to run, why buy a fancy car and nice new clothes?"

"Fancy! It was a used car. And I'll pay it off—all I charged was the down payment."

Today, this afternoon, it's a different Marya. No makeup, big eyes, no cynicism. Her voice is full of breath. She says, "I'll convert for you, Jacob. My mother's Jewish, I told you. We'll have beautiful *shabbes* nights. I'll light the candles for you."

It's when she talks like this that he feels sick. He knows the risk he's taking—not the bad guys with guns and money, assuming any of that's true, and not the danger to his career: Jacob has confidence in his ability to convince people he can work at a very high level. The real risk is to his soul. He's running a guerrilla operation into a dark no-man's land—a covert action. The Hasidim speak of entering into evil in order to reclaim the holy sparks. But isn't that putting a fancy façade on a kind of desire he's never come close to before?

What *is* it about erotic love? Why do you yearn so uncontrollably to touch the arch of the foot, her bare upper arm, the hollow where the collar bone meets the neck, the soft down of earlobe? Why, when she puts on a silk scarf, does it become a sacred object? Her eyes, when you can stand to look into them, why do you get so lost? What *is* this?

Over and over he tries to puzzle it out. Is he with Marya for the innocence he is persuaded is hidden in her, or for the wildness she lets loose in him? Maybe, worse, it's her darkness he hungers for, and if, by pretending this is some kind of holy enterprise.... Yet there are times, sitting or lying beside her and settling into the hum of meditative consciousness, when he can feel the borders of his energy open like a million gates, and he touches the humming edges of her, takes her in, blurs her soul with his. This isn't erotic; it's something more.

More dangerous.

In his mind's eye, all the way across the country in Brookline, his father shakes his head. *You don't know what you're letting yourself in for. A crazy woman! A good boy like you.* Now a fantasy comes to Jacob, lying with Marya, this afternoon: a vision of Pinhas the son of Eleazar the priest invading the tent where an Israelite man was lying with a Midianite woman, a worshiper of Baal, and skewering both of them through the belly with his spear. This was in the portion he read ten years ago on, God help him, the day of his bar mitzvah. Imagine that spear plunging down through him, through her, their blood soaking the motel mattress.

But then there was the talmudic story he learned long ago at his Jewish high school in Brookline. Once a wealthy merchant heard about a beautiful courtesan who charged 400 gold *denari* as her fee. He sent her the gold and appeared at the appointed time. She had built bed upon bed, the top one covered in gold, with ladders of silver and gold, and she, having disrobed, lay on the highest bed, and he began to climb, but he kept tripping on his *tzitzit*—the ritual fringes he wore under his garments—and he wouldn't remove them. Finally the fringes struck him square in the face and he fell to the ground. When the great beauty saw him lying there, she slid down and sat beside him. "What blemish did you see in me?" she asked. And the merchant: "You are the most beautiful woman I have ever seen, but my fringes, which the Lord has commanded us to wear, are like witnesses against me." So the courtesan asked the name of his teacher and his town, and when he had gone she gave away all that she possessed except her golden bed coverings and traveled across the sea to the merchant's town and asked the merchant's rabbi to teach her. She became his proselyte and married the merchant and covered their marriage bed in the gold cloth.

Fables of the erotic Other.

Jacob has fantasies of her redemption. He sees her hovering at the edge; she's taken him there, and he's looked over. In the middle of a loft in Soho, an old factory floor turned into living space, with no lights in the growing dusk, stands a big Harley that had been brought up in the factory elevator. Young men and women dressed in black sit rocking to music he does not know, listening, or not listening, stoned, and, in a back room, shooting up. Nobody says much. He looks for Marya—where has she gone? Upstairs, somebody says. He goes after her. A guy tying off; Marya helping. "I'm out of here," Jacob says, his face hot, hot. She runs after him, catching up halfway down the street. "You're all I've got," she cries.

The night they met he'd been dragged by a friend to a gallery opening on the west side. He must have been gawking, not at the paintings but at this forbidden beauty, for suddenly she was standing beside him, saying softly, "Well? So, do I pass?" A black suit, skirt high, mauve thighs, under the jacket a mauve silk chemise.

"You want to go for a drink?" she asked. "Whoever you are, I've decided I can talk to you."

She loved it that he was an observant Jew, a student of Talmud. She loved it that he was going to do poverty law after he passed the bar. "I'm not used to people like you."

The people she *was* used to: when Marya was twelve, she told him, her stepfather started to come on to her. Then he asked her to do a series of little jobs—flying to Paris, coming back with a suitcase: a child, well-dressed, sweetly smiling for the customs inspectors. And so then he had her trapped. She dropped out of school. A couple of times she tried to kill herself—once, she cut her wrists ("look, Jacob") and got sent to a clinic. When she came back, it started all over. That's when she began a career as a model—turning down a full scholarship to Princeton so she could make her own money and get away. And she did—but from time to time the bastard still forced her to serve as a courier.

"And you can't get away?"

"I'm a weak person, Jacob. I'm a slave, but I want to be free."

That first night they made an unspoken pact. He would rescue her; she would let him. And she would teach him things.

God knows, she's kept up her part of the bargain—taught him to swim in the depths, taught him how hard it is for someone to change, taught him not to believe half the things she says. The feelings may be real; the stories are something else again. Once her roommate in the West Village, Carol, said to him, "You're a good guy, Jacob. If you ever want to know about our friend Marya, just ask me." He's never asked; he's never dared.

That afternoon Marya tells him good news— Ralph Lauren wants her for a shoot in Malibu. And there's the possibility of a TV commercial. She'll do some modeling, she tells him, pay off the sporty Supra, see what she can work out with her stepfather's "money men," then she'll be back East. "I know you can't wait for me. You've got your classes. You go home, Jacob. Things will cool off. I'll join you soon as I can."

He believes and doesn't believe. Anyway, is it so much better modeling for Ralph Lauren than being a courier for money or diamonds or whatever? Trading on skin and smile? When she comes back from shoots—say, in the Bahamas—her look is distant, cheap. Anyway, he's surprised and not surprised the next day when he returns to the motel from morning prayers—7 A.M. in a small sanctuary at the rear of a synagogue—and she's gone. She's packed up, hasn't left a trace except an old *People*, a lipstick discarded in the bathroom trash, silk panties under the bed. The scent of her, everywhere. And a note, scribbled a little more crudely than her usual graceful calligraphy:

> Sweetie,
>
> I'm crying as I write this. I think I'm being followed again. I saw someone downstairs. I'm scared. I'm not dragging you into this, baby. If they catch up to me, we're dead. Especially you, because me they need—and I don't care anyway. About me. You think I'm kidding? Just remember Cary Grant helping Eva-Marie Saint up the head of some dead President on Mt. Rushmore—dissolve into him helping her onto the top bunk in a train compartment. We'll get together again, I swear it, when I clear this up. Okay? Don't forget about what it's like, you and me. Only when you're part of me am I whole. Please, leave L.A. I'll see you soon in NYC. I know this is crazy. You've been so, so beautiful.

Where could he look for her? It's a wild goose chase, ending in humiliation. But he finds himself driving slowly along Rodeo Drive in Beverly Hills, because that's where she likes to browse. Yesterday, that's where she'd taken him, store after outrageously expensive store, still wearing the dress from Saks that she'd charged on his credit card. She tried on outfit after outfit, and because she knew how to move, to turn, to present herself, and because she was so honeyed of skin, so soft-eyed, her smile so warm, the saleswomen loved her, made a fuss over her, didn't blink when she told them she was "desperate" for a nice dress for London, where he, her husband, was being transferred, or that she needed something she could wear for a few months until she grew...too large. He let her blab. Later he asked, "Why?" "Oh, for fun. Jacob, for godsakes, don't always be a prune." She squeezed his hand. "Honey? I don't mean *always.*"

Cruising Rodeo Drive, he stops in at a couple of places. They haven't seen Marya. "Should we hold that cashmere dress for her?" "No, I'm afraid not." He stops at a bookstore where her friend Gwynn works, but Gwynn hasn't seen her, either. He walks along the esplanade overlooking the beach in Santa Monica, hoping to see her far below among the exercisers. He thinks about calling her roommate Carol in New York, but Carol must be at work.

Without Marya, the motel is even bleaker than before. In the mid-afternoon he rests on the remade bed, calls the desk to prepare their bill—yes, he knows he'll have to pay for another night. He'll take the red-eye to Boston, see his parents for a couple of days, stay for *shabbes.* His mother will light the candles, she'll bake challah. He'll daven with his father.

Ten minutes from leaving for the airport, she calls. "Jacob? Oh, thank God. Everything's going to be okay." The car, not to worry—she's found a buyer in New York, Carol's boyfriend, he's willing to pay what she paid. "So if you can just drive east with me...."

"And those big bad men running after you to kill you?" he says, laughing.

"Stop. You think it's funny? I'll tell you all about it. I think it's all cleared up." She exhales a groan, as if to say, thank God—there's all sorts of things I'm not telling.

Scrunching the phone between neck and shoulder, he keeps packing his suitcase, silent.

"Don't believe me. Oh, baby...it'll be so nice, the two of us. And you've got a week before classes."

She wears tight jeans, she wears high-heeled boots and a cowgirl shirt. It makes Jacob wonder who the guy is: her new stylist. In the back of the little red Supra she has a suitcase of clothes; up front, her purse and a backpack with vitamins, her CDs and tapes—a high-end stereo system was one of the goodies she'd put on his MasterCard. While he drives, she leans back, boots crossed on the dash, and sings along with Willie Nelson. Some guy, for sure, Jacob thinks. Does it bother him? Yes; but he actually likes her in this just-folks mode.

He drives east through the hills, up into the mountain pass on 15, snow mounded dirty along the roadside but shining white higher, on the peaks, then down onto desert flats with overlapping lines of mesa in the distance. Dead land, brutal. Into the crotch at Clark Mountain and down again, then flat, bare country along the line of the Mojave into Nevada, the rock hills closing in on the little red car, then opening to let it pass. You're wearing no makeup, not even eye makeup. I like the look. The last thing he wants is to make her self-conscious. He wants her to find a place in herself where she's comfortable. She's blathering now about her mother. About Nina, her mother's lover, who's never trusted her. "I mean the way you trust me, Jacob."

"Trust you? I *don't* trust you, honey. I just believe in how beautiful you could be. How beautiful you are under the lies."

She laughs. "You see? You're so damned honest with me. You keep me straight, Jacob."

"But I don't."

"Well, no one could. You come close."

"You run away."

"Don't get tiresome on me. I swear to God I won't ever run away from you again. You hear me, honey?"

"I thought you had a modeling job in Malibu." She shrugs. On the long, terrible desert road to Vegas she pulls him to her by a clutch of his curly hair and kisses his cheek. "Jacob? I'm trying to be the person you see. You understand?" She closes her eyes. Something hovers over the road ahead; not a bird but a sheet of newspaper, whisked by a dust devil.

"Wait a minute." It dawns on him: "You said Nina? So your mother has a woman lover? What about that guy—the stepfather? *Is* there a stepfather, Marya?"

He can feel her churning, rehearsing something. She says, "My mother—she swings both ways. Anyway, stepfather isn't exactly the case."

"No?"

"Truth is, the guy I told you about, he was my mother's boyfriend. He's the one I was a courier for. His friends are the guys who were after me."

"And now they're not?"

"We made a deal."

"Marya, please." He waves away her story. "So you weren't abused?"

"Oh, I was, Jacob. I was. But not by him. He never came on to me. Actually…it was my *grandfather*, okay? My father's father." She looks for his reaction; he's not reacting. "You don't have to believe me," she says, sounding hurt, sitting up and reaching into her backpack for a cigarette. But Jacob holds his nose, shakes his head; she grunts a laugh, puts the cigarette back.

"Stepfather, grandfather—the point is you experienced abuse. I do believe that."

"Stop talking like a textbook. You know, mister, I hate that in you. 'Experienced abuse.'" She slumps down, pouting. He glances over at her, now this beautiful little child again, and feels grown-up, heavy. "I was *pawed.* The old son of a bitch put his fingers etcetera…. I had to do my own grandfather, okay? Then it got *worse,* got really bad, they sent me to a therapist. Don't believe me. You know, most kids who go through that, they're nauseated by sex, they get weirded out when a guy touches them. But that's not me. I get drunk on sex."

"Don't brag."

"You think I'm bragging? I'm like an addict. But with you—with you I feel almost whole, like it doesn't overwhelm me. Jacob? Do you love me?"

He takes a long, long time—a mile, two miles of desert, while they're both silent. Then she blurts out a laugh. "Just testing. Pulling your chain, baby."

"Yes, I suppose. I suppose I do love you. I mean, I'm in love with you. So what?" His face hot with anger. "So what?"

"Nah—nah—you just like the little things we do."

"Just shut up, stop that, will you, with the phony toughness."

"What are you doing here, anyway? Okay, okay." She spurts a laugh. "I know. You're here because I begged you, because you know the idea of driving all the way across this lousy country makes me want to kill myself."

"Too many things do that."

"I guess. So, you do love sick little me." She slips out of her boots and puts her feet in his lap and rubs her heels in figure eights. Her head tilts to the side, her long hair spilling over her shoulders. She holds golden strands in her fingers—like *tzitzit,* he thinks. "I'm your little adventure into bad places. Aren't you lucky?"

"Stop—I'm driving." He pushes her feet away, and she laughs and lifts her foot up to his neck, tickles his neck with her toes.

"You won't marry me, Jacob?"

"I won't marry you."

"You see? Listen, I'd convert. Anyway, I told you, my mother is a Jew."

"Even if you were a Jew, how could I marry you? Maybe I'm in love with you—"

"Sure, sure."

"But marriage? I think about children. I think about bringing up children decently. The way I was brought up. Frankly, honey, I'd have to be crazy."

"Crazy, see, that's the only kind of love. *L'amour fou,* right? The way you were brought up? You were brought up to be a wuss, Jacob. See? *I'd* have to be crazy to love *you.* Hey, suppose I cut off all my hair and wore a wig and became a good Jewish wife?"

"Oh, baby. It would just be another costume."

"Well, thanks, mister. Jesus, I asked for honest, I get honest. You really think I want to marry you? You boring creep." She opens her window, stretches to open the back windows. Desert wind blows through. It's a statement. He lets it blow.

"What *do* you want from me?" Jacob asks. He feels so sad this minute for her—for the boots, the sexual pizzazz, the image of her wildness that keeps her going, keeps her, maybe, from breaking apart and keeps her from putting herself together. *Teshuvah,* a turning. Looking over at her, he's overcome by tenderness.

When did he start to love her? Until today, he's never told her, but he's known it for weeks. What a joke—that he flew to L.A. to rescue her. The truth is, he couldn't stand her not being with him. Face it. At times, he hates her. But when he's alone, he can't stop remembering her eyes. The night she called him, babbling and weeping—she'd tried to kill herself and got scared, needed him to get her to the emergency room. By the time he ran the seven blocks to her place, she'd already thrown up the pills. She cried as he held her all that night; she made him believe in her longing for a real life.

Las Vegas fifty miles. Forty miles.

"Look, Jacob. Cattle? Is that a herd of cattle?" As they get closer, he can see: "No. It's ATVs or motorcycles. A posse of thrill riders."

They're driving through desert and desert and desert now, and under the flat blue sky the monochrome plainness says to him, *This is it, this is all there is, everything else we invent.* "Marya? Have you ever been to Las Vegas?"

"Omigod yes," she said. "And Jacob, don't let me gamble."

"Let's drive on through. Okay?"

"Or maybe gamble just a little?"

Their left rear tire starts to thump. Tup-tup-tuptup-tup. The car floats a bit but there's no danger. He lets a couple of trucks shake by and pulls over onto a broad, flat gravel breakdown lane. Something about this he doesn't mind—what the hell, it gets them out of the car, into desert, and he can do what he's good at: handle things, real things, tires.

"I've got my cell," she says, digging through her purse.

"It's nothing," Jacob says. "It's easy. I'll bet we've got one of those little emergency spares; it'll take us to a station." He pops the rear hatch and moves her suitcase so he can lift the cover over the spare tire.

"Jacob?"

"It's here. They couldn't sell it to you without a donut."

"Hey, but listen, Jacob?"

He's unbolting the small tire. The desert wind blows hard.

"Jacob!"

Her eyes look a little crazy. He stops, wipes his hands on his jeans.

"What?"

"Look, Jacob. This is so stupid, but—that's not a working spare. Please—let me use my cell."

"It's fine." He taps the tire. "It's a little soft, but it'll do."

"No it won't, Jacob. Believe me."

Now he stops and really listens. He's already grim. "Why not?"

"Because the tire's a fake. I mean, it's got a plastic frame to make it look real."

"Why? Why would anybody do that?"

"Oh, figure it out, goddamnit!"

He bends down, shakes the tire a little, finishes unbolting and lifts. At the bottom is a patch. "Better leave it," she says.

"Oh." He steps back as if there were a bomb in the trunk.

"Here's the thing. It's no big deal. I promised some guys I'd drive it east for them."

"Or *I'd* drive it east."

"I swear to God, Jacob, I really sold them the car, they're taking the whole thing—the car, the stuff, and I'm out of it. I leave them the keys and take an envelope from some doorman on 68th Street and walk away. Then I can pay you back. See, they're afraid of flying the stuff east. This is easy. Who's gonna look?—and if some asshole does take a look, there's a spare. It fooled you, right?"

"It fooled me."

"You think I needed you so you could drive? I told you why I wanted you here. Honey? Jacob? Friend?"

She puts out her hand, he pushes it away. "Use your cell," he says. He re-bolts the tire, sits in the passenger seat, tilts back, closes his eyes.

She drops him at the airport outside Vegas. They don't even say goodbye. He flies to Boston, spends a couple of days in the house he grew up in, the room he grew up in, now a guest room but with his tournament Frisbees still in a row on the wall and in the closet his old computer, his expensive baseball glove still good enough to save for his children, thousands of baseball cards, strata of childhood going back to a couple of stuffed animals and his first yarmulke and his kid drawings. Framed, covered by glass, a painting of a Torah scroll done as part of preparing for his bar mitzvah. He takes off his shirt, lies on his old bed with the carved wooden headboard, looking up at the ceiling, hands cradling his head.

His parents don't ask questions. His mother looks in, brings a piece of carrot cake, tea. He goes with his father to shul the next morning; afterward they stop at a deli for bagels. Jacob breathes in the smells of his childhood, breads and sliced meats, pickles. His father, balding, overweight, has taken to breathing heavily, and Jacob worries about his heart, although the rhythmic sighing somehow comforts him. Max Gershom riffles out onto the Formica a sheaf of papers. "I've been doing some checking on this friend of yours. You want to hear?"

Jacob shrugs. Sure. His father is an executive headhunter who works out of his home. So he knows how to search. He likes to say, "I'm a kind of detective, except the people I turn up are happy to be found." Now he clears his throat. "You're well rid of her. First of all, no Marya Gilbert graduated from Hunter High in New York City. Period. Also, I find no Marya Gilbert listed anywhere as a model or an actress. Of course," he says, holding up his palms, "maybe I'm not looking in the right places. If Ralph Lauren came to me as a client, it would be to find him a marketing director, not a model."

"So what did you find?"

The waitress puts down bagels and coffee. Jacob's father shoves the papers to one side and loads his bagel with cream cheese.

"That's the point—I found nothing. I found an e-mail address and a phone number. You tell me she lied to you? You bet she lied. You want to hear what she told the car salesman?"

"You talked to the car salesman?"

"Yes. In Queens. I'm like a bulldog—you know me, Jacob. From what you said about the Supra? Easy. So you want to know what she told him? He remembered her really well on account of her beauty—those were his exact words. She told him you were undergoing chemotherapy, you had maybe six months to live, and she was buying the car to take you to Maine, to your family home."

Jacob laughs so loud all the customers turn to look. "What a bullshit artist."

"The guy was really concerned about you." His father leans forward, the smile disappears. "Jacob—you're not sick, are you?"

"Dad! Of course not. You've got to understand how needy she is."

"You're well rid of that one," his father says again. He reaches a hand over the table and rubs Jacob's cheek.

Jacob takes the fast train to New York. He's just pulling out of New Haven when the first call comes in on his cell phone. He picks up but stays silent. "Jacob? Please, Jacob? Jacob, you bastard! *Jacob*?"

He imagines her driving through Nebraska and Iowa and Kansas with no one to lie to, no one to give her back a self. She's sitting in her fancy little car in the middle of desert, of prairie; she pulls over to the side of the interstate, the big trucks whipping by and shaking the Supra. She sits in the pretty red car by herself, weeping. Now she drives again, seventy, eighty, more, music blasting. Waking up in some chintzy motel and not knowing where she'd got to the night before. She must be terrified. She's knocked out, she pops pills, uppers to keep her going through the long day, playing her stack of CDs loud to let the music carry her. She's crying without an audience. Once in a while she stops for coffee and takes off her sunglasses, sees the men seeing her, her beauty reflected in their look. She smiles, puts the sunglasses back on, heads outside.

He works all afternoon, all evening, in the apartment he shares off Bleecker. Second semester in law school begins next week. He feels enormous relief, the virtue in anger, cleaning her out of his system. He feels he's gotten away with something. But groggy with fatigue, almost asleep, the room dark except for the city lights reflecting off his ceiling, he sees her driving through the dark of the Midwest, needing him.

All day she's called; he's turned off the phone. Next day there are long messages on voice mail; he erases them without listening.

Then she stops. Now, in her absence, he remembers her sadness more than her falseness. Remembers the times her eyes grew wide as if to show him that her defenses had dropped away. *This is who I am.*

When he gets home, he calls Carol. "Is it okay if I drop over before Marya gets back, pick up my things? I left a sweater."

Remembering the night he ran through these streets to save her, he walks self-consciously past bars and stores to Christopher Street. It's getting on toward dusk, but the sun has escaped the clouds in Jersey and as it drops it sends a rosy haze through lower Manhattan. He looks south, where two giant towers are not there to catch the sunset.

Carol lets him in, lets him look around, gives him a plastic bag for books and the sweater Marya borrowed, the shirts he'd left. She's a lean, plain-looking young woman with a nice smile; Jacob feels comfortable in her presence. He can sit on her kitchen counter, legs dangling, drinking tea. Her dark hair is cut very short; she's in jeans and a heavy sweatshirt with the name of a gym. That's where she'd met Marya—they kept the same workout schedule. He talks with her about her job in her father's construction company, learning to estimate bids. They talk about law school. As he's leaving, his clothes in a shopping bag, he stops; this is the real reason he came over. "Carol? You said once you could tell me about Marya."

"Right. Well. You could probably tell *me* things. You must know everything by now."

"Her lying?"

"I've had it up to here with her lying," Carol says. "Not to mention, she hasn't paid any rent in three months. Anyway, when she's back, she's moving out. She'll be staying with that weird friend of hers, Ian. You know—the motorcycle in the living room?"

"I remember."

"I'm advertising for a new roommate. Sane, this time. But that's not what I meant. I meant…the modeling. You do know, don't you?"

"Not really." He remembers her regret at his regret that she couldn't do more with her life. When she'd come back from some Caribbean resort, after doing a commercial for a line of clothing, she was in particular grief. *If it weren't for you, Jacob....* "She doesn't much like doing it, I know that."

"Doesn't like modeling?.... Well, she's hardly *done* any modeling. You understand?"

"No."

"No? Well, I guess you could call it private modeling. You didn't know? For rich men. Not a lot of them. Two that I know of. She'd go away for a weekend. You see?"

He says he'd rather not talk about it.

But on the way home the new knowledge sinks down into him like a virus into a computer, altering memory, freezing the programs. Fragments come up to consciousness. Messages left on his answering machine. Her weeping over the phone after she got back from Aruba. He notices his jaw is clenched; he must be angry.

A couple of nights before the start of class there's another call. Her voice is cool and a little sloppy from drink, or drugs.

"Jacob, pick up? Jacob, if you get this, well, listen. I'm back. Jacob? I got rid of the Supra. I've got the money for you.... Well, look—here's why I'm calling. Remember you said to me a couple of times, you said if I needed to get to the hospital, I mean if I went *ahead* with it, okay?—and then I changed my mind and called you?—you'd get me there. Like the night you ran over to my apartment when I took the pills? The joke is, I didn't really take the pills that night, I just needed you. But now you need to get me to the hospital, baby. I really did it this time, and Ian's not home—you remember the guy with the Harley?—and I'm scared. Jacob? If you don't get this...no loss. Really. Certain people will be relieved. Including me. If you don't call back, I won't bother you again." And she recites Ian's address, Ian's phone number.

He's silent. He's thinking of calling 911—let them take her to a city hospital and pump her stomach. But it's just one more phony story. He's silent.

"I got rid of the car and the funny tire.... Come on, I know you're there, you bastard! Okay. Maybe you don't think I'm so beautiful down deep anymore? Well—maybe you're right. So...maybe goodbye. Jacob? Are you there, Jacob? Pick *up,* Jacob."

She took pills," he tells his father over the phone. "Her friend Ian found her this morning. And she'd shot up with something. That's what Ian told Carol, and Carol called me. She died on the floor, trying to get to the bathroom, maybe, or get help. I don't know."

"What a terrible thing to do to you. I've got no sympathy. She left you with that? Jacob, let her rot in hell!"

"Dad?"

"I've got no sympathy, Jacob. That's unforgivable."

"Dad? Let me explain something—I was *home* last night."

"You were home. So. You heard the message? When?"

"When she called, I was right there."

Now his father is silent. Jacob can hear him breathing heavily. It's no comfort. "And you didn't pick up?"

"No. I was sure it was another con. More manipulation."

"So you didn't pick up?"

"I would have called 911. But she was such a liar. Those weekends she was modeling...."

"So you didn't come to the phone, you didn't call back? Oh, Jacob. How awful for you. How you must feel. Listen. Probably, even if you got to her or called, she must have been so full of bad drugs." Silence again. "Oh, Jacob, Jacob."

"Dad? Listen. Suppose it was to get back at her."

"That's not you, Jacob."

"Or suppose I couldn't stand it, being without her, so I wanted her to do it. So I wouldn't be tempted."

"Why do this to yourself?"

"Or worse. Dad? This is what scares me the most. Maybe it's something in me? Something I wanted to get rid of?"

"You think I don't get what you're saying? But the long and the short of it is you didn't know. Period. Jacob, you didn't know. So. I'm coming down to see you tomorrow. Okay?

It's a month later—a gray winter morning, early morning, in Brooklyn. Jacob has withdrawn from classes for the semester. For almost no rent—he helps out a little, painting, running errands—he lives with the Presslers, a family of Orthodox Jews in Flatbush, and studies with a hasidic rebbe he knows.

As he walks along the street, he talks to himself. Always, his lips are moving, in murmured prayer or conversation; it dulls and softens the world.

He's chanting morning blessings as he walks to Reb Pinhas's, past stores still closed-up, past well-dressed men hurrying to a minyan somewhere before taking the subway to work. Past the stores for Jews, the stores for non-Jews. From a trio of young black men walking to the subway he gets hard, contemptuous looks. This shocks him—as if they knew all about him and Marya. Then he remembers what he's wearing—black hat, black suit, the ritual fringes symbolizing the commandments tying him to the Torah and hanging down outside his pants; the beard. He hunts his reflection in the window of a kosher butcher shop. Even to myself I look foreign; must be the costume.

Reb Pinhas runs a little *shtibl*—a shul and a house of study—in a pair of adjoining brownstones; the walls have been broken open in places to make a single building. The lower floor, just below street level, has been converted into a room for prayer and study. The books and the dark paneling give the room a brown appearance; it's drafty, chilly, especially first thing in the morning. The room is too dim for study; in the cones of light from the desk lamps you can see a snowstorm of dust motes, you can smell hot dust. Old books line every wall, floor to ceiling. Two pairs of students in their late teens, early twenties, are talking in that yeshiva mix of Yiddish, English, Hebrew, and Aramaic. Always their hands are talking—fast, fast. At one of the study desks they're examining a text, chanting and talking, chanting, pointing, talking.

In the far corner, in the half-dark, Jacob davens alone, his fedora tilted back on his head, the prayer book resting on his chest as he stands and rocks. Everyone is in black and white. White shirts, black pants, shoes, jackets, yarmulkes, fedoras. Everyone is bearded. Jacob's beard has come in thick, curly, black.

Reb Pinhas comes down from his office upstairs to take part

in the service. He's a balding man, not old but with the appearance of age, his bushy gray beard streaked with peculiar cords of pure black. He's fat, not overweight like Jacob's father but pasty-fat, his skin puffy, pale, every breath comes hard, and when he sits he has to draw himself down slowly into the leather library chair that looks as if it finished its best days fifty years ago. Someone has mended a crack with duct tape.

"I want to see you upstairs in my office," Reb Pinhas says to him after morning prayers.

A month ago, when he first told him the story, Reb Pinhas nodded, nodded, and, eyes closed, sighed.

"I hope you don't come to me so I can accuse you," the rabbi said, smiling. "No. Of course not. But I think I see why you stay away from your parents. You think, Reb Pinhas won't let me off the hook. It is said in *Berakhot,* in the place where penitents stand, not even the perfectly righteous can stand. So. We both know it's not a hopeless situation. You tell me you intend to say kaddish for this woman? I know you know, this is not customary."

"As if she were my sister."

"So we'll study the texts."

Study is what he's good at.

This morning, in the rabbi's room, it's study he first asks about. "So. How's it going?"

"Good."

"Good is good. But I notice things. I watch you. You're a little embarrassed by your study partner, isn't that right? And you're embarrassed that you're embarrassed?"

Jacob flushes. He is aware of his impatience. Shlomo, his study partner, can say only what the authorities have said about a text, sheep-like citations and over-reliance on the traditional principles of interpretation. When they study Psalms, Shlomo knows many by heart, but what can he say about them except "Oh, my…oh, my"? So Jacob, who has plenty to say, plays teacher. "We're learning together," Jacob tells Reb Pinhas.

"He is a very good soul."

Jacob, nodding, hears in his head Shlomo reciting in the

Hebrew, "As for me, my feet were almost turned astray, very nearly were my steps washed aside." Isn't that enough? This isn't supposed to be Yale! He is a broken soul trying to break more, break all the way.

"I pray for God to help me turn."

"Of course."

"But, Rabbi?" His breath feels trapped in his chest. At last he says, "Sometimes when I pray, I look down and the whole room feels askew. I mean it's tilted—like an expressionist theater set. I'm afraid I'll fall."

Jacob doesn't expect the rabbi to understand "expressionist theater." But Reb Pinhas says, "You know, that's exactly the kind of thing I was afraid of. So tell me: You want to be one more *meshugene* in Flatbush?"

They laugh together.

"I'm serious." The rabbi raises a finger and wiggles it again like a metronome. "You think you can redeem yourself by showing God how much you suffer? Mr. Gershom: crazy is another costume. Like your nice black hat. You think God cares about a costume?"

"No."

"That's right—no. I'm asking you, please, Jacob: do not concentrate on your own gestures. You understand me? And when you find yourself doing so, say, 'God! I am now in a place dangerous to my remembrance of You. Help me, that I not forget You.'"

Jacob nods, nods, gesture of submission.

"And then, Jacob, just…just live, study Torah with us. Say 'Good morning, Reb Pinhas.' Help out the family where you live. That's your *teshuvah,* your turning, you understand me?"

He nods. Even now, he feels like a liar. Because he nods and nods and doesn't say, Listen, Rabbi, I'm sitting studying gemara and she comes to me, and the whole of my side opens up to take her in. Every day, for an instant, he remembers touching her, that dangerous landscape.

Help me, that I not forget You.

He murmurs to himself, sitting in the basement with his eyes staring at a page of Talmud. Suppose Marya isn't dead at all. How does he know, except for Carol's call? I didn't see a body, did I? I didn't speak to the police. He's afraid to look up and out through the basement window, afraid he'll see a little red car. And wouldn't he just run to her, fringes flying.

Of course, if she were alive, the mark on his soul would be almost as dark. It was still a test—and he failed. But he begins to wonder. He considers calling Ian, but revulsion wells up too strong. One evening, in black coat, black hat, *tzitzit* dangling from under his belt, he takes the F train into Manhattan, drops in on Carol. She has a new roommate, a graduate student at NYU. "I'm glad you're here," Carol says. "A letter came for you a week ago. I didn't know where to reach you."

> Dear Sweetie,
>
> Here's the money I owe you. For reasons I won't go into, I had to disappear last month. But I didn't want you to worry or pray for me or something. When things settle, I want to be with you. You think we could be together? I can understand why you didn't come that night. I almost took the pills. I did. I filled the tub and lay there with the bottle of pills beside me but I just couldn't do it—maybe because you've taught me my life has possibilities. You think? Just so you know the truth. And I do love you, baby.

That's all. He passes the letter to Carol, and Carol starts cursing, until her roommate has to hold her, crying and cursing. Jacob closes his eyes, breath comes like rain, so deep. "Carol, it's okay. It's better."

"Better! Let her fall under a train, the bitch! And I've been feeling so bad about kicking her out!"

A money order is enclosed. Jacob considers tearing it up; but on the subway back to Brooklyn, he decides that it is, after all, his own money. He will treat it as a blessing from God. Back in the basement, when he looks up from his text, he sees legs walking by outside, cars passing, no little red Supra. Another blessing—the room, thank God, stops tilting. And now his lips don't move so often as he walks down the street.

Winter is almost done. It's a Sunday. This morning he is prepared to jack up the back porch of the Presslers' house. It's the kind of work he used to do every summer when he was in college. The porch leans badly, one outside corner more than a foot lower than the other. With the help of one of the kids, he's moved the contents of the porch onto pallets in the backyard and covered everything with polyethylene. Now, mid-afternoon, he rests on his bed. It's the first day he's been able to open the window of his room more than a crack; lying on the bed, he feels spring air wash across his chest. He closes his eyes. Is he remembering a motel in Venice, California? Not as far as he could tell you. But the breath of air makes him shiver; eyes closed, he feels Marya lying beside him on the bed, the length of her cleaving to him, flesh to flesh. Oh, just for a moment.

The air washing over him, he thinks of it as the air of freedom. Well, there's freedom and freedom. For instance, Passover is coming. On Passover we are to feel as if we, personally, are being liberated from Egypt. The root of *mitzrayim,* the Hebrew word for Egypt, means a narrow place. Hasn't he been trapped in a narrow place? And now, in spite of feelings he still can't control, isn't he freer? Lately, he's been able to talk to his mother and his father about his life here, to consider plans. He's planning to come to them for Passover.

But suppose that little red car of hers…?

A soft tap at the door. It's Mrs. Pressler, calling in her soft voice, "Jacob? Jacob, there's a telephone call for you."

Originally appeared in Commentary, *October, 2003*

Blue House

The blue house, modern colonial in a Boston suburb, had been sick a long time, the house doctors said, but nothing showed until the heavy rains of April, and then leaks, leaks sprang—a bedroom wall developed a grotesque blister, swelled like an abscess until Monroe poked it, and then the skin broke open and yellowish water ran down the wall. The source of that leak was found; another turned up. The carpenter shook his head, looked mournful, dug with a pocketknife into rot: a new roof was needed; structural lumber had become punk, so part of the roof framing would have to be replaced. Roof and then one sill, clapboards near the foundation. "At least the house won't catch fire," Joanna laughed, soothing. Bravado: we can take our knocks.

And then one afternoon a telephone call came from New Jersey, and the roof didn't matter. Sheryl was Joanna's daughter-in-law, married to Joanna's son from her first marriage, Ted. A landscape architect, Sheryl had been on the Jersey Turnpike, driving out to a tree nursery. It had been raining; a trailer truck jackknifed in front of her car. She swung to avoid it, State Police said, but clipped the rear of the trailer and went through a guardrail and down a run-off ditch.

Joanna's son Ted was consulting in Minneapolis that day, a Friday. Ted and Sheryl's fourteen-year-old, Sam, got called up to the principal's office. "What did I do now?" he asked the guidance counselor who, silent, accompanied him. Joanna got a call at noon from a friend of the family. No rush—we can take care of him awhile, the woman said. A competent, kind woman—she'd already spoken to Ted, gotten in touch with the rabbi, the funeral home. But in an hour, Joanna and Monroe were on the road—Newton, outside Boston, to Orange, New Jersey.

That beautiful, beautiful girl. Monroe didn't care a hell of a lot for Ted, Joanna's son, but he loved Sheryl. He was embarrassed the way his body would bloom when he simply hugged her hello, goodbye—nothing more, nothing even cooked-up in his imagination. Sheryl was half his age; Monroe kept even his fantasy life under observation. Sunday, the funeral, Ted bewildered, looked middle-aged; Monroe, who never cried, cried. Joanna, Monroe, Ted, poor Sam, sat shiva in the split-level in Orange. Friends congregated for services, brought food. Monday, Monroe, who had to teach at Tufts, took the train home; Tuesday, Ted flew to LA—though "poor Ted didn't look capable of conducting business evaluations and consultations," Joanna told Monroe over the phone.

"Is he crazy? Business? The man's got a son."

"Dear?" A long, breathy silence. "Dear? Sam's coming to us."

He could feel a diatribe brewing in his chest. He kept his mouth shut. What could he say without showing contempt for Joanna's son—for Joanna as a mother? "I see," he said at last.

Sam brought baggage with him to Boston: a duffel, a couple of suitcases, cartons of stuff. "Monroe?" Joanna whispered. "The boy hardly said a single word the whole trip."

At first, the kid, Sam, went through the house like a ghost. It was hard to look at him: skinny kid, his shoulders slack, zombie head with ragged spikes of hair; a force field surrounded him: nobody got through. It hurt. Monroe couldn't play grandfather, Joanna couldn't play grandmother. They had a grieving, silent, teenager ghost, *blue* ghost: a blue plastic tarp hanging over the joists and spacers of the living room cast its tint on furniture and faces.

Monroe's fingers tingled, throbbed, when he looked at Sam, that's how much he wanted to comfort the boy—rub his shoulders, pull him against his chest. Monroe's a big, shaggy man with gray hair; he's overweight, slow-moving, with a head Rodin could have sculpted—nose thick like an architectural ornament, grand forehead—like Rodin's head of Balzac. Sam wouldn't look his step-grandfather in the eyes. *Maybe*, Monroe thought, *maybe because my eyes are sad. Maybe that's why Sam avoids them.* Or maybe it's just a dark time, the blue house itself sad.

To Monroe it was as if Ted were responsible for the blue pall over the house. Some father! What's wrong with that pipsqueak? To dump his son! And if Sam has to live separate from his father, wouldn't it be better for him to live with a friend in Teaneck than dislocate him this way? As weeks go by, Monroe realizes why Sam agreed to live with his grandmother and step-grandfather: from his friends he couldn't hide so well.

Sam, combat boots, cargo pants, shuffles in dirty sneakers over the polished wood floors, leaving scuffmarks and scratches. Ghost with heavy sneakers. But how can you chide the kid? Chide?—can you even talk to him? He won't talk about his mother, won't let his grandmother give him a hug. Nor will he go with Monroe to synagogue to say Kaddish. "This is not optional," Monroe explains, speaking just above a whisper to soften the judgment. "It's for your mother, for your mother's soul. You're an adult Jew, Sam." But when Sam shrugs and avoids his eyes, Monroe leaves him alone. He'd press the boy, but Joanna gives him a look: *Don't start trouble.* It says: *Sam doesn't need to be guilt-tripped.* And a deeper message adds…*any more than Ted.*

Don't get Monroe started on Ted. "A tragedy has happened," Monroe whispers to Joanna one night. "Sam is bound to suffer. But Ted doubles the tragedy. He runs away, the little fart."

"Are you saying we shouldn't have my grandchild here?"

"I'm *saying* he needs his father. Or maybe not. What he needs is a decent father."

Sam fathers himself. He gets himself up and out to the school bus in the morning; at night he stays in his room. Doing homework? Listening to music on his headphones, letting music wash out his brain? He walks around the house with headphones on, cord trailing. They hear the thump, thump of the bass. They're too respectful of his feelings or afraid of his judgment to barge into his room. Only at dinner do they see him without headphones. He stays quiet, head down. Monroe says the blessing after the meal, while Joanna lays a hand on Sam's arm to insure that he won't leave and start trouble; then the boy goes upstairs and shuts himself in.

Bags and boxes sit in the hall outside Sam's new bedroom.

God knows, at his age Monroe Lichtenstein has no time or energy or patience for being father to another child, and that's what it comes down to. Ted is on the road most of the time—in Seattle one day, Dallas the next. He calls, promises to call and forgets, calls. He'll come by for weekends when he can get away. *Don't do us any favors.*

For both Monroe Lichtenstein and Joanna Levin, it's been a calm second marriage. Conflict they deal with by retreating to their private rooms—Joanna to her studio, Monroe to his study—till resentments cool. Monroe's own children are grown—he married young first time around—Shira an illustrator in L.A. , Michael a lawyer in Denver. Both were easy kids. As a young academic on the make, he didn't spend a lot of time with them. Now, he's barely in touch, sees each of them and the children a couple of times a year; remembers birthdays, sends presents. His ex-wife is a lot closer to their kids. Suddenly to have to handle a child in the house, a "difficult" (the word they keep hearing from family friends, school authorities back in New Jersey) fourteen year-old boy…?

Joanna is a gifted painter, representational, successful—in the sense that she makes a steady income from her work; people like putting up her oils and watercolors and digital paintings of gardens and rocky landscapes. Their own walls are decorated with her art. Now, at almost sixty, she's been taken up by a few museums. Monroe is grateful to Joanna, he admires her as a painter and—in a traditional sense—as a homemaker. If there are to be flowers on the table, a new silk throw over a chair, she's responsible. He's grateful she rescued him ten years ago from a post-divorce midlife of stuffy insularity. He could have turned into the crotchety academic—petulant and small-minded—his academic enemies think him. With her help he feels he escaped. They bought the house together, wanting a place where they could each have a studio and where children and grandchildren could stay. He's looked forward to retirement from teaching soon, an elder life of writing, of travel with Joanna to museums, to rocky coasts and gardens where she can sketch.

Last year, at sixty-three, he received a lifetime achievement award from a division of the American Psychological Association for his work on issues of trauma and reconciliation. His books and essays line a special shelf over the landing between first and second floors, and above the books, the photograph of him smiling, receiving the award. As a social psychologist he sits on national committees; a few months ago he was invited to the White House for a conference—and declined, not wanting to be associated with the present administration. He wants to feel free to continue to write his bitter critiques of the damage this administration is doing to the social fabric.

Suddenly, at sixty-three—to be father to a teenager. Well! What kind of fathering has Sam ever had? Monroe remembers the day last spring Sam became bar mitzvah (at least Sheryl had been alive to see that). On the bimah, Ted Levin, in his brand-new thousand-dollar suit, grinning foolishly from self-consciousness, had stumbled through a transliteration of the blessing of the Torah. Later, Monroe said to Joanna: "I wish *I* could have taught your grandson."

"Oh, Monroe, he did just fine."

"What could it *mean* to him—when his own father…?" Then, for the sake of peace in the home, *shalom bayit*, he kept silent. Driving into Boston now, he says aloud what he can't say to Joanna: "Big shot in a Lincoln Town Car. Uch!" How did Joanna bring up such a white-bread, money-hungry son? She'd blame her first husband.

Well then?—now he has an opportunity to teach the boy, and the boy won't talk to him.

They're living in a blue haze, the three of them. It's like being under tropical waters; when the sun is shining—not too often this spring—you wouldn't be surprised to find schools of fish floating by above the couch, over the glass table in the living room. Monroe thinks about *repair*—it's hard enough to repair a house. The heart is something else again. He's an expert on rituals of reparation in societies that have undergone civil wars, genocide—like Bosnia and Rwanda. That's his field of scholarship and his fieldwork. What rituals are there for Sam's loss?

Constant uncertainty. What do you do? Do you call Sam on his rudeness?—the way he doesn't answer questions or answers with a contemptuous shrug, the way he ignores advice—*Think you ought to take a raincoat, Sam*—Sam doesn't even acknowledge the suggestion; he walks out the door in a tee shirt. After the first week, Sam has walked the house less like a ghost than a malign spirit. Monroe lets him be. Yet he doesn't believe a laissez faire attitude toward children is good. Here's his spiel: Children need structure. They need to be taught responsibility to other people. We live in moral chaos in America. Look at the models a teenager is offered! Rap punks proclaiming self. Sports heroes selling cell phones and fancy jeans. Pseudo-religious glow of expensive toys—cars, clothes. Against a culture of vulgarity and triviality parents have to weigh in, making it clear that it's not the children who are the enemy. But Sam isn't ready for moral lessons.

"He's angry," Monroe says. "With his father away, we're all he has to witness his anger. He needs to be shown he can depend on somebody and be an unholy terror and we'll survive and take care of him."

"You think so? And that's going to help him get through this?"

"Not to help him get through it. How can he get over it or past it or through it? But *bear* it." Monroe knows from his work in Rwanda: Sam needs ways of grieving that connect him to people.

In his office, between classes, or waiting for his favorite doctoral student to come in, he closes his eyes and whispers, "Dear God, please dear God, help us figure this thing out." Behind his eyes he sees himself teaching Sam, becoming the wise nurturer.

Before dinner tonight, he says the simple blessing over the bread but adds, "Dear God, we're remembering Sam's mother Sheryl. We're full of remembering. Please hold her in Your love." Sam looks up, startled, and Monroe is pretty sure he's thinking of bolting the table. Monroe puts out a hand on his shoulder to steady him.

Monroe's idea is to model a conscious, reverent grieving, to build it into Sam's life. He watches Sam scarf down his meal, mumble, "…b'excused…" and not waiting for an answer, slip away. Monroe finishes his meal and his blessing. Joanna runs upstairs after Sam. Monroe hears blurred conversation, staccato interchange. "There's no *way*," Joanna says shrilly, in a voice Monroe barely recognizes, as she follows Sam down the stairs. He's out the front door. *Slam*.

"I think we've got our hands full," she says, sitting down, keeping her tone even, calm. But she sounds apologetic: as if she's to blame—it's her son's child.

"I guess Sam's got his hands full."

"Ted says he's always been trouble."

"Ted." They stare at the door. "So where does he think he's going tonight?"

"He wanted me to drive him to the Big Mall. Maybe I should have driven him. He said he's going anyway."

"The mall? On a school night! And you let him go? How does he expect to get there on his own?" Monroe is on his feet. He lumbers out onto the front steps and, too late, calls, "Sam! Sam, you come back here."

The Big Mall—"Big" has become part of its unofficial name—is on an overcrowded secondary road next to the "Little Mall". There's a Wal-Mart, a Staples, a Borders, a supermarket, a Cineplex—twelve theaters. Indoors, the usual suspects. Among all the works of man, it's the place Monroe most detests. Not when he thinks rationally, no. There's a lot worse—the torture chambers and jails of various dictators, the backroom factories where suicide bombers are provided explosives, the fancier factories where cluster bombs are produced for armies. But the mall—it's the cathedral of a dark religion, with services to…well, to the god of commodity lust. It drives him crazy to see teenagers work twenty hours a week, then take the money and (like some poor drunk son of a bitch who works his butt off for a distillery, then drinks up his wages before he gets home) spend it in the same mall for something to help them feel…cool. *Cool*: there's a word, an attitude toward life, Monroe wishes he could blot out. *Cool* is definitely not a Jewish—or Christian—value.

So he does not walk through the mall tonight with an open heart. He walks armed with his vision. He goes *Oh, oh, oh my God* as he passes The Sharper Image, Media Play, The Gap. He's grieving—without asking the customers at the mall if there's anything to grieve about on their behalf. He sees people as starving—this is the thing—to have radiance in their lives, to give their isolated lives meaning, and isolated lives can't manufacture meaning. So some cheap second-rate holiness is sold to them; instead of cross or six-pointed star they wear the logos of brands.

Sam he can't find. He's not listening to CDs, not eating junk food. Then he tries a video arcade: martial arts games, killing games, with highly sophisticated graphics and wrap-around sound. You're in a dogfight between jet planes; you're killing sci-fi monsters in a cavern. Sam is sitting at a console—*JET-STRIKE*—guiding his jet on a bombing run through anti-aircraft fire. His hair spiked with goop, he's blowing up radar stations, ammunition dumps, and when he hits they blow apart with Hollywood sound effects and ringing bells and a score flashes on a screen above.

Monroe rehearses what he can say to Sam after the game ends. But says only, "Good score. You've got fast fingers."

Sam shrugs.

"Sam? Let's get some ice cream and go home, okay?"

Sam puts two quarters into the coin slots and the next bombing run starts up off the deck of a carrier. Crackly voice says to the pilot, "On my mark, three, two, one…" and the cockpit view shows them whizzing down the deck, slingshot up into the air. And here's the shore, the jungle; the jet hugs the tops of the trees to avoid radar and—watch out!—that's a surface-to-air missile battery trying to target Sam, but Sam takes evasive action and hits back with a missile under the wing, and the battery explodes in noisy bits of flame and debris. The imaginary children of mothers who cleaned their ears and worried about their education become body parts. Monroe has seen real keening mothers. Sam evades the debris and his mission keeps going. His score rises, rises. Monroe realizes he's been employing body English to keep the jet safe. He shakes his big, hairy head.

The jet takes a hit on the flight back, but it's able to land on the deck of the carrier, and Sam sits back, not wrung out by the mission but numb, dead again. Zombie man. And the torture of seeing the boy so blank, so cut off, eats at Monroe. Here's an antidote that doesn't work or works for only the five minutes of play—and it's not *play*, it's the hard work of making oneself feel alive.

"Please?" Monroe says. Sam is reaching into his pocket for more change. Monroe takes a chance, touches the back of the boy's hand. "Please, Sam. It's so empty, this make-believe violence. The kick doesn't stay with you. It's not real rebellion. It won't keep you high."

"Who said I'm getting high?"

"You think I don't know about grief?"

"You think you know everything. It's a game. I just got nine thousand points."

"Will you look at me?"

Challenged, Sam looks—not as if Monroe is an almost-grandfather, a fellow Jew, fellow human being, a feeling subject; Monroe is an object of perception, dead wood, a thing. Anything he says will be heard as an attempt to manipulate Sam. Monroe reads in the boy's eyes: *fucking shrink, old faggot.* All this happens in what?—two, three seconds?—time enough for Monroe to see and to question his own seeing: *Who knows what the boy is really thinking?*

"I did my homework," Sam says. "Why can't I have some down time? Some mall time? It's my life, Mr. Lichtenstein."

"'Mr. Lichtenstein'?"

"*Monroe.* Okay? You think you're my *grandfather*? Like, '*Grandpa*'?"

"No. Better—because I've got some distance, you understand me?"

"I'm not stupid."

"No. Absolutely. You're smart. See, if I were your grandfather

I'd feel hurt, and I'd be ashamed of having a grandson with a mouth like yours. But with you I look at a boy I *like*—and I do, I like you, Sam—somebody else's boy, and he's acting out, not grieving straight. He's looking in the wrong places for relief."

"That's bullshit. That's plain bullshit, *Monroe.* Just because I like going to the mall? I always liked the mall, *Monroe.* My mom let me. She took me."

"And hitchhiking? Hitchhiking at night, a fourteen-year-old. You could get into the wrong car one time."

"Oh, come on. I know about those things." He reaches down and unzips a pocket on the leg of his cargo pants. In his hand, out of sight, down below the level of the console, he palms a hunting knife, long stainless steel blade folded into its black polymer handle.

Monroe has been standing, Sam sitting at the controls. But now Monroe has to sit down in the booth beside Sam, *has* to—he's woozy. A knife! Carries a knife! *Where do you start?* Well, you start by taking the knife away. He puts out his hand, palm up.

"What?" He knows. "*What*? My knife?" Sam's voice breaks register, the way it did last fall at his bar mitzvah, and Monroe remembers, this is a kid, just a kid. He keeps his hand held out and looks steadily at the boy until the knife drops into his hand. He knows, Monroe, he had nothing to back up that request. He wasn't going to wrestle the knife away from Sam. Relieved at this acknowledgment of his authority, he says, "Nice knife. Real good steel. I don't mean you can't take it with you when you go in the woods."

"Like, wow."

Sam needs the tough tone to cover his giving in. So Monroe ignores it. "Let's go home."

"'Home,'" the boy repeats.

Monroe can bear the sarcasm. Sadness he can handle, too. But in May when the blue polyethylene tarp gets folded up and, in the gaps between rainy days, the roof is finished, the house begins to feel worse than sad, feels closed-in, harder to bear. It's not blue anymore, but it grows thick with tension that announced itself, Monroe thinks, when Ted spent the weekend with them.

Ted comes on as the exciting high roller. Almost leading-man good looking, Irish-handsome, he walks as if he knows it. He brings presents—a hand-held video game for Sam, an expensive wine for the house. He acknowledges the grief they all feel, bows his head, but then lifts it with a smile—as if to say, Monroe imagines, there, now, we've got that out of the way. This seems even more callow than Monroe expects. Now the salesman charm as he describes his week on the road, working with three companies in the Northwest. But the peculiar thing is, Sam isn't buying. He stays sullen, sulks, skulks, answers his father's questions in grunts. Monroe can't make it out. Sam picks up the video game and sits there by himself. But Ted keeps at him. He's brought a Frisbee; he takes it out of the trunk of his rental car and entices Sam into a game. And just before time for lighting candles, Monroe hears Sam laughing—laughing!—at Ted diving for a toss.

They come inside to make Shabbos. Suddenly, Ted is a guy too busy for bullshit—he sits, deadpan, arms folded, while Joanna lights the candles and Monroe says Kiddush over the wine. Ted's hot to get out, take the boy to the movies at the mall. Monroe says, "Now it's up to you to bless Sam." Ted grins at the thought—says, "Okay, Monroe. Well, sure. Bless ya, kid."

Passive aggression, the punk son of a bitch, Monroe says to himself. Monroe puts his own hand on Sam's messy hair, says the blessing in Hebrew and in English—*May the Lord bless you and keep you*...and sees Joanna's mouth purse up, like *Why must you make a big deal of this? Is it absolutely necessary to put my son down?* And Monroe thinks, *Shalom bayit, peace in the home—especially on Shabbat*—and says nothing. They hurry through dinner. The blessing after the meal he makes once father and son are off to the mall.

"So. Are you proud of yourself?"

"Please. I'm trying hard to say nothing."

"Yes," she says. "And we can all hear you trying."

Sam doesn't mourn; he broods—worse after his father leaves. He begins spending time with new friends from middle school. Monroe he avoids, even avoids Joanna. Some evenings, Ted calls, and

Monroe can't stand the one-way conversations; Sam's end just "Uh huh. Uh huh."

Monroe keeps his opinions to himself. But increasingly, increasingly, he feels alone in this house. The house is silent too much. Oh, it makes its noises, some—a slammed door, dishes clattering in the sink—meant as coded communication. Each of them—Monroe, Joanna, Sam—is living a dream, and the dreams don't know each other.

The house is built to give them space, lets them live separately, each in a room. But even so it cramps Sam, who begins to stay away after school, to take the school bus to "the library". He's really playing hacky-sack in front of the store near the center of town that sells CDs and comics. Four of them, six of them, foot the little leather sack, and nobody has to talk. They're older kids, but Sam is tall, looks sixteen. He's good with his feet, a soccer player; his mother used to coach his travel-team—she'd played in college. And one of them knows this older guy who works at the gas station, and when he gets off, he buys a couple of six packs for the kids and they split them up in the alley behind the CVS and stuff the cans in the pockets of their floppy prison jeans and Sam and the others head for the town conservation area and sit at the edge of the stream and finish the beers.

And one afternoon they get a little stupid. A kid from another school, local Catholic school, comes through the conservation area on a mountain bike and he acts uneasy, so they chase the bike, five of them, just to scare him, and maybe they push the bike and the kid falls, the bike on top of him, and cuts his head and his leg and he's bleeding and cursing, and hey—nobody means anything so they walk away and let him get back on and ride off. "We better get the hell out of here." They dump the cans in the trash barrel but Sam, who doesn't much like the stuff, still has a full can in his backpack. When the cop cars head them off at the entrance to the conservation area, two of the kids take off through the woods. One cop says, "I know that tall one, I know his mother, we can pick him up later." All that's left is three kids, stinking of beer and looking guilty. And Sam is caught with the full can, and the other kids give him a look—*Asshole*!

Joanna's home, so she has to go down to pick him up, and he's being charged with assault and illegal possession of alcohol. She calls Monroe at Tufts, and he calls their lawyer in town. And at dinner Sam is even more silent than usual.

Monroe says quietly, "Before it gets worse, I want us to have a talk with Rabbi Bamberger."

"A rabbi? Why?" Sam says. "You think you're gonna get me to see some rabbi?"

"Monroe? Please?"

"Crap! You can't get me to see a rabbi." And suddenly, in Sam's singsong whine, Monroe hears the song of the victim. Sam's strategy is to see himself—make you see him—as victim. The banged-up boy isn't real, the beer isn't real: *I'm being abused; trouble is being dumped on me.*

It's still light out. The sun's down, but the sky is amazing—mauve, orange, pale blue through the effluence of Boston. The little dining area faces the light. It's so sad: if you were to look at the three of them in this warm room, Joanna's lush tropical landscape on the wall, her family brass samovar glowing, a roast chicken golden in the center of the table, you'd envy, you'd think, ah, what a beautiful family scene. Almost corny, Monroe thinks. And look!

"Monroe, what did the lawyer say?"

"Well...Sam's not going to see any time in Corrections, but—Sam?—they're going to want to keep you out of the town center." He speaks in a low voice, working hard not to dump blame.

"They can't do that. No way. This a free country?"

"They *can* do it. It's accept that or worse. Sam...your actions create limitations on your own freedom. Your freedom is contingent upon your acting like a responsible person."

Sam rolls his eyes, and, listening back to his own words Monroe hears how stuffy they must sound. Sam takes an apple from the fruit basket. From the knife block he chooses the twelve-inch chef's knife, the biggest they have, and brings a cutting board back to the table. He cuts a slice *snap* on the board, pops it in his mouth, narrow so he can cut more often. Snap. Snap. "Why is it such a big deal, *Monroe*?" Snap onto the board. "Dad lets me drink beer. I don't even like beer. I didn't push the kid. Little whiner. We didn't do anything. He got scared and fell. It's not fair, Grandma."

"Honey, I know you didn't mean to hurt the boy. But we can't help worrying. We're responsible for you."

"Look, Sam. I'd like you to see this from that boy's point of view," Monroe says. "You're biking through the woods and all of a sudden—"

Joanna heaves a breath; Monroe's meant to hear it as exasperation. "Oh, Monroe, this is no time for philosophical discussion."

"Oh? When *is* the time?"

"The little whiner. Sure, you take his side. Listen, I'm sorry the kid got hurt. Nobody was trying to hurt him. You think I meant to?"

"Can't you understand why I think we should see the rabbi, Sam?"

"Sure. So he can give me a lecture when you're finished giving me a lecture." Sam's not slumping now. He's stiff, sitting straight up, alert. Monroe remembers him at the *JET-STRIKE* console.

"I think you need a grounding. This is not something a Jew does."

"You mean I'm grounded."

"That, too. But no—a grounding. You're floundering—all there is out there is emptiness. It won't hold you. I'm worried for you."

"I don't know what you're talking about. I hate you. Can't you ever stop talking?"

"You think you're rebelling? You're becoming exactly what society wants you to become: it's a trap, Sam. *Me, me, me*—that's not rebellion."

"You don't hate your grandfather," Joanna says.

The sky has lost color. Monroe goes outside to look at the iris beginning to open. When he returns the table's cleared and he sits down to sing in a whisper the blessing after the meal. Afterwards, he sits thinking of words to say to Sam—words, words, as if, were he to find the right words, Sam would be able to see his own chaos for what it is, would hold his grief in his hands and know it for what it is. Monroe knows better, knows he's a word junky. There's no beautiful argument in the world that would change Sam's life. He sits and sits and can't stop rehearsing words to say, and while he says them, a boy is falling off a cliff.

That's when he decides to say nothing at all. Joanna goes off to email her gallery in New York. Sam is in his room. Monroe turns out the lights and goes upstairs. Book in hand, he knocks at Sam's door. He feels his own heart thumping. Just a kid—so what if he kicks him out? He knocks again. But Sam doesn't answer; Monroe has a fantasy that he'll walk in and the boy will be popping pills, shooting up heroin, slicing his wrists. But it's only that the headphones are so loud and knuckle taps can't compete with the thump of bass. Sam doesn't offer to remove the headphones, Monroe doesn't ask. It's like visiting someone who's inside a glass box. Still, it is a visit. He's not kicked out. He sits in the broken-down easy chair that came with the house, wasn't good enough for the last family to take with them, was too useful for Joanna and Monroe to discard. It's got a nice standing reading lamp to one side. So he smiles at Sam, not a real smile but an indicator that he's here and friendly. And now he reads a published essay by one of his ex-students.

And this goes on for half an hour, an hour. Sam changes the music on his Discman; Monroe gestures once, his hands holding an invisible glass, his eyebrows shaping a question.

"No, thanks."

He reads the essay carefully enough to be able to email a generous sentence or two to his ex-student, quickly enough to forget it the next day. And he turns to Dostoyevsky, *The Possessed*. He's somewhere in the middle, and it's only after a chapter goes by that he realizes yes, there's a connection for him, connection with Sam, the danger of…what? Dostoyevsky (crazy anti-Semite, but he knew a lot) would have called it nihilism. Monroe wants to speak to Sam about the Covenant of the Jewish people with God. *How important you are, Sam.* But he continues to say nothing.

Thump of the bass of Sam's headphones. Driving Sam around town, he's let him play that ugly music on the radio—Gangsta Rap—wanting to hear what it's all about. The lyrics he can make out say, essentially, *I'm so cool and so tough—I'm a hotshot, baby. You better not fuck with me.* The rapper doesn't mourn a mother. He's cool alone-alone. What insupportable narcissism. If you're party to a Covenant you don't have to lug such a dreary burden. The thing that makes you special makes us all special. He won't say any of this to Sam. He sits with him.

And the following evening the same. He sits; after awhile goes downstairs for a pitcher of ice water, some cookies. Between CDs, Sam says, "You think you're my policeman?" Monroe shakes his head. Once, looking up from his homework, Sam says, "What's *indigenous*?" Monroe tells him. Later: "What's *incorporeal*?" At nine-thirty Sam says, "Better get ready for bed." Joanna calls, "Monroe?" Closing his book, he puts a hand on Sam's shoulder. "If you'll let me, I'll come back to say the Bedtime Shema." Sam scrunches up his eyebrows—"Huh?" "Last blessing of the day." Sam shrugs.

A big, big victory, Monroe thinks, that shrug. And he's grinning as he goes downstairs to Joanna's studio.

"Just *what* are you saying to him?" Joanna asks.

"I'm just sitting with him. He doesn't need *saying*."

"I'm here, too," she says. "I need saying."

"Your father's coming next weekend," Joanna announces. Monroe's just poured morning coffee, Joanna's fixing eggs for Sam. It's going to be one beautiful spring day.

"*No*."

"What do you mean 'No'? *No* meaning what, honey?"

"I don't want to see him."

"Well, dear," she soothes, "we'll have to think about it calmly—when we're not in a hurry."

"Grandma? No! I don't want him here. Does he have to come here? Please?"

"I don't want you to be late for school, dear."

He's gone, slamming the door behind him. Joanna, in jeans stained from paint and garden dirt, looks at Monroe with fury. "I know this makes you very happy."

"Well, you're wrong."

"I know you can't stand Ted. You've never liked him."

"What have I said?"

"I can read you like a book." Monroe sees himself in Joanna's eyes—big butt in sloppy chinos, complacent, smug; is that what she sees? What bookshelf has she put him on? What's the title?—He'd like to toss that book in the garbage, offer another, *The Book of the Kindly Grandfather* perhaps, or *The Book of the Loving Husband.* Is he a loving husband? There are moments. But what he remembers, what he sees in his inner eyes, is swimming with Sheryl and Sam in a pond on the Cape, Ted off shopping with his mother. When was this? Last summer! He's flooded by the memory, feels his legs in the water, feels the rich thrill of the cool water on his beach-baked body. It's one of the National Seashore ponds of Wellfleet, way back in the woods—you have to know the sand roads to get you there. Sandy-bottomed, clear, full of tiny fish, fringed with reeds and water lilies. Standing up to his neck, talking with Sheryl about nothing special while Sam dives for a sight of pond fish, Monroe felt, feels now again, the *contact*: molecules of water touching Sheryl touch the molecules of water touching him. It isn't erotic, not exactly; he's conjoined with her in a single field.

All this in a few seconds. And all over again he's washed through and through in sorrow for the loss of her. That splendid bright amusement of her eyes.

Well? And aren't there times when he's no more separate than that from Joanna? Well, yes, maybe...but surely not this minute. She sits, hands clasped in front of her, sipping sourness. He sees what she'll look like as an old woman. He feels himself erase the image; the pursing of her mouth is a statement: *you think I'm a weak mother.* And isn't she right? Doesn't he see Ted as her product, a factory-second, let off the hook too easy as a kid?

"You want some more coffee?"

She won't look his way.

He goes up to his study to prepare his keynote address for a summer conference in Switzerland—a paper on the re-establishment of community after an outbreak of genocide: guaranteed to put his private griefs into perspective.

No class today. Without a word to Joanna, slipping out of the house, in fact, so she doesn't ask, he drives down to the middle school to pick Sam up at three. He gets there early, goes to the office to check in, finds bus #3 and waits.

Kids come out mostly by threes and fours; Sam is alone. He's been warned, even before his court hearing, he can't hang with the older kids in town center. But nobody said he couldn't have friends. Tall, skinny, big-eared, hair spiked, he looks a little weird as he crosses the parking lot to the busses; Monroe's worried for him. He needs a friend.

"Sam—get in." Shuffle, shuffle, scuff, eyes on the pavement. They walk over to the Taurus and as soon as he's in, Sam switches on a rap station. Angry ugliness at your service all day, no charge. Monroe fantasizes snapping off the radio, slamming the kid up against the post, and reading him his wrongs. Oddly, he also sees himself putting a big hand around Sam's skinny shoulder, hugging him to himself; sees them weeping together. He neither slams nor hugs; he sucks breath, turns the music up but keeps his body from rocking to its rhythm—obscene *davening* to a strange god.

"I'm not answering questions."

"So? Then we'll listen to the music."

"I'm not talking about him."

"Your father?"

Sam lifts up his knees so that his sneakers are on the seat. Monroe ignores. The town goes by. It's mid-May, early blossoming done. Everybody's been planting. In the front-yard borders late tulips are still strong, and now the irises are coming on and pansies have taken off. The dirt's been churned up; it's weeded and breathing. Young greens have darkened almost to their summer monochrome. It's almost comical how out of place it is, this angry music.

"Where do you think you're taking me? Monroe? I'm not talking to a rabbi."

"No rabbi—I'm buying you a damn ice cream. Can you put up with that?"

"So what do I have to do?"

Monroe just bobs his head to the beat.

"Okay, then. Well, sure."

It's the first day Monroe needs to put on the air conditioning. After the car cools, he shuts off the AC, opens the windows wide. Thump of the bass: an old lady crossing the street turns around, offended by the noise, and, surprised to see an older man driving, gives him a harsh look.

"I guess it's not her music," Monroe says.

Sam laughs. As the car heads down the street, Sam picks himself up and, like a big dog, sticks his whole head, spiked hair and all, out the window. Monroe says "Careful" but just for himself, too quietly to be heard by someone with his head in wind. And Sam sits back down. They park. Sam lets himself be steered by Monroe into Friendly's; they sit in a booth and eat ice cream.

"You want to ask about my dad?"

"You want to tell me?"

"I guess you know they were going to get a divorce?"

"A divorce? No. I didn't."

"They were. Grandma knows. So they were fighting about stuff. Right the night before. They were yelling half the night."

"The night before your mom died?"

"They were fighting practically all night. It sucked big-time. I couldn't even sleep."

Monroe kept silent. He shook his head.

"So Mom didn't get much sleep. You *see*?"

"I see. So you think it was his fault?"

"Maybe. Yes."

"Does he know you heard? Have you talked to him?"

"I won't talk to him, the bastard. I'll never talk to him again. He killed her, that's the truth."

"I hear a trailer truck jackknifed. Not much you can do about that."

"Yeah? Well, yes you can. It's reflexes. Right? And suppose you didn't get any sleep?"

"Oh, Sam. You imagine how bad he must feel, your dad?"

"I hope so. Okay?" Sam sits chewing a cuticle; Monroe notices how raw the boy's fingers are. Sam looks up. "I said I don't want to talk about it."

"Okay…. So that's why you were so strange when your dad came."

"I feel lousy I even talked to him. Mom would have lived. Don't *you* think? Come *on*."

"Maybe. Sam, we didn't know anything. How hard for you. You've been holding all this?"

"Grandma knows. Now cut it out. Stop."

"Okay."

"It was about *me*," he hisses. "They were fighting over *me*. He was yelling at her he wanted joint custody. You see now he doesn't give a shit about living with me? He wasn't gonna give in, that's all. I'd never have lived with him. Now he better stay away, I'll kill him, the lousy bastard."

"Will you kill him?"

"No…but he better stay away."

On the way back to the car, Monroe wants to put his arm around the boy. It's so clear he needs an arm. And so clear it would be a mistake to touch him: if Sam feels soft, vulnerable, if he cries, he'll just end by getting furious. They pull down their seat belts. "Thanks, Sam."

"For what?"

"Look." He turns off the engine. "I deal with tragedy a lot, Sam. That's what I do. I work in countries where neighbors slaughter neighbors. This is also a tragedy. Everybody's suffering. If you need something, please, you tell me what to do, how to help, okay?"

A shrug.

"Okay, Sam?"

Joanna is sending out a stack of postcards announcing a gallery show. She stops, slams her hand down on the lapboard. "You know why I didn't tell you? You'd judge him. You're so judgmental these days. I suppose it comes with being a genius with a lifelong achievement award."

"Oh, please."

"That's why your own children stay away. You think you're a model father, Monroe?"

He feels a weight in his chest; he sits down, says nothing.

"And you can't judge him, I know you're judging him, don't you dare, Monroe. You don't know what she was like."

"What was she like?"

"Please! For one thing, always nagging. You don't know what he went through. He didn't talk to *you* about it."

And he says, "I'm sorry you didn't tell me, Joanna. How you must see me. But all right. So? What do we do if he comes?"

"*If*? He's coming! Ted's my son. If he wants to visit his child, well, this is my house, too."

"Of course it's your house. What is all this about? What are you so angry about?"

"Sometimes it feels like just your house. Monroe, the famous psychologist."

Some years ago he took a stress-reduction course. He learned to breathe. He learned to close his eyes and breathe. That's what he does now. And when he opens his eyes she's gone, lapboard and all, as if he's made her—poof—disappear. Later, he takes down the framed photo of receiving his Lifetime Achievement Award at APA. It's put in a drawer.

It's Shabbos, and usually Monroe looks forward to blessings and songs. Tonight he hopes Ted's plane gets in late, and Joanna can light the candles and he can say the blessings without that smug face to ruin it for them. And where's Sam? Ten minutes before they are to begin, he calls out a warning—"Get dressed up, get ready, put away your work. Sam?"

No Sam.

And Ted's brand-new red Chrysler convertible, rented, Monroe understands, to excite Sam, pulls into the driveway; Ted gets out and calls out, as if hollering at a ballgame, "Hey, Sam, hey, kiddo, Sam? Come take a look what I got for you!"

No Sam.

Ted locks the car and carries his bag in, stows it in the guest room. "Hey, Sam?" He scrunches up his eyes at his mother. "So? Christ—I busted my hump to get here before sunset—isn't that when you get started, Monroe? Where'd he go? Didn't you tell him I was coming?" Ted stands at the glass doors between dining room and living room, hands outstretched to the jambs like Samson ready to crumble the temple. He looks around as if they're hiding Sam.

Monroe says, "Come in, Ted."

"Please, Monroe, dear..."

"It's okay, Ted. It's time to make Shabbos. Let's bring some peace into this house." He shuts his eyes, tries to imagine disgust and judgment washing out of him.

"Exactly," Joanna says. "Shabbos is no time for argument."

They stand around the table; Ted leans on his knuckles, weight on one hip carelessly—*I'm being polite but this isn't my thing*. Joanna lights the candles and, eyes closed, says the blessing, beckoning the light of peace to her. There's no child to bless, and Monroe doesn't have the heart for singing. He's imagining the worst. And since the worst is not preventable, he starts scanning a mental map of the town for Sam. But at the same time he's welcoming the Sabbath: he recites Kiddush over the wine and blesses the bread; they sit and break challah together. Monroe puts a hand on Ted's shoulder. "He told us what happened. The fight you had that last night before she died. Ted? Listen. I can imagine how you feel."

Ted's still in his business suit; he's loosened his tie. Now, maybe to give himself time, or because he's going to say things you can't say so well in a suit, he undoes the tie and folds it into his jacket pocket, takes off the jacket and hangs it over his chair. Then he says, "Listen—it was nothing. Nothing happened. It's not such a big deal. Don't make a big deal out of it, okay? Pass the fucking chicken, Monroe."

Monroe soothes, says gently, "Sure, sure. People fight. I'm just saying it *is* a big deal for Sam. You need to know that."

Ted rubs his cheek to soothe himself. That he needs soothing gives him permission to speak up. "I frankly don't see where you get off talking to my kid about it. What gives you the right? Just because you're a big deal psychologist? That really bothers me, Monroe. That pisses me off."

Joanna says, "Please, oh, please, it's nothing—every married couple..."

"And Mom—I told you in confidence, Mom."

"I didn't speak one single word, dear. Anyway, it's not relevant, whatever fight you had. It was a truck, for godsakes. That's all. It's tragic enough. Please!"

"So what's Sam talking for? I expect a little loyalty. Talking behind my back. Jesus."

Victims and victims. It's dark, now. All you can see in the back yard are the silhouettes of garden and hedge. They eat in silence. Sam's still gone. Now Joanna puts her dish in the sink and goes upstairs to call the one boy in Sam's class who might know something.

By themselves, they fiddle: Ted with crumbs of challah, which he rolls into a ball; Monroe with the silver, which it's crucial to set precisely at right angles to the edge of the table. "I think I'll wait to hear about him," Ted says, "then maybe I'll get the hell out of here."

Monroe shakes his big shaggy head. "You come with me tonight."

"What's the point? He's telling me something real loud."

"Sure he's telling you something. But what is it he's telling you?"

"What do you think? He's telling me to keep the hell away. Maybe you think sympathy will help. It won't. It'll stuff him full of self-pity. No. You know what's going to happen to that kid? I'm going to find a really tough prep school, maybe a military academy."

No, he's not. But Monroe knows better than to argue. He thinks of the committee on Reconciliation in Bosnia—you had to let the bitter speeches be made. It wasn't the end of dialogue; you had to let them come. And those were real victims. He knows it's the saying, not the doing, Ted needs. He's talking to himself, talking himself into gutsing it out, defining himself as a solid man and solid father. "Let's take your convertible, Ted. If we find him, won't he love that car!"

There are three long lines at the multiplex cinema; the lines snake back along lanes hemmed in by webbing attached to brass posts, and wind back behind that past a Pizzeria Uno and a Footlocker. Overhead, the icons of movie glory. Past the main food court, the video arcade is crowded. At the sleek console Sam's flying his jet again, skimming the jungle canopy, evading a missile battery and rending the enemy into shards of noisy death. Sam looks comically outsized, skin and bones in a baggy tee shirt. The pilot's backpack, sleeping bag, air mattress sit at his feet. Where was he intending to sleep tonight?

Explosions, explosions—points accrue on the screen above. Until he sees his father. Suddenly the plane goes wild, gets hit by a surface-to-air missile, another, and goes down in jungle. A new plane revs up on the flight deck of a carrier. Sam looks up, furious, furious not at his father—at Monroe. *Why can't you leave me alone?* Monroe puts a hand on his back. "Sam? Take it easy." Sam takes up his pack, sleeping bag tied on top, air mattress on bottom, and puts it on his shoulders, and he's out of there, bumping through the kids, the families, the couples. But he's not running, not trying to dodge them. Monroe is relieved to see that the boy's posture is making a statement. He's stomping through the mall, shoulders stiff, to show how truly bummed he is.

He storms past dream images of the satisfying life—past the sleek technology of The Sharper Image, past windows with designer jeans or hundred fifty dollar sneakers.

"Sam!" Ted calls out. "Wait up, will you please? Please?"

So Sam waits. He's got a load to lay on his father; of course he waits up. But his neck is pressed forward—*Come* on*, I haven't got all night.* Ted catches up, and from a distance Monroe watches Ted's hands conducting a symphony of explanations and Sam's face turned away to examine some interesting window. Oh, but he's listening.

They go out into the parking lot. Monroe, walking ten feet behind, can only imagine the conversation or lecture or whatever it is. He hears the peaks of Ted's words; he hears "…how terrible I feel?" At this, Monroe feels an effusion of tenderness for the two of them, for father and son.

Now they stop in front of the rented car. Sam slips off the backpack and Ted puts it in the trunk. Ted stands in front of the car, the shiny red convertible, hands spread open, as if he were presenting a fabulous star to an audience. The audience isn't having it. No smile from Sam. All right—admit it: it kind of pleases Monroe that Sam's not impressed.

"You said you were driving a sports car. This is no sports car. Just a big convertible."

"It's what I could get. Give it a try," Ted says. "Go sit in the driver's seat."

Sam tries it. He sits at the controls and holds the wheel. He nods; he lets slip a tiny grin. "Cool." He slides over and Ted gets in. Monroe slips into the back. Long time since he's sat in an open car. He sits in the middle, spreads his arms over the whole back seat.

And now, as Ted guns the engine and the car floats off, Monroe remembers, blown by the warm night air in the open car, cool water on his skin, the Wellfleet pond that afternoon with Sheryl. Feeling in-the-swim: connected. A couple of nights ago he heard Sheryl's voice very clearly just as he was falling asleep. It said: *I've always cared for you, Monroe. What are you going to do about it?*—just the voice, so audible he was embarrassed—what if Joanna hears! He couldn't get back to sleep. Aach, romance with the dead! But it's not a question of romance. The dream was of his longing: *you don't have to live a life of separation. You are held.*

In Monroe's presence Sam can't let himself be seen as giving in to his father—not an inch; he sits crammed against the door, gap between them big as possible. Ted can't let himself be seen as pleading. Monroe taps Ted on the shoulder. "Please—let me off here by the trailhead. It's just a mile, nice spring night; I want to take a walk before I turn in."

From the side of the quiet road, he watches the slick red car zoom off and become taillights, hissing to silence. He enters the wood-chip trail in the dark; he's used to this. Without a flashlight he feels feral, belonging to these woods. It's damp, it's cool on his face. There's a mossy smell. As he draws closer to the house, he slows his pace. He doesn't belong there. By the time he gets home, Joanna's in bed; light's off in their bedroom. Sam must be in bed. Under the guest room door a crack of light shows Ted is up. Monroe sits downstairs not-reading the book on his lap.

Some time during the night it begins to rain; he wakes, relieves himself, goes back to sleep. In his dream the house is leaking again. There are pails and pots everywhere to catch the water. In the morning he wakes to see water staining the bedroom rug! Had he known in his sleep? Water has stained the cream-colored rug, left streaks down the bedroom wall behind their bed. Joanna comes out of the bathroom. "Nice surprise to wake up to, isn't it?"

She'd deny it, but he's sure: she's blaming him. "It's the dormer. I'll call Noonan. He should have checked the roof over the dormer."

When Sam comes down to breakfast he keeps his eyes on the linoleum. No one's looking at Monroe—Joanna keeps busy making pancakes, expressing her irritation with him, he's sure, by the way she scrapes the pan with plastic spatula. He's already called Noonan—he could tell her that—but it's not the leaking roof that's between them. Ted comes down in his phony, breezy way, rubbing his hands, volume pumped up, "Smells great, Mom. I love that old smell. Banana pancakes!"

"You can have blueberry if you'd rather."

"Me, I'll have whatever Sam's having."

Ted grins at Monroe. You and me, *a couple of good buddies, couple of pals.* Along with the grin, a fixed bright look right in the eyes. A little maniacal, this All-American, Joe-Six-Pack look. *It's to show he's not afraid to meet my eyes.* Then the eyes dart off and stay away.

But it's Sam's looking away, looking anywhere else, that bothers him. Saddens him. And then it dawns on him: last night, when they went back to the house, father and son, they made a deal. Now Sam feels ashamed of having caved in. Monroe's sure: Sam is going to leave us. Yes.

Monroe's chest grows heavy; he slumps with the weight.

Meanwhile, they eat pancakes and talk about the Red Sox.

Well, what else can the boy do? But Monroe feels as heavy as if he were losing a lover.

Ted is talking pancakes. "Like a ten on the Fabuloso scale," he says. Then he says, "Mom, Monroe, we've got something to tell you. It's gonna take a couple of weeks to set things up, but Sam and me, we've decided he'll be living with me. But I want you to know, both of you, how grateful we are for everything you guys've done."

And Monroe, Joanna, say *Sure, Of course, Best thing,* and Joanna hugs Sam around his shoulders. Monroe says, very quietly so that Sam will know he means it, "Sam, that's really great. You'll see your friends."

"You've got to take care of that skinny father of yours," Joanna says. "I'll teach you to make pancakes before you go."

And Sam's gone. They're living once again under blue polyethylene, this time in their bedroom. The roofers are hammering on their heads with a nail gun. Other times, it's very quiet in the house. Joanna doesn't like music when she's working. So Monroe puts a Discman on his belt and walks around with headphones playing Schubert and Mahler. But once or twice he puts in a CD Sam has left behind, some mumbling arrogant fool demanding recognition over a heavy bass, and he cuts up veggies to the beat.

Like a bruise or a swollen ankle, the tenderness day by day diminishes, until, by the time the roof is nearly fixed, he and Joanna are civil, even kind to one another. They try to keep in touch with Sam, but it's Ted they wind up speaking to. Ted feels he has to show them how upbeat he is. When Ted calls, Monroe says *Hello*, says *Great, Ted, great*, and lets him talk to Joanna.

He feels the gap; she feels the gap. They bracket it off and do their work.

It takes a month before Sam calls him. It's been a muggy, cloudy day and then it rained, rained *big-time* as Sam would say. It's cleared up. He's sitting on the deck—he's toweled off the table and chair—preparing next semester's class; Sam calls not on the house phone but on his cell.

"Hi...Monroe?"

"Hey, Sam."

And now, silence; breathing, breathing. And "Well..."

"Are you okay?"

Sam's okay. Just wants to say hello. *Yeah, really, I'm okay. My dad? Well, actually*, actually Ted is on the road and Sam's staying at a friend's house. And he's been thinking.

"Thinking?"

"You know, like that junk at the mall, what a lot of phony garbage." And Sam goes on giving Monroe what he thinks Monroe wants to hear. Still, it's a gift, right?—the thought that counts.

"I just plain miss you, Sam," Monroe says flat out.

"Uh huh."

Monroe wonders: What does this *uh huh* mean? He says, "You're gonna be a smart guy, Sam. A smart rebel—I promise."

But getting off the phone, as he sits amid the debris of his teaching, it's not Sam the rebel he misses—just Sam. Late June, late sunset through the trees in front of his house, through his neighbors' trees. The light, after such a rain, is very clear. Workers are all done. No gaps in the protection above them. But the house is too quiet. He reads till it's almost dark; they eat late these days. When he goes into the kitchen, he finds Joanna establishing her palette of colors: red and yellow peppers, wonderful aubergine, sweet green of scallions. He, when he cooks, just dumps things together and chops. He admires her artist's eye and her patience. He sits with a glass of wine and feasts his eyes.

After a while she turns from the counter and raises her eyebrows. "Pretty," he says. This pleases her. Then they stare at one another and don't know what to say. And for a long moment, they look at one another. And look. The brightly lit kitchen keeps out the dark but makes what's outside look darker. They look at one another. Who knows whether they're meaning the same thing in this look? Who knows whether they're in the same room in the same house? What they share is a gap, a silence. And this is the way it is.

Vertigo

Here is a man stripped of much of what he thought of as his life. His son is dead, his work is gone, his mother fading, his daughter off in college and when they speak on the phone they have nothing to say. This summer, this fall, he seems deep in dream. He's thick, this Daniel Bergoff: thick-jawed, balding, a chunky, strong man, a one-time wrestler, with body hair and long heavy eyebrows half gray, half black, not someone you'd expect to be a dreamer. A gorilla, dreaming? He'd been comptroller and chief financial officer for a high-tech company in Cambridge, someone more likely to think numbers and protocols than to take in light on barn and field and trees, not a candidate for revelations.

But for months now he's been walking, walking and sitting, watching afternoon light playing on barn and field and trees and on the water of the pond, Walden Pond. Thoreau's pond—well, hardly that, with its smoothed-out trails now railed off for handicap access, sandy beach and timbered steps, the hum of traffic on Route 2, but still full of beauty. He's been praying from the siddur or sitting, eyes shut, watching the little monkey of the mind do its tricks.

He breathes in beauty. He remembers the visit. One night, four months ago, late spring, after the unveiling of his son's stone, he had a dream, and in the morning he told Shayna about it. "I was wrapping myself in my *tallis,* and the fringes became feathers, the *tallis* became wings that lifted me. Of course I didn't make up the image. In the morning prayer, when you put on your *tallis*—it's compared to sheltering wings."

"It sounds like a healing dream," she said. "Beautiful. I should have such dreams."

He felt it was a mistake to tell her—it might keep the angel away. The next night he wanted the dream so much he couldn't get to sleep. But when he finally slept, the wings were around him again, or he was wearing the wings, only the whole atmosphere was full of danger. This time he kept the angel to himself.

Of course, you could say his strangeness, his silence, the visitation itself—they were simply his ways of grieving, of coping. Gabe: killed just over a year ago. The first anniversary of his dying, the *yortzeit,* was last spring. And upstairs Daniel's mother, Gertrude, barely complaining now about her arthritis, murmurs old love songs in a husky voice ruined by cigarettes, as if she were the ghost of Edith Piaf, of Lotte Lenya. At eighty-five, she's slipping into forgetfulness; remembers, forgets. She still walks a little, still cooks a little. She's writing family history on her own laptop. She can still do that, though sometimes she forgets how to turn off the machine. Or else she sits by the window, open a crack to let the smoke out, and nods to herself. This was a woman who wrote a witty syndicated column that at its peak was picked up by over a hundred newspapers. Now, old. Her skin smells sweet.

Sometimes he hides upstairs, sitting in Mother's room in an old easy chair his daughter Celia made him drag home from the dump when she was a kid. Until Gabe went off to Dartmouth, this was Gabe's room; maybe that's another reason Daniel sits there. When his mother began to wither a few years ago, her crusty, haughty selfhood to soften, and she moved in, Gabe's room seemed best. Gabe hadn't minded; when he came home he slept in the study.

Gertrude Bergoff: old bones, with a little puffed belly under her blue housedress, she's calmer than in Daniel's memory she's ever been. Even her wrinkles seem to have relaxed; her face seems youthful. "So? How's your day?" she asks. "Fine. Fine, Ma." And sometimes she remembers about Gabe and they shake their heads. But sometimes she asks, "When's your Gabe coming home from school? Isn't he late? He's playing soccer?" And he reminds her, "No, Ma. He's not playing soccer. Remember what happened to Gabe? Remember? The accident?" And she begins to cry. "Oh, no, not Gabe, it couldn't happen, Danny, Danny"—as if learning for the first time all over again, and he comforts her. He rubs her back in big circles the way he'd once rubbed Gabe's back. "God should only take me soon," she says.

Sometimes he pokes through the closet, still Gabe's. His school papers. His soccer awards, papers from the summer he interned at the State House in Boston. His baseball cards, thousands of cards. When he was eight, nine, ten—that's where his birthday money, his Chanukah money went.

Daniel's mother smiles at him, one eyebrow tilted up in an irony that no longer bites. He sits with her, his eyes in soft focus. Or he picks up a photograph Gabe took and tries to locate himself in those eyes, as if by yoking his look to Gabe's, he can reach him in the world-to-come. With his mother he can be as strange as he wants—she thinks it's ordinary. Otherwise, he hides his strangeness as best he can.

He can't hide it from Shayna. It's a Friday morning. Leaning against the kitchen counter, her clear gray eyes gazing steadily, brows raised in a pretense of amusement, she watches him knead dough for challah, pressing knuckles and rolling out with the heel of his hand, turning the ball, and again. She lowers her head and stares at him over granny glasses. It's probably a gimmick she's picked up as a guidance counselor, and though he's no teenager he shrinks like a kid from meeting her glance. "We need to talk about this, Danny."

"Talk about what? Nothing's wrong."

She puts her hands on his shoulders, kneading them as he kneads the dough, turning him to face her. She raises a lecture-finger. "This peculiar retirement—that's the problem. You? You're too young to retire. You're not even sixty. So—you know what you're like? You're like some Olympic athlete who suddenly quits training. All those muscles are revved up aching to be used, and soon they're just aching, full of acid."

"Maybe I'm in training for something else."

"In training! You're in mourning is what you're in. In your sleep, I've heard his name. You turn over and curl up away from me. 'Gabe, Gabe....' Many nights, Danny."

He shrugs. Well? Isn't it true for both of them? Didn't he hear Shayna crying just last week behind a shut bedroom door? He closes his eyes but keeps kneading the dough, heel of his hand, roll it under, heel of his hand, until the dough resists, a fat lady's earlobe. He puts it into the yellow bowl.

"Look, look at you. Half asleep. Brooding all the time. If you're brooding, where are the eggs?—oh, come on, Danny, that's a joke. Or baking bread. What is this, what are *you* doing baking bread? Or organizing the garage?—God knows in our twenty years in this house did you ever clean once without being nagged? Please. Honey. Call Rabbi Shulberger. Go work for the Hesed committee. You've got so much to offer, Danny."

A year ago last April they lost Gabe, their first-born, a senior at Dartmouth—car crash late at night, someone else driving, too much to drink, Gabe asleep, killed instantly. He remembers calling the inn to cancel the reservations they'd made for the weekend of his graduation.

For months, coping meant being willing to get up in the morning. Meant being willing to bear looking at Shayna, making the loss real again by seeing it in her face. The thought of sex nauseated and depressed him. This made no sense, but it was true. He wrote in a notebook about Gabe, about the hole in the heart, but the cavity, cleaned out, left a bigger cavity, more decay. He remembered failures as a father—impatience, irritation, and how could he make reparations? Let's be honest: there were times with Gabe.... Oh, he was never like his own father, never roared his rage directly. The old rage, knotted up, got transmuted into judgment. The judgment in my eyes—Gabe suffered from that, surely. My lousy little failures of soul.

He prays. He also works out daily at the gym. He's bought an expensive single scull and rows on the Charles. He takes a course in Hasidism at the synagogue; they study the words of the Baal Shem Tov as written down by his disciples. Rabbi Shulberger explains *devekut,* cleaving with all of yourself to God: this is a state he can't imagine.

To keep occupied, he's begun day-trading in commodities, and he's performed consistently well, even in this bear market. When he meets someone at the gym, instead of saying, "I'm retired," he can say, "I'm a commodities trader." He's taken enough of an interest to read books on the mathematics of the markets. What a peculiar thing, not ever to lay eyes on the commodities he trades. He doesn't trade commodities at all, only paper certificates, and not even those but pixels on a screen representing mathematical curves. Fiction upon fiction.

Again and again these days, his father's heavy, worried face comes to him; he sees beads of sweat wiped away by a dirty handkerchief. He can almost smell his father's self-disgust. A couple of times when Daniel was in his teens, his father had gotten past snarling, past blaming other people, sat in his big red poppa chair and wept, blew his nose in that handkerchief. *Danny, you got a bum for a father!* In that guttural, raspy, tough-guy voice, not even his own voice but one he needed in order to let his guard down. A bum for a father. What did he mean a bum? Money. He meant money, that's all. He couldn't bring home enough money. At those times of self-exposure, Daniel would forget how much he hated the man, would sit on the edge of the chair, put his arm around his father's shoulder. *Dad, Dad, it's okay....*

He'd been a tough, resisting boy. When his father yelled and threatened, Daniel fought back. He was always better with words; his father was afraid of his words. And Daniel could sense the last possible moment, the moment before his father would shove him or hit him, to retreat to his room, where he locked the door, shrank inside himself into a knot made of iron. Face down on his bed, he throttled, bit his pillow, tightened his jaw like a bulldog. And in this way Daniel lost the war, for he still has this knot of cold iron inside, has to lug all the rage of his father. Poor bastard, he says to himself, poor bastard, meaning his father, meaning himself.

When his father died, he hadn't been able to bring himself to say kaddish. He'd rationalize—what would it mean to Dad? Nothing. So now, as if in compensation, almost every day for the eleven prescribed months, he has said kaddish for his son.

Retire? How do you retire from your childhood? Here he is, a half-century later, still hiding in his room—now, his study—or in his mother's room. No meetings with the CEO, no reshuffling of the company's portfolio. No budget statements, no negotiations over lines of credit. He takes walks.

On his walk along Walden Pond one late spring morning over a carpet of last year's leaves and new moss, he'd stopped and, staring at the water, staring at the pattern of tiny wind ripples, felt a dizziness that began in his stomach—like when a plane hits clear-air turbulence and suddenly drops fifty feet. It was like staring at one of those 3-D pictures that appear to be flat patterns of color but, gazed at in soft focus, suddenly melt and reveal a three-dimensional architecture to get lost in.

He closed his eyes as he was pulled in and through, traveling a tunnel of inner space that let him out as suddenly as it sucked him in. And there he was at the same water, pond's edge, staring. Same water, same trees in early green, but everything pulsing with its own intent, each fragment, bark, leaf, water expressing its own self, its special speech, to his self. Nothing to do with angels. Still, he imagined himself held by wings, tips of feathers framing his view of water, patterns of pollen on its surface, fallen tree, moss and lichen on damp rock. These very things.

It wasn't wholly unfamiliar. When he was getting his MBA at Harvard in the seventies people used to put on funny, prismatic glasses and pretend to be tripping. It was like that. Or like the day he found himself in a total eclipse of the sun without knowing it was happening, and the light grew thin and strange. Or remember what it was like to smoke dope? Say you're walking along a path through the woods. Stoned, you let the path lose its role as a way to get you from point A to point B. You almost lose the illusion of continuity and experience a series of separate moments that are—well, simply what they are.

He wasn't afraid that morning at Walden; in fact, he tried to intensify the vision. But that simply made him aware of the effort, and the numinous quality fell away. So over these months he's learned to breathe in what he sees, not to push it, and these are the times he really sees, his eyes and ears caressed the way a swimmer is caressed by water. There's a hum associated with this way of being, the blood in the ears perhaps, or a shimmer at the edges of things. His breath eases, deepens, as if he were asleep, but colors are more vibrant, and everything seems to sing about itself. He breathes deep and sits, and if, at these times, he thinks about Gabe, it isn't a terrible thing. Gabe enters as breath.

This vertigo he feels—what is it but the wooziness caused by the leap between worlds? When he was a child lying in the dark in a churning house, he'd float away from his parents' guttural whispered fights by burying his head under a pillow and staring at the window (apartment building across the courtyard, mauve light from city streets) until the window bent and shrank to the size of his thumbnail and he pulled back, afraid the window would become a pinhole and he himself tiny enough to pass through and away. Then there was the sound of a car horn or a cough or hissed curse from the other room, and he'd be back.

Now, if he shrinks himself down, first there's the vertigo and then he can almost enter the light. He has to become very small. He is barely there; Gabe is barely not-there. He strains to find the place where they both exist.

Mornings this fall, during the Days of Awe between Rosh Hashanah and Yom Kippur, Daniel walks at Walden, but now he's taken to sitting on a rock off the path. He brings a cushion protected by a plastic bag and sits. He drifts off, returns. Nice here, uncomplicated. All through the previous month, then through the High Holy Days and until the end of Sukkot, they have been reciting Psalm 27 in the synagogue:

> One thing I asked of the Lord, one thing I shall seek
> To live in the house of the Lord all the days of my life....
> He will hide me in His haven on an evil day.

Sounds like a good deal to him. This is the time of year when we're told to take stock, a time of turning. The year turns, we are to turn our lives toward God. But is he turning? Or is he simply hiding on an evil day? The thing about hiding is it brings you right back to what you're hiding from. Sitting, he sees Gabe—his beautiful face. At first, this brings peace. But only at first.

Mid-winter the year Gabe died, Daniel drove up to Dartmouth and spent a couple of days hanging out. He can't stand motels, so Gabe gave up his bed and slept on a camping mattress on the floor.

Lying in the dark, Daniel asked about courses, about grad schools. They laughed about the dress Celia had chosen for her high-school prom. Lights from college paths played on the concrete-block walls, on the blown-up photo of FDR that Gabe had tacked up in his room at home just after his bar mitzvah. Before they said good-night, Daniel said to him, "Gabe? It's been pretty great being your father." He knew it embarrassed Gabe to hear things like that, but he said it anyway.

There came a long silence. He hadn't expected that. It grew thicker, more dangerous. Half a minute. A minute. He sighed, he yawned, to break the silence. Gabe spoke.

"Dad? You know I love you a lot…but when I was a little kid, it wasn't always easy being your son."

"I was too hard on you?"

"Not that. No. Most of the time, you were so kind. But then I'd screw up in some way that bothered you, and you'd get choked up and not yell but get hard like a wall, hard as ice, Dad, your eyes so cold—you'd turn your face away, I couldn't reach you to make things right. After a while you'd be okay—for you it was over, but not for me. I'd be left holding a lot of stuff I couldn't put down anywhere. You've mellowed, you know. Gotten sweet in your old age—just kidding, just kidding. And…well, Dad, I know how to handle you."

"You always knew that," Daniel laughed. Then: "How come you never spoke about this?"

Gabe had no answer. Daniel knew better than to press.

From down the hall, ugly music. Thump, thump, thump of the

bass. Laughter. He could hear Gabe trying to get comfortable on the camping mattress. It took a long time to get to sleep that night.

In the morning they embraced and Gabe went off to the library, Daniel drove home. And that was the last time he saw his son. Now he's left holding a lot of stuff, nowhere to put it down. He still speaks to Gabe, but does anyone answer? Can the vertigo take him to a place where they're both present? On the Day of Atonement, Yom Kippur, fasting all day in synagogue, he can't put it down, can't make it up.

It's the first holiday season that Celia hasn't spent with the family; too busy with her studies to fly home, she attends services at Swarthmore. Maybe her absence makes Celia more a presence for Daniel, for right after Sukkot he flies to see her. What's the good of being retired if he can't take off a couple of days? Why has it been so hard to call? Walking around Walden Pond, he says "Celia" into his voice-activated cell phone, but then kills the call. He sucks up a huge breath to quiet his heart. "Celia," he says again, as if he's angry at the phone.

She meets him at the Philadelphia airport, Swarthmore just a half-hour away. He enjoys it that she's the driver—pretty little blue used Corolla they bought for her—and he can relax and look over at her. He sees her freshly, as if she's not his child—tall as he, taller when sitting in the car, long-waisted as she is. She's bony-lean like Shayna, her eyes wonderfully clear, her beauty formed: a young woman. "I can't get over it."

She glances over at him. "Over Gabe? You can't get over Gabe, Dad?"

"No. No. I mean *you*—look at you, you're all grown up and lovely." She twists down the corner of her mouth, an old gag, and, without turning from the wheel, thumps him hard on the chest.

While she takes classes, he wanders—the Swarthmore campus another haven, specimen trees in full color. The gardens, fall-pruned, are sad, but the sky is clear and blue. He sits on newspapers on the damp lawn and watches breath pass through him, world to world. At her cross-country practice he puts on sneakers and runs alongside of her but soon he's heaving breath and she leaves him behind.

Dinnertime, Celia takes him to the eating hall and introduces him to a blur of names and faces. They make a fuss over him, and since they don't know him from Adam it makes him feel that Celia is loved around here. Later, in the dark, bundled up against the cold evening, they walk to the library and she tells him about her courses, the a-cappella group she's joined, and later, both carrying books, they walk back to her dorm. She shows him a few papers. Over her bed is Gabe's blown-up photo of Roosevelt. On the opposite wall is a blown-up picture of Gabe.

Celia works at her desk. Her long black fuzzy hair is rolled up and pinned out of the way. He remembers Shayna getting tired of running after her with a hairbrush, Celia refusing to cut it off, him laughing, the mediator. Her roommate's staying with a friend tonight so he can have a bed. He sits on the bed trying to read, but gets stuck like an old phonograph needle on one passage. Thump of a bass, somebody's stereo; laughter from the hallway. Roosevelt, battered at the edges, above her bed, Gabe looking at him from the wall across. Tournament Frisbees form a pattern on one wall, a collage of ski posters on another—she and Gabe were both skiers from the time they were four or five. She looks up. "Dad? What is it? You look incredibly moony."

"Who, me?"

She turns from her computer screen to face him. "My pop. My soda pop." She does the old stuff—runs her fingers through his thinning hair, rubs his shoulder.

"I wonder, Celia. Do you ever feel in contact with him?" It's only after he's said this that he knows he's been rehearsing it all day.

"No."

"Never?"

"Sometimes I dream about him, but that's all."

"Good dreams?"

"Not bad ones. I can't remember.... You never used to talk like this."

"No?"

"And since Gabe died, do you know we've hardly talked about him at all? In fact...this whole visit is amazing to me. When you called, I got a little nervous. I'll tell you what I thought. That maybe Mom or you were really sick God forbid or something. Because we never talk."

"Celia? Gabe said I came down hard on him, judged him. He said I could get like ice."

"Well, maybe you were like that sometimes with Gabe—you know, fathers and sons? On me you were always easy."

As if he's praying, he rocks, rocks, to the thump of the bass. "Honey?" he says. "This is going to sound peculiar: I've been trying to reach him."

"What does that mean, Dad?"

He shakes his head as if it's impossible to say, then says, "If I can leave my self behind, maybe I can get to the place...where we're both present."

"Oh, Dad. Dad." She came over and hugged, hard, then held him at arm's length and looked into his eyes. "Have you talked to Mom about this?"

"A little."

"You ought to talk to Mom. She's lonely."

The morning after Yom Kippur, while Shayna sleeps, he goes back to Walden. Here, at the pond, he finds, sitting on a stump he's covered with a pillow, he can let things go. Maybe Celia helped. It becomes soothing to breathe-in morning light, brackish water, the weave of pond surface this morning, leaves of yellow and now burnished reds of oak obliterating the path—breathe them in so they seem suffused with their origin. It's as if he's a little drunk. The humming in his blood suffuses pond, leafy path. Under his ribs the tug of fear—he'll go too far; this Daniel will disappear—and the opposite fear: this way of seeing will disappear.

He watches words, not his own, babbling through him, watches...nothing; there's no one to *do* the watching. As he sits, eyes shut, there's a vertiginous lifting, from above his body he can look down and see himself sitting, Daniel looking down at Daniel. He's above himself, outside the map. This is too much. At once—whoosh—he's back in his house of bones.

How long was he outside himself? A few seconds? No time at all? But he thinks about it all the time. In his office at home, playing with a pencil, he remembers, as if still from above, a sitting fool who's lost his son. Well, so many have lost their sons. *Kindertotenlieder:* songs of the death of children. But that doesn't make it inconsequential. Loss and loss, intensified by all the parents keening in chorus for all the children. He could have said this a year ago, ten years ago. But now, feeling part of one great wave of grief, he finds some of the burden lift: it's not merely his.

He can't stop replaying the moment. He sticks to his study or walks at the pond, shies away from Shayna, cancels lunch downtown with his old friend Morris Goldman. Why? Out of fear it might show? Out of fear he'll lose the understanding?

One afternoon, returning from the pond, he says hello to Shayna, just home from school, and stops in at his mother's room upstairs. But his mother's not there, or in the bathroom, or listening to music downstairs. Where could she be? Sometimes she takes a walk, but never alone. Hurrying downstairs, he calls, "Shayna, Shayna, where did Mom go?"

"She's not upstairs?" Shayna gets up from her laptop and they hunt through the house. No Gertrude. No Gertrude anywhere. "She could have had a stroke," Shayna says. Then: "Don't panic," in a flat, frozen voice, her voice of panic. Daniel goes for his car; Shayna stays home to wait for a call.

Gertrude's usual walk, always with him or with Shayna, is two blocks away to a local park. She sits and feeds the ducks, pets the dogs. Not today. He reaches Shayna on his cell phone. No, she says, no one's called home. "Should we call the police?"

"Not yet. I'm heading up the road toward town."

He's still on the line with Shayna when he spots his mother standing at the black iron fence to the playground, leaning a little on her cane but looking fit and determined. "There she is. We'll be home in a couple of minutes." Daniel pulls alongside and lowers the window. "Ma? You want to get in, please?" He opens the door for her.

"Daniel. How nice. I thought I'd go find Celia in the playground." She points—the playground where Celia and Gabe used to swing and slide, fixed up now with colorful plastic play units but otherwise the same. "Your father and I haven't seen her all day."

He says, "Celia will be home soon, Ma. For Thanksgiving. We'll have a big turkey." He gets out of the car and stands by the entrance to the playground and looks.

She looks blankly, blankly; then her eyes take focus. She snorts. "Don't you condescend to me, Mister," she says, glaring, hands akimbo. "Don't you think I know where Celia is?" Now, thrusting up her chin, she's playing Rosalind Russell, Bette Davis. He's a boy again and she's telling him a thing or two. "So, my son. You caught me in a little gap? At my age, that's permitted."

"Sorry, sorry, Ma."

"Look at the way the time goes, my darling." Softer, now. "Suppose I did slip into a slightly different time. So what? Don't be such a coward. That's just the way things are. Your father, before he died, half the time he was in another world. You couldn't talk sensibly to him for five minutes in his last years. And Celia was such *a lovely* little girl. Only this very morning wasn't she six years old? Look at her there—"

Gertrude points with her cane. Daniel follows. There's a girl with dark hair tied up in a pony tail, there on the swings. Trick of the eyes, trick of the light?—it's Celia, she's six years old, and the big boy pushing from behind, that's Gabe, age ten. It's my distance vision, playing games. But Daniel doesn't want to lose it. He knows, doesn't he, that Celia's a young woman at Swarthmore, outside Philadelphia? But he knows, too, that all he has to do is leave his mother, walk into the playground, and, if he doesn't look back, he'll find them there, age ten, age six.

Instantly, as if he were only in a reasonable, shared world, he says, "Ma? She's *still* lovely."

Gertrude picks up on the last word. "And what about your mother?" She lifts her penciled, Rosalind Russell eyebrows at him. She presents him with her face, as if it were a portrait of herself. There!

"Oh, lovely, too."

"Well? Am I *not a* bit of all right?" They laugh together. He takes her arm and leads her to the car. Just before she steps in, they both look back at the girl on the swing, the boy pushing. She nods. She sits down in his car, the *grande dame,* and says to her chauffeur, "Home, Mister."

Shayna's making out reports for the Department of Social Services. She's sitting over her laptop, papers spread out on the dining-room table, and looks at him over her glasses, perched half-way down her nose.

"You know what?" she says when he tells her about the playground, "I feel that way all the time, Danny. That's just our ordinary loss of children. Our little girl Celia—that terrific sweetness, remember?—playing on those swings?" She takes off her glasses and folding them neatly, places them on her papers. "Listen, I know, I should count my blessings that Celia has grown up into a marvelous adult, and I do—but I still miss that little girl. So. Your poor mother. Time crumples up for her? Maybe she's lucky."

"What I'm thinking is—you know—well, maybe it's a form of communication?"

"Oh, baby." Shayna pulls off her computer glasses and stands up as if she were to meet a friend coming to the door. "Oh." She looks at him with her clear, severe look, then, softening, puts her arms around his neck. "You mean a message from Gabe using your mother? Danny? Is that what you mean?"

"I didn't say that at all," Danny says, face hot. He tries to slacken, but the fortress of bones keeps resisting. At this moment he deeply understands what he has always known, that in this terrible time he has her, has had her all the way—but what in God's name does she have? He makes himself hug back.

The next afternoon he drives back to the playground. The big kids are still at school; only little ones, two of them, are playing on the colorful plastic climbs and slides. Their mothers, standing nearby, talk together. It's a sunny day; bundled in sweater and parka, he's buffered against the cold.

He sits on a wooden platform—part of a structure where big kids climb—crosslegged, his back against an upright. It's like a giant chair, like the chair on which Alice sat. He closes his eyes. In his mind's eye he can see the old equipment, heavy aluminum, where

Gabe and Celia swung, slid, seesawed, spun. And then, as he opens his eyes, well, there are these hoops of light to be considered. What about them? Each of them might be an angel…or just a trick of perception. Hoops of luminescence float or seem to float, and the objects themselves are surrounded by this pulsing light, as if light loved the things of this world.

It's making him dizzy. Gone limp inside, he isn't breathing but being breathed. His face hot with blood, head humming with blood, a high-pitched keening. The leaves are falling. He knows that.

Gabe—why, Gabe is just through those trees over there. So he takes a little walk. He knows he can join his son just past the trees. But trees, they just give way to trees. A path into the conservation area, and beyond the little woods, a wooden barn and hayfield. There's nobody conserved in these woods. He might get small and small, might dissipate his being and then—what if there's nothing, or nothing like a son? Suppose his eyes blur with tears, with light; instead of Gabe, all there is is light's confusion. Just some father, some body, that's all, stumbling through piles of yellow, orange, red maple leaves drying in the late fall sun. Leaves fall, adding vertigo to vertigo, until they make a bed for someone.

Crumpling the dry leaves, he lies down in his bones until the dizziness passes, but then it's so comforting to lie here on this bed that he closes his eyes and sleeps. No angels, no children, and all the scattered energy of light calms down like the leaves. It's okay here. Leaves like feathers.

Don't worry; in a while he'll get up. He remembers where he lives. He'll go home, and if Shayna's lonely, sitting at her laptop, he'll try to comfort her. The leaves are like camouflage; sunlight of late afternoon speckles the leaves and, past the woods, barn and hayfield. Soon, Daniel will step back inside the map, lug his bones home.

Originally appeared in Commentary, *December 2004*

Soap Opera

David, who had once wanted to create the most beautiful house in the world, trained and practiced as an architect, but there's not much call for original architecture in the hill towns of Western Mass. At fifty he's settled for work as senior designer and project manager for a construction company doing high-end commercial projects. He makes good money, and at least his own house is beautiful—demanding as a lover, this two-hundred-year-old house in the hills. But worth it.

Coming home tired, pulling off muddy work boots, he has his cranky father to take care of, ex-TV actor languishing in the guest room. *How you doing, Dad?* Not so great; late seventies, often out of sorts. *All day,* he says, *you stick me in front of the goddamn television.* The quaver in his voice means he's kidding, playing a role. Hey—he's too hip to think of himself as helpless. The day he came to live with them, a year ago, not long after David's mother died, he strode in, Stetson tilted back on his head. Wealthy rancher from the badlands of New York City. "Well, sonny boy, I came to straighten you kids out." The old luster, the old phony charm. But in a couple of months, it faded. So it's not *just* a joke now, the complaint that he's been discarded. If David pleads, *Dad, I keep telling you we'll take you any morning to a senior center,* the old man quavers, *What? So you can get rid of me?* So David backs away, goes into the kitchen to listen to his wife's victories and frustrations at the high school where she's head of the math program.

His current construction project is in Western Mass. near Springfield, half an hour from home. It's dark by the time he leaves in the late afternoon; headlights pick up patches of congealed early snow along Route 91. Driving into the small clump of houses in the hills, he finds the road blocked off by a police car. Policeman in a winter parka waves him off. David lowers his window: "I *live* down here. Okay I drive through?" Only then does he notice smoke rising just around the curve. "Whose house?"

The policeman points. "Over there—Bromowitz."

He pulls over, sets the brake and runs up the road in his heavy boots. The rear corner of the house, the addition where his father lives, is smoking. Firemen, local police. Water. Two men are hosing down the rear of the house. "My dad's in there. He's an old man."

"We've got him," a big man with a clipboard says. "He's okay—he's in the ambulance up the driveway, they're giving him oxygen, but he's okay. He's fine."

"Thank God."

The man looks flatly at David. "It seems he kind of started it."

"The fire?"

"He covered a lamp with a quilt and got underneath. Like a bed warmer. He said his family wouldn't give him any heat. The shade must have buckled and the quilt caught."

"He could have burned himself up."

"No kidding. Real lucky. His hands got a little singed trying to put it out."

No heat. Why, that dumb bastard! When all he had to do was turn up the damned thermostat! Or put on a sweater! At once his anger shames him. He sucks breath. Dad's an old man. So he got a little befuddled.

Fury explodes: *That stupid sonofabitch!*

David hurries over the water line, through a huge puddle drowning the driveway. Water keeps playing over the rear wall. As an architect, he can't help but see the skeleton under the soaked clapboard siding. The house is basically okay. The room that burned is an addition to the old Colonial. If something had to go, well, thank God it's just that room. Walls will have to be ripped out, the room gutted to its structural members. New walls, new floors. But at least not the original house. He breathes deep, breathes deep, smells the acrid tang. And now, with gratitude to God who resides in all things: in fire, in walls, in these noble firemen and their fat hoses, he lets water gush from his mind to drench the poor walls.

He raps at the rear doors of the ambulance. A young man in EMT uniform opens. "My dad's in there." The man holds the door open. His father sits up on the gurney, skinny in his pajamas and a robe. He's still a handsome man; once a *professionally* handsome man, his long face has slumped and his beaked nose has become more prominent. "You see what happens when you're stingy with the heat?" So: ha!—it's a lesson, not a mistake. David rubs his father's shoulder. "I'd better make sure you stay warm, Dad. Next time maybe you'll build a campfire in the living room."

"Smart ass." Harry Bromowitz pokes the EMT. "My son's a smart ass."

"Don't worry. It's not a huge problem, Dad. We're insured."

"Insured! Right. So you see?" Harry says to his son. "Hah?"

You see. You see? Ah. Now he gets it: a few months back, he remembers, his father nagged them to make certain the house was insured for replacement value.

"Look at my hands!" He holds them out, swathed in bandages.

"You poor guy. Are you hurting?"

"As if you give a shit!"

"You taking him to the hospital?"

"Nobody's taking me to no goddamn hospital."

"Okay, Dad. Let's see what the fireman says."

"We should take him and check him out."

"Nobody's taking me to no goddamn hospital."

"Okay, okay," David soothes. "How are his signs?"

"Good. But see, we're responsible now your dad's in the ambulance."

"Listen. We'll make a bargain. Listen, Dad. I'll ride with you, and we'll sign a release soon as they check you out. I promise. Please, Dad?"

But Harry Bromowitz isn't having any of it. "Just tell your boss I refuse." And to David: "These guys just want insurance to pay for the ambulance." With hands made clumsy by the bandages, he puts on the winter parka somebody brought him and he's out the door. David holds his hands open in apology.

"Tough old guy," the fireman sympathizes. "You got your hands full. I guess he was a pretty famous actor, your father? He told me about it."

"I'll bet he did. Not *that* famous: daytime TV. And not that tough—he loves to talk tough."

The water's shut off. One truck leaves. Three firemen stick around, walk back and forth, guest room to screened-in porch, through the empty frame of what had been a slider, retrieving and piling up damaged things, undamaged things, checking for hot spots underneath. Among the undamaged things, Karen's collection of math texts, their son Michael's skis, their daughter Sheila's quilting materials. Two firemen stretch and staple plastic over the slider to keep out the cold. Nice of them—they're not required to do that. David thanks them.

Michael and Karen must be driving home from basketball practice. On his cell, David calls her cell, but it's turned off; he leaves no message. His father is sitting in the car, engine running, to keep warm. "You can come in now, Dad. Firemen said. Heat's on again."

He's pouting, won't look at David. He sits, bundled up in a parka, arms folded, a thin man with a little pot belly. His body has shrunk over the past few years.

Only one fireman is left, the big man with the clipboard. David goes in, staples up more plastic. Not much water has spilled over into the rest of the house, but the smell, it's everywhere.

His father has come in behind him. Now he stands in the kitchen, shaking his head. "You smell that sour, damp, lousy stink, Davey? Some kind of goddamn burnt plastic. My lungs don't need that. I can't stay in this house."

"Okay, Dad. Don't worry. We'll stay at my friend Ari's a couple of days. Remember Ari? The rabbi?" He wants to keep the old guy calm. But he knows this is the end of having him with them. The thought of getting rid of this father of his feels like a secret bounty.

His father is sorting things saved from the fire. But there's not enough satisfying aggravation in this; he goes to the pile of soggy and charred clothing, books, papers, bedding, and says "Just look, just *look*, would you? I just *bought* this sweater!" And he squeezes the water out of the sleeve as if to choke it. And it's totally futile; the sweater's gonzo. "Aach!" he groans. David's own jaws have begun to ache, he has a headache that really belongs to the old man. The problem, as David sees it, is that he can't fully separate himself. He feels the sour stink of his father's humiliation; staring at his father's bandaged hands, David winces at the sting of fire on his own hands.

David goes to the door a few seconds before the green 4-Runner with its scrape along a rear bumper turns onto their road. How does he know they're coming? He knows. David waves, smiles BIG, holds up an *okay*-circle of thumb and forefinger. Michael jumps from the car before it stops. "Oh, shit, oh, shit!"

"Careful!" David yells. Michael charges inside, returns while David's telling Karen the details. "It's just Sheila's room," Michael says. "Boy, everything stinks bad."

Their computers, David's violin: undamaged. The new living room furniture, the new kitchen: just fine. Thank God, Harry got to the phone right away.

"We sleeping here tonight?" Michael asks.

"No, we'll stay with Ari—Rabbi Pearl. Go give Amy a call, tell her what's up, okay?"

Standing on the muddy kitchen floor, Karen shines her sweet, slightly plump face up at David, looks steadily into his eyes. She doesn't have to use words: (1) It's hard, but aren't we blessed to have one another, to have lost so little? (2) Harry has to move. He's your father, but do we have a choice? She hugs him hard. "I still think of it as Sheila's room. I'll call her tonight."

They share, he thinks, a giddy, secret sense of freedom: now they've got to send the old man to a retirement community. Oh, Harry's going to hate it. He'll yell. But what doesn't he hate? When didn't he yell? The very first memory David has of his father is that of a red-faced screamer. He feels the hot sweat coating his father's cheeks. This must be almost fifty years ago. Maybe his sister Rose had done something; or Mom; or David himself. His father had a baseball cap in his hand. Yelling, he began twisting it; then he clamped the brim between his jaws and began to rip. This excess was meant to indicate, *Look how upset you've made me!*

In the kitchen Karen is sorting through what's been saved. Sheila's room/guest room/Harry's room, a room attached to the original house, has become the place they put things they didn't know what to do with. Well. Now they have fewer things to put. "*This* is sad," she says, holding up a bag of baby clothes they'd saved for when Sheila got married. "But I can wash the clothes, I can save most of them." She's using a contractor's bag in a 45 gallon barrel for things less precious. But every once in a while she's sidetracked into fussing over forgotten skates. "I'm never going to let it get like that again."

Harry Bromowitz, still in winter parka over pajamas, goes to the fridge and pours himself a glass of his special soy milk with vitamins. "Where we going to eat tonight?"

"Out," David says. Listening back to himself, he's surprised. He's not a man of one-word answers; he must be angry. David turns to the pile of saved things. "You need help?"

Karen shrugs, leaves the kitchen; he sees anger at Harry in the hunch of her shoulders.

"I never expected the damn thing would catch fire so fast," Harry says.

"I know, Dad. Of course not. But why didn't you just turn up the thermostat?"

"What kind of junky material you buy for a quilt?"

This is the kind of question Harry is famous for. If he bangs up the car, he blames your steering system; if he drops a glass, he complains about its design. David chortles.

"I mean," Harry explains in a hoarse whisper, "all I *meant* to do is put a little *char* on the damn thing."

"You what?"

"To *show* you a thing or two."

"You did what? Show us what?"

"What I have to go through around here for heat, get it? So all right—maybe it was dumb. But the damn thing went from a little singed to a big fire in no time."

Not the kind of thing to tell the insurance company. Or even Karen. David closes his eyes. The stupidity stuns him. Then he sees through his father's eyes: *I'll let them know how goddamn cold it was! See? 'We could've had a fire,' I'll tell them.* Theater! Except they *did* have a fire. And this is not, let's face it, senility. Just the selfishness his mom, his brothers, and David had to put up with all through their growing up.

Harry Bromowitz was made for daytime TV. Back in the sixties he was on two or three soaps at the same time—second leads, small parts—and commercials. It used to turn David's stomach to switch on TV and see his absent father playing a kind, loving family man. Those days, when he was, say, fifteen, Michael's age, Harry Bromowitz—TV name Harry Brunell—was all over network television, one piece of junk after another. Nobody ever heard of him, but he sure as hell had work. Once in awhile he appeared in an off-Broadway play, and David, Mom and Steve would drive in from New Jersey and camp out afterward at Dad's pied-à-terre on a side street in the West 70s.

"Nothing," Harry says, "happened to my scrapbooks. That's one good thing."

Ari is rabbi in their tiny regional synagogue; he plays cello in the community string orchestra for which David plays violin. Once or twice a month, separate from rehearsals, the two of them get together to play, usually in this room, Ari's music room. He's shaped like his cello, Ari—two hundred soft pounds on a man five foot nine, who works out in a gym only on days he feels a bit uneasy about his weight.

David is sorry about the dangerous pounds but is comforted watching Ari sink into the overstuffed chair in the music room.

"Of *course* you'll have to settle him somewhere else. After this? There are pretty decent residences around here. Not cheap. You know Sara Klein from shul? She just moved her mother into a very nice place."

David nods. "Financially, we can manage. When Dad made money as an actor, he squirreled it away in annuities. And you know, it's not as if he was ever much of a father. A lot of the time he lived in that little apartment of his in New York. We'd go into the city to visit him, and sometimes Dad would have 'forgotten' to hide the last bottle of perfume or the last silk slip and Mom would see it and there'd be tears and whispers. She'd hiss, *And I'm fool enough to answer your fan mail? I should have my head examined!*"

"Why did she?"

"She was a great wife to that man. She made books of his clippings. Of course she should have left him."

"So, you're feeling guilty? He almost burned down your house, and you can't face it that you need him to live elsewhere? Isn't that taking the mitzvah of honoring parents a bit far?"

David doesn't answer this. "Ari? I'm too old to be fighting with my father."

"No one's that old. So, Dave, you want to play the Beethoven?"

"Coming, coming, Dad," David calls when the old man sings out, "Davey? Davey?"

Surrounded by bookshelves with Ari's collection of Jewish books, in old bindings a lot of them, a substantial sacred library, Harry, unshaven, sits up in bed, wrapped in a wool blanket, an Indian. "My book! Hey! We forgot my damn book on Winchell."

"We didn't forget. It's in the car. Actually, Karen remembered. One minute." David goes out into the dark for the book. Out here it's cold! Well below zero. He wishes, in spite of the cold, in spite of the dark, he could walk off awhile into the night. But he gets the book, goes back, pausing by Michael's door to wave. "You okay?"

Back in his father's room, handing him the book, he tucks the blanket around him, asks, "You still cold?" He worries about his father's circulation—maybe that's what makes him cold. He imagines a stream of sluggish blood. For Ari's house is even warmer than David's—kept at just below seventy. David sits on a chair by the bed.

"Ahh. I'm used to a lot of heat in New York. I'm still a New Yorker at heart."

"Funny. And here I thought it was New Jersey we lived in."

This is a dig: *You never really lived with us.* Harry picks up on it. "Yeah. You think I was a lousy, absent father? I was busting my ass for you kids."

That does it. As he hears the tough-guy self pity in his father's voice, David becomes Righteous Judge. "Now you listen! Listen! When *were* you my father? Even when you managed to come home on weekends and you'd play ball with us or we'd go for a hike, the four of us, like a family. But it was bullshit, Dad. Just one more role. Harry Brunell playing Family Man."

"Can't stand your old father, can you? You still got a chip on that shoulder of yours."

A fury comes up in David's throat; his cheeks grew hot, and he stands up above the bed. "As if it's *my* problem. You ruined my mother's life with your whoring around. You almost burn down a two-hundred-year-old house, and you have a right to complain?"

The old Indian loses ten years and his blanket. He sits up tall on the edge of the bed, waves his hands at David as if brushing away flies. "Whored around? Who whored around? I never whored around. Or maybe once or twice, but that's all." He leans forward, bony legs in long johns sticking out like weapons. "All right, kiddo. I'm going to tell you things you know nothing about." Now he pauses, nodding to himself to build the drama.

"You don't have to."

"Well, I'm going to tell you. You want to know why I was away so much of the time?"

"Please, let's just forget it, Dad."

"No. I want to tell you. You got a beef coming. This is the real story. Years and years, for years and years, there was a woman all right, just *one* woman, my love, Nancy, *that's* what was going on, Davey. It's about time you knew—you and your sister Rose. I'm sure you'll get on the phone to Rose and blab about me. Nancy Collins: she was on Broadway. She was an actress."

"You're telling me you were with one special woman in the city? All that time?"

"See? Hah! Surprised, aren't you?" Harry looks gleeful, his eyes slitted. "Special! The love of my life. Years and years we were just like married. Nancy had her little apartment, but whenever I was on 73rd Street, she was there. Like married. Don't worry, I felt lousy enough about your mother. She deserved better, your mother." Now he sits on the bed and folds the blanket around him, this time full of dignity, as if he were wearing royal robes.

The room is dim and full of silence, but soon, in their common imagination, this woman Nancy enters the room, and David's mother enters. "Well, Dad," David says very quietly. "I guess I have things to tell you, too. Another little secret."

"Everybody's got secrets. What?" he whispers, "You been playing around, Davey?"

"Me? No! I was never going to tell you. But now…I feel different. It's Mom."

"What? Your mother? Don't make me laugh. She could never keep a secret, your mother."

"You say she deserved better. Well, you remember a man named Steve Margolies?"

"Vaguely. A New Jersey lawyer. Receding hairline. Yeah? So?"

"All those years, Mom was with Steve Margolies. Of course we weren't supposed to talk about it. We weren't supposed to know. Mom was very discreet. Afternoons, they met, or evenings when she pretended to be at PTA meetings. But we knew."

"What? What kind of crap is this? What do you mean 'she was with'?"

"It's okay, Dad. You don't have to believe me."

"This is horseshit. When was this?"

"Well, actually, it was as long as you had the little place on 73rd. Maybe longer. It wasn't easy to keep you in the dark. But," David says, "it wasn't all that hard either—because you were in New York so much. It was a little refuge of love for her."

"'Refuge of love'? Don't make me laugh. When was this? When you were a kid?"

"*Maybe*," David says, "*even before*." And with this, he makes his exit. His triumphant exit. And before he's over the threshold David repents his little piece of theater, repents his need to get back. Why does he need to get back at a seventy-eight-year-old father? He goes down the hall to see Karen feeling giddy and terrible.

Giddy and terrible because he's hurt his father—and because it's none of it true. He's invented for that poor mother of his, his poor, loyal, decent mother, a different life. A little joy. He sees Hannah Bromowitz dolled up in Persian lamb-fur hat, silk scarf at the throat. Okay, okay, erasing that as impossible, he sees her in the plain navy wool muffler she really wore, but loving a romantic shadow man in a fifties' fedora, someone who thought she was precious as he, David, thought she was precious. Precious but too dumb-faithful ever to take a lover. He and Rose became her life; those PTA meetings just PTA meetings. From the PTA, from the sisterhood at the synagogue, she had a few women friends, no one very close. Why *couldn't* she have found a lover? She was a smart, beautiful woman, no question. Why keep Dad's pictures framed along the stairway wall?

He says nothing to Karen. He says nothing to Ari.

The next morning his father won't come out for breakfast. Before running off to school, Karen gets him his special cereal and soy milk, his arthritic meds and his vitamins, but Harry Bromowitz isn't interested. *That story. I'm killing my father*, David says to himself, and he wants to tell Karen, but she's so busy, rushing to get out to work while being sociable to Amy. So David's stuck with it, and all morning, between taking Michael to school, calling Maguire Construction to explain his absence, calling his insurance company, meeting with an insurance adjuster at the house, conferring with Karen between her classes, all morning it's there, his father's secret, his own great lie, and the longer he's away from his father, the less judgment he feels. Life, he says. It's just life. A mantra: *just life*. He imagines his father going off to a nursing home and dwindling into senility and weakness, deteriorating and dying. And it'll be his doing, David's doing. What good will that suffering do for his mother, who all her life, like Karen, tried to assuage other people's suffering?

Harry eats a little lunch, thank God. Some homemade soup.

David comes to take away the bowl. In his mouth like murmured prayers are rehearsed words taking back the story. *I lied, Dad. She never thought about taking a lover.* But his father won't look at him. During the afternoon David buys fiberglass insulation and nails temporary studs onto the inside of the house, staples up the insulation between the studs, covers the wall with old sheets and Indian bedspreads. It looks okay. As long as it has to be redone, he'll design a big sun room, lots of glass. But that can wait for spring; till then, they'll manage. And the smell is bearable.

Cold as it is—he's turned the heat way down—he opens a couple of windows a crack to air the house out. They could move back in tonight, but he thinks he'll give it another day. Tomorrow's Friday. Ari will be leading Friday night services in town; no Shabbos rest for the rabbi. David and Karen would like to get out of the Pearls' way and be at home for Shabbos.

Back at Ari's, he tells no one.

"Dav…ey? Dav…ey?" A long moaning of the name as if someone had died.

He comes in and brings his father the afternoon local newspaper. "What, Dad? What is it, Dad? Don't you want to get up? It's not good for you to lie around like this."

"Don't these people have a television? These old Jewish books! They smell of fish."

"Fish!" David laughs. He helps his father out of bed. Harry gets dressed, whining only once—for a shirt he wishes he had. David keeps rehearsing words. *It never happened, Mom was faithful.* Harry puts on a sweater and looks himself over in the mirror over the dresser. "Your father used to be a damn good looking guy. Look at me now, all bones…I'm the wreck of myself."

This gives David a heavy jolt of irritation. When Harry talks of himself in third person, it drives David nuts. He says, "So tell me, Dad. She's dead, this Nancy of yours?"

"I don't think so. Naw. I'd have heard. Definitely I'd have heard. Mutual friends."

"She's married?"

"She's a widow. She's got some decent money."

"Nancy's a widow?"

"She lives with her daughter in Atlanta. So what?"

"Well, Dad, it's obvious. Why don't you call her? Why don't you go see her?"

Harry holds up his palms, king from a tragedy. This is a put-on and not a put-on. "Go see her?" he asks in quavering cry. He points at the mirror. "Looking like this I should go see her? You think I'd let her see me looking like this?"

"Come on. She probably doesn't look like a chorus girl herself."

"She was never a chorus girl." Harry pulls the bandages from his hands, wincing.

"You know what I mean."

"Hell, the woman's fifteen years younger."

"You want me to call her for you? It's warm in Atlanta."

"You keep your nose out of it. If I want to call, I'll call. You just want me out of your hair." He dumps the bandages in the wastebasket and looks at his hands. "Not bad, not too bad."

Back in their borrowed bedroom, David tells Karen half the story: *his father's mistress*. This upsets her. *That spoiled little boy*, she says. *Your dear mother*, she says. And he means to tell her the other half—his lie about his mother. The life she never had. But it feels so foolish, so shameful and infantile, that he can't get the words out.

Friday, David's back at work but gets away early, picks up his father at Ari's and gets home just after Michael, just before Karen. The pocket in the hills where the house sits is in deep shadow. The top of the hills glow with last light. Harry gets out of the car and trudges into the house, not looking at the hills, not looking at his son. He sure doesn't belong here, David thinks. *We* don't belong here either, he thinks, except maybe Michael. But then, as Jews, we carry our world with us. Thank God, Mom gave me that. Dad—he's more an alien than Karen and I. No world he can carry with him into exile.

"Pretty clever," Harry says, "the way you fixed up the wall with that Indian junk—what are they—bedspreads?"

Oh! The big shot, his proprietary tone, as if David is his employee. It's dusk, half an hour past candle-lighting time, but Karen calls them together and they make Shabbos in the kitchen, blessing the candles, the wine, and a challah Karen bought in Greenfield on the way home. David blesses Michael, though he has to reach up five inches to lay hand on head. Karen and David avoid using the phone on Shabbos but make an exception for Sheila. They always call her in Ann Arbor, and especially tonight. They want her to know they're back in the house and things are normal.

Except they're not normal. Karen, who usually knocks herself out cooking on Thursday night for Shabbos just thaws a vegetable stew for dinner. There are trash bags and boxes full of things waiting to be stored, restored. There's the faint bitter odor. There's Harry staying in Michael's room. Harry wants his son to know how deeply this is affecting him, this revisionist history of his marriage. He makes sure David can hear him suffering from time to time. Big sighs are ordinary enough from Harry, and the subdued groaning is meant to be heard, but soon the old man is weeping and muffling the sobs in pillow or arm. Karen leans across the table. "Poor Harry. I've been thinking about him. I think Harry feels deeply ashamed, but he can't let himself feel it. It's not just the fire. He knows what a terrible father he was. Like when a child feels guilty and acts worse and worse, plays the bad boy he feels he is. I think the fire was that kind of acting-out."

"Let me go see what I can do for him." And alone with his real secret, clutching the lie under his shirt, like the wolf under the Spartan's, David goes in to see him. His father is sitting up in bed, reading glasses low on his nose. David's eyes get wet with shame or sudden love. Big hardcover art book on his lap for a desk, Harry is writing a letter, which he hides against his chest. "Yeah? So what do you want?"

"Hey, Dad."

"*Maybe.*"

"Maybe? Maybe what?"

"*Maybe* 'Dad'. Maybe I'm your Dad. How the hell would you know?"

"Oh, I was just trying to get back at you." And now, not knowing he's going to keep on lying, he adds to the lie. "She...well, she didn't even *know* Steve Margolies until I was about ten."

"Oh yes, she did. Sure she did. She knew him. Sure."

"But not as a friend. Not as a friend, Dad. Not as far as I know."

Harry doesn't answer. He goes back to his letter. "Letter to Nancy?" David asks.

"Is that your business all of a sudden? You know, I'll tell you something, Davey. You want to know something? I'm goddamned glad about it, really. This other life of hers. Because frankly, I was no kind of husband for your mother. I was a bum in that particular department. So Hannah had a little adventure in her life? Fabulous. Why should I complain? Am I right?"

"Sure. You're right, Dad. You are."

"She had her life, I had mine. Terrific!"

"It lets you off the hook, huh?"

"You bet your ass, Davey boy. Exactly. No more feeling so damned guilty." Harry Bromowitz blows his nose into a tissue. "You don't know how big this is. I think back about those weekends and I understand a few things. Why I felt the way I felt. It all makes sense. I've been thinking and thinking. The whole story is clearer now. Here I figured she was plain crazy for me. I was this bad boy, but she had a heart for me. This is a whole different story. She was trying to make up for her business with this Margolies fellow. And I think about parties—this guy Margolies was so super-charming to me, and I didn't get it. Why the hell didn't you tell me this before?"

It's dark outside; it's Shabbos, time for peace. David has no story which can make his father's long desertion dissolve. "Well, Dad," David says, mollifying, "it's all guesswork. We don't really know what happened. Maybe nothing happened. Who's to say? We were kids."

But Harry isn't listening. "My whole married life—I've got to see it differently. You understand? Suppose I had acted like a real husband—like you with Karen. Then maybe our life together, Hannah and me, would have been a different thing." He puts down the book and the letter and pats the bed. "Sit down. I'm not mad at her."

"But Dad, I'm saying, I don't really know anything. Don't blow it out of proportion."

"Sure, sure. But it all makes sense. You remember those long weekends she shipped you and Rose out to friends while she flew down to Florida to stay with her Aunt Sarah?"

"Sure. I used to stay with Alex. The Kadens."

"Right. With Alex. Exactly. Well? Did you ever meet that 'aunt' of hers? Right! Neither did I. What aunt? I've been thinking and thinking since you put the bug in my ear. And remember how I'd call evenings and she'd be at a meeting? She was at one hell of a lot of meetings."

"Well, she was lonely, Dad. So she did volunteer work."

Harry waves a hand in front of his face—no more talk about it. "See this letter? This letter is to Nancy. Suppose we *do* get together. Suppose she comes for a visit. Would that be okay?"

His father seems like an eager child when he speaks. He's not whining. And the sentimental catch in his throat. David realizes: my father is in his element.

In bed that Shabbos night, as they touch one another, Karen and David, as they stroke one another, preface to making love, David says, "Remind me to tell you something later on, honey. It's a peculiar story." But after love, they sleep, just sleep, and it's not until the morning, over coffee, that the story gets told, his lie upon lie. "It's a soap opera," he says. "So schmaltzy." He looks out the window. It snowed last night, making everything fluffy white and gorgeous. It's so quiet. The refrigerator hums; that's all. Michael's asleep on the couch. Harry's awake in Michael's room; every once in awhile they hear him moving around. "I've been thinking: Suppose we wind up taking care of the two of them. Aach!"

"Why invent hypothetical troubles?"

"Maybe it's disloyal to my mother, having this woman here. Maybe I'm making things all right when they weren't all right. Honey? They were pretty terrible."

"He's almost eighty years old. Can you undo the past?"

"Karen, but that's just what I've done. I've undone his past. And if we have her here, this Nancy, I'm giving him permission to rewrite *our* past. To make everything normal."

"Honey, is that so bad?"

"You know, I wish it were true, the story about my mother."

"I guess I'm not such a stickler for truth."

"If I were so in love with the truth, you think I'd make up such a story?"

She leans across the breakfast table and kisses his rippled forehead.

One evening a couple of weeks later, the whole family goes to Bradley (between Springfield and Hartford) to meet the plane from Atlanta. It snowed heavily the night before; snow is banked high on the sides of Route 91; it's slow going. David, Karen, Michael and Harry stand among the families and the limo drivers holding up cardboard signs lettered in marker. Harry hasn't looked this good in years, David notices. He's wearing his broad Stetson. Maybe he's afraid she won't recognize him; maybe he wants to hide his white hair. How long has it been? With ten minutes to go, Harry can't stop talking. How we met (across a crowded set). How we tried to be "just friends". How beautiful she was. Now he comes down to earth again and, holding up a hand like a traffic cop, says, "No more beautiful than your mother. Your mother was a great beauty," he assures David, and David, who needs no such assurance, says to himself, What is this? Am I crazy? Marriage broker for my own foolish father? He feels a headache, oh, here it comes, puffing up like a sluggish locomotive behind his eyes.

"We began an affair," Harry says, "but then, because I was married and it was plain hopeless for us, she broke away and wouldn't see me. And she married. And her daughter came along. Time passes, time passes, lots of looking and longing on the sets of a couple of soaps, understand? And then we started up again. Afternoon rendezvous when we weren't taping. We were both of us in love with theater. So when she could slip away from her husband and her little girl, we'd take in a show and sit holding hands in the dark. There was usually a way to get free passes."

Harry is looking down the bright tunnel toward the gates. "I can't tell you," he says in a dreamy voice, "how relieved I am about your mother. That she had her own friend. Even if this Steve Margolies was a boring shmuck. I only wish I'd known before."

It's almost time. He rushes to the bathroom. While he's gone, a clutch of passengers comes through the barrier. An ornate lady in jeans and fur coat, wearing gold and lots of makeup, looks around, looks around. But then she waves at someone else—a grandchild? And Harry's back. He's spotted David staring at the woman. He points an accusing finger at his son. "That bimbo?" he laughs. "So that's what you think of your father's taste in women, huh?"

The locomotive presses in at full throttle. David closes his eyes.

"There she is, coming now," Harry calls out. "You see? What did I tell you?"

That's Nancy? Here's a lady in a tweed coat, mauve wool muffler at her throat, rolling a carry-on behind her. Nancy's lean like a dancer, walks like a dancer. She must have been a beauty once. She's still, in middle age, still a beauty. The ravages of time / the fine sculpting time accomplishes: it depends how you look at it. She's no ingénue, but beautiful in a regal way, big eyes with subtle eye shadow, a broad, strong mouth, a Hepburn (Catherine, Audrey) boniness to her face. Her short hair is colored auburn. David sucks in a giant breath to accommodate the blood rushing to his face as it always does when he's embarrassed or excited. What *is* this? Then he gets it: he's so identified with his father he's experiencing her as if he were Harry. David feels embarrassed for his father, that this attractive, well-dressed woman, rather elegant woman, so outclasses Harry. She's in another league. What would she want with an old, crabby actor in love with his scrapbooks?

David turns to his father. Surprise—Harry stays back, smiling, shy. Karen's the one who comes forward. "You must be Nancy Collins. I'm Karen Bromowitz. Welcome." Karen gives her a hug. "Let me introduce you to David and Michael." Nancy is polite, *So nice you could have me*—but she looks past them. "Hello, Harry."

"Hello, my heart," Harry says. They look and look at one

another; Nancy's eyes are glistening. She shakes her head. "How many years?" he asks.

"Oh, Harry. Over twenty years. Almost a quarter century."

"You! Here I thought years were supposed to matter—you don't look any different. What is this—some kind of miracle?" Harry takes the handle of her carry-on. Karen tugs at David's arm. *Stay back.* David, turning to Karen and Michael, mugs amazement—open mouth, hands outspread —at all this tender charm. Michael's giggling; Karen gives him a severe look, then catches the giggle. But up ahead, Harry Brunell and Nancy Collins don't seem to be aware.

"It's like my dad's playing the role of Sleeping Beauty," he tells Ari a couple of days later. Sunday evening. They're driving in one car to orchestra rehearsal, Ari's van, cello in back. "She's the prince—in this case the princess—who wakes him up. He's a new man, our Sleeping Beauty. He's got the same wattle under his old chin, same bags under his eyes. But all of a sudden he's not crabby, he's alive, a charmer. His voice is full of television honey. For godsakes, yesterday he put on boots and parka and took a walk into the hills with her. You remember how cold it was yesterday? Remember we couldn't warm up the shul? I came home from services to find they'd gone for an actual walk. And no complaints when he came back with her. Of course, he's showing off."

"And this bothers you?"

"No. No, I'm pleased. Except I don't want her fooled and stuck with the guy."

There are things he can't say to Ari: How much he likes talking with Nancy when his father isn't around. Which isn't often. He likes her show business stories—she played Nellie Forbush (*South Pacific*) in a national touring company; she was nominated for a Tony. When her daughter was born, she stopped. "First, I let it slide, and then I gave it up. Same time I gave up your father. Well, actually, no: I gave up your father again and again. Like cigarettes."

"You and Dad. I guess it was a big thing for both of you."

"Big? Oh, God. Oh, my God. David, my dear, no one will ever know."

"He's not…a young man," he says, and means also, *But you, oh, you're still a beautiful woman.* Not all that much older—thirteen years—than he himself. The mauve silk scarf at her throat may disguise skin no longer so firm, may blur facial lines with its subtle color, but it isn't the scarf and the soft, romantic clothing she wears that make her look so full of life. It's in the way she walks across a room. It's in her eyes. She projects this lovely, calm, silent spirit, so that sitting in her presence soothes him. He takes to walking through a room she's left and breathing the perfume.

Nancy's visit is meant to be for a weekend, but on Saturday they invite her to stay on, and on Monday Nancy drives Karen to work so she can take the car for the day. That night Nancy prepares salmon in white wine, baked in parchment, fragrant with herbs. The room is lit by candlelight glowing off the old, oiled pine. "I was her sous-chef," Harry says, patting the back of her hand. "One time on set we cooked together. I mean make-believe cooked. Nance, you remember what that was? Were we married on that show?"

Are they making love? Not likely. Unless…during the day? But the question implies a different way of seeing Harry. Karen has lent Nancy her study as a bedroom. She'll need it back, but for now Karen's willing, because adding Nancy to the family makes their lives less complicated, not more. For now Harry's not demanding, not complaining. When a light snow hits, he bundles up in layers and shovels the walk! One night he and Nancy put on a show—their version of an old soap, played for laughs. He's a wise doctor, she's a mother whose son has been arrested for driving while drunk. Michael pops up and plays the kid. Laughing, David keeps the fire going.

"Harry's such a good actor. Such a pro," Nancy says. "We all knew it. He was never recognized by the men who could give him big parts, but working actors deeply admired him." Stories of Harry. "At first, we went on live," Nancy says. "I remember one day an actor began to flub. He couldn't read the cue cards. Drunk, I think. Harry took over, helped us improvise around the man. Anyway, at the end, each of the folks on set went over to Harry and hugged him or shook his hand."

When he's at work, David thinks about Nancy a lot. He'll be checking specs for the construction of a bearing wall and there she'll be in his office in her wools and silks, and he'll say to himself, *I can't be in* love *with her,* and he'll say, *It's just part of my war with Dad.* But oh, the grace she's brought into the household. He looks forward to coming home. Evenings, before dinner, pushing back table and chairs, she does yoga in the living room. After giving up the theater, she taught yoga, even had a studio for a few years. At first David just gawks. The lady in lycra. But this becomes too embarrassing, and the second night, he changes into exercise clothes and joins her. His own yoga is rusty, klutzy. She doesn't try to teach him; he copies her moves.

It's as if they're all on stage, Nancy director; they have each other for audience. The roles call for kindness. When Harry asks about the rebuilding—When the hell is it going to start?—and makes a dig, "Ahh, cobblers' children—the last to get shoes," one look from Nancy, head tilted in disapproval, shuts him up. Often, she tilts her head to one side like that: "Harry?" That's it, that's plenty. Whatever he's been saying, he stops. He grins at her. This, David prophesizes, won't last.

Every night Harry dresses up for dinner. One night, a blue silk shirt and maroon velvet waistcoat, Nancy's gifts. "Where did you get anything so gorgeous?" Karen asks. "On line," Nancy says. "They came in two days. Isn't the man beautiful?"

She puffs Harry up a little; otherwise, there's a no-nonsense severity about her; it's part of why David trusts her. One night she and David are washing up after dinner. She puts the last plate into the dishwasher, leans back against the sink, sponge in hand. "I see you looking at me, David. You're always looking at me. Are you saying to yourself, 'This woman stole my father from me'?"

"No. That's not why I look at you."

"Why do you?"

"I see what my father sees in you."

"That's very sweet."

"But I think I see you more truly than he can."

"You look so much like Harry when you're embarrassed. Your eyes, your long face—like a hound. So, David? You wonder why I put up with Harry? I do know what I'm getting into."

At the Shabbos table, a couple of weeks after Nancy first came, Harry taps his glass with his knife. "Folks, Nancy and me, we're going down to Florida. We're going to go stroll hand in hand on a beach in Florida—at least till the flowers decide to fly back to Massachusetts."

Nancy adds, "You've been wonderful. Karen. David. Michael. It's time to see how we do on our own."

"So you see? You see? There's still an *our*," Harry says. "Can you believe it? Here I am seventy-eight years old, and after a quarter century my girl still says '*our*'."

"'Girl'! What a real fool you can be, Harry. 'Girl'!"

And Harry, grinning at being chastised, says, "Yeah. I know, I know."

Amazing! A Harry who can acknowledge foolishness? That night David can't sleep. He comes downstairs and sits in front of the fire, stokes the embers and adds a couple of logs. He thinks about their destructive fire; he thinks about his father's call for warmth. Since Nancy arrived, has he said a single word about the heat? Here's another story: the fire as a call for attention, a call for forgiveness, a call for warmth?

Story piled upon story. And he, David, what is he? Oedipus smitten with a surrogate mother figure? That's something he'll be able to laugh about with Karen—but...not just yet. Story on story. Michael said tonight, after Harry and Nancy had gone off for a walk, "I think I understand Grandpa. Such a great story. The guy was bored, he had nothing left, he needed a little fire in his life. Fire, get it? Then, kaboom, this woman comes and everything changes. He's in a romance, it's great, he's young and hot again. It's really a cool old story out of Hollywood."

David's picture of Harry is buckling, a Picasso cubist portrait. As he drives Harry and Nancy down to Bradley, bags in the trunk, Harry at his side looks like a million dollars in his camel-hair coat. Sitting at the wheel, glancing over at his handsome father, David has a moment of insane identification: part of himself will be flying down to Florida tonight.

Lights of the runway glow just past the fence. A jet coming in for a landing whines left to right a few hundred feet over their heads. He drives them up the departure ramp to American and lifts their bags from the trunk. Harry says, "Don't think you're getting rid of me this easy. Nancy and I, we're just on a vacation. We'll see. Okay?"

"Anytime. Both of you. Any time."

Nancy laughs. "Your father's giving himself an escape hatch, David, dear."

Harry throws up his hands. "See? She knows everything." He hugs David; kissing him, he whispers, "Listen, Davey—I'm real sorry about that fire. You tell Karen."

Goodbye, goodbye. David kisses Nancy's cheek. Call us, remember to call us…

Back on the airport access road, at first he feels relief, lightness. On the radio, a blues by Coltrane. But then—how peculiar—tears well up, and his breath is hot. Why tears? Hasn't he gotten just what he wanted? He has. Thank God his father is off his shoulders. But a heavy knowing sits in his chest: Of course. His father, flying off—it's replaying the old story, his father deserting him. He's a kid back in New Jersey, his father is off somewhere, his mother down in the dumps.

That's true. But just around a corner of his mind, there's something more.

It's not until he's made the turn onto I-91 North that—ahh!—it comes to him with a jolt—ahh!—such a jolt he has to pull over to the side of the road and take deep breaths. Acid, rising to his throat, burns. It's that lie of his, giving his mother a lover. A useful lie that moved his father to get off his behind? But suppose—suppose it wasn't a lie! After all, there *were* so many nights, especially as he grew older, she was out of the house. Suppose all that time there *was* someone. Maybe not Margolies. That name came to him out of the blue. But someone. He pictures his mother's face as she's heading off to one of her meetings. She's full of life, of nervous good humor. He sees her bend down, apply lipstick in front of the hall mirror. "So? How do I look? Please, dear," she says before he could answer, "don't wait up for me. In case the meeting runs late." Dad's right: there were so many meetings. And those long weekends he was deposited with the

Kadens. Who *was* this favorite aunt of hers? Why didn't Aunt Sarah ever come for a visit?

He looks in the rear-view mirror as he pulls out onto the road. Oh! He's got to call his sister Rose, he thinks, driving along to Miles Davis on Public Radio. What does Rose remember?

He sees his mother leave the table, close the door of the bedroom to make a phone call. Mostly, she called from the kitchen, from the living room. But there were times....

If that's true—well, it changes his whole childhood.

When he gets home, Michael is doing homework. Karen's correcting exams. It's peaceful, but he's stirred up. If he tells Karen, she'll make light of the clues—well, hardly *clues* at all. Nine P.M. He has to wait at least an hour till Rose is through with her family's dinner out in Seattle.

She answers on the first ring. "Let me get off the other line," she says.

He's been rehearsing for an hour. The story tumbles out: the fire, Nancy's visit, the lie that may not be a lie... "So? Tell me. What do you remember?"

"Not that much," Rose says. "I don't even know any Steve Margolies. But don't you remember how we used to tease her when she'd go out?"

"No. Tease about what?"

"Oh, Davey. You know. That man—the man who was her doctor. I can't remember his name. He'd pick her up in his Lincoln to take her to meetings. You don't remember that?"

"Vaguely. Yes, vaguely."

"When Mom would look down-in-the-mouth, we'd get mad at Dad and imagine she might marry that man. We said, what a good dad he'd make. Maybe I remember better because I used to wonder about the nice clothes she wore, and the pearls—for a meeting? Davey? I always guessed."

He says nothing to Karen. He sits in his study and puts Dvorak on the stereo, listens over the headphones Karen bought him for Hanukkah. But it doesn't work; he shuts down the music.

If only he could call his mother.

She's sitting at the kitchen table. It's morning. Maybe he's home with a cold. Her coffee cup is empty, two cigarette butts are crumpled in her saucer; the sour smell of tobacco fills the kitchen. He sits across from her with hot chocolate or tea she's made him, grieving together with her about her life, not knowing how to relieve her sadness. Lover or no lover, it must have been hard for her, especially back then, when a woman felt so defined by her husband. Even in his absence, she organized the clippings about Harry the clipping service sent her. He sees them in neat piles on the kitchen table. She looks up: "When you're older, I can tell you a few things that will surprise you." She said that so often. Was having a lover one of those things? Maybe there was someone else to comfort her. If so, that guy, too, failed to assuage her sorrow. What to do with this revised childhood?

He turns to his desk. He begins sketching the new room.

Karen comes in with a cup of tea and puts it on his desk. "So," she says, "they must be halfway to Florida by now. Nice having our house back." She looks over his shoulder. "Is it this house you're drawing plans for?"

He's going to make it really beautiful, he tells her, build a bigger room on an expanded foundation, add on a small conservatory for her orchids and seedlings and, "we'll have an enclosed porch—see here?—that looks out on the garden and the hillside."

"Beautiful! It'll be just beautiful."

She's unambivalently happy; for David it's not so simple. This house feels a little empty. It makes him remember their house in New Jersey.

Say it's a weekend night and his mother is stuck there alone with him and Rose. Stuck is how it feels, the energy is stuck. He can't help her. Emptiness weighs down the house. The television spreads noise to lift the weight, but fails. Television reminds them of the absent Harry. David hates the bastard; but he longs for him to show up. And sometimes, unexpectedly, Harry does show up. And it's as if there's a sudden infusion of light; everything glows. Those nights—probably, he sees now, it's times Nancy can't get away from her family—his father walks in with a garish superfluity of flowers, candy for him and Rose, a huge steak from the city an inch and a half thick. "Let's broil this baby," he sings, and wings the wrapped, raw steak like a football to David. Replaying the scene, David feels in his own chest the unease, the emptiness, his father must feel and blusters to fill. But for the time being his father does fill it, for himself and for his family; the house lights up, it's a living house.

Maybe his mother has been cooking; without a word, laughing, her face flushed, she sets aside the food and puts up water for potatoes, rubs the steak with crushed garlic and pepper, turns on the broiler. She goes upstairs to change and do her hair. Soon the kitchen is hot and pungent with charred, rare steak. Harry's singing show tunes, Rose accompanies him on piano, and David, giddy, runs for his violin. False, all false, each of them showing the others how much life there is, what a real family they are. No way to rewrite that.

Now he's left, David, with a hole in his heart. All these years later. Isn't that strange? As if he were the phony blusterer. The hole, an empty room awaiting a father. You can write all sorts of stories about that time, turn your life this way and that, but stories won't fill that room. No matter how you tell what went on, you can't get rid of it, can't fill it, can't burn it down. He's sitting in his own study trying to draw a new room, trying to remake himself, to father himself. When spring comes he'll build, God willing, a room full of light. But it won't fill the hole in his heart.

Friends

He saw her first at his doctor's office over on Park Avenue, his regular doctor he'd been with for years. Saw her a couple of times. Ben Abrams liked the way she smiled at the receptionist. And when she smiled, he liked the funny little space between her two front teeth. A sexy imperfection.

He was dying; she was blooming. That's the way it was.

Dr. Peretz' waiting room was carpeted in warm beige wool; light from table lamps was golden; the walls were paneled and the chairs were like those in his sister's house in Great Neck. Even in those days—this was 1953—you paid for professional warmth. Well, and why shouldn't he pay? I'm telling you this because it influenced the way he saw her. You know how in films of the thirties they covered the lens with a silk stocking to soften the skin? She was, after all, in her late thirties, only a few years younger than his wife, and in 1953 that wasn't so young. Maybe the lighting helped him uncover her innocence; for he saw her as painfully innocent. Not a New York matron. For instance, she wore no pancake makeup; maybe a little eye liner, that's all. She wore a white blouse with pearl buttons and a black wool skirt. Very simple, very plain, but high quality goods. He owned and ran a small, high-end dress company on 38th Street; he knew material.

Then he saw her around the neighborhood. Ben Abrams lived at 25 West 81st, just across from the Planetarium, and some evenings when he came home from work he'd have to take the damned dog for a walk because Carol had a meeting with the sisterhood at their temple. He'd walk around the block till the cocker *kocht*, and sometimes stop at Sheffrin's Delicatessen and have them make up a roast beef sandwich to take home. And once, there she was, coming out of the pharmacy on 82nd, and once in the early September dusk he saw her walking alone in the Planetarium park, and he had the strong desire to cross over to her. What would she say if he came over out of the blue like that? Not that he would. Some men were like that, but it wasn't in his makeup, godforbid. Besides, he was too old for her. For that matter, he was too old for Carol. Sixty-one. According to two separate doctors—Dr. Peretz and a specialist—he wasn't going to make sixty-five.

Which was, frankly, almost acceptable to him. He was tired of dresses, and Carol wasn't much company. He'd gotten married in his mid-thirties to a very young woman, and as she grew up and her undergraduate sweet sexiness fell away, he found he'd married someone he basically didn't respect. He thought her callow, a little shrill, a frantic shopper. And how come he hadn't seen those qualities in advance? Sex was the one-word answer. Sure. But not just sex—it seemed smart, too, to marry into Carol's family. He'd been head salesman, and the old man had liked him, had brought him home when Carol was just out of high school. An old story. He married the family business.

Thank God, their children were grown up and out of the house; Larry would be a lawyer this coming June; Sylvia was engaged to be married to a very nice young man. Ben hoped he could stick around for Larry's graduation, for Sylvia's wedding. But at least Larry would say Kaddish for him; not every day, but maybe once a week. And Carol? Would she take time off from shopping and fund raising for Hadassah to say goodbye at the hospital? Ahh, Carol was the way she was. He wished he could talk to her a little better. What did they talk about?—a new couch, a television, a vacation trip. But maybe at the end things would change in that department. At the end. Pain, he was definitely afraid of. He was afraid of pain, but over the years he'd squirreled away some potent pain killers, never mind how, and had a little understanding with his doctor to look the other way.

Still, still, he felt old yearnings when he saw this woman in the park. She looked so sad. He imagined she was lonely. She didn't even have the excuse of walking a dog. For him, seeing her was almost a religious event, seeing her in a little blue wool hat tilted to the side like a beret. She wasn't pretty like a model. Small face but a full mouth and her hair wild, black, curly, worn too long for someone out of her teens, hair held in some kind of check with a barrette. He and she must be sharing breaths of the same molecules of air—though only he knew. He heaved a great breath. There in the dusk between them in the little park with the black iron railings, God hovered between them. It's true! "Come on, Beast," he said to the cocker spaniel, "let's go on home."

Beast's real—Carol-given—name was Champagne. Carol was home when he got back, wearing a new outfit—from Henri Bendel, he guessed. The dresses his company made, though expensive, she'd never wear. "Oh, Champagne, Champagne!" Crouching, she cradled the dog's head in her arms, a young girl again. Then, embarrassed at her own gushing over a dog, she touched Ben's cheek—"So how did your day go?"—and turned away to pour them cocktails. He knew better than to waste his time telling her; it would just irritate him to see she wasn't listening. "And you?" he asked. And she nodded and handing him a drink, went into the bedroom to change.

On Saturdays after Shabbat morning service and a nosh, he liked to wander through one of the museums. This particular Saturday he was alone—his old friend Howard Stein couldn't make it—and Ben found himself facing a lion. This was years before the Museum of Natural History charged admission, before it grew slick and exciting and you had to queue up on a Saturday. It was before shooting specimens was problematic. The lions moved him, and so did the great blue whale that hung in a room the size of half a football field.

And all by herself on a polished granite bench in front of an African scene, a family of zebras and a solitary giraffe by a watering hole, was the same pretty woman. Thin, slight, in profile a delicate oval of a face, like an old cameo. It was her serious look that made him think of the cameo. The point is, it wasn't a social look; it was private. He wasn't used to quiet, serious eyes, especially on a woman. Not even on his sister, whom he knew better than he knew himself. Women charmed; they demonstrated for someone's benefit how happy, how angry, how melancholy, they were. They struck poses. Yes, much more than men. And it wasn't their fault, their dependence; this was, after all, a world ruled by men. The war had changed that, but it seemed worse now than before.

He sat at the other end of the granite bench and stared through the big window at the giraffe and zebras. In peripheral vision she must have seen him turn to her; she turned to him and raised her eyebrows. "I couldn't think where I knew you from," he lied. "It's Dr. Peretz, the waiting room."

"Oh. Yes. That's right." She smiled and closed her eyes a moment and folded her hands. "Dr. Peretz. Yes."

Oh my.

Was she laughing at him, knowing he'd seen her in the neighborhood? Had she seen him with Beast? He was flustered. Not wanting to be caught doing so, he searched her fingers; yes, she wore a diamond ring, a gold wedding band. Well, good. He wasn't about to start something. But maybe—why not?—they could talk. If anything, her rings made that easier. He avoided her dark eyes, waved at the glassed-in display cases. "I love these. They're works of art. Sit long enough you can walk around inside. People confuse this with Africa. I know better. But for what it is, I like it—I like coming in from modern New York City and seeing such creatures."

"It's a refuge."

"Like a sanctuary. I mean in shul. You're Jewish?" And the question gave him permission to look her over. She looked Italian, Greek, but yes, she said, she was Jewish. An Iranian Jew.

They walked past the scenes of Africa, went to India to look at tigers. Ben said, "It's sad, of course. Rich men with nothing better to do but shoot these creatures, and so a museum is built to lend purpose to the shooting. I feel a little shame coming in here. Jews don't hunt. Do you know any Jewish hunters?"

"It has more to do with class," she said. "It's an upper-class activity. And a *sign* of class."

"I suppose you're right," he said.

There was a pleasure to this; pleasure especially in acceding to her. Taking her seriously. She had the habit of pausing, considering, before she spoke. It was amazing how precious their talking seemed, as if each phrase were surrounded by a fringe of light.

"You have children?" he asked.

She had. She and Gerald had three boys, the oldest a junior in high school, the youngest in seventh grade. So they talked about their children, and because they lived just around the corner from each other, they made a time to walk through the park the following week. It was what he thought about all week on the subway ride to work, home from work. But he was a busy man, it was a busy fall season, thank God, plenty of re-orders. Most of the time he forgot about Shira.

"So? Do you think we can get away with this?" he asked her some weeks later.

"But what are we getting away with?"

"Exactly."

Her husband Gerald played bridge very seriously on Saturday afternoons; her boys were busy with friends and sports. And Carol met with the sisterhood. So Ben and Shira met at the museum, walked in the park on nice days, or in one of the museums when the fall grew cold and damp. They never talked about spouses. She told him about her boys. Once she let him know when she was taking the youngest for a haircut, so he could see the boy. Before shul on a Saturday morning, he walked over to Amsterdam and half hidden by the spiraling barber pole, he peeked in the window.

Though his eyes weren't perfect, he could spot her blue beret as she climbed the steps to the museum. Sometimes she wore a cashmere scarf in pale mauve that flowed into the beret. As they walked, the soft scarf lifted in the wind and touched his face. Once they went to a restaurant on Broadway for tea. It was there he told her about his condition. Slowly, you see, he was dying.

"We're all dying," she said.

He held his hand to his heart. He tapped his fingers to his chest.

"Oh, Ben." She nodded. "And here we are just getting to know each other."

He was impressed that she didn't try to undo his dying with words of hope or comfort. "You know what I worry about?" he asked.

"What?"

"You'll think this is foolish. When we hardly know each other. I'm embarrassed to say. I worry that I'll die, Shira, and you won't even know."

She closed her eyes and nodded. "That would be sad. But you know what? I don't think it'll happen. No. And Ben? It's better you don't call me. It's perfectly innocent, but please. Gerald's mother lives with us. She's always home. A good woman, but you know…"

"Don't worry," he said.

Ben Abrams was trim, always well dressed. He met Shira in the expensive suit he wore to synagogue. More and more she was becoming his sanctuary, his Sabbath rest. But there was unease, too. September, October, he was between tans—he'd lost his summer tan and hadn't yet been to Florida. Before he joined her Saturday afternoons, he rubbed his cheeks to bring the color back.

He was, it's true, vain about his looks. Handsome as a young man, spoiled by women—clothes models, buyers—now he looked distinguished; diplomat or senior military man more than dress manufacturer. Tall, lean, a handball player until this medical business began, his short hair thick and mostly dark. He was gallant with her, opening doors and paying little checks for tea after they'd taken their walk. She wasn't strong, could walk even less than he, and she didn't have age or a bum heart as an excuse. He was protective, sheltering; she was submissive, letting him choose the walk, the café. She enjoyed being held by him, supported, affirmed. He took her small arm through the Persian wool coat to lead her across Columbus Circle. His fingers brushed back a lock of hair that had tumbled down over her ear. On the Sabbath we are enjoined to speak words of holiness. He felt, walking home alone after leaving her, that they had spoken holy words.

Shira needed no support when they talked ideas. He hadn't her level of education; he felt his mind was badly trained, and on a daily basis it got exercised with dummies who knew only one thing—money. He loved her intellectual fervor; he didn't mind knowing less than she or caring less than she. For instance, she mourned the deaths, that past June, of Julius and Ethel Rosenberg. He'd hardly thought about it; if asked, he'd have said he considered their execution a mistake, but thought they must have done something. The government had evidence it couldn't talk about. But he liked it that it grieved her so much, liked the lines at the corners of her eyes, her sigh of sympathy for the Rosenberg children, and at once he took on the grief.

He was so much older, but she knew things he didn't know. An art student as a girl, she knew so much about painting, and when they went through the Met, she explained things. And then music—well, he knew show tunes, jazz; she was a serious violinist and had studied composition. He wished they could attend a concert together, but he was afraid to make the suggestion.

But one lovely November day when the sun was strong, she brought along her violin in its canvas case, and when they were alone, in the bare Shakespeare's Garden by the castle and little pond, he sat on a bench and she stood and played for him, she played Brahms. The sound was lost in the cool air, but he sat close to the violin and listened. *Oh*, he said. *Oh my*. She put away the violin, they walked. There was nothing green in November, and this was years before the park was restored—it was bleak, seedy, full of trash—but they walked its paths like adolescent lovers.

She had to get home before the boys did. That cut short their afternoons. "Some time soon, I'll have to cook for you," she said. "I'd love to cook for you." It would never happen.

At home, these past weeks, Carol seemed different, more present, greeting him with attention when he came home, cooking with care. She fussed over the table. There were candles, flowers. She wore even more makeup than usual. "You're all dolled up," he said. "Well, I'm not some yenta," she said. "How many women my age look the way I look?" She meant that she dressed young, hadn't taken on the matronly look of the other women in their temple. How peculiar. Maybe, he thought, she'd become aware of his growing distance and that made her uneasy—though God knows why she'd care. Maybe she *knew*—not that there was very much to know. He found himself hiding from her, hiding more than his knowing Shira. He walked around the apartment with his eyes cast down to avoid hers. He certainly wouldn't talk about his condition, afraid that if he told her he was dying, she'd sympathize, and it would bring them closer; *close* he wanted to save for Shira.

But why had Shira grown close to *him*? This he couldn't fathom. Was she looking for a father? Her father had died some years ago. Her husband was in his early forties, successful in real estate. Maybe he was a terrible husband; she never said. If she spoke of him, she spoke kindly. But one Saturday she took Ben's hand across the table and caressed it, held it to her cheek. Like a lover?—yet they'd never even kissed. Maybe he had it all wrong. Maybe it was rather as a kind older friend, an uncle, that she felt close to him. He touched her cheek. Her small face, dark eyes, shone with tears. Tears? Did she love him? It would be so foolish to love him, this dying businessman. What was there to love?

Often he felt there were things she wasn't saying. Secrets. As if she was trying to tell him something, ask him something. Often. But she never did. And it seemed that the more she saw him caring about her, the less forthcoming she was. Yet when they said goodbye and she went home to her family, each time she'd tell him, "It's so good to talk to you."

The first time he bought a present for her, a little Cornelian shell cameo, an idealized classical profile set in gold on a delicate gold chain, on that Saturday afternoon she didn't show up. But she called him at work on Monday; maybe she could get away one evening in the middle of the week. There were things to talk about. He called a small hotel on the East Side and made a reservation for Wednesday. He was going out of town, he told Carol. In their long marriage, never had he done such a thing. And even now, it might come only to friendship; probably, it should. *Probably* he was lying to himself. No, *definitely* he was lying. He knew it was only because he was dying that he could do such a thing, as if approaching death entitled him. What did she want to tell him? Was her husband being unfaithful? Did she want to start a new life with him? What—a life of a year or two? It seemed hopeless.

They were to meet at the Russian Tea Room on 57th Street. He was there before her. His poor heart was beating like a kid's. Sitting over a glass of wine, he fingered the gift box in his jacket pocket. He looked at himself in the mirrored wall—the ruin of the athlete he'd been. Faded. Still handsome, he thought, but only in clothes. If they became lovers, would they undress in the dark? And would he be a good enough lover for this woman so much younger? He promised himself he'd be very tender, very slow; the sex would be speech.

But she didn't come and didn't come, and he couldn't call. He sat an hour and went off to the hotel and stayed a terrible night alone.

He couldn't call, and she didn't call him at work. Maybe it was for the best. But shouldn't she write him at least? She didn't write, and the following Saturday afternoon, she didn't meet him at the museum. The lion was stuffed skin. It was too cold to walk in the park. He went back home.

Carol must be home. He could smell recent cigarette smoke as soon as he came in. The cast recording of *South Pacific* was on the turntable. Maybe the one thing he shared with Carol—besides the children—was their love of Broadway musicals. He'd heard this record enough to know a scratch was coming, and at once he headed to the phonograph to tap the needle as it stuck.

"Carol?"

She was fussing in her closet in the bedroom, reorganizing. Clothes and more clothes on the bed. "I thought you were with your women friends," he said. "Fundraising or something."

"Oh, Ben." She put down on the bed several hangers with dresses, jackets, skirts. "Ben, I can read you like a book. You think I don't know what you think of me?"

"That's not entirely true," he said. "It's wonderful that you do good work for the temple."

"Please. Sit. I have something to tell you." She took a long inhale. This was a year when cigarettes punctuated sentences. "You always said I should have married someone my own age."

He sat. He felt a miracle was about to happen.

"I'm a very romantic woman," she said.

"I've never denied it. So. Are you saying you've got a…boyfriend?"

"A 'boyfriend'—please!"

"And do I know this man?"

"You know him very well. It's Arnold Mankin from temple. You know Arnie. Look. I've waited a decent amount of time. The children are out in the world. Why go on like this?" She saw him looking at the clothes laid out on the bed. "Don't worry, I'm not leaving this minute. We'll wait until after the wedding. When Sylvia is settled. Don't you think that's a good idea?"

"Absolutely a good idea," he said. "Definitely. So…what are you doing with the clothes?"

"I'm bringing a few things over to Arnie's. Don't worry, officially I'll still be here. There's plenty of time." She put her arm over Ben's shoulder. "It's not been all bad," she said.

Now it became urgent for him to reach Shira. But if he called, what would he say to her husband? In 1953 men and women were rarely "friends". If she wanted not to see him again, he should understand and be grateful for their time together. Enough. But she lived around the corner, and so he began taking Beast for walks past her apartment building. Carol had left him with the dog—this Arnie of hers—Arnie couldn't stand dogs—and so Ben had the excuse for walks. He stared past the doorman deep into her lobby. He walked in the little park by the Planetarium. He stopped in at the shops along Columbus Avenue—the pharmacy, the deli, the A&P.

At work he'd ask Sally, his receptionist, "Has anyone called?" No one had called. The fall line was selling well; they were showing the spring line. He was thankful he was busy. Sitting down a little dizzy after a discussion with the head cutter, he found it very funny and blurted a laugh: he might die before Carol had a chance to leave. It seemed like a joke. How surprised she'd be. The kids would never know there'd been a problem between them. Just as well. But Shira—Shira would never know he'd died, and that wasn't so funny. Should he write her? Suppose her husband picked up the mail. The last thing he wanted was to get her in trouble.

But after awhile, after almost a month and frankly it wasn't getting any easier, he called, he had to call. If her husband answered, or her mother-in-law, well, he was selling Hoovers.

But when a strange voice, a woman, answered, he simply hung up. Days passed, and he called again. And this time, when a woman answered, he asked, "Is Mrs. Ullman available?"

"I'm sorry, but Mrs. Ullman," the voice said, "has passed away."

"Passed away?"

"My son is sitting shiva for her this week. We're sitting shiva. You're a friend?"

"An acquaintance."

"Then you know. From cancer. And so the children will grow up without their mother," she sighed. "We're sitting shiva until Friday. A service at our house seven-thirty tonight, tomorrow night."

Getting off the phone, he looked out the office window onto West 38th. A gray late December morning, dirty snow lumped between cars. Down in the street Cadillac pushers—the young men who rolled metal carts with high frames and racks of clothing—rolled their carts alongside the traffic. It was a furious morning. Cabbies, truck drivers honked. He could hear the whining and rumbling of machines from the factory floor. He locked the door to his office. He removed his shoes. He sat on the dusty floor. He couldn't have said why. He said in Hebrew, *Blessed are You...the true judge. Dayan ha'emet.* He sat on the floor and tried to weep, but it was as if the source of his tears were gone. Quietly he keened, a high-pitched howl that might have sounded like a cutting machine, a drill from somewhere—no one bothered him.

That evening he worked late, grabbed a sandwich at the deli across the street, and took a taxi uptown to pay a shiva call. He wept dry-eyed in the cab. He could hide, he felt, within the minyan. Nobody would know him, nobody would ask.

A young boy answered his ring. "I'm very sorry for your loss," Ben said, taking a yarmulke from a box by the door. From another box, a prayer book. The apartment was crowded, full of the odor of too many perfumes. Behind the boy came an older woman—the voice on the phone, Gerald Ullman's mother, he was sure. A big-boned woman about his own age. "I'm very sorry for your loss," he said. She sighed and put a hand to her heart.

"A dear woman," she said. "You knew my daughter-in-law well?"

"Just from the doctor's office," he said. "But she was very kind. We talked."

"So fast," she said. "So fast. A few months." She sighed the way his own mother used to sigh. "Such courage. Never did she talk about being sick. At the end…well, you can imagine…. The rabbi should be here any minute. Let me introduce you to Gerald before the service."

"That's really not necessary," Ben said.

A red-eyed young man with a scruff of mourner's beard stood up. "You knew my wife?"

"Just from the doctor's office, Dr. Peretz on Park."

"Oh. We thank you for coming." Gerald seemed so young, a good-looking man with curly reddish hair. A strip of black cloth was pinned to his lapel.

"May you be comforted," Ben said, "among the mourners of Zion and Jerusalem." Why, he could be this man's father. And in the oddest way, he felt toward him like a father, or at least an uncle. In his presence, Ben's tears welled up; his eyes blurred. He wanted to comfort.

A small woman in black was sitting alone in a corner. Shira's mother? Clearly, she had been crying; her face was blotched; she was nodding to herself. One of the boys took her by the hand and led her to the folding chairs. Gerald, the children, a sister, friends, began to take seats.

The mirror over the couch was covered. A shiva candle glowed on the mantle over the fake fireplace. Bowls, platters of fruit, cakes, cheeses, crackers were squeezed onto the table in the dining room, but that was for after the service, and the family grew uneasy. Where was the rabbi?

"I'll call. You have the number?" his mother asked Gerald.

Mrs. Ullman went off to call and a minute later came back, stood in the archway, and rocking her head, fingers to lips, announced, "Rabbi Berger is very, very sorry. He can't be here tonight. His wife says he thought only tomorrow night he'd promised." Silence. Who could lead?

This was a house of secular Jews. There were twenty, thirty friends and relatives; not a single prayer leader. "We don't need a rabbi," someone said. But that wasn't an offer. Again, silence.

Ben said, "If you wish…I'd be honored to lead." Not that he was a big *macher* of a prayer leader, but often he'd led a service in a house of mourning.

"Thank you, thank you," Gerald said.

He stayed in his seat. "Welcome. I'm Ben Abrams. I didn't know Shira well. But I know what a wonderful woman she was. We're going to begin the evening service. Please open your books to page fifty-seven. We rise for the *Barekhu*…"

Chanting and murmuring the Hebrew, he felt giddy both with grief and irony. When they came to the Mourners' Kaddish, he said the words with the family, helping the family, who needed the transliteration at the back of the book. The second time, when only the immediate family should say the Mourners' Kaddish, Ben, without the right to do so, led the prayer. *Yitgadal v'yitkadash shemei raba*…. He imagined that he was the real husband, saying Kaddish for his wife of many years. And then he had the peculiar idea that he was saying Kaddish for himself as well.

As prayer leader he asked Gerald, would he like to say a few words about Shira?

Gerald started to tell how they met, but he couldn't speak. To collect himself, he took up a photo album, let the pictures help tell his story. "Here's Shira when we first met. She was nineteen, studying painting at the Art Students' League on 57th. Look how beautiful she was. I was studying engineering. Then—here, this picture—I was at Pratt and Whitney and we had Michael…"

So. Their too-brief life together. A marriage. For Gerald, Pratt and Whitney during the war, then into management and upper management. And Shira took care of the boys and sometimes still painted. She was "an original", he said. That painting over the couch, of a landscape in patches of green and gold, that was hers. But what her life was like, Gerald didn't say. "She was a wonderful mother to these boys," he said, cupping the head of the two older boys with his hands. Strange—he didn't complete the cliché, *wonderful* wife *and mother.* Did the omission mean anything?

The boys didn't speak. Friends spoke about her gentleness, her reserve. Her mother could say only, "my beauty, my baby," and fall to weeping, comforted by a grandson. Gerald told anecdotes of Shira and the boys. Ben didn't speak; he was an outsider. Her real life, whatever it was, was here; he had no place in it, and that was right. But if he had spoken, what would he have told them? "She was a kind, gentle woman. I hardly knew her." He would not have said, "I loved her."

In a century—a century!—*hardly*; in just a blink of the eye, someone looking back at their lives wouldn't be able to say who had died first. While Gerald talked, Ben imagined himself and Shira as star-crossed lovers in a story, dying together. Or no, not star-crossed: secret man and wife. But of course, no one *would* look at their lives; for the world it would be as if they'd never met at all. He closed his eyes and instantly saw her in blue beret and Persian lamb coat. *But we met.*

There is a kind of seeing, he thought, in which the facts of our biographies don't define us; in which tender afternoons sustain their shape. When two people love one another, he thought, even for a little while, maybe a new soul comes into being. At any rate, that's how it feels. Maybe one soul for Gerald and Shira, one soul for Shira and me. Or maybe I'm just fooling myself. Love? Maybe she needed the comfort of being with someone going through what she was going through. Even—even if she just couldn't tell him. How he wished she could have told him.

The Lord is my shepherd, I shall not want...Ben sang it softly in his husky voice, in the Hebrew; then they read it in English. Gerald Ullman shook his hand, thanked him for leading. "I don't know how we would have managed."

"It was my honor." He held Gerald's hand in both his own. He wanted to hold Gerald in his arms. But this wasn't done between men in America in 1953.

When he got home that night to an empty house, he opened the box and held the cameo up to the light of his bedside lamp. He put on his reading glasses to see it in focus. What did a Victorian profile with stylized classical hairdo have to do with the face of Shira, an Iranian Jew? He felt sad and foolish. And now, what could he do with it? Put it in a desk drawer? He held the cameo in his palm and ran his thumb over the ridges of the lady's cool face. There was no one here to judge him. So what if he's a fool? He hung the chain around his neck and felt the pendant against his chest. That was the way he went to sleep.

Voices

Words come to him at the edge of sleep.

Hebrew. Bits of daily prayers, of daily blessings. Fragments in English, voices, many voices, no one he knows: *inasmuch as...the forlorn ones...adversary song*. A sign of sleep to come. But it's not his own sleep he's entering. It's somebody else's dream. He's listening in. Whose dream is this? And in the daytime: Gliding down the mile-long hill on his drive to the clinic, voices in his ears, obscure gestures, pure lilt and syntax. He invents a political thriller: a receiver has been sewn into a subcutaneous pouch of a spy. Then who's on the other end of the line, whispering mischief? He's had schizophrenic patients who firmly believed such things. Or maybe messenger angels—*malachai*—with words of prophecy? I don't think so, thanks all the same.

Sam Krassner has an investment in the dynamics of individual unconscious processes—a costly investment—a PhD in psychology and years of clinical training. This training says: you may not know what's happening, but you can bet a soul-struggle is going on. Something worked on, worked out; it's residue of battle he's hearing at a distance. But suppose the voices are nothing personal. Think of all the griefs he's privy to every day. In his private practice in Northampton, Massachusetts, he hears subtle suffering like his own: spouse, sibling, parents; guilt, grief, rage. At the clinic, the same, but compounded with intermeshed griefs of class and race he resists taking inside. Or perhaps they *are* inside, the words duplicating themselves in him like a virus—sorrowing, raging words no longer tied to particular voices.

And they *are* waves, for they can't be distinguished. Look. One client at the clinic, Barbara Hammond, yes, sure she's neurotic, enacts "narcissistic injury," but mixed up with so many other troubles—she's obese and diabetic; ashamed of herself as a physical being, she can't get a decent job, doesn't believe she could be trained for anything even if she had money for training, and this assumption that she's a dead-end person humiliates her further, so that, as she expects, she is demeaned by her out-of-work husband, who debases her when he bothers coming home; and in turn she demeans her children, who enact their humiliation by doing dismally in school, continuing the pattern. A circle of pain. Circles overlap circles. And it's not just personal. Powerless, does Barbara even care that she is represented in the State Legislature by a guy who consistently votes against funding the social services that might help her change her life?

Sam wonders: maybe the words he hears are of love needing to be expressed. Isn't it true he has to keep his clients' suffering at bay? You might call it a sensible professional attitude, but that's not it. After all, he can effect so little change; he resists feeling for Barbara or, say, the enraged counterman, or the mother of a boy with terminal cancer. He stays outside the poverty and chaos of these lives. What good would it do to open his heart? But maybe his heart has a different opinion.

Sam's life is stuck. Is that why the voices have been busy? He makes this discovery: if on his noontime walk he sits on a bench and, closing his eyes, holds his cell to his ear, pretends to be on the phone, he can listen to voices under voices. Like in a busy restaurant. Sometimes a phrase from a news report, sometimes Blessed Are You O Lord, or murmurs so ambiguous he doesn't know in what language. The quieter he gets, the deeper the place from which the voices seem to come. It's as if he had a surveillance microphone and could keep extending its focus further and further through crowds of talk—fifty feet, a hundred, a hundred fifty.

It's after a certain therapy session with Barbara Hammond that the words seem to tell him that he should do something. What happens is this:

Hot September day. Barbara comes in, heaving as always her 250 pounds side to side, falling forward hip to hip. A beauty about her in spite of the weight, she reminds him of an enormous blues singer. Today on one hip she hefts a three-year old, her youngest, and sits in the upholstered chair, child in her lap. Yards and yards of material in that flowered summer dress; the child floats in it. Barbara says sorry, sorry, sorry, last minute my neighbor called, she's sick, can't take Alicia, so you mind? We went over this when you first came in, Dr. Krassner says. But…you're here, and at least—he laughs—your other two children *aren't*. Sure. It'll be all right this time, Barbara.

Sweet child, sweet little girl, hiding her face in her mother's great breasts, beautiful child, much darker than Barbara, almost pure African. He listens to Barbara, humiliation upon humiliation, her husband staying out for days, comes home to use her *like a toilet*; and the case worker you sent me, that spy, his eyes so suspicious I'm getting away with something.

"Barbara—Do you really think *I* sent you that caseworker?"

"*What do I get away with? You tell me. What?*" Barbara has a powerful sense of drama. *Why am I supposed to keep on going? You tell me*. Even when she's demeaned, neglected, bruised, she's the star of her sad show; there's a certain glory in that, a certain power. How, Sam wonders, do you interrupt her performance to get at the real grief that fuels it? His attention wanders to the child, who peeks at him from time to time, hiding in the dress, popping out to grin, and then becomes absorbed in folding the flowered cloth of her mother's lap into a soft-sculpture flower.

Does Barbara feel his attention float away? When he asks her, "So, Barbara, let's put things together: how do you see your options?" She says, "Well, Doctor, I'll tell you." And doesn't tell him. "It's hard to figure out your choices?" he probes. "Oh no. My 'options'? Well, we've got a friendly little gas pipe in the apartment. We cook with gas. You ever hear that, Doctor? Cooking with gas? How about *not*-cooking with gas. That's one option. Course, when the kids are out. What d'you think of my option, Doctor?"

"Barbara, don't you even play with that idea. If I think you really mean something by it, you know I'm going to have to do something about it."

"You scare the shit out of me. I'm scared this PhD white guy going to lock me away someplace where they feed me and dope me up and I watch the television all day." Her face softens. At times she looks like a big teenager. So odd, this mix of relaxation and despair! She slumps in her chair; he's wary she'll put her feet up on his desk. Rivers of the big summer flowers in her dress flow over the arms of her chair. He imagines her flowing over the room, drowning him.

"You have children, Barbara. When you have children, you lose your right to kill yourself."

"Nice to know I used to have rights."

"They're your riches, those three kids. You understand me?"

"Riches! Well, sure, I do see your point. Thanks for the warning, Dr. Krassner. Don't you worry. I'm just messing with you, Dr. Krassner. I'm gonna become a great writer."

"A writer?"

"I told you I'm in a writing class, a workshop, uh huh—and teacher thinks I'm *good*."

"If you told me, it didn't register. Tell me about it."

She tells. Her eyes get swallowed by all that fat; made tiny. Perception = interpretation: the way you see contains within it the meaning for you. For instance, her eyes. Isn't he saying she can't see, can't see or be seen? That she's hiding? And her beauty—for he thinks of her as *beauty buried in fat*. Barbara is only thirty for godsakes! He peels away the layers of fat, like unwanted marble of a sculpture, and imagines her ten years ago, before the children. Her skin soft as the skin of her child. Wanting to touch Barbara, wanting to soothe her, he reaches out to her little girl. As if *there's* the full beauty, undisguised. The child shrinks away, but Barbara sweet-talks her, "You go right ahead now, honey. The doctor means to be nice," and says to Krassner, "Her name is Alicia."

"Alicia," he says. "Hi, Alicia."

Now he has a problem: he's made himself vulnerable. Alicia lets him take her hand, and still shrinking into her mother's breasts, she grins at him. He says, "Your riches, Barbara."

"Yeah? And I guess I'm too stupid to figure that out?"

Embarrassed, he says, "What a lovely little girl." He'd take her home in a minute, begin the whole process of parenting all over. He wants to make sure this child is safe, whole. His own children are grown, one in college, one in Boston. Ah, honey, honey.

So that's the session. She tells him pieces of her story: a neighbor who makes the building shake with heavy bass from his stereo and sells stuff out of his apartment—drugs, computers, TVs. Scares her, kind of people come around. Next time I'll come alone, Doc. It's okay, he says. Alicia makes me understand what it's like for you. He asks himself: does Barbara get anything out of these sessions except to tell stories, to vent griefs? It lets her get other help—daycare, help with her diabetes, food stamps, maybe training. Barbara hauls herself to her feet. The office is air conditioned, but there are quarter-moons of sweat at the armpits of her flowered dress. It's a nice dress, picked up, she told him, at a survival center. But those big flowers!—wrong costume for a big woman. She kisses Alicia, and Sam Krassner imagines she's kissing him goodbye.

After she's gone, he stands at the mirror in the men's room, staring at his own physical being, his creaturely self. It's not to contrast himself—healthy, thank God, slim except for an insignificant pound or three of thickness at his waist from too much sitting, his mustache and sideburns beginning to gray; why, if he removes his rimless glasses he looks almost handsome in his own eyes—it's not to contrast himself with Barbara. Rather, what he feels is their common physical being: his flesh, hers. It's as if they're both standing in front of the mirror in odd communion.

It's after that session, on the way home, Springfield to Amherst, he hears words in a sentence. You know how you turn around in the street at the thump of a bass and an angry voice coming from somewhere—oh, from *there*, you say, open convertible, two guys with stocking caps and an attitude, sound system meant as a weapon against the world. It's that much not-in-his-head. The words clear enough but meaning what? STRICT PROCEDURE. Or maybe it's CONSTRICTED PROCEDURE or STRICTLY PROCEED. If these words are coming from an angel, he wishes the angel would be less mumbly. But still, doesn't he know? Oh, he *knows.* Barbara. He takes the next exit, drives under the highway and enters heading south. He's sweating with anxiety—that he's onto something / that he's a little crazy. He calls the clinic, gets Barbara's phone number, her address, directions. He calls his wife's voice mail at her office. "Sheryl, it's four-thirty. I've got a problem with a patient. I may be late getting home. Sorry."

This is against all the rules, strictures about professional distance. It's not as if he's never heard gestures of suicide, mostly a way of saying, Listen, I'm in *that* much desperation. You don't go running to a patient's house. He's in the middle of a fairy tale. He saves, heals, transforms.

It's a run-down neighborhood but not as damaged as he'd imagined. Some houses are boarded up, their front yards littered, and most freestanding houses are in need of paint and upkeep. But there are renovated apartment buildings and quite a few places attended to with care and work. It looks like a neighborhood coming back. Critics say "gentrified," but what's happening—his patients tell him—is that some young family is struggling to make payments and have enough left over for repairs and paint; husband, wife, kids spend their weekends fixing up the place. He admires the little trees held straight by wire on the front lawns. Look at them leafing in sweet, young green as if they were champions of the forest. He feels the beauty and dignity of these loved houses.

But Barbara Hammond lives in an old red brick apartment building, not renovated, four floors high, next door to a one-story flat-roofed building: a bar. Barbara's mentioned the place; it's one of the bars where her husband goes to liquor up before he can get himself to go home for a conjugal visitation. Nice life. He's scared for her—but scared, too, for himself: it's like visiting hell. No voices now. He's on his own. Mission or *mishegos*? There's no need for the buzzers just inside the big front glass door cracked corner to corner, because the inside door, bulwark against invasion, is askew, won't close, as if someone strong got real mad one night. But he pushes Barbara's buzzer, expects no answer. His heart is thumping. It's all he can do to push the front door open and walk into the dimly lit foyer and up the dimmer stairs. A smell of clammy walls. Graffiti on the ceiling over the stairs; highly stylized, unreadable. One word, F U C K, clear enough. Music thumps from somewhere. From somewhere, a talk-show voice. From somewhere, a hip-hop beat. Up to the second floor and up again. He walks softly as he can. Barbara's on the third floor. At her door he smells for gas. But suppose she's sealed the crack under the door.

He knocks. "Barbara?" Louder. "BARBARA?"

"And who the fuck are you?" A slow voice from the stairwell behind him.

He speaks back into the semi-dark. "She's my client. I'm a little worried about her."

"Yeah? And just what you worried about?" It's a wiry black man in overalls over a Red Sox sweatshirt, inspecting, glowering, long pry bar in hand. Well—reasonable suspicion, Krassner think—but feels interrogated, threatened.

"I'm not even sure she's home. I saw her at my office a couple of hours ago—just want to make sure she's okay. I guess she's probably not home. She's probably not home yet."

"She's home. I saw her come in." The man sucks at his lower lip. "I'll go get us a key. You stay cool." He hurries off. Krassner keeps on knocking till he's back. "I'm kind of a superintendent," the man says. "I keep my eye on things. I got a key just in case."

"I'm Sam Krassner."

"Uh huh. I'm Emet Brock. What? You a social worker?" But he doesn't wait for an answer. He uses the key. Door's on a chain. "Ah, hell." In a minute he's back again with a bolt cutter, and in another minute, Krassner holding it taut, Brock has broken the chain, and they're in.

Clothes clutter, toy clutter, food clutter, a smell, not gas. Brock takes the lead. No one in the living room, no one in the first bedroom. In the second, half off the bed, there she is, knocked out, puke all over her flowered dress and on the bedside table three plastic vials from the pharmacy, empty. An intense, sour smell fills the room. "Oh, God!" Krassner gets close, puts his fingers to Barbara's throat. Brock is already at the phone. Krassner opens a window, realizes he hasn't been breathing, finds towels, wipes up the worst of the mess. The thing is to get her moving. He's not so strong, and Brock is a small man. They have to lift 250 pounds. "Give me a hand," he calls.

The woman is dead weight. I mean, put her on her feet, she'd collapse into a lump on the floor. Brock on one side, Krassner the other, they each wrap an arm over their shoulders and heave her to a sitting position. "Maybe if she gets vertical," Krassner says, "she'll throw up some more. More she throws up the better. You know where her kids are?"

He starts down the stairs after the attendants meaning to follow the ambulance to Bay State Medical—but what good? It's the kids he has to think about. He yells down the stairwell, "If she wakes up, tell her I'm checking on her kids!" He turns back; from her apartment calls the hospital to let them know what's going on, calls Marty Shire, her caseworker from DSS. This is her caseworker's job—to follow up, to take care of the kids. By now it's after six. But he doesn't leave. He pokes through the livingroom. A giant TV-stereo commands the room like an altar—or the Ark of the Covenant. With the rack of music and videos, it takes up a wall. Above it, a framed poster of Martin Luther King. He's afraid he'll find drugs, afraid because she's told him she'd stopped using and he believed. But all over the room he sees books. Books from the Springfield Public Library, from used bookstores. Novels, books of self-help. She hadn't told him she was reading.

He gets a pail from the kitchen closet, fills it full of hot, soapy water, and best he can, scrubs up. He feels like an idiot. What's he doing it for? Well, for the kids, so they don't come back to a stink. It's when he's dumped the pail into the toilet, cleaned his hands, is about to go home, a girl walks in, eleven, twelve, must be Barbara's oldest. And there he is, pail in his hand, he's got to be the one to tell her. And at this point he doesn't even know if her mother's alive. He thumbs his mental Rolodex for her name. "I'm Sam Krassner. I've been trying to help your mother. Your mother's sick right now."

The girl's in jeans and a tee shirt, name of some band splashed in red across her skinny chest. She backs toward the door. Sam Krassner puts down the pail and holds out his hands, palms up, mudra of innocence. "Hey, you don't have to be scared. I'm your mother's friend. Your mother is in the hospital."

"Mr. Emet?" she calls, and Brock, behind her by the door, says, "I take it from here, Doc."

"I *told* you I heard someone in here," she says to Brock.

And Krassner explains, explains as if he were doing something wrong—I'm just trying to help, keep you kids out of foster care, because that's what'll happen, and—honey, you're Denise, right?—Do you have a grandma or an aunt you can stay with a few days? Emet Brock is shaking his head. "You don't know their Daddy," he says. Sitting on the sagging sofa, he folds his arms. "Their daddy comes back here to check on the kids, well you better run, mister or you be on the evening news. You just try telling him you're a *social worker*—" These last words he says in parody of a school principal or a pastor or a professor.

"—I'm not a social worker, I'm a psychologist, a therapist."

"You a white man around his family. No offense. You want to help, better help by *phone*."

Denise is trying to get words in—My mother's in the hospital? What hospital? What happened? Brock stands up, puts a hand on her shoulder. "What's your auntie's name, you know, lady comes see you a lot? Where she live?"

"My mother do something to herself? She try something? She always talking."

"Your mother took too many pills. We'll call the hospital, find out what's going on. But we need to get hold of your auntie," Sam Krassner says. "And your brother and your little sister. Can you help? Your brother's in daycare, right? Where's daycare? And Alicia—where's Alicia?"

He goes with Brock—they follow Denise to daycare to pick up Mickey, then to their neighbor's to collect Alicia. (*Remember me, Alicia? You came to my office?*) Denise becomes transformed from little kid to family leader. She's up front, holding both kids' hands as they go around the corner to Jackie, who's an aunt, it turns out, only by love. At the corner near the bar, three young men watch them pass. Krassner, a little frightened, keeps his eyes on the kids. Looking at the three kids from behind, he feels hopeful; if they're this beautiful, it's got to be hopeful.

He's saved a life. Mazeltov! The rabbis tell us in *Pirkei Avot* that to save a single life, it's as if you saved a whole world. Not bad work for a hot September day. But now he feels responsible for her in a new way. Well, of course. He is. Tendrils have grown between them.

Driving back to Amherst at dusk, he's sure what Sheryl will say. *If I were you, I'd stay out of it now.* But when he gets home and microwaves his dinner and tells her his story, she sits by him and runs her fingers through his hair and says, "Well, my big, old hero Superdoc. You must feel terrific. So will she be all right, this Barbara?"

"Oh, yes. We got to her in time, thank God. But will the *kids* be all right is another question. Can Barbara be a real mother? I don't know what to make of her."

"So tell me—this Barbara, she's beautiful?"

"Not the way you mean. There's something about her. But only thirty and so damaged."

"How did you know in the first place?" she asks. "Something she said in the session?"

"Well, she played with the romance of killing herself, but she's done that before." He smiles at her, a smile he knows she'll know is phony, and he imagines coming clean, telling her about the voices. *Your husband's hearing angels.* "It's your husband's therapeutic intuition."

"Oh, bullshit, my darling. I think I'll decide to be jealous. She must be breathtaking."

"Right." She's kidding and not kidding. He knows where it's coming from: their old friends, maybe closest friends, the man, a psychiatrist, six months ago he ran off with his patient, broke apart their lives—his daughters', his wife's, his own. They haven't even heard from him.

"Well, you stay out of it now," she says, as if summarizing a long discussion they never had.

He answers with the Jewish mudra of acquiescence: lower lip out, shoulders up to ears, neck retrenched turtle-like, hands open, see?—no weapons. But not answering in words, he hasn't committed himself. And how can he stay out? The kids, those kids. And what about the protocols of a professional attitude to the sufferer whose suffering he's supposed to assuage?—those protocols were developed partly to protect healers from their own need to rescue, the need that got them into the profession in the first place. They make sense. You can't help people when you bring your own noise into the room. Then, too, you need to be a model of calm, of *shalom*, for people who are not calm, whose lives feel like chaos. It's not bad, this professional style. But sometimes he feels its cost and burden. Now he's not thinking of Barbara the patient but of Barbara the sufferer and Barbara's kids, and the community that needs to hold those kids.

The voice he heard in his car today doesn't care a damn for professional detachment.

Between private patients from his office in Northampton, he helps the way Emet Brock suggested, by phone, checking with Barbara's social worker, talking to the aunt, finally talking over the phone to Barbara herself, who, still under "observation," stoned on tranquilizers, speaks in the language of irony: It's ironic she's alive, ironic he wants her to live. *You like my life so much, why don't you take it up and live it for me, let me be, Dr. Krassner?* Selfish! So unbelievably selfish, he thinks. Hard not to condemn her. He has to remind himself: even the outrageous selfishness is a gesture, a masochistic gesture like twisting a knife into her own flesh—see how worthless I am?

It's under the engine noise on his drive over the Connecticut to Amherst and his health club that he hears a voice again. But all it says is "LISTEN." To what? He pulls over by a farm stand, buys some corn, sits in his car waiting. Listens, he listens, *Shema,* and nothing comes, and it doesn't matter. Because he knows damned well what it wants him to do. "Listen" can mean "obey"—*you listen to me.* Listening, he turns the Subaru around and re-crosses the river, heads down 91 toward Springfield. *Holy One, protect us all.* On cell he calls Barbara—no answer; calls Jackie Chambers, the "aunt." She works till five at the desk of a hotel in West Springfield. To her voice mail: "Listen. Are the kids okay? Are they with you? I've got a little time—think I'll drop in. If it's not a good time, call my cell." And his number.

Five o'clock. Driving to Springfield he gets an idea: pizza for the kids! He imagines the three of them gobbling a pizza. From the road he calls the only pizza place he knows in Springfield—just a few blocks out of his way—and drives to Barbara's with a big white box. No answer to his ring, so he tries Brock, who comes out to the vestibule, holds the crooked inner door open. Late afternoon sun floods the little space between inner and outer doors, lights them both up. Krassner holds the white box on his palm like an offering. "Pizza's for the kids. They here?"

"Well, well. You the pizza man."

"That's it. Barbara been back?"

"Not so I seen. Maybe the kids are with that aunt. I thought I warn you to stay off. Look—it don't matter to *me* you come around here, but that husband of hers, well he's a crazy fucker. Just I don't feel like cleaning up your blood off these stairs," he says, pointing over his shoulder.

"Thanks."

Brock smiles a funny, crooked smile. Is Brock razzing him, ragging him?

"I'll try not to drip."

"Man thinks I'm kidding. You'll see. No pizza for me?"

"Afraid not. Got to go find the kids."

"So long, pizza man."

Same three young guys standing on the corner near the bar. They stop talking as he passes. They stare. In the infinite depth of a single instant he wants to smile a big smile their way but keeps his face blank, knowing it would be a smile of fear defended against by a pretence of innocence. It would be saying, *There's no such thing as racism in your lives, or if there is, please recognize that I'm not any part of it. Don't think of me as white. Don't take out your anger on me*. But he's got a couple of patients at the clinic in their mid-twenties. He knows too much about their anger to pull off that smile of innocence. The whole story of race relations is present at this almost-interaction. This same instant he fantasizes: if he weren't on a mission he might hang with them on the corner, talking about their lives, his life; but in fact his whole life he's never hung out on a corner—not with black, not with white—swigging beer or wine or whatever's in those paper bags. He avoids eye contact, but one of the young men says in high tenor, almost falsetto, "That pizza for *me*?"

Now he can smile. Passing them, he heaves a breath, feels their eyes on his back as he comes to Jackie's building. It's been renovated with Federal funds—new windows, new doors, new sheetrock, new plumbing and electricity. He buzzes, gets buzzed in. Jackie's apartment is on the third floor; as he climbs he can hear Alicia's laugh. Jackie's standing outside her half-open door with her arms folded. This is a real good looking woman, about Barbara's age, maybe thirty, but lean, athletic, clear-eyed. Her hair is set in cornrows, the cornrows lifted into a crown—no, a *tiara*, a black tiara. Just home from work, she's still in a suit, gray polyester, and a white blouse. When she remembers him, her eyes soften, she steps inside and opens the door all the way. Denise comes out to stand at Jackie's shoulder, and Mickey and Alicia peek from the living room. Krassner calls out, "It's just the Pizza Man!" Then, to Jackie, "I hope you don't mind if they eat a snack."

"Mind! Think I feel like cooking?"

They clear the table in the kitchen where Mickey and Alicia were drawing. Jackie takes out plates. "How about for you?"

"No, thanks. How's Barbara?"

She stops, silverware in her hand, and meets his eyes. He's not expecting so direct a look; he's the one who glances away. "You stick around, you see for yourself," she says. "You understand, there's a lot to that woman, Dr. Krassner. She's so smart, you wouldn't believe."

Krassner nods; his eyes well up—not professional at all. He asks the kids, "Pizza okay?"

"Great," Mickey says, hunched over his eating.

"Who am I?" he asks Alicia. "I'm 'The Pizza…'"

"The Pizza Man!"

And the Pizza Man sits at the feast pulling at his mustache, resting his bifocals on the tip of his nose to look at them—a guest, not partaking, a Pizza Man who wishes he'd bought two pies. Mickey is making a jet plane out of his slice, then crashing the plane into his mouth.

Just for this crazy moment Krassner's got a second family.

Rap at the door, Barbara's here. She looks doughy, dowdy, glazed. It doesn't take her half a minute to put down a plastic bag she's brought from the hospital, to take off her man's windbreaker and play the role she's scripted for today. In this role, she's very calm, she draws out her words, pitch rising and falling as if she were singing. "My baby's eatin' pizza," (or is it "My babies eatin' pizza"?) To most people walking into Jackie's kitchen, Barbara would appear a happy, loving mother. Krassner hears it as role, opera, tragedy, *Madame Butterfly*, *Medea*; it scares him, his heart gets pumping, and Jackie knows, too—she puts her arm around as much of Barbara as she can manage, kisses her cheek and steers her toward a chair. Barbara isn't having any of it. She shakes Jackie off. Her head's waving, rocking, she's using the rocking to build up whatever internal energy she can muster for an explosion, Krassner's sure. He's seeing *crazy*. No—*gestures* of crazy. "Barbara, we're all here. Your beautiful children and Jackie and me, we're all here, dear."

Dear! So intimate, so outside permissible language for therapy. It's as if one of his disowned voices broke into his own speech. He flushes; Barbara doesn't seem to have heard. She's on stage, mad tragedy-queen. *Watch out.* Denise stops eating and stands behind her mother, rubs her shoulders, her neck, says, "Still a slice left, Mama." Barbara's rocking. "But what?" she asks, "are we doing here? What we doing in my good friend's house? Beautiful Jackie. Finish up, children. I'm your mother come back from the dead to bring you up best I can. I know, I know what *you* doing here, Dr. Krassner. You think you gonna take these children away from their mother?"

"The opposite, Barbara. I'm trying to keep you together."

"We just goin' home," she says in almost a drawl, not her own urban, Northern speech.

Jackie says "Barb, honey? Why don't you stay awhile? Dr. Krassner's just leaving."

"I *am* leaving," he says. "But talk to me, Barbara. Will you be able to handle things? Are you taking medication? What did they prescribe? Please. Can you just talk to me so I'm not uneasy?" He's lying. If he wants information, he can call her social worker, the hospital, the admitting physician. What he wants is to see, Can she be here in the room with him, talk coherently?

Barbara says, sings, "You got a kitchen knife, Jackie honey?"

"What you need a kitchen knife for?"

"That's right. Maybe I don't." She lifts Alicia from her chair and plants kisses over her neck, her cheeks; she takes Mickey by the shoulder and when he finishes his slice and gets up, she buries his face in her belly. Denise is talking with her eyes to Jackie, and Krassner doesn't know the language. But talk of knives and her textbook gestures of decompensating, of a psychotic break he reads in her eyes—don't they mean he needs to hospitalize this patient, get in touch with Barbara's social worker and with Crisis Services? Of course—except these *aren't* gestures of real madness; they're gestures meant to indicate madness.

"I'll walk you home."

"What a gentleman my doctor is!" Barbara says to Jackie. "You want to come along, too? Or you think I can get around the fuckin' corner in one piece?"

"You know I believe in you, sweetie. Stop messing around, will you? You scaring your kids, honey. Just remember what you showed me."

"What?"

"Your writing, your journal. You know."

"Good days and bad days, baby. This definitely not one of my good days." But Barbara laughs, thank God, a full-lung laugh, not the quote of a laugh, not a crazy laugh, just the real thing.

All at once, Denise shepherds her mother and the kids toward the door. Mickey leans down to the kitchen table to grab Alicia's crusts in one hand, then takes his mother's arm with the other. Alicia burrows against her mother, Krassner says "Home, home, home," as if a celebration were going on, and since it's anything but a celebration, he feels false as hell, weighed down with sadness he can't show. No need for voices to tell him anything; no need to be a prophet: he knows in his own bones the way this will play out.

The three young men are gone as they turn the corner, but in front of Barbara's building one man is waiting, leaning against the pilaster to one side of the door, and right away Krassner sees it's not Brock and he knows who it must be. He's in for it. *You damned fool*, he says to himself.

Eugene Hammond hovers tall above Barbara. Nightmare man, Krassner's nightmare, hulking, thick-necked, his eyes bloodshot, his skull shaved bald, his clothes stained, sloppy.

"Daddy!" Alicia yells. Mickey goes, "Hi, Daddy," but without enthusiasm. Denise doesn't say hello. Barbara says, "My Eugene!"—which she pronounces *YOU-gene*. So much going on in this moment. If he could tease it apart, Krassner thinks as he snatches the looks in their eyes, it would contain a bitter history of whites and blacks, a history of power and powerlessness, of men and women. *Maybe I'll die here*. He's silent; he knows the last thing he should do is speak.

Eugene Hammond speaks. "They told me you were hanging out with this white guy." Very calm—the calm spooks Krassner, and at once Denise is weeping. Hammond says, "What *you* cryin' for? What's this got to do with you, girl?" Then, to Barbara—"Told me you messing around and it does look like."

"This is my *doctor*, Eugene. You get the fuck away. You the last thing I need just now."

"Maybe I'm the last thing you gonna see. Look at this doctor of yours. He's pissing in his pants, your Jew doctor."

Krassner says in a gentle voice, "Mr. Hammond, Mr. Hammond, here's the story. I'm trying to keep your family in one piece. All right? Your wife's been in the hospital. You know that?"

"DID YOU HEAR ME TALK TO YOU?" Hammond points his finger into the air between them, rap, rap, rap. Krassner is silent. Now, almost a whisper: "I didn't say shit to you, Mister. You lucky if I don't kill you with my hands. And you, crazy woman. You pill woman. Oh. You *some* kind of mother."

Barbara makes a fist and thump, thump thumps hard at the side of her head. Denise tugs her arm and holds it against her own chest like holding a lover. She hasn't looked at her father. Hammond gestures to them like a contemptuous traffic cop waving along a line of cars, and one by one they pass by and into the building. Suddenly Brock's there in the vestibule. "Eugene, m'man, you just let the good man go home now."

Hammond stands at the cracked glass door and stares Krassner down. "Go home? He damn lucky if he gets home tonight. Why he here? Fuck he want here?" Turning, pressing his chest up against Krassner, he whispers, "When you be come and hearing me invite you to my house?"

Brock laughs. "C'mon, man. Your point's made, Eugene."

Hammond steps back; Krassner stumbles back; now Hammond turns and, brushing past Brock, disappears into the dark foyer. Brock comes out onto the stoop and shakes his head, shakes his head. "I know," Krassner says. "You told me."

Sheryl, home just before Sam, assumes he's been at the club and has had a different sort of workout. He kisses her in passing, retreats to his study with a mumble, "Something I got to do…" and there *is* something: he calls Marty Shire, Barbara's caseworker, writes notes about Eugene Hammond for a report to the Massachusetts DSS. He's legally, of course, a "mandated reporter" of abuse, of neglect. But it's not a clear case. Barbara's been shoved against the wall a couple of times, or so she tells him, but mostly she's been terrorized. The children, she says, Hammond hasn't touched. Neglect he surely can report, must report. But how do you report chaos, terror, whispers of the makings of a tragedy?

Now, while Sheryl clatters in the kitchen, he sits, his office a synagogue, his laptop a prayer book, and stares into the pixels and the cloudy white of the screen. He's hungry for a voice not his own. All at once his heart softens, breath comes easy, and a voice does come, barely audible, more a keening like the song of blood in his ears. Now a word, "*commence,*" but the voice neglects to tell him what he's to commence. What good is such a voice? Now again, a word, all by itself, "*tender.*" To *be* tender? To *tender* his resignation? To resign himself? To soften?

At dinner he tells Sheryl about Hammond. She presses her fingers to her lips. She looks down at the food. It disturbs him: she doesn't even tell him to back off, to be careful. Her silence scares him. He clears the dishes, rolls up his sleeves, stacks the dishwasher.

His hands are still damp when he hears yelling outside—someone yelling. At once he knows it's Eugene Hammond. He opens the window to hear. "Krassner. You! *Doctor* Krassner!" Hammond stands in the driveway, tee shirt over baggy jeans. "I'll be right there, *Eugene!*" he calls, pronouncing the name Barbara's way, then shuts the window and goes into Sheryl's study. She's looking out through the slats of the blinds. He lays his hand on her nape, soothes, soothes. "Don't worry. Don't get frightened."

Her fingers at her lips. "You're going to call the Police, aren't you? You want *me* to call?"

"Wait. Sheryl. I call the Police and there's no stopping it, like a roller coaster it'll just go down, down into tragedy. The poor man's in agony."

"Don't try to be such a saint, Sam. I'm calling 911." But she just sits there in the mauve yoga pants she always wears at home, fingers rubbing her cheek. He feels a surge of anger against her for her fear and helplessness.

Sam is at the door. He's in slacks and an open shirt. The night spring air is sweet from someone's garden. Hammond stands under a tree, washed in the glare of a security light. The light distorts his features into a monster mask. As Krassner steps outside, Hammond yells, "What's the matter? You think you come to my house I can't come to yours? You address in the phone book, Krassner. So? YOU FUCKING MY WIFE, *DOCTOR* KRASSNER?" This he bellows so the neighborhood can hear. But it's not that kind of neighborhood. Even Hammond's bull voice won't carry through the trees of these two-acre lots. However…it will carry clearly enough to Sheryl.

His own voice Krassner can't find. What's he to say? *No, no, I'm not messing with your wife?* Bad idea—just get him started. Maybe Hammond's brought a gun, a knife. God knows fists would be sufficient. Hammond has him by thirty pounds and twenty years, and to say that's a joke—even as a young man he'd have stood no chance. He can't speak. But a muscle lets go. Maybe it's his very helplessness that eases him. He knows—*knows*—he won't need to think about it; *words will be available.* They may not change anything, but they'll be there. Krassner can breathe. Grateful, he plunks himself down on the brick steps leading to his front door. "Want to sit and talk, Eugene? You want a soda?"

"Too damn late to talk. Think you talk your way outa this, doctor?" But they're in dialogue. Hammond moves no closer. "She tell you all about me, she tell you what a bastard I am?" Not waiting for an answer—"You tell her to leave me? That what you tell her? She say you do."

"She'll say things. She's full of pain. You are, too."

Hammond peers across the lawn. "You crying? Look like you crying."

Krassner hadn't been aware. "Well? It gets me."

"What kind of motherfuckin' doctor cries?"

Krassner ignores. "And your kids, Eugene—what about them?"

"Crazy woman, what she gonna do to my kids?"

"Both of you, Eugene. What's all this battling going to do to your kids? You've got beautiful kids. Look, you want to split a soda?"

"She gets me crazy. I go crazy. I can do things." So peculiar!—like an old Jewish mourner, he shuts his eyes and rocks his head side to side.

"Why don't you can come to my office tomorrow and talk? I bet we can bypass the usual bureaucracy. You know? Maybe we can change things. I'd like to try."

"Can't change shit. Can't. Change. Shit."

Here's this powerful man standing by the maple tree, looking as if he could make a world with his big hands, and he says this. He's trapped in his story. Trapped in his words. And they're not even his. *They've been whispered to him the way words were whispered to me.* Sam Krassner wants to give him new words. "Can't change a lot of things," Krassner says. "Might change some. Beautiful kids. It's worth trying."

But Hammond shakes his head. "Too *late* for that shit. See, you don't know." And he turns away, picks up the baseball bat he's stowed by a tree on the front lawn, and goes back to his rusting Camero. He doesn't look back. He opens the trunk, puts away the bat, he's gone.

At once Sheryl comes out onto the front steps. "Thank God," she says. "You did well."

He's feeling a little sick. Heart pounding, he takes Sheryl's arm and they walk back into the house; without asking, she pours him a shot of bourbon. "You did really well," she says.

Her eyes are shining; kind, quiet eyes—they're why he first loved her. Still, he's irritated; she makes him feel he simply manipulated the man. "We'll see," he shrugs. "He says it's too late. Maybe it's not." He doesn't tell her that the words came to him, weren't really his, weren't tools of manipulation. An angel's words, an offering. "Did you call 911?"

"I was afraid what could happen if he heard a siren."

The bourbon helps. In Krassner's inner eyes this angry man comes in and talks, and through the words they come to know one another; Krassner no longer white repressor; Hammond no longer the latest incarnation of drunken Cossacks who made Krassner's ancestors flee the Pale. Back at his desk, not knowing he's going to call, he picks up the phone and dials Barbara. No answer and no answer. He calls her friend. Jackie's at home, her voice flat. "Just wanted to touch base," he says.

"Barbara's still at the hospital. At Bay State. They're doing okay."

"What? The hospital? I don't know anything, Jackie. What? She try to kill herself again?"

"*No*. I was sure you must know. Right after you left their place, they went upstairs, and that Eugene, he picked up a baseball bat and came after her, the kids were screaming, and Denise, poor baby, she tried to protect her mama, she hugged her so Eugene couldn't get at her."

"Oh, my God. Oh, my God."

"The bastard kept swinging his bat. If he hit Denise on the head, she be dead now. Broke her collarbone, broke her wrist, maybe some ribs. Man there, superintendent, he saved her life."

The Police are out looking for Hammond. Krassner calls to let them know Hammond came to his house; then he sits. What good are those damn words? An angel's voice? What good? Is he really puppet to an angel? Maybe it's the other way around—he's got this angel puppet on his lap and pretends the words are coming from a holy place. Krassner, accomplished ventriloquist, doesn't move his lips. But it's the ventriloquist who writes the dialogue.

Next evening he visits Denise in the hospital. Her father didn't hit her head, but her face looks swollen, puffy. He won't embarrass her by staring. He tells Denise how brave she was.

She cries "Mister. You get out! Please! You made enough trouble." She won't look at him. She curls away into a small thing, faces the white curtain separating beds.

Saturday, after Shabbat services, he visits Hammond in jail in Springfield. "You minded your business," Hammond says, "I wouldn't be here now. You lucky I don't kill you.... You got cigarettes for me?"

"You want me to get you cigarettes?"

"I won't smoke your cigarettes."

Barbara he can't find at all. She's not with Denise; she doesn't come to the clinic. More grief: the caseworker's report—Barbara went after Hammond with a knife—went for him *first*. This blurs the story. His eyes blur when he reads the report. A knife. He thinks: failure; total defeat. If she's lucky, Denise will live with Jackie; the little kids will end up in foster care. He thinks about taking Alicia and Mickey into his own home; but Sheryl would be furious if he asked.

He can't sleep; exhausted, at eleven he crashes as if drunk—into darkness, random language, but, wide awake at midnight, he can't remember what he dreamed, makes himself a snack and reads. At work snippets of voice; he shoves them away.

"What happened to that poor woman?" Sheryl asks. He shrugs. He knows Barbara's out of his program, can imagine the rest. He'd like to blame Sheryl—but for what? Lack of faith, he supposes, now that he himself has none. He thinks about those kids in foster care. Mickey, Alicia. He sees a tunnel of dark air, a dark wind spout, carry them away as shadows. Finally—two weeks later—he asks Sheryl, "What about taking those kids? Temporarily. If DSS allows."

"That's so generous," she says. "Really, Sam. But impossible. Anyway, that man scares me too much. When he gets out, a few months, maybe just a few weeks, you don't think he'd come after you? If you've got his kids? A white doctor taking his kids away?"

So he stays in touch with Jackie Chambers. She's his only source. "Barbara? She's living with her mother. She's…not in great condition."

"Look. Jackie. The younger kids. You think there's any way they could stay with you for awhile? Suppose I sent you a small check every month?"

"You saw my place, Dr. Krassner. Real nice of you though."

Words come at the edge of sleep. *Genuflect…Cognizance.* He's wide awake, hunting for meanings. Suppose after all an angel—so what? What good are an angel's words when someone takes a baseball bat to a child? Midnight, but he calls Barbara's number. The phone's disconnected, and when he calls Emet Brock next day he finds out she doesn't live there any more. "You were right," he says to Brock.

Brock soothes. "You tried. This not about *you*, Doctor."

All day these are the words he hears. *This not about you.* He protests to Brock in his head, *I didn't think it* was *about me.* But on the way home from the clinic he turns off Public Radio, pulls into a Wal-Mart parking lot. *Or did I? Think it was about me?—How I failed.* My story.

Everybody's got their story. Eugene has his, Barbara hers; this is Sam's story—blabber to wrap the heart in. He blurts a sad laugh, and it comes to him what he's been hearing all these weeks. It's like half-hearing a television play from the next room and only a few of the words slip through. That's what he's been hearing—fragments of a story, a word here and there. Whose story? At just this moment, with a gasp in his belly as if a roller-coaster were starting down, down, he slips through a crack between stories. In this gap the words fly like eagles below you in a canyon, floating, far beyond your willing, on the thermals. They're not his, the words; it's not his story.

A few weeks later he finds on his list of appointments at the clinic:

4 P.M.—Barbara Hammond.

A couple of minutes late, she enters in a flurry; late, he surmises, so she *could* enter in a flurry and get through embarrassment. A pulse in his temple beats. "Good to see you," he says.

She wears the same floral dress; she sure doesn't look like spring, but she's fixed her hair like Jackie's, in a braided tiara—maybe, he thinks, it was Jackie fixed it for her. She's living with her mother and her stepfather. It's not the ideal situation, but she's got a job. Her caseworker came through for a change. "Nothing great. Doing home care for a couple of old women."

He holds back his questions: *The knife, what about that knife?* He says, "That's wonderful."

"Try it."

"And the kids?"

Denise is still with Jackie, she says; the others are kind of with Barbara—"Actually, they're with my mother till I show I'm okay."

"Are you okay?"

"If I were okay…" She leans forward till he can feel the warmth of her breath, "…you think I'd be here looking at *you*?"

In the place between stories, they lean back and have a laugh together.

Originally appeared in Missouri Review, *Fall 2005.*
Will be included in Pushcart Prize Anthology, *2007*

The Promised Land

A Sunday Cruise

It's a Sunday. Samuel Rosen sits in sunshine, sunshine, sunshine, taking a beating from the salt wind, on a fighting chair high up in the fishing tower of his son's big boat. But he's not fishing. Sundays, Peter insists on floating him around in the yacht.

He laughs, suddenly, a big laugh. *My son the captain*!

Samuel's remembering a joke his mother, God rest her soul, used to tell him: a nouveau-riche Jewish businessman buys a yacht and invites his mother to see. He stands on the bridge in his brimmed and braided captain's hat and calls down, "Nu, mama, so do I look like a captain?" "To me, my darling," she says, "certainly you look like a captain. But to a *captain* do you look like a captain?" Old story about assimilation, its point almost lost—hardly any comic contradiction remaining between Jew and yachtsman.

He laughs aloud and is ashamed at the laugh, knows it's his way of standing apart from his son—remembering this joke from sixty years back.

Samuel's son Peter, he wouldn't get it. He's at home on *The Promised Land*, his fifty-five foot cabin cruiser, small yacht really, built of fiberglass and polished, imported woods. Or if he does get uncomfortable, it's not a question of Jew/WASP nor a question of class. A boat this big, he's terrified he might scrape the hull; last year he snagged an unmarked chain and it wound up costing him a couple of thousand dollars. Berthed at Marina Del Rey, *The Promised Land* rides level on stabilizing bars; it's air-conditioned, powered by two giant inboard engines yet almost silent when you sit in the main cabin. You can cook a small standing rib roast in the galley oven; one night, Ruthie did just that. The four staterooms, finished in cherry, are like small bedrooms in an elegant hotel; there are three heads, the flush a purr, a living area with soft lighting and TV, stereo. The music, which no one but Peter controls, is piped all over the ship.

Peter controls and Peter worries. In baseball cap with the logo of some dot.com, he can run the ship from the bridge or the fishing cockpit where Samuel sits, set fifteen feet up above the deck. At his command are radar, sonar, Loran systems. With computer, he can plot a precise course and the instruments can serve as his skipper. *The Promised Land* is an expensive toy that uses the same abilities and obsessive need to control that he employs in his work. Weekdays, he worries about corporate strategies; weekends, on the boat, when he's not on the phone for work, he tinkers with electrical panels, charts, depth of channels. He keeps track of tide and weather. When he goes into a harbor it's like a military operation, eyes narrowed, shoulders tense, and Samuel looks at him, bewildered; saddened that his child should have grown into this tense adult. *What did we do wrong*?

It's difficult for Samuel to know (twenty-five feet above the calm water, rocking gently through a long arc of sky) how to love this big, graying-haired son of his. At forty, Peter is so self-contained. Samuel hears him down below on the bridge. He hears the radio picking up a conversation between boats. *Do I know my own son*? When he was a child, even when he'd come home from college, Samuel would make him pancakes. Pete loved pancakes soaked in syrup. Or as they walked up Broadway together to pick up bagels on a Sunday, Samuel would shmooze and philosophize, and under cover of language he'd pat Peter's back or wrap an arm around his shoulder, sing Cole Porter songs till Peter would say, "Pa, Pa, please!" They'd laugh. And he'd buy him things on impulse—electronic gadgets, a translation of Psalms, whatever.

But now, oh, Peter is so hip, so L.A. cool, his voice a flat, mellow monotone; anything New York in the voice is gone. There seem to be no open places to touch now, no way to give him anything. Peter knows just what he wants and puts in a call on cell to get it. Now Samuel is the one being given.

First of all, a home. With Hannah gone, Pete's mother, Hannah, dead almost a year now, Pete came to his father: "What d'you want to be stuck in New Rochelle for?" Well, the fact is, he didn't, Samuel didn't. When it came right down to it, except at his shul he had few friends, and some of these he lost contact with when Hannah died, others when he retired from teaching at Sarah Lawrence. And then his dear friend the rabbi was nudged into retirement by some of the younger families, and Samuel said to himself, Well, Abraham was already seventy-five years old when God said to him, "*Lech lecha... Go from your land, from your relatives, from your father's house, to the land that I will show you.*" Samuel would only be seventy next month.

On the other hand, unlike an Abraham he feels, to all intents and purposes, already dead. Don't get me wrong. He's in pretty good shape. Mornings, he gets up with energy, and if his joints ache a little, so what? He does his stretching exercises and gets to his study. *Still...* still, he's ready enough to follow Hannah when the time comes. After all, listen. After all, *what*? I mean how *long?*—a few more years of this consciousness? Set it against the mouth-gaping immensity of God's time, before he awoke into consciousness, after consciousness ends. A drop in the bucket. And the thing is, that's okay with Samuel. It's been more than a year since Hannah's death, but the loss of her and the lacerations of the two horrific years of her dying haven't closed up. Maybe he can only cope with the loss by denigrating the loss. He wonders: What's so beautiful about this world? Is it really worth God's while? There's God, always, but when Samuel blesses, it's with a little irony. *I'll bless because You say so. But I'll tell You frankly....* So death, death doesn't scare him a whole lot; he doesn't feel any need to suck desperately the last bit of juice in the glass, mostly ice by now. It's all right; to reenter God's time is all right. And this way of seeing changes things. God's radiance hovers over the sad world. You float up here above the ocean in this extraordinary light without worrying about getting anywhere. He's where he is to get.

From this death before dying he finds himself looking down at a world that doesn't bear closer scrutiny. Is, frankly, unbearable. The fifteen months of Hannah's decreasing abilities, increasing pain, sobered him forever. Samuel remembers a character in Dickens, his loved ones in coffins under the ground, who yet "did not make a coffin of his heart." Hannah's slow dying seems to have flayed a layer of skin from Samuel. Isaiah prays to remove the foreskin around our hearts. But then, how keep going? He asks every day of God, How do *You* keep going? If it's unbearable to me, what can it be for You? Take the child soldiers kidnapped into service, forced to prove their loyalty by being brought through their home village and, drugged into numbness, told to slaughter family, friends—or are themselves killed by the other children. He's read the accounts.

And so on.

Still…it makes him uneasy, to be inside this—well, this clarity of light, to feel the sea rocking the boat, to feel a wind misting his face, and then—*not* to feel all this as blessing? It's peculiar in fact. In fact, there's something wrong, unholy, with how little he's moved. As Wordsworth says, "*…I see, not feel, how beautiful it is…*."

"So am I fooling myself?" he asks the Holy One this afternoon, asks in a whisper, his lips barely moving (old city trick so you don't look crazy) as he puts on a yarmulke and prepares to pray *Mincha* way up here above the ocean. "I'm not saying I haven't got work left to do with this soul You've given me. God knows."

They're cruising south towards Newport, parallel to the coast; Peter's down on the bridge with his charts. Samuel's grandson Dan is playing cards with Ruthie in the main cabin. Up above, Samuel whispers his afternoon prayers, swaying as the boat sways, when he hears footsteps on the ladder leading up to the tower. To avoid discussion he stops, puts yarmulke in shirt pocket. Peter in his white boat shoes, white shorts. Samuel in an open white shirt, long beige pants.

"You're okay up here, Pop? Some people get sick."

"I'm an old sailor. From before you were born."

"Look how clear Catalina is from up here. Pretty. Some Sunday we'll check it out. Pop? Ruthie gave me an idea. Look—you've got time on your hands. Isn't that right?"

"What? You think I'm bored, Pete?"

"No, no, you sit around reading, you fix things—you're terrifically handy, Pop, I never realized—something breaks, boom, you fix it. In L.A., you call somebody, and it's three months before he comes. We're grateful, Ruthie and I. And you study. But I wish you had a friend or something. So anyway, Ruthie had this idea. How would you like to prepare kids for Bar Mitzvah—You know, teach them their Haftorah—a few of Danny's friends are ready. One family especially, they're looking for someone right now. It's not a money thing, but it's like psychoanalysis—people take it seriously if they have to pay."

"The boy is serious about spiritual study?"

"Jeremy? I know his family is making a big deal out of the Bar Mitzvah. Good kid, Jeremy Siegel. You'll like him. And the thing is...we want Danny to be better friends with Jeremy. Ben Siegel has fantastic contacts in finance."

"Let me ask you something Peter. At the same time, maybe I could teach Danny?"

"Please. Pop. Don't make an issue. Okay?" Peter's hands are raised, palms out, an image half surrender, half karate-readiness.

Father and Son

Peter's recently turned forty, a tennis player, just missed taking top singles in his club's master's category. He doesn't look at all like his dad. Peter's tall like Samuel, but an athlete, big shoulders, thick neck. His cheekbones are broader than his father's. He played baseball in high school, could have made the team at Penn but needed to work. He's beginning to look distinguished, his wavy black hair silvering at the temples. The pugnacious edge to his face has softened, his eyes are more open, his walk has eased. His look says, *I don't need to shove myself into the world. I get where I want without forcing the issue.*

Samuel's always wondered where this muscular American came from. He himself is slightly stooped, not from age but always, as if he were surrounding, protecting, the hollow of his chest, embracing an invisible fate even if convinced the fate was not a pleasant one. Or maybe…as if the weight on his shoulders was too much for such a narrow chest. He's long, a Don Quixote. His eyebrows float up in sadness, and his head, his whole self, nods back and forth, as if affirming, This is it, is life, it's what we've been given. Ludicrous to thrust oneself forward.

All right. This was always something of a con. It covered up a shrewd, secret aggression. With no noise, he did pretty well in academic life, didn't he?—as scholar and teacher of nineteenth century novel, he wrote essays—an often-reprinted essay on *Daniel Deronda*, a respected book on George Eliot. And for the past ten years, he was Dean of Graduate Studies. But his stooped stance isn't so much a con since Hannah died, may her soul rest in peace. The nodding, nodding, the submission—they seem…well, just himself. He has no kudos to win; he prays, he studies.

Abraham in L.A.

Getting back to Abraham—California doesn't seem like a land God *sends* people. Yes, sure, it's a land overflowing with milk and honey. *But*…so why is there a "but"? Why is he suspicious of comfort and sunshine? Why does it make him sad to stroll along the "boardwalk"—cement, really—that runs along the beach, under the Santa Monica Pier, down to Venice, stroll and see the hard-muscled, well-tanned young men and women skate by? If you asked Samuel, he'd shrug, laugh at himself. If he trusted you (not many people, old friends, in that category) he'd say, "It's emptiness, it's meaninglessness—*nada*—and everybody—you see, this is what's so bizarre—*agrees* about the emptiness but nobody even worries. It's…cool. Now, you see, it's one thing for God to be *murdered*" (he's thinking of Nietzsche's *Zarathustra*). "It's another when God is simply not invited to the party."

And then the family, his own family, his *toledot*, his descendents: look at this boat, for instance—and then what about the house—Peter has been adding to a house that seemed to Samuel already ridiculously large for his small family. Just the three of them—Peter, Ruthie, Danny, just turned twelve—in a house four thousand square feet. Already there was a guest suite where Samuel could stay. Now, Peter has added two thousand square feet more. Rooms, "living areas," more rooms. Plus pool, and terrace, and irrigated lawn, a green carpet on a slope overlooking the tops of trees and roofs of houses. For what? All surface. Nowadays there is a delight in *surface*—no, *more*: a backlash against critiques that depend on an orientation to depth, ultimately to God, to the Holy. Well…too bad, thinks Samuel. No way he'll fall for that!

Peter is, if not close, decent to him. Ruthie is positively kind, making sure he's included in conversations and meal planning, taking him to meet their friends, thanking him (too much) when he stays with Danny so they can go out to a party. Friday nights, they let him say the blessings over the candles, the wine, the challah. Ruthie doesn't keep kosher, but they eat mostly vegetables and rice anyway, and she buys kosher chickens to keep him happy. She's so busy—at home a lot, but busy writing scripts turning children's stories into animated half-hour TV shows. He makes allowances for the kitchen, that it hasn't been kashered. He makes do. He uses his own set of dishes and keeps away from her shellfish and bloody meats.

And Danny—Danny listens to his stories. A great virtue in a grandson! Already twelve years old, he should be studying for *his* Bar Mitzvah, but—"Look, pop, he's just not interested. Okay?" He leans over Samuel, standing beside the table. "*Okay*?"

"You mean *you're* not interested. Let me tell you something. Maimonides—Rambam— says, 'Just as a man is obligated to teach his son, so is he obligated to teach the son of his son, as it is said, Make them known to your sons and the sons of your sons.'"

This was two nights ago, a Friday evening in October, a week after Sukkot. Danny has cleared the dishes. The candles have been burning down, and by himself at the table, for all of them, Samuel has said the *Birchat Hamazon*, the blessings after the meal.

"I guess, sure," Peter says, "he picks it up from me."

"'*Veshinantam levanecha*'...'You shall teach the words intently to your children.'"

Peter lets the words sit between them for ten, fifteen seconds. "I guess in that case—I guess you didn't do too good a job on *me*, Pop."

"No. Those days, I didn't know my *tuchas* from my elbow."

"Well, you see?"

"I *do* see. You can't imagine how I regret. I was rebelling against your grandfather. And my awful cheder in Brooklyn where they yelled and slapped. I didn't want to impose. Even me, I myself was hardly observant. But now, I regret. You can't imagine."

Peter puts a hand on his shoulder. "Hey. You know—you didn't do such a bad job, you and Mom." And he grins and opens his hand as if to hold in it this showplace of a house and, beyond, the landscaping lit by outdoor spots; holding in his hand, as an offering, *himself*. Samuel tries not to offer up a sigh—it's his sighs Peter especially can't stand.

Listen: here's what Samuel is *not*: he is not an immigrant, he's no ancient Jew from a shtetl or even from an Orthodox community in Brooklyn. So many stories, a couple of generations back, about the conflict between father and son, the old Jewish way, the new, assimilated way. The son forgets the old ways; the father rends his clothing. But that's not it. Samuel *himself* is assimilated, a professor of English literature. By the late sixties, when Peter was born, Samuel had stored his tefillin and prayer book in a box on the top shelf of a closet. That was not only revulsion against the severity of cheder and home; it was a conscious political gesture. There were more important things to consider: protest against the war in Vietnam, organizing to build a new society. His congregation was composed of political comrades. Laws of *kashrut* seemed absurd—well, he'd never kept kosher since he left his parents' house. Anyway, Hannah wouldn't have stood for it in those days. Assimilated, hip, he experimented with drugs, even had a brief affair Hannah never discovered. It was only when Peter was already in his teens—too late, too late—that he came back.

It happened when his father died. Then, the next year, his mother. And while he had a sister in Chicago who'd stayed observant, he felt he should be the one to say Kaddish. At first, only once a week; then he grew hungry: once a week wasn't enough. He found an Orthodox morning minyan and stumbled through the prayers until the prayers came back. And then, he began taking Shabbat more seriously. He began by lighting the candles and saying the blessings. Peter, coming home from Yale, would roll his eyes and grin when Samuel, in skullcap, would press a hand on his head and bless him on a Friday night. And little by little, little by little. *Baruch Hashem*, as a child he'd had good training; soon he was leading services, chanting Torah. It was Hannah who asked—this was 1985, 1986—*If you like, we can make the kitchen kosher—Would you like?* Not so easy; she was working full time as a school psychologist.

But we did it, he thinks. It's hypocritical to be critical of Peter. It's my own fault.

In this part of L.A., Samuel has no shul to walk to on the Sabbath. Or yes, there *is*—a long walk, too long by Jewish law, and for years now, he'd been *shomer Shabbat*, keeping the Sabbath as well as he could. But all right, the first Saturday morning, he walked, to check it out. The synagogue, cantilevered audaciously on a hillside, looked, God-forbid, like a Las Vegas nightclub. The slick architecture and expensive materials said that the life of the spirit was enjoyable, uplifting…and expensive. This was no shul; it was a *facility*!—a place for weddings and Bar Mitzvah banquets, with a big kitchen and an elegant sanctuary. A Torah scroll from Czechoslovakia, saved from the Holocaust, was a museum piece behind glass in a gold-framed cabinet. A choir sang, in banal New-Age harmonies, made-up hymns about love! The *Shema* itself they hoked up with a schmaltzy melody, poor second-cousin to *Fiddler*. He queried the young rabbi, Rabbi Levine, about the peculiar order of the service—a revised order. "We are blessed by having a dramaturge in our congregation," the rabbi told him. A dramaturge? "To shape for our contemporary congregation a deeply religious experience. But tell me—you can chant Torah for us?"

"I'll get back to you."

But so what?—Twenty minutes drive away there's a real minyan that meets weekday mornings at seven. And that's where he goes. He prays *Shacharit* with a lawyer, a few retired men, a carpenter, a jazz musician, a doctor at U.C.L.A. Wrapped in tallis, wearing, on arm and forehead, the black leather boxes filled with the precious words, tefillin his father gave him at his Bar Mitzvah, he feels like a Jew. Saturday, since he feels uncomfortable driving, he leads his own Shabbat service for a congregation of one.

He looks forward to teaching this Siegel boy. What he should have given his son, his grandson Danny—*Baruch Hashem*, he can at least give this stranger.

The First Tutorial

Jeremy comes to the house on his own—by bike. Small for his age. But Samuel remembers the psalm: "Not the strength of the horse does He desire nor the swift legs of men." On the little oak table in Ruthie's conservatory, the boy slaps down a Xerox of his Haftorah, the passage of prophecy by Micah he will be chanting. It's in Hebrew, in English, and in transliteration line for line. They shake hands, but Jeremy doesn't look at Samuel; he aligns and realigns the pages. Among orchids and giant tropical plants, here's old Sam Rosen, long, stooped and skinny with a little paunch, a knitted skullcap over his bald spot, and here's Jeremy Siegel, twelve, small and plain skinny, skullcap over his hair. He's got a long, pale face. His hair, like Danny's, is Marine-short, and his ears stick out; he's wearing jeans, big sneakers, broad dark sunglasses, but, *Baruch Hashem*, when he takes them off, his eyes don't match the wished-for all-American look. Soft eyes, soft. Wounded, he looks; he looks wounded. Or is that my *mishegos*? Samuel looks and nods, looks and nods. The boy keeps his eyes on the text.

Samuel taps a forefinger to the stapled xeroxed pages. "So tell me—what's this?"

"It's—you know—what I'm supposed to memorize."

"For what?" Samuel asks, pretending bewilderment.

Jeremy gives a Look, like Who is this guy? "For my bar mitzvah."

Samuel keeps himself from laughing at the look. He keeps playing dumb. "Ahh! Congratulations. You'll be a bar mitzvah. So you'll put on your first tallis, you'll be wrapping yourself in the mitzvot, the commandments. Tell me: you understand what that entails, Jeremy? You go to Hebrew school?"

"Uh huh. I started last year. I read but slow."

"You've talked to your rabbi? Who is your rabbi?"

"Rabbi Levine—you know, the synagogue near here?"

Samuel closes his eyes. "I've met him." It's at this point that he becomes aware of a rustling in the living room that adjoins the conservatory. The glass door's ajar. Almost hidden in a big leather reclining chair, his grandson Danny is reading. All Samuel sees is his big basketball sneakers up on a hassock. Now, Danny has a big desk in his own room, and that's where he usually does his homework. In fact usually, in the afternoon, he's out roller blading or playing basketball. He's at the verge of developing an underarm odor, keeps sniffing for it, hopeful. He swaggers around but unconvincingly, as if he hasn't quite got it right, hasn't grown into his own imagined body. So he's gawky, not as cool as he'd like, a little uncomfortable under the eye of an invisible camera. He'd like to be a jock. So why is he interested in what's going on out here? Just in case, Samuel raises his voice to the level of a chant. "Jeremy, I'm not talking about your skill of reading Hebrew. I'm talking about growing up a Jew. Tell me, does your family keep the Sabbath?"

At first Jeremy doesn't answer at all. He screws up his face, he shrugs. Finally: "Sometimes we light candles and say a blessing."

"Good. *Baruch Hashem*. You know, I'd like to meet your father and mother."

"Sure. But they're both real busy."

Jeremy looks at him with big, steady brown eyes. And the

look, its vulnerability, so different from the California-cool eyes he sees everywhere, does something to Samuel to end his arrogant catechism. It goes to his heart, this softness. "You see—Jeremy—I want this to be real for you. Okay? Look: believe it or not, you don't even need to chant a Haftorah passage to be a Bar Mitzvah. You just need to come up for an aliyah. You come up to the reading of the Torah and say a blessing. I could teach you that in ten minutes. It's just a custom, chanting Haftorah."

"You're not going to teach me? My Dad said…"

"I understand. Sure, I'll help you with the cantillation. But first we work on what it's all about. Otherwise, why bother? —No matter what your parents say."

In the next room, the big sneakers uncross, re-cross.

The Tenth Tutorial

They're sitting among the orchids and tropical plants. Who needs a conservatory in L.A. ? For Ruthie it's just a tiled glassed-in patio, pretty, and the odor that Samuel assumed to be flowers turns out to be mostly the perfumed spray that moistens the orchids. While Dan, sitting at the conservatory table, half listens to the lesson, half does math, Jeremy in yarmulke half-closes his eyes—because it's the only way he can get the cantillation right—and sings, sings beautifully so it hurts, though without *Yiddishkeit*—more like a boy soprano in a Cathedral—the introductory blessing to his Haftorah portion. Like a boy soprano and maybe—maybe a little like a café singer singing of gone love. Because really, what can the boy know? What are his models? How many times has he been to shul in his life? And what kind of shul? But his voice is so sweet, so tender, that Samuel's eyes fill with blessing, and he reaches out and touches Jeremy's cheek. "Nice, nice."

Dan and Jeremy grin at one another.

All right, Samuel's embarrassed. Ordinarily he's no gusher. But *this*: like rain falling on parched earth. To feel the *blessing* of this blessing! But now, *ah hah*, something uncomfortable grabs his insides and tugs: So tell me, mister—*who's* been the one painting by the numbers, blessing by rote? Not this boy with his big, serious eyes and tender voice.

Out of the corner of his eye, warped through a bit of water, he sees Peter leading through the living room a small portly man in running suit. Jeremy's father. What's left of his hair is curly, graying, loose, damp—he's been exercising. Peter's smiling, Ben Siegel's smiling, smiling. "Rabbi, rabbi. A pleasure to finally meet you—I'm ashamed I've been too busy. So, is my son behaving himself?"

"*Baruch Hashem*, your son is a fine boy. He's learning very well."

"One smart kid, isn't he, rabbi?"

"Very…. Danny and Jeremy, *both* smart. But Mr. Siegel, I'm not a rabbi."

"*Ben*. Call me Ben." And he says for Peter's benefit, "This kid I'm grooming for Stanford." And then to Samuel—"You…were a lit. professor, am I right?"

"At Sarah Lawrence."

"Good school. Wait a minute. —Jeremy, Danny?— you two guys go take a walk for a few minutes. Okay, Peter?" And he waits till the boys are gone. "'Not a rabbi, huh?' You know, it's funny—that's just what I thought," Ben Siegel says. "*Just* what I thought. But…with all this religious business he's bringing home…."

Samuel, Ben, Peter sit at the glass-topped conservatory table. Samuel can see Peter's cool dissolving. Peter's grinning. Oh, Samuel has known that uncomfortable grin for about four decades; today it makes him furious. He'd like to slap it off his face. As if thousands of years of Jewish history have ended up in this son of his, laid-back businessman with amused, wry look, embarrassment for his own father. *Wait*—wait till the Bar Mitzvah—he owes that to Jeremy—then (he says to himself) fly back to New York, go live on the West Side near Columbia, go live in Brooklyn, somewhere it's not so odd to be a Jew.

"Pop can get just a little carried away," Peter says, patting Ben's shoulder.

Samuel is grim. "'Religious business'? So? Something wrong with that? What do you suppose he *should* be bringing home?"

"A *skill.* Okay? Like piano. A skill." He speaks into the circle of forefinger and thumb looped to contain, to frame, each point. "So he can be initiated into the tribe, you know what I'm saying? It's a big day. All the relatives! My relatives, my wife's relatives. Big expense, big party, but look Mr. Rosen, let me put it like this: If I feel like sending my kid to a yeshiva, I got the wherewithal. You get me?" All said heartily, as if he's joking, *pretending* to be annoyed. When it's quite clear to Samuel that it's the *pretense* that's the pretense. "But *other than that*, hey—you're doing one great job, the boy's taking it seriously. Not like those lousy classes at the synagogue."

"*Piano.* Exactly, Mr. Siegel. Suppose I were teaching your boy piano. Wouldn't I want him to feel the music inside the music, the music under the notes? What kind of teacher would I be, I just taught the notes?"

Peter laughs, pretending it's light banter passing back and forth.

"I'm glad we had this little talk," Ben says. "*Look.* My son's telling me he wants *tefillin* for his Bar Mitzvah. Tefillin! You kidding? No offence, but that's left over from the Middle Ages. It'd spook me out just having them in my house." Now, having spoken with professional toughness, Ben softened. "Otherwise...I love what you're doing. Amazing! You know a hell of a lot about motivation, I'll say that. I could use a guy like you in my business. Just go a little easy, okay?"

A Party in the Hills of Malibu

A Sunday afternoon. Ben Siegel's party—Jeremy's parents are moving up, literally, into the expensive rocky hills of a canyon above the ocean. No house yet, but plans have been approved, the site cleared; construction is about to start. Tonight will be a fortieth birthday party for Ben's wife Elaine; and this house, Ruthie tells him on the way, is Elaine's *dream*. Ruthie's voice slides half an octave down the word. Samuel thinks of a Haftorah trope.

Samuel expects a picnic. But—"Better dress up a little," Peter says. "Open shirt, nice pants. And Pop? Please, if it's okay with you—no yarmulke?"

Boating doesn't make Samuel sick, but this ride in the back of Peter's Mercedes, up switchbacks into the rocky hills, does it. Brutal rocks look ready to fall on the car. Switchback, switchback, switchback. A little dizzy when the car stops, he sucks in a deep breath; as he lifts himself from the car, he finds a young man in a black shirt standing above him, holding the door. Behind their car is another, and another valet waiting. Two more valets, Hispanic, all in black pants, white shirts, stand by to park the cars.

It's been a warm day, but up here it's cool—he's glad he wore a jacket. Peter leads them to an arched trellised gate that's been set up, like a flowered trellis in a thirties' movie about country life, to establish an entrance. Here are three really massive black men in open white shirts—they look like football players, weightlifters. Any one of them you'd turn in the street to look at, that big. They're wearing walkie-talkies on their belts, like pistols. A white guy with a list on a clipboard takes names, lets the Rosens pass under the trellis.

It's not a bare site; a house was built here in the twenties, a big stone house, recently burned down, and so there's a wonderfully irregular brick path, and the plantings are beautiful and well established—giant cactuses, palms, and succulents, twenty-foot ficuses, a massive thicket of bougainvillea, and California greenery Samuel can't name. Posted on a leaning fat sycamore, a sign,

H a p p y B i r t h d a y, E l a i n e!

The giant plants, obviously planted yet in a wild, rocky place, look like something out of *The Wizard of Oz*. So it's as if he's suddenly entered into a Technicolor dream. And in fact, it has the quality of movie set. Platforms have been hammered together, leveled on concrete blocks; actual living room furniture, rented, or maybe borrowed from some back-lot warehouse, has been clustered into imagined open-air "rooms," bars set up, young men and women tending, black-shirted waiters cruising with trays of food. The tang of a platter of spicy shrimp, darker pungent scent of sausages in pastry rolls. *Treyf.*

Beyond, an enormous walled tent has been set up for dinner—maybe fifty, sixty yards long! It's such a big place it doesn't seem crowded, but there must be a hundred guests. *More.* Samuel guesses—thirty thousand dollars? No, *ludicrous!*—easy fifty thousand. Maybe twice that. Beyond the tent, a rough lawn slopes down, clipped from wild grasses, and a little wooden stage for the music later on. And past the stage, the lawn comes to a point, like the prow of a land ship, then a steep declivity and across the canyon, other hills, and past the hills, a snip of ocean.

He's critical of such expense. What a difference money like that could make for fifty, a hundred families in L.A. But, frankly, he's also impressed. To go to the trouble of setting up outdoor rooms, with coffee tables and leather sofas—rooms with invisible walls and invisible ceilings. From a tree limb hangs a large ornate picture frame, empty: the implied picture: the landscape beyond. And he's impressed by these young successful people sitting on the sofas—film producers, high-tech executives, entertainment lawyers exchanging business cards, negotiating lunches. It's a party, but a lot of people seem to be walking off by themselves, talking to themselves—actually into cell phones. Considered as a whole, all right, it's a Fellini scene of capitalist excess. Still, when he looks at the faces one by one, when he presses between clusters of black shirts and stops to listen in on conversations—admit it!—he finds intelligence, energy. They talk about e-business, of course, and financial moves by Time-Warner and Intel, but also about their children's schools, and debt relief for undeveloped countries.

He gets into a conversation with a young man with one gold moon earring who directs a television series—robotic machines that battle one another. But then two women in white linen come over, lovely looking women with hardly any makeup, and conversation changes to the spiritual benefits of some fabulous resort in the desert. "When the mudpacks go on you practically leave your body," one woman tells the other. At the fringe of another conversation, he hears someone say, "I've read that half the young boys in sub-Saharan

Africa will die of AIDS." To which a young woman drawls, "Well, *I've* never understood people wanting to *travel* to Africa," as if the chief point were her perspicacity in choice of tourist destinations. But the others in her little group *don't* nod agreement; they glance at one another, raising eyebrows, recognizing her foolishness.

As if this were Italy in the twenties, nearly everyone's wearing a black shirt. And the black pants, black jackets—what you'd expect among the Orthodox in Brooklyn.

This is no simple birthday party, Samuel sees that right away. It's a celebration of some acquisition. Is Siegel a senior partner? A broker? Everyone else, he's sure, must know what's going on. Now he sees, hanging from the branches of a eucalyptus, a Calder-like mobile made up of laminated posters with the new logo—a stylized eye held in palm of stylized hand, and bordering the eye at the top, echoing the arc of the cupped palm, the words: I-CON/TACT. The logo is everywhere: on cactuses, the walls of the tent, inside, outside, and hugely on the rear of the stage. And stapled on tree trunks, Velcroed to rocks, a slogan against the mauve background of a sci-fi space ship entering a space station: WE BRING THE WORLD TO YOUR DATA PORT....

Past an empty swimming pool, tiled by hand, tile by tile, perhaps seventy-five years ago, he finds the central "living room," and here, on a table like an altar, stands a great black television thin as an attaché case, and beside it, flat black speakers, like manufactured monoliths. They're like beautiful sculpture. A video camera has been set up to look out from this hill into the valley, all the way to the ocean, and as you turn it, the picture on the video changes, zooms in on houses and boulders: a virtual landscape to compete with the real.

Samuel feels nausea. It's too beautiful a day to let himself get this sour. He closes his eyes in distaste and walks and breathes the way Hannah, who did yoga for years, always tried to teach him. But his breath comes hot. He has nothing to say in this crowd. Off by themselves on the lawn near the prow of the cliff, back-lit by the late afternoon sun, Jeremy and Danny are tossing a Frisbee back and forth. Big, athletic kid, skinny little kid. Samuel waves at the two of them, walks past them to the edge, and in the face of the rocky fingers of canyon stretching to the sea, rocky cliffs with a few jutting houses but no slogans, puts on yarmulke and begins murmuring *Ashrei*, "Happy are those who live in Your house…"—the great psalm of praise he prays every day, one line for each letter of the *aleph-bet*. He knows what he's doing: singing a music that can beat down this imposition of commerce—worse than commerce, *unreality*—onto God's world.

That's *not* what he's doing. Please! He's trying to wrap himself in some kind of comfort, because he feels particularly bleak, particularly alone today. He praises because he can't feel any reason to praise. He's fearful, high on this cliff edge, no one here. Hannah, if she were with him, would make for him, as she always did, an alternative world he could stomach living in. Even when they snipped at each other. Which was often. Even when he grew petulant. Peculiar—or maybe not at all peculiar—that surrounded by beautiful landscape, high-energy people, a feast, he should feel this down, this alone. He misses Hannah. He aches, missing her. He remembers things. Moments. His memory has never been all that hot. Hannah used to say, "Remember that dumb little café near Pont Neuf where they served those awful croissants we laughed over, said McDonald's could do better?" and he, no, he couldn't remember a thing, while she could tell you the color of the plate!—could laugh about a chip gouged out of its edge! But here's the strange thing: now that she's not with him, he recalls moment after moment of their time together, can feel how the sun slanted in, feel the menu card stock in his fingers. More: he even remembers what was on the menu, the font of the print. One day it's like that for Paris, one day for a moment in New York.

The sun is low over the sea; he squints. Hannah would have gotten such a kick out of being here. They would have laughed together.

What kind of life is this? He sways in the wind. And all this time the words of *Ashrei* tumble from his lips.

"Grandpa? You're praying, Grandpa?" Danny joins him, Jeremy, too. They're curious. Or being kind.

"I'm praying *Mincha*—Remember we learned? '*Mincha*,' afternoon service? Before sundown—and look how low the sun is.

Jeremy—you remember, we talked about '*Ashrei*'? We thank the Holy One for the world He has made according to His will. 'You open your hand and satisfy the desire of every living thing.' It's *God* brings the world to our data ports, Mister. Look—look how beautiful"—and like some old Charlton Heston take-off of Moses at the Red Sea, he lifts his arms wide to the view, chuckling at himself.

And at once the prayer becomes true: *Happy are those*...it's as if this is his ship; and of this ship, for the moment, he's captain, and yes, *happy*—it's beautiful, isn't it, God's world. It's a world you'd be loathe to leave sooner than necessary. To feel this so suddenly! It's the boys. Gawky twelve-year-old boys who walk cool but with tender eyes.

He can't help but add, "Too holy, this world, to desecrate—boys, you understand 'desecrate'? To make *un*holy—with those phony advertisements!" Now, having gotten started, oh!—he's furious! "'I-CON/TACT.' You *hear*, boys? They're building a temple to an *icon*. Exactly! 'I' as an icon, an idol. And whose world *is* this? Huh? What *chutzpah*! Do they think they really own it? Are they really going to bring it to your 'data port'?"

Danny doesn't get it. But Jeremy says. "Dad's slogan? It's weird."

"Come," says Samuel. "Never mind me, I talk. Sit down with me. We'll talk Torah together and be in His presence. 'Blessed be the Holy One by Whom all this came to be!'"

Then why do I need to rail like this?

If Samuel had turned at that moment he would have seen the boys exchange a Look, seen them wave at the small, thick man walking toward them across the lawn. But eyes shut, high drone of wind making a peculiar harmony, Samuel davens, rocking slightly back-to-front, spilling out fragments of Hebrew—psalms—praises to hold and protect them.

Danny says, "*Hey, Grandpa*?" and Jeremy says, "*Mr. Rosen*, it's my father!"—and their voices are at the same emotional pitch, bespeaking an intimacy that surprises (pleases) Samuel even before his eyes are open; he hears in the voices an urgency to protect—to protect *him*! They're worried, they're warning. This intimacy, he knows at once, comes from many conversations.

And Ben Siegel is with them. His jacket is a soft gray wool; he's wearing a black silk vest, black slacks, black shirt and tie. "Mr. Rosen. So—what are you doing at my party without a drink in your hand? I'm told that's against the law in Malibu. Only kidding. Maybe you don't drink."

"I drink, I drink. A little later, Mr. Siegel."

Siegel tilts his head and narrows his eyes, looks at Samuel the way you'd look at a peculiar object. "Now, tell me, Mr. Rosen. A beautiful day like this, is this a time for prayers? Whatever are you doing?" A sharp laugh. "I caught you saying prayers out here, am I right?" And, not waiting for an answer, he closes in until Samuel can smell the whiskey on his breath. "Hey." A shrug. "It's your business if you feel like praying—hah!—on *Sunday*? Like the goyim?—but Jeremy I'll take with me. People I want to introduce the kid to."

They walk off. Jeremy looks back and waves, hiding the wave from his father. Samuel says nothing. But in his heart he recites in the Hebrew from the prayer at the close of the Amidah.... *To those who curse me, may my soul be silent.*

And, *Baruch Hashem*, it *is* silent.

Danny's looking at Samuel. He picks up small stones and throws them off the cliff into the valley. Keeps looking. "Grandpa?" Samuel raises his brows. "I was wondering. You think, as long as you're teaching Jeremy, you could teach me?"

"Teach you?"

"The whole business. All the stuff. So I could do a Bar Mitzvah?"

"A Bar Mitzvah! That's a big undertaking, Danny. It means learning—"

"—Sure—"

"I'd have to speak to your mom and dad."

"Talk to *Mom.*"

At this, Samuel laughs, and Danny picks up the laugh, and back and forth they carry it awhile like a secret puppy you sneak home and hide. "No, but Danny, seriously..."

"Dad said *no way*. He said all the synagogues are booked way, way in advance, and anyway, we're not even members."

"Danny, that's inconsequential. You don't need to do it on a Saturday. If you're serious, you come to my minyan in the morning, get used to it, and when it's your birthday, on a Monday morning, you go up for your first aliyah. That's all. Danny, it's everything *else* that matters. It's learning the mitzvot, living a Jewish life, living a sanctified Jewish life—that's what matters."

Danny shrugs. They're sitting cross-legged. Danny's throwing stones.

"So? All right. You want the whole megillah, like Jeremy? Okay, Danny. It's possible. Rabbi Levine needs a good Torah reader at his shul—a chazzan. My voice isn't what it used to be, but good enough. I'll bet I could make a deal with Levine. Let me talk to your dad."

Music Illumining the Soul

By dinnertime it grows dark. At a large circular table, one of maybe fifteen tables, he sits with seven or eight strangers, thirty years younger, who speak to him with respect, then talk to one another in a verbal shorthand about dot.coms and IPOs that leaves him out as if they were speaking a foreign language. Lotus flowers float in glass bowls in the center of circular tables eight foot in diameter. Hannah would *love* this party. She'd be on the phone to all her friends for days. She'd notice the dresses, the hairstyles. She'd say to him, how *beautiful* this site is; he'd say to her, How can a Jew live this far from a Jewish community? And she'd make fun of him. A pleasure.

There are birthday toasts to Ben Siegel's wife, Elaine. Afterwards, lanterns light the way to the prow of lawn where the temporary stage has been constructed. The music is already playing when Samuel wanders down. He can hear drumming, a *tabla*, the whine of a harmonium, a high, male voice swooping up and down. "It's that really cool group from Pakistan," someone says.

Cushions have been arranged in front of the stage; some guests sit cross-legged on these, some stand behind. The singer is sweating; he's a giant fat man in white—they're all wearing soft white pants, white jackets or shirts—and he's gesturing with his hands as if he were telling them all something funny, something tender, full of wonder. His eyes close and the perspiration pours down his cheeks, and every couple of minutes he wipes his face with a handkerchief. His repeated lifts and falls, the soarings into high tenor, are speech at the edge of becoming ecstatic cries.

What kind of music? Samuel has never heard music like this. It's like hearing the blues for the first time. Fingertips rap a tabla faster than seems possible. The singer's face is radiant. The singer listens to the tabla, head cocked to one side, answers in a brief phrase, long, feminine fingers gesturing *Is this what you mean?*—listens, answers, goes off into a long flight, half wailing, half laughing, eyes shut, eyes wide again. The harmonium grounds his song, and the harmonium player sings chorus, sometimes hovering over the singer, sometimes doubling his song. Around him in the dark, the guests nod their heads. It's sacred music, he's sure. Sufi music. He looks for Danny and Jeremy, spots them off to one side, takes up a cushion and sits beside them.

The fat singer is offering a love song to God; of that, Samuel is certain. He wants to believe he *gets* it, wants to believe this L.A. moneyed crowd can't possibly get it. Well, it's true that for some, yes, it's background, they aren't listening, they stand in clumps talking. But the ones who *are* listening, why, they're intent, not talking, eyes narrowed; heads nodding to the music. That beautiful young woman near him—rocks, rocks, eyes closed. Davening.

Samuel takes Danny's hand in the dark, holds on. The singer reminds him of a great cantor, but so intimate, so personal! On Yom Kippur the cantor chants a heartbreaking prayer of his own unworthiness to stand before God on behalf of his congregation. This singing is a little like that, though the feeling is different: is joy. Tonight it's Samuel who feels unworthy. Sitting in the dark, holding his grandson's hand, he is aware of feeling distaste for his judgmental, isolated old-man self, as he stares past the stage to the prow of land, small lanterns marking out the edge where lawn becomes cliff, looks past, down the valley, to lights of canyon houses, silhouettes of rock clefts, lights of boats on the Pacific a few miles farther on.

To be this old and still so petty! My soul not illumined. Dark, grim with death. Sour, still, with Hannah's death. It's as if the music—music from another tradition—is teaching him where he could be. How his soul could become light, enlightened, could dance.

He needs to speak to Peter. He needs to make it up.

Samuel hears someone in the dark behind them: "Hell of a lot of money to be made in world music." This, he ignores.

He wants to make it up to Peter—as if the music, the prayers and bitter loneliness at the cliff edge—have been, partly, a form of discourse about Peter and himself. *My son, my son,* he thinks, to prime himself as he leaves the boys, walks over to Peter and Ruthie across the lawn, rehearsing regret but saying only, "That was *some music.*" He sits down on a cushion in the dark. "Pete, do you know the poetry of Rumi?" Then, not wanting to embarrass him, he says, "Rumi was a mystical Sufi poet, thirteenth century, he wrote poetry of spiritual ecstasy. Like these songs."

Peter comes close to his father's ear and whispers in a parody of a tough-guy voice, "Listen, Pop, I hate to spoil the romance, but one of Ben Siegel's companies—one of I/CON's subsidiaries—produces world music. This is just classy promotion is what it is."

Blood flushes Samuel's face; his good intentions come crashing down. He says, too loud, "Why do you insist on cheapening it?"

"Shh. Pop. Pop. Hey."

"Peter?" Ruthie says quietly.

"Sorry. Sorry…"

"Come," she says, "we have to get home. It's late. Danny's got school." She waves Danny over. "Go say goodbye to Jeremy and catch up, all right, honey?" Now, she tugs at Peter's sleeve; they pass through the huge tent and down the brick path. But Peter stops in the middle of the brick path. People are leaving, new people coming. Mouth to his father's ear he whispers, this time without pretense of parody, "You know what this party is about, Pop? It's about money and power."

Ruthie squeezes Samuel's arm to comfort. "*Please,* Peter."

Samuel stiffens. "You know something, Peter? You're too old for this."

"For what? Tell me, for what am I too old?"

"To prove how grown up and tough you are. Why do you still have to fight me?"

Peter's laugh explodes over the brick path, lit now by hanging Japanese lanterns. "*I* fight *you*? Haven't you got it upside down? You're the one. *You changed all the rules.*"

"Peter, please," Ruthie says.

"When I was a kid, you wanted me to work hard, make a success. Well, I made a success. I made a success, Pop. You're supposed to be proud. Instead, you got new rules, and my life is no damned good, I see it in your eyes. I can knock myself out for you, nothing's good enough."

"The whole point is, they're *not my rules.*"

"'The whole point is' *you* think *you* know what the whole point is! Nobody knows the 'whole point'! God's rules, huh? Says who? Says who! Some rabbis two thousand years ago?"

"*Well*!" Samuel steps back and laughs. "You know, this is the first decent fight we've had, Pete. You know that? It's been little snide, cool digs, you to me or me to you, Ruthie trying to make peace. Ruthie, dear, it's all right. This is a good New York fight."

"'New York'—there you go—more snobbishness," Peter says.

This, Samuel grants.

"Why fight at all?" Ruthie says.

"And God has given you one additional commandment: *Thou shalt demean thy son.*"

"Ha ha! Nice! Peter, dear, if I've done that, I regret it. It's been my terrible failure. I get obnoxious, I know it—a judge pretending to be a prophet."

At this, Peter laughs—*my father the prophet!* They stand grinning at one another.

"The thing is," the prophet says, "I can't stand it—people think the world is made up *by* themselves *for* themselves. Listen: We received a great vision: *the world according to His will.* We can live by that vision—or choose not to."

Ruthie lets them go ahead; she waits for Danny to catch up to her.

Peter laughs. "So—God wants us to be more Jewish?"

"That's *not* it. No! *That's not it.*" He stops on the brick path, tugs at Peter's jacket collar to turn him around. "Those Sufi musicians tonight, *they* know. It's not a question of *Jewish*. I'm saying, it's *not okay,* this way to live—whatever you call it—America, California. I can't be 'tolerant.' It's *not* just another, equally valid, way to live—it's *empty*…"

"What exactly does 'empty' mean?"

"The way a holograph is empty. It's getting suckered into pseudo-hungers for things, it's feeding a voracious narcissism. *Voracious*, Pete! Because it *cannot* be satisfied. It's a *virtual* world. *Icons.* That's the only world they bring to your 'data ports.' And it hurts me to see you caught up in it. Listen—there's another kind of life, where you try to line up in accord with the orientation that's *built in*—like iron filings over a magnetic pattern? And that is a *superior way to live*. Get it? *Superior*. Sanctified. And if that's lost, it doesn't matter, Jew or gentile."

"You were never like this when Mom was alive. So angry."

"You're right," he sighs. "She soothed me, your mother. I see more darkly since I watched her die."

Peter walks along quietly beside his father. Then he says quietly, "You did. Dad? I mean *watched*. I know. I came at the end, but you were there alone with her every day." He puts his arm over his father's shoulder; Samuel permits it to remain. They continue up the brick path.

Behind them in the dark, music starts up again. Tick-tick-a-tick of the tabla, singer's wail. It's carried over loudspeakers through the darkness. The path is lit by lantern, but overhead the trees are dark, so that it feels as if they're inside a cave. "I see more darkly, yes—but also more *truly*. Those last months, I wanted to plug my ears. But I felt I was supposed to listen." Samuel lifts his brows, and it makes him feel for a moment as if he's lifting above the path into the dark. A giddy feeling. Reaching over, he touches Peter's cheek, as if to ground himself.

They're almost to the entrance when Ben catches up to them. "No! You leaving so early?"

Ruthie is right behind him. "Ben, it's a *lovely* party, but there's school tomorrow."

Ignoring her, Ben says, "Mr. Rosen? Can I see you a minute?" He speaks low so Danny can't hear. "Don't mind me—my clowning—I had a bit too much to drink this afternoon."

Samuel shrugs. "It's of absolutely no consequence." And that's true. What matters, after all, is Jeremy. Siegel is apologizing because he requires his services. Who cares about this *grubyom*? Samuel is grateful he'll be able to teach the boy; maybe, *Baruch Hashem*, both boys.

"But I spoke out of turn. You're not offended?"

Samuel shrugs, stays silent. Clearly, Ben is waiting for reassurance, so it's a terrible silence. The tick, tick-a-tick-tick of the tabla over speakers set in the rocks underlines the silence.

Now what happens can't be expressed as dialogue. What matters is gesture and expression seen in extreme close up, its significations understood—the action seen in slow motion, even frame by frame. For example, now Ben smiles at Peter, lifts the corners of his lips while his eyes stay hard; it's *apparently* a smile of camaraderie: *He's a handful, your dad.* But oh, it's making a demand. Debts are being called in. For Ben is surely not willing to be humiliated. The apology expressed a kind of *noblesse oblige*; not accepted, it becomes a sign of weakness. Tonight, especially, here on this beautiful land at the top of the canyon, he sees himself as some kind of feudal lord of California, a newly-minted aristocrat, to whom Peter is vassal. Ben knows that Peter's firm needs an infusion of new capital, and unsecured capital isn't all that easy to come by these days.

But Peter gives him back a blank stare. He doesn't know how Ben insulted Samuel, but he can imagine. It must have been ugly if Ben feels he has to acknowledge it as insult. Ben won't let Peter go, Ben's smile freezes, he's upping the stakes, *demanding* response, a shared smile, that's all, and though knowing the cost, Peter keeps refusing. Even at this instant, while Peter is almost breathless from the effort of resisting Ben's demand, another piece of him is already skimming mental lists for alternative financial contacts.

Ruthie is worried. "Dad? Time to go."

Samuel just turns away, but as he continues up the path, he looks back at the great tent lit by candles, floating above the trees.

Ben calls after him, "I saw you enjoying the music."

Peter turns. *Now* he can be polite. "My father was just saying—"

But Ben won't let him finish. "Hey. That's religious music, your old man *should* like it. We got lucky. They happened to be starting an American tour. They're for real, these guys. Big shots back home in Pakistan."

And that should be that. Good night, good night. Only something peculiar happens. Maybe because Ben is nervous, feels unsupported by Peter, and because Samuel remains silent? Ben blurts a laugh—a cynical little laugh. To Samuel's ears, the laugh is mean, caustic. *You think I give a damn if you accept my apology? You think you mean a damned thing to me? I can buy you and sell you.* It's meant to communicate contempt, but Ben doesn't expect to get called on it.

"That music," Samuel says, turning back to face Ben Siegel, as Peter tugs at his elbow, "It moved me. It moved me. *Very* much. But—how can I put this —? You just *rented* it. It's like your black silk shirt, Mr. Siegel, or that silk vest—a little touch of style you put on...."

Ruthie puts her arm around Samuel's shoulders. "Dad, Dad, please, we do need to get home. Another day you can have this discussion."

But Peter, in for a penny, in for a pound, says, "Oh, let Pop alone. He'll just be a minute."

Having to speak loud over the music, Samuel says, "And here's the thing, Mr. Siegel—at some level you *know* it, that's the trouble, so it looks foolish on you. A costume. Or an alien from another planet speaking colloquially, you understand?—but not quite getting the intonations right."

Now Peter: "Pop! Enough, Pop."

"Mr. Siegel, you're like a Jewish Gatsby. You try to become special, glorious. And let me tell you frankly, that's not going to happen. But even if it *were* to happen, what would you have? What? Is this what you really want your life to be about?" This feels so good to say—and immediately Samuel regrets saying it. He feels a whirring in his ears from the rush of the fight.

Ben blurts another laugh, turns to Peter, another try. "You got some peculiar father. What's wrong with this guy? He getting a little funny in his old age?"

"I don't see anything peculiar," Peter Rosen says. "My dad is just a little outspoken, Ben. But Ruthie's right—it's time for us to go home." He takes his father's elbow and steers him away, and when they're at the trellised gate, Peter stops them—out of earshot of the young man with the lists of names and the drivers standing around having a smoke. "He's pretty peculiar himself."

"I'm sorry, Pete. That cost you. I know it."

Ruthie goes up to the parking attendants to hand them the ticket for the car. She's shaking her head. But Peter sings a laugh that harmonizes with the singer's cry. "Well, you are really something, Pop.—What a mouth on this guy!" he calls to Ruthie. Then—"Oh, you—you old prophet! Listen, I've been wanting to cut that phony down for months."

"I'm ashamed. For your business—you need him. And it's not just that. Me, I need to stop judging so much. It's a real disease. I give everybody grades for living. I'm ashamed."

Danny doesn't get it. He keeps asking, "What happened? Grandpa? What?"

The Promised Land

We're back on *The Promised Land*; it's January but warm, a clear Sunday; Peter's cruising toward Catalina, where he promises everyone a marvelous brunch at a restaurant overlooking the ocean, and he's making time to keep his reservation. It's choppy; they're clipping the waves.

No piped-in music today—Peter's made a deal with Samuel, who's in the main cabin teaching Torah cantillations to Jeremy and Danny. Instead of a yarmulke, Samuel is wearing one of Peter's baseball caps, logo of the Dodgers. And Samuel has agreed to fishing on the way back; Peter's got several heavy rods rigged and strapped up like aerials on the fishing tower.

Small accommodations like these have been made, nothing said; for instance, Samuel shows an interest in the boat. Occasionally he takes the helm and lets Peter correct him. Occasionally, he watches TV without lecturing the family about false gods. Fridays, he's taken to baking and blessing the challah. In fact, he's taken over most of the shopping and cooking, spent a day kashering the kitchen—which they pretend they know nothing about. Ruthie's grateful—she has plenty to do without cooking.

Oh, there are times—Samuel knows—Peter can't stand being in the same room with him.

Today, there's *shalom bayit*, peace in the house. Or on the boat, this massive venture skipping over the waves.

In the main cabin, Samuel is struggling to keep Danny on pitch, then to get Jeremy to link the tropes, to put phrases together legato, not as a disconnected series. The two boys are learning different Haftorah passages, but Jeremy is learning to chant some of Danny's, Danny Jeremy's. how did it happen? Samuel has no idea. Somehow, there—last week—was Jeremy for his lesson. There was Danny. "Dad says okay." Samuel hasn't questioned. The boat slams a swell, another. The xeroxed sheets slide along the table. "Let's stop for today and go up on deck," Samuel says. "Let's end with a *niggun*. You've almost got it, *both* of you. You should be very pleased."

He works them too hard, he thinks, these L.A. kids in jeans and baggy crew-necked shirts. But they do love learning these *niggunim*, melodies without words that seem to say…everything. Mostly a sad music. This, the music says, is how life is. And that's how it leaves him when the boys grab a Coke and turn on the TV. The melody shaping his breathing, he goes up on deck, climbs to the fishing tower.

Peter is steering a course from the upper cabin; he's been teaching Ruthie how to program the computer memory for navigation. Above, in the fishing tower, alone, floating above the ocean like the gulls, Samuel picks up the *niggun* in his head, then hums aloud, but after a minute it simply comes apart, turns into a keening, like the cry of the gulls, a keening, a howling no one below can hear, but he feels ashamed—Still, after a year? *What kind of faith*?—and then one of Hannah's deep breaths, and again into the *niggun*, a melody that knows more than he knows, knows what we go through. The music doesn't try to cope in any way—except to love the sad world and let the singer know it *knows*, knows for all of us. It holds us, or it breathes us.

Port ahead: Catalina. Boats streaming towards, away. A ferry sounds its horn in warning as it lumbers out of its dock. Over a loudspeaker he hears Peter's voice: "Dad? Come on down from there while we're docking." *Aye, aye, Captain*. Samuel climbs down to the deck of *The Promised Land*; the melody still in his head, he rejoins the family.

Originally appeared in Virginia Quarterly Review, *Summer, 2003*

Acknowledgments

Thanks to my readers and teachers, especially my wife Sharon Dunn, Neal Kozodoy, Fred Robinson, Bill Roorbach, George Cuomo, Rabbi Eddie Feld, Rabbi Sheila Weinberg, Thane Rosenbaum, and to writers I've learned from, including Saul Bellow, Grace Paley, and Alice Munro.

About the Author

John J. Clayton

John J. Clayton has taught modern literature and fiction writing at the University of Massachusetts, Amherst since 1969, and has also taught as Visiting Professor at Mt. Holyoke College. His stories have been published in most major periodicals and have won the *O. Henry Prize*, *Best American Short Stories*, and the *Pushcart Prize*. His second collection, *Radiance*, won the Ohio State University award in short fiction and was a finalist for the National Jewish Book Award in 1998.

Clayton has edited six editions of an anthology, the *Heath Introduction to Fiction*. He has also written a good deal about modern fiction, including *Gestures of Healing*, a psychological study of modern British and American fiction. His *Saul Bellow: In Defense of Man* won awards in literary criticism. He has published criticism on various twentieth century writers including D.H. Lawrence, E. L. Doctorow, and Grace Paley. His third novel, *Kuperman's Fire*, will be published in spring, 2007.

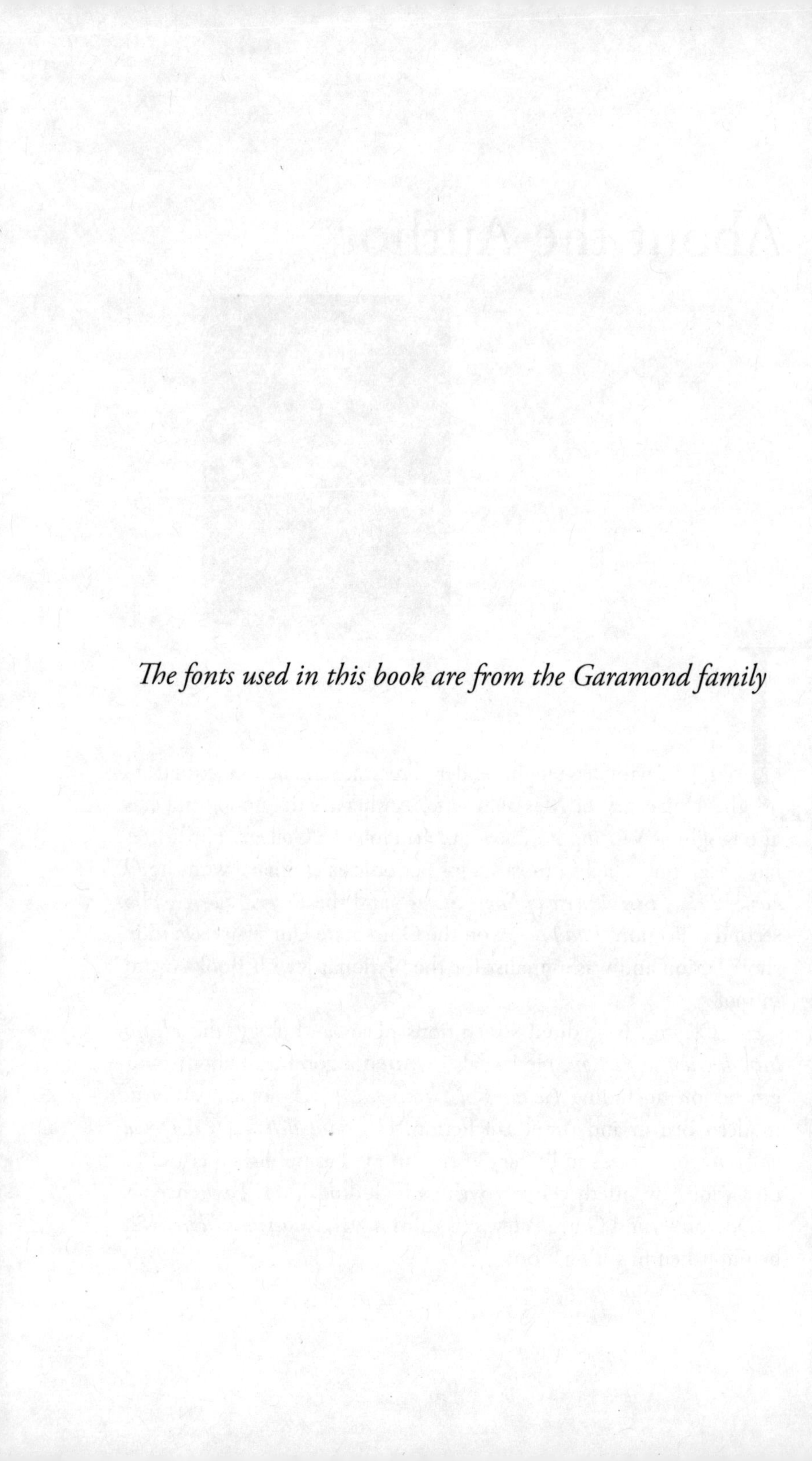

The fonts used in this book are from the Garamond family